P9-CNH-204

BLOOD
AND
HONOR

G·K
Hall
&Cº.

Also by W. E. B. Griffin
in Large Print:

Behind the Lines

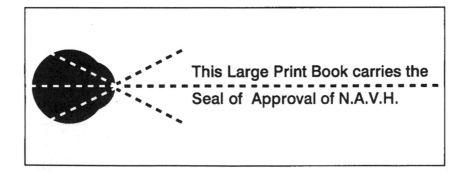

This Large Print Book carries the
Seal of Approval of N.A.V.H.

BLOOD
AND
HONOR

W.E.B. Griffin

G.K. Hall & Co.
Thorndike, Maine

LANCASTER COUNTY LIBRARY
LANCASTER, PA

Copyright © 1996 by W. E. B. Griffin

All rights reserved.

Published in 1997 by arrangement with G.P. Putnam's Sons.

G.K. Hall Large Print Core Collection.

The text of this Large Print edition is unabridged.
Other aspects of the book may vary from the original edition.

Set in 16 pt. Plantin by Minnie B. Raven.

Printed in the United States on permanent paper.

Library of Congress Cataloging in Publication Data

Griffin, W. E. B.
    Blood and honor / W. E. B. Griffin.
        p.   cm.
    ISBN 0-7838-8125-8 (lg. print : hc)
    1. United States.   Marine Corps — History — Fiction.
    2. World War, 1939–1945 — Fiction. 3. United States —
    History, Military — 20th century — Fiction.   4. Buenos
    Aires (Argentina) — Fiction.   5. Large type books.   I. Title.
    [PS3557.R489137B57   1997]
        813'.54—dc21   97-7602

LAN 28.95   SIMON + SCHUSTER SV

I would like to thank Mr. William W. Duffy II, formerly of the United States Embassy in Buenos Aires, and Colonel José Manuel Menéndez, Cavalry, Argentine Army, Retired, who both went well beyond the call of duty in helping me in many ways as I was writing this book.

W. E. B. Griffin
Buenos Aires, 13 December 1995

Foreword

Nation at a Glance

A federal court will decide this week whether or not former Nazi SS Erich Priebke will be extradited to Italy. A year ago, Priebke admitted to having participated in the murder of 335 civilians in the Ardeatine caves in Rome during World War II. San Carlos de Bariloche Judge Leónidas Molde agreed to Priebke's extradition after Italian courts petitioned the Argentine government to send Priebke to Italy to face murder charges.

Page 2
The *Buenos Aires Herald*, Buenos Aires, Argentina
July 4, 1995

PART ONE

I

[One]

Estancia San Pedro y San Pablo
Near Pila, Buenos Aires Province
Republic of Argentina
2105 4 April 1943

The concentration el Coronel Jorge Guillermo Frade was devoting to the inch-thick document on his desk was interrupted by what sounded like the death agony of a water buffalo being stomped by an elephant.

Frade, a six-foot-one, 195-pound, fifty-one-year-old, still had all of his hair (including the full mustache he had worn since he was commissioned Sub-Teniente — Second Lieutenant — of Cavalry) and all of his teeth; but in the past five years he had found it necessary to wear corrective glasses when reading. He removed his horn-rimmed spectacles, sighed audibly, and looked across his study at the source of the noise.

It came from the open mouth of a heavyset man in his late forties who was sitting sprawled in a leather armchair, sound asleep. He, too, wore a cavalryman's mustache.

He was Enrico Rodríguez, who had left Estancia San Pedro y San Pablo to enlist in the Cavalry to

9

serve as Sub-Teniente Frade's batman. They had retired together twenty-five years later as Colonel Commanding and Suboficial Mayor (Sergeant Major) of Argentina's most prestigious cavalry regiment, the Húsares de Pueyrredón.

During their long service together, el Coronel Frade had grown familiar with Suboficial Mayor Rodríguez's snoring. Tonight's was spectacular, which meant that Rodríguez had been drinking beer. For some reason wine and whiskey did not seem to affect Enrico the way beer did. Wine made Enrico mellow; whiskey very often sent him in search of feminine companionship; but beer — even two beers — made Enrico sleepy and turned on the snoring machine full blast.

For a moment el Coronel Frade seriously considered picking up his metal wastebasket and dropping it on the tile floor of the study. That would bring Enrico out of his slumber — and the chair — as if catapulted.

He decided against it. It had been a long day, and Enrico was tired.

He looked at his watch, and at the inch-thick folder on his desk, and decided to hell with it. He too was tired, and they had to drive back to Buenos Aires.

He slid his glasses into the breast pocket of his tweed jacket and stood up, then picked up the inch-thick folder and carried it to an open, wall-mounted safe. After placing the document on one of the shelves, he shut the door, then turned a chrome wheel that moved inch-wide steel pistons into corresponding holes in the frame; finally, he spun the combination dial.

The safe itself was concealed from view by a movable section of bookshelves. When closed, these gave no indication that anything was behind them.

Frade swung the bookcase section back in place and tiptoed out of the simply furnished study, so as not to wake Enrico. He then went down a long, wide corridor to his apartment. There he sat on the bed and with a grunt removed his English-made riding boots. That done, he removed the rest of his clothing and tossed it on the large bed.

He went into his bathroom and showered and shaved. When he went back into the bedroom, Enrico was there.

"There is an operation, I am told," Coronel Frade said. "The surgeon goes in your throat — or maybe it's the nose — cuts something, and then you don't snore."

Enrico looked uncomfortable.

"I am told the operation is relatively painless," Frade went on straight-faced, "and that you don't have to spend more than a week or ten days in the hospital, and that you can eat normally within a month."

"You should have woken me, mi Coronel," Enrico said.

"And disturb the sleep of the innocent?"

"I have fueled and checked the car, mi Coronel," Enrico said, changing the subject. "Rudolpho and Juan Francisco will precede us in the Ford."

"No, they won't," Frade said. "There is no need for that."

"It is better, mi Coronel, to be safe than sorry."

"We will go alone," Frade said.

"Sí, Señor," Enrico said.

"Have a thermos filled with coffee, please," Frade ordered. "I don't want you to fall asleep on the way to Buenos Aires."

"Sí, Señor," Enrico said.

"Wait for me in the car," Frade said. "I won't be a minute."

Enrico nodded and left the bedroom.

The car was a black Horche convertible touring sedan, painstakingly and lovingly maintained by Enrico, often assisted by el Coronel. Some of the reason for their loving care was that parts for the Horche were not available at any price. The Horche Company was no longer making luxury automobiles, but rather tank engines for the German Army. And some of it was because el Coronel was extraordinarily fond of this automobile.

He rarely let Enrico drive it. Tonight was to be an exception.

"You drive, please," el Coronel ordered as he walked quickly down the wide steps to the verandah. "I want some of that coffee."

"Sí, Señor," Enrico said.

He opened the front passenger door, closed it after Frade stepped in, then went around the front of the car and got behind the wheel.

"Pay attention to the road," Frade ordered. "Stay well behind anything ahead of us until you're sure you can pass without having it throw up a stone and hit our windscreen."

Enrico had heard exactly the same order three or four hundred times.

"Sí, Señor," he said.

Enrico drove slowly until el Coronel had poured coffee into a mug, closed the thermos bottle, and put it on the floor. Then he pressed more heavily on the accelerator.

Two miles down the road — still on estancia property — his headlights picked up an object on the road. As he took his foot from the accelerator, el Coronel ordered, "Slow down, there's a beef on the road."

It was indeed a beef, lying crosswise in the center of the macadam.

El Coronel swore. He could not have told anyone within five hundred head how many cattle roamed Estancia San Pedro y San Pablo, but he was always enraged to find one of them on the road, victim of an encounter with a truck.

Enrico applied the brakes more heavily. The Horche took some time to slow from 120 kph. And he knew that if he went on the shoulder at any pace faster than a funeral crawl, el Coronel would have something to say.

The roof was down, and as Enrico started to pass the beef, el Coronel stood up, supporting himself on the windscreen frame to take a good look at it.

As he did this, Enrico noticed movement on the side of the road. He was wondering if somehow his headlights had failed to pick out more beeves when he saw the muzzle flashes.

And then something hit him in the head and he fell onto the wheel.

The Horche veered left, crossed the road and the shoulder, and then came to a stop against a fence post.

Two men ran up to the car.

El Coronel Frade was on his knees on the front seat, searching for the .45 automatic pistol he knew Enrico carried in the small of his back.

One of the men shot him twice, in the face and chest, with both barrels of a twelve-bore side-by-side shotgun.

El Coronel Frade fell onto Enrico's back and then slid down it, coming to rest between Enrico's back and the seat.

The man with the Thompson submachine gun

looked at the bloody head of Suboficial Mayor Enrico Rodríguez, Cavalry, Retired, and professionally decided that shooting him again would be unnecessary.

[Two]

Wolfsschanze
Near Rastenburg, East Prussia
2130 5 April 1943

The license plates of the Mercedes sedan bore the double lightning flashes of the SS. As it approached, a Hauptsturmführer (SS Captain), a Schmeisser submachine gun hanging from his shoulder, stepped into the floodlight-illuminated roadway and rather arrogantly, if unnecessarily — a heavy, yellow-and-black-striped barrier pole hung across the road — extended his right hand in a signal to stop.

He wore a leather-brimmed service cap with the Totenkopf (death's-head) insignia. Behind him, wearing steel helmets, their Schmeissers in their hands, an Unterscharführer (SS Sergeant) and a Rottenführer (SS Corporal) backed him up. Between two narrow silver bands around the cuffs of their black uniform sleeves, the silver-embroidered legend "Adolf Hitler" identified them all as members of the Liebstandarte (literally, "Life Guard") Adolf Hitler, Hitler's personal bodyguard.

The Hauptsturmführer approached the Mercedes, raised his arm straight out from his shoulder in salute — the passenger in the rear seat wore the

14

uniform of a Standartenführer (SS Colonel) — and barked, "Heil Hitler!"

The Standartenführer raised his right arm, bent at the elbow, to return the salute, then reached in his pocket for his credentials, which he extended to the Hauptsturmführer.

"Standartenführer Goltz to visit Partieleiter Martin Bormann," he announced. "I am expected." (Partieleiter — Party Leader — Bormann, as Hitler's Deputy, ran the Nazi party.)

"Be so good as to have your driver park your car, Herr Standartenführer, while I verify your appointment," the Hauptsturmführer said, as he opened the rear door of the Mercedes.

Goltz stepped out of the Mercedes. Above the two silver bands on his tunic cuffs were the silver letters SD, identifying him as a member of the Sicherheitsdienst, the security service of the SS.

He stood waiting in the road as the Hauptsturmführer went into one of the four buildings of the Guard Post South. Not even a Standartenführer of the Sicherheitsdienst was passed into Wolfsschanze ("Wolf's Lair," Adolf Hitler's secret command post) without being subjected to the most thorough scrutiny.

A minute later, the Hauptsturmführer returned, and again gave the stiff-armed Nazi salute.

"If the Standartenführer will be so good as to follow me, I will escort him to his car."

"Thank you," Goltz said, again returning the salute with his palm raised to the level of his shoulder.

The yellow-and-black-striped barrier pole rose with a hydraulic whine, and the two passed through what was known as the "outer wire" of Wolf's Lair. The compound, four hundred miles from Berlin and about four miles from Rastenburg, was an oblong approximately 1.5 by .9 miles. The outer wire was guarded by both machine-gun towers and machine-gun positions on the ground and by an extensive minefield.

Just inside the outer wire perimeter — separated as far as possible from each other to reduce interference — were some of the radio shacks and antennas over which instant communication with the most remote outposts of the Thousand Year Reich was maintained.

A Mercedes sedan, identical to the one Goltz had just left, backed out of a parking area inside the outer wire and up to the now raised barrier pole. A Rottenführer jumped out, opened the rear door, and raised his arm in salute.

SS officers in charge of security had decided it was more efficient to require Wolf's Lair visitors to leave their cars outside the outer wire, and transfer inside the wire to cars from the Wolf's Lair motor pool. Doing so obviated subjecting the incoming vehicle to a thorough search. It also spared the visitor the waste of time such a search would entail, not to mention the time of the SS personnel who conducted the search.

As soon as Standartenführer Goltz was seated in the back of the Mercedes, the driver closed the door, ran around the front of the car, and slipped behind the wheel.

The road passed for three-quarters of a mile through a heavy stand of pine trees, with nothing visible on either side. Then, in the light of the full moon, behind a Signals Hut on the left, railroad tracks came into sight. A parallel spur, Goltz saw, held the Führer's eleven-car private railway train. A moment later, on the right, ringed with barbed wire and machine gun emplacements and towers, the first of the two inner compounds of Wolf's Lair came into sight. This one held, essentially, the personnel charged with the administration and protection of Wolfsschanze.

There were buildings assigned to the Camp Commandant and his staff; the headquarters of the battalion of Liebstandarte troops, and their barracks and mess hall; a second mess hall, dubbed the Kurhaus ("Sanitarium"); and a thick-walled concrete air-raid bunker, dubbed "Heinrich," large enough to hold everyone in the compound.

Past the first inner compound and to the right, lining the road for half a mile, were other small buildings that housed the second level of Thousand Year Reich officialdom. Here, spreading out from the Gorlitz Railway Station, were the offices of Foreign Minister Joachim von Ribbentrop; Albert Speer, Germany's war-production genius; GrossAdmiral Karl Doenitz, the Commander in Chief of the Navy; senior Luftwaffe officers; and another mess and another huge concrete bunker.

Across the road, ringed by barbed wire and the heaviest concentration of machine-gun and antiaircraft weaponry, was the Führer's compound itself.

Inside were no fewer than thirteen thick-walled concrete bunkers. The largest and thickest, not surprisingly, was the Führerbunker. Across the street from it were two other bunkers. One housed Hitler's personal aides and doctors; the second housed Wehrmacht aides, the Army personnel office, the Signal Officer, and Hitler's secretaries.

To the east Reichsmarschal Hermann Göring had both an office building and his own personal bunker. Between these and the Führerbunker was a VIP mess called the "Tea House." Nearby were the offices and bunker assigned to Field Marshal Wilhelm Keitel, titular head of the High Command of the Armed Forces (OKW). He shared his bunker with Generaloberst (Colonel General, the equivalent of a full — four-star — U.S. Army General) Alfred Jodl, the chief of the Armed Forces Operations Staff, and Admiral Wilhelm Canaris, Chief of the Abwehr, the military intelligence service of the OKW.

Once, when they were alone, Reichsleiter Martin Bormann had explained to Goltz that while Jodl was important enough to be given space inside the Führer's inner compound, he was not important enough to have his own bunker.

Bormann — who was deputy only to Hitler in running the Nazi party — of course had his own bunker, as did Josef Goebbels, the diminutive, clubfooted genius of Nazi propaganda. But Bormann's staff also had their own bunker, while Goebbels's staff did not. Although bunkers were provided for servants, liaison officers, and official visitors, Goebbels's underlings privileged to be in the Führer compound had to find bunker space for themselves.

Standartenführer Goltz believed that Wolfsschanze — rather than Berlin — provided the best clues to judging who stood where in the pecking order. And nothing he had ever seen — here, or in Berlin or anywhere else — had caused him to question the very senior and very secure position of Martin Bormann. That perception had provoked an interesting decision: Where did his loyalty lie? With Heinrich Himmler, who as head of the SS was his own direct superior? Or with Martin Bormann, with whom he had been close since the early days?

It would have been nice if the question had never come up. But when Himmler had assigned him as SS-SD liaison officer to the Office of the Party Chancellery — in other words, to Bormann — it did.

As Goltz was aware — and Bormann was equally aware — Himmler fully expected him to study Bormann and his immediate staff for signs of anything that Himmler could report to Hitler. And Himmler trusted him to do so. Goltz went a long way back with Himmler, too.

The question for Goltz had boiled down, finally, to what would best serve the Führer himself. For one thing, Goltz understood that while the Führer should be above politics, this was unfortunately not possible. And he understood further that while Reichsprotektor Himmler certainly could not be faulted for his untiring efforts to protect the Führer, Himmler was not above using the information that came his way for his own political purposes.

Bormann was, of course, no less a political creature than Himmler, and certainly just as willing to use information that came his way for political purposes. The difference was that Martin Bormann had no purpose in life but to serve the Führer, while Heinrich Himmler's basic purpose was to serve the State. Himmler would argue, of course, that Adolf Hitler and the German State were really one and the same thing, but in the final analysis, Goltz did not think that held water.

Thus, in a hypothetical situation, if Hitler were forced to choose between Bormann and Himmler, Goltz had no doubt that he would choose Bormann.

And so, even before he reported to Martin Borrann's office in the Reichschancellery, he had decided that his SS officer's oath required that he transfer his loyalty from Himmler to Bormann. In his mind, he had no other choice.

At the same time, he had come to believe that what had begun as a selfless act of duty — bread cast onto the water — was going to pay dividends. For one thing, Hitler had often confided in Bormann his suspicions that not all cowards and defeatists were in the Armed Forces. That the Führer was referring to the SS was a not unreasonable inference.

In Goltz's professional opinion, as a security man of some experience, defeatists and traitors were indeed in the highest echelons of the Army, just waiting for a chance to seize power, depose the Führer, and seek an armistice with the enemy. It was Himmler's job, the job of the SS, to ruthlessly root these men out. He had found some. But the Führer was correct in suspecting that he had not found all.

It logically followed — it was a question of numerical probability — that if there were X number of defeatists and potential traitors in the Army, then there were Y number in the Navy, Z number in the Luftwaffe, and even XX number in the SS. Goltz believed that the ratio probably was geometric. If there was one traitor in the SS, there were probably two in the Luftwaffe, four in the Navy, and eight in the Army.

In Goltz's view, Hitler might well pardon Himmler for not finding all the traitors in the Army, or even those in the Navy and Luftwaffe, but the first traitor uncovered in the SS would look to the Führer like proof that Himmler was incompetent . . . or even disloyal himself.

And it reasonably followed that if the Führer

decided that Himmler could no longer be trusted, then the Führer would not place a good deal of trust in Himmler's immediate underlings either. If Himmler was deposed — and this was far from inconceivable, if one remembered Röhm* — so would be those immediately under him.

And who would be better qualified to replace Himmler than Standartenführer Josef Goltz, who had not only been in the SS at senior levels long enough to know how that agency should operate, but who all along — literally since the days of the Burgerbraukeller in Munich — had been the trusted intimate of the faithful Martin Bormann?

The Mercedes stopped at the first of the entrances to the Führer compound. Obviously, the Hauptsturmführer at the gate in the outer wire had telephoned ahead not only to Bormann's office, but to the SS officer in charge of Führer compound security; for an Obersturmführer (First Lieutenant) was waiting for him.

"Heil Hitler!" he barked. "It is good to see the Herr Standartenführer again."

"Well, look who's here!" Goltz said, although he did not remember meeting the tall, good-looking Obersturmführer before. "How have you been?"

"Very well, thank you," the Obersturmführer said. "If you'll come with me, Sir, I will escort you to Reichsleiter Bormann's office."

"How kind of you," Goltz said, and followed him into the Führer compound, this time returning the guard's salute with an equally impeccable straight-armed salute.

---

* On Hitler's orders, Ernst Röhm, one of his oldest friends and head of the Sturmablietung (SA), was murdered by the SS June 30, 1934, on "The Night of the Long Knives."

[Three]

Wolfsschanze
Near Rastenburg, East Prussia
2200 5 April 1943

There were, of course, no windows in Bormann's office. Behind the oak paneling was several feet of solid concrete. On one wall hung an oil portrait of the Führer. Facing it on the opposite wall was a monstrous oil painting of the mountains near Garmisch-Partenkirchen. It had been a gift to the Führer, and he had given it to Bormann.

"I'm really sorry I kept you waiting, Josef," Reichsleiter Martin Bormann said, sounding as if he meant it. As he spoke, he stepped from behind his desk to greet Standartenführer Goltz. "How was the trip?"

Bormann was a short and stocky man, wearing a brown Nazi party uniform decorated only with the swastika brassard on his right sleeve and the Blood Order insignia pinned to his right breast. (The Blood Order decoration, awarded to those who participated in the — failed — 1923 coup d'état in Munich, was of red and silver, surmounted by an eagle, showing a view within an oak-leaf wreath of the Feldherrnhalle in Munich, and bore the legend "You Were Victorious.")

"Very long, Herr Reichsleiter," Goltz replied, returning the firm handshake.

"Well, at least you won't have to drive back to Berlin. I've arranged a seat for you on the Heinkel."

A Heinkel twin-engine bomber had been converted to a transport for high-speed service between Berlin and Wolf's Lair. Only six seats were avail-

22

able, and they were hard to come by unless spoken for by someone very high — Keitel, Göring, Bormann, or the Führer himself.

"Wonderful. Thank you."

"Reichsprotektor Himmler was kind enough to tell me early this morning that he had received word from Buenos Aires that a certain highly placed Argentine met a tragic death at the hands of bandits," Bormann said, getting immediately to the point that most immediately concerned Goltz, "and that he felt you could now travel to Buenos Aires without raising any suspicions that you were personally involved."

A faint smile crossed Goltz's lips. Oberst Karl-Heinz Grüner, Military Attaché of the Embassy of the German Reich to the Republic of Argentina, had sent a radio message to Himmler reporting the death of el Coronel Jorge Guillermo Frade. A copy of that message was delivered to Goltz in Berlin an hour before Himmler saw it. Goltz had immediately called Bormann.

"I did not, of course, tell him that I had already received the same information," Bormann went on. "I *did* tell him that was good news, as I had finally received the last signature on the document, and suggested he order you here personally to pick it up. He told me that you were already en route."

"Everyone has come on board?"

"Canaris last, of course," Bormann said, smiling, and walked behind his desk, pulled open a drawer, and handed Goltz a business-size envelope. Goltz took from it a single sheet of paper, folded in thirds, and read it.

Nationalsozialistische Deutsche Arbeiterpartei

Berlin 1 April 1943

The bearer, SS-SD Standartenführer Josef Goltz, has been charged with the execution of highly confidential missions of the highest importance to the German Reich.

In his sole discretion, SS-SD Standartenführer Goltz will make the nature of his missions known only to such persons as he feels may assist him in the execution of his missions. Such persons are —

1. Directed to provide SS-SD Standartenführer Goltz with whatever support, of whatever nature, he may request.

2. Absolutely forbidden to divulge any information whatsoever concerning SS-SD Standartenführer Goltz' missions to any other person without the express permission of SS-SD Standartenführer Josef Goltz, including communication by any means whatsoever any reference to SS-SD Standartenführer Goltz' missions to any agency of the German Reich, or any person, without the express permission in each instance of SS-SD Standartenführer Josef Goltz.

M. Bormann
Reichsleiter Martin Bormann
NSDAP

Keitel
Wilhelm Keitel
Feldmarschal

H. Himmler
Heinrich Himmler
Reichsprotecktor

Doenitz
Karl Doenitz
Grand Admiral

JvR
Joachim von Ribbentrop
Foreign Minister

Canaris
Wilhelm Canaris
Rearadmiral, Abwehr

Goltz raised his eyes to Bormann.

"A very impressive document, Herr Reichsleiter," he said. He refolded the letter and put it back in the envelope. "Do I understand that I am to keep this?"

Bormann nodded.

"While you were on your way here," Bormann said, "Reichsprotektor Himmler called again, to inform me that he had obtained a seat for you on the Lufthansa flight leaving Templehof for Buenos Aires tomorrow."

Goltz put the envelope in an inside pocket of his uniform.

"You don't seem too happy to hear that," Bormann said. "Is duty about to interfere with your love life, Josef?"

"I never allow duty to interfere with my love life," Goltz replied. "What you see is a mixture of anticipation, curiosity, and unease, Herr Reichsleiter."

"Unease about what?"

"I hope you're not placing too much confidence in me."

"Modesty doesn't become you, Josef. And you know how important this endeavor is."

"I will, of course, do my best."

Bormann nodded.

"I had a thought," he said, moving to another subject, "when they told me you were at the outer wire, and again while you were waiting. Vis-à-vis von Wachtstein."

"Oh?"

"I have a feeling his son might be very useful to us. Particularly if the Generalleutnant himself were participating in the endeavor." (A Generalleutnant is literally a lieutenant general, but is equivalent to

25

a U.S. Army — two-star — major general.) "I won't say anything to him, of course, until you have a chance to look at the situation in Buenos Aires and let me know what you think. But why don't you pay a courtesy call on him now, Josef, ask if there is something you could carry for him to his son — a letter, perhaps?"

"A very good idea," Goltz said. "I was, what shall I say, a little surprised at how close the von Wachtsteins are to poverty. If we are to believe the Generalleutnant's estate-tax return."

"Perhaps he dug a hole with his paws and buried a bone or two in it for a rainy day. After all, he is a Pomeranian."

Goltz smiled.

"While he is preparing whatever he wishes to send — give him an hour, say — you come back here and we'll talk."

"Yes, Sir."

"He's across the road, but I'll send you in my car so you won't have to walk."

"That's very good of you."

"In lieu of a drink, Josef. I'm taking dinner with the Führer, and I don't want to smell of alcohol."

Goltz chuckled. The Führer was an ascetic man who neither smoked nor drank. There was an unwritten law that those privileged to be in his presence also abstained.

Generalleutnant Graf (Count) Karl-Friedrich von Wachtstein was a short, slight, nearly bald fifty-four-year-old, the seventh of his Pomeranian line to earn the right to be called "General." Originally a cavalryman, he had joined the General Staff as an Oberstleutnant (Lieutenant Colonel) eight years before.

When war broke out, he went into Poland at that rank but assumed command of a Panzer regiment when its colonel was killed in his tank turret during an unexpectedly difficult encirclement maneuver. His Polish opponent, they later learned, had instructed his troops to save their rifle fire for officers who gallantly exposed themselves in tank turrets. Afterward, he was promoted to colonel.

He went into Russia commanding a tank regiment, and was fairly seriously wounded. When Generaloberst Jodl heard this — von Wachstein had worked under Jodl as a major — he decided that the Army could not afford to have an unusually bright general staff officer killed doing something as unimportant as commanding troops in combat, and ordered him back to Berlin. With the transfer came a promotion to Generalmajor (literally, Major General, but equivalent to a U.S. Army — one-star — Brigadier General).

Earlier this year, in February, following a shakeup in the General Staff after the Sixth Army's surrender at Stalingrad, he was promoted Generalleutnant, with the additional honor of having the Führer personally pin on his new badges of rank.

"What the General Staff needs, Jodl," the Führer had said at the small promotion ceremony in his bunker, "is more general officers like Graf von Wachtstein and myself — men who have been exposed to fire."

Hitler had won the Iron Cross First Class — an unusual decoration for a lowly corporal — in the First World War, and was fond of reminding his generals that, unlike many of them, he had been tested under fire.

"Hello, Goltz," von Wachtstein said, returning Goltz's salute with an equally casual raising of his arm from the elbow, palm extended. "What can I do for you, beyond offering you coffee?"

"Coffee would be fine, Herr Generalleutnant," Goltz replied. "It was a long ride from Berlin."

Von Wachtstein mimed raising a coffee cup to his lips to his chief clerk, Feldwebel (Technical Sergeant) Alois Hennig, a tall, blond twenty-two-year-old.

"Jawohl, Herr Generalleutnant," Hennig said, and left them alone.

"Reichsleiter Bormann is in conference," Goltz said. "I thought I would pass the time paying my respects to you."

"Bormann is a busy man," von Wachtstein said.

"I'm about to go to Buenos Aires."

"I'd heard something about that."

"I thought of your son, of course, when I received my orders."

"I'm sure he would be delighted to show you around Buenos Aires," von Wachtstein said. "By now I'm sure he is familiar with everything of interest. Most of that, unless he has suddenly reformed, will be wearing skirts."

"He does have that reputation, doesn't he? Have you heard from him lately?"

"Not often. The odd letter. He was apparently asleep in church when they went through that 'Honor Thy Father' business."

Goltz chuckled.

"And then the mail is erratic, isn't it? I thought perhaps I could carry a letter for you."

"That would be very kind, but irregular," von Wachtstein said.

"Even if it came to anyone's attention — and I

28

can't see how it would — I don't think there would be any serious questions about someone in my position doing a small service to an old friend."

"I would be very grateful, Goltz, but I don't want to impose on our friendship."

"It would be no imposition at all."

"When are you leaving Wolfsschanze?"

"Whenever the Heinkel leaves. The Herr Reichsleiter got me a seat on it."

"There is something," von Wachtstein said. "In one letter he complained that he has only one set of major's badges . . ."

"That's right, he was promoted, wasn't he?"

". . . and spends a good deal of time carefully moving them from one uniform to another. I could probably get a set or two here. . . ."

"I'd be delighted to carry them to him."

"Thank you."

Feldwebel Hennig appeared with two cups of coffee on a wooden tray.

"The African coffee, Herr Generalleutnant," he said. "Unfortunately, about the last of it."

"You're a bright youngster, Hennig," von Wachtstein said. "I have every confidence that you will be able to steal some more somewhere."

"I happen to have a source of coffee, good coffee," Goltz said. "I'll tell my office to send you a couple of kilos with the next messenger."

"And I was not really glad to see you, Josef, when you walked in here. I shamelessly accept."

"Friends should take care of one another, shouldn't they?"

"A noble sentiment."

As Hennig was setting the tray down, one of the three telephones on von Wachtstein's desk rang. Hennig moved to answer it but stopped.

"It's the red line, Herr Generalleutnant," he said.

A red-line telephone — so called because the instrument was red — was another symbol of status in Wolfsschanze. There were only fifty red-line instruments. The special switchboard for these had been installed so that Hitler and very senior officials could talk directly to one another without wasting time speaking to secretaries. Those who had red-line telephones were expected to answer them themselves.

"Heil Hitler, von Wachtstein," he said, picking it up.

"Canaris," the Chief of the Abwehr identified himself. "I understand Standartenführer Goltz is with you?"

"Yes, he is. One moment, please, Herr Admiral," von Wachtstein said, and handed the phone to Goltz. "Admiral Canaris."

"Yes, Herr Admiral?" Goltz said, listened a moment, and then said, "I ask the Herr Admiral's indulgence to finish my cup of the Herr Generalleutnant's excellent coffee." There was a pause, and then, chuckling, "I'll tell him that, Herr Admiral. Thank you."

He handed the telephone back to von Wachtstein.

"Admiral Canaris said that if you have excellent coffee, you have the only excellent coffee in Wolfsschanze, and it is clearly your duty as an old comrade to tell him where you found it."

"Actually, Peter got that for me in North Africa. He ferried a Heinkel over, and brought that back with him."

"Maybe he wasn't asleep in church after all," Goltz said. "May I suggest you get your son's rank badges as soon as you can, and if you're going to send a letter, write it as soon as possible. Within the hour."

"You're very kind, Josef."

"Not at all. After all, since you served me the last of your African coffee, it is the least I can do."

"Please give my regards to the Admiral," Generalleutnant von Wachtstein said.

[Four]

Admiral Canaris was preoccupied. He did not acknowledge Goltz's salute, and although he looked up when Goltz entered, Goltz felt that his mind was far away.

But then, suddenly, he felt Canaris's eyes examining him coldly.

"This won't take long, Standartenführer," Canaris said. "But I have a few things to say to you before you leave for Argentina."

"I will be grateful for any direction the Herr Admiral may wish to give me."

Canaris ignored that too.

"One. I agreed to the elimination of Oberst Frade with great reluctance. But in the end, I decided the risk that he would assume the presidency was unacceptable. It was entirely possible, in my judgment, that he might well have had sufficient influence to obtain a declaration of war against us — especially in the period immediately following the seizure of power by the Grupo de Oficiales Unidos. The implications of that should be obvious. Not only does Germany need Argentine food

31

and wool, but as Argentina goes, so will go Uruguay, Paraguay, Chile, and probably Peru."

"I understand, Herr Admiral."

"His elimination, Standartenführer, was not without price. I know the Argentine Officer Corps. While the great majority of Argentine Army officers are sympathetic to the National Socialist cause, they will deeply resent the elimination of Oberst Frade. Not only was he a popular figure, but the Argentines are a nationalist people. They understandably resent an action like that occurring on their soil. Meanwhile, it is to be hoped that in time the necessity of our act will be understood, and later accepted. The goodwill of the Argentine Officer Corps is an asset we cannot afford to squander; and I admonish you, Standartenführer, to do everything possible to avoid further antagonizing them."

"I understand, Herr Admiral."

"For that reason alone, I did not sign your mission order until after the elimination had taken place. I did not want you suspected of any responsibility for it. That, in my judgment, would have been the case had you been in Buenos Aires at the time the elimination was carried out."

"I understand, Herr Admiral."

"Two. Regarding the *Reine de la Mer* incident. The Portuguese government has protested — has von Ribbentrop gone into this with you?"

The Portuguese vessel *Reine de la Mer* (really a replacement, replenishment vessel for German U-boats) was sunk in Argentine waters — by Americans, everyone believed but could not directly prove.

"I received a Foreign Ministry briefing, Herr Admiral."

Canaris looked at him for a long moment. "Well?"

"I was informed that the Portuguese government has in the strongest possible terms protested the sinking to the United States government. I was further informed that the Americans deny any knowledge of this."

"The Portuguese have also protested strongly to the Argentine government," Admiral Canaris added. "More important, the Spanish Foreign Ministry called in the American ambassador to express their 'grave concerns' about the *Reine de la Mer*, and made it clear that there would be 'grave consequences' if anything like that happened in the future to a vessel flying the Spanish flag."

"So I was informed, Herr Admiral," Goltz said. "The Spanish said they would regard such an attack as 'an unpardonable act of war.'"

"Since the Americans do not wish to see the Spanish join the Axis, Standartenführer, one would think that would be enough to make them think twice about attacking a Spanish-registered vessel in Argentine waters. Or even boarding a Spanish vessel on the high seas to search for contraband. Were you briefed thoroughly on this by the Navy?"

"I was informed during my Navy briefing: That the replacement replenishment vessel will sail from Sweden, via the English channel, directly to Buenos Aires. That she will notify both the German and British authorities she is bound for Argentina. And that she will have the Spanish flag on her hull floodlighted at night, so there can be no mistake as to her nationality and neutral status."

"And?"

"That five other Spanish and Portuguese vessels

33

will be crossing the Atlantic toward Argentina at the same time —"

"*Not* at the same time!" Canaris interrupted impatiently.

"I misspoke, Herr Admiral. Pardon me," Goltz said. "At twenty-four-hour and forty-eight-hour intervals *ahead* of the *Comerciante del Océano Pacífico*."

"The idea is that the Americans, who expect us, of course, to send a vessel to replace the *Reine de la Mer*, will board any suspicious vessel. We have taken steps to make sure their agents in Spain and Portugal believe the other ships are suspicious. The moment the Americans stop Ship One, the vessel will radio that it is being boarded. The Portuguese or Spanish will immediately summon the American ambassadors in Lisbon and Madrid to protest. If the Americans sight the *Comerciante del Océano Pacífico* — who will be doing her very best to avoid being sighted (she'll sail far into the South Atlantic, and then approach Buenos Aires from the south) — perhaps they will not be so eager to stop her after this has happened two, three, or four times."

"I thought it was a clever plan, Herr Admiral," Goltz said.

"It is overly complicated, and enormously expensive, and I would not give it more than a fifty-fifty chance of succeeding," Canaris said coldly. "It was justifiable only in that a replenishment vessel is essential for submarine operations in the South Atlantic."

"I understand, Herr Admiral."

"Two of three members of the OSS team which took out the *Reine de la Mer* left Argentina immediately afterward. The team leader, Oberst Frade's son, and a man named Pelosi. Pelosi returned four days ago. . . .”

“I had not heard that, Herr Admiral.”

“There was a radio from Oberst Grüner. He's a good man. He has someone in the Foreign Ministry. Pelosi now has diplomatic status, as an assistant military attaché. My feeling is that he was returned to assist a follow-on OSS team which will probably be sent when the Americans learn we have replaced the *Reine de la Mer*.”

“The third man of the OSS team? The Jew?”

“He is still in Argentina, working covertly. The Americans apparently feel he can garner information from the Jews in Buenos Aires. Shipping information, that sort of thing. The head of their FBI in Buenos Aires is also a Jew. I have the feeling Ettinger, the Jew, may be working for him, and no longer is connected with the OSS. In my judgment, that OSS team — they are of course known to the Argentines — has ceased to exist as an operational unit. Thus I believe we can count on the OSS sending an entirely new team down there when the Americans learn the *Océano Pacífico* is on station. When that happens, it may be necessary to eliminate them. This of course has to be done very carefully — referring to my earlier remarks about not antagonizing the Argentine sense of nationalism. The first OSS team down there was eliminated with great skill by Grüner — there was not even notice of it in the newspapers. Please tell him I expect the same sort of first-class work when the time comes to deal with the next OSS team to show its face.”

“Of course, Herr Admiral,” Goltz said with a smile.

Canaris looked at him curiously, as if surprised

that his words could have been interpreted in any way as amusing.

"May I ask a question, Herr Admiral?"

Canaris waited for him to go on.

"The third member of the former OSS team. You say he is working with the Jews in Buenos Aires? Is there a possibility —"

"That he will put his nose into the source of our special funds?" Canaris interrupted. "Yes, of course there is. If that happens, you have permission to eliminate him, taking the same great care I've been talking about."

"And not before, as a precautionary measure?"

"I'm getting the idea I am not making my point about Argentine sensitivity, Standartenführer. Let me make it again. You will do nothing that might even remotely annoy the Argentines unless there is absolutely no other option. We want them to think of us as allies in the war against communism, not, for example, as the kind of people who come to their country and blow up ships or eliminate people. Now, is that clear?"

"Perfectly, Herr Admiral."

Canaris looked at him coldly, as if wondering why someone with such visibly limited mental powers could be entrusted with the mission he had been given.

"Three, Standartenführer," Canaris went on after a long moment. "I have supported from the beginning the idea of acquiring property in Argentina for operational purposes. As a matter of fact, the concept was originally mine. If my recommendations had been listened to as far back as 1937, we would already have property in place. Not only for the immediate operation planned, but for other purposes. I repeated these recommendations at the time the *Graf Spee** was scuttled, and again nothing was done. The result of that inactivity is now obvious. Here we are embarked on an operation far more important than anything else I can think of — important to the very existence of the Thousand Year Reich. And we're starting from scratch so far as acquiring property is concerned. Not to mention that we have been unable until now to even seriously plan to repatriate the *Graf Spee* officers, something that should have been done three years ago."

Goltz could think of no tactful way to respond, and said nothing.

"I want you to clearly understand, Standartenführer," Canaris went on, "that I view the property you will acquire as a long-term asset, not something which can be, so to speak, expended in the course of the repatriation operation. Do you understand that?"

"I understand, Herr Admiral."

"Good," Canaris said. He extended his hand. "That's all I have. Thank you for coming to see me. Good luck."

Goltz saw in Canaris's eyes that he had already been dismissed.

---

* On December 13, 1939, in what became known as "The Battle of the River Plate," the battle-damaged German pocket battleship *Graf Spee* was driven into the harbor of Montevideo in neutral Uruguay by the British and New Zealand cruisers HMS *Ajax* and HMNZS *Achilles*. Intense diplomatic pressure from England and the United States forced the Uruguayan government to order the *Graf Spee* to leave the harbor within the seventy-two-hour period called for by the Geneva Convention, or be interned. On December 17, 1939, at the personal order of Adolf Hitler, the *Graf Spee* was scuttled just outside Montevideo to keep her from falling into British hands. The German community in Buenos Aires, 125 miles across the river Plate, chartered a fleet of small boats and took her crew to Argentina, where they were interned.

II

[One]

Café Lafitte
Bourbon Street
New Orleans, Louisiana
1535 5 April 1943

The bar was crowded, smoke-filled, hot, noisy, and reeked of sweat and urine. Most of the patrons were servicemen, and most of these were sailors, sweating in their blue woolen winter uniforms. A pair of Shore Patrolmen stood just inside the door, each holding a billy club in one hand and a paper cup of soft drink in the other.

As the young man in a tieless white button-down collar shirt and a seersucker jacket elbowed his way toward the bar, he was aware that he was getting dirty looks from some of the sailors. He thought he knew why: *Hey, what the hell are you doing out of uniform, when here I am, three weeks out of Great Lakes Naval Training Center and about to go out and save the world for democracy?*

The last thing in the world the young man — who was twenty-three years old, and whose name was Cletus Howell Frade — wanted to do was find himself in a confrontation with a half-plastered nineteen-year-old swab jockey. It seemed to be the

38

final proof that coming in here for a Sazerac cocktail was not the smartest thing he had done today.

He knew for a fact that the Café Lafitte made lousy Sazerac cocktails. But ten minutes before, when he first got the idea to have a symbolic farewell Sazerac, and in the Café Lafitte, which was supposed to have been in business since Christ was a corporal, it seemed a good idea.

The bartender, a corpulent forty-year-old with a stained white apron around his waist, looked at him, his eyebrows signaling he was ready to accept an order.

"Sazerac, please."

"I got to see your draft card," the bartender said in what Clete recognized to be a New Orleans accent.

"What?"

"We're cooperating with the authorities," the bartender said. "Gotta see your draft card."

Clete took out his wallet and removed a plastic identification card — not a draft card — and handed it to the bartender. The bartender examined it carefully and compared the face on the photograph with the face of the young man standing before him.

He did not seem wholly satisfied, but he handed the card back, said, "I thought you had to wear your uniform," and turned to make a Sazerac.

Clete was about to put the card back in his wallet when he felt a hand on his arm. He turned and saw one of the Shore Patrolmen standing beside him, and the second SP standing behind the first.

"Could I have a look at that, please?" the SP said politely, but it was a demand, not a request.

Clete nodded and handed it to him. The SP went through the business of comparing the photograph on the card with Clete's face, then held the card over his shoulder so the other SP could have a look.

"It looks, Sir," the SP said, "like you're out of uniform. Could I have a look at your orders, please, Sir?"

Clete reached into the inside pocket of the seersucker jacket and came out with a single sheet of mimeograph paper, folded twice. He handed this to the SP, who unfolded it.

"Paragraph seven authorizes me to wear civvies," he said.

The SP found Paragraph 7, read it, and then showed the orders to the SP standing behind him and stuck out his lower lip, registering surprise.

"I never saw orders like that, Sir," the SP said. "But I guess it's all right. Sorry to have troubled you, Sir."

Clete smiled and nodded, and put the orders back in his pocket. Then he turned back to the bar as his Sazerac was served.

He laid a five-dollar bill on the bar, then picked up his Sazerac and took a sip. It was a lousy Sazerac, as he was afraid it would be. When he was a student at Tulane he'd had enough of them to become a judge. And had painfully learned that the second would taste better than the first, the third better than the second, and the fourth would strike one treacherously in the back of the head, causing one so stupid as to drink that many to lose not only inhibitions but often consciousness and all memory of what happened subsequently.

Sazerac drinking had another facet, he thought, as he took a second sip. When fed to a well-bred young woman, taking care to administer the proper dosage — an overdose usually produced a number of unpleasant side effects, ranging from nausea to unconsciousness — quite often produced both a diminishment of inhibitions and a concomitant urge to couple.

Get thee behind me, Satan! he thought, when he realized the direction his mental processes were taking him. *That sort of thing is in your past. You are no longer free to nail any female you can entice into a horizontal position. Your watchword, like that of the goddamn U.S. Marine Crotch itself, is now* Semper Fidelis, *always faithful.*

He drained his glass, and felt the alcohol warm his veins. He picked up his change, shouldered his way back out of the Café Lafitte onto Bourbon Street, and headed toward Canal Street, where, he thought, with a little bit of luck he would find a taxi.

[Two]

3470 St. Charles Avenue
New Orleans, Louisiana
1905 5 April 1943

The taxi dropped Major Cletus Howell Frade off at the curb before a very large, very white, turn-of-the-century ornate, three-story frame mansion on St. Charles Avenue, the tree-lined main boundary of the section of New Orleans known as the Garden District.

He crossed the sidewalk, opened a gate in the cast-iron fence that separated an immaculate lawn from the street, and walked up the brick path onto the porch, fishing for keys in his pocket. Before he could put them in the lock, the leaded-window door swung inward.

A silver-haired, very light-skinned Negro butler wearing a gray linen jacket smiled at him.

"What were you doing, Jean-Jacques? Peeking through the curtains, waiting for me?"

"I just happened to be looking out the window, Mr. Cletus," Jean-Jacques replied. "Miss Martha's here, Mr. Cletus."

"Miss Martha," the former Martha Reed Williamson, was Clete's aunt and the widow of the late James Fitzhugh Howell. Her husband had died instantaneously of a cerebral hemorrhage en route from the bar to the men's room of the Midland Petroleum Club shortly after Clete had flown his Wildcat off the escort carrier USS *Long Island* onto Guadalcanal's Henderson Field.

"She is?" Clete asked, surprised. He had said goodbye to Martha in Midland three days before. "The girls?"

The girls were his cousins, Elizabeth (Beth), who was twenty-one and about to graduate from Rice, and Marjorie, who was nineteen and in her sophomore year at that institution. Miss Martha became pregnant with Beth shortly after she took into her bride's home the two-year-old son of her husband's sister, Eleanor Patricia Frade, deceased. She raised Clete as her own, and her daughters and her nephew always thought of themselves as brother and sisters.

Jean-Jacques shook his head, "no." Clete was disappointed. Marjorie and Beth seemed to be less a royal pain in the ass recently than earlier on.

"Miss Martha drove up from Houston," Jean-Jacques said. "Got here just after you went to town. Must have gotten up in the middle of the night to start out."

He pointed at a Kraft paper bag in Clete's hand.

"You want me to put that in your room for you? They're in the library, and I know he and Miss Martha *have* been peeking out the curtains looking for you."

"He" was Cletus Marcus Howell, master of the house, Chairman of the Board of Howell Petroleum, and Clete's grandfather.

"No, thanks, I want another look at it."

"Anything I can get for you?"

"No, thanks," Clete replied, and then changed his mind. "Yeah, there is. I just had a god-awful Sazerac, and I'd like a good one."

"My pleasure," Jean-Jacques said. "One Jean-Jacques Jouvier world-famous Sazerac coming right up."

Clete crossed the wide foyer and entered the library.

A tall, pale, slender, sharp-featured, silver-haired man glowered at him. He was wearing a superbly tailored dark blue, faintly pin-striped three-piece suit, with a golden watch chain looped across his stomach.

"Well, look what the cat dragged in," the Old Man said. "Ran out of rotgut in the Vieux Carre, did they?"

"Grandfather," Clete said, and walked to his aunt Martha, a tanned, stocky, short-haired blond woman, and kissed her cheek.

"He had no way of knowing I was coming," she said, defending him.

"What brings you here?" Clete asked.

"What do you think? I wanted to see you before you left," Martha said.

"I'm flattered," he said.

"You know Mr. Needham, I believe, Cletus?" the Old Man said.

43

"No, Sir, I don't believe I do."

Mr. Needham was a bald, nearly obese middle-aged man who had removed his jacket and rolled up his white shirtsleeves so that he could more easily practice his art.

He was standing before an oil portrait of Cletus Howell Frade in a Marine Officer's dress-blue uniform. He turned to look at Clete, smiled, wiped his hand on a rag, and extended it to Clete.

"I'm honored to meet you, Sir," he said. "A genuine privilege to meet one of our country's heroes."

Clete looked uncomfortable.

"How do you do?" he said, then: "I didn't know you could do that."

"Do what?" his grandfather asked.

"What's the word? 'Fix'? 'Change'? Go back and change one of those once it was done."

"Of course you can. That's an oil portrait, not a photograph," the Old Man said.

"I'm really glad you're here, Major," Mr. Needham said. "I want everything to be just right."

He pointed to Clete's dress-blue tunic, laid out, complete to Sam Browne belt and officer's saber, against the back of a red leather couch.

"I had Antoinette bring that down from your room," the Old Man said. "Mr. Needham had little difficulty changing your rank insignia to a major's. Your decorations — including that Navy Cross you somehow forgot to tell me about — posed more of a problem."

"It looks fine to me," Clete said after comparing the tunic with the nearly complete work on the portrait. "I'm really impressed with someone like you, Mr. Needham. I can't draw a straight line."

"How is it, Cletus," the Old Man pursued, "that

I had to learn of your Navy Cross from Senator Brewer?"

"What's the name of that play? *Much Ado About Nothing*?"

"They don't hand out the Navy Cross for nothing," the Old Man said. "You can tell us about it now."

Jean-Jacques appeared with four Sazeracs in long-stemmed glasses on a silver tray.

"Saved by the Sazeracs," Clete said, taking one. "Thank you, Jean-Jacques."

"I don't recall asking for a Sazerac," the Old Man said.

"Not to worry, Jean-Jacques," Martha said. "If he doesn't want his, Mr. Needham, Cletus, and I will split it."

"I didn't say I didn't want it, I said I didn't remember asking for it," the Old Man said. "Thank you, Jean-Jacques."

Needham took his glass and raised it to Clete.

"To your very good health, Sir," he said.

"Thank you," Clete said.

"Hear, hear," the Old Man said.

Clete sipped his Sazerac, then set it down and opened the brown paper bag, taking from it a pair of binoculars.

"What have you got there?" the old man asked.

"A pair of Bausch and Lomb 8-by-57-mm binoculars," Clete replied. "I just bought them. I'm sure they're stolen."

"What in the world are you talking about?"

"You asked what I have here, and I'm telling you."

"If they're stolen, where did you get them?" Martha asked.

"In a pawnshop on Canal Street."

He saw that the stolen binoculars now had the Old Man's attention. With a little bit of luck, that would end the questioning about the Navy Cross.

"Why do you think they're stolen?" Martha pursued.

The moment Clete saw the binoculars in the pawnshop he knew they were stolen. For one thing, there was a burnished area (freshly painted over) by the adjustment screw where the Navy customarily engraved *USN* and the serial number. For another, the price was right, and finally the pawnshop proprietor was exceedingly reluctant to provide a bill of sale. He reduced the price even further on the condition that Clete take possession without paperwork.

Instead of a sense of outrage at the theft, Clete felt a certain admiration for the thief. It had been his experience as an officer of the Naval Service that the three most difficult things to steal from the Navy were pistols, binoculars, and aviator chronographs.

When he was in Washington, where he had spent most of the last six weeks, he would not have been at all surprised if some dedicated, and outraged, Marine Corps supply officer had shown up at Eighth and Eye* — or for that matter, had burst into OSS Headquarters in the National Institutes of Health Building — and demanded either the return of his Corps-issued Hamilton chronograph or payment therefore, since he was no longer in a flying billet.

The first time he was shot down, he parachuted into the waters off Tulagi and was rescued by a PT boat. As they roared back to the "Canal," her

---

* Headquarters, USMC, is at Eighth and I Streets in Washington, D.C.

skipper suggested to him that if he put the Hamilton into his pocket, it might be considered "Lost In Combat."

Since a small gift of a government-issued chronograph to a fellow officer of the Naval Service whose vessel had plucked him from shark-infested waters seemed appropriate, Lieutenant Frade took that Hamilton off his wrist and gave it to him, together with his saltwater-soaked .45 Colt automatic and its holster.

He was, of course, issued another Hamilton chronograph and another .45, but only after a dedicated supply officer (literally during a Japanese strafing raid on Henderson Field) offered him the choice of either paying for both, or signing a two-page document swearing, under pain of perjury — the awesome punishments for which were spelled out in some detail on the form — that they had really and truly, Boy Scout's Honor, cross my heart and hope to die, been lost in combat.

He had paid. The Hamilton on his wrist now was still on some supply officer's books somewhere.

"Look here," Clete said. "You can see where someone ground off 'USN' and the serial number."

Martha looked, and then the Old Man looked.

"If you believed them to be stolen, why did you buy them?" the Old Man asked, incredulously.

"I wanted them," Clete explained reasonably. "You can't just walk into the optical department of Maison Blanche and buy them anymore. The Navy takes all that Bausch and Lomb can make."

"The morality of the question never entered your mind?" Martha asked, with a tolerant smile.

"Oh, but it did. Since they had already been

stolen, I decided the higher morality was to make sure they were put to use by a bona fide commissioned officer of the Naval Service, such as myself, rather than, for example, by some tout watching the ponies run at the racetrack."

"You have a screw loose, you know that? Your deck of cards is at least four or five short of the necessary fifty-two. A genetic flaw from your father's side," the Old Man said, and then had what he thought was a sudden insight. "You're pulling our leg, right? Taking advantage of an old man and woman who trust you?"

"Pulling your leg about what?"

The Old Man looked at him suspiciously, then changed the subject.

"Tell me about the Navy Cross," he demanded. "The Senator said the citation was very vague."

"You really want to know?"

"No. Not really. Why should I care how my only grandson earned the nation's second-highest award for gallantry?"

"I'd like to know too," Martha said.

"Well, there I was, cruising along at ten thousand feet, with nothing between me and the earth but a thin blonde . . ."

"Oh, God!" Martha said.

"Spare us your vulgar sense of humor, if you please," the Old Man said sternly, but unable to keep a smile from his lips. "You will have to excuse my grandson, Mr. Needham. He frequently forgets we tried to raise him to be a gentleman."

"I'd venture to say, Mr. Howell, that the Major is simply being modest," Mr. Needham said.

"I suppose that's possible," the Old Man said, visibly pleased. "Unlikely, but possible." He changed the subject: "Well, at least we've had the chance to make sure the portrait is technically accurate, haven't we? There was a problem of time. My grandson returns to duty tomorrow."

"Oh, is that so?" Needham replied. "Where are you going, Major? Or isn't a civilian supposed to ask? 'Loose Lips Sink Ships'?"

"Actually, I'm going to Buenos Aires," Clete said. "And, so far as I know, that's not a military secret."

"Buenos Aires?" Needham asked.

"It's in Argentina," the Old Man offered helpfully.

"About as far from the war as you can get," Clete said.

"Thank God for that," Martha said.

"Cletus has been appointed Assistant Naval Attaché at our embassy there," the Old Man said.

"That sounds very interesting," Needham said. "I don't know anything about Argentina, except, you know, what is it they call their cowboys?"

"Gauchos," Clete said.

"And lovely dark-eyed señoritas . . ."

"And some lovely blue-eyed señoritas," Clete said, thinking of one of the latter in particular.

"Oh, really?" Martha said, picking up on that. "Has your blue-eyed señorita got a name?"

"You sound like you've been there before," Needham said, sparing Clete from having to respond to Martha.

"Yes, I have."

"Unfortunately, he was born there," the Old Man said.

"Really?"

Clete gave the Old Man a warning look. The Old Man met his eyes defiantly, but after a moment, backed off.

"I hope you haven't made plans for dinner, Cletus," the Old Man said. "For reasons I can't imagine, Martha just told me she wants to go to Arnaud's."

"No, Sir," Clete said. "I was planning to have dinner here, with you."

"Another indication that you're not playing with a full deck," the Old Man said. "Why in the world would you prefer to have dinner with me, as opposed to having dinner with a young woman very likely to be dazzled by your uniform and medals?"

"Because you are my grandfather, and despite some monumental flaws of your own, I would rather spend time with you than anyone else I can think of except Martha."

The Old Man looked at him. Tears formed in his eyes. He turned and went to the wall and pulled the call bell.

Jean-Jacques Jouvier appeared almost immediately.

"Call Arnaud's," the Old Man ordered, his voice sounding strange. "Tell them I require a private dining room for three at eight. Tell them — understanding this dinner is important to me — they may prepare whatever they wish. Arrange for the car at 7:45. And when you've done that, bring us another round of Sazeracs."

Jean-Jacques nodded and left the room.

The Old Man looked at Clete, then pointed at the uniform tunic on the red leather couch.

"Since it's already off its hanger, would it be inconvenient for you to wear that?"

"Not at all," Clete said. "Is Arnaud's offering a discount for servicemen?"

"I don't know," the Old Man said. "But now that you've mentioned it, I'll be sure to ask."

[Three]

Arnaud's Restaurant
The Vieux Carre
New Orleans, Louisiana
2030 5 April 1943

When the 1938 Durham-bodied Cadillac pulled up to the over-the-sidewalk canopy of the French Quarter Landmark — it was said that the Marquis de Lafayette wanted to dine at Arnaud's but couldn't get a table — one of the proprietors, who was functioning as the maître d'hôtel, and a waiter came out the door.

"I was hoping you'd change your mind, again, Mr. Howell," the proprietor said as the Old Man, grunting, stepped out of the car.

"I'd heard business was bad, but I wasn't aware it was so bad you had to stand on the street shanghaiing customers," the Old Man said.

Clete laughed.

"Stop that," Martha said. "The last thing you want to do is encourage him."

"You remember my daughter-in-law, of course, Edward?" the Old Man asked.

"Of course. Nice to see you again, too, Mrs. Howell."

"And my grandson?"

"Of course. Miz Howell, Mr. Frade."

"That's *Major* Frade, Edward. What did you think he's wearing? A doorman's uniform?"

"It's good to see you, too," Clete said, shaking hands.

"For reasons I cannot fathom, Mrs. Howell wished to have dinner here tonight, and my grandson went along with her. Personally, if this were to be my last meal in New Orleans for a while, I could think of half a dozen other places besides your greasy spoon," the Old Man said.

"Well, we'll try to see that Major Frade doesn't go away hungry."

"That'll be a pleasant change," the Old Man said, and, following the waiter, walked into the restaurant. The proprietor, Martha, and Clete smiled at each other, shaking their heads. The proprietor bowed Martha into the restaurant ahead of him.

"Would you like anything special?" the proprietor asked Clete. "All I heard was that the dinner was important to him. I didn't know who."

"How are the oysters?" Clete asked.

"Compared to what?" the proprietor asked.

"Hey, this is me, not my grandfather." Clete chuckled.

"How would you like them?"

"On the half-shell."

"These are nice, you'll like them," the proprietor said. "I was going to suggest on the half-shell."

The little procession moved past the long line of people waiting for tables and on to the rear of the lower dining room. The Old Man, who had been taking half a dozen meals a week in Arnaud's since he was twelve, was one of the rare exceptions to the rule that Arnaud's did not accept reservations. A small room with a curtained door was waiting for them, the table set up elaborately, including a candelabra. Three wine coolers held napkin-wrapped bottles.

The proprietor took a bottle of champagne from one of them, skillfully popped the cork, and poured.

"I don't recall ordering champagne," the Old Man said.

"It's for Mrs. Howell and Major Frade," the proprietor said. "They, at least, appreciate a nice glass of wine."

"Major Frade also expects a serviceman's discount."

"Tonight the serviceman's discount, one hundred percent, applies to him and any of his lady guests. All others, of course, either pay or wash dishes."

"If I have to pay, I will have a glass of water and some rolls and butter."

"With the greatest of pleasure," the proprietor said. "I will feed the *porc Lafayette au beurre noir* I had prepared for you to the cats in the alley."

"If you prepared it, it's probably *chat Lafayette au beurre noir.*"

"It wouldn't matter if it was; you couldn't tell the difference," the proprietor said. "I will leave you now, closing the curtain, so my paying customers will not see what I have hidden in the back room."

"Thank you," Clete said, raising his glass.

"Not at all," the proprietor said. "My mother always taught me to be kind to the ill-bred, especially those on the edge of senility."

"I told your father he was making a terrible mistake when he allowed you to wear shoes and told me he was going to try to teach you to read and write," the Old Man said.

"Bon appétit!" the proprietor said, and left them.

"He's not his father, of course," the Old Man said, "but he does know food."

A waiter appeared with an enormous silver bucket full of iced oysters, put on a heavy canvas glove, and began to shuck them.

"Is everyone having oysters?" he asked.

"Of course," the Old Man answered.

The Old Man waved them into chairs, sat down himself, and from an array of condiments began to concoct a sauce of ketchup, lemon juice, horseradish, and Tabasco.*

"I saw him on the 'Canal, did I ever tell you?" Clete said.

"You saw who on Guadalcanal?"

"Ed McIlhenny. He was a lieutenant. Platoon leader."

"He's back."

"Is he all right?" Clete asked quickly, concern in his voice. The return of a Marine to the United States from Guadalcanal more often than not meant that he had suffered a wound too serious to be treated in the Pacific.

"According to his father, as fit as a fiddle, and as proud as a peacock about being promoted to captain. His father asked about you, by the way."

"I hope you told him they made me a major; that'll take the wind out of Ed's sails."

"I did, in fact, mention it in passing," the Old Man said. "That took some of the wind out of his father's sails, too."

He gave the cocktail sauce a final, satisfied stir with a spoon, then pushed the bowl to the center of the table. Clete dipped an oyster in it and ate it with satisfaction.

* Tabasco is manufactured on Avery Island, Louisiana, by the McIlhenny family. The McIlhenny who served with the First Marine Division on Guadalcanal ultimately became president of the company, and retired from the Marine Corps Reserve as a Brigadier General. On his death in 1994, he left a substantial portion of his fortune to the Marine Academy, a Marine Corps–connected boarding school for boys.

"How do they eat their oysters in Argentina?" the Old Man asked.

"They're not big on seafood down there," Clete said.

"The reason I asked is that once I prepared a sauce like that for your father. He turned three shades of green, and I thought for a moment he was going to faint," the Old Man said, obviously cherishing the memory.

"They don't spice their food very much," Clete said, hoping that the Old Man's comment was not the opening line in a conversation about his father.

"I was wrong when I asked you, with Needham there, about your Navy Cross," the Old Man said. "I know what you did down there was classified, and I shouldn't have asked."

Clete shrugged, signaling it didn't matter.

"You can tell us now," the Old Man said. "We're alone."

Clete put another oyster in his mouth and shook his head resignedly.

"The Senator told me," the Old Man went on, "that the citation read, 'for conspicuous gallantry, above and beyond the call of duty' —"

"They all say that," Clete interrupted.

" '. . . at great risk to his life.' "

"I didn't hear that part, either, honey," Martha said. "Can you tell us about it?"

"I'd rather not," Clete said.

"Please, Clete," Martha said.

"The Germans were supplying their submarines from a neutral vessel in the Bay of Samborombón — in the river Plate estuary," Clete said, knowing there was no way he could get out of an explanation. "We took it out."

" 'Took it out,' meaning you sank it?" Martha asked.

Clete nodded.

"How?"

"That's classified."

"The last time I looked, it was not this side of your family which could be fairly suspected of being Nazi sympathizers," the Old Man said.

"That's not true, Grandfather, and you should know better."

"If it walks like a duck and quacks like a duck, it's a duck."

"OK. And this *is* classified. I could get in a hell of a lot of trouble if they found out I'd told you about this."

"Our lips are sealed."

"We found the allegedly neutral supply vessel — it was flying a Portuguese flag. Tit for tat, the United States violated Argentine neutrality by sending a submarine into Samborombón Bay, Argentine waters, and the sub took out the supply ship."

"There's more to it than that. They didn't give you the Navy Cross for finding a Portuguese freighter."

"Yes, they did."

"How did you find it?"

"With an airplane."

"Where'd you get an airplane?"

"It was my father's."

"He's changed sides, has he?" the Old Man asked, and then went on without giving Clete a chance to reply. "You said 'was.' Past tense. What happened to the airplane?"

"It went in the drink."

"It crashed?" Martha asked.

Clete nodded.

"It was shot down, is what you mean, right?" she pursued.

Clete nodded again.

"You went out and found this German ship in an airplane, right? What kind of an airplane?"

"A Beech stagger-wing."

"You went out in an unarmed civilian airplane, knowing full well you were going to get shot at, and probably shot down. Am I getting close?"

"You're a regular Sherlock Holmes."

"Not 'probably' shot down. *Almost certainly* shot down. That's why they gave you the Navy Cross. And promoted you to Major. You did what you saw as your duty, thinking you were going to get yourself killed. Modesty is a virtue, Cletus, but there is such a thing as carrying a virtue too far."

"Have another oyster, Grandfather."

"And what are you going to do down there now? The last time I spoke with Colonel Graham —"

"The *last* time you talked with *Colonel Graham?*"

Colonel A. F. Graham, USMCR, was a Deputy Director of the Office of Strategic Services (OSS) and Clete's immediate superior officer.

"— he was pretty vague about what you're going to be doing, in addition to being the Assistant Naval Attaché, I mean."

"I'm surprised he talked to you at all," Cletus said.

"It turns out that not only does Howell Petroleum ship a lot of product on that railroad he used to run, but also that we have a number of mutual friends," the Old Man said.

"Senator Brewer, for example?"

"Him too, I suppose. His name never came up. And furthermore, as a favor to the OSS, I'm still carrying that Jew on the Howell books as an oil-depot expert. Of course, Graham talks to me. He knows where I stand in this war. Unlike some other kin of yours, I want *our* side to win."

"I know how you feel about my father . . ."

"I should hope so."

". . . but I cannot sit here and by keeping my mouth shut tacitly agree to your characterization of him as a Nazi, an Axis sympathizer."

The Old Man snorted.

"This is Clete's last dinner," Martha said entreatingly. "Do we have to get into it over Clete's father?"

"Who's fighting? I'm just calling a spade a spade."

"And I don't like your characterization of Ettinger as 'that Jew.' Christ, *you* had him to the house as *your* guest!"

"He's an Israelite, isn't he? What's wrong with that?"

"I give up."

"I have no idea what I've said that could possibly offend you," the Old Man said.

A waiter appeared with small bowls filled with a reddish liquid.

"Crawfish bisque, Gentlemen," he said.

"Wonderful, he said, changing the subject," Clete said.

"Fine. You were telling me what you're going to be doing for Colonel Graham in Argentina."

"Whatever I'm told to do," Clete said. "I expect to spend a lot of time on the canapé-and-idle-conversation circuit."

"In other words, you're not going to tell me,"

the Old Man said.

"Right."

"Why didn't you just come right out and say it was none of my business?"

"It's none of your business," Clete said, laughing.

"OK. That's settled. What about Henry Mallín? Do you see much of him?"

Enrico Mallín, an Anglo-Argentine called "Henry," was Managing Director of the Sociedad Mercantil de Importación de Productos Petrolíferos (SMIPP). Howell Petroleum, especially Howell Petroleum (Venezuela), was his primary source of crude petroleum and petroleum products.

"From time to time," Clete said, as a very clear picture of Señor Mallín's daughter, Dorotéa, came into his mind's eye.

"It might pay you to cultivate him a little," the Old Man said. "I've seen some very interesting geological reports about — where is it the whales are?"

"Patagonia?"

"*Patagonia*. This war isn't going to last forever, and I would be very interested in your opinion of Mallín. Is he, in other words, the man we should have down there to set up exploration for us?"

"You're thinking of doing exploration down there? In *Argentina?*"

"I said 'we' and 'us,' " the Old Man said.

"You would actually invest *your* money in *Argentina?*"

"By the time this war is over, it will in all likelihood be *your* money . . ."

Damn him! He didn't say that to elicit my sympathy, but he is an old man, and he damned well might be dead before the war is over.

". . . and if that comes to pass, I want you to remember that I told you that oil is like money. It doesn't matter where it comes from; it can be converted into cash."

"I'll try to remember that," Clete said.

"Don't be smug from a position of ignorance, Cletus. Try to remember that, too. You really don't know what this war is all about, do you?"

"In my ignorance, I've been under the impression we're fighting this war because the Japs bombed Pearl Harbor."

"Why did they bomb Pearl Harbor?"

"That's where our Pacific Fleet was."

"Don't you know, or are you being flip?"

"Tell me."

"We're fighting the Japanese — and for that matter, the Germans — over oil. Did you know that the Soviet Union has the largest oil reserves in the world?"

"No, I didn't," Clete said, genuinely surprised.

"The Russians have oil, the Germans want it — need it desperately — so they went to war. Did you know that the German Army and Air Force are already using synthetic petroleum — they make it from coal — for twenty-five percent of their needs?"

"Where did you hear that?"

"From Colonel Graham," the Old Man said. "The Germans have damned little of their own petroleum reserves. Most of the crude they're using, they're getting from Romania. Did you know that?"

Clete, more than a little chagrined, shook his head, "no."

"You probably also thought that Royal Dutch —

60

Shell — was getting its crude from windmill-powered pumps set up in tulip beds next to the dikes in Holland, right?"

"Either there or from the Permian Basin," Clete said. "We — *Uncle Jim and Martha* — put down . . . Christ, I don't know, thirty, forty exploratory holes for Shell outside Midland."

"You got that right, at least," the Old Man said.

"Sir?"

"You said '*we* put down holes.' Right. Howell Petroleum put down exploratory holes on a participatory basis with Royal Dutch. Some of them even came in. Yes, *we* did, since the last I heard, Howell Petroleum is owned by the Howell family."

"I know that," Clete said, holding up both hands, palm outward, to shut him off.

Two waiters and a busboy appeared. Their appearance did not shut up the Old Man either.

"And when the Good Lord sees fit to take me, with the Howell stock your mother — may she rest in peace — left you, and with what Jim — may he rest in peace — left you, and with what you're going to get from me, *you're* going to be the majority stockholder, so we're not talking in the abstract, here, Cletus, we're talking about real money!"

"Yes, Sir."

One of the waiters ritualistically poured a half inch of a red wine in a glass for the Old Man's approval. He picked it up and sipped it.

"Well, this is better than the vinegar you tried to foist off on me the last time I came in here," he said.

"My day is now complete," the waiter said.

"And that," the Old Man said, pointing to a sauce-covered pork tenderloin the other waiter was

61

slicing, "is presumably the French fried cat?"

"Indeed it is, Sir," the waiter slicing it replied. "When Old Tom got himself run over, we carefully preserved his carcass for a special occasion like this."

Clete, smiling, picked up his wineglass and took a sip.

"I'm going to miss you," he said.

"When I'm gone, you mean? And well you should. I'm going to leave you a very rich young man."

"I meant now, when I go to Argentina."

"Oddly enough, I will miss you, too," the Old Man said. "We were talking about oil, or money, which is really the same thing."

"We weren't talking. You were delivering a lecture."

"Royal Dutch has production all over the Far East," the Old Man resumed his lecture. "There is no oil in the Japanese islands. The Japanese need oil, the Dutch have oil that can be stolen. Ergo, another war."

Christ, he's probably right. I don't know. When he starts off on one of these lectures to the ignorant, he makes me feel as if I'm thirteen years old and have just flunked World Politics I.

"If the Germans can hang on to the Russian oil reserves, which means they can simply steal the Russians' oil, fine for them. They don't need Argentina. But if they can't hang on to free oil, they're going to have to get it somewhere. They are in a fine position to barter with Argentina. Germany, like the United States, is industrialized. Argentina isn't. The German factories turn out things Argentina needs — automobiles, trucks, electricity-generating systems, locomotives, that sort of thing —

and Argentina pays for them with crude oil. You getting the picture?"

"But Argentina is not producing enough oil for its own needs," Clete said. "Isn't that why Howell is shipping them both crude and products?"

"I'm not talking about *now*, Cletus, I'm talking ten, twenty years down the pike, long after I have gone to my reward. You've got to start thinking about that *now*. With Jim gone to his reward, you're going to have to take over Howell for me when I go."

"No," Clete said. "Not necessarily. Odds are that Marjorie or Beth will latch on to some oil type. Or both of them will. Houston's full of them."

"No, Clete," Martha said. "He's right, for once."

"Of course I'm right," the Old Man said.

"Jim and I talked about it," Martha said. "The way his will was written — and mine — the girls get the preferred stock, and that income, but you'll get Jim's and my voting stock, and control of the company."

"He never said anything about anything like that to me," Clete said. The conversation was making him uncomfortable.

"He thought there would be time, we both did, when you came home after the war."

There was a moment's silence, and then Clete decided to change the subject. "You're talking as if you think Germany might win the war, Germany and Japan."

"Will German tanks roll down Pennsylvania Avenue in Washington? Or will Jap soldiers bayonet people and rape women in Beverly Hills like they did in Nanking? That's highly improbable. But I'll tell you what is possible — an armistice. The First

World War ended with an armistice, why not this one?"

"I never even thought about an armistice," Clete thought aloud.

"You know what happened at Stalingrad?"

"I don't know what you mean."

"The Germans lost a whole army there. Six hundred thousand men and all their equipment."

"That many? I never thought about that, either. I don't think we had forty thousand Marines on Guadalcanal."

"Can you imagine what would have happened here if you had had to surrender on Guadalcanal? If forty thousand Americans had been killed? Roosevelt would have been impeached — which might not be such a bad idea, come to think of it. And we're a hundred and eighty million people. There are about seventy million Germans. Six hundred thousand is almost one percent of seventy million."

"What's your point? You've lost me."

"My point is this," the Old Man said. "Somewhere, right now in Germany, there are people — important people, and whatever you want to say about the Germans, they aren't stupid — who are facing the facts. If they are losing one percent of the total population in just *one* battle, and the war is nowhere near over, then it's time to get out of the war."

"I don't think Hitler is in any danger of getting himself impeached," Clete said. "He's a dictator, remember?"

"You've read *The Decline and Fall of the Roman Empire*. A lot of big-time dictators suddenly found themselves out of a job when their people had had enough." The Old Man drew his meat knife across his throat. "Remember that?"

"I think the word for that is 'regicide,' " Clete said softly. "Killing the king."

"Well, I'm impressed. Maybe you did learn something at Tulane after all."

I didn't learn that word at Tulane. I learned it in Buenos Aires, when Peter von Wachtstein translated the letter from his father, in which Generalmajor von Wachtstein announced that his officer's honor required that he commit the act of regicide.

You're right, Grandfather. We're not talking in the abstract here. We're talking about real people actually committing regicide.

"Always stand pat on sixteen, you mean?"

"I was trying to be complimentary," the Old Man said. "Sooner or later, and I think sooner, Hitler will be deposed. As soon as that happens, the Germans will seek an armistice, and we'll give it to them."

"President Roosevelt called for unconditional surrender at the Casablanca Conference."

"If the Germans offer an armistice, we'll take it," the Old Man said, dismissing Roosevelt's pronouncement. "And once that happens, and the Japanese realize that they're all alone, they'll ask for one too."

"I don't agree with that at all. Japs don't surrender. We learned that on the 'Canal."

"If the Emperor tells them he's decided there should be an armistice, there'll be an armistice," the Old Man said flatly. "Anyway, for the sake of argument, indulge me. The war is over. Germany wants to barter manufactured goods for Argentine crude. I would be happier if they were bartering with us, but that looks unlikely."

"Wait a minute, you're losing me."

"I would like to barter our crude to Argentina, our *Venezuela* crude — preserving our own oil reserves — for American manufactured products, but that's not about to happen."

"Why not?"

"Germany will make them a better deal. They really will need crude. And so will the Japs. They'll sell them an equivalent washing machine, or automobile, for less than we will."

"So where does that leave us?"

"Out in the cold, unless we get in on the ground floor when the Argentines start developing their oil fields. If we get in on exploration and production first, we can take a percentage of whatever they produce. So we're back to where this conversation started. It will behoove you, Cletus, to pay attention to Henry Mallín. He could be very important to us."

"I'm going down there as a Marine, as the Assistant Naval Attaché, not to cut an oil deal."

"Funny, you always struck me as being smart enough to walk and chew gum at the same time. All I'm asking you to do is be nice to Henry Mallín for our own selfish purposes."

"I give you my word as an officer and gentleman by act of Congress that I will be the essence of charm and goodwill toward Enrico Mallín."

If not for the reasons you want me to.

The Old Man looked at him for a long moment, then nodded.

"This boiled cat isn't as bad as it smells, is it?"

"Not if you wash it down with enough of the vinegar."

"You go easy on the vino when you get down there, Cletus. And I don't want you earning any more medals. You've done your fair share in this

66

war, and then some. Let somebody else do their share. You just go out — what did you say? — on the canapé-and-idle-conversation circuit and sit out the rest of the war. I want you back in one piece. I want a male great-grandchild."

"Well, I could start to work on that the minute I get down there. I have seen —"

"I'm not so foolish as to try to tell you to keep your pecker in your pocket. But carry on with somebody you won't have to marry if you get her in the family way. One Argentine in-law in my lifetime has been more than enough."

"If it wasn't for my father, I wouldn't be sitting here with you."

"Possibly not, but your mother, may she rest in peace, would be. She could have had her pick of any one of —"

"Strange," Clete interrupted the Old Man, "but I seem to recall hearing all this before."

"All right," the Old Man said. "Just don't write me a letter and tell me you've found some female down there you want to marry."

"That's highly improbable."

"It better be impossible," the Old Man snapped, and then suddenly his entire aura changed. He looked old and vulnerable, not delightfully feisty.

"Clete, if there is one thing that would break my heart, kill me, it would be if you were to get seriously involved down there. It would kill me if you married an Argentine. Your mother did that, and look what happened to her."

"I have no plans to marry anybody in Argentina," Clete said.

That is the truth. I would like to, but it's simply out of the question.

"Don't change your mind," the Old Man

snapped, his feistiness returning as quickly as it left. "That's a hell of a long airplane ride for an old man to take with a bullwhip to beat some sense into you. Which I assure you I would do."

Clete shook his head. "I'm terrified," he said.

He sensed that he would remember the old man's momentary vulnerability for a long time, perhaps forever.

What the hell's the matter with me? The question is moot. It is because I love her that I can't marry her. The worst thing I could do to her, in my line of work, is marry her. Make her pregnant. Leaving her a widow with an American child would be a hell of a lot more rotten thing to do than what my father did to my mother.

III

[One]

3470 St. Charles Avenue
New Orleans, Louisiana
2305 5 April 1943

The Cadillac turned off St. Charles and stopped while the chauffeur opened the gate. When it did, they could see lights burning behind the drapes of the library of the Howell Mansion.

"It must be the new maid," the Old Man said. "Jean-Jacques knows better than to throw money away lighting empty rooms."

"Or there may be somebody in the library," Clete said, "who's afraid of the dark."

"Somebody in the library? At this hour?" Martha asked doubtfully.

"There's a car at the curb," Clete said, gesturing toward a black Ford Fordor.

The Old Man did not follow the gesture.

"My guests park their cars inside the fence, on the drive," the Old Man said.

Jean-Jacques opened the portico door to admit them.

"Colonel Graham is in the library, Mr. Howell," he said, "with two other gentlemen."

"Is he really?" the Old Man said, and headed for

69

the library. Clete followed him. After a moment's hesitation, Martha followed Clete.

Afterward, Clete was to remember that his reaction to the unexpected appearance of Colonel Graham was curiosity. He had no concern that something might have gone wrong — much less a premonition that disaster had struck.

"Well, hello, Graham," the Old Man said. "Jean-Jacques get you everything you need?"

"Mr. Howell," Graham said. "Clete."

The Deputy Director for Western Hemisphere Operations of the OSS was a short, trim, tanned, barrel-chested, bald-headed man in his fifties. He was as well-tailored as Clete's grandfather and wore a neatly trimmed pencil-line mustache.

"A sus órdenes, mi Coronel," Clete replied — "[I stand] at your orders, Colonel." — primarily to annoy the Old Man. Although his grandfather spoke fluent Spanish himself as a result of his years in Venezuela, he devoutly believed the world would be a far better place if everybody spoke English.

The Old Man flashed Clete a dirty look.

"I don't believe you know my daughter-in-law," the Old Man said. "Mrs. James F. Howell. Martha, this is Colonel Graham."

"I've heard a lot about you, Colonel," Martha said, offering him her hand.

"Have you really?" Graham said, looking at the Old Man. "It's an honor to make your acquaintance, Ma'am."

"Not that you're unwelcome at any hour, of course, Graham," the Old Man said, "but curiosity . . ."

"I apologize for the hour," Graham said, "but it was unavoidable. I'm afraid that I'm the bearer of some very bad news."

"Is that so?"

"Clete, I have to tell you that your father is dead," Graham said.

"Oh, Clete, honey, I'm so sorry!" Martha said, and touched his cheek.

"What happened?" Clete asked after a moment.

"We don't know much, and what we do know we haven't been able to verify. It seems there was a robbery attempt last night on the estancia highway. Your father resisted and was shot to death. I'm very sorry."

"What about Enrico?" Clete asked without thinking.

"Enrico?" Graham asked, confused.

"Enrico Rodríguez, my father's . . . sergeant," Clete said. "He never goes . . . went . . . anywhere without him."

"Clete, I just don't know," Graham said.

"Cletus, I'm sorry," the Old Man said. "I —"

"Those sonsofbitches," Clete said bitterly. "They couldn't get me, so they got him!"

"We don't know that, Clete," Graham said.

Clete snorted.

"What do you mean, 'they couldn't get you'?" Martha asked, horrified.

"Nothing," Clete said.

"I want to know," Martha went on, "what Cletus meant when he said they tried to get him!"

Graham, visibly uncomfortable, looked as if he was carefully framing a reply.

"If you're thinking about telling me this is none of my business, save your breath," Martha said.

Graham looked at her directly for a long moment before deciding that she could not be cowed.

"An attempt was made on Clete's life, Mrs.

Howell," Graham replied. "Obviously, it failed."

"An attempt was made on his life? By whom?"

"In Clete's case, we have reason to believe it was the Germans," Graham said.

"Christ," Clete said. "We *know* it was the Germans. And it was the Germans who killed my father."

"We don't *know* that," Graham argued.

"I'll damned sure find out when I get down there."

"We have to talk about that, Clete," Graham said.

"What do you mean, talk about it?"

"This unfortunate development opens a number of other possibilities for us," Graham said, "which we really should not — I'm truly sorry, Mrs. Howell — discuss in your presence."

"Us meaning the OSS?" the Old Man interrupted.

"Yes," Graham said, simply.

"I don't know what the hell you're talking about," Clete said.

"We've been thinking —" Graham began.

"We is who?" the Old Man interrupted, and when Graham looked at him in shock and annoyance at the interruption, went on: "And don't tell me this is none of my business, Graham. We're in my library, and I have been involved in this whole business from the beginning. And for that matter, so has Mrs. Howell, so don't try to exclude her, either."

Graham's face was stiff for a moment, but then he smiled and shrugged.

Then he turned to one of the men who came with him, a slim man in his thirties, who wore his hair combed straight back and, like Graham, sported a pencil-line mustache. "Delojo," he said, "this is one of those circumstances we were talking about when it is necessary to deviate from procedure."

Delojo nodded but did not smile.

"Excuse me," Graham went on. "Mrs. Howell, Mr. Howell, may I present Lieutenant Commander Frederico Delojo, U.S. Navy, and Mr. Quinn?"

Quinn was a stocky, pale-skinned Irishman, also in his thirties.

Delojo offered his hand first to Martha and then to the Old Man. When the Old Man shook Delojo's hand and then Quinn's, he made it clear with the gesture that while he was willing to be civil, his patience was being strained.

"You were saying, Graham?" he challenged.

"You understand, I'm sure, Mrs. Howell, Mr. Howell, that we are dealing here with highly classified material affecting national security —"

"Get to the point, Colonel," Martha interrupted. "I sit on the National Oil Production Board. I have a TOP SECRET security clearance."

"Yes, I know, Mrs. Howell," Graham said. "But you are *not* cleared for OSS information. May I continue?"

"Go ahead," she said.

"I want both you and Mr. Howell to understand that severe penalties, including the death penalty, are provided for the unauthorized disclosure of material classified by the OSS as TOP SECRET. Do you both understand that?"

"I'll take that as a recitation of some bureaucratic drivel you feel compelled to make," the Old Man said, "rather than a threat. If I thought you were threatening me — or my daughter-in-law — I would have to do something about it."

73

"Grandfather . . ." Clete said.

"It's all right, Clete," Graham said. "Actually, Mr. Howell, in this case I was referring to Director Donovan and myself when I said 'we.' "

Colonel William J. Donovan, a Wall Street lawyer, and winner of the Medal of Honor in World War I, had been named Director of the OSS by his longtime friend, President Franklin Delano Roosevelt.

"I'm tempted to call Bill Donovan right now and tell him you're down here threatening me," the Old Man said.

"Go ahead," Graham said. "I'm sure you have his number —"

"Damned right I do," the Old Man interrupted.

"And equally sure that he would tell you what I have just told you."

He pointed to the telephone.

The Old Man looked at him.

"Get on with what you have to say," he said. "I reserve the right to call Donovan at my convenience."

"Of course," Graham said.

Clete could see in Delojo's and Quinn's eyes — their faces remained impassive — their surprise at encountering people who were not awed either by the Director of the OSS or by his Deputy.

"OK. Let's start at the beginning," Graham said. "When Clete went to Argentina the first time, his cover was that he had recently been medically discharged from the Marine Corps, and that his purpose in visiting Argentina was to see that the petroleum products shipped by Howell Petroleum down there were not diverted to the Axis."

"And I went along with including — what's his name? Pelosi — *Pelosi* and Ettinger in that little charade," the Old Man said. "Let's not forget that."

Graham stared at him for a moment, looked as if he was going to reply, and then changed his mind.

"The idea of sending Clete back to Argentina as the Naval Attaché came after the *Reine de la Mer* incident," Graham said. "There were two justifications for that —"

"The *Reine de la Mer* is the name of the ship Clete was responsible for sinking?" Martha interrupted.

"I'm disappointed, but not surprised, Major Frade, that you saw fit to discuss this with Mrs. Howell," Graham said, looking into Clete's eyes.

"Colonel," Clete said, coldly angry, "I don't regard either my aunt or my grandfather as threats to national security."

"Neither do I," Graham said. "But that's not the point, is it? They did not have, do not have, the right to know."

"When do we get to the point?" the Old Man snapped.

"The death of el Coronel Frade makes Clete's continued presence in Argentina even more important," Graham said. "Will you grant that point, or should I elaborate?"

"If I didn't think that my grandson's presence down there was important to the war effort, I would never have gone along with any of this," the Old Man said.

"There are a number of people in Argentina who are distinctly unhappy with Clete's presence there. Starting — I don't know if you are aware of this, Mr. Howell — with Admiral Montoya, who is Chief of the Argentina Bureau of Internal Security. Montoya did not expel Clete from Argentina only

75

because el Coronel Frade went to him and exerted the pressure necessary to dissuade him."

"Cletus did not tell me that," the Old Man said. "I wondered why they didn't throw him out of the country."

"To get back to the Naval Attaché business," Graham said. "As Naval Attaché, Clete would have had the protection of diplomatic status. While he could have been declared persona non grata, this could not have been done without his father's knowledge, and, furthermore, would have caused the usual diplomatic response: We would have expelled an Argentine diplomat of equal, or superior, rank. Under those circumstances, there was, we believed, little chance that he would be expelled. Those circumstances have changed. Coronel Frade is dead. Those who don't want Clete in Argentina will be perfectly happy to have their Naval Attaché here — for that matter, any Argentine diplomat — expelled tit for tat."

"Meaning, the minute Clete gets down there, he'll be shipped out on the next plane?" Martha asked. "While I suppose this will open my patriotism to some question, that really wouldn't bother me at all. It seems to me that he's already done more than one young man can reasonably be expected to do. Let somebody else take his chances down there."

"Martha, come on!" Clete said.

"It would bother us a great deal. We would be losing the most important intelligence asset we have in Argentina."

"The way you're talking, it's a done deal," the Old Man said.

"There is an option," Graham said. "Argentine citizens cannot be expelled from Argentina. And

Clete is an Argentine citizen."

"He's an *American* citizen. He just had the misfortune of being born down there," the Old Man said.

"Under Argentine law, he's an Argentine," Graham said flatly.

"What are you suggesting, Colonel?" Martha asked.

Graham did not reply directly.

"Furthermore, under Argentine law, on the death of his father, as the sole heir, he comes into possession of everything his father owned."

"He doesn't need his father's money," the Old Man said. "He's got enough money in his own right."

"It would be perfectly natural for Clete to go down there to claim his patrimony," Graham said.

"If he claims he's an Argentine," the Old Man said, "and they catch him doing work for you, there's a word for that: treason. What do they do to traitors in Argentina, Colonel?"

"Am I permitted to join this conversation?" Clete asked. "Since it concerns me?"

"What?" Graham asked.

"What's this business about me being — what did you say? — 'the most important intelligence asset' you have in Argentina? How do you figure that?"

"There's going to be an attempted coup d'état. You know that. The G.O.U. is behind it. You know that."

"The what?" Martha asked.

"It stands for Grupo de Oficiales Unidos," Clete said. "Group of United Officers."

"Colonel Frade was the President of the G.O.U., and the source of most of its money," Graham said.

"What's that got to do with Cletus?" Martha asked.

"We think he will be in a position to get close to whoever will replace his father. The G.O.U. officers were all close friends of his father. He will be in a position to influence —"

"And if this coup d'état fails," the Old Man interrupted. "Then what happens to Clete? They stand him against a wall?"

"If things go wrong, we'll get him out of Argentina," Graham said.

"How are you going to do that?" Martha asked.

Graham pointed at Commander Delojo.

"He'll get you out. He'll take your place as Naval Attaché . . . and that will still be cover for the OSS Station Chief in Buenos Aires."

"How?" Clete asked, looking at Delojo.

"Whatever it takes, Major," Delojo said. "Hopefully, we can still get that airplane into Argentina. That would make things easier, of course. But if necessary, I'll get you out, airplane or no airplane. Into Paraguay, Uruguay, or most likely Brazil. If anything goes sour, Colonel Graham has made getting you and your team out my first priority."

The airplane — a Beechcraft Expediter* — was to have been a gift from the President of the United States to Colonel Jorge Guillermo Frade. Officially it was an expression of Roosevelt's admiration for Colonel Frade as an Argentine leader. It was also intended to replace Colonel Frade's Beechcraft stagger-wing — now on the bottom of Samborombón Bay; for that aircraft had been "in the service

---

* The Beech Aircraft C-45 Expediter was a small (six-passenger) transport aircraft, powered by two Pratt & Whitney "Wasp Junior" 450-horsepower engines. It had a maximum speed of 215 m.p.h. and a range of 700 miles.

of the United States" when Clete was shot down flying it. And incidentally it would give Clete wings to look for the next "neutral" merchant ship the Germans would send to supply their submarines.

Clete thought that whole idea was bizarre, and had told Colonel Graham so: His father was virtually certain to reject the "gift" the moment he heard about it. And if the chances, with his father alive, of getting the airplane into Argentina had been a hundred to one against, now, with his father dead, they were nonexistent.

"Cletus," Martha asked incredulously, "you're not actually considering going along with this?"

"Martha, I'm a serving Marine officer," Clete said. "I go where I'm ordered to go."

"Cletus, I absolutely forbid you to have anything to do with this," the Old Man said.

"Grandfather, I'll tell you what Uncle Jim would have told you. This is my decision, no one else's." He looked at Martha. "Martha, you know that."

"I know I wish neither one of you had ever heard of the Marine Corps," she said.

"My wife said much the same thing when I came back on active duty," Graham said.

"And she probably suspected, at your age, that you would be behind a desk, wouldn't you say, and not involved in something like this?" Martha said acidly.

"Martha, that was a cheap shot!" Clete said.

"I'm surprised that a 'serving Marine officer' like you, honey, hasn't heard what they say about 'all's fair in love and war,' " she said. But then she added, "But you're right. I had no right to say that. I'm sorry, Colonel."

"No apology is necessary, Mrs. Howell," Graham said. There was a moment's silence, and then he went on. "You're not being ordered, Clete. If you go under these changed circumstances, you go as a volunteer."

"There you go!" the Old Man said.

"When do I go?" Clete asked.

"Tomorrow. As scheduled. Commander Delojo will be on the plane day after tomorrow. We sent a cablegram, in your name, asking that your father's funeral be delayed until you can get there."

"You were pretty sure that he'd go along with this," Martha said.

"I was," Graham said.

"You're not going, Cletus," the Old Man said. "That's that."

"I'm going, Grandfather," Clete said, and turned to Graham. "How am I supposed to have heard about what happened to my father?"

"In a Reuters news story, which we made sure was picked up by both the *New York Times* and the *Washington Post*."

"OK," Clete said. "And who did I send the cablegram to?"

"Your uncle Humberto," Graham said. He turned to the Old Man. "You may have noticed, Mrs. Howell, that your nephew is very good at this sort of thing. He can take care of himself. He'll be all right."

"I pray to God he will be," the Old Man said. "But right now I think he's as insanely irresponsible as his father was."

"Goddamn it!" Clete flared angrily. "Grandfather, not one more nasty goddamned word from you about my father! Not tonight! For Christ's sake!"

The Old Man did not back down.

"Or what? That wasn't some sort of a threat, was it?"

"Colonel," Clete said, "give me ten minutes to gather my gear."

"Where do you think you're going?" the Old Man asked nastily.

"Out of here," Clete said.

"You're going to apologize, Marcus Howell," Martha said firmly. "And not utter one more word about Clete's father. Or I'm leaving with him. And it will be a cold day in Hell before you see me or the girls again. And that's not a threat, that's a statement of fact! You ought to be ashamed of yourself!"

For a moment, it looked as if the Old Man was going to hold his ground. Then he cleared his throat.

"Cletus, you know that I would never say anything . . ." he said.

"That's not an apology!" Martha said, coldly angry.

"If you believe an apology is called for, consider that one has been offered," the Old Man said. Then he saw the look in Clete's eyes. "Cletus, please. Don't let us part like this. Please stay."

Clete didn't reply.

"It's up to you, honey," Martha said. "We both know that's about as far as that nasty old man is capable of going."

Clete looked at the Old Man.

"Not one more goddamned word!" he said. "Not tonight. Not ever!"

The Old Man held up both hands at shoulder height, palms outward, in a gesture of surrender. Then he looked at Colonel Graham.

"You will please pardon this unseemly display of

81

intimate family linen," he said.

Graham did not reply directly.

"We need a few minutes alone with Major Frade," he said. "And then we'll be on our way."

The Old Man thought that over a moment.

"I think," he said finally, "that you would probably be more comfortable in here. Martha, would you like to come to the sitting room with me?"

Martha walked to the door, waited for the Old Man to pass through it, turned and smiled at Clete, and then went through the door. She closed it after her.

"Sorry about that," Clete said, looking somewhat sheepishly between Graham, Quinn, and Delojo.

"Commander Delojo and Mr. Quinn have read your dossier," Graham said. "I think they understand the situation."

Clete nodded.

"Mr. Quinn has an Argentine passport for you," Graham said, getting down to business. "The idea is that you will try to enter Argentina with it. If there is difficulty with that, then you will produce your diplomatic passport. They'll have to accept that, and that will give you at least a day or two in the country. We'll play it by ear from there. There will be somebody from the embassy meeting the plane. They may hold you in Immigration. . . ."

"I have an Argentine passport," Clete said, as if he had just begun to pay attention.

"I didn't know that," Graham said, and added, disapproval in his voice, "You never mentioned that in your debriefings."

"My father got it for me," Clete said.

"Well, that's one problem out of the way," Quinn said. It was the first time he had spoken.

"How does this change of plan affect my team?" Clete asked.

"You remain in command of your team, of course," Graham said.

"And Ashton's team? The Radar team?" Clete asked.

Another OSS team was being sent to Argentina. It was commanded by someone Clete had not met, but who he suspected was another of Donovan's socialites — his name was Captain Maxwell Ashton III. Ashton's team was equipped, Clete had been told, with the very latest radar. After Clete had arranged for a place on the shore of Samborombón Bay where it could be set up, it could locate the German replacement vessel within a hundred yards, at night, or in the most dense fog.

Once that had been done, the plan went, an American submarine could enter Samborombón Bay at night, running with just enough of its conning tower out of the water to provide Ashton's radar with a target and to allow its radios to function. It would then be directed to a position near enough to the German vessel to make a sure one-shot torpedo kill.

Clete thought that plan was almost as bizarre as the airplane "gift" to his father, and with only a slightly better chance of success. Getting the radar into Argentina at all was going to be difficult, and getting it from wherever they managed to land it to Estancia San Pedro y San Pablo without being discovered would be even more difficult.

And if the radar Captain Maxwell Ashton III and his team were bringing with them was anything like the radar on Guadalcanal, it would not be capable of locating anything with a hundred-yard degree of accuracy — if it worked at all.

He devoutly hoped he was wrong. If there was no radar — and it now seemed absolutely impossible to get a replacement for the Beech staggerwing — they would be worse off than they'd been before. He would have to try to locate the German ship with one of the Piper Cubs on Estancia San Pedro y San Pablo, then guide a submarine to it the way he'd done with the Beech. And after their experience with the Beech, the Germans were almost certainly going to be prepared for another nosy airplane.

"We learned yesterday that they are in Brazil. Commander Delojo will coordinate the infiltration of the team with you and Captain Ashton."

"And what about the airplane?"

"That's in Brazil too. Available to you and Commander Delojo as you feel necessary."

"You're not being very clear, Colonel, about who's in charge," Clete said.

"The Part One of the basic plan remains in effect," Quinn said. "You — your team — will locate and identify the replenishment vessel when it arrives on station. As far as Part Two is concerned — infiltration of the new team into Argentina — that will be coordinated, as Colonel Graham just told you, between you and Commander Delojo. Part Three, elimination of the replenishment vessel, is something we're still working on."

"In other words, SNAFU, right? Situation Normal, All Fucked Up?" Clete said, a little bitterly.

"Wait a minute, Major," Delojo said.

"You wait a minute, Commander," Clete snapped. "Without an airplane, I have no goddamned idea how I can find the replenishment vessel. And with my father gone, I have no idea how I can get an airplane into Argentina."

84

"We were thinking of the light aircraft on your father's estancia," Quinn said.

"I should have said a decent airplane. A *capable* airplane. The only airplanes on my father's estancia are Piper Cubs. I need that C-45."

"You found the *Reine de la Mer* with your father's Beechcraft," Delojo argued.

"And got shot down. I'm not going to try that again."

"That may be necessary," Delojo said.

"Aside from the fact that it would be suicidal, Commander," Clete said, "it would not work. If the Germans can talk the Argentines into looking the other way again when they anchor another replenishment ship in Samborombón Bay, the Argentines are also going to look the other way when the Germans shoot up any airplane — or any boat — that comes anywhere near them. We're going to have to go with the original idea of identifying the ship by aerial photography. And you can't do that with a handheld camera in a Piper Cub."

"I think Clete's right," Graham said. "We're going to have to get that C-45 into Argentina somehow. For the sake of thinking about that, Clete, could you conceal that airplane on your father's estancia if we just flew it, black, no markings, into Argentina?"

Clete thought that over.

"The landing strip on my father's estancia isn't lighted," he said. "Which means that it would have to be flown in during daylight hours. I think Martín would hear that an unmarked airplane had landed before it could be pushed into the hangar."

"Who's Martín?" Delojo asked.

"You don't know?" Clete asked, a tone of disgust in his voice. "He's the Bureau of Internal Security guy in charge of watching me. And probably of watching you, too, as soon as he hears you're in Argentina."

"Well, then, we're going to have to do some thinking about this, aren't we?" Graham said.

"And, this being the situation," Quinn said, "this brings us back to inserting Ashton's team by parachute, doesn't it? Which was my original thought on the question."

"I think Clete's original objections to that remain valid," Graham said.

"Sir, with respect," Quinn said, "we drop Jedburgh teams into France and the lowlands every day."

"We're talking about Argentina, not France," Clete said. "It's a hell of a lot farther from Brazil to Buenos Aires Province than it is across the English Channel."

"And whatever chance Clete might have to influence the new government — presuming that goes well — would be destroyed if it came out that we were parachuting OSS teams into Argentina," Graham said. "I repeat, Clete's original objections to that remain valid. It is not an option at this time."

"Yes, Sir," Quinn said.

"I think you had better message Brazil to have the team prepared to infiltrate from Brazil across the Uruguay River into Corrientes Province," Graham said.

"Yes, Sir."

"You work, Clete, on getting the airplane into Argentina, and I'll work on it at this end."

"Yes, Sir," Clete said.

"And also, until Delojo has time to get his feet on the ground, you be thinking about infiltration across the Río Uruguay."

"Yes, Sir."

"Anything else, Clete, that we should talk about here and now?"

"Colonel, the priorities," Clete said. "What's more important, me getting close to the Grupo de Oficiales Unidos or taking out the replenishment vessel?"

"That decision is going to have to come from the President," Graham said. "There has been enormous diplomatic pressure about the *Reine de la Mer*. And what he might decide today might very well change tomorrow."

"Great!" Clete said.

Graham stood up and put out his hand.

"Good luck, Clete. We'll be in touch."

[Two]

Centro Naval
Avenida Florida y Avenida Córdoba
Buenos Aires
2110 5 April 1943

A dark-blue 1939 Dodge four-door sedan pulled to the curb and a man stepped out of the backseat. The man — tall, fair-haired, light-skinned, in his mid-thirties, and wearing a light-brown gabardine suit — leaned down and put his head in the open passenger-side front-door window.

"Come back for me in an hour and a half," he ordered the driver, a somewhat younger man in a nearly identical suit.

"Sí, mi Coronel," the driver said.

The man then turned and quickly mounted the shallow flight of stairs on the corner of the building and pushed his way through the revolving door of the Centro Naval.

"Buenos tardes, mi Coronel," the porter manning the guest-book table said, and then, when el Teniente Coronel Alejandro Bernardo Martín had finished signing in, reached into a table drawer and handed him a small envelope.

"Muchas gracias," Martín said.

He turned his back to the porter and quickly checked the flaps for signs of tampering. Finding none, he tore the envelope open. It contained a single sheet of paper. It was blank. He turned it over, and the other side was blank too.

He jammed the sheet of paper and the envelope into his trousers pocket and turned back to the porter.

"Marching orders," he said with a smile. "If Señora Martín should telephone, please tell her I am in compliance with her orders."

"Sí, mi Coronel," the porter said, exchanging a knowing smile with the doorman. Another wife-mandated shopping mission. It happened all the time. The Avenida Florida, between Avenida Córdoba and the Plaza San Martín, holds a number of department stores, ranging downward in size and prestige from the Buenos Aires branch of London's Harrod's to tiny one-man closet-size vendors.

Martín, shaking his head as if in resignation, passed back through the revolving door, turned onto Avenida Florida, and started toward Plaza San Martín. He turned into Harrod's and quickly bought a pair of socks. Though he didn't need them, they came packed in a readily identifiable Harrod's paper bag. He then left, turning right again onto Florida and walking briskly toward Plaza San Martín. After one other stop, to buy a copy of *La Nacion*, he walked to the end of Florida, crossed the street that circles the Plaza San Martín, and went into the park.

He ambled down the curving paths between (and sometimes under) the massive, ancient Gomero trees — some said to be four hundred years old — and then sat down on one side of a double bench. A tall, good-looking man in his twenties, who was wearing both the uniform of a Capitán of Cavalry and the *de rigueur* cavalry officer's mustache, sat on the other side of the bench, facing away from the Círculo Militar toward the River Plate.

Martín took a quick look at the Círculo Militar. The magnificent Italian-style building had been built in the late nineteenth century as a private residence by the owners of *La Prensa*, the second of Argentina's major newspapers. They had subsequently given it to the Army, as a small token, some said, of the family's admiration for that body. Others snickered knowingly when this explanation for the donors' multi-million-dollar generosity was offered.

Martín picked up *La Nacion* and opened it.

"Nothing," he said softly. "It is not in either the house on Díaz, or in the guest house on Libertador."

The Capitán, whose name was Roberto Lauffer, could not resist shrugging, but he looked the other way and covered his mouth with his handkerchief before he replied.

"Then it has to be at Estancia San Pedro y San Pablo," he said.

"I can't get anybody in there," Martín said. "And even if I could, I don't have the combination to the safe. And it's a Himpell, German, built like a battleship. The only way to open it without a combination would be with a blowtorch. Or explosives."

"The dealer?" Capitán Lauffer asked.

"Don't you think I tried that?" Martín said icily. "One of the many advantages of a Himpell safe is the ease with which the combination can be changed by its owner."

"You don't think anyone else has the combination? Suboficial Mayor Rodríguez?"

"I think el Coronel Frade had the only combination, and in his mind, not written down somewhere," Martín said.

"I will relay this to General Rawson," Capitán Lauffer said.

"I'll give you something else to ruin his dinner," Martín said. "Humberto Duarte got a cable an hour ago from el Coronel Frade's son, asking that the funeral be delayed until he gets here."

"He's coming back?"

"He will leave Miami tomorrow on the Panagra flight" — Pan-American Airways–Grace Airlines.

"And Duarte will delay the funeral?"

"Of course he will."

Capitán Lauffer exhaled audibly.

"I will so inform General Rawson," he said.

"The room has been inspected for listening devices, but . . ."

"I understand," Lauffer said.

"I think that's everything for now," Martín said.

"Yes, Sir," Lauffer said, rising. He then walked through the park toward the Círculo Militar.

When Teniente Coronel Martín assumed his duties with the Ministry of Defense's Bureau of Internal Security as "Chief, Ethical Standards Office," he was given responsibility for keeping an eye on the Grupo de Oficiales Unidos. For the G.O.U., it was correctly suspected, were planning a coup d'état against the regime of President Ramón S. Castillo.

In the meantime, Coronel Martín's relationship with the G.O.U. had changed. A new set of circumstances had forced him to choose sides. On the one hand, he now accepted that his hope to remain apolitical and perform his services for whoever was constitutionally in office was wishful and naïve. And on the other hand, he realized that he had chosen the right side, at least morally. Whether right would prevail was entirely another question.

In this light, he saw that his duty now was to prevent those with ties to President Castillo from learning more than was absolutely necessary about the activities of the G.O.U.

The worst possible contingency was that OUTLINE BLUE would fall into the hands of President Castillo's supporters. For OUTLINE BLUE was the detailed plan for the coup d'état, complete in every detail, including the names of the officers involved and the roles they would play; *everything* except for the date and time of execution.

In view of the danger, only one complete copy of OUTLINE BLUE was assembled. This was entrusted to el Coronel Jorge Guillermo Frade, who had written most of it and was el Presidente of G.O.U. Frade was now dead, assassinated, Martín believed, at the orders of the German Military Attaché, acting on orders from Germany. His assassination served two German purposes — to keep Frade from becoming President, and to remind other senior Argentine officers that Germany could punish its enemies as well as reward its friends.

But preventing Frade from becoming the next President of the Argentine Republic, Martín believed, was the primary cause of the assassination. For if the coup d'état succeeded, that would have happened. The Germans did not want the President of Argentina to lead the nation away from its current status, which was Neutral, leaning heavily toward the Axis, to Neutral, leaning toward the Allies. Or worse: leading Argentina to a declaration of war against the Axis.

Six months before, the Germans, with reason, considered el Coronel Jorge Guillermo Frade a friend. He was a graduate of the German Kriegsschule — literally, "War School." It was, roughly, the German military staff college, combining the American Command & General Staff College and the War College, and he was known to hate the United States in most of its aspects.

That changed within a matter of weeks, when the norteamericanos, in a brilliant ploy, dispatched to Argentina an Office of Strategic Services agent, who was, among other things, a Marine Corps aviation officer who had fought in the Pacific. More important, he was the son, estranged from infancy, of el Coronel Jorge Guillermo Frade.

The Germans then made the tactical blunder of attempting to assassinate the son. The attempt failed, and the son went on to carry out his mission, the sinking of the *Reine de la Mer*.

For Frade, blood proved stronger than the political belief that the Germans were fighting a near holy war against godless communism. He not only assisted his son in the sinking of the *Reine de la Mer*

— by making his airplane available to find the ship — he also used his influence to ensure their escape from the country if they were caught trying to destroy the *Reine de la Mer* — by obtaining, for instance, Argentine passports for the OSS team.

Probably as bad, from the German point of view: el Coronel Frade was quoted in both *La Nacion* and *La Prensa* as believing the Allied statement — which the Germans of course denied — that Germans had imprisoned several hundred thousand Jews for use as slave laborers. In fact, he went on to state he was convinced that the number of Jews in concentration camps was well over a million.

When el Coronel Frade's sudden, unexpected, and well-known change of sides became apparent to the Germans, Martín believed, the decision was made to assassinate him.

The death of Frade not only saddened Coronel Martín — he genuinely liked him — it brought with it serious problems. If, in the course of normal postmortem activities — which would include going into el Coronel Frade's safe-deposit boxes and personal safes — the Operations Order fell into the wrong hands, the coup d'état would fail and those involved would be exposed. People involved in a coup d'état are either saviors of their country or traitors.

Martín didn't think Castillo would actually stand all those involved against a wall, or even see that all of them would be tried by court-martial and sentenced to long prison terms. Just perhaps the dozen or so people of the inner circle. But however short the list of the inner circle, one of the names there would certainly be Teniente Coronel Alejandro Bernardo Martín's.

Martín forced this uncomfortable line of thought from his mind and turned to the business immediately at hand. He was too deeply involved now to get out, even if he went directly to Castillo and exposed everyone. And he knew he was simply incapable of doing that. It was a question of honor. He had made his choice, and he would have to live with it.

Although he had been in the intelligence and counterintelligence business long enough to know that nothing should surprise him, he was nevertheless surprised that the sweep for listening devices of the room where Minister of War Teniente General Pedro P. Ramírez was about to take dinner with el General Arturo Rawson had found nothing. That was the meaning of the blank sheet of paper in the envelope at the Centro Naval. And he was equally surprised that the Federal Police were showing no interest in the meeting itself — at least none he could detect. For it was Ramírez's responsibility to order the coup; and if the coup succeeded — now that Frade was dead — Rawson was likely to be the next Presidente of the Argentine republic.

It occurred to Martín that perhaps the meeting had been called off, and for some reason this had not been brought to his attention. Or it could be that the Federal Police had not been able to place a microphone in the building. Getting caught doing so would have been very embarrassing. If he were the Federal Police official charged with watching General Ramírez he would be very careful not to anger him: the coup d'état might succeed.

With all that in mind, he decided to wait until Ramírez and Rawson actually appeared. And so he read *La Nacion*, and glanced frequently across the street at the Círculo Militar.

At 2130, Teniente General Pedro P. Ramírez arrived in his official car before the ornate gates of the Círculo Militar, seconds after the private 1940 Packard 220 sedan of General Rawson.

General Ramírez, seated in the rear of the Mercedes with his aide-de-camp, Mayor Pedro V. Querro, graciously signaled Rawson's chauffeur to precede him through the gates of the imposing mansion. This caused General Ramírez's chauffeur — who was not used to giving way to other vehicles — to suddenly and heavily apply his brakes.

Martín almost laughed out loud as Mayor Querro, a tiny, immaculate, intense man with a pencil-line mustache, a look of outrage on his face, abruptly slid off the slippery dark red leather seat onto the floor. General Ramírez fared better; he managed to keep his seat by bracing himself against the back of the front seat. Shaking his head in amused disbelief, Martín neatly refolded his *La Nacion* and, carrying the Harrod's paper sack containing the unneeded socks, started back for Avenida Florida and the Centro Naval.

[Three]

Neither General Rawson nor his chauffeur was aware of General Ramírez's and Mayor Querro's difficulty retaining their seats and their dignity. The chauffeur dropped Rawson off at the entrance, then drove into the mansion's interior courtyard to park the Packard.

Rawson, a good-looking, silver-haired man in his

fifties, with a precisely trimmed mustache, was wearing a well-cut, somewhat somber dark-blue business suit. He stood beside the entrance and waited for Ramírez and Querro, who were in uniform — green tunics with Sam Browne belts, pink riding breeches and highly polished riding boots. Except for their leather-brimmed caps, with their stiff, gilt-encrusted oversize crowns, Ramírez and Querro looked not unlike U.S. Army cavalry officers.

"Arturo," General Ramírez greeted him, touching his arm affectionately.

"Mi General," Rawson replied, nodding at Mayor Querro.

"You are getting a little chubby," Ramírez said. "We will have to find something useful for you to do, take some of that off."

"I am, with a long list of exceptions, entirely at the General's service," Rawson said.

Ramírez laughed, and the three passed through doors held open for them by neatly uniformed porters.

Inside the building, at the foot of a curving flight of marble stairs, another porter (like most of the Círculo Militar's employees, a retired Army sergeant) stood by the Register in which members of the Círculo Militar were supposed to sign their names on their arrival.

Aware that neither General Ramírez nor General Rawson ever complied with that regulation — or with any other they found inconvenient — and that the Membership Committee would not say anything about their breach of that rule — or of any other rule — the porter inscribed their names in the Register.

"Where have you put el General?" Mayor Querro

asked, somewhat arrogantly, as Ramírez started up the stairs.

"In Two-B, mi Mayor," the porter said.

"With a little bit of luck, there will not be a gaggle of women next to us," Rawson said.

"With a little bit of luck, perhaps there will be," Ramírez said. "Women in groups not only don't listen to each other, but to anyone else, either."

Rawson laughed, as he was expected to, and wondered if Ramírez was getting a little nervous.

Why not? When one is plotting a coup d'état, and the details of that operation may soon be on the desk of the man you hope to depose, one may be excused for being a little nervous.

Two-B, on the second floor of the mansion, was a small private dining room, with a table capable of comfortably seating ten guests. Four places had been set, with an impressive display of silver and crystal, at opposite ends of the table. A sideboard was loaded with bottles of whiskey, half a dozen kinds of wine, two silver wine coolers, and appropriate glasses.

Capitán Lauffer, who had been inspecting the wine, came to attention when the two general officers entered the room, as did two waiters in brief white jackets.

"Here you are, Roberto," Rawson said. "I think that when it's my time to pass through the pearly gates, you'll have gotten ahead of me there, too, and will be holding them open for me."

"Mi General," Lauffer said, and bowed his head toward General Ramírez.

"How are you, Lauffer?" he asked, smiling. He then turned to one of the waiters and pointed: "And put everyone at one end of the table," he ordered. "I don't want to have to shout at my guests."

Both waiters quickly moved to obey.

Rawson looked around the room, then put his hand to his ear and looked questioningly at Lauffer.

"El Coronel Martín, Sir, tells me the room is clean. He also suggested discretion, Sir."

Rawson nodded, satisfied that the room was indeed free of listening devices. He knew Teniente Coronel Martín to be a very knowledgeable, and reliable, security officer.

"Did he find anything?" Mayor Querro wondered aloud.

"I think he would have said something, Sir," Lauffer said.

"What else did he have to say?" Rawson asked.

Ramírez waved his hand in a gesture signaling Lauffer that he should not answer in the presence of the waiters. Lauffer nodded his understanding.

Querro walked to the sideboard, waited until he had Ramírez's attention, and then pointed at a bottle of Johnny Walker Red Label scotch.

"If that's champagne, I'd rather have that," Ramírez said, indicating one of the coolers with his hand.

One of the waiters moved quickly to take a bottle of champagne from the cooler and started to peel off the metallic wrapping at the neck.

"I think that's what I'd better do, too," Rawson said. "What for you, Lauffer?"

"Nothing, Sir. Thank you."

"Oh, have a glass of wine," Ramírez said. It was an order, and Lauffer understood it.

"Thank you very much, Sir," he said.

The champagne was poured and offered on a tray by one of the waiters.

"Thank you," General Ramírez said, taking a glass, and then adding, "Please leave us now."

He took his glass and walked to the ceiling-high French doors that overlooked Plaza San Martín and its ancient, massive Gomero trees.

Rawson sipped his champagne and waited for Ramírez to turn to him. When he did not, he walked to the window and stood beside him.

San Martín, Belgrano, and Pueyrredón, Ramírez thought, *stood a hundred and thirty years ago, looking at those very same trees, looking out onto the River Plate, and deciding to pay the price, whatever it was, to see Argentina free and democratic. Is that what we're doing? Or will we be just one more junta in a long line of juntas who decided they were the salvation of Argentina? And were, more often than not, wrong.*

"You seem very pensive, mi General," Rawson said.

"I suppose I am, but if you are asking, 'Are you having second thoughts?' the answer is no," Ramírez said, and met Rawson's eyes. "I regret the necessity of having to do what we have no choice but to do; but el Presidente has made it quite clear he has no intention of leaving office, no matter how the election turns out."

"No man is good enough to govern another man without that other's consent," Rawson said.

"Are you quoting someone?" Ramírez asked.

"Abraham Lincoln."

"Ah, Lincoln! Honest Abe. What did they call him, 'The Great Emancipator'?"

---

* José de San Martín, "The Great Liberator" Manuel Belgrano, and J. M. de Pueyrredón are revered as the fathers of Argentina.

"I asked myself if that isn't what we — with the best intentions — are about to do ourselves? Govern without consent?" Rawson said.

"And what did you answer yourself?"

"Depending on how you look at it, we intend to either preserve or restore democracy," Rawson said. "If we do that, we are right. If we don't, if we seize power and then retain it — for whatever noble reason — we will be no better than Castillo."

"Anything else?"

"More North Americans were killed in Lincoln's Civil War than were killed in the First World War, more than they will probably lose in this one. I don't even like to think what would happen here if what we plan turned into a civil war. Look at Spain . . . brother against brother, God only knows how many thousands, hundreds of thousands, died over there."

"Argentina is not Spain," Ramírez said sharply, and then, more softly, "So you are having second thoughts?"

"I had second thoughts. The conclusions I drew you just expressed with some eloquence: 'I regret the necessity of having to do what we have no choice but to do.' And I deeply regret that Jorge is no longer here to lead us."

"I asked myself what would happen if we did nothing," Ramírez said. "Just do nothing. Castillo might get reelected. That's unlikely, but possible. Or even if he seizes power rather than step down. What real harm would that do? Aside from the obvious answer that he and his cronies are robbing the treasury dry —"

"We are in agreement," Rawson interrupted him. "*We* regret the necessity . . ."

"Yes, we have had this conversation before,

haven't we, Arturo?" Ramírez said. "Let's put philosophy away for a moment and hear what Lauffer has to tell us."

Lauffer, who had been waiting near the wine coolers for a summons, walked to them.

"Our friend," he said quietly, "believes what we are looking for is very likely in the country."

Ramírez grunted. He had suspected that all along.

"In any event, what we seek is not in Buenos Aires in either house," Lauffer said.

"I didn't think it would be," Rawson said. "What about the money?"

"We are proceeding in the belief that the money will be with OUTLINE BLUE, mi General."

"Either house?" Ramírez asked.

"The one on Avenida Coronel Díaz, or el Coronel's guest house across from the Hipódromo on Libertador," Lauffer clarified.

"If there *is* someone listening to this conversation," Rawson said, "and he has half the brains he was born with, he already has figured out who, and what, we're talking about. Can we stop acting like characters in a bad movie?"

Ramírez looked at him, and after a moment shrugged.

"What does Martín have to say about finding what we're looking for at Estancia San Pedro y San Pablo?" he asked.

"He said, Sir, that seems impossible. Getting in the house at Estancia San Pedro y San Pablo by itself would be difficult. And there is a good safe . . ."

"A Himpell, in the shrine," Rawson said.

"What?" Ramírez asked. "What *shrine?*"

"You never saw the shrine to the blessed

101

norteamericano?" Rawson asked.

"I don't know what you're talking about," Ramírez said.

"Jorge had a private library at Estancia San Pedro y San Pablo," Rawson said. "More or less full of photographs and other material devoted to his son. The safe is behind the books. A portion of the bookcase moves outward."

"Why do you call it a shrine?"

"That's how I think of it," Rawson said. "I meant no disrespect, either to God or to Jorge. . . ."

"Where do you suppose the combination to that safe is? Do you suppose Señora Carzino-Cormano might have it?" Ramírez said, getting back to the subject.

Claudia Carzino-Cormano's only slightly smaller Estancia Santo Catalina bordered Estancia San Pedro y San Pablo.

"Coronel Martín believes only Coronel Frade had the combination," Lauffer said.

"Well, it wouldn't hurt to ask her," Ramírez said, paused, and went on. "God, if he'd only married her! Why in God's name didn't he marry her! They were living in sin for years! If they had married, even if she didn't have the combination, she could have ordered the safe opened."

"He didn't marry her because he wanted to leave everything he owned to his son," Rawson said. "I thought you knew that. But that's neither here nor there. We have to deal with the situation as it is. What are our options?"

"Send el Coronel Martín to Estancia San Pedro y San Pablo with orders to open the safe — even if he has to use explosives," Mayor Querro said.

"You don't really think we could do that without attracting the attention of the Policía Federal, do you, Pedro?" Ramírez said sarcastically. "And that, for obvious reasons, is the last thing we want to do."

"Another option," Rawson said, "is to do nothing about the safe. . . ."

"Hope no one gets into it before we act?" Ramírez asked. He thought that over a moment, then went on. "Assemble another complete Operations Order, you mean. That's possible, I suppose."

"What other choice do we have, mi General?"

"Sir, we need the money," Querro said. "What about that?"

"Damn!" Ramírez said.

"Sir," Lauffer said uneasily, "el Coronel Martín asked me to tell you that there has been a radio from the son —"

"From el Coronel Frade's son?" Rawson interrupted.

"Yes, Sir. Asking to delay the funeral services until he can get here. He leaves Miami tomorrow."

"Wonderful!" Ramírez said. "And the first thing he's going to do is head right for that safe!"

"Why do you say that?" Rawson asked. "I can't believe that Jorge discussed OUTLINE BLUE with him."

"I'm not so sure about that," Ramírez replied. "But that's not what I meant. What I meant was that, under the law, the moment Jorge died, everything he owned became the son's patrimony."

"I'm not sure that's so," Rawson said. "He's an American. For one thing, we can deny him a visa."

"He doesn't need a visa, he's an Argentine."

"He's not an Argentine. My God, he served in the American Navy!"

"Corps of Marines," Ramírez corrected him. "But he was born here and is legally an Argentine.

He has an Argentine passport. Jorge got him one just before he became involved with blowing up the *Reine de la Mer*."

"We could *detain* him," Rawson said.

"On what pretext? The Americans would howl in outrage, and Castillo would wonder why we did that. About our only choice is to appeal to him — maybe Claudia Carzino-Cormano could appeal to him — to let us carry out the work his father began."

"And if he says no?"

Ramírez shrugged.

"I'm open to a better suggestion," he said.

"He's close to Señora Carzino-Cormano," Rawson said. "And he knows her relationship to his father."

"What I suggest is that we treat him as an honored guest who has suffered a terrible loss, and as soon as possible have Claudia talk to him. Does that make sense to you?"

"Sí, Señor, of course," Rawson said.

"I'll go see Claudia tonight," Ramírez said. "I know she's in Buenos Aires."

"If nothing else, perhaps Claudia can keep him away from the safe until after we act," Rawson said, warming to the idea. "We don't need OUTLINE BLUE. We just have to keep Castillo from laying his hands on it."

Ramírez grunted thoughtfully.

"But as Pedro pointed out, we cannot put OUTLINE BLUE into operation without the money. We're going to have to get into that safe," he said. "Blowing it open is a last resort. Which means we have to deal with the son. Agreed?"

"Sí, mi General," Rawson said.

"The possibility exists, Señor, that Suboficial

Mayor Rodríguez has the combination," Querro said. "If he does, it would solve a lot of problems."

"As I understand it, he is in the hospital being guarded by the Policía Federal. Any conversation any of us might have with him would be recorded," Rawson said.

"It's agreed, then," Ramírez said, "that we will deal with the son, through Claudia. Is that correct?"

Rawson nodded.

"And now I suggest, gentlemen," Ramírez said, closing the discussion, "that we have our dinner."

"Sí, mi General," Lauffer said, then walked to the door and pushed the button that would summon the waiters.

IV

[One]

Avenida Pueyrredón 1706, Piso 10
Capital Federal,
Buenos Aires, Argentina
0755 9 April 1943

While there were many things in Argentina Hans-Peter Freiherr (Baron) von Wachtstein had come to admire, from the food to — especially — the women, the Argentine concept of time was not among them. It was not a question of whether an Argentine would *ever* be on time, but instead, of how late an Argentine was going to be, a period that ranged from a minimum of fifteen minutes to an hour.

Argentines ascribed this character flaw to their Spanish heritage, but that was so much nonsense. Peter had been to Spain. He knew Spaniards regarded their timepieces as instruments of civilization rather than as decorations for the wall and/or jewelry for the wrist.

When this casual disregard for an agreed-upon schedule was tied in with another national character flaw, forgetfulness — such as forgetting the door key to the place where they were supposed to be long minutes before — Peter, normally a placid, sometimes quite charming young man, tended to lose his temper.

In the situation at hand, his maid — a Paraguayan Amazon who outweighed him by at least thirty pounds — had agreed to daily present herself at his apartment at 0700, to prepare coffee according to the ratio of beans to water that he had laid out, to awaken him at 0715, and to have coffee, two soft-boiled eggs, rolls and/or bread, marmalade, and butter waiting for him when he came into the dining room at 0730.

He did not think it was too much to ask, and consequently was more than a little annoyed when his slumber was disturbed by the unpleasant grinding of the service-elevator door opening on his floor, followed almost immediately by the unpleasant clanging of the service-entrance doorbell. When he consulted his wristwatch, it indicated 07 : 54 : 45.

The facts spoke for themselves. She was not only fifty-four minutes late, again, but she had forgotten her key, again.

Peter, who was a blond, blue-eyed, compactly built twenty-four-year-old, jumped out of bed. Pausing only long enough to snatch a towel from where he had dropped it on the bedroom floor and wrap it around his waist — he slept naked — he walked quickly out of his bedroom.

The apartment was furnished with heavy, Germanic-looking furniture, rented, like the apartment itself, from an Ethnic German-Argentine family who were happy to make these available at a very reasonable price to a man like von Wachtstein. They considered this act a small contribution to the war effort and the Thousand Year Reich.

He walked quickly through the living room to the kitchen and finally reached the service-entrance door, rehearsing all the harsh and unkind things he was going to say to Señora Dora.

After some trouble with the lock — during which the bell clanged twice, impatiently, in his ear — he got the door open, swung it wide, and was struck dumb.

His caller was not his maid, but a black-haired twenty-year-old Argentine female of extraordinary beauty named Alicia Carzino-Cormano. He had known Alicia socially since the previous December and in the biblical sense for approximately fifteen days.

"Liebchen!" he finally blurted.

"May I come in?"

He stepped back from the door and she walked past him. He closed the door, reached out his hand, and touched her shoulder, whereupon she turned to him, came into his arms, rested her face against his chest, and clung to him desperately.

"Liebchen, what's wrong?"

"I'm frightened," she said.

"About what?"

"Everything," she said.

Well, that makes two of us.

She pushed away from him and smiled up at him.

"Sorry," she said.

"Don't be silly," he said. "Sorry for what?"

"I'm supposed to be at mass," she said. "Confession and then mass. That's what I told Isabela. Mother really sent me here."

"Why?"

"Humberto called Mother very late last night. Cletus arrives here this afternoon. Mother thought you'd want to know, and she didn't want to use the telephone."

I don't suppose it's very likely Cletus has the combination to his father's safe, but I'm grasping for straws.

"Yes, of course."

He leaned down and kissed her, very chastely, on the forehead.

"I'd better put some clothes on," he said. "Dora is an hour late. She's liable to walk in any second."

She nodded.

"You want to make some coffee? I won't be a minute."

She nodded again, and smiled.

He walked back to his bedroom and began to take clothing from his closet. He sensed he was not alone, and turned.

Alicia was standing in the bedroom door.

"Do you think they're going to try to kill Cletus, too?" she asked.

Probably. And this time they may succeed. Coming back here was insanity.

"I don't think so, sweetheart," he said. "And Cletus can take care of himself."

"They will, you know they will," Alicia said, and he heard her voice starting to break. And then she ran into his arms again.

"He'll be all right, baby," Peter said, stroking her hair, hoping he sounded far more confident than he felt.

"I've been thinking," Alicia said. "About Brazil."

"That's just not possible, sweetheart," Peter said. "We've talked about that."

They had talked about it in her mother's apartment immediately after the murder of el Coronel Jorge Guillermo Frade. She wept then, too. It was the second time he had seen her weep. The first time was the afternoon at Estancia Santo Catalina, when she became a woman and told him she was weeping with happiness.

In her mother's apartment she wept with grief over the loss of el Coronel Frade. Understandably. For most of her life he had filled the role of father for her. But that wasn't the only reason she wept. The primary cause of her misery was that Hans-Peter von Wachtstein, whom she loved, was a German, a German officer, and she could see nothing in their future but grief and misery and probably death.

She announced through her tears that the only hope they had was for him to desert, to cross the border into Brazil, and turn himself in. Brazil would treat him as a prisoner of war. Though this would separate them for now, he would live through the war; and after the war, they would be together.

He knew then that Alicia, who was as hard-headed as her mother, would not be satisfied with a "Sorry, that's just not possible" answer. He had to tell her why it was not possible for him to desert. Not everything, of course, not the truth, the whole truth, and nothing but the truth. But some truths, and some major omissions.

He told her that he had been charged by his father with salvaging a portion of what was already becoming the ashes and rubble of Germany, so that the people who lived on the von Wachtstein estates in Pomerania would have enough to rebuild their lives once the war was over.

He told her that it was a matter of honor for his father and himself to do so; that they had an obligation, as von Wachtsteins, to do what they could for the several thousand people who depended on the von Wachtsteins to care for them, as von Wachtsteins had cared for their people for centuries.

He told her that he had brought a large amount of money with him — in U.S. dollars, Swiss francs, and English pounds — when he came to Argentina.

He told her that Cletus Frade had asked his father's help in investing the money secretly, and that el Coronel Frade and his brother-in-law, Humberto Valdez Duarte, the banker, were helping him not only in that, but also in moving more money out of Germany through Spain and Switzerland into Argentina, and that he simply could not abandon the project.

He told her that if he deserted, his father would almost certainly be arrested and placed in a concentration camp.

He did not tell her that if it came to the attention of the Sicherheitsdienst of the SS that he and his father had been hiding money outside Germany, they would both be tried by a Nazi court, all the family lands and other property would be confiscated, and they would both be executed.

He did not tell her that Humberto Valdez Duarte had come to him as soon as he could after the murder of el Coronel Frade to tell him there was a major problem regarding the financial transactions: el Coronel Frade held all the records for these in the safe at Estancia San Pedro y San Pablo. Unless they could get into the safe before it was opened by officials of the Argentine government, the transactions would come to light . . . and the records would be turned over to the Germans by German sympathizers.

He also did not tell her — or Humberto Valdez

Duarte — that there was another document in el Coronel Frade's safe, a letter from Generalleutnant von Wachtstein to his son. Nor did he tell them that if this letter came to light, Generalleutnant von Wachtstein would be put to death by garroting, unless he died first of torture during the SS interrogation.

Schloss Wachtstein
Pomern

Hansel —

I have just learned that you have reached Argentina safely, and thus it is time for this letter.

The greatest violation of the code of chivalry by which I, and you, and your brothers, and so many of the von Wachtsteins before us have tried to live is of course regicide. I want you to know that before I decided that honor demands that I contribute what I can to such a course of action that I considered all of the ramifications, both spiritual and worldly, and that I am at peace with my decision.

A soldier's duty is first to his God, then to his honor, and then to his country. The Allies in recent weeks have accused the German state of the commission of atrocities on such a scale as to defy description. I must tell you that information has come to me that has convinced me that the accusations are not only based on fact, but are actually worse than alleged.

The officer corps has failed its duty to Germany, not so much on the field of battle, but in pandering to the Austrian Corporal and his cohorts. In exchange for privilege and "honors," the officer corps, myself included, has closed its eyes to the obscene violations of the Rules of Land Warfare, the Code of Honor, and indeed most of God's Ten Commandments that have gone on. I accept my share of the responsibility for this shameful behavior.

We both know the war is lost. When it is finally over, the Allies will, with right, demand a terrible retribution from Germany.

I see it as my duty as a soldier and a German to take whatever action is necessary to hasten the end of the war by the only possible means now available, eliminating the present head of the government. The soldiers who will die now, in battle, or in Russian prisoner-of-war camps will be as much victims of the officer corps' failure to act as are the people the Nazis are slaughtering in concentration camps.

I put it to you, Hansel, that your allegiance should be no longer to the Luftwaffe, or the German State, but to Germany, and to the family, and to the people who have lived on our lands for so long.

In this connection, your first duty is to survive the war. Under no circumstances are you to return to Germany for any purpose until the war is over. Find now some place where you can hide safely if you are ordered to return.

Your second duty is to transfer the family funds from Switzerland to Argentina as quickly as possible. You have by now made contact with our friend in Argentina, and he will probably be able to be of help. In any event, make sure the funds are in some safe place. It would be better if they could be wisely invested, but the primary concern is to have them someplace where they will be safe from the Sicherheits-dienst until the war is over.

In the chaos which will occur in Germany when the war is finally over, the only hope our people will have, to keep them in their homes, indeed to keep them from starvation, and the only hope there will be for the future of the von Wachtstein family, and the estates, will be access to the money that I have placed in your care.

I hope, one day, to be able to go with you again to the village for a beer and a sausage. If that is not to be, I have confidence that God in his mercy will allow us one day to be all together again, your mother and your brothers, and you and I, in a better place.

I have taken great pride in you, Hansel.

Poppa

Keeping the letter had been insanity. Simple common sense dictated that he should have burned it immediately after reading it. But he was reluctant to do so, feeling that it was likely to be the last word he would ever have from his father. And further, el Coronel Frade encouraged him to keep it.

"It will be important, Peter, after the war," el Coronel said to him. "Not only personally for you, but to counter the argument that every German, every German officer, supported Hitler and the Nazis."

El Coronel Frade offered to keep the letter for him, and Peter gave it to him. And now there seemed to be a very good chance that it would wind

114

up in the wrong hands.

Peter was stroking Alicia's hair with his left hand, while his right hand held her back. As he did this, he became aware of the warmth of her back, and then the pressure of her breasts against his chest. He kissed the top of her head, tenderly.

Christ, I love her. Which, under the circumstances, is probably the worst thing I have ever done to a woman.

He became aware of the warmth of her breath against his chest, and her fingers on his naked back, holding him close to her. And then that her breath had become uneven, shuddering, and that the muscles of her back were tensing.

He pushed his body away from hers as he felt the warmth of her belly through the towel.

She took her left hand from his back and raised it to his face. He looked down at her.

"Christ!" he said.

She raised her face to his and kissed him hungrily. Her hand slipped off his face, down his chest, and there was a sudden violent movement as she jerked the towel off his body.

It was only when he heard the knock at the door, and Dora's voice calling, "Señor! Señor!" that he vaguely remembered hearing the telephone ring.

"What is it?" he called.

"El teléfono, Señor. El Coronel Grüner, Señor."

Alicia was lying on him. He felt her breasts rubbing against his chest as he reached for the bedside telephone.

"Guten Morgen, Herr Oberst."

"I had the odd thought, von Wachtstein, that if you had nothing better to do today, you might wish

115

to come to work. Loche will be there shortly."

The line went dead.

Peter looked at his watch. It was twenty past nine.

"What is it?" Alicia asked.

"Grüner. He's sending his car for me."

"What time is it?"

"Nine-twenty."

"What happened?"

"What *happened?*"

"You must think . . ."

"I think I love you, is what I think," he said, and squirmed out from under her and got out of bed.

The clothing he had so carefully laid out on the bed — a tweed jacket, gray flannel trousers, a stiffly starched white shirt, and a finely figured silk necktie — was in a heap on the floor, mixed with Alicia's dress and lingerie.

He dressed quickly and sat on the edge of the bed to slip his feet into tan jodhpurs. Alicia moved on the bed. He felt her arms around him, and then she moved farther and he found her breast in front of his face. He kissed her nipple.

"I want to wake up every morning for the rest of my life like this," she said.

"Liebchen!"

"God, I love you so much!"

He disentangled himself and stood up.

"I'll call you later," he said, and headed for the door. Then he stopped and went back to the bed, sat down, and put on the other jodhpur. As he did so, Alicia kissed the back of his neck.

There had always been a fantasy in Russia. Going back to civilization. Being warm. Bathing in unlimited hot water. Having all you wanted to eat, especially beef and fresh vegetables. Having a young

116

beautiful naked sweet-smelling woman in your bed. Even more fantastic than that. Having a young beautiful naked sweet-smelling woman in your bed because she was in love with you, not because it was a feather in her hat to wave in the faces of her peers around the Hotel am Zoo, or the Adlon, for having bedded a wearer of the Knight's Cross.

Well, you've had it all, Peter. The fantasy come true. But it's not what you thought it would be like, is it?

Günther Loche was sitting in the living room.

"Guten Morgen, Herr Freiherr Major," Loche said, standing up and coming almost to attention. He was a muscular, crew-cutted, blond, twenty-two-year-old, who was wearing a suit that seemed two sizes too small for him. An Ethnic German — he had been born in Argentina to German immigrant parents and was an Argentine citizen — he was employed by the German embassy as driver to the Military Attaché, Oberst Karl-Heinz Grüner. Loche considered it a great honor to be of service to von Wachtstein, for Major von Wachtstein was everything he wanted to be. A very young major, a Luftwaffe fighter pilot, the recipient of the Knight's Cross of the Iron Cross, and, from what he'd seen, a smashing success with the ladies.

"Good morning, Loche," Peter said.

"I have taken the liberty of ordering coffee for the Herr Freiherr Major," Günther said, pointing to a cup and saucer.

"Thank you very much," Peter said.

If you weren't so stupid, Günther, I think I would loathe rather than pity you.

When Peter arrived at the Embassy, both

117

Grüner and First Secretary Gradny-Sawz were waiting for him. Three days before, Grüner told him, a radio message from Berlin had alerted them that "a distinguished personage," not further identified, had departed Berlin aboard a Condor aircraft of Lufthansa, the German national airline, for Buenos Aires, "for liaison with the Ambassador." That morning there had been a second message, this one from the German Consulate in Cayenne in French Guiana, informing the Embassy that the Condor had departed Cayenne and could be expected to land in Buenos Aires at approximately 1500 hours.

"Which causes all sorts of problems for me, of course," Gradny-Sawz, who was in charge of protocol, said importantly. "Whoever our distinguished visitor is, he's arriving in the midst of all the folderol the natives have laid on to bury Oberst Frade."

Gradny-Sawz was a tall, mildly handsome forty-five-year-old with a full head of luxuriant reddish-brown hair. The hair, he believed, was his Hungarian heritage. As he frequently told people, flashing one of his charming smiles, he was a German with roots in Hungary who happened to be born in Ostmark. (When Austria was absorbed into Germany in the Anschluss of 1938, it officially became Ostmark.) He would usually manage to add that a Gradny-Sawz had been treading the marble-floored corridors of one embassy or another for almost two hundred years, first for the Austro-Hungarian Empire and now for the Thousand Year Reich.

"Yes," Peter said. "I can understand that."

"So, Peter," Gradny-Sawz said, "we've decided that you will meet the distinguished personage at the airfield. Using Oberst Grüner's car and driver."

"Yes, Sir."

"In uniform, Peter," Grüner said.

"Yes, Sir."

"A *complete* uniform, meine lieber Hans," Gradny-Sawz added. "Modesty is a fine thing, but distinguished personages should be reminded that some of us who are waging war on the diplomatic front have also seen combat service."

That was a reference to von Wachtstein's Knight's Cross of the Iron Cross, which he had received from the hands of the Führer himself, and Gradny-Sawz's own Iron Cross First Class from service in the First World War.

Luftwaffe pilots and Wehrmacht infantry and panzer officers joked that the award of the Iron Cross First Class to well-born junior officers attached to the General Staff Corps was usually automatic if they had gone three months without contracting a social disease or making off with the mess funds.

"Yes, Sir."

"Oberst Grüner will arrange suitable accommodations for Herr Distinguished Personage at the Alvear Plaza, to which you will carry him from the airport. I will suggest to the Ambassador that he entertain Herr Distinguished Personage at dinner, at which time it will be decided whether or not Herr Distinguished Personage will accompany us to the Edificio Libertador for the official visit. You, my lieber Hans, are invited to the latter. Wearing your Knight's Cross. You are not invited to dine with the Ambassador."

"Yes, Sir."

"And I will stay here and try to coordinate everyone's schedule with the natives."

"Will you want me to send someone with you to handle the diplomatic pouches?" Grüner asked. "Or can you handle both?"

"I can handle both, Sir."

"You'd better be going then," Grüner said. "I told Loche to bring my car around and wait for you."

"Jawohl, Herr Oberst."

[Two]

Aboard Pan American-Grace Airlines
Flight 171
The *Ciudad de Natal*
Above Montevideo, Uruguay
1505 9 April 1943

There was a break in the cloud cover. Through it, 11,000 feet below, they could see Montevideo. But when they moved out over the river Plate toward Buenos Aires, the cloud cover closed in again, and there was nothing beneath them but what looked like an enormous mass of pure white cotton batting.

Buenos Aires was 105 miles away. At 165 miles indicated, call it forty minutes. Ten minutes out over the 125-mile-wide mouth of the River Plate, the First Officer looked at the Captain, and the Captain nodded.

They were flying a Martin 156, a forty-two-passenger flying boat powered by four 1,000-horsepower Wright Cyclone engines. The First

120

Officer took the plane off Autopilot, made the course correction, then retarded the throttles just a tad, worked the trim control, and then put it back on autopilot.

They would make a long, slow descent for the next twenty-five minutes, and with a little luck, break out of the cloud cover at, say, 4,000 feet, with Buenos Aires in sight.

Two minutes later, the *Ciudad de Natal* slipped into the clouds, and there was nothing to be seen through the windshield but an impenetrable gray mass.

Ten minutes after that, with the altimeter indicating 8,500 feet, they broke out of the cloud cover. Now they could see the River Plate beneath them, and here and there a dozen assorted vessels, small and large, some under sail, and some moving ahead of the lines of their wakes. Neither the Captain nor the First Officer could see whitecaps; their landing therefore would probably be smooth.

"Tell the steward to pass the word we'll land in twenty minutes," the Captain ordered. Then he added, "I'll be damned, look at that."

The First Officer looked where the Captain was pointing, out the window beside his head.

"I'll be damned," the First Officer unconsciously parroted when he found what had attracted the Captain's attention.

A thousand yards away, on a parallel course at their altitude, was a very long, very slender, very graceful aircraft. It looked something like the Douglas DC-3, particularly in the nose. But it had four engines rather than two. It was painted black on the top of the fuselage, and off-white on the bottom. On the vertical stabilizer and on the rear of the fuselage were red swastikas, outlined in white.

"Is that a Condor*?" the First Officer asked.

"I can't think of anything else it could be," the Captain said.

"He's come a hell of a long way in something that won't float," the First Officer said, a touch of admiration in his voice. "Nice-looking ship, isn't it?"

The Captain grunted, then said, "Tell the steward to ask that ex-Marine to come up here."

The First Officer nodded and got out of his seat.

They met the ex-Marine, a good-looking kid, in Weather Briefing in the Pan American terminal in Miami. The Weather Briefing facilities were off limits to the general public, but there he was — dressed in a tweed jacket, tieless button-down-collar shirt, gray flannel slacks, and cowboy boots — standing in front of the wall-size maps holding the latest Teletype weather reports in his hands.

There was a brief conversation:

"I don't think you're supposed to be in here, Sir," the pilot said.

"Probably not," the young man said. "But I used to be an aviator, and I like to check the weather between where I am and where I'm headed."

"Used to be?"

"I used to be a Marine," the young man said.

"Where are you headed?"

* The Focke-Wulf 200B Condor, first flown in 1937, was a twenty-six-seat passenger airplane, powered by four 870-horsepower BMW engines, built for Lufthansa, the German airline. The 200C was a military modification, turning the aircraft into an armed, long-range reconnaissance/bomber aircraft.

"Buenos Aires," the young man replied, and then, when he saw the look of surprise in the Captain's eyes, added, "Probably with you. Panagra 171?"

"Right," the Captain replied. "What's it look like?"

"Not a cloud in the sky," the young man said. "Which probably means we'll run into a hurricane thirty minutes out of here."

"Let's hope not," the Captain said, and added, "See you aboard," which ended the conversation.

The Captain, as was his custom, checked the passenger manifest with the steward before takeoff. It was often useful to know who was aboard, whether some Latin American big shot, or some exalted member of the Pan American hierarchy. The Captain had once carried Colonel Charles A. Lindbergh in the back, the man who had not only been the first to cross the Atlantic alone, but had laid out many — maybe most — of PAA's routes to South America. If he had not checked the passenger manifest that day, he would never have known "Lucky Lindy" was aboard, and would have kicked himself the rest of his life for blowing the chance to actually shake the hero's hand and offer him the courtesy of the cockpit.

The steward reported that there was nobody special aboard 171 that day, just the usual gaggle of diplomats and Latins of one nationality or another. No Americans this trip. The captain wondered what had happened to the ex-Marine who said he was going to Buenos Aires.

When he took his ritual walk through the cabin, he saw him.

"I thought you were an ex-Marine," the Captain said, stopping by the Marine's seat. "The steward

123

said we're not carrying any Americans."

"You don't have to be an American to be a Marine," the Marine said. "I'm an Argentine citizen. Going home."

The Captain was curious about that, but to ask any questions would be close to calling him a liar. And he knew Customs and Immigration carefully checked all passengers.

"Well, we'll try to get you home quickly and in one piece," the Captain said, and then his curiosity got the better of him. "Not as fast as — what did you fly in the Marine Corps?"

"Wildcats, F4F's," the young man said, and then, as if he sensed the Captain's suspicions, added, "with VMF-221 on Guadalcanal."

"These boats aren't as fast as a Wildcat," the Captain said with a smile, now convinced the young man was what he said he was. "But a hell of a lot more comfortable."

Because he had made the flight before and was thus really aware of how long it took to fly from Miami to Buenos Aires, Clete Frade had stocked up on reading matter in Miami.

He hadn't bought enough. When the steward came down the aisle to softly inform him that the Captain requested his presence in the cockpit, he was reading the April 1, 1943, edition of *Time* magazine for the third time.

It reported that the American First Armored Division was almost at the Tebaga Gap — whatever the hell that was — in Tunisia; that the Red Army had retaken Anastasyevsk, in the Kuban, north of Novorossiysk — wherever the hell that was; maybe near the Russian oil fields the old man had talked about? — and that 180 Japanese bomber and fighter aircraft operating off aircraft carriers and from the Japanese base at Rabaul had attacked Guadalcanal and Tulagi in the Solomon Islands, and that further attacks were anticipated.

He knew damned well where Guadalcanal and Tulagi were.

There was something unreal about sitting here in a leather-upholstered chair drinking champagne when people he knew — unless they'd all been killed by now — were climbing into battered, shot-up Grumman Wildcats to go up and try to keep the Nips from dumping their bomb loads on, or strafing, Henderson Field, Fighter One, and the ammo and fuel dumps on the 'Canal.

He drained his glass of champagne, unfastened his seat belt, stood up, and made his way forward to the cockpit.

"I thought you would be interested in that," the Captain said, jabbing his finger in the direction of the Condor making its parallel approach.

Clete Howell stared.

"Jesus," he said. "What is that?"

"I think it's a Condor," the Captain said, and then, attracting the engineer's attention, he called, "Charley, isn't there a pair of binoculars back there somewhere?"

"Yes, Sir," the engineer replied, and pulled open a drawer in his console, rummaged through it, and came up with Zeiss 7 x 57 binoculars. He stood up and handed them to the Captain, who handed them to Clete.

"Nice-looking bird," Clete said a minute or so later, taking the binoculars from his eyes. "I wonder where it came from."

"We were just talking about that," the Captain said. "Probably from Portugal, then from somewhere in Africa, and then across the drink to French Guiana. Wherever he came from, with the fuel he would have to have aboard, he can't be carrying much."

"That's the first German airplane I've ever seen," Clete said.

"They used to have regularly scheduled service before the war," the Captain said. "And I think I remember hearing that they sold Brazil a couple of those. Aerolineas Brasília, or something like that. But that's the first one I've ever seen, too, and I've been coming down here for a long time."

"It would be almost a shame to shoot down something that pretty, wouldn't it?" Clete said, thinking aloud.

The Captain chuckled.

"Put such thoughts from your mind," he said. "You're out of the Marine Corps and back in neutral Argentina. From here on in, when you see a German, all you can do is look the other way. Or maybe say, 'Buenos días, Fritz.' "

Clete chuckled, then said, "Look, there he goes. I guess he'll land at El Palomar." In 1943, El Palomar was the civilian airport on the outskirts of Buenos Aires.

The Captain looked. The Condor was banking away to the right.

"Pretty bird, isn't it?"

"Thank you, Captain. I appreciate your courtesy," Clete said.

"My pleasure," the Captain said. "Welcome home!"

[Three]

Sea Plane Terminal
River Plate
Buenos Aires, Argentina
1525 9 April 1943

When Panagra's flight 171 appeared in the sky, obviously about to land, Mayor Pedro V. Querro, to Capitán Roberto Lauffer's carefully concealed amusement, became nearly hysterical.

"Lauffer," he ordered in a fierce whisper, "the boat's not here! Call them! There's a phone in there!" He pointed to the Customs and Immigration shed. "Ask where the hell it is!"

"Sí, Señor," Lauffer said. "Who should I call, Señor?"

Generals Ramírez and Rawson looked at the two of them.

"The School of Naval Warfare! They promised me a boat! And it's not here!"

"Is that what you're looking for, Mayor?" General Rawson asked, pointing.

A highly varnished speedboat was five hundred yards away, splashing through the swells on the river's muddy water. The flag of Argentina flapped at its stern and some sort of naval pennant flew from a short flagpole on the bow.

"That would appear to be it, Señor," Querro said.

"I personally have found the Navy to be very reliable," Rawson said, and winked at Lauffer, whose father, a friend, was a retired Naval officer.

The speedboat arrived at the quay before the two boats moored there — the Customs and Immigration boat and the larger boat that would take off

127

the passengers — began to make their way out to meet the Martin flying boat. By then the aircraft had landed, and was in the process of turning around to taxi to the buoy that it would be tied to.

Meanwhile, the speedboat stopped in the water, the coxswain having apparently decided to wait until the other boats had left. When he saw that, Mayor Querro signaled almost frantically for it to approach the quay, then turned to Lauffer.

"Well, Lauffer, are you waiting for a formal invitation?" he said, then hurried down the stairs and jumped onto the Customs and Immigration boat to wait for the Navy speedboat.

Lauffer descended the stairs and joined him.

"What's going on?" one of the Customs officers asked.

"The Minister of War," Querro announced grandly, gesturing toward the quay, "is personally meeting a distinguished passenger on the Panagra flight."

As soon as the Navy speedboat came close, Querro jumped into it, then turned impatiently to wait for Lauffer.

"Out to the plane!" Querro ordered the moment Lauffer had stepped aboard.

The coxswain immediately gunned the engine, which almost caused Querro to lose his footing.

Pity, Lauffer thought. The idea of Querro taking an unintended bath in the River Plate had a certain appeal.

Lauffer was looking forward to meeting Señor Cletus H. Frade, about whom he had heard a good deal but had never actually seen. Lauffer had been in the Army for seven years without hearing a shot fired in anger. According to what he'd heard, Frade fought at Guadalcanal, was twice shot down, and downed seven Japanese airplanes. All before he came to Argentina, where he apparently bested two assassins sent to kill him, and then was responsible for the sinking of an armed cargo ship.

"Distinguished passenger, my ass," Querro said softly. "If I had my way, he'd never make it from the plane to the shore."

"Sí, Señor," Lauffer said.

Clete Howell looked out the window, now splashed with water, as the Martin 156 taxied in a sweeping turn from the end of its landing roll toward the buoy where it would be moored.

Is it really, on a flying boat, a "landing roll"? Land planes roll, on their wheels, until they're slowed down enough to taxi. Flying boats, which have no wheels, obviously can't roll. So what do flying boat pilots call it? "The landing slow-down"? Or maybe "the landing splash"?

Who cares? What difference does it make?

That's the champagne working on me. I had damned near a whole bottle, which wasn't too smart, since I may have to use my brain when I get to Customs and Immigration carrying an Argentine passport, issued here, which does not have an Exit Stamp. What am I going to say if the guy asks me how I got out of the country without an Exit Stamp?

Damn! Colonel Graham should have thought of that!

What the hell, when all else fails, tell the truth, or something close to it. I left Argentina on my American passport, duly Exit Stamped.

The forty-odd other passengers aboard Pan American–Grace Airlines Flight 171 all seemed to be out of their seats, collecting their cabin baggage.

Three boats were headed out from shore, obviously to meet the flying boat. There had been two the last time, a Customs boat and a graceful, narrow, varnished wooden powerboat. Pan American Grace had permanently chartered it from the owners of a fleet of substantially identical boats in El Tigre, a Buenos Aires suburb that Clete's father had described to him, accurately, as "an undeveloped Venice."

The one leading the procession looked like a Navy boat of some sort, sort of an admiral's barge, carrying two officers.

Obviously to meet some big shot. I wonder who?

The admiral's barge reached the flying boat before it was tied up, and then moved close.

Those are Army officers, not Navy. What's that all about?

The hatch in the side of the fuselage opened, and the two officers came aboard. One of them, a small and intense major, spoke somewhat arrogantly to the steward.

That major's a feisty little bastard. Why are small people like that?

The major came down the aisle, shouldering past the passengers collecting their belongings.

Jesus, he's coming to me!

"Teniente Frade?" the little major asked, with a patently insincere smile.

"*Señor* Frade," Clete said.

"I was led to believe you served as a Teniente in the Norteamericano Corps of Marines, Señor."

"I served as a major in the U.S. Marine Corps, Major."

Clete thought he saw amusement in the eyes of the good-looking captain standing behind the major.

130

"*Mayor* Frade, I am Mayor Querro, who has the honor of presenting the compliments of Teniente General Ramírez, the Argentine Minister of War."

"How do you do?"

"This is Capitán Lauffer, Mayor Frade."

"How do you do, Capitán?"

"I have the honor of presenting the compliments of General Rawson, mi Mayor," Lauffer said. "And may I offer my condolences on the death of el Coronel Frade, under whom I was once privileged to serve?"

"Thank you very much," Clete said.

"If you will give your baggage checks to Capitán Lauffer, Mayor Frade, he will deal with that. I will take you to General Ramírez."

"What about Customs and Immigration?" Clete asked.

"Capitán Lauffer will deal with that. Will you come with me, please?"

As soon as the admiral's barge moved alongside the quay, Major Querro jumped out, then extended his hand to assist Clete in leaving the boat.

Clete ignored the hand, more because he thought being assisted offered more risk of taking a bath than jumping out himself.

Major Querro motioned for him to precede him up a flight of stairs cut into the massive stone blocks of the quay.

A half-dozen ornately uniformed senior officers, coronels and generales, of the Argentine Army were lined up at the top of the quay behind an officer whom Clete recognized — he had been introduced to him by his father — as General Pedro P. Ramírez, the Argentine Minister for War.

Ramírez marched over to Clete, saluted him

crisply, then put out his hand. The others raised their hands to the leather brims of their high-crowned uniform caps.

"Señor Frade," Ramírez said, "please accept the most profound condolences of the Ejercito Argentina" — Argentine Armed Forces — "and my personal condolences, on the tragic loss of your father, el Coronel Jorge Guillermo Frade."

"You are very kind, mi General," Clete replied as Ramírez emotionally grasped his hand.

One by one, the other officers identified themselves and shook Clete's hand. One of them, a General Rawson, he also recognized, and remembered his father telling him they were old friends.

"Our cars are here, Señor Frade, if you will come this way?" Ramírez said.

A crowd of people stood behind a barrier waiting to greet the incoming passengers. One of them Clete recognized — a slight, somewhat hunch-shouldered, thickly spectacled man in his late twenties wearing a seersucker suit and carrying a stiff-brimmed straw hat and a briefcase. His name was H. Ronald Spiers, and he was a Vice Consul of the Embassy of the United States of America.

As two policemen shifted the barrier to permit General Ramírez and his party to pass, Spiers stepped forward.

"Mr. Frade?"

Clete stopped.

"I am here on behalf of the Embassy, Mr. Frade," Spiers said. "To offer the condolences of the Ambassador on your loss, and to assure you the American Embassy is prepared to do anything within our power to assist you in any way."

"That's very kind of you," Clete said. "Thank

you very much, but I can't think of a thing right now."

"We are ready to assist in any way we can," Spiers said.

"Thank you very much," Clete said, and offered his hand.

Spiers has a handshake like a dead fish, Clete thought, *but at least Colonel Graham will know, as soon as a message can be encrypted and transmitted, that I not only got into the country without trouble, but am being treated like the prodigal son returning.*

General Ramírez seemed to be annoyed at the delay.

Outside the building stood a line of official cars. Ramírez led him to the largest of these — a soft-top Mercedes limousine, said to be identical to that provided for field marshals in the German Army.

"Your father is lying in state in the Grand Salon of Honor in the Edificio Libertador," General Ramírez said when they were inside. "We can go there directly, if you like. Or if you would like to compose yourself, we can go to your father's home."

"What happened to my father, General?"

"Banditos," General Ramírez replied, exhaling. "They blocked the road near Estancia San Pedro y San Pablo. Your father, who had the courage of a lion, apparently resisted, and was shot to death."

Well, that's the official version, apparently. Now I have to find out what really happened.

"And Suboficial Mayor Rodríguez? Was he with my father?"

"Yes."

"And how is he?"

"He is in the Argerich Military Hospital," Ramírez said. "He will recover."

"If you please, General, I would like to see him."

"Of course. I will arrange it."

"I mean now, Sir."

Ramírez looked at him thoughtfully for a moment, then nodded.

"Whatever you wish, Señor Frade," he said, and leaned forward on the seat to give the driver his orders.

"For whatever small comfort this might provide, Señor Frade," Ramírez said, "the people who did this outrageous act did not get away with it. They were located by the Provincial Police and died in a gun battle which followed."

Clete's mouth ran away from him.

"He who lives by the sword shall die by the sword," he said sarcastically, mentally adding, *And dead men tell no tales, right, like about who hired them?*

The sarcasm was not apparent to General Ramírez.

"And if we are to believe the Holy Scripture," he said, "they will burn in hell through eternity for their mortal sin."

V

[One]

El Palomar Airfield
Buenos Aires, Argentina
1535 9 April 1943

Sometimes a Condor flight came twice a month, most often once a month, and the last flight before this one had been five weeks ago. Whenever he went to meet one, Major von Wachtstein was always relieved and a little surprised that the Condor had made it at all. He knew aircraft: Before coming to Argentina he had flown in Spain with the Condor Legion, and with fighter and fighter-bomber squadrons in Poland, Russia, and France, and had commanded a squadron of Focke-Wulf 190s defending Berlin.

It was one hell of a long flight from Berlin to Buenos Aires, and the shooting down of transport aircraft of the enemy was just as legal under the Geneva Convention as torpedoing their merchant ships.

First, the Condor had to make the 1,436 miles from Berlin to Portugal. There were few places over Germany, and fewer over occupied France, where one could not reasonably expect to encounter an Allied fighter.

The skies over neutral Spain and Portugal were safe, but fifteen minutes out of Lisbon toward Dakar, in French West Africa on the next leg of the flight, the Condor lost the protection of Portuguese neutrality. To avoid Allied aircraft certain to be alerted to its departure by Allied agents at the field, it had to fly far out into the Atlantic. Now that the Americans were in Morocco, that was a real threat.

It was about 1,800 miles from Lisbon to Dakar. Marshal Petain's officially neutral Vichy French government had no choice but to permit a German civilian aircraft to make a fuel stop at the Dakar airfield. But once the Condor left Dakar, the danger of being shot down was replaced by the danger of bad weather and running out of fuel. It was 2,500 miles from Dakar to Cayenne in French Guiana on the South American continent, and another 2,700 miles from Cayenne to Buenos Aires.

To avoid detection and interception on the Cayenne–Buenos Aires leg, the Condor had to fly at least one hundred miles off the coast of Brazil. Brazil had declared war against the Axis powers, and the Americans had given them some armed long-range maritime reconnaissance aircraft. On that leg the Condor faced dangers both from enemy aircraft and from the hazards of an incredibly long flight. Only a few years before, any aircraft that had successfully completed a flight of that distance would have made headlines. It was still a magnificent achievement.

Major Freiherr von Wachtstein privately thought the Condor flights were an exercise in idiocy. For one thing, they required a great deal of fuel. And the Condor, like any aircraft, had a finite weight-carrying capability. The unavoidable result was that

136

when the Condor took off there was very little weight available for either passengers or cargo. Usually the planes arrived carrying only half a dozen passengers, a dozen or so mailbags, and the diplomatic pouches.

He thought, again very privately, that there were only two reasons for making the Condor flights at all, and both were connected with the convoluted thinking of the upper hierarchy of the National Socialist German Workers' Party. First: Someone as important as Reichsmarschal Hermann Göring, head of all things in aviation in Germany, the Luftwaffe (Air Force), and Lufthansa (the national airline), probably felt that maintaining the flights increased — or at least maintained — Nazi prestige.

The effects on Nazi prestige when an Allied fighter pilot — inevitably — got lucky, happened across the pride of Germanic aviation, and shot it down had not occurred to *Der Grosse Hermann*.

The second reason, even more convoluted, and thus even more likely in the Nazi never-never-land, was that the Condor often carried high-ranking members of the Nazi hierarchy aboard. It was a matter of prestige for them to fly aboard a Condor; they would seem much less important if they traveled abroad on a civil aircraft of a neutral power.

As Peter von Wachtstein stood behind the fence, watching the Condor taxi up to the terminal building, the face of the pilot was familiar. They had flown together in Spain.

A stairway was pushed out to the plane as the pilot shut down the engines. Argentine Customs and Immigration officials stationed themselves at the bottom, and the passengers began to debark.

First off was a tall, well-dressed, good-looking, sharp-featured man in his middle forties. A moment later — still holding his diplomatic passport importantly in his hand — he marched through the gate in the fence, made directly for von Wachtstein, and greeted him somewhat abruptly: "You are?"

"Major von Wachtstein," Peter replied.

"Oh, yes," the man said, his tone suggesting that he was very familiar with just who Peter was and where he fitted into the hierarchy. "In my luggage, I have a letter and a small package for you from your father."

"Oh, really? How good of you, Herr."

"Standartenführer Josef Goltz at your service, Major," Goltz said with a smile.

Major von Wachtstein came to attention and clicked his heels.

"Excuse me, Herr Standartenführer," he said. "I had no way of knowing who you are."

"My movement here was of course classified," Goltz said. "No offense was taken, Major."

"The Herr Standartenführer is very kind," Peter replied.

A very tall, well-dressed, olive-skinned man with prominent features walked through the gate and joined them.

"Colonel, this is Major von Wachtstein, of our embassy," Goltz said.

"I have the pleasure of the Major's acquaintance," the tall man said, offering Peter his hand.

"What a pleasure to see you again, Colonel Perón," Peter said, saluting — the old-style, fingers-to-the-temple salute, now officially out of favor — and then shaking the Colonel's hand.

"And have you found here what I said you would find, Major?"

"What you told me, mi Coronel, was an understatement," Peter said, in absolute sincerity.

"I told this young man," Perón chuckled, "that it would not surprise me if he found our young women extraordinary, and that the reverse might also be true."

"Is that so?" Goltz said with a somewhat strained smile, then looked at Peter and added, "I had rather expected First Secretary Gradny-Sawz to meet me," Goltz said. "We are old friends."

"I'm sure that the First Secretary did not know you were on the plane, Herr Standartenführer," Peter said.

"But if not Gradny-Sawz, then Oberst Grüner," Goltz said.

That did not surprise Peter, who knew that Military Attaché Grüner was, in fact, in the service not only of the Abwehr (the Intelligence Department of German Armed Forces High Command) but the Sicherheitsdienst as well. Grüner himself had actually confided this to von Wachtstein, and he had also been warned about it by Ambassador Manfred Alois Graf von Lutzenberger.

Military attachés are always intelligence officers, although the diplomatic community invariably pretends this is not the case. Grüner's role as SD officer for the Embassy was thus a covert role within a covert role. It was one more manifestation of the Through the Looking Glass land of National Socialism that Peter von Wachtstein had only recently come to understand and loathe.

As a soldier, the scion of an ancient family of Pomeranian warriors, he found it a strange mixture of the comical and deadly. It was literally suicidal to criticize any facet of it.

"The Oberst was charged by First Secretary Gradny-Sawz with handling the Herr Standartenführer's arrival," Peter said. "He thought that I could safely be entrusted with meeting the unidentified very important personage arriving on the Condor, while he saw that your hotel accommodations were both suitable and ready for you."

Goltz looked at him coldly for a moment.

"I presume you have a car, von Wachtstein? I have offered Colonel Perón a ride."

"Oberst Grüner's car and driver are at your service, Herr Standartenführer."

"I can call, and have someone come meet me," Perón said.

"Don't be silly. I knew the embassy would send a car for me. Where am I going, von Wachtstein?"

"A suite has been taken for you at the Alvear Palace Hotel, Herr Standartenführer. Oberst Grüner will be there waiting for you."

"And how will you get to town?" Perón asked.

"A bus is here, Sir, to take the crew, the mail, and diplomatic pouches. I'd planned to go with that. I regret, Sir," he said, turning to Goltz, "that regulations require that I sign for the diplomatic pouches here. It will take a few minutes to get them through Customs. If the Herr Standartenführer doesn't mind waiting, I would be happy to accompany the Herr Standartenführer —"

"Thank you very much, von Wachtstein, but that won't be necessary," Goltz — far too important a personage to be forced to wait around anywhere for anything — interrupted him. "My luggage?"

"I would be happy to see the Herr Standartenführer's luggage arrives safely at his hotel."

"Splendid. You are most obliging, von Wachtstein."

"It is a privilege to be of service to the Herr Standartenführer," von Wachtstein said.

"I'm sure we shall be seeing more of you, Major,"

Perón said. "While I am sure you have met some of our beautiful women, I'm sure you haven't met all of them. Perhaps we can have dinner."

"It would be a great privilege, mi Coronel," Peter said.

He led them to Grüner's Mercedes, saw them safely inside, closed the door, and rendered the Nazi salute as the car drove off.

"Scheisskopf" — shithead — he muttered more than a little bitterly. And then, his diplomatic *carnet** in his hand, he made his way through the Customs and Immigration section, out to the tarmac, and climbed up the movable stairs into the Condor.

The pilot, copilot, and crew chief were still in the cockpit, their laps covered with the mounds of paperwork made necessary both by arrival in a foreign country and to ensure that maintenance personnel had a complete list of items to inspect, replace, or repair.

"Well, Peter," the pilot said, "I thought that was you standing out there showing all the signs of your dissolute and immoral life among the Argentines."

"That sounds like jealousy, Dieter," von Wachtstein said, shaking hands with the pilot and nodding at the copilot. "How was the flight?"

"Wonderful. There's nothing I like better than spending an hour in the air with all the LOW FUEL lights lighting up the cockpit."

"Was it that bad?"

"Not really. We had at *least* thirty minutes' fuel remaining when we sat down."

Both knew that on a 2,800 mile leg, a thirty-minute reserve of fuel at an average airspeed of 220

* A photo identification card in a leather wallet issued by the Argentine Foreign Ministry.

miles, which meant a reserve of 110 miles, was so small as to be meaningless. Or suicidal.

"And when we came out of the soup just now, we almost ran into an American China-Clipper flying boat," the copilot said. When Peter turned to look at him, he added, "I don't have the privilege of the Herr Freiherr's acquaintance." He put out his hand. "I'm First Officer Karl Nabler, Herr Major."

"Peter, please," von Wachtstein said. "I stand in awe of your balls, Sir."

Nabler chuckled. "Because of the low fuel, you mean? It wasn't really only thirty minutes. I made it closer to an hour's reserve."

"For flying with Dieter, is what I meant. I've always believed that at a certain age, old birdmen should be forced to retire."

"You can kiss my ass, Peter," the pilot said.

"What did you almost run into? A China Clipper?"

"I think it's a follow-on model to the China Clipper — bigger engines, for one thing," the pilot said. "Anyway, when we came out of the soup, there it was, a four-engine Pan American flying boat with a great big American flag painted on the fuselage."

"And you didn't consider it your National Socialist duty to try to cut its tail off with your propellers? Shame on you, Dieter."

"That would have been nice, Peter," the pilot said, something in his eyes telling von Wachtstein that jokes of that nature were not wise in the presence of the copilot, "but I decided that the safe arrival of Standartenführer Goltz and Colonel Perón were really more important to Germany than one downed China Clipper."

"And I wasn't sure where we stood, neutrality-wise," the copilot said, making it clear that he didn't consider it insane to try to cut the vertical stabilizers off an enemy civilian transport with one's propellers. "I think that we were within what Argentina claims as its territory."

"Yes, and they take their territorial claims very seriously," von Wachtstein said. "It could have proved embarrassing, whether or not you succeeded."

"Karl, why don't you get the diplomatic pouches out of the baggage compartment?" the pilot suggested, handing him a set of keys. "So that Peter can sign for them and get them off our hands?"

"Yes, Sir."

"I'll give you a hand," Peter said, and stood to one side so that the copilot could get out of his chair.

The copilot walked past him, and Peter started to follow.

"Peter?" the pilot called, and Peter turned. "Have a look at this, will you?"

Peter leaned over the pilot's shoulder. The pilot handed him a thick, well-sealed envelope. Peter glanced at it quickly, just long enough to recognize that the address — "H-P v. W." — was in the handwriting of his father, then stuffed it quickly into the inside pocket of his uniform tunic.

The letter from his father sent in the custody of Standartenführer Goltz was obviously a decoy, sent because a Generalleutnant with connections in high places could be expected to ask someone like Goltz to carry a letter to his sole surviving son — despite specific prohibitions against doing so. It would be thought odd if he hadn't asked the favor.

The letter he had just taken from the pilot was

143

a real letter. Its contents would probably get both of them shot, or more likely garroted, if it wound up in the hands of the SD or Gestapo.

"Thank you," he said.

The pilot nodded.

"Watch what you say around Nabler, Peter," the pilot said. "He still thinks Adolf pisses lemonade."

Major Freiherr Hans-Peter von Wachtstein nodded, then turned and left the cockpit.

[TWO]

```
Dr. Cosme Argerich Military Hospital
Calle Luis María Campos
Buenos Aires
1655 9 April 1943
```

As the convoy of staff cars rolled through the gates of the hospital, Clete had several thoughts, some of them irreverent and on the edge of unkind.

There was absolutely no reason for all these brass hats to be following them. But they had apparently been told to accompany Ramírez to the Panagra terminal to meet him, and nobody had the balls to leave without further orders. And the term "brass hat" was really more appropriate here, where the headgear of the senior brass was both enormous and heavily encrusted with gilt decoration, than it was in the States, where most general officers he had seen had worn soft fore-and-aft caps.

I'll bet those hats weigh more than a steel helmet. These guys probably go home at night with one hell of a headache, groan loudly as they take off their caps, and then have their wives massage their necks.

The guards at the gates, wearing German-style steel helmets, wide-eyed at the parade of brass hats in their cars, snapped to the Argentine equivalent of Present Arms — holding their Mauser rifles vertically, at arm's length, in front of them, where Marines held their rifles so close to their chests that they nearly touched their noses.

I was no better. The first time I saw a general up close I was a little surprised he didn't have a halo.

This place is bigger than I remember. What the hell, it's the Argentine equivalent of Walter Reed Army Hospital in Washington, so why not? The difference, of course, is that probably the only wounded soldier in the whole place is Enrico. Unless some Argentine boot shot himself in the foot on the Known Distance Range.

"Mi General," Clete said, turning to Ramírez. "I know that you and your officers are busy men. I can manage by myself from here."

"Señor Frade, with your kind permission, my officers and I would be honored to accompany you to where your father lies in honor in the Edificio Libertador."

"Your kindness, mi General, honors both me and my father."

Ramírez nodded and then raised his left hand in a gesture Clete had learned was common in Argentina and signified, "it's nothing," or "don't be silly."

The Mercedes pulled up before the main entrance of the white masonry nine-story building. Two helmeted guards brought their Mauser bolt-action rifles to Present Arms. Ramírez's aide-de-camp jumped out of the front seat and opened the rear door for Clete. Meanwhile, a gray-haired man in uniform trousers and a white medical jacket he was still in the process of buttoning came through the ten-foot-high bronze and glass doorway.

He saluted Ramírez.

"A sus órdenes, mi General," he said. "I had no word —"

"Señor Frade," Ramírez interrupted him, "may I present el Coronel-Médico Orrico, who commands Dr. Cosme Argerich Military Hospital? Coronel, this is Señor Frade."

Orrico offered his hand.

"I'm sorry we have to meet under such a tragic circumstance, Mr. Frade," he said in perfect, British English. "I was privileged to call your father my friend. Please accept my sincere condolences."

"Thank you very much, Doctor," Clete said.

"Mr. Frade wishes to see Suboficial Mayor Rodríguez," Ramírez announced.

"Of course," Orrico said, and motioned for them to enter the building.

"How is he?" Clete asked.

"Very fortunate," Orrico replied. "It could have been, should have been, a good deal worse."

"Speak Spanish, please," Ramírez ordered curtly, then looked at Clete and smiled. "My English, you will forgive me, is quite bad."

"Not at all," Clete replied in Spanish.

They boarded an elevator and rode to the sixth floor. When the door opened, a man in civilian clothing was sitting in a very uncomfortable-looking upright chair. Hanging from the back of the chair was a .45 automatic pistol in a shoulder holster. He stood up and came to attention.

A cop, Clete decided. *One of el Teniente Coronel Martín's men? Or Policía Federal?*

Orrico led them down a wide corridor to a room, outside of which sat another guard, this one with

146

his .45 barely concealed in a holster on his belt. And he, too, came to an Attention-like position as Orrico pushed open the door.

A hospital bed, cranked up so that its occupant could sit up, held a heavyset, closely shaven and shorn man in his forties. He was bare-chested, and there were bandages, some of them showing blood, on his chest and arms. His head was heavily bandaged, including one covering his left eye. He was Enrico Rodríguez, late Suboficial Mayor of the Húsares de Pueyrredón cavalry regiment of the Argentine Army.

When he saw Clete, he dropped the newspaper he was reading and tried to get out of bed.

"Stay where you are, Enrico," Clete ordered, walking quickly to him.

"Mi Teniente," Rodríguez said, his voice breaking, "I have failed el Coronel. I have failed you!"

"Don't be absurd," Clete said. He turned. "May I have a moment alone with the Suboficial Mayor, please?"

"Of course," Orrico said.

Clete had the feeling that Ramírez didn't like the idea, but he left the room with the doctor.

Suboficial Mayor Rodríguez was now sobbing.

Clete put his arms around him, felt his throat tighten and his eyes water.

"What happened, Enrico?"

"They were waiting for us about two kilometers from the house at Estancia San Pedro y San Pablo, where the road curves sharply?"

Clete nodded to show he knew where Rodríguez meant.

"They put a beef, a carcass, in the road. When I slowed to go around it, they opened fire. . . ."

"Banditos?"

Rodríguez snorted contemptuously.

"Banditos like the 'burglars' on Libertador," he said.

"They were killed, I'm told, by the Provincial Police."

"They were killed so they could not be questioned by the clowns," Rodríguez said. He customarily referred to the agents of the Bureau of Internal Security as "the clowns."

"Go on."

"Thompsons, I think," Rodríguez said, professionally. "There was too much fire for pistols. I was hit . . ." — he pointed to his head and the bandage — ". . . the bullet must have hit the window post first, or just grazed me."

"Or hit your head and bounced off. My father always said you were the most hardheaded man he had ever known," Clete joked.

"The doctor told me the bullet dug a trench as deep as a fingernail. There was a lot of blood. They probably thought I was dead . . ."

"You were lucky," Clete said.

". . . and the car ran off the road and hit a tree. And when I came to" — he broke into chest-heaving sobs again — "el Coronel was in heaven with the angels, and your blessed mother and my sister."

Clete was surprised at the emotion that came over him. He hugged the older man tightly and only after a long moment found his voice.

"Enrico, mi amigo," he heard himself saying, "in the Bible it is written that there is no greater love than he who lays down his life for another. You did that. You failed neither my father nor me."

I sounded like an Argentine when I said that. I never said anything so corny on Guadalcanal, and Enrico is not the first weeping man I've tried to talk out of feeling responsible for someone else's death. But that came out naturally. What is that, my Argentine genes?

"And in the Bible it says, 'an eye for an eye,' mi Teniente," Rodríguez said.

"I wish you'd stop calling me that," Clete said.

"Whatever you wish, Señor Cletus."

"How about 'Clete'?"

"Whatever you wish, Señor *Clete*."

He simply doesn't understand what I'm asking. That he regard me as a friend, as I regard him. Not as an officer, not, for Christ's sake, as el Patrón. *To hell with it. That can wait.*

"Is there anything I can do for you? Anything I can get you?"

"I wish to pray at the casket of el Coronel," Enrico said. "To beg his forgiveness."

"He has nothing to forgive you for," Clete said.

"And to go with him to his grave."

"I'll arrange for that."

"They tell me it will not be possible," Enrico said.

You will pray at his casket, Enrico, and go with my father to his grave if I have to carry you on my back.

"I'll arrange for it," Clete said firmly.

"Gracias, Señor Clete. Is it fine?"

"Is what fine?"

"Where your father lies in honor. Is it fine and dignified?"

"I don't know. I came here from the plane. That's next."

"Señor Clete, you must go to your father and pray at his casket!"

"Just as soon as I leave here," Clete said.

He put out his hand to Enrico, and then, instead, wrapped his arm around his shoulders.

General Ramírez was waiting, looking a little

149

impatient, outside the room.

"Mi General," Clete said, "Suboficial Mayor Rodríguez wishes to visit my father where he lies and to accompany the body to the grave. Is there a problem with that?"

Ramírez hesitated. "There are, of course, problems of security, Señor Frade."

"Whoever killed my father has no reason to cause harm to Suboficial Mayor Rodríguez."

"Of course," Ramírez said. "I will see to it."

You know as well as I do, don't you, mi General, that "banditos" didn't kill my father?

"I am inappropriately dressed to go to the Edificio Libertador, mi General. May I impose further on your time by asking . . ."

"By now your luggage will be at the house," Ramírez said. "It will be no imposition at all on our time, Señor Frade."

"Thank you," Clete said. "And with your permission, mi General, I would like a private word with el Coronel-Medico Orrico."

"Whatever you wish," Ramírez said, his tone making it clear he was displeased.

Clete took Orrico's arm and led him twenty yards down the corridor.

"Was my father brought here?" he asked.

Orrico nodded.

"Was there an autopsy?"

Orrico nodded again, looking uncomfortable.

"I wish to speak to the physician who performed the autopsy."

"I had that sad duty."

"What was the cause of death?"

Orrico hesitated, then met Clete's eyes.

"Multiple wounds from shotshell pellets to the chest and cranium. We removed twenty-five dou-

150

ble zero pellets from the body, which — together with what I believe are two entrance wounds — makes me believe he was shot twice with a twelve-bore shotgun. Either wound, in my opinion, would have caused instantaneous death. Your father did not suffer, Mr. Frade, if that is any comfort."

"Not very much, mi Coronel," Clete said. "But thank you very much."

He touched Orrico's arm, turned, and walked quickly back to General Ramírez.

[Three]

Alvear Palace Hotel
Avenida Alvear
Buenos Aires
1730 9 April 1943

Oberst Karl-Heinz Grüner, the Military Attaché of the Embassy of the German Reich to the Republic of Argentina, was a tall, ascetic-looking man who looked older than his forty years.

He was not surprised when notified that Standartenführer Josef Goltz would be making a "liaison visit in connection with security matters" to Buenos Aires, only that the "liaison visit" was so long in coming. The *Reine de la Mer* had been blown up on December 31, 1942, three and a half months before.

There was no question whatever in his mind that no matter how long the list of matters about which Goltz wished to liaise, the first item on it would be the destruction of the *Reine de la Mer.* It would therefore seem to follow that Goltz would have come as soon as possible after that disaster.

Germany's submarine operations in the South Atlantic were critically important to the war effort. Neutral Argentina was growing rich providing both the Allies and the Axis with beef, leather, wool, and other agricultural products.

Under international law, a neutral country's merchant ships bound from one neutral country to another could not be torpedoed. Thus, Germany-bound supplies were shipped in Argentine and other neutral bottoms to neutral Portugal or Spain, then transshipped by rail through occupied France to Germany.

England, of course, was also free to use neutral merchantmen as far as Spain or Portugal, and sometimes did so. But there was no way to transship by land cargoes from Spain or Portugal to England, and the moment a merchantman, neutral or otherwise, left a Spanish or Portuguese port for England, it was fair game for German submarines.

The Allied solution to this problem was to use their own merchantmen. These sailed up the Atlantic Coast of South America under the protection of Brazilian warships, and then of the U.S. Navy, until the ships could join well-protected England-bound convoys sailing from ports on the Gulf of Mexico and on the Eastern seaboard of the United States.

Consequently, the best — often the only — place where German submarines could attack England-bound merchant ships was on the high seas between the mouth of the River Plate, when they left protected Argentinian/Uruguayan neutral territory

152

and before they came under Brazilian Navy protection.

It was a very long way — more than 7,000 nautical miles — from the submarine pens in Germany and France to the mouth of the river Plate. As a practical matter, submarines on station in the South Atlantic could not return to their home ports for replenishment. Under the best conditions it was a forty-day round trip, and submarines returning to the South Atlantic arrived already out of fresh food and low on fuel.

Replenishment ships, stocked with everything the submarines needed, were the obvious solution. But either German Navy or civilian cargo vessels ran the great risk of being interdicted and sunk, either en route to the South Atlantic or while on station on the high seas, waiting to replenish submarines. And "neutral" merchantmen serving as replenishment vessels weren't the solution either, as any "neutral" vessel suspected of being a replenishment vessel was shadowed by Allied warships on the high seas and off the Uruguayan and Argentine coasts.

The solution to the problem was to take advantage of Argentine neutrality — with the secret support of some high-ranking Argentine officers.

A Spanish-registered merchantman was secretly loaded with fuel, torpedoes, and other supplies in Bremen. It returned to Spain, and then sailed from Spain for Buenos Aires, as a neutral vessel bound from one neutral port to another, and thus safe from Allied interdiction.

It anchored "with engine problems" within Argentine waters in the Bay of Samborombón in the river Plate estuary. With the Argentine Navy and Coast Guard looking the other way, submarines were able to take on fuel, weapons, and fresh food and then resume their patrols.

It didn't take the Americans long to figure that out.

Reluctant to violate Argentine neutrality by sending warships into Argentine waters to take out a "neutral" merchantman, the Americans turned to covert operation. They sent a team of OSS agents to blow the ship up. But when they arrived, Grüner's contacts in Argentine intelligence warned him of the presence of the OSS team, and later identified them.

Argentina, Uruguay, and Paraguay had a criminal element quite as vicious as any in Berlin or Hamburg. Grüner had little trouble contracting with a group of Argentine smugglers to eliminate this OSS team on the river Plate, and then with a group of Paraguayans to eliminate the Argentines when they went to Paraguay "until things cooled down."

The Americans then sent a second team of OSS agents to Buenos Aires, and again they were identified to Grüner by German sympathizers in the Argentine military. Though Grüner attempted to eliminate the team chief, the attempt failed. And shortly after the replacement replenishment vessel — the Portuguese-registered *Reine de la Mer* — arrived in the Bay of Samborombón with a fresh cargo of torpedoes and fuel, she was blown to bits, taking to the bottom with her a submarine that was tied up alongside taking on fuel. There were no survivors.

Grüner didn't know exactly how this was accomplished. But he suspected the infiltration into Argentina of a team of U.S. Navy underwater demolition experts — with the assistance of el

Coronel Jorge Guillermo Frade. Frade also doubtless helped the team in its exfiltration from that country.

It was a monumental disaster for submarine operations. The *Reine de la Mer* had managed to refuel and otherwise replenish only one submarine before it was destroyed. Afterward, Grüner had no idea how many other submarines — he guessed ten, or perhaps a dozen — were ranging the South Atlantic counting on replenishment in Samborombón Bay.

What those submarines did when they were advised that fuel and food — not to mention torpedoes or ammunition for their cannon — were not going to be available in the South Atlantic was unpleasant to think about.

Even the obvious — heading for the submarine pens on the coast of France — was not possible for some of them. They did not have the necessary fuel for the twenty-day voyage.

There were options, of course. There are always options. They could rendezvous at sea with other submarines. Those with reserve fuel could share it with those whose tanks were empty. As a last desperate measure, one submarine could theoretically tow another.

Grüner had heard nothing of what actually happened. The German embassy in Buenos Aires was told only what it was necessary for it to know. Significantly, Grüner thought, there had been no word of a replacement for the *Reine de la Mer*. Which probably meant that none was en route. There was a possibility, of course, that the completely unexpected — and catastrophic — loss of the *Reine de la Mer* had so upset people that Buenos Aires would learn of a replacement vessel only when it entered Argentine waters.

It was also possible, of course, that a midocean rendezvous had taken place, with the submarines receiving at least fuel from the tanks of German surface warships, or perhaps even from merchantmen, German or otherwise, which would at least get them back to the sub pens in France.

But for all practical purposes, the destruction of the *Reine de la Mer* had brought submarine operations in the South Atlantic to a halt.

El Coronel Jorge Guillermo Frade had been one of the most powerful men in Argentina. It was scarcely a secret that he had been the power behind the Grupo de Oficiales Unidos, who were reliably reported to be about to stage a coup against the government of President Ramón S. Castillo. At one time, Frade, a close friend of General Pedro P. Ramírez, the Argentine Minister of War, had been thought to be, like Ramírez, very sympathetic to the German cause.

That had changed. In an unexpectedly masterful stroke on their part, the Americans sent in Frade's long-estranged son. Blood, Grüner knew, was indeed stronger than water, and he himself knew the strong emotion — mixed pride and love — a father felt for a son who was a heroic aviator.

Grüner now acknowledged that he had allowed that knowledge to color his judgment. Young Frade had turned out to be more than a son sent to tug on the heartstrings of a father from whom he had been long separated. He was also a professional intelligence officer. The bodies of the two highly qualified assassins sent to eliminate him, and the blown-up *Reine de la Mer*, were absolute proof of that.

After a good deal of thought, Grüner decided that Goltz had waited to come to Argentina until the operation to eliminate el Coronel Jorge Guillermo Frade was carried out. If Goltz had been in Argentina, some would suspect he was involved in that. Because of the implications of the Frade elimination, and of his own and Ambassador von Lutzenberger's objections to it, Grüner also decided that the order to eliminate Frade must have come from higher up — perhaps from Canaris or Ribbentrop. But he wasn't sure. In his experience, highly placed SS-SD officers were very good at arranging for fingers of suspicion to point at other people.

There would be a long list of other items on Goltz's agenda, of course, matters that interested the upper echelons of the Nazi hierarchy.

This secondary list would start with questions concerning how long it had taken him to deal with the problem of el Coronel Jorge Guillermo Frade once the order to eliminate him was given. This would be followed by the ritual inquiries into the level of devotion to the Führer personally and to National Socialism generally by members of the Embassy staff from Ambassador Manfred Alois Graf von Lutzenberger downward.

Goltz and his superiors would also be interested in what he had done, and was doing, to aid the escape and repatriation of the officers of the *Graf Spee* who had been interned in Argentina since the ship was scuttled.

Getting the officers out of the internment camp and back to Germany was of personal interest to Abwehr Chief Admiral Wilhelm Canaris, who had himself escaped from Argentine internment during the First World War. Oberst Grüner was very sensitive to this; Canaris was not only his superior officer in the Abwehr, but an old friend as well.

157

He was sure that Canaris had been satisfied with his report on the sinking of the *Reine de la Mer*, and that Canaris would not hold him personally responsible for it, or for the failed elimination attempt on the OSS team chief. Things go wrong, honest mistakes are made; in his report to Canaris he had admitted his culpability.

He'd admitted further that he should not have presumed that Coronel Frade's son was the naive amateur he had believed him to be, and that he also should have presumed Frade would help his son, regardless of his sympathy for the German cause. Canaris would understand. But that did not mean that others high in the Intelligence and Espionage hierarchies of the Third Reich would be satisfied with his explanations, or with the time it took him to comply with orders to eliminate el Coronel Frade.

"Herr Oberst," Günther Loche announced loudly as he pushed open the door to the suite Grüner had taken for the visiting liaison officer, "Standartenführer Goltz!"

Grüner liked Loche, a civilian employee of the Embassy known as a "local hire," because he was just smart enough for his driving duties — in other words, not too smart to the point where he would take an interest in matters that were none of his business.

His parents had immigrated to Argentina after the First World War and went into the sausage business, where they mildly prospered. More important, they were as devoted supporters of Adolf Hitler and National Socialism as anyone Grüner had ever met. And there was something else: Günther's father, who had served on the Western Front

158

in the First World War and had few illusions about combat service, was delighted that Grüner had convinced Günther that he could make a greater contribution to National Socialism by serving as his driver than by "returning to the Fatherland" and volunteering for military service.

"Welcome to Argentina, Herr Standartenführer," Grüner said, raising his arm in the approved Nazi salute. "Oberst Grüner at your service. I hope it was a pleasant flight?"

"A very long flight, Herr Oberst," Goltz said, returning the salute. The two men shook hands and unabashedly examined each other.

They were of equal rank. Tonight, of course, at dinner at the Ambassador's residence, Standartenführer Goltz would have the place of honor, and be seated at the head table next to the Ambassador and across from the Ambassador's wife. Ordinarily, although he was senior in grade by almost two years to Grüner, he would be seated far below him at a formal dinner table. Protocol, which for some reason had always fascinated Grüner, held that branch of service was the first consideration, then the rank of the individual.

In terms of protocol, the Army was the senior service, followed by the Navy, the Air Force, and then the SS. This was a source of annoyance to many members of the SS. Since their mission was the protection of National Socialism and the Führer himself, they felt that the SS should be the senior service, and that SS officers should not be relegated to a distant corner of an official table. None of the other services agreed, of course.

Grüner had come to understand and appreciate the necessity for protocol and to understand why it rankled the SS. Many senior SS officers had

159

never worked their way up through the ranks, and that situation was getting worse. To curry favor with — or ensure the loyalty of — high-ranking bureaucrats and even prominent doctors, lawyers, and businessmen, these people were being given honorary officer's rank in the Allgemeine SS. This carried with it the privilege of wearing the black SS uniform and the cap adorned with death's-head.

At a formal dinner, serving SS officers had precedence over honorary officers. So everyone at a dinner could look down the table and see who was a serving SS officer, and who was a bureaucrat or businessman dressed up like one.

Grüner found a certain justice in the dictates of protocol, and had taken pleasure that every time the SS wanted the system changed, it had been frustrated by those who wanted it left as it was.

Goltz had at least once been a serving officer. Although they had never seen each other before, Grüner knew a good deal about him. In the same out-of-normal-channels envelope in which he had notified him of the identity of the SS liaison officer who would visit Argentina, Admiral Canaris had included a copy of Goltz's Abwehr dossier.

Grüner had learned that Standartenführer Josef Luther Goltz was a Hessian, born in 1897 in Giessen, forty miles north of Frankfurt an der Main. He was called up with his class of eighteen-year-olds in 1915, and served four months in the trenches on the Western Front with the 219th Infanterie Regiment. While recuperating in Weisbaden from wounds, he was awarded the Iron Cross Second Class, as well as selected for Officer Training School.

On graduation he was posted to the Sixteenth "List" Bavarian Infanterie Reserve Regiment — in which Corporal Adolf Hitler won the Iron Cross First Class — and served in it until the Armistice in November 1918. During that time he was wounded twice again, promoted Captain, and also awarded the Iron Cross First Class.

Obviously, Grüner thought as he read the dossier, *if Lieutenant or Captain Goltz encountered Corporal Hitler in the trenches, he treated him well, or he would not be a Standartenführer.*

Immediately demobilized after the Armistice of 1918, Goltz returned briefly to school, but after less than a year at Munich University, he dropped out. He then found employment driving a streetcar for the City of Munich. And in 1921, he joined the Sturmabteilungen (the SA, the private army of the Nazi party, commonly called the "Brown Shirts," commanded by Ernst Röhm) of the just-renamed (from "German Workers' Party") Nationalsozialistische Deutsche Arbeiterpartei (National Socialist German Workers' Party).

Grüner remembered this now, seeing the "Long Service" Nazi party pin in Goltz's lapel.

In 1924, Goltz left Civil Service to work full-time for the Nazi party. And in 1929, he left both the SA and the employ of the Nazi party to reenter government service, this time as a policeman. In 1933, he was commissioned into the SS as a Hauptsturmführer, the equivalent of a captain. His promotions thereafter came rapidly.

After reading Goltz's dossier, Grüner decided that Goltz was an obviously bright, well-connected, and thus dangerous man. Looking at his face now, he saw nothing to change that opinion.

"I think you'll be comfortable here," Grüner said, gesturing around the suite.

"I'm sure I will be," Goltz said. "At what time,

if you know, would it be convenient for me to present my respects to the Ambassador?"

"The Ambassador requests the pleasure of your company at dinner at the residence . . ."

"How kind of him."

". . . at eight P.M. Following this, the Ambassador suggests that you join the official party which will go to the Edificio Libertador to pay our respects to the late Oberst Jorge Guillermo Frade."

Goltz's face now showed interest.

"Oh, really?"

"Günther, would you wait in the corridor, please?" Grüner ordered.

"Jawohl, Herr Oberst," Günther said, came to attention, clicked his heels the way he had seen Major von Wachtstein do, and left the room.

"Oberst Frade," Grüner said, pausing to light a cigarette, "a prominent Argentine, was tragically murdered during a robbery attempt three days ago."

"So I've heard," Goltz said. "Murdered by robbers, you said?"

"Yes. They were quickly detected by the Buenos Aires Provincial Police, and died in a gun battle during an attempt to arrest them."

"That question was one of the matters I had wished to discuss with you, Herr Oberst," Goltz said. "There was some question —"

"I must temper my desire to immediately comply with my orders," Grüner said, aware of the direction Goltz was taking him, "as I am sure you will understand, Herr Standartenführer, with other considerations."

"There are those in Berlin who felt you questioned that decision, Herr Oberst."

"Both the Ambassador and I felt that it was

unnecessary, Herr Standartenführer, and perhaps even unwise. I cannot, of course, speak for the Ambassador, but I still feel that way. A moot question, anyway. Oberst Frade is no longer with us."

"The thinking in Berlin — of your superiors and mine — to which I was privy, was that the solution ordered would not only have the obvious benefit of making sure Oberst Frade was not in a position to cause Argentina to declare war on Germany, it would also make the point that the enemies of Germany, no matter how highly placed, are not immune to German retribution."

Grüner did not reply.

"You question the wisdom of that decision, Herr Oberst?"

"I never question my orders, Herr Standartenführer. But I consider it my duty to advise my superiors of my best judgment on any issue before them."

"Of course. And your candor, as well as your professionalism, Herr Oberst, is both admired and respected in Berlin. But in this case, certainly you are willing to concede that you were . . . what shall I say . . . that you erred on the side of caution?"

"Time will tell, of course, Herr Standartenführer."

"What if I told you that Oberst Juan Domingo Perón was on the Condor with me?"

Grüner shrugged.

"We can, I presume, credibly deny that we were in any way involved in Oberst Frade's tragic death at the hands of robbers?"

"With the assassins dead, there is no way that any connection with us can be proved, Herr Standartenführer. Credibly denied, yes. But that is not quite the same thing."

"Oberst Perón is a member, a powerful member, of the G.O.U., is he not?"

"He is."

"Wouldn't you agree that for Perón to replace Frade as a power in the G.O.U. is to Germany's advantage? After the coup d'état, in particular?"

"Oberst Perón and Oberst Frade were intimate, lifelong friends, Herr Standartenführer. That was one of the points I raised."

"And it was duly noted," Goltz said, although he could not remember that being mentioned in Berlin. "I concede that may be no immediate problem. But since you tell me that we can credibly deny knowledge of the incident, and since time passes . . ."

"Today's Pan American flight from Miami brought with it Oberst Frade's son, Herr Standartenführer. I rather doubt that he will keep from Oberst Perón his suspicions regarding those responsible for his father's death, or that he will permit the subject to simply pass into memory."

"Certainly the Argentine authorities are aware that he is an OSS agent? Who violated Argentine neutrality with regard to the *Reine de la Mer*?" Goltz asked.

"I'm sure that Admiral Montoya is fully aware of those facts."

"And that won't get him expelled from the country? I'm surprised they let him in."

"Keeping him out would have been impossible."

"How so?"

"He entered the country on an Argentine passport."

"How can he do that?" Goltz asked, surprised and annoyed.

"He was born here. Under Argentine law, he is

an Argentine. He is apparently claiming both his inheritance and his Argentine citizenship."

"Are you telling me that a word in the proper ear cannot expose that charade? And have him expelled?"

"Finding the proper ear may be difficult, Herr Standartenführer."

"That's your job, Herr Oberst!" Goltz said, his temper flaring.

"When Oberst Frade's son arrived at the Pan American terminal, Herr Standartenführer, he was greeted by a delegation of senior Argentine military officers, headed by the Minister for War, General Pedro P. Ramírez, and Major General Arturo Rawson. Both men were close friends of Oberst Frade. I rather doubt that would be of much use to whisper in either of their ears that expelling Oberst Frade's son would be a good thing."

"The Americans arranged for that?"

"I don't think so. I think it was General Ramírez's own idea. Both to show respect for the late Oberst Frade and to send a signal to those responsible for his death that the officer corps of the Argentine Army is displeased."

"That's an unexpected development."

"I was disappointed, but not surprised. Oberst Frade was a highly respected officer. Perhaps even a beloved officer."

"We will have to have a long talk about this," Goltz said. "But I would prefer that the Ambassador and Gradny-Sawz participate. This is not the time."

"I am at your disposal, Herr Standartenführer."

"You were telling me about tonight?"

"The Ambassador suggests that you join the official party to pay respects to Oberst Frade at the

165

Edificio Libertador. Inasmuch as the Ambassador and the First Secretary will be in uniform, you might wish to wear uniform yourself."

Goltz considered that. "It may require pressing. . . ."

"I'm sure that will pose no problem," Grüner said. "May I suggest you wear uniform to the Ambassador's residence?"

"Yes," Goltz agreed.

"Following dinner the senior Embassy officers will meet at the Residence, and we will all go to the Edificio Libertador. That shouldn't take long. There is a Corps Diplomatique line. You sign a guest register, enter the Hall of Honor, pay your respects at the casket, then to members of the Frade family in an adjacent room, and have a glass of champagne with the Argentine protocol officer in another adjacent room. After that you are free to go. The Ambassador will bring you back to the hotel."

"What, exactly, does 'pay one's respects at the casket' mean?"

"This is a Roman Catholic country. The custom is that you kneel — a prie-dieu is provided — at the casket and offer a prayer for the quick reception of the deceased into heaven."

"Are you a Catholic, Herr Oberst?" Goltz asked, almost suspiciously.

"I was raised Evangalische" — Protestant — "but I rarely enter a church except when duty requires. There will be a funeral service tomorrow for Oberst Frade at the Basílica of Our Lady of Pilar, with interment to follow in the adjacent cemetery. It's called Recoleta. I don't know whether the Ambassador would like you to attend that or not."

"I'll discuss that with him tonight," Goltz said. "I am not fond of either funerals or church."

"The diplomatic service of the Reich sometimes requires that one do things one would rather not," Grüner said, and immediately was sorry.

Goltz was liable to interpret the remark as referring to the Frade action, and in fact Goltz looked at him strangely.

"How do I get from here to the Residence?"

"I would be happy to take you there, but that will mean I will have to stop by my house to change into dress uniform. The other option is to have Major von Wachtstein accompany you. A third option would be to go to the Residence by yourself. In my car. You would be in Günther's hands. He is both a capable driver and speaks Spanish, which may prove useful to you."

"Of the three options, I would prefer to inconvenience the Major," Goltz said.

"The Major works for me," Grüner said. "What pleases you would be convenient for him."

"Perhaps if he came by here in time to take me?"

Grüner went to the door and motioned Günther into the room.

"Do you know where the Major is, Günther?"

"The Herr Freiherr is seeing to the Herr Standartenführer's luggage, Herr Oberst," Günther said. "He should be here any minute."

"Then it's solved," Grüner said. "I will leave you here in Günther's competent hands until von Wachtstein shows up, and then see you at the Residence."

Günther smiled at what he perceived to be a compliment.

"You have been most kind, Herr Oberst," Goltz said.

"It has been my privilege, Herr Standartenführer," Grüner said, and offered both his hand and the Nazi salute.

Goltz returned it, and Grüner started to walk out of the room.

"Oh, there is one more thing," Goltz called after him. Grüner turned to look at him. "I have to go to Montevideo, as quickly as possible. How difficult a trip is that?"

"I presume, Herr Standartenführer, that you have visas for both Argentina and Uruguay?"

Goltz nodded.

"In that case, it is a rather pleasant trip. One catches a boat downtown, at ten at night, has dinner aboard, goes to a very nice stateroom, and wakes up in downtown Montevideo."

"That's the quickest way?"

"One can drive. There is a ferry across the Río Uruguay at Gualeguaychú. It is about a six-hour drive, but one can, obviously, leave when one wishes."

"There is no quicker way?"

"We have a Fieseler Storch, Herr Standartenführer. Von Wachtstein flies it. I'm sure it would be at your disposal."

The Fieseler Storch was a two-seat, high-wing observation and liaison aircraft powered by a V8 Argus AS 10c.3 240-horsepower engine that provided a top speed of 109 m.p.h. and a range of 400 miles.

"And how long would it take by Storch?"

"That would depend, Herr Standartenführer, on how much of the journey one was willing to make over water. As the crow flies, one hour and thirty minutes. That route is essentially over the Río de la Plata. The Río de la Plata ends fifty miles north

168

where the Río Uruguay begins. By flying north and then south over land to Montevideo, perhaps three hours."

"Be so good as to ensure that the Storch is available, should I need it."

"Of course, Herr Standartenführer. Is that all, Herr Standartenführer?"

"Thank you again, Herr Oberst."

Grüner left the room.

Adding his reaction to their brief personal contact to his impression of the dossier he had read in the Sicherheitsdienst headquarters in Berlin, Goltz decided very much the same thing about Grüner as Grüner had decided about him: Grüner was obviously bright and well-connected, and thus dangerous.

Goltz decided he was going to have to be very careful dealing with Oberst Grüner in the accomplishment of his mission.

VI

[One]

1728 Avenida Coronel Díaz
Palermo, Buenos Aires
1730 9 April 1943

A 1940 Ford Fordor sedan was parked at the curb before the massive cast-iron fence. Two men were sitting in it.

More cops? Clete wondered. *Or Martín's men?*

The enormous bronze lights beside the double doors to the mansion were draped in black, and black wreaths were fixed to the wrought-bronze metalwork that protected each of the double doors.

A dignified, silver-haired man in his sixties, dressed in a gray frock coat with a black mourning band around the sleeve, opened the door to them. Antonio had been el Coronel Jorge Guillermo Frade's butler for longer than Clete was old.

"Señor Cletus, my prayers that you would arrive in time to say farewell to your father have been answered," he said.

"I am here, Antonio," he said "Would you offer General Ramírez and the other gentlemen something to drink — coffee, whiskey, whatever — while I change? My luggage *is* here?"

"You have been unpacked, Señor Cletus," Antonio said.

"Where did you put me?" Clete asked.

"In the master suite, of course, Señor Cletus," Antonio said. "Should I show you the way?"

"I know where it is," Clete said. "Please take care of my guests." He turned to General Ramírez. "I won't be long, mi General."

"Take whatever time you need," Ramírez said.

As Clete crossed the marble-floored foyer and went up to the second floor on the left branch of the curving double stairway, he remembered two descriptions of the mansion. His father had told him that his mother referred to the place as "The Museum" and refused to live there. And his father himself had described it as "my money sewer on Avenida Coronel Díaz."

It was like a museum, both in its dimensions and in the plethora of artwork, huge oil paintings and statuary that covered the walls and open spaces. The first time he saw the building, and the artwork, he had the somewhat irreverent thought that two subjects seemed to capture the fascination of Argentine artists and sculptors: the prairie — here called *La Pampa* — at dusk, during a rainstorm; and women dressed in what looked like wet sheets that generally left exposed at least one large and well-formed breast.

He really wished that Antonio had put him in one of the guest rooms — there were certainly enough of them — instead of in his father's suite. Its four rooms spread across the rear of the house, with windows opening on a formal, English-style garden surrounded by a wall.

When he reached the double doors to his father's suite, he stopped, his hand actually raised to knock.

"That's no longer necessary, is it?" he asked aloud, and pushed down on the bronze lever that opened the right door.

Inside was a living room, one of the few places in the house that seem to have been furnished with anyone's comfort in mind. To the right was a book-lined office. Straight ahead was the bedroom, with a dressing room to one side and a bath to the other. The furniture everywhere was heavy, and the couches and armchairs seemed to him to be constructed lower to the floor than such furniture in the States.

He took off his jacket and tossed it on the bed, then went into the dressing room.

"I wonder where they hid my stuff?" he asked aloud.

He slid open the first of a line of doors along the right side of the dressing room.

"I'll be damned," he said.

The closet held the three suits and three sports coats he had brought with him, and on separate hangers half a dozen pair of trousers. He took from a hanger a brand-new, nearly black, faintly pin-striped suit — one he had dubbed, when he bought it in Washington, "my diplomat's uniform" — carried it back into the bedroom, and tossed it on the bed.

It got through to him that his entire clothing wardrobe looked very lonely in the large closet.

He went back into the dressing room and slid open the adjacent door. That closet was absolutely empty, and so was the one next to it. On the other side of the room, a closet with shelves for God Only Knows how many shirts now held only the dozen new shirts he had purchased — like two of the suits — for his diplomatic assignment, along with half a dozen other shirts. The closet next to that held the three sweaters he had brought with him — on shelves that would accommodate fifty. The final closet held his dozen sets of shorts and skivvy shirts, plus his shoes and boots — including his favorite, battered, ancient pair of cowboy boots, which someone had already made a determined, if unsuccessful, effort to shine — and his half-dozen neckties and two pairs of suspenders.

The last time he saw the dressing room, the closets were crowded with his father's clothing. El Coronel Frade was something of a clothes horse. Now it was all gone. He wondered where.

He picked out a necktie and linen, and suspenders — the salesman in Washington had insisted on calling them "braces" — and after a moment's indecision, his new pair of "dress boots," and carried everything into the bedroom, where he tossed it all on the bed.

The enormous bathroom, marble-floored and -walled, as large as Clete's bedroom in the old man's house on St. Charles Avenue, was even worse. His battered Gillette safety razor, comb, brush, toothbrush, toothpaste, and half-empty bottle of Mennen's After Shave lotion were laid out to the left of the washbasin, a depression two feet across in a twenty-foot slab of marble. On the other side of the basin was arrayed an obviously new sterling silver version of the Gillette in a silver case, and in the event that wasn't acceptable, a set of seven ivory-handled straight razors. There was a shaving brush and a wooden tub of English shaving soap; two different kinds of bath soap; an array of bottles of what he presumed were after shave and cologne; a matched set of hairbrushes and a tortoiseshell comb that looked large and sturdy enough to do a horse's mane.

A thick terry-cloth bathrobe was laid out farther down the marble slab. And a chrome stand near the glass door to the shower held four towels and a washcloth.

Clete stripped, picked up one of the bars of soap and his Gillette, and opened the shower door. He showered quickly and shaved, using the bath soap, a time-saving device he had learned in his first year at Texas A&M, where cadets were allotted about five minutes each morning for their personal toilette.

He came out of the shower and took a towel — a warm towel; the chrome stand was obviously a heating device — and dried himself. He looked at the terry-cloth robe, decided there was no time for that luxury, and walked naked out of the bath into the living room to get his underwear.

A uniformed maid was standing there, a young woman with her hair drawn back severely under a lace cap, who had pushed a serving tray into the room. When she saw him, she flushed and modestly averted her eyes.

"Sorry," Clete said, grossly embarrassed, and retreated into the bathroom for the terry-cloth robe.

Modestly covered, he returned to the bedroom.

"Antonio was not sure if you would prefer coffee, tea, or whiskey, Señor Frade," the maid said, indicating the cart, which held silver coffee and tea pitchers, three bottles, and all the accessories.

"Coffee, please, and that will be all," Clete said, went to the bed for his underwear, and again retreated to the bathroom.

The maid was gone when he came out again.

Coffee had been poured and was waiting for him on a small round table. He took a sip, grimaced at its strength, put the cup down, and went to the tray.

He picked up a bottle of Jack Daniel's, uncorked it, and took a healthy swallow from the neck.

Then he dressed quickly, returning a final time to the bathroom to tie the necktie and brush his hair.

The uniform caps of General Ramírez and the other officers were lined up in a row on a table in the foyer. He found the officers themselves sitting comfortably in the couches and armchairs of the downstairs reception room. They all rose to their feet when he walked in.

[Two]

Ministry of Defense
Edificio Libertador
Avenida Paseo Colón
Buenos Aires
1845 9 April 1943

There were both ceremonial and functioning guards on the wide steps leading up to the entrance of the fifteen-story Edificio Libertador. The ceremonial troops were in a uniform* that dated back

* White breeches, dark-blue coats, high black leather boots, and what resembles a silk top hat. The hat dates back even earlier, to 1806, when a volunteer force was recruited and led by thirty-four-year-old General Juan Martín Pueyrredón to resist a British attempt to occupy Buenos Aires. Pueyrredón seized a British mer-

to Argentina's War of Independence (1810–16). They were armed with rifles and sabers of the period and stood at rigid attention, seeing nothing, like the guards at Buckingham Palace. A dozen other soldiers, in present-day German-style uniforms and steel helmets and armed with Mauser rifles, were shepherding a long line of people into the building.

The Marine officer in Clete Howell Frade — remembering that the soldiers who march perpetually guarding the Tomb of the Unknown Soldier in Arlington Cemetery allow absolutely nothing, not even the President of the United States, to disturb their ritual — wondered if the ceremonial guards here would salute the Minister of War. They did not, but the sergeant in charge of the other detail scurried quickly both to salute Ramírez and to quickly open a door for them.

Clete followed Ramírez across the lobby of the building to a corridor to the right. The line of people he had seen outside was obviously headed in the same direction.

To my father's casket? Why does that bother me?

As Clete followed Ramírez past it, the shuffling line moved slowly through a corridor. The corridor was lined with foreign flags, their flagstaffs resting in heavy bronze, vaselike holders. The Stars and Stripes looked strange somehow, as just one flag among many. He spotted the German flag, with its

---

chantman in the harbor. Its cargo included top hats, which Pueyrredón issued to his troops — primarily gauchos from the Pampas — as the only item of uniform he had available. Four years later, together with generals Manuel Belgrano and José de San Martin (revered as El Libertador), he led the war for liberation from Spain, which concluded with the July 19, 1816, Proclamation of the Congress of Tucumán, declaring the United Provinces of La Plata to be free of Spain and to be the Argentine Republic.

swastika, and the Japanese, with its red-ball "rising sun," similarly lost among other flags and flags he could not remember seeing before. He smiled, remembering that the Air Group parachute riggers on Guadalcanal had made a very nice buck, indeed, turning out on their sewing machines Genuine Japanese Battle Flags for sale to gullible replacements and dogfaces.

They probably use this place for diplomatic receptions, he decided. *If you show up, they haul your flag out of the corridor to make you feel welcome.*

The corridor ended at another enormous set of double doors, also guarded by soldiers in ordinary uniforms. Only one of them was open, and as they approached, a sergeant stopped the shuffling line and motioned for Ramírez, Clete, and the officers trailing behind them to enter the room. In turn, Ramírez signaled for Clete to precede him.

He found himself in an enormous, marble-floored and marble-walled room that reminded him of photographs he had seen of Hitler's Reichs-chancellery in Berlin. He started to walk across the room to the end of the shuffling line of people, but Ramírez stopped him with a gentle tug at his sleeve.

It took several minutes for the last people in the shuffling line to pass by the casket at the far end of the room, but finally Clete could see it. It was on what looked like a table draped in black velvet. Hanging from the ceiling above — *which must be fifty, sixty feet high, at least,* Clete thought — was a huge Argentine flag three times as wide as the casket was long.

That has that golden-face-in-a-sunburst centered on the blue-white-blue stripes, Clete thought, *which makes it a military flag. The ordinary flag has just the stripes.*

Behind the casket were massed twenty or thirty normal-size Argentine military flags in holders placed so close together that the flags formed a blue and white mass.

At each corner of the casket, facing outward, head bent, his hands resting near the muzzle of a butt-on-the-floor Mauser cavalry carbine, stood a trooper of the Húsares de Pueyrredón, in full dress uniform.* Behind the casket was a Capitán of Húsares, head bent, his hands resting on his unsheathed saber.

Ramírez touched Clete's arm, a signal that he was supposed to approach the casket. He walked alone, uncomfortably, down the one hundred feet or so toward it. When he was halfway there, he heard a faint order being given, and was surprised to see the troopers and the officers, in slow motion, raise their heads and then bring their weapons to Present Arms, the troopers with their carbines held at arm's length in front of them, the Capitán with his saber also held upright at arm's length.

He remembered his father, who'd had more than a couple of drinks at the time, telling him that he was not at all surprised that he had "done well" in the Corps, since the blood of Pueyrredón — of whom Clete had never heard before that moment — "coursed through his veins."

That salute is as much for me, as the great-great-grandson, or whatever the hell I am, of Pueyrredón, as it is for my father.

* The dress uniform of the Húsares de Pueyrredón — Pampas horsemen turned cavalrymen — features a bearskin hat and a many-buttoned tunic bedecked with ornate embroidery clearly patterned after that of the Royal & Imperial Hungarian Hussars of the Austro-Hungarian Empire.

He felt his throat tighten, and his eyes watered.

For Christ's sake, control yourself. You're a Marine officer, and Marine officers don't weep!

He reached the closed, beautifully carved solid cedar casket. An Argentine flag was draped over the lower half of it. His father's high-crowned, gold-encrusted uniform cap and a blue velvet pillow covered with medals rested on the upper portion.

Where the hell did you get all those medals, Dad? Argentina's never been in a war. So far as I know, you never heard a shot fired in anger.

Except one, of course. El Coronel-Medico Orrico said death came instantaneously.

He dropped to his knees at the prie-dieu.

I don't want to think of you inside that casket, Dad. I've seen what happens to people when they take a load of 00-buckshot in the face.

I'm sorry my coming here got you killed.

I'm sorry I spent most of my life thinking you were an unmitigated sonofabitch.

I feel sorry as hell for myself because I will never get to know you better.

I really hope that Enrico was right, and that you're with the angels and my mother in heaven.

And I swear to God, Dad, I'll get the sonsofbitches who did this to you.

He rose to his feet. As he did, he heard the Húsares Capitán murmur another order. He looked at him. The Capitán was starting the slow-motion routine of changing from Present Arms to whatever the hell they call that head-bowed, hands-on-weapon position.

Clete snapped his right hand to his temple in a crisp salute. There was surprise and maybe displeasure in the Capitán's eyes.

Well, fuck you, Capitán. I'm an officer, you're an officer, and my father was an officer. If I want to salute, I goddamn well will salute.

He held the salute until the Capitán had rested his hands on his saber again and started to incline his head. Then he made a precise left-face movement and marched away from the casket.

The Capitán who had come aboard the seaplane, now wearing a Húsares full dress uniform, and who Clete decided was probably a couple of years older than he was, stood by a door at the side of the room. He motioned to Clete, and Clete went through the door and found himself in a small room furnished with heavy, leather-upholstered furniture.

"May I offer you a small refreshment, Mayor Frade?" the Capitán asked.

Sure. Why the hell not? A couple of canapés, how about a cucumber sandwich and a deviled egg?

The Capitán held a bottle of Johnny Walker scotch in one hand and a bottle of Martel cognac in the other.

"The cognac, por favor, Capitán," Clete said.

The snifter he was handed a moment later was half full of liquid. He had just taken a healthy swallow and was beginning to feel the warmth spread through his body when generals Ramírez and Rawson came into the room. Ramírez took a handkerchief from his pocket and dabbed at his eyes.

"A soldier is not supposed to show emotion," Ramírez said. "But when you saluted . . ."

Well, at least he didn't disapprove. That makes me feel better.

Ramírez pointed a finger at Clete's snifter, as a signal to the Capitán to get him one.

"What we will do, with your permission, Señor Frade," Ramírez said, "is wait for the other officers to join us. Then, if you think it is appropriate, we will raise our glasses a final time in the presence of your father."

"I think he would like that, mi General."

"And then I will turn you over to Capitán Lauffer, who is General Rawson's aide-de-camp," Ramírez said, inclining his head toward the Húsares Capitán. "He will be with you until after the interment tomorrow. If there is anything you need that the Capitán cannot provide, please get in touch with me."

"You're very kind, mi General."

"Not at all. Your father was a lifelong friend, and I can't tell you how sorry I am, how ashamed, that this terrible thing happened to him."

The small room gradually filled with the officers who had been following them around since Clete had gotten off the plane. When Capitán Lauffer had provided each of them a brandy snifter, Ramírez raised his own glass high.

"Gentlemen, I give you our late comrade-in-arms, friend, and distinguished Argentinian, el Coronel Jorge Guillermo Frade."

They all raised their glasses and drained them — surprising Clete, who thought they would take a small ceremonial sip. Then, apparently in order of rank, with Ramírez doing so first, they each shook Clete's hand, expressed their condolences a final time, and left the room.

"Capitán, what did you do wrong?" Clete asked Lauffer. "You seem to be stuck with me."

"It is my privilege, Señor. I served under your father."

"Well, I think you can go home after you take

me back to the house. All I'm going to do, frankly, is have another stiff drink and go to bed."

Capitán Lauffer looked uncomfortable.

"I don't think that's what you had in mind, is it?" Clete said.

"I thought perhaps you might wish to call on your aunt and uncle, Señor."

Christ, I forgot all about them!

"La Señora de Duarte left here only minutes before you arrived," Lauffer said. "She asked me to tell you that she waited as long as she could, but she had an appointment with Monsignor Kelly, some final points about the Mass and interment tomorrow."

"Thank you," Clete said. "The embarrassing truth is I completely forgot about my aunt and uncle."

"Under the circumstances . . ." Lauffer said.

"And so, if you would be so kind, I would appreciate a ride over to the Avenue Alvear."

"My car is out in back," Lauffer said. "It will save you passing through the crowd in front."

I also forget Dorotéa. Jesus Christ! And Tony and Dave Ettinger. And Peter. I really want to see him. And with Capitán Lauffer hanging around, how am I going to be able to?

And — Jesus H. Christ! — Claudia! She wasn't married to him, but if anybody feels worse about my father than I do, it's Claudia, and I didn't even think of her until just now.

[Three]

Alvear Palace Hotel
Avenida Alvear
Buenos Aires
1930 9 April 1943

Anton von Gradny-Sawz, First Secretary of the Embassy of the German Reich to the Republic of Argentina, was wearing his heavily gold-encrusted diplomatic uniform when the top-hatted doorman pulled open the door of the Embassy's Mercedes sedan in the arcade of the hotel.

Gradny-Sawz was more than a little annoyed that he had learned only an hour before that the "distinguished personage" who had arrived on the Lufthansa Condor was Standartenführer Josef Goltz. It was another instance of Ambassador von Lutzenberger not electing to tell him information he believed he was entitled to know. In this instance, it was particularly galling because he and Josef Goltz were not only old friends but had worked together in the uniting of Germanic Austria with the Reich.

He could only hope that his old friend would believe him when he said he would have been at the airport to greet him when he arrived, and to take him into his home, if only he had known he was coming.

Early on, when he was a relatively junior officer in the Foreign Ministry of the Austrian Republic, Gradny-Sawz decided that Adolf Hitler and his National Socialists were the one hope of the *Deutsche Volk,* and that Austria should "return" to the German fatherland.

After he had made this judgment, a visiting German officer, a Sturmbannführer (SS Major) by the name of Josef Goltz, somewhat delicately brought up the subject of Austria becoming part of the Reich, and of the way this might be accomplished. Gradny-Sawz understood that this was that opportunity which comes but once in one's lifetime, and took the chance. He assured Goltz that he was in complete agreement with Adolf Hitler's plans for the German people and would do whatever he could to bring Austria into the Thousand Year Reich as soon as possible.

He had bet on the right horse, he liked to somewhat smugly think. In 1938, with not a little assistance from Anton Gradny-Sawz, the Austrian Republic fell in an almost bloodless coup d'état, the Wehrmacht marched on Vienna, and Austria became Ostmark.

Grateful for his services, the German Foreign Ministry "absorbed" Gradny-Sawz — with a promotion and decoration "for services rendered." In January 1940, he was assigned to the Embassy in Rome as Third Secretary for Commercial Affairs. In 1941, he was assigned to Buenos Aires as First Secretary.

In Buenos Aires, he saw it as his mission to do whatever he could to see that Argentina declared war on the Allies, and if that proved impossible, that Argentine neutrality be tilted as much as possible to the advantage of Germany.

"Wait here," he ordered his driver. "I will be back directly."

The doorman was displeased. There was room for only three or four cars under the hotel arcade. Because Gradny-Sawz's Mercedes blocked one of the spaces, the traffic flow would be impeded. But there was nothing he could do. The Mercedes carried the CD insignia and Corps Diplomatique license plates. Diplomatic status gave one the privilege of parking wherever one elected to park.

Gradny-Sawz marched into the lobby and stopped by the desk to inquire as to Standartenführer Goltz's room number. When he had it, he ordered, in not very good Spanish, "Be so good as to inform the Standartenführer that I am on my way up. I am First Secretary Gradny-Sawz of the German Embassy."

"I know who you are, Señor Gradny-Sawz," the desk clerk said in a tone that bordered on the insulting.

Gradny-Sawz climbed the second flight of stairs and entered the elevator.

When Gradny-Sawz knocked, Major Freiherr Hans-Peter von Wachtstein opened the door to Goltz's suite.

Gradny-Sawz was relieved to see that von Wachtstein was in full dress uniform, complete to the Knight's Cross of the Iron Cross hanging around his neck. He was sometimes negligent about this. Gradny-Sawz was willing to grant him the benefit of every doubt — he was, after all, a fellow nobleman — but sometimes he seemed unable to grasp that he was now assigned to diplomatic duties, with concomitant responsibilities vis-à-vis dress and other matters of protocol.

"I hope you have been taking very good care of Standartenführer Goltz, Hans-Peter," Gradny-Sawz said.

"I have been doing my best," Peter said. "I thought we would see you at the Residence."

Goltz came out of the sitting room, curious to

see who was at the door. Anton Gradny-Sawz raised his right arm in the Nazi salute.

"Heil Hitler!" Gradny-Sawz barked.

"Anton, my old friend!" Standartenführer Goltz cried happily, went to him, and embraced him. "You're just in time. Major von Wachtstein and I just opened a bottle."

"Josef," Gradny-Sawz said, taking Goltz's arm as they walked into the sitting room, "if you had not become so important, the Ambassador would have told me it was you arriving, and I would have been at the airport with a bottle of champagne, to take you to my house."

"I know you would have," Goltz said. "But security . . ."

"Well, at least we'll move you out of here tonight," Gradny-Sawz said. "I'll have von Wachtstein take care of it."

"Will it wait until tomorrow? I'm just a little worn out."

"Moving may wait, but what we might find when we get there tonight, Josef, might not be there tomorrow."

Goltz took his meaning.

"I thought you might be getting too old for that sort of thing, Anton."

"God, I hope not!"

"In that case, I think I just may have to impose on the already abused Freiherr von Wachtstein."

"Sir?" Peter asked, coming into the room and hearing his name.

"Hans-Peter," Gradny-Sawz ordered, "would you see that the Standartenführer's luggage is packed and moved to my home?"

"Yes, Sir."

"The Standartenführer and I are old and dear

friends," Gradny-Sawz said. "We can't have him staying in a hotel."

"Yes, Sir."

"And be so good as to call my houseman and tell him we'll be there directly after paying our respects at the Edificio Libertador, and to make sure everything is in order when we arrive."

"Yes, Sir," Peter said. "I was just about to introduce the Standartenführer to the very fine native champagne."

"Well, by all means, continue," Gradny-Sawz said. "It's quite good. It's not a good German *Sekt,* of course, but every bit as good as any French I've ever had."

Peter poured the champagne.

"Welcome to Argentina, Josef!" Gradny-Sawz said, touching his glass to Goltz's, and then, after a moment, to von Wachtstein's.

"Hear, hear," von Wachtstein said.

"Nice," Goltz said, tasting the champagne.

"Their wine is nice, and so is their beer," von Wachtstein said. "And their beef! Magnificent!"

"And so, according to Oberst Perón, are the women?" Goltz said. "Or were you just being diplomatic, von Wachtstein?"

"No, Herr Standartenführer, I was not being diplomatic. Their women are magnificent."

"Aryan?"

"I never thought about that before," von Wachtstein said. "I'm not sure where the Spaniards and the Italians fit in as Aryans. The majority here are Spanish or Italian. Some Germans, some English, even some Slavs. Poles, for example."

"If I were you, von Wachtstein, I don't think that I would take some Spanish or Italian beauty home to Poppa in Pomerania."

187

Von Wachtstein laughed.

"I'm not ready, Herr Standartenführer, to take some Berlin blonde of impeccable Aryan background home to my father."

"Nor would I if I were in your shoes. Enjoy life while you can. Before you know it, you'll be as old as Anton here."

Anton Gradny-Sawz's smile was strained.

"I think we had better leave," he said. "It's time."

"I'll see that the Standartenführer's things are packed, and take them to your residence, and then come to the Residence."

"You're a good man, von Wachtstein," Goltz said, smiling at von Wachtstein and touching his arm.

He went to the mirror by the door, put on his black brimmed cap with the death's-head insignia, and adjusted it twice before he was satisfied.

Peter closed the suite door after them, helped himself to another glass of champagne, and waited for the maid's knock. When she arrived, he showed her what he wanted done. He then told her he had business in the lobby and would wait for the luggage in the lobby bar, and left the room.

When he got on the elevator he told the operator to take him to the roof garden. Once there, he stood in the line waiting before the maître d'hôtel's table. And when he reached the head of the line, he replied to the maître d's surprised look at seeing him both in uniform and alone by announcing he had to make a quick telephone call.

The maître d' picked up the telephone. Peter gave him a number, which the maître d' repeated, then handed the receiver to Peter.

"This is the Duarte residence," a male voice announced.

"Señorita Alicia, please," he said. "Señor Cóndor is calling."

"I will see if the lady is at home, Señor," the butler said.

He didn't know if there were listening devices on the Duarte line; there might be. There were almost certainly listening devices on the line in Goltz's hotel room. But even if someone was listening to the Duarte line, no suspicions would be aroused, unless Alicia, in her naïveté, said something she should not. He had arrived in Buenos Aires speaking fluent Spanish. Since then he had worked very hard to acquire the Porteño (Buenos Aires Native) accent and idiom. Cóndor — which they had chosen as a *nom d'amour* from the Argentine national bird, and because he was a pilot — was a fairly common name. It was unlikely that any telephone monitor would find one more call from a young man to Señorita Alicia Carzino-Cormano suspicious, or that Señor Cóndor was a German officer.

"Hola?"

Every time he heard her soft, somehow hesitant voice, his heart jumped.

"How are you?"

"How do you think I am? Where are you?"

"In the roof garden of the Alvear."

"I mean, really?"

"I mean, really."

"I thought you said you had to go to work."

"I am working. I am carrying the luggage of a distinguished personage. Later, I'm part of the official party which will go to the Edificio Libertador to pay our respects to el Coronel Frade. . . ."

"Oh, Peter!"

"I should be free after that. About ten, I think."

"Well, I can't leave here, obviously, and you can't come here."

"The Duartes have told me I am always welcome," he teased.

"Cletus is here," Alicia said.

"Cletus is there?"

I've got to see him. How the hell am I going to arrange that?

That was the last thing in the world he expected to hear.

"Not *here*. Right now, no one seems to know where he is. But he's in Buenos Aires. He'll probably, certainly, come here sooner or later. In addition to everything else, Mother is frantic."

"How do you know he's in Buenos Aires?"

"Someone called Beatrice Duarte and said that she saw him at the casket . . . at Edificio Libertador. He was with General Ramírez."

Well, if he's with Ramírez, everybody in Buenos Aires will know he's back.

"If you see him before I do, would you tell him to get in touch with me, please?"

"Of course," Alicia said, then: "Cariño,* he's not in danger, is he?"

"I don't think so."

Not as long as he's with Ramírez, anyway. And maybe not for a day or two, until Grüner has time to set up another assassination.

"Peter, I'm worried for him."

You and me both, Schatzie. **

"He'll be all right," von Wachtstein said.

"I'll see you tomorrow," she said.

"I love you."

---

* Porteño: Sweetheart, darling, or equivalent.
** Berlinerische: Sweetheart, darling, or equivalent.

"Yes, of course, I feel the same way."

"Somebody's there?"

"Yes, certainly."

"Isabela?"

"Yes."

Isabela was the elder of the two daughters of Señora Claudia Carzino-Cormano. Clete referred to her as "El Bitcho," Peter remembered with a smile. The feeling was mutual. Isabela loathed Clete, and she was not very fond of Peter either, which he suspected was because he had shown no interest in her from the moment he had laid eyes on Alicia.

"Stick your finger in her eye," Peter said.

"That's a very good idea, if somewhat impractical. Thank you for calling. Goodbye."

He hung up and looked up and saw the maître d' examining his extended index finger. Then he mimed sticking it in his eye.

"Mother or sister?" the maître d' inquired.

"The sister."

"I will pray for you. Sisters are more dangerous than mothers."

"Thank you," Peter said. He slipped the maître d'hôtel a bill and got back on the elevator. He rode to the main floor, took a seat in the lobby bar, ordered a beer, and waited for either the maid or a bellman to bring him Standartenführer Goltz's luggage.

191

[Four]

1420 Avenida Alvear
Buenos Aires, Argentina
2105 9 April 1943

The Mercedes pulled up to the heavy gate in the twelve-foot-tall wrought-iron fence. As it did so, a police sergeant, one of three policemen standing on the sidewalk before the mansion, put out his hand and ordered it to stop.

An officer in the uniform of the Húsares de Pueyrredón was not an ordinary citizen, but the sergeant's orders had been explicit. He was to ensure that no one intruded on the privacy of the mourning Duarte family.

"Are you expected, mi Capitán?" he asked politely when Lauffer rolled down the window.

"We are expected," Lauffer replied, and added: "This is Señor Frade."

"Thank you, Sir," the sergeant said, saluted, and signaled for one of his men to open the gate.

The door to the mansion was opened by a maid; but a butler, a black mourning band on his arm, appeared the next moment.

"Señor Frade," Lauffer announced. "To see Señor Duarte."

"I will announce you," the butler said. "May I show you into the reception*?" He met Clete's eyes. "You have my most sincere condolences on the loss of your father, Señor Frade."

"Thank you," Clete said.

---

* The day-to-day Spanish of middle- and upper-class Argentines is heavily laden with British terms. Living rooms are called "the living"; dining rooms, "the dining"; reception rooms, "the reception," et cetera.

Clete and Lauffer followed the butler across the foyer to a double door. He opened the door and bowed them through it, then closed the door after them and began to climb the stairs to the second floor.

"Cletus!" a svelte woman in her fifties cried, rising out of one of the armchairs and walking quickly to him. She was dressed in a black dress with a rope of pearls its only ornamentation. Her luxuriant black, gray-flecked hair was parted in the middle and done up in a bun at the neck.

Señora Claudia de Carzino-Cormano kissed Clete on the cheek.

"I'm not entirely sure I'm glad to see you," she said, and then changed her mind. "Yes, I am. Oh, Cletus!"

She wrapped her arms around him and rested her face on his chest.

His hand on her back could feel her stifling a sob, then she got control of herself.

"What are we going to do without him, Cletus?" she asked.

He shrugged and made a helpless gesture with his hands.

Claudia then acknowledged the presence of Capitán Lauffer.

"Good evening," she said. "Despite the circumstances, it is good to see you."

"It is always a pleasure to see you, Señora," Lauffer said.

When Claudia stepped away from Clete, she was replaced by Alicia, who was dressed and made up almost identically to her mother. The only difference Clete could see was that instead of pearls she wore a golden cross on a chain around her neck.

"Oh, Clete, I'm so sorry," she said.

She kissed Clete somewhat wetly on the cheek and then, while hugging him, whispered, "Peter wants you to call him."

"OK," he said very softly, so that her sister, Isabela, who was approaching, could not hear him.

Isabela, two years older than Alicia, wore her black hair piled on top of her head. A diamond-and-emerald brooch was pinned to her black dress. She was tall, lithe, and finely featured. Isabela was even better looking than Alicia, Clete often thought, but unfortunately knew it.

She did not embrace Clete, and her kiss, he thought, was the sort of kiss a bitch like Isabela would give to an alligator when good manners required her to go through the motion.

"Cletus," she said.

"Isabela," he replied.

"Would you like something to eat? Drink?" Claudia asked.

"Yes, I would," he said. "To drink."

"I'll ring," Alicia said.

"There's whiskey here," Claudia said. "In that cabinet. Whiskey, Clete? Capitán?"

"Please," Clete said.

Claudia went to a huge cabinet, which opened to reveal a complete bar.

"You'll have to ring," Claudia said. "There's no ice."

"Straight's fine," Clete said.

"Maybe for you," Claudia said. "Send for ice, Alicia." She looked at Clete. "I don't think I've ever seen you looking so elegant."

"I bought this to be my diplomat's uniform," he said.

"You will stay now? At your embassy, I mean?"

"I declined the appointment. But I will stay."

"Meaning what, Cletus?"

"I entered Argentina on my Argentine passport," he said. "I have, in a sense, come home."

"Oh, my!" Claudia said.

"Your Argentine passport?" Isabela said. "But you're a norteamericano."

"Isabela, I was born here," Clete said. "I'm as entitled to an Argentine passport as you are."

"I never heard of such a thing!" Isabela snorted.

"I'm sure there's a lot of things you haven't heard about," Clete said.

"Don't you two start!" Claudia said. "I couldn't stand that."

"Sorry," Clete said.

"Your father is in the Edificio Libertador," Claudia said.

"We just came from there."

"I'm sure he would like it, but I found it rather macabre."

"It was impressive," Clete said. "But, yeah, I think el Coronel would like it."

A maid appeared with a bucket of ice.

Too soon to be in response to Alicia's sending for someone, Clete decided. *Somebody decided we would need a drink.*

"Your aunt Beatrice was over there all day. She came back not an hour ago. We are to have a small — family, I suppose — dinner."

"How is she?" Clete asked.

"She's not here," Claudia said. "She's in the arms of Jesus and/or morphia."

"Mother!" Alicia said, shocked.

"I'm sorry, I shouldn't have said that. Forgive me."

195

There was a barely audible tap on the corridor door, and when Humberto Valdez Duarte turned his head to it, he saw the door open just wide enough to show his butler's face, his eyebrows asking permission to enter.

Duarte, a tall, slender man of forty-seven, who wore his thick black hair long at the sides and brushed slickly back, held out his hand, palm outward, and shook his head "no."

He quickly swung his feet off his wife's delicate, pink and pale-blue silk-upholstered chaise longue, on which he had been resting with a cup of coffee, and walked out of the bedroom and through the sitting, to the door.

"Señor Frade is here, Señor," the butler said.

"Thank God!" Duarte said softly.

"I put him, and Capitán Lauffer of the Húsares, in the reception, with the Carzino-Cormanos."

"Fine. Please offer them whatever they wish, and tell them the Señora and I will join them shortly."

The butler nodded, then withdrew his head from the door and closed it softly.

Duarte went back into the bedroom. Beatrice Frade de Duarte was sitting before her vanity in her slip, brushing her long black hair. She smiled at him in the mirror. His wife was six months older than he was, a tall, slim woman with large dark eyes and a dazzling smile.

"What was that, cariño?" she asked.

"Cletus is here."

"Oh, *good!* In time for dinner."

"He has Capitán Lauffer of the Húsares with him. What would you like me to do about him?"

"Invite the Capitán to join us, of course. I've

always liked him, and you know how fond Jorge was of him."

"Would you like me to go to them now, or wait until you're ready?"

"You go down now, of course, offer my apologies, and tell them I'll be there shortly."

He walked to the vanity, smiled at his wife in the mirror, touched her head, and finally bent over and kissed it. She smiled and put up her hand and caught his.

Then he turned and left the room.

The fact that his wife had developed serious emotional problems did not cause Humberto Valdez Duarte to love her less, he often thought, but rather the opposite. Sometimes — like now — he felt a tenderness for her that was surprising in its intensity . . . a desire to wrap her, figuratively and literally, in his arms and to continue to protect her from all unpleasantness.

They had known each other all of their lives, and had married at twenty-one, on Humberto's graduation from the University of Buenos Aires. While everyone agreed that the marriage was a good one, uniting two of Argentina's most prominent families, there were some raised eyebrows at the time — even some whispers — about their tender ages. People of their social position usually married no younger than twenty-five, and often later. Unless, of course, there was a reason.

The whispers died thirteen months after their marriage when Beatrice gave birth to their first — and as it turned out, only — child, Jorge Alejandro.

The first indication of emotional problems came when Beatrice's postpartum depression required the attention of a psychiatrist.

Now that he thought about it, there had been

indications of emotional difficulty all along, most often manifested in Beatrice's detachment from reality — her unwillingness to accept the existence of anything unpleasant — coupled with a growing religious fervor. She began to go to mass daily about the time Jorge started school, and developed an unusually close relationship with her confessor, Padre (later Monsignor) Patrick Kelly.

Humberto often wondered what she had to confess. When he went, infrequently, to confession, there was generally some act or thought for which he really needed absolution. Try as he could, however, he could think of nothing Beatrice might want to confess more sinful than possible unkind thoughts about one of her friends, Jorge's teachers, or her brother, Jorge Guillermo Frade. The latter seemed most likely. Having un-Christian thoughts about her brother was very understandable.

During the six months since Jorge Alejandro had been killed, he had confessed the same thing many times.

Jorge Alejandro idolized his uncle from the time he could walk. Children are prone to adore indulgent uncles, especially when the uncles are dashing cavalry officers and superb horsemen, and who delight in making available to nephews the toys — fast cars, highly spirited horses, firearms, airplanes — their parents would just as soon they not have so early in life, or ever.

But neither he nor Beatrice could bring themselves to deny Beatrice's brother the company of his nephew. After Jorge Guillermo Frade lost his wife — and for all practical purposes, their son — he never remarried. And it was clear that he really loved Jorge Alejandro . . . saw him as a substitute for the son he had lost.

In his third year at St. George's School, Jorge Alejandro firmly announced that he had no intention of becoming a banker — with the clear implication that in his view banking was a profession about as masculine as hairdressing and interior decorating. He announced that instead he intended to follow his uncle to the Military Academy and become an officer — after all, he carried the blood of Pueyrredón in his veins. There was nothing Humberto, who was Managing Director* of the Anglo-Argentine Bank, could do about it except hope that Jorge Alejandro would find the discipline at Campo de Mayo too much to take.

That hope did not materialize. Like his uncle, Jorge Alejandro was appointed Cadet Coronel during his last year at Campo de Mayo. And like his uncle — by then el Coronel Jorge Guillermo Frade, commanding the Húsares de Pueyrredón Cavalry Regiment — he was commissioned into the cavalry. Almost certainly because of his uncle's influence, he was "routinely" assigned to the Húsares.

All that was well and good, but what el Coronel also did was arrange for Capitán Duarte to be posted to the German Army as an observer. For this Humberto vowed he would never forgive him — now, of course, he was sorry about that. Logic told Humberto that el Coronel would rather die himself than see any harm come to Jorge Alejandro, but the facts were that el Coronel arranged for Jorge Alejandro to go to Germany as an observer, and that he was killed at Stalingrad. The godless Communists shot down an observation aircraft that he was flying, against regulations for a neutral observer.

* In Argentina, as in Europe, the term is equivalent to "President" or "Chief Executive Officer."

Beatrice's nervous problems grew worse, naturally, when Jorge went to Europe. And when word of his death reached them, it pushed her over the edge. And so, one of the apartments in their house was turned into what was really a psychiatric facility. It was complete to a hospital bed with restraints, and nurses on duty and doctors on call around the clock. After a time, she came out of it — with Monsignor Kelly reminding her that suicide is a mortal sin, and the doctors keeping her in a chemically induced state of tranquillity.

Meanwhile, in what Humberto regarded as a cold and calculated public relations gesture, and Beatrice as an act of great Christian charity and compassion, the Germans returned Jorge's remains from Stalingrad, escorted by a highly decorated Luftwaffe pilot from a very good German family.

Jorge's remains and Major Hans-Peter von Wachtstein of the Luftwaffe arrived in Buenos Aires at almost the same time as another highly decorated aviator. The second dashing young hero was an American Marine. In what Humberto regarded as a cold and calculated diplomatic move, the Americans sent him to Argentina primarily because he was Jorge Guillermo Frade's long-estranged — from infancy — son. It was common gossip — at least before Cletus arrived — that el Coronel was probably going to be the next President of the Argentine Republic, and the norteamericanos were certainly aware of this.

Though Cletus Howell Frade was, of course, his and Beatrice's nephew, Humberto confessed to Padre Welner, a Jesuit — not to Monsignor Kelly, who had already heard too much of his private affairs through Beatrice — that he had selfish and un-Christian thoughts about him, and was afraid he hated him, for no reason except that Cletus was alive and Jorge Alejandro was dead.

Jorge Alejandro was buried in the family tomb in Recoleta Cemetery with much ceremony — including an escort by the Húsares de Pueyrredón and the pinning of the Knight's Cross of the Iron Cross to the flag covering his casket. In her chemically induced tranquillity, Beatrice seemed more interested in the postinterment reception at the house than in the burial of their only child.

The same night, the Germans tried to murder Cletus Frade. The official story was that Cletus came across burglars, but there was no question in Humberto's mind that the same Germans who solemnly honored Jorge Alejandro at the Basílica of Our Lady of Pilar in Recoleta Cemetery cold-bloodedly ordered the assassination of his cousin on the same day.

Beatrice accepted the burglar story without question. And later, when her brother died at the hands of "bandits," she was even further removed from reality. She was absolutely incapable of believing that the charming German Ambassador, Graf von Lutzenberger, or the even more charming Baron Gradny-Sawz, his first secretary, were capable of displaying bad manners, much less ordering the assassination of her brother.

In fact, she made a point of personally inviting both of them to the postinterment reception they were holding.

Under the circumstances, Beatrice's dissociation from reality was probably a good thing. Humberto did not want to see her again as she was when word of Jorge Alejandro's death had reached them. It broke his heart.

And there were practical considerations, too.

Gradny-Sawz was delighted that Beatrice made von Wachtstein a welcome guest in their home. (The young German airman had remained in Buenos Aires as the Assistant Military Attaché for Air at the German Embassy.) Gradny-Sawz considered himself an aristocrat. Thus he saw this relationship between the aristocratic young officer and the prominent Duarte family — and consequently the Anglo-Argentine Bank — as both natural and of potential use to Germany. At the same time, he didn't have the faintest idea that the real relationship between von Wachtstein and the Anglo-Argentine Bank had absolutely nothing to do with furthering the interests of the Nazis, but the reverse.

When Humberto pushed open the door to the reception, Cletus Frade was sitting on a couch beside Claudia Carzino-Cormano, who was holding his hand. When Cletus saw his uncle, he stood up.

Humberto went to him. Although Cletus had made it quite clear that norteamericanos regarded any gesture between men more intimate than a handshake as damned odd — even between uncle and nephew — he embraced him, kissed both of his cheeks, and then embraced him again.

"Cletus, I am so very sorry."

"Thank you."

"God has seen fit to take my son, and your father," Humberto said. "May they rest in peace. And God, I like to think, has given us each other. I will now regard you as my son, and ask that you think of me as your father."

Oh, shit. He means that. That's bullshit, pure and simple. So why do I feel like crying?

Clete found himself embracing his uncle.

"And how is Aunt Beatrice?" he heard himself asking when they broke apart.

"I have come to believe that God, in his infinite mercy, has chosen to spare Beatrice the pain she would feel under normal circumstances. I think you take my meaning."

Clete nodded.

In other words, what Claudia said was right on the money. She's in the arms of Jesus and drugs, and you know it. You poor bastard.

"Beatrice will join us shortly," Humberto said, then turned to Claudia and her daughters, kissing them each in turn.

"Do you have everything you need?" he asked.

Everybody nodded.

"I think I will have a little taste, myself," Humberto said, and made his way to the cabinet bar. "Beatrice will be along in a minute, and then we can have our dinner."

VII

[One]

```
1420 Avenida Alvear
Buenos Aires, Argentina
2145 9 April 1943
```

Beatrice Frade de Duarte appeared in the library a few minutes after her husband. She was immaculately turned out, and the soul of refined hospitality. And quite obviously mad.

She kissed Clete on the cheek as if she had seen him only a few hours before, gaily kissed the Carzino-Cormano females, complimented them on their dresses and hair, and then called for champagne.

"Champagne increases one's appreciation of food," she complained, "but whiskey simply makes one gluttonous."

Claudia Carzino-Cormano, smiling brightly with a visible effort, squeezed Clete's upper arm painfully.

When the champagne was served, Beatrice toasted, "Good friends. They are always such support at a time like this."

Clete thought Alicia was going to cry.

After Beatrice carefully paired them off — Humberto with Claudia, Capitán Lauffer with Isabela, and Clete with Alicia — they went into the dining. She began the dinner conversation with the announcement: "This is probably the wrong time to say this — Cletus would have to get a special dispensation from the Cardinal Archbishop to waive the year's mourning period — but I always suspected that my late brother hoped that Cletus and Isabela would be struck by Cupid's arrow. I think of you, dear Claudia, as family already. Their marriage would make it official."

"Well, you never know what time will bring," Claudia said quickly, to forestall any reply from either Isabela, who rolled her eyes, or Clete.

Throughout dinner, Beatrice chattered on happily about her idyllic childhood with her brother on Estancia San Pedro y San Pablo. The highlight of all this was the story of el Coronel's burial casket.

"Poppa somehow came into a stock of cedar," she said, turning her brilliant smile on Capitán Lauffer. "Which, unless I am mistaken, is not grown here. Or if it is, this was of an exceptionally high quality. I have no idea where it came from, to tell you the truth. But, *anyway,* there it was, in one of the buildings some distance from the big house, and one day Poppa saw it and decided he wanted to be buried in a cedar casket."

"Is that so?" Capitán Lauffer replied politely.

"So he asked one of the foremen to find someone who knew how to make a casket. The foreman came up with a man from one of Poppa's estancias in Corrientes. . . . Do you know where Corrientes is, Cletus, dear?"

"No, Ma'am," Cletus confessed.

"It's in the north. It's bounded by Brazil, and

Paraguay, and, in a tiny little corner in the south by Uruguay."

"Is it really?"

"You must go there, Cletus, and soon."

"I'd like to."

"You have property there. It was your dead father's, and now, of course, it's yours. It was of course Poppa's. Poppa was your grandfather, but you never knew him. He was taken into heaven before you were born. Your father and I inherited from Poppa, of course, but when I married your Uncle Humberto, your father bought out my share."

"Is that so?"

"As I recall, the property in Corrientes was rather extensive. Five or six estancias and something else, some kind of a business. . . ."

"*Three* estancias, my darling," Humberto said with a banker's certainty. "The tea plantation, and the refrigerico" — a slaughterhouse and meatpacking plant.

"Yes, I knew it was something like that. *Anyway,* long before we were there, the Jesuit fathers were there, bringing the Indians to the blessed Jesus. You can still see the ruins of what they built. You really must see those ruins, Cletus, it would be very educational for you. *Anyway,* the Jesuits — this was hundreds and hundreds of years ago — taught the Indians whose souls they had saved crafts, among them wood carving."

"Is that so?"

"And that wood-carving skill has stayed with the people after all these years, even though there are hardly any Indians at all left. Long after the Jesuits were expelled from Argentina. Can you believe that?"

206

"It's hard to believe, Aunt Beatrice."

"But it's *true*. You can get the most beautiful carved things in Corrientes. *Anyway,* there was a man on one of the estancias who was a really good wood carver, so Poppa had him sent to Estancia San Pedro y San Pablo, took him to the place where he had stored the cedar he'd acquired, and told him to make a casket."

"Really?"

"And the man did. And when Poppa was taken into heaven, your father remembered that Poppa was always talking about being laid to rest in his carved cedar casket, so he went looking for the casket Poppa had made. And do you know what he found, Cletus?"

"No, Ma'am."

He drained his wineglass, and Claudia gave him sort of a warning look.

El Coronel got really drunk when they buried cousin Jorge, and she doesn't want a repetition of that from me. And she's right. If this keeps on much longer, I'm going to be either drunk or crazy.

"Casket after casket after casket. A *dozen* caskets!" Beatrice announced happily. "Maybe more. Maybe fifteen, or sixteen. But at least a dozen. *Anyway,* so what had happened, you see, is that when the man who carved the casket finished, and no one sent him back to Corrientes, and there was a lot of cedar left over, he made another casket, and when he finished that, another. Isn't that amazing?"

A maid appeared at his side with a bottle of Cabernet Sauvignon. Clete covered his glass with his hand, and got a quick pursing-of-the-lips kiss from Claudia as his reward.

"Absolutely amazing," he said.

"This went on for . . . I don't know. Humberto, darling, for how many years did the wood carver make caskets?"

"Several, my darling."

I wonder how in hell he puts up with this, day after day?

"*Anyway,*" Beatrice went on relentlessly, "finally he ran out of cedar and asked someone, one of the foremen, what he wanted him to do next, and that was the first your father knew about all the caskets this man had made. Whatever happened to the man, Humberto, do you recall?"

"I don't know where he is now, my precious. I know he stayed on at Estancia San Pedro y San Pablo for a long time. He did all the carving in La Capilla Nuestra Señora de los Milagros."

"Yes, that's right. I'd forgotten. Now, Cletus, I know you've been there. Your father buried Señora Pellano from Nuestra Señora de los Milagros."

The Chapel of Our Lady of the Miracles, which was equipped with two priests, seemed to be a wholly owned subsidiary of Estancia San Pedro y San Pablo. Clete remembered his father telling him that 1,400 people lived and worked on the estancia, whose 84,205 (more or less) hectares (one of which equals 2.47 acres) surrounded the small city of Pila, in southeast Buenos Aires Province.

"Yes, Ma'am."

"*And* in one of Poppa's carved cedar caskets. Your father was really fond of Señora Pellano, Cletus. Otherwise he would have buried her in an ordinary casket — after all, all she was was a servant — instead of in one of Poppa's carved cedar caskets."

"My father was very fond of Señora Pellano, Aunt Beatrice."

"*Anyway,* all of these caskets just sat there in the building on San Pedro y San Pablo until we needed one for Señora Pellano. We couldn't put my Jorge Alejandro in one, you see. I forget why, exactly, but Monsignor Kelly said it wouldn't be a good thing to do, and I never question the Monsignor's judgment, but when Señora Pellano was taken into heaven, we used one for her, and now that your father has gone to be with all the angels and your blessed mother, Cletus, we are going to lay him to rest in one. I thought it looked so *handsome* in the Edificio Libertador. Many people commented on it."

"It is a magnificent casket, Señora de Duarte," Capitán Lauffer said politely.

"Well, *anyway,* it's going to be a long, long time before anyone in *this* family has to go out and buy a casket," Beatrice said, and then changed the subject: "Capitán Lauffer, did you think to bring a schedule of events with you?"

"I have one in the car, Señora."

"Well, after dinner I think we should go over it with Cletus, don't you? To see if he approves?"

"I think that would be a good idea, Señora," Lauffer said, looking at Clete, his facial expression indicating that he was sorry but under the circumstances he had had no choice but to agree with her.

The schedule of events turned out to be something like an Operations Order: Viewing of the casket at the Edificio Libertador would cease at 10:30 P.M. that night. At 1 A.M. the body would be moved to the Basílica of Our Lady of Pilar, which was adjacent to Recoleta Cemetery. It would be carried there on an artillery caisson of the Second Regiment of Artillery, and accompanied by a mounted escort of the Húsares de Pueyrredón.

Clete wondered about that, but he quickly saw the logic of it. When they buried Cousin Jorge Alejandro, his casket was moved in the same way the six or seven blocks from his parents' house to the Basílica. Because that happened during the day, it caused a monumental traffic jam. Moving his father's casket from the Edificio Libertador to the Basílica, which was at least two miles away, would be logistically impossible in the daytime, unless closing down the business center of Buenos Aires was acceptable.

The Basílica would be opened to the public from 8:00 A.M. until 10:00 A.M. for viewing of the casket, and then closed. Seating of official guests would begin at 11:00 A.M. Nuns from the Convent of the Sisters of the Holy Cross would provide appropriate choral music from 11:00 until 12:00, when the mass would begin. The mass would be celebrated by the Cardinal Archbishop of Argentina, assisted by three bishops, a monsignor named Kelly, and one lowly priest, Padre Kurt Welner, S.J.

Following the mass, the casket would be carried by officers of the Húsares de Pueyrredón from the Basílica to the Frade tomb for interment.

Following the interment, Señor and Señora Humberto Duarte would receive mourners, by invitation only, at their residence at 1420 Avenida Alvear. Because of a shortage of parking, it was suggested that mourners move by foot to the Duarte home. A limited number of automobiles would be available to accommodate the immediate family, the aged, and the infirm.

"I think, Capitán Lauffer," Beatrice asked thoughtfully, "that it would be appropriate for Cletus to be at Our Lady of Pilar from about nine o'clock until the final viewing is over, don't you?"

Lauffer looked at Clete.

"May I respectfully suggest, Señora, that would be Señor Frade's decision?"

Beatrice looked at Cletus.

"Yes, of course, Aunt Beatrice," Clete said.

"But now, Beatrice, we have to send Cletus to bed," Claudia Carzino-Cormano said firmly. "He must be exhausted."

"I am a little tired," Clete said.

"You poor boy," Beatrice said, kissing Clete's cheek. "Of course you must be, with all you've had to do today."

[Two]

1728 Avenida Coronel Díaz
Palermo, Buenos Aires
2330 9 April 1943

"I know dinner was very difficult for you, Capitán," Clete said to Lauffer as they sat in his car before the door of what his father had called "the money sewer." "I appreciate your understanding."

"Don't be silly," Lauffer said automatically, then blurted, "I felt more sorry for your uncle than your aunt."

Clete grunted.

"I shouldn't have said that," Lauffer said. "Forgive me."

"I was thinking exactly the same thing," Clete said. "Christ, he must have the patience of a saint."

"He loves her very much," Lauffer said. He put

out his hand. "You must be exhausted."

"Yeah."

"I will be here at eight-thirty to take you to the Basílica," he said. "Would that be all right?"

"Fine."

"Or I could be fifteen, twenty minutes late. Delayed in traffic."

Clete smiled at him. "I really appreciate that," he said. "But I think I'd better be there at nine."

"Eight-thirty, then," Lauffer said, and reached across Clete to open the door. "Sleep well."

The moment he stepped out of the car the door to the mansion opened. He saw Antonio, the butler.

The perfectly trained servant, Clete thought. *He didn't open the door until he was sure I wanted it open.*

"Good evening, Señor Cletus."

"Good evening, Antonio."

"Is there anything I can get for you, Señor?"

"No, I don't . . . Yes. I'm not sure I have an un-messed-up shirt for tomorrow. Is there someone . . . ?"

"Your linen has been gone over, Señor."

"In that case, you can't do anything for me except say 'good night.' "

"Would you like me to have your suit refreshed?"

Clete looked down at the creases in his trousers. "It looks fine to me."

"I'll have the laundress touch it up," Antonio said. "Your father took great pains with his appearance."

Was that a shot at me, el slobbo? Or was "touching up" the son's suit a last service to el Coronel?

"Thank you," Clete said.

"You have had several telephone calls, Señor. All from, I believe, the same lady. She did not

212

choose to leave her name."

Well, I know who that is, don't I?

"If she calls back, put her through. Even if I'm asleep."

"Very well, Señor."

"Good night, Antonio."

"Good night, Señor."

Clete started up the wide stairway.

He found the bed had been turned down. A pair of pajamas were laid out on it.

What do I do, put them on and toss and turn all night? Or sleep in my skivvy shirt, which will make me appear both ungrateful to the staff and boorish, as well?

He stripped to his underwear, then carried the suit to the sitting and left it on a chair so the laundress could find it. That done, he returned to the bedroom, closing the door after him.

He was brushing his teeth when the telephone rang.

Tinkled, he thought. *The telephones here don't ring, they tinkle, as if the bell is powered by a run-down battery.*

There was an ornate, French-style telephone on the huge marble sink.

"Hola?"

"Clete?" Dorotéa's voice made his heart jump.

"Hi, Princess."

"I've been trying for hours to get you."

"How did you know I was here?"

"Your grandfather called Daddy. Daddy told me."

"How are you?"

"I'm all right," Dorotéa said. "Clete, I can't tell you how devastated I am by what happened to your father, how sorry I am for you."

"Thank you."

She seems hesitant about something. Distant.

"I have something to tell you, Clete."

"Tell me."

"Not over the telephone. I want to be looking at you when I tell you."

"Tell me now, and look at me later."

"Damn you! This is very important."

"So what do you want me to do? I don't suppose you can come here. Do you want me to come there?"

"God no! Daddy would have kittens."

"OK. Then what?"

"Where are you going to be first thing in the morning?"

"At nine o'clock, I'll be at the church."

"Our Lady of Pilar?"

"Right."

"Will you be alone?"

"I don't think so, but we can find someplace to talk, if that's what you're asking."

"All right, I'll see you there."

"Fine."

"Cletus, I am so sorry for you."

"I'll be all right."

"I'll see you at nine, or a little after," Dorotéa said, and the line went dead.

He put the ornate receiver back in its cradle.

"Clete, my boy," he said aloud, "I think you have just received Part One of a 'Dear John' communication, with Part Two to be delivered in person at zero nine hundred hours. Shit!"

Well, what the hell did I expect? She just turned nineteen years old, for Christ's sake. Before me, she was really the Virgin Princess. I was the first, quote, real man, unquote, in her life. Nineteen-year-old girls routinely fall in love with, quote, older men, unquote,

214

and if the older man is a sonofabitch, as I certainly was, sometimes even let them into their pants.

"Cletus," she will say, "I will always love you. But I have met someone else. He is my age. I didn't want to fall in love with him. It just happened. I can only hope that you can understand. I never wanted to hurt you."

Whereupon, as a gentleman should in such circumstances, I will touch her shoulder in a brotherly way, sincerely announce that of course I understand, wish her and the boyfriend all possible happiness, and tell her I will never forget her either.

Which is true. I'm in love with her — or think I am. I never felt this way about anybody else before — but that does not add up to us living happily ever after in a vine-covered cottage by the side of the road. What I should be is grateful that Juan or Pancho or whatever the fuck the sonofabitch's name is has come into her life, getting me out of it without causing her any pain. Or getting her killed, which would have been a genuine possibility. And if these bastards do succeed in killing me, which is also a geniune possibility, it will be easier on the Princess. I will have been just one in a long line of her ex-boyfriends, not her lover or, Jesus Christ, even worse, her fiancé.

Shit!

He walked out the bath into his bedroom and looked at the bed.

I don't want to get in there. That's not my bed, it's my father's bed, and I don't care if they have gone to great pains to remove everything that was his from his apartment, it's still his apartment and his bed.

And for some reason, I'm not at all sleepy. Probably all the alcohol I didn't have, and all the coffee — strong enough to melt the teeth of a mule — I did.

Tony! I have to see him, and I have to see Ettinger.

And Peter. I really want to see Peter. He knows who ordered the assassination of my father, and I think he'll tell me.

He went to the dressing room and quickly pulled on khaki trousers, a polo shirt, and a tweed jacket. He hadn't gotten as far as taking off his boots, and getting dressed took less than a minute.

When he went through the sitting, his suit was already gone. He went down the wide stairs, then to a corridor under them. Just off that was the stairwell to the basement garage.

Half a dozen cars were in the garage, but none was in the place reserved for his father's beloved Horche.

I wonder where that is? Do the cops have it?

He went to a 1940 Ford station wagon, parked between an ancient, immaculately maintained Rolls Royce sedan and a small Mercedes sedan. The Ford was locked.

"Damn!"

"Señor?"

He turned to find a middle-aged man in his shirtsleeves.

"May I help you, Señor?"

"Can you get me the keys to this?" he said, pointing to the Ford.

"I would be pleased to conduct the Señor anywhere he wishes to go," the man said, pointing at the Rolls Royce.

"Just get me the keys to this, please," Clete said.

[Three]

Avenida Pueyrredón 1706
Capital Federal, Buenos Aires,
Argentina
0005 10 April 1943

When Clete drove past Peter's apartment building looking for a place to park, he saw the doorman sitting behind his tiny desk in the lobby, his hands folded on his stomach, sound asleep.

He thought it very likely that the doorman got a weekly envelope from Teniente Coronel Martín of the Bureau of Internal Security in exchange for a report on who rode up to Piso 10 and when and how long they stayed.

Or perhaps two envelopes, the second from the Policía Federal. Or maybe even three. Peter told me that there are two obscure flunkies at the Embassy who really work for the Military Attaché, who is really, in addition to his other duties, the counterintelligence officer. They're probably keeping an eye on Peter, too.

If I go up to see Peter — or just ask the doorman if he's at home — that means Martín — and probably the Policía Federal and Colonel Whatsisname . . . Grüner . . . will hear about it. I can't risk that, so what the hell do I do?

Don't try to see Peter tonight, obviously.
Shit.

But then the doorbells caught his eye. The doorbell system was mounted on a marble pillar outside the lobby — Clete had never seen anything like it anywhere but in Buenos Aires. There were buttons for each apartment, and an intercom. You pushed the proper apartment number, identified yourself, and if the person called wanted to let you in, he pushed a button operating the solenoid-controlled lock on the plate-glass door leading into the lobby.

The question is, Clete decided, *can Sleepy in the lobby see who's pushing the bells if he wakes up?* He looked. *He can, if he wakes up. But even if he does, he won't know what button I've pushed. I can at least talk to Peter, if not go up to his apartment. Tell him to call me, or something.*

He parked the Ford around the corner and walked back to the apartment building. The doorman was still asleep.

It took three long pushes at button number 10 before there was an annoyed, even angry, "Hola?"

"Clete."

There was just a moment's hesitation.

"Go around the corner, to your right," Peter's metallic-sounding voice said.

Clete turned from the doorbell system on the marble pillar and walked away. The doorman was still asleep. To the right was in the opposite direction from where he had parked the Ford.

He turned on his heel, went to the Ford, and started driving around the block. No pedestrians were on the sidewalk, and so far as he could tell, no one was sitting in any of the automobiles parked along the curb on Avenida Pueyrredón. On his second pass past the apartment building, he saw Peter walking quickly toward the corner.

He drove by him, flicked his headlights, and pulled to the curb. Peter jumped in the front seat, and Clete drove off.

"See if anyone's following," Peter ordered.

There were no headlights in the rearview mirror.

"Nobody," Clete said. "Where should we go?"

"There's a bar on Libertador that's usually crowded this time of night," Peter said. "Just past the American Ambassador's residence, by the railroad bridge. It's called 'The Horse.' "

"How are you, my friend?" Major Freiherr Hans-Peter von Wachtstein of the Luftwaffe said to Major Cletus Howell Frade of the U.S. Marine Corps.

"How do you think?" Clete replied, raising his glass of Johnny Walker to touch Peter's.

They were sitting at a small table on a balcony overlooking the ground-floor bar and restaurant of The Horse. When they started up the balcony stairs, they got an odd look from the waiter, who could not understand why two young men would go to the nearly deserted balcony when at least a half-dozen attractive, and unattached, women were sitting at the bar.

The two had met the previous December. When Clete first came to Argentina, his father turned the Guest House over to him — "Uncle Willy's House" across from the racetrack on Avenida del Libertador. After a trip to Uruguay, where he had acquired explosives to blow up the *Reine de la Mer* — never used, as it turned out — Clete returned to the house to find Peter sitting in the sitting room, sipping his fourth glass of cognac as he listened to Beethoven's Third Symphony on the phonograph.

Either because she didn't know that Clete was staying in the house, or because she was so detached from reality that she did not consider that a Luftwaffe officer and a U.S. Marine Corps officer were officially enemies, Beatrice Frade de Duarte

219

had ordered von Wachtstein to be put up in the guest house.

It was then well after midnight, and there was nothing the two young officers could do but declare that a temporary truce existed between them. They sealed the truce with a glass of cognac, and then another. And several more.

And then it became apparent that they really had a great deal in common. Both were fighter pilots, which provided an immediate bond between them. Peter had heard of the exploits of the greatly out-numbered Marine fighter pilots on Guadalcanal, and had an understandable fellow fighter pilot's professional admiration for someone who had been one of them. And Clete had heard of the ferocious valor of German fighter pilots defending Berlin from waves of B-17 bombers and had a fellow fighter pilot's professional admiration for someone who had been one of them.

By the time they staggered off to bed, they were friends.

But this truce ended very early the next morning when an Argentine officer, learning that the two enemies were under the same roof on Liber-tador, appeared to remove von Wachtstein from the difficult situation before one tried to kill the other.

Later, when von Wachtstein learned that it was Oberst Grüner's intention to "eliminate" Cletus Howell Frade — by then identified as an OSS agent — von Wachtstein, after a painful moral battle with himself, decided he could not stand silently by and watch it happen. He warned Clete that an attempt would be made on his life.

Clete, forewarned, was able to deal with the as-sassins when they came to the Libertador house.

The equation, so far as Clete was concerned, was simple. He owed von Wachtstein his life, and told him so.

Shortly afterward, Peter received from his father the letter in which he told him that he was required by honor to join the small group of German officers who saw it as their duty to kill Adolf Hitler, and that he had done so. From the tone of the letter, it was clear that Generalleutnant von Wachtstein fully expected to lose his life and was prepared for that.

Peter was not surprised. He had by then already smuggled into Argentina the equivalent of half a million dollars in Swiss francs, English pounds, United States dollars, and Swedish kroner. His father had given him this money to safeguard in Argentina until the war was over. When his father did this, he explained that "a friend" in Argentina would not only help him invest the money, but would also receive more money from other sources to be safeguarded.

The friend turned out to be Ambassador Manfred Alois Graf von Lutzenberger. Soon after he was so identified, the Ambassador informed Peter that getting money to Argentina was only the beginning of the problems they faced. Protecting the money and investing it was very risky. All over Argentina there were Nazi sympathizers who would quickly report anything suspicious to Grüner and his operatives. In Nazi Germany, illegal foreign financial transactions were considered treason. The penalty for treason was the execution of the traitor, all members of his immediate family, and the confiscation of all lands and property of whatever kind.

Reluctantly, but with no other choice that he

could see, Peter went to Clete for assistance. And Clete in turn went to his father, carrying with him Generalleutnant von Wachtstein's letter to Peter. The letter so moved el Coronel Frade that he wept. And he immediately enlisted his brother-in-law, Humberto Valdez Duarte, Managing Director of the Anglo-Argentine Bank, to deal with the secret investment and safekeeping of the money.

"Saying I'm sorry about your father seems pretty damned inadequate, Cletus."

Clete shrugged his understanding.

"Tell me what you know about what happened," he said.

"I didn't know about the details," Peter said. "But I was aware that something like that was going to be attempted. I tried to tell your father that. . . . I'm terribly sorry, Clete."

"Why?"

"I suppose I don't enjoy the complete confidence of Oberst Grüner," Peter said. "Oh, you mean why did they . . . ?"

"Kill my father?"

"The order came from Berlin. Both Grüner and the Ambassador tried to stop it. Grüner for professional reasons — he knew how angry your father's friends would be. Von Lutzenberger? I'll give him the benefit of the doubt and say he happily went along with Grüner's objection that it would cause trouble. What I think — and this is only a guess — is that there were several reasons for the assassination. One, they didn't want your father to become President of Argentina. Two, they couldn't let the destruction of the *Reine de la Mer* go unavenged. You were in America . . . your father

222

was here. What do they call that, 'two birds with one stone'?"

"Christ!"

"Three," Peter went on, "they wanted to punish your father for changing sides, to make the point that traitors can expect to be punished. Four, they wanted to frighten the Grupo de Oficiales Unidos, make the point that they have the ability to assassinate anyone who gets in their way."

"But Grüner gave the order, right?"

"Grüner *carried out* the order."

"What's the difference?"

Peter shrugged.

"I'm going to get that sonofabitch," Clete said evenly.

"If you could get him, which might not be easy to do . . ."

"I'm going to get that sonofabitch!"

". . . all that will happen is that they will send somebody else in, even before they persona non grata you out of Argentina," Peter said. "As a matter of fact, there's already somebody here."

"Excuse me?"

"I spent most of the day with Standartenführer Josef Goltz."

"What's a Standartenführer?"

"Colonel, in the SS," Peter said. "We had a Lufthansa Condor flight today . . ."

"I saw it. It was making its approach as we came in," Clete said. "Good-looking plane."

". . . and he was on it. I thought it was significant that he left Berlin right after we cabled them about what had happened to your father."

"You think he's the man who ordered —"

"I don't *know* that," Peter said. "It's possible. He's some sort of a big shot, I know. Just before he came here he was at Wolfsschanze . . ."

"Where?"

"Hitler's headquarters — it means 'Wolf's Lair' — near Rastenburg, in East Prussia. That it even exists is supposed to be secret. And he's Sicherheitsdienst."

"What does that mean?"

"The Sicherheitsdienst — SD — is the secret police, the elite of the SS. Sicherheitsdienst plus Wolfsschanze adds up to two Very Important Nasty People."

"How do you know he was at . . . what did you call it?"

"Wolfsschanze," Peter supplied. "Because he brought me a letter from my father. My father's stationed at Wolfsschanze. A letter and some major's insignia."

"What's he doing here?"

"I don't know. I know he's meeting with the Ambassador, Grüner, and Gradny-Sawz tomorrow morning," Peter said. "And I know he wants to go to Uruguay — Montevideo — as soon as he can. He wants me to fly him there in our Storch, but he doesn't like the idea of going direct, over the Río de la Plata."

"I know the feeling," Clete said. "Every time I'm out of sight of land, I imagine my engine is making strange noises."

"I didn't like crossing the English Channel," Peter said. "Anyway, I suspect, as anxious as this guy is to get there, he'll tell me to take the over-solid-earth route."

"Why is he so anxious to get to Montevideo?"

Peter shrugged.

"He didn't say," he said, then changed the subject: "Clete, I have a real problem."

"What's that?"

"You remember that letter I got from my father? The one your father translated for you?"

"What about it?"

"Don't bother to tell me I should have burned it," Peter said.

"It's still around?" Peter nodded. "Why, for Christ's sake? If Grüner gets his hands on that . . ."

"I won't blame it on your father," Peter said. "But he . . . I didn't want to burn it. Your father thought it would be a good thing to have after the war."

"So you kept it."

In your shoes, I would have done the same thing.

"Your father was keeping it for me."

"Where?"

"I don't know for sure. In some safe place. Probably with the records of the investments. And I don't like to think what would happen to a lot of people — Ambassador von Lutzenberger and maybe even your uncle Humberto — if those records fell into the wrong hands."

"Where do you *think* they are?"

"Did your father have a safe at Estancia San Pedro y San Pablo? Or some other place besides the obvious . . . bank safety-deposit boxes, for example?"

"I don't know. Seems likely. But I don't know. I'll ask Claudia."

"I don't think there's a hell of a lot of time."

"I understand," Clete said. "Maybe Enrico knows. I'll ask him, too."

"Be careful, diplomatic immunity or not," Peter said.

"I don't have diplomatic immunity."

"You don't?" Peter asked, visibly surprised. "Alicia told me you were going to be the Assistant Naval Attaché."

"That changed. I came back here on my Argentine passport."

"But you're still OSS?"

"I'm still what?"

"Sorry."

Clete shrugged.

"I was asking as a friend, concerned for your welfare. You understand that, I hope?"

Clete nodded again.

"You can count on them trying to kill you, you know that?" Peter said.

"When I was in fighter school, the instructors kept harping, 'watch your back, watch your back, watch your back.' I didn't know what they were talking about then, but eventually I got pretty good at it."

He looked at his watch. It was quarter to one.

"I'll see Claudia in the morning," he said. "And Enrico. They should have an idea where my father would put something he didn't want anybody else to get at."

"I better go home," Peter said.

"I'll drop you."

"You go, I'll finish my drink, then catch a cab."

"OK."

"This might be a good place to meet, if we have to."

"Sure. What'll we call it, in case anybody is listening, as they probably will be."

"It's The Horse. Let's call it The Fish."

They looked at each other. Clete stood up and put out his hand.

"It's good to see you, amigo," he said. "But do

me a favor, will you?"

"Certainly."

"Try to walk like a man when you leave. The waiter is three-quarters convinced that we're a pair of fairies."

"What the hell, we've been up here by ourselves, holding a whispered conversation, doing everything but holding hands, what do you expect him to think?"

[Four]

Recoleta Plaza
Buenos Aires, Argentina
0145 10 April 1943

There was no answer when Clete rang the bell of Tony Pelosi's apartment in a run-down building in the heavily Italian La Boca* district.

He's probably out with Maria-Teresa, damn him!

Though Clete thought it was a dump, Tony had selected his apartment primarily because it was close to the Ristorante Napoli. Its proprietor, Señor Alberghoni, had a daughter named Maria-Teresa. Tony was in love . . . not a very smart thing for someone in Tony's line of work to be, Clete thought.

He drove back through downtown on Avenida del Libertador, then headed for Belgrano, where Et-

---

* "The Mouth," so called because it is the mouth of the Riachuelo Industrial Canal opening on the river Plate. Shipping tycoon — and second husband of Jacqueline Kennedy — Aristotle Onassis got his start operating a small ferry across the Riachuelo Canal.

tinger had an apartment on Calle Monroe (Monroe Street). Just before he reached the Avenida 9 de Julio, there was a traffic holdup of some sort. He crept along for a block or two, and the jam cleared. As he passed Avenida 9 de Julio, he looked up and saw the source of the trouble.

What looked like half a squadron of cavalry, each splendidly mounted trooper holding a lance, was moving at a walk. He couldn't see an artillery caisson, but he thought there was only one reason cavalry would be moving through downtown Buenos Aires at this hour. He checked the Hamilton chronograph. It was twenty minutes to two. The schedule of events called for the casket to be moved, starting at one.

He accelerated, drove three blocks farther, and turned left, reaching Avenida Alvear as the lead troopers of the cavalry came into sight. He drove ahead of them to the park that fronts the Recoleta Cemetery and the Basílica of Our Lady of Pilar, stopped, and got out.

He stood in the shadow of the Recoleta Cemetery wall and watched the procession arrive. The maneuver had obviously been planned carefully and rehearsed, for it went off like clockwork.

The procession stopped by the front of the church. A half-dozen troopers in the lead of the procession dismounted, and the reins to their mounts were given to the troopers beside them. The dismounted troopers then marched to the head of the procession and held the bits of the horses of the commanding officer and the detachment of eight officers riding immediately behind him. They dismounted and marched to the caisson, where they unstrapped the casket, shouldered it, and marched into the church with it.

Two minutes later, they came back out, remounted, waited for the horseholders to regain their mounts, and then did a column left at the walk back toward Avenida Alvear.

Clete waited until the last of them had left, then got back in the Ford and returned to Avenida del Libertador.

He wondered if Enrico had been able to get out of the hospital to go to the Edificio Libertador.

He hoped so, but it was too late to do anything about it if there was a hitch in that plan.

I'll make damned sure he's at the funeral tomorrow, if I have to go to the hospital and get him myself.

[Five]

As he drove back past The Horse — which he now thought of as The Fish — on Avenida del Libertador, he had a sudden thought:

There's a secret compartment in Uncle Willy's desk. Did my father know about it? Would he hide Peter's father's letters and the records Peter was talking about in there?

It was an uncomfortable thought. He had discovered the secret compartment by accident when he lived in Uncle Willy's house. It held some of Uncle Willy's secrets: a large collection of glass slides showing a number of Frenchmen and Frenchwomen — the ladies were a bit overplump, and the gentlemen were wearing nothing but mustaches and black socks — performing various obscene sexual acts on one another.

On the one hand, the chances that his father even knew about the secret compartment were remote. And even if he did, would he use the secret compartment to conceal important documents? But on the other hand, it might be just the place his father would choose to use, because it was so unlikely. And the secret compartment was certainly large enough.

What the hell, I'm practically right in front of the place. It will only take me a minute to look. And Peter is obviously scared shitless, with reason, that somebody will find his father's letter.

Directly across Libertador from the racetrack, he stopped before the cast-iron gates of a large, turn-of-the-century masonry house. The gates carried both the house number — 4730 — and the crest of the Frade family. He blew the horn, and thirty seconds after that there was a glow of light as the basement garage door opened. A moment later, without question, a stocky, middle-aged man started to pull the gates inward.

What Clete thought of as "Uncle Willy's house" had been built by his granduncle Guillermo, a bachelor and near-legendary ladies' man. Uncle Willy's apartment on the top floor was actually one very large room stretching the full width and length of the building.

It was designed with two objects in mind: Wide windows opening on Avenida del Libertador provided Granduncle Guillermo with what amounted to a comfortable private box for watching the horse racing at the Hipódromo across the street. And when the curtains were drawn, he had comfortable quarters for entertaining lady guests. According to Clete's father, there were an awesome number of these.

Clete's connection with the building went back to his birth. According to his father, his mother flatly refused to live in "The Museum," the Frade mansion on Avenida Coronel Díaz, and moved into Uncle Willy's house. When her time came, she left Uncle Willy's house for the hospital, where she was delivered of a male infant named Cletus Howell — after her father — Frade.

He drove the Ford down a steep ramp into the basement garage, thinking, *Just as soon as I can, I'm getting out of the Museum and coming back here.*

A second stocky man walked up to the car. Clete almost didn't see him, his attention having been caught by two cars already in the garage. One of them — a 1941 Buick convertible coupe — was his. It was as glistening as it had been in the showroom of Davis Chevrolet-Buick in Midland, Texas, the day Uncle Jim had made it plain to him that only fools drove convertibles, and the best he could expect for a graduation present was something sensible, like a Chevy business coupe.

The second car was his father's Horche convertible touring sedan, the joy of his life. El Coronel's extraordinary attachment to his Horche was well-known, and a source of amusement to his friends.

Enrico had told Clete that from the moment el Coronel — "as nervous as a first-time father" — watched the massive automobile being lowered to the dock from the *Dresden* of the Hamburg-Amerika Line, only three people were ever behind its wheel, el Coronel himself, Suboficial Mayor Enrico Rodríguez, and Cletus Howell Frade.

Clete thereafter made a point of asking to drive the car whenever they rode in it, and then of driving it in a manner to cause his father to hang on with white knuckles.

I really should have buried him in that, Clete thought. *He really loved that car, and he died in it.*

Even in the dim light, Clete could see the shattered windshield, and the bullet holes in the massive hood and doors.

"Enrico, mi Teniente," the stocky man said, "will be here shortly. He rode with el Coronel to Our Lady of Pilar."

"He *rode?*"

"Sí, mi Teniente."

Jesus Christ, his wounds are still bleeding!

"I just came from there. El Coronel is safely inside the church."

The man nodded.

"I wish to see Enrico when he comes," Clete said.

And then I will take the stupid sonofabitch back to the hospital, where, with a little luck, they'll be able to fix the damage he did to himself by getting on a horse in his condition. Jesus, I hope I can get him out again for the funeral!

As he walked to the interior stairs that led to the kitchen, he saw where the stocky men had been sitting, in armchairs obviously moved to the garage from somewhere upstairs, and that beside the armchairs were two double-barreled shotguns.

Three women were in the kitchen when he pushed open the door. One of them was middle-aged, and the other two were younger. The two younger ones were in maid's uniforms.

Christ, with nobody living here, why do we need two maids and a housekeeper?

Oh, yeah, El Coronel told me he used this place as a guest house before I showed up. It's probably full of people here for the funeral.

The kitchen was clean and cheerful, and the tiles on the floor were spotless.

Clete had a sudden, sickeningly clear mental image of the tiles by the kitchen table, thick and slippery with the blood of Enrico's sister, Señora Marianna Maria Dolores Rodríguez de Pellano, who had been the housekeeper.

"Her murder was unnecessary," el Teniente Coronel Alejandro Bernardo Martín explained at the time. (He'd come to the murder scene to see how it affected Argentine security, not to investigate the crime.)

"But on the other hand," Martín added, "from the viewpoint of the would-be assassins, it was the correct thing to do. The dead make terrible witnesses, and the government can only execute murderers once."

A voice interrupted these thoughts.

"I am Señora Lopez, Señor Frade. The housekeeper. Can I get you anything?"

"No, thank you. I'm going to go upstairs for a minute, and then I'm going to wait for Enrico in the sitting."

"I have laid out some things in the sitting for our guest, Señor Frade. If there is something else you would like, just ring. And there is whiskey and ice and soda."

"Thank you," Clete said, and smiled at her.

Did she say "our guest," singular? That's surprising. I would have thought this place would be full of people for the funeral.

He rode the elevator to Uncle Willy's apartment on the top floor. There was evidence that somebody was staying in the room, and it made him a little uncomfortable to be an intruder.

Screw it. All I'm going to do is check the secret compartment in the desk.

He walked across the room to the massive desk, and opened the secret compartment without difficulty. There was nothing in it at all.

Not even Uncle Willy's naughty pictures.

Somebody's been in there. Who? When? And did they find just the dirty slides? Or, presuming it was here, Peter's father's letter?

Damn!

He got back on the elevator and rode it back to the foyer. When he entered the sitting, he saw that a plate of sandwiches and other finger food had been laid out on a table beside a coffee service and half a dozen bottles of hard liquor.

He made himself a scotch and soda, looked for and found a cigar in a humidor, and then slipped into an armchair. He looked around the room. There was a change since he had left: The oil portrait of a Thoroughbred was no longer hanging over the fireplace. (Granduncle Guillermo had raised the horse from a colt, and had won a great deal of money on it.) In its place hung a large oil portrait of a beautiful young woman in an evening dress with an infant in her arms. The woman was Señora Elizabeth Ann Howell de Frade, and the infant was her firstborn, Cletus Howell Frade.

Clete had last seen it hanging in his father's private library at Estancia San Pedro y San Pablo.

I wonder why he brought it here?

Well, it means he came here when I was in the States, which suggests that goddamned letter may be here — or was here — after all.

He found a match, and was in the slow process of correctly lighting the cigar when the door opened.

It was Enrico, in a Húsares uniform.

The bandage on his head is leaking blood. Christ only knows what he looks like under that Student Prince Graustarkian uniform jacket.

"Mi Teniente . . ."

"I asked you not to call me that," Clete snapped.

"Señor Clete . . ."

"What in the name of God were you thinking riding a horse in your condition?"

"I rode with your father in the cavalry all our lives, Señor Clete. It was my duty to ride with him tonight."

"And what are you going to do, for Christ's sake, when I die? Follow me to the cemetery in an airplane?"

Not only could Enrico not immediately counter the logic of that remark, but there was a chuckle of appreciation from a previously unseen spectator.

Clete raised his eyes from his still not fully and properly ignited cigar and saw a tall man in uniform. Not of the Húsares. He didn't recognize anything about this one except the epaulets, which carried the insignia of a coronel.

Clete stood up.

"According to Enrico, you are quite a soldier yourself, Señor Frade. Therefore, you should know that arguing with a determined Suboficial Mayor is a waste of time and breath. One has the choice of giving in or having him shot."

"I'm tempted to do the latter," Clete said. "Or at least to chain him to his bed."

The tall colonel walked to him and put out his hand. "Perhaps levity is out of place," he said. "But on the other hand, I've heard that laughter often occurs spontaneously when pain is at the point of being unbearable."

"You have the advantage of me, mi Coronel," Clete said.

"Forgive me. But I have heard so much of you over the years, and tonight, from Enrico, that I feel I know you. Your father was my best friend, from our first day at the military academy. My name is Perón, Juan Domingo Perón."

"How do you do?"

"I have just, with great embarrassment, realized that I find myself an uninvited guest in your home, Señor Frade."

"My father's best friend will always be my honored guest," Clete heard himself say.

Where the hell is this flowery language coming from? It just pops into my mouth. And not, I don't think, because I'm speaking Spanish, and not English. I have never been a charmer in either language.

He turned to Enrico.

"Take off your jacket and sit down," he ordered, pointing to a chair.

"Señor Clete?"

"You heard me," Clete said. He walked to the pull cord and jerked on it. When the housekeeper appeared a moment later, Enrico, with some difficulty, was still in the process of taking off his tunic.

She sucked in her breath when she saw Enrico's bloodstained undershirt.

"I'm going to need bandages, and tape, and cotton wool, and alcohol, or some other antiseptic," Clete said.

"Sí, Señor," she said, and quickly left the room.

"What I should do, Enrico, is call for an ambulance and send you back to the hospital."

"I am all right, Señor Clete."

Clete looked at him, felt a wave of emotion for Enrico's dedication to his father, and went to the whiskey bottles, poured an inch and a half in a glass, and handed it to him.

"With a little luck, you'll choke to death on this, and I won't have to worry about you anymore," he said.

"Gracias, Señor Clete," Enrico said, and added: "I saw you outside Our Lady of Pilar."

"You're lucky I didn't see you," Clete said.

The housekeeper and one of the maids appeared with what Clete had asked for.

Clete unwrapped the bandage on Enrico's head. Dried blood had glued it to his skin. After some thought, Clete decided it would hurt him less to jerk it off than to pull it. He did so. Enrico winced but made no sound.

He winced again as Clete mopped at the blood with alcohol-soaked cotton wool. It wasn't as bad as he thought it might be. The stitches sewing the wound together had not pulled loose. The wound itself, as Enrico had told him in the hospital, was actually a half-inch-wide, two-inch-long canal gouged out of his flesh. He washed it carefully, then applied a fresh bandage.

"You have done that before," el Coronel Perón said as Clete was applying the fresh bandage.

"Once or twice," Clete said. "This is one of those famous wounds — 'another half an inch, and that's all she wrote, Charley!' "

"Excuse me?" Perón said.

"He's lucky he's alive," Clete said. "Another half an inch, another *quarter* of an inch . . ."

He bent over and looked for a fingerhold on one of the bandages on Enrico's upper chest. "On the other hand," he went on, "the head wound probably kept him alive. It knocked him out, and with all the blood, those murdering bastards thought he

237

was already dead and not worth a round of 00-buck."

He jerked the bandage off. Enrico grunted.

"At least the banditos who did this soon paid for it," Perón said. "Saving yourself and the rest of the family the pain of a trial, and the government the expense."

"*Banditos,* my ass," Clete flared, aware that he was now sounding more like himself. "*Assassins* is the word, mi Coronel. The fucking Krauts couldn't get me, so they went after my father and Enrico. And got my father."

There was no reply for a long moment, long enough for Clete to finish washing Enrico's wound and to turn to find a fresh bandage.

"By 'Krauts' I presume you mean Germans?" Perón asked, somewhat stiffly.

"That's right."

"Enrico told me that was his belief," Perón said. "But I am frankly surprised that you give credence to something like that."

"I believe it because it's true," Clete said evenly. "And the reason the bastards are dead, mi Coronel, is because dead people can't testify about who hired them."

"Argentina has long been plagued with banditos," Perón said.

"These bastards may have been banditos, but they were working for the Germans."

"Your father was a friend of Germany, Señor Frade. He had many German friends. He was a graduate of the Kriegsschule."

"Yeah, well, one of his German friends ordered his assassination. Another of them — or maybe the same sonofabitch — ordered my assassination. That time they got Enrico's sister, Señora Pellano."

"In that tragic incident, as I understand it, you killed both of the burglars. Did you do that so they would not be able to testify in court?"

What the hell's the matter with you? You don't like hearing the truth? Well, fuck you, Colonel!

Watch your temper, Clete!

"I had to kill one of them," Clete said evenly. "The second, I am ashamed to say, I shot because I lost control of myself when I saw what they had done to Señora Pellano. I now regret that very much. If I hadn't lost my temper, we could have made the sonofabitch tell us who paid him."

There was another long silence. Perón said nothing at all until Clete had finished replacing all of Enrico's bandages.

"Obviously, Señor Frade," he said finally, "you believe what you have said. I find it difficult — impossible — to accept. But I will look into the matter, and put the question to rest for all time."

Watch what you say, Clete! Not only was this guy your father's best friend, but pissing him off isn't going to accomplish anything.

"I would be grateful if you would, mi Coronel," Clete said. "And I have another service to ask of you."

"Anything within my power, Señor Frade."

"Would you see that Suboficial Mayor Rodríguez gets to Our Lady of Pilar tomorrow? By automobile? I will see to it that there are seats with the family for my father's best friends."

"Of course."

"You go to bed, Enrico, and try not to do anything else stupid between now and tomorrow."

"Sí, mi Teniente. Gracias, mi Teniente."

"If I can't get you to call me by my name, at least get the rank right," Clete said. "I was discharged from the Marine Corps as a major."

Clete saw Perón's eyes light up with that announcement.

Is that why I said that? So Perón won't dismiss me as just one more young, and stupid, lieutenant?

"You're very young to have been a mayor," Perón said.

"Yeah, well, we were in a war. Promotions come quickly when there's a war. Enrico, is my Buick drivable?"

"Yes, of course, mi Mayor."

"I think I'll take it with me," Clete said. "I took a Ford station wagon from my father's house. Do you think one of the men downstairs could drive it back for me? They may need it tomorrow."

"You came here alone?" Enrico asked, horrified.

"Why not?"

"Mi Mayor," Enrico said, shaking his head at Clete's stupidity. "The men downstairs will see you safely to el Coronel's house."

Clete put out his hand to Perón.

"I am delighted to have the privilege of your acquaintance, mi Coronel."

Perón grasped his hand firmly.

"The pleasure is mine, Mayor," he said. "I regret the circumstances."

VIII

[One]

```
The Basílica of St. Pilar
Recoleta Plaza
Buenos Aires
0915 10 April 1943
```

It was necessary for Antonio to really shake Clete to wake him, and even after a shower and several cups of coffee with his breakfast, he still felt groggy and exhausted.

As he had announced he would, Capitán Lauffer appeared at eight-thirty.

En route to Our Lady of Pilar, Clete told him about Enrico climbing out of a hospital bed onto a horse to escort his father from the Edificio Libertador to the Basílica, and also about meeting el Coronel Perón.

"He and your father were great friends," Lauffer said.

"So he said."

"He just came back from Germany."

"Excuse me? What did you say?"

"He just came back from Germany. He was on the Lufthansa flight yesterday."

"What was he doing in Germany?" Clete asked.

Lauffer shrugged. "I'm afraid I don't know."

Well, that explains that "difficult — impossible — to believe" bullshit he gave me last night, doesn't it?

"Is Perón involved in this Grupo de Oficiales Unidos business?"

"Señor Frade . . ."

"Do you think you could bring yourself to call me 'Clete'?"

"I would like that. My Christian name is Roberto."

He offered Clete his hand.

"Clete," Lauffer said, "one of the difficulties we have in Argentina with norteamericanos is that you have a tendency to ask questions that shouldn't be asked, and are impolitic to answer."

"In other words, he is," Clete said. "Is that why he came back? Because the G.O.U. is about to move?"

Lauffer looked at him, smiled, and shook his head.

"I don't know anything about the G.O.U."

"You are being deaf, dumb, and blind, right?" Clete challenged with a smile.

"But if I were a betting man, and I knew that one man was involved with the G.O.U., I would wager his best friend was."

"OK. That's good enough. Thank you for your nonanswer. And since you don't know anything about the G.O.U., I suppose you can't tell me if it's loaded with Nazi sympathizers?"

"I wonder if you are asking that question personally or professionally."

"Professionally?"

"There is a rumor going around that you are really an agent of the OSS."

"Of the what?"

"You never heard of the OSS, of course?"

"Not a word."

"Then I suppose it's also not true that you are the man who blew up the *Reine de la Mer*."

"The what?"

"As an officer of the Argentine Army, of course, I was horrified to hear that the American OSS violated the neutrality of Argentina by blowing up a neutral ship in our waters."

"As, of course, you should have been. The Americans blew up a Nazi ship, you say? Do you think they had a reason?" Clete asked, smiling.

"My father, however — he is a retired Admiral of the Armada" — Navy — "does not share my views. He said something to the effect that he was surprised it took the Americans so long to do what the British should have done in the first place, and that he hoped whoever did it not only got away but received an appropriate decoration."

"You can tell your father, if what you say is true, that something like that probably happened."

Lauffer smiled back at him. "A decoration and a promotion to Mayor?"

"Something like that," Clete said.

"So far as Nazis being within the Grupo de Oficiales Unidos: I would suspect that if such an organization really exists, it is not controlled by those who sympathize with Germany, or, on the other hand, by those who sympathize with the British and the norteamericanos. It would be concerned with Argentine internal affairs."

Clete was disappointed when he looked out the window and saw they were at the rear of Recoleta Cemetery; he preferred not to end the conversation just now.

When they reached the church* itself, a line of people had already formed to view the casket when the church was opened. Clete wondered how many of them had known, much less admired, his father, and how many were there out of simple curiosity.

Lauffer knocked at a side door, which was opened by a monk in sandals and a brown robe.

"This is Señor Frade," Lauffer said, and the monk opened the door all the way and pointed to the interior of the church.

The casket — el Coronel's uniform cap, his medals, and the Argentine flag back in place on top — was in the center of the aisle near the altar. And the honor guard was present, too, preparing to go on duty; their officer-in-charge was checking the appearance of the troopers. When he saw Lauffer, he came to attention and saluted.

There was a tug on Clete's sleeve, and he turned to see another brown-robed monk, extending a large key to him.

"The key to your tomb, Señor," the monk said.

Clete looked helplessly at Lauffer, and the monk picked up on it.

"We have moved your grandfather, Señor, and made the preparations for your father. I would like your approval of the arrangements."

"Moved my grandfather"? What the hell does that mean?

Lauffer, seeing Clete's confusion and hesitation, nodded.

"Thank you," Clete said to the monk.

"I'll go with you. I knew this was coming, and brought a torch," he said, exhibiting a flashlight.

* The Basílica of Our Lady of Pilar (completed 1732), on Recoleta Square, is considered the most beautiful church in Buenos Aires.

They followed the monk out of a side door of the church and into the cemetery. Ornate burial grounds were not new to Clete. Because of the water table, belowground burial in New Orleans is virtually impossible. The result of that over the years has been the construction of elaborate above-ground tombs covering hundreds of acres.

The Old Man called the cemeteries "Marble City," allegedly to keep the bodies from floating down the Mississippi, but really erected to impress the neighbors. The worse the scoundrel, the larger his tomb.

But there was nothing in New Orleans like Recoleta Cemetery. Here even the smallest of family tombs resembled marble churches, and there were acres and acres of them, side by side.

He had been here once before, the day Cousin Jorge Alejandro was laid to rest in the Duarte tomb.

They came to the Frade tomb. It was about the size of the Duarte Tomb, about thirty feet wide and twenty feet deep. Wrought-iron-barred glass doors offered a view of the interior, which was set up like a church altar.

The monk reclaimed the key.

"With your permission, Señor Frade," he said, and unlocked the door.

I'll be damned. I think he expects me to go inside.

He looked at Lauffer, his eyebrows raised in question, and Lauffer smiled, nodded, and handed Clete a flashlight.

That was nice of him to think about that, but I won't need a flashlight in there. I can see well enough, and I don't intend to stay long.

He followed the monk into the tomb. He looked around. There was a large Christ on the cross — *either a statue or more likely a bronze casting* — on the wall of the tomb above the altar; a large, formal

245

cross — *I wonder if that's gold? Probably not; if it was gold, somebody would climb the cemetery walls at night and steal it* — and several other gold — or at least gold-plated — objects beside it on sort of a shelf against the wall. Two of them were filled with fresh flowers. *Nice touch.* Everything rested on a — *what do you call that, an altar cloth?* — sheet of finely embroidered linen. *That's fresh from the laundry.* A similar but larger cloth covered a marble table, three feet wide and eight feet long, two feet from the altar against the wall. *In a church, that's where the priest would have the wine and wafers for Holy Communion.*

He turned to the monk, wondering if it would be appropriate to comment on the nice furnishings, or maybe to thank him — *he had the key to this place, he's probably responsible.*

The monk was on his knees, not praying, but instead lifting a section of the tomb floor. The floor, Clete noticed for the first time, was of steel. *Like in the center of a bridge, where they put a section of steel like that, with holes, to keep cars from skidding when there's ice.*

What the hell *is he doing?*

With a grunt, the monk pulled a five-foot-square section of the floor loose, and with an effort pushed it to the side of the room, resting it against a wall.

Then he took a small flashlight from the folds of his robe, put it in his mouth, and backed into the hole in the floor. When only his chest was above floor level, he took the flashlight from his mouth.

"Be careful, Señor. Sometimes the ladder is slippery."

Does he expect me to go down there? What the hell is down there, anyway?

When the monk disappeared from view, Clete

went to the opening and stared down. A metal ladder, looking like something you'd find on a destroyer, went down as far as Clete could see.

At least three decks.

He shrugged — *what the hell?* — and backed carefully into the hole. Lauffer's flashlight was too large to put in his mouth, so he had to put it in his pocket. There was just enough light for him to find the round rungs of the ladder with his feet. He started to climb down.

He found himself in a room as large as the altar room above. There was no altar. Instead there were shelves on all four sides of the room, four high, each holding a wooden casket. Most of them were full-size, but he saw three smaller caskets, one tiny. Children's caskets, and a baby's casket. On the wall in front of him, where two shelves would ordinarily be, he saw another Christ on a cross.

The monk was descending farther into the ground. Clete followed him.

There's no smell of death in here. A musty smell, and the smell of wood, that's all.

The thought triggered a clear and distinctly unpleasant memory of the sweet smell of corrupting corpses.

Shit!

Clete climbed down after the monk through three more burial chambers, each full of caskets on shelves, and then to a fourth chamber. In this one, all but two of the casket shelves were empty.

I guess this is where el Coronel will go. How the hell are they going to get that casket down here?

The monk flashed his light on the two shelved caskets. Both were massive and polished like good furniture, Clete saw, but not identical.

I'll be damned! That's one of those cedar caskets

247

Beatrice was raving about!

"We have moved your grandfather here, Señor Frade," the monk said, laying his hand on one of the caskets. "Beside your grandmother."

"I see," Clete said.

"I will now leave you to your private prayers for the repose of the souls of the departed," the monk said, and started for the ladder. He stopped. "I suggest you be careful with your torch. If you drop it . . . very little light gets this far down."

He waited until Clete had taken his flashlight from his pocket and turned it on, then offered a final word of advice. "You might find it convenient to place the torch under your belt. And mind the ladder!"

"Thank you," Clete said.

The only thing I want out of this place is me! But, shit, I can't just follow him immediately.

You've been around dead people before. Stop acting like a child.

He flashed the light on the caskets, noticing for the first time that engraved bronze plates were on them.

> ## MARY ELIZABETH CONNERS DE FRADE
>
> ### 1861–1916

"Mary Elizabeth Conners"? That doesn't sound Spanish. What did the monk say, "beside my grandmother"? Mary Elizabeth Conners is — was — my grandmother? She bore my father? Changed his diapers, for Christ's sake? Suckled him? An Englishwoman? Or an Irishwoman?

He flashed the light on the other casket.

EL CORONEL

GUILLERMO ALEJANDRO FRADE

1857–1919

My grandfather, another el Coronel Frade.

Clete saw in his mind's eye el Coronel Alejandro Frade's pistol. His father had given it to him as a Christmas present reflecting his heritage. It was a Colt .44–40 single-action, often fired, most of the blue gone, a working gun, not a decoration. On one of its well-worn grips, inlaid in silver, was the crest of the Húsares de Pueyrredón, on the other the Frade family crest.

To judge by the gun, my grandfather was apparently a real soldier.

El Coronel — why do I think of him that way, rather than "Dad"? — told me his father died the year before Dad *came to New Orleans and married my mother.*

Did some monk bring my father down here when his father died, to show him where his grandfather had been moved? What the hell is that "moved" business, anyway? Moved from where, and why?

Sorry, Grandpa, Grandma, I'm an Episcopalian, and I don't know what kind of a prayer I'm supposed to offer for the repose of your souls. If I knew what to say, I would.

I've been down here long enough.

Curiosity got to him before he reached the next level, however, and instead of climbing higher, he stepped off the ladder and moved around the chamber, looking for one casket in particular. He didn't find it on that level, although he came across a surprising number of people whose names were non-Spanish-sounding. Even some Germans, which he found disturbing, but mostly English. Mawson. Miller. Evans.

He found the casket he was looking for on the next level.

> ## JORGE GUILLERMO FRADE
>
> ### 1850–1915

Uncle Willy's in there. Horse breeder, swordsman of national disrepute, and collector of dirty pictures. Maybe I do have some of your genes in me, Uncle Willy. God knows, I like horses, whiskey, and wild, wild, women, and I looked at every one of your dirty pictures the night I found them.

The discovery of Uncle Willy's casket somehow pleased him, and when he realized that, he was uncomfortable. He returned to the ladder and climbed upward again.

In the chamber immediately below ground level, where there was enough light from above to see more clearly, an ornately carved casket caught his eye — angels blowing trumpets; a hooded woman carrying a limp body, presumably to heaven — and he stepped off the ladder and looked for the name-plate on it.

> ## MARIA ELENA PUEYRREDÓN DE FRADE
>
> ### 1812–1858

Jesus Christ, Pueyrredón's daughter! My what? My great-grandmother? This is the reason I got that saber salute from the Capitán of the Húsares de Pueyrredón at the Edificio Libertador yesterday. Down here, that's like being related to George Washington.

He touched the limp body the hooded woman was carrying, tenderly, almost reverently, then climbed back on the ladder.

Why do I suspect that Colonel Graham knows more about my family tree than I do? He's a clever son-ofabitch, and damned well knows that nobody's going to easily throw Pueyrredón's great-great-grandson out of Argentina.

When he put his head through the hole in the upper-chamber floor, he could see out of the tomb. Specifically, he found himself looking farther than decency allowed up the marvelously formed, silk-stocking-clad legs of a young woman in a black dress.

He had two thoughts, the first of them not very relevant:

There seems to be plenty of silk stockings down here. I wonder why there's such a shortage of them in the States? Women are painting their legs in the States, including a line down the back of the leg, so it looks like they're wearing stockings.

His second thought, since he had recognized the legs, was more to the point.

Jesus, Dorotéa! I forgot all about her. Somebody must have told her where I was, and she came to personally deliver Part Two of the Dear John letter she started on the phone last night.

Christ, I'm going to miss her!

He came out of the hole. Dorotéa had been waiting for him. He gave her a wait-a-second signal and turned to the monk to thank him for the tour of the family tomb.

And suddenly, on seeing the embroidered cloth-covered table, it was as if his brain, which had been out of gear, suddenly dropped into high.

They're going to put el Coronel's casket on that table. That's what he meant when he said they had moved my grandfather. He was here, for God only knows how long, until today, or yesterday. The casket of the last one to die goes on display in front of the altar for however long it takes for the next family member to croak.

The next one to croak is very likely to be me.

Jesus, what a weird custom!

Christ, I better say something to Tony, leave a letter of instructions or something. I don't want to go on display in here!

Or do I? What's wrong with being with my father and Uncle Willy?

Jesus Christ!

"Is everything to your satisfaction, Señor Frade?" the monk asked.

"Perfectly. I am in your debt, Sir, for your thoughtfulness."

"Your father, Señor Frade, your family, have always generously supported the Recoleta Cemetery."

That's a pitch for money. I'll be damned!

What the hell do I say to him?

I'll have to ask somebody — Humberto — about giving them money. How much and to whom.

"Again, I thank you for your thoughtfulness. And I will never forget it."

The monk smiled, turned, bowed before the altar, and walked out of the tomb.

Clete followed him. He saw Lauffer, standing twenty yards away, motion to the monk to join him.

He thinks I want to be alone with the pretty girl. What did General Lee say at Appomattox Courthouse? "I would rather die a thousand deaths . . ."?

"What do you say, Princess? How's tricks?"

"I really wish you wouldn't call me that," Dorotéa said in British-accented English.

"Sorry. You said you had something on your mind, *Dorotéa?*"

"This is probably the worst *possible* place, at the worst *possible* time, to tell you this," she said. "I'm really sorry."

Oh, I don't know. This is a cemetery. Shouldn't dead love get a decent burial?

"What is it, Prin . . . *Dorotéa?* I probably won't be nearly as upset as you think I'm going to be."

She moved close to him and looked into his eyes.

"We're going to have a baby," she announced softly.

Even as he spoke the words, looking into her eyes, he knew the question he was croaking — "Are you sure?" — was unnecessary.

"Of *course* I'm sure."

"Oh, Princess!"

"Does that mean 'Three cheers, hurrah!' or 'Oh, my *God!*' "

"Princess, you really surprised me with this one."

"In other words, 'Oh, my *God!*'?"

"I thought I was going to get a Dear John," he said.

"I have no idea what you're talking about, Cletus. What's a 'Dear John'?"

"It's a letter a girlfriend writes her boyfriend in the service. 'Dear John, I'm sorry to tell you this, but someone else has come into my life.' "

"Sometimes you are a *bloody ass*, Cletus," Dorotéa said angrily, and loudly enough so that the monk turned. "I love you, and until this moment I was laboring under the delusion that you loved me, too."

"Princess, I love you more than my life," Clete said. "When I thought I was going to lose you, I wanted to jump in the goddamned River Plate."

She looked at him. Her tongue came out and licked her lips in a nervous gesture he found exquisitely exciting.

"Yes," she said.

"Yes what?" he asked, confused.

"Yes, I will marry you. Or wasn't that a proposal?" she asked, a naughty glint in her eyes.

"It was," he said. "But I don't think this is the place to get on my knees."

"Or the time. You had better wait a couple of days before you ask Daddy for my hand. And speaking of the devil, so to speak, what he thinks I'm doing is trying to find the loo, so I'm going to have to go back."

She stood on her tiptoes and kissed his cheek.

"I would really like to put my arms around you and really kiss you," she said. "But not here with the monk watching. Can you wait?"

"I don't have any choice, do I?"

"None," she said brightly, turned, and walked away.

She's not wearing a girdle under that dress. She really has a magnificent fanny. And as far as that goes, a magnificent everything else, too.

And she's carrying my child!

Why couldn't you keep your pecker in your pocket, you stupid sonofabitch?

Capitán Lauffer raised his eyebrows questioningly: *Don't you think you should be getting back to the church?* Clete nodded and walked to him.

[Two]

1420 Avenida Alvear
Buenos Aires, Argentina
1215 10 April 1943

"Would you like something to eat, Cletus?" Humberto Valdez Duarte asked, walking over to where Clete stood at the bar set up in the downstairs reception, helping himself to a bottle of scotch.

Is that just good manners, or an expression of concern for my welfare, or is he worried that I'm going to climb into a bottle the way my father did when they buried Cousin Jorge Alejandro?

"I'm all right, thank you. Can I fix you one of these?"

"There is supposed to be someone . . ." Humberto said impatiently, and looked around the empty reception. A door leading to the butler's pantry opened as he watched, and two barmen in starched white jackets came through, carrying a large, galvanized tub filled with ice and various bottles. "Ah, there they are!"

He waited until they had placed the tub behind the bar, then ordered: "I'll have one of those, please."

"Are you all right, Cletus?" Humberto asked.

Just peachy-keen, Uncle Humberto. I have just watched my murdered father being buried, and have been standing here thinking that if I hadn't shown up down here, he would still be alive. And also thinking that heading the list of shitty things — sins, if you like — I have done in my life is impregnating an innocent nineteen-year-old. Fucking up not only her life, but that of a child, too.

"I'm fine. Thank you."

The barman handed Humberto his drink. He nodded his thanks, then raised the glass.

"To Jorge Guillermo," he said, "May he find your mother in heaven as beautiful as he remembered her."

Clete touched his glass.

"And the horses be fast, and the champagne properly chilled," Clete said.

Where the hell did that come from?

Humberto chuckled and took a sip.

"Yes," he said.

"I watched the Húsares de Pueyrredón move him from the Edificio Libertador last night," Clete said. "I think el Coronel would have been pleased with his funeral."

"He loved parades," Humberto said. "Particularly if he was leading it."

"He was too goddamned young to die," Clete said. "And like that!"

"Yes," Humberto said. "Cletus, that brings up a somewhat delicate matter."

"What's that?"

"The reception will start in about fifteen minutes. There are already people arriving."

Clete nodded and waited for him to go on.

"There will be a reception line . . ."

"Can I get out of that?"

". . . and among the guests expected are Ambassador von Lutzenberger and members of his staff from the German Embassy. I believe Major von Wachtstein will be among them."

Clete's eyebrows shot up, but he said nothing.

"We see a good deal of Ambassador von Lutzenberger and his staff socially," Humberto went on. "Your aunt Beatrice added many of them to our list after their many courtesies to us when Jorge

Alejandro was brought home. She is especially fond of Major von Wachtstein. There are, of course, certain advantages to the situation."

"I'm not sure I'm up to standing in a reception line and smiling at the murdering sonsofbitches."

"I think everyone will understand that you are indisposed."

"Is that what I am, 'indisposed'?" Clete said, and then, softly, "Speaking of Germans, I saw Peter von Wachtstein last night."

"Was that wise? If you were seen . . ."

"We weren't," Clete said. "He's very concerned that my father had some records . . ."

"The records of certain financial transactions," Humberto said. "I'm very concerned myself."

"Plus a personal letter from Peter's father."

"I know about the letter, too."

"But you don't know where they are?"

"They're most likely in your father's safe at Estancia San Pedro y San Pablo," Humberto said. "God, I hope they are!"

"I don't know what safe you're talking about."

"It's in your father's study."

"I'd like to get in it as soon as possible. Who has the combination?"

"I was hoping you would have it."

"No. I didn't even know there was a safe until just now."

"Well, I know Claudia doesn't have the combination," Humberto said. "She asked me for it."

"Why does she want it?"

"I simply presumed there were personal things — letters perhaps — that she didn't want anybody else to see. Wanted to get them out of the safe before you started going through it."

"So how do I get in it?"

"Right now, I don't know. Let me think about it. But for the moment, unless you want to see the Germans, you'd better get out of here."

"Where do I go?"

"The upstairs sitting," Humberto said. "I will instruct the servants who is to be taken there to pay their respects to you privately. The Mallíns, for example. And there is an American officer . . ."

"An American officer? Do you have his name?"

"Teniente Pelosi," Humberto said. "I have his card." He handed it to Clete.

ANTHONY JOSEPH PELOSI

First Lieutenant, Corps of Engineers
Army of the United States

Assistant Military Attaché
Embassy of the United States of America

"I really want to see him," Clete said. "But I don't want to make it obvious. Wait until the place is full of people, and then send him upstairs."

"Certainly."

"Make sure he doesn't get away. He may think I don't want to see him."

"I understand," Humberto said.

"Right," Clete said. "Humberto, thank you. And when this is all over, I really need to talk to you."

"I was about to say almost exactly those words," Humberto said. "There are business matters that need immediate decisions. Perhaps we can find the time over the weekend. We will *have to find* the time over the weekend. Can I show you the way?"

"I know where it is, thank you."

Suboficial Mayor Enrico Rodríguez, in Húsares de Pueyrredón uniform, jumped to attention when Clete walked into the upstairs sitting, startling Clete enough that in a Pavlovian Marine officer's reflex, he barked, "As you were!"

"Mi Mayor?" Enrico asked, baffled.

"One, stand at ease, Enrico, and two, stop calling me 'Major.' "

"Por favor, mi Mayor," Enrico said. "My last service to mi Coronel."

"What?"

Enrico turned to the table beside him.

"Mi Mayor," he said, "I present to you the saber and decorations of the late el Coronel Jorge Guillermo Frade!"

He extended to Clete a saber, together with its accoutrements, and the pale-blue velvet medal-covered pillow that had lain on the casket.

Clete's throat tightened and his eyes watered. He came to attention.

"Muchas gracias, Suboficial Mayor," he said, and took them with as much military decorum as he could muster. When he looked at Enrico he saw tears running down his cheeks.

Clete turned, found a table, and laid the saber and the pillow on it, then turned to Enrico, who was standing at the Argentine equivalent of Parade Rest.

"I think that what my father would prefer now, Enrico, is that his friend and his son have a drink to him, rather than stand here weeping like women."

"Sí, mi Mayor, I think he would," Enrico said. He snapped to attention and then relaxed, as if he had been dismissed. He walked to a small bar that had been set up. "English whiskey, Señor Clete, or norteamericano?"

"Just as long as it's wet," Clete said.

[Three]

The official delegation of the Embassy of Germany to the funeral mass and interment of the late el Coronel Jorge Guillermo Frade had arrived at the Basílica of Our Lady of Pilar in two automobiles, and it was presumed that the suggestion that mourners walk the half-dozen blocks down Avenida Alvear to the reception at the Duarte mansion did not apply to them.

Ambassador von Lutzenberger did not invite Standartenführer Goltz to ride with him and Frau Ambassador in the Embassy Mercedes. On one hand, this surprised First Secretary Gradny-Sawz, for it would be the polite thing to do vis-à-vis a visiting dignitary of Goltz's stature, he thought. But on the other hand, it pleased him, for it allowed him to be with Goltz. Major Freiherr Hans-Peter von Wachtstein also rode with Gradny-Sawz and Goltz in the second, slightly smaller Embassy Mercedes.

The police passed them through the barriers blocking Avenida Alvear without question, but the gates of the mansion were closed, and it was necessary for them to get out of the cars on the curb.

A barrage of flashbulbs went off. Gradny-Sawz glanced around, saw an unruly crowd on the sidewalk, and quickly decided what was going on. Though the police had tried to keep the journalists from Buenos Aires newspapers a respectable distance from the mansion, the journalists had jumped over the police barricades and were overwhelming the half-dozen policemen at the fence gate. They saw a good picture, and were going to risk a policeman's angrily swung baton to get it.

After paying what Gradny-Sawz thought was probably the shortest courtesy call possible, President Ramón Castillo was leaving the mansion with a small entourage just as the American Ambassador with his entourage — Gradny-Sawz saw Vice Consul Spiers and the American military attaché — started inside.

An exchange of handshakes was of course required by protocol, and that in itself would be a good news photograph. But this act was taking place as Ambassador von Lutzenberger also started to enter the mansion. A photograph of the President of Argentina shaking hands with the American Ambassador while the German Ambassador waited his turn was a photograph worthy of the front page, and would probably be seen all over the world.

And God was with Germany, Gradny-Sawz decided, as the American Ambassador walked into the mansion. At least three photographs got a shot of Castillo shaking hands with von Lutzenberger while, back to the camera, the American Ambassador, trailed by his staff, marched away.

That photo would almost certainly appear on the front pages of *La Nacion*, *La Prensa*, and *Clarin*, the major Buenos Aires newspapers. With a little luck, it would be transmitted by cable all over the world.

The American Embassy Press Officer had somehow managed to make the major Argentine newspapers aware that the late Oberst Frade was survived by his son, Cletus Howell Frade, of New

Orleans, Louisiana, USA and Buenos Aires. *La Nacion* had further described the son as "Teniente Frade, USMC"; and *La Prensa* as "Major Frade, U.S. Navy." The *Buenos Aires Herald* — as expected, considering their close connection to the Americans — had reported that Major Cletus H. Frade, USMC, Retired, a hero of the Battle of Guadalcanal, had flown from his home in Texas, USA, to attend his father's funeral. Major Frade was expected to remain in Argentina, the nation of his birth, and was, under Argentine law, an Argentine citizen.

The photograph of President Castillo shaking Ambassador von Lutzenberger's hand, in Gradny-Sawz's professional judgment, would affect Argentine public opinion far more effectively than the best public relations efforts of the Americans.

It was, of course, a shame that Ambassador von Lutzenberger was not a more imposing figure physically. Von Lutzenberger's uniform was, of course, even more heavily gold-encrusted than that authorized for First Secretary Gradny-Sawz. It was, Gradny-Sawz thought, as he usually did on occasions like this, no fault of Graf von Lutzenberger that he was fifty-three, sharp-featured, small, skinny, and almost entirely bald. But the result was inevitable: Von Lutzenberger looked somehow comical in his uniform, like a member of the chorus in an operetta.

The police soon managed to get the press back behind their barricades, and Gradny-Sawz, Goltz, and von Wachtstein walked quickly to the gate in the fence. And Ambassador Graf and Frau Grafin Ambassador von Lutzenberger were waiting for them just beyond the servants checking invitations at a table set up inside the door.

There were only two people receiving. Señor and Señora Duarte. Gradny-Sawz wondered where the son was; he had been at the church earlier, and it had been reported to him that he had also gone to the Edificio Libertador.

"Permit me, Señor Duarte, and Señora," von Lutzenberger said, "to offer the most profound expression of condolences on the tragic loss of el Coronel Frade on behalf of the German government, and my wife, and myself personally."

"How kind of you," Humberto said.

"My brother is now in heaven with the blessed Jesus and all the angels," Beatrice said, almost cheerfully.

"You know my wife, of course," von Lutzenberger said. "And First Secretary Gradny-Sawz. May I present Standartenführer Goltz? Herr Standartenführer, these are my friends Señor and Señora Duarte. Señor Duarte is the managing director of the Anglo-Argentine Bank."

Goltz clicked his heels and bowed, then bent over Beatrice's gloved hand.

"I am honored, Sir and Madam," he said, "to meet the parents of the courageous officer who gave his life in the war against Bolshevism."

Beatrice did not seem to hear him.

"Good afternoon, Peter," she cried happily.

Peter von Wachtstein clicked his heels and bowed.

"Señora," he said.

Beatrice pushed between Frau Ambassador von Lutzenberger and Standartenführer Goltz to clutch Peter's hand and offer him her cheek.

"And we are going to see you over the weekend, aren't we?" Beatrice said. "You'll come to the estancia for the memorial mass?"

"I hope to have that privilege, Señora," Peter said.

"You'll sit with us, of course. I'll tell Señora Carzino-Cormano," she said, then kissed his cheek again before resuming her place in line to shake the hand of Gradny-Sawz.

"Anton," she said, gushing sincerity. "Thank you for coming."

"Thank you having me, my dear Señora," Gradny-Sawz said, and the German delegation was through the line.

A white-gloved servant showed them the door of the reception. Another servant stood just inside the door holding a tray of champagne glasses.

"The bar, gentlemen, is at the rear of the room," he said.

They all took champagne and moved into the reception.

Goltz turned over his shoulder.

"What was that about, von Wachtstein?" he asked. "With our hostess?"

Ambassador von Lutzenberger answered for him: "There is to be a private memorial service, family and friends only, for Oberst Frade at his estancia on Sunday. To which, apparently, our von Wachtstein has been invited. Since he escorted the remains of Hauptmann Duarte to Buenos Aires, the Duartes seem to have almost adopted him."

"How interesting," Goltz said.

Fascinating. Von Wachtstein has developed a friend-ship, a close friendship, with the people who run the Anglo-Argentine Bank. That may prove very useful indeed.

264

[Four]

Clete's first visitors in the upstairs sitting were Señora Claudia Carzino-Cormano and her daughters. He had been sitting slumped in an armchair with a drink, reading with disbelief the *Buenos Aires Herald*.

It was clear to him that the front-page story — which described him as a hero of the Battle of Guadalcanal, retired from the Marine Corps as a Major, and an Argentine citizen — had come directly from the typewriter of the Information Officer at the American Embassy. He wondered if it had been written at the Ambassador's orders, or whether Colonel Graham had something to do with it. That seemed unlikely, but Graham routinely did unlikely things.

Accordingly to other stories in the *Herald*, the Germans and the Japanese were retreating on all fronts after suffering severe losses, Hitler was about to fall on his knees and beg for mercy, and Emperor Hirohito was next in line.

The last he had heard, the Germans were still occupying most of the landmass of Europe. And the Japanese were still in Singapore, and for that matter, the Philippines, plus all the little Pacific islands from which the Marine Corps would have to remove them, in fighting that was going to be at least as bloody as it had been on Guadalcanal.

He wondered how the readers of the *Herald* reconciled the optimistic news reports on the front page with the two and a half pages of obituaries, often with photographs, of the Anglo-Argentines who had been killed fighting with His Britannic Majesty's Royal Army, Navy, and Air Force all over the world. Three Anglo-Argentines, he noticed,

265

had been killed fighting with His Royal Australian Air Force in New Guinea, another place from which the Japanese obviously had no plans of retreating.

When he saw Claudia enter the room, he dropped the newspaper on the floor beside him, jumped to his feet, and went to her.

"How're you holding up, sport?" he asked, although through her black veil he could see in her eyes and the strain on her face the answer to that.

She pushed the veil off her face and hugged him and tenderly kissed his cheek.

"So far, not bad," she said. "At least I'm not drinking my way through it."

She indicated the whiskey glass he had left on the wide arm of the chair.

"My first," he lied, and she snorted.

Alicia kissed him, and then Isabela made smacking noises as far from his cheek as she could manage.

"You all right, Enrico?" Claudia asked, and went to the bar. "Do as I say, not as I do," she said, and poured a half-inch of scotch in a glass and tossed it down.

"Life will be empty without el Coronel," Enrico said.

"You have Señor Cletus to take care of now," Claudia said.

"With my life, Señora," Enrico said simply.

"I wondered how you were going to handle Beatrice asking the Germans to come here," Claudia said.

"I'm indisposed," Clete said. "Humberto set this up."

"They're downstairs, exuding condolences and charm," she said.

Clete looked at Alicia. She nodded, signifying that Peter von Wachtstein was among them.

"We don't *know* that the Germans are responsible . . . ," Isabela said.

"Jesus Christ, Isabela, not you *and* el Coronel Perón . . . ," Clete flared.

Claudia touched his arm to stop him.

"What did you mean, about Colonel Perón?" Claudia asked.

"I stopped by Uncle Willy's house last night. He was there. And having just come back from Germany, he finds it impossible to believe that . . ."

"Juan Domingo was your father's best friend."

"So he said."

"And you got off on the wrong foot."

Clete shrugged.

"He's going to be at the estancia over the weekend. You really should make an effort to get to know him."

"You mean come out there? Why?"

"You didn't know there's going to be a requiem mass at Nuestra Señora de los Milagros for your father on Sunday?"

"Not until just now, I didn't. What's that all about?"

"The people on the estancia naturally expect it. And there will be a number of other people. Your father's — our — close friends. A private mass, so to speak, as opposed to what they did here today. There will be about forty people, counting wives and family."

"And I have to go, naturally?"

Going out there would give me a chance to go to the radio station. And the sooner I do that, the better.

"Of course you must, Cletus. You're the new Patrón of Estancia San Pedro y San Pablo. You'd better start getting used to that."

"That's not going to be easy."

"The people of *your* estancia, many of whom have never seen you, will expect to see *their* Patrón there."

"OK. Anything to get out of my father's bedroom in the museum," Clete said, and quickly added, "Sorry, I didn't mean that the way it came out."

"I know," she said, then went on: "There's something else, Cletus. There are some papers in your father's safe that belong to General Rawson. He'll be staying with me at Estancia Santo Catalina, and I'd really like to have his papers for him when he arrives."

What kind of papers?

"Oh?"

"You do have the combination to the safe, don't you?"

And that was just a little too casual a question.

"I've never even seen the safe," Clete said "Enrico, what do you know about el Coronel's safe? Where's the combination?"

"Only el Coronel knew the combination, Señor Clete," Enrico said.

"Well, then, I guess General Rawson will have to wait for his papers until we can get a locksmith out there," Clete said. "Or we could blow it open, if the papers are that important."

Claudia did not find that amusing.

"I just can't believe that your father didn't write the combination down somewhere," Claudia said. "Would you mind if I looked for it?"

Yeah, as a matter of fact, I would. I don't understand why, but the idea bothers me. Why do I have the feeling, Claudia, that you would rather that I don't see what's in the safe?

"If this is important to you, Claudia, as soon as I get out there, I'll call you, and we'll look for it together," he said.

"I'm . . . the girls and I . . . are driving out to Santo Catalina tonight," Claudia said. "I thought I'd go over to San Pedro y San Pablo tomorrow and see if I could find the combination. If you have no objection to my looking for it, that is."

I can't have her getting into the safe before I do. I don't want her looking through the records of what Humberto has been doing for Peter.

And have I just been sandbagged? Is that persistence innocent, or because she knows damned well I'm not likely to tell her no again, no matter how politely? And what is in that safe that she — and General Rawson — don't want me to see?

"Does 'G.O.U.' mean anything to you, Claudia?" Clete asked.

He could see in her eyes that she knew what it was.

"What do you know about the G.O.U.?" she asked.

"Not nearly as much as I would like to," he said.

"Clete . . . ," she began, and stopped when a servant opened the door.

"Señor Frade, Señor Mallín and his family wish to pay their respects."

"I'll leave you, Clete," Claudia said. "This has been a very long day for me."

She gave him her cheek to kiss.

"I need to talk to you, too, Claudia," Clete said, thinking of Dorotéa.

"Call me when you get to San Pedro y San Pablo," she said, and then, "Let's go, girls."

They left the room, exchanging quiet greetings with the Mallíns as they came in.

IX

[One]

1420 Avenida Alvear
Buenos Aires, Argentina
1320 10 April 1943

Clete walked to the door to greet the Mallín family.

Enrico Mallín was forty-three years old, six feet two inches tall, and wore a full mustache. "Henry" met and married his wife, the former Pamela Holworth-Talley, while taking a degree at the London School of Economics. And they had two children: blond, fair-skinned, lanky "Little Enrico," their fifteen-year-old son; and Dorotéa. In her black dress and veiled hat, Clete thought, she looked more beautiful than any female he had ever seen.

Clete was aware that Enrico Mallín believed his daughter had shown an interest in Clete that was inappropriate for one of her tender years, purity, and standing in the community.

If you could, Henry, you'd have paid pro forma *respects to Beatrice and Humberto and taken your family out of here as quickly as possible. The only reason you're up here to smile at me is because your business is dependent on the crude and refined petroleum products it gets from Howell Petroleum, and you don't want to risk offending the Old Man's grandson.*

What the hell, if I was in your shoes, I'd probably feel the same way about me. Me being too old for your innocent nineteen-year-old daughter — which is true — isn't one tenth of what's wrong with Cletus H. Frade as a suitor. After what they tried to do to me — what they did to my father — only a lunatic would want his daughter — or any member of his family — within five miles of me.

"Good afternoon, Señor Mallín. How good of you to call," he said politely.

"Our sympathy for your loss should go without speaking, Cletus. Your father was a magnificent man, who will be sorely missed."

"Thank you."

"Mrs. Mallín," Clete went on. "How are you, Ma'am?"

"For the fifty-fifth time, Clete, *please* call me 'Pamela,' " Señora Mallín said, and gave him her cheek to kiss. "I'm so sorry about el Coronel."

"Thank you," Clete said.

"What do you say, Enrico?" Clete said, and punched Little Enrico, man-to-man, on the arm.

"I am very sorry about your father, Cletus," Little Enrico said.

And then Clete turned to Dorotéa.

"And the lovely Señorita Mallín," he said, putting out his hand. "How have you been, Dorotéa?"

"Very well, thank you, all things considered," Dorotéa said. "I'm very sorry about your loss, Clete."

"Thank you."

"And how is your grandfather, Cletus?" Henry Mallín asked.

"Mean as a rattlesnake, as usual," Clete said, immediately regretting it. The Argentine — and particularly the Anglo-Argentine — sense of humor was markedly different from that of Texas and Louisiana.

Little Henry made a noise somewhere between a chuckle and a giggle.

His father glared at him, then moved the glare to Clete.

Clete smiled at the man who was blissfully unaware he was about to become both a grandfather and a father-in-law.

"My grandfather asked me to extend his best regards to you and your family, Señor Mallín," he said.

"How kind of him."

"May I offer you some refreshment?"

"No, thank you. We must be going. We wished to pay our respects."

"It was very kind of you."

"Clete, you come to see us, lunch, dinner, or just to visit, just as soon as you find time," Señora Mallín said, to her husband's discomfiture.

"Yes, do that," Dorotéa chimed in mischievously. "We have *so* much to talk about."

Her father headed for the door, followed by Little Henry, his wife, and Dorotéa. Without realizing he was doing it, Clete went after them, his hand reaching to touch Dorotéa's shoulder as if with a mind of its own.

She turned, looked into his eyes, then touched her lips with her fingers and moved the kiss to Clete's lips. Clete didn't think either her father or her brother saw this, but he knew her mother did. She looked at Clete, asking without words what that was all about.

Clete met Dorotéa's mother's eyes, nodded his head, and shrugged.

I am forced to confirm herewith, Señora, your worst

suspicions and fears. Well, maybe not your worst suspicions and fears.

"Oh, my!" Pamela Mallín said. "Oh, *my!*" And then scurried quickly down the corridor after her husband.

Clete watched them for a moment and then turned.

Enrico was standing there, startling him, and then mystifying him. He was simultaneously solemnly winking at Clete and tapping his temple with his index finger.

What the hell is that all about?

"It is here, Señor Clete," Enrico said.

"What's there?"

"The combination to el Coronel's safe."

"Oh, really?"

"If you would like, I can drive out there tonight and bring the contents of the safe to you."

Clete's next visitor interrupted the conversation. And again startled him.

"Christ, where did you come from?" Clete blurted.

First Lieutenant Anthony J. Pelosi, Corps of Engineers, Army of the United States, had come through what a moment before Clete believed to be a solid, paneled wall.

"What we will do, Enrico, is leave for San Pedro y San Pablo very early in the morning," Clete said. He waited for Enrico to nod his understanding, then gave in to his curiosity and went to examine the door.

A masterpiece of fine carpentry — *or is it cabinetmaking?* — it blended invisibly with the paneled wall when closed. Only on close examination could Clete find a toe-activated panel that functioned as a doorknob.

"It leads to the kitchen," Tony Pelosi said. "Your uncle sent me up that way."

He was a swarthy, short young man who had two weeks before celebrated his twenty-first birthday. His muscular arms and chest strained the tunic of his pink and green Class "A" uniform.

The insignia of the Eighty-second Airborne Division was sewn on the sleeve of his tunic, and the breast carried silver parachutist's wings and two medals. One was the Silver Star medal, the third-highest award for valor, and the other announced that the wearer had served in the American Theater of Operations. It was automatically awarded after ninety days of service. Pelosi's sharply creased pink trousers were bloused around the tops of highly polished parachutist's jump boots.

Tony, Clete thought, *is probably the only man in the U.S. Army, Navy, or Marine Corps who has won the Silver Star for service in the American Theater of Operations, which is defined as the continental United States and South America, theoretically far from any shots fired in anger.*

"How are you, Tony?" Clete said, turning to him and shaking his hand. "I went looking for you yesterday. You weren't home."

"I was probably standing in line at the Edificio Libertador," Tony said. Italian emotions overwhelmed him. The handshake turned into an embrace. "Jesus, Clete, I'm sorry about your dad."

"Thank you," Clete said.

After the emotional moment passed, Tony, looking a little embarrassed, went to Enrico.

"How are you, Sergeant Major?" he asked.

"Mi Teniente," Enrico said. Visibly torn between saluting an officer and embracing him, he finally did both.

"You all right?" Tony asked when Enrico finally released him.

"I am fine," Enrico said.

"He is not," Clete said. "He took what was probably a .45 slug — it gouged a three-inch hole in his head — and he took 00-buckshot in his chest and arm."

"Jesus!"

"I am fine," Enrico repeated firmly.

Tony turned to Clete.

"I couldn't get into Our Lady of Pilar this morning, Clete. No invitation."

"Sorry, I didn't think about that."

"But after the mass was over, I went in and lit a candle for him, and after that I went to the tomb and said a little prayer."

"Thank you, Tony."

"And after that I came here. And had trouble getting in, no invitation. But I threw a fit, and waved my diplomatic carnet around, and finally the cop outside caved in."

"I just didn't think about getting you invitations, Tony. I'm sorry."

"Christ, you had enough on your mind, Clete. Don't apologize."

Clete decided to lighten the conversation.

"You look like a recruiting poster," he said. " 'Join the Airborne and see the World.' "

Tony did not react well to what Clete hoped would be a joke.

"I thought wearing my uniform was the right thing to do," he said. "And when I saw those fucking Krauts downstairs in theirs, I was glad I did. Sorry, if you think that was wrong."

"It was the right thing to do, Tony. My father would have appreciated you wearing your uniform, and I do."

"OK," Tony said, accepting what he recognized as an apology, then moving to what was on his mind: "The Ambassador got a SECRET cable last night saying that Lieutenant Commander Frederico J. Delojo, the new Naval Attaché, would be on the Pan American flight today. You want to tell what that's all about?"

"How did you get access to a SECRET addressed to the Ambassador?"

"I seduced one of the crypto guys," Tony said. "A real feather merchant from Iowa or someplace like that. Buck sergeant."

" 'Seduced'? Or 'corrupted'?" Clete interrupted, smiling.

"Whatever. I showed him my OSS ID. He practically pissed in his pants. Anything you want to know about cable or radio traffic to the Embassy, just ask me."

"And you're not worried he'll tell anybody you . . . seduced him?"

"I told him we shoot people who identify OSS agents," Tony said. "And he believes me."

"Maybe we can make a spy out of you yet, Tony," Clete said.

Tony flushed with Clete's approval.

"You going to tell me about Commander Delojo? *You* were supposed to be the Naval Attaché. What's going on?"

"Not here, Tony," Clete said. "You remember where my father's house is?" Tony nodded. "OK. Give me twenty minutes to get out of here. I'll catch a taxi over there —"

"Your Buick is here, Señor Clete," Enrico interrupted.

"You had it brought here?" Clete asked, surprised. "Why?"

"It attracts less attention to carry a shotgun in a private car than in a taxi, Señor Clete."

"So it does," Clete said, smiling. "It's in the basement?"

"Sí, Señor Clete."

"OK. Tony, anytime in the next twenty minutes, go down to the garage in the basement. I'll make an appearance downstairs, and meet you there."

After Tony realized that Enrico was hurt worse than he was willing to admit, he finally persuaded him to take the front passenger seat in the Buick, but only after he argued that using the shotgun from there would be easier than from the back, if using it became necessary.

Clete came to the garage a half hour later, having taken longer to do his manners in the reception than he imagined. The exit from the basement garage let them out behind the house, on Avenida Posadas, and they were thus able to avoid the crowd still on Avenida Alvear.

When he adjusted the rearview mirror, Clete noticed a car, an English Ford, called an "Anglia," pull away from the curb and follow them. When he reached Avenida del Libertador and turned left, the Anglia was still on his tail. There was no question they were being followed.

He considered, and immediately dismissed, the idea that it might be another set of German-sent assassins. There hadn't been time to plan something like that, and he didn't think even the Germans would try to kill the son on the same day he buried his father.

But who is trailing me? And why? To keep track of my movements, or to protect me?

The route to the Avenida Coronel Díaz took them past the residence of the Ambassador of the United States of America to the Argentine Republic. The American flag flew over the four-story mansion, whose grounds took in most of the block.

Primarily to keep Enrico from finding out they were being trailed — *God only knows how he would react* — Clete leaned across him and pointed out the statue of George Washington in the park across from the Ambassador's residence.

"George Washington, Tony. You ever see that before?"

"Yeah," Tony replied without much interest.

"He had bad teeth," Clete announced.

"What?"

"While I was futzing around Washington, I drove over to Mount Vernon," Clete said. "They've got his false teeth on display. They're *wood*. Jesus, he probably couldn't eat anything but mush."

"No shit?"

"If they had shown me those wooden choppers when I was a kid, they wouldn't have any trouble getting me to brush my teeth."

"Between bullshit lectures on how I was supposed to behave 'as a member of the diplomatic community' and that crypto class at Camp A. P. Hill, I didn't have any time in Washington to do anything but piss and brush my teeth," Tony said.

Clete laughed.

"Wooden teeth, Señor Clete?" Enrico asked in disbelief.

"Wooden teeth, Enrico," Clete said.

The Anglia stayed with them until they turned

into the drive of the house on Avenida Coronel Díaz, when it drove slightly past the house and pulled to the curb.

I will have to keep in mind that Enrico didn't spot that car. He's good, but he's not perfect.

[Two]

1728 Avenida Coronel Díaz
Palermo, Buenos Aires
1545 10 April 1943

Tony looked around in exaggerated awe as they passed through the hotel-size foyer of the Frade mansion.

"You're going to live here? Won't you be a little cramped for space?"

"I'd like to move back into the house on Libertador, but there's a colonel named Perón staying there."

"Who's he?"

"My father's best friend. He just came back from Germany."

"What was he doing in Germany?"

"I have no idea," Clete said, "but he told me he finds it impossible to believe the Germans were involved in my father's assassination."

"Oh, shit!" Tony said. "Clete, my back teeth are floating."

"Over there," Clete said, stopping on the first step of the stairs to the second floor and pointing. "Unless you can wait until we get upstairs?"

"Over there will do very nicely, thank you very

much, Major, Sir," Tony said, and walked quickly to the restroom.

Enrico touched Clete's arm.

"Señor Clete, we are being followed by the clowns. One of their cars, an Anglia, followed us from Avenida Alvear."

"You didn't say anything."

"We don't have to worry about the clowns any longer, Señor Clete. El Coronel Martín is now one of us," Enrico said, and then asked, "You did not notice that we were being followed?"

Clete shook his head, "no."

"You must be on the lookout for such things," Enrico said. "A car following you may not be a clown car."

"You're right."

Tony came out of the restroom a moment later, a look of satisfaction on his face, and the three of them continued up the stairs.

Once they were in his bedroom, Clete rang for a maid, ordered drinks and something to nibble on, then changed out of his suit and into a pair of khakis.

"OK," he said, walking back into the sitting from his bedroom to find Tony drinking from the neck of a bottle of Quilmes beer. "I feel better. I really wanted to get out of that suit."

He spotted a silver wine cooler filled with ice and beer and took one, dismissing the maid's offer of a glass, and the maid herself, with a smile and a waved hand.

He slumped into an armchair facing Tony.

"How was your leave?" Clete asked, taking a sip of his beer.

"We came all the way over here to talk about my leave?"

"Indulge me, Tony. I've had a bad couple of days. This is the first time I've had a chance to sit down and relax."

Tony gave him a strange look, then shrugged.

"Very nice," he said. "My *leave* was nice. I could have done without those bullshit briefings in Washington. And the crypto school was worse."

"They were necessary, I suppose. I went through them too."

"Not the crypto school, you didn't," Tony corrected him. "Or the aerial photography school."

"What did you tell your family?"

"I told them what the OSS told me to tell them. We're building a secret air base in Brazil. I'm handling the demolitions."

"They believe you?"

"Yeah. My mother said a novena to thank God for getting me out of the Eighty-second Airborne, where I was liable to have to do something dangerous."

"Obviously, you didn't wear your Silver Star in Chicago."

"I didn't get it until I went to Washington."

"Did you tell your family about Maria-Teresa?"

"If I told my mother I'd found a girl down here, she would think Maria-Teresa has a ring in her nose and runs around in the jungle wearing a grass skirt and no shirt."

"As long as she's Italian and Catholic, what's wrong with the ring in Maria-Teresa's nose?"

"I want to marry her, Clete."

"Is that a statement, or are you asking for advice?"

Tony shrugged.

"Tony, I spent the last two hours on the plane rehearsing the speech that I was going to give to

281

break it off with Dorotéa," Clete said. "It was a good speech, but I never got to use it. I'll be happy to give it to you. The major point is that we're in the wrong business to get married."

"It sounds like you changed your mind."

"The situation changed," Clete said dryly, and then added: "Dorotéa's pregnant."

Tony raised his eyebrows. "When did you find that out?"

"This morning," Clete said.

"Her father will shit a brick," Tony said. "He doesn't like Americans in general, and you, Ettinger, and me in particular."

"I don't think he will be beside himself with joy," Clete agreed. "And neither will my grandfather."

"What's he got against Dorotéa?"

"He hates all Argentines."

"Jesus, Clete. What are you going to do? Marry her?"

"I don't really have any choice, do I?"

"Now I see what you mean about having a couple of bad days," Tony said. "When are you going to marry her?"

"I just found out this morning that she's pregnant, for Christ's sake! Nobody knows but Dorotéa, me, and now you."

"Where are you going to live?" Tony asked, and from the tone of his voice, Clete understood that it was not an idle question.

"You really think those bastards would come after her?"

"They got Señora Pellano," Tony said. "She was an innocent bystander."

"I hadn't thought about where we'll live. Either here — it would be safer than Libertador — or at the estancia."

"She'd probably be all right here," Tony said practically. "This place is built like a bank. But the estancia would be better, obviously."

Clete didn't want to think about, much less talk about, the danger Dorotéa was going to find herself in. He changed the subject again.

"Is Maria-Teresa pushing you to get married?"

"She's a good Italian Catholic. Good Italian Catholic girls can't go to confession and get absolution unless they swear to God that they'll stop . . . you know. If they don't get absolution, they can't take Holy Communion. That kind of pushing. She hasn't said anything."

"You haven't told her what you do, I hope?"

"Her father thinks the *Reine de la Mer* blew up by itself; that all the talk about Americans taking it out is bullshit. I sit there nodding my head in agreement. Maria-Teresa thinks I'm sort of a clerk for the Military Attaché at the embassy. So does he, by the way, the Military Attaché."

"He's giving you trouble?"

"Not trouble. He's a colonel, I'm a lieutenant. When colonels have things they don't want to do, and there's a lieutenant around, the lieutenant does them. Last week, I inventoried the Embassy Post Exchange."

"No kidding?" Clete asked, chuckling. "That's right. He doesn't know you're OSS, does he?"

"I was told to wait until you got back and tell him. But I don't know. They gossip like fucking women around the embassy. I think everybody there knows you're OSS. And some people know I was here before."

"Commander Delojo will get him off your back."

"Are we back to him, I hope?" Tony said.

"OK. Sorry, Tony. I needed a minute. Your

fearless leader has feet of clay."

"What the fuck does that mean, 'feet of clay'? I've always wondered."

"You know, I don't know," Clete confessed. "It probably means I'm telling you that you see in me a lot more than you can expect to get."

"I don't know," Tony said thoughtfully. "I mean, aside from nearly getting Mrs. Pelosi's baby boy killed, doing something that nobody in their right fucking mind would even think about trying to do, what have you done so wrong?"

"You want me to start with the replenishment ship?"

"Why not?"

"There's not really much more on that than when you left Washington," Clete said. "We're getting lots of intelligence about ships headed in this direction. The last count was five of them. Nothing specific, nothing solid, on any one of them."

"Maybe they're sending five so we can't take them all out."

"Graham says that's not likely. For one thing, the Germans don't have that many torpedoes."

"How does Graham know that?"

"They've got a good idea of how many the Germans can make, and they're not all that hard to spot when they're being moved. Graham thinks that one of the five ships is the replacement; the others are decoys. The real ship, Graham says, may not be one of the five we know about."

"What about the airplane? How are you going to get that into the country now that . . ."

". . . my father can't arrange it?" Clete furnished, "I don't know. Graham may come up with something. It's in Brazil, and so is the other team.

They've been told to prepare to infiltrate across the Uruguay River into Corrientes Province, near some town called Santo Tomé. Until Delojo gets, quote, his feet on the ground, unquote, that's something else I'm supposed to figure out how to do, get them — and all their goddamned equipment — from there to here."

"Tell me about Delojo," Tony said. "What's this business all about that you've retired from the Marines — I saw that story in the *Herald* — and this Commander Whatsisname has become the Naval Attaché?"

"Graham convinced me I would be more useful if I came back here as an Argentine. Out of the Marines, and as an Argentine. That way, presuming this coup d'état they're planning comes off, I'm supposed to be in a position to influence the new government."

"But if you came back as an Argentine . . . How did you manage that, by the way?"

"I've got an Argentine passport."

"A real one?"

"A real one. File this away. I've got Argentine passports for you, Ettinger, and the Chief, too. Or I did. Where are they, Enrico?"

"In the safe at San Pedro y San Pablo," Enrico said. "I did not want Señora Carzino-Cormano to see them."

And I goddamned sure don't want General Rawson — or, for that matter, Claudia — to see them. I've got to get into that goddamned safe before she does!

"I don't understand any of that," Tony said.

"Just before we took out the *Reine de la Mer*, my father got us passports in case we had to leave Argentina in a hurry."

Tony nodded his understanding, then asked:

"But if you came here on an Argentine passport . . . Christ, you're *not* traveling on a diplomatic passport?"

"No."

"You realize what that means? If I get caught doing something I shouldn't be doing down here, all they can do is throw me out of the country. Christ only knows what they'll do to you. I can't believe you were dumb enough to go along with that."

"None of us had diplomatic passports the first time we came down here. Ettinger still doesn't have one."

"We had *American* passports. They'd think twice before standing an American citizen in front of a wall. An Argentine? You're likely to get yourself shot on general principles."

"I don't think that's likely."

"Everybody with enough brains to find their ass with one hand knows we're OSS, Clete. Who does Graham think we're fooling?"

"I don't think Graham thinks we're fooling anybody."

"Then what?"

"Our team, Tony — presuming Captain Ashton's radar gets here, and works — is going to have very little to do with taking out the replacement replenishment ship, except for using our radio to communicate with the submarine. Graham hopes everybody will be so busy watching us, they won't be looking too hard for another team."

"And what if Ashton can't get his radar in here?"

"Then we'll have to locate the ship."

"With a Piper Cub?"

"Unless I can figure out some way to get the C-45 into Argentina."

"How's the other team going to take it out?"

"You weren't briefed?"

"You explain it to me."

"Graham will let us know the name of the ship as soon as he finds out. Then we find out roughly where it is in Samborombón Bay. Once we do that, Ashton can keep track of it with his radar. Then they send in another submarine to sink it."

"And if Captain Ashton and his magic radar can't get into Argentina? Or his radar doesn't work?"

"I think it will work," Clete said. "The problem is getting it into the country."

"You know as much about radars as I do," Tony said. "Zero. On the other hand, the Chief knows all about them. When I told him this nutty idea, he didn't know whether to laugh or cry. He says there's no radar in the world that can locate a ship within a hundred yards."

The Chief was Chief Radioman Oscar J. Schultz, USN, formerly of the USS *Alfred Thomas*, DD-107. Chief Schultz volunteered for OSS service when he learned during a "Courtesy Call" of his ship to Buenos Aires that the team's radioman, Sergeant David Ettinger, couldn't handle all that had to be done by himself.

"I think he's wrong. If he's right, I'll go out and find it with one of the Piper Cubs."

"If they were going to send us out to light it up again, you'd tell me, right?"

"That's not going to happen. But — if I can figure some way to get the C-45 into the country — we'll probably have to take pictures of it."

"Don't bust your ass trying to get that C-45 into the country," Tony said. "One trip like the last one is enough for me, thank you. And what is this

287

picture-taking bullshit all about, anyway?"

"The idea, I think, is that if we have photographs of the ship actually supplying a submarine, then when we take it out — either with another sub, or with bombers, whatever — and the Portuguese or the Spanish start screaming, they can show them the pictures, and say, 'Yeah, we sank it. This is why, fuck you.' "

"Let me get this straight. What you're saying is that all we, *our* team, has to do is find the new ship, take pictures of it supplying a submarine, and Ashton and his team will do everything else."

"They will use our radio to communicate with the sub," Clete said. "But yeah, until something else comes up, and it probably will, that's about it. What I'm supposed to do is try to tilt Argentina — influence the people who will run Argentina after the coup — toward the United States. Or at least keep them from tilting the other way. If I don't do something stupid, I don't think that will get me in serious trouble. I don't intend to blow up the Casa Rosada, Tony." (The Casa Rosada — "The Pink House," so-called because of its color — is Argentina's seat of government.)

"That's all?" Tony asked in disbelief.

"That's it."

"What's my relationship to Commander Whatsisname?"

"None. He knows who you are, of course. But I am still in command of our team."

"Ettinger and the Chief, too?"

Christ, I didn't think to ask Graham about the Chief. The Chief is assigned to the Office of the Naval Attaché, and Delojo's liable to assume he belongs to him. And Graham didn't say anything. And Graham avoided the question when I asked him about my rela-

tionship with Delojo. Damn!

"Until I hear otherwise, the Chief is part of our team. We need him to run the radio station. Ettinger can't run it by himself."

"Where do you get your orders? From Delojo? Doesn't a commander outrank a major?"

Absolutely. Is that why Graham avoided my question, because I should have understood that? But he didn't *answer the question. So fuck him, until it's spelled out, I* do not *take my orders from Delojo.*

"That doesn't apply here," Clete said. "I get my orders from Graham."

"Jesus, you had me worried there for a minute."

"Don't rub it in his face, but if he starts something you don't like, tell me, and I'll stop it. I don't think it will happen. When he gets here, I'll make sure he understands that you, Ettinger, and the Chief work for me."

"Good."

"How are they, by the way? I went looking for Dave, but he wasn't home."

"He's at the radio station. They're fine. I go out there every couple of days — when I'm not inventorying the PX, or some other bullshit — and bring them cigarettes, stuff from the PX, et cetera, and their mail."

"They stay out there?"

"The Chief does. Ettinger spends most of his time in Buenos Aires. The estancia is a good place for us to meet."

"I'm driving out there first thing in the morning. I'll come out to the station to see you and Ettinger and the Chief, but I don't want either you or Ettinger to come to the house. They're having another funeral service for my father, for the people on the estancia. And a lot of people will be out there that I don't want to see you and start wondering."

"Right. These people that are going to be out there? G.O.U.?"

"You know about the G.O.U.?"

Tony nodded.

"Yeah, Leibermann told me. They're about to overthrow the government."

"Who told you?"

"Milt Leibermann. They call him the Legal Attaché, but what he really is is the FBI guy. And *he* knows who we really work for. And he wants to talk to you, too, just as soon as possible."

"Oh, Christ, Tony!"

"Something wrong?"

"I have specific orders about that. I am, which means you are, to have as little contact, preferably none, with the FBI."

"Why not?"

"Wild Bill Donovan and J. Edgar Hoover don't like each other."

"Come on, it has to be more than that."

"Congress gave Hoover — the FBI — authority to conduct intelligence and counterintelligence operations in the Western Hemisphere. Hoover believes that includes covert activities — what we did, in other words. But the President gave the OSS responsibility, worldwide, for intelligence, counterintelligence, and special operations, which means open and covert sabotage, espionage, everything. Since South America is included in everybody's definition of the wide world, Donovan thinks Hoover's walking on his grass here. And vice versa. Graham was serious about this. Stay away from the FBI guy."

"He's a nice guy, Clete."

"Stay away from him, Tony. That's an order."

"Yes, Sir." Tony shrugged. "But I really think you ought to see him, Clete."

"Maybe later."

"I told him I'd try to get you to meet him in the Café Colón at half past nine," Tony said, uneasily. "He said he'll be there."

"You mean tonight?" Clete asked incredulously. "What gave you the idea you have the authority to make appointments for me?"

"I thought you wouldn't mind, Clete."

"Well, I goddamned well do!"

"OK," Tony said, chastened and chagrined. "It won't happen again, Clete."

Damn! There's already enough bad blood between the FBI and the OSS. If I don't show up to meet this guy, it will get worse.

"Where the hell is the — what did you say, Café Colón?"

"Café Colón," Tony confirmed. "Right behind the Opera.* There's a basement. He said he would wait for you there."

"How's he going to recognize me?" Clete wondered aloud, annoyed.

"He's got a picture of you."

"You gave him a picture of me?" Clete asked incredulously.

"He had one. He showed it to me. It shows you getting out of a cab at the National Institutes of Health."

"Jesus Christ! The FBI's running around taking pictures of people in the OSS in Washington?"

Tony shrugged.

"I guess so. He had your picture."

* Buenos Aires' Teatro de Colón, on the Avenida 9 de Julio, is one of the world's largest opera houses.

"I'm going to meet this guy . . . what did you say his name was?" Clete said.

"Leibermann."

"I am going to meet Mr. Leibermann of the FBI, and as politely as possible let him know I am not interested in making new friends. And you don't ever do something like this again, OK?"

Tony nodded, accepting the rebuke, then asked, "You see the SS guy at your uncle's house?"

Clete shook his head, "no."

"Bird fucking colonel of the SS. Fancy black uniform, with skulls on the collar. I can't believe they had the balls to show up there."

"If they didn't show up, it might look like they had something to do with my father's murder," Clete said. "And speaking of wearing that, you look like a recruiting poster. But wearing that Silver Star isn't too smart. What are you going to say if somebody asks you what you got it for?"

"I thought about that. I wore it for your father. If it hadn't been for him, I wouldn't be around to wear it. And I figure they took him out because of how I got it, what we did. And I figured nobody here knows what the fuck it is anyway. The Argentines give out medals for not missing Mass three months running."

Clete chuckled.

"What are you going to do about what happened to your father?" Tony asked.

"What do you mean by that?"

"Well, I figure it was either this SS guy or the Military Attaché, Grüner, who ordered your father killed. Your friend von Wachtstein probably knows and would tell you."

"So?"

"You know that plastic explosive we got in Uruguay and never used? I used a little bit of it, just to see what it would do. A piece about this big, Clete" — he held up his fist, thumb extended — "rigged by somebody who knew how . . ."

Jesus Christ, he's serious!

"Forget it, Tony!"

". . . say in a telephone . . ."

"Hey, I said no."

". . . would blow his fucking brains out his other ear."

Clete shook his head back and forth.

"Your father was a good guy, Clete. He saved my life. They shouldn't be allowed to get away with what they did to him."

"Thank you, Tony, but no. And I mean that. I mean thank you, and I mean no. Not now, anyway."

"Let me know if you change your mind," Tony said. "I consider it a matter of honor."

Clete glanced at Enrico and thought that Enrico would think Tony had both a splendid idea and the proper attitude concerning revenge.

There was a discreet knock at the door, followed immediately by the appearance of Antonio.

"Pardon me, Señor. A Señorita Mallín has called. I have asked her to wait in the reception while I saw whether or not you were at home."

"Oh, ho!" Tony said, smiling and winking at Clete. He glanced at his watch. "I've got to get out of here anyway. And let the BIS guys go home to their wives and kiddies."

"What?"

"The BIS has been following me around ever since you got here. You didn't notice the Ford Anglia following us over here from Alvear?"

Clete shook his head "no" and looked at Enrico.

"Yeah, well, trust me, there was. And they're parked across the street now."

"Get out of here, Tony," Clete ordered. "And you too, Enrico."

"I will change out of my uniform for the last time," Enrico said, rising to his feet. "After I put el Teniente into a taxi."

"Please show Señorita Mallín up, Antonio," Clete said.

[Three]

The door opened, and the No-Longer-Virgin Princess came in. She was now wearing a tweed skirt and a powder-blue sweater.

She looks like the Tulane homecoming queen. Nicer. The time I dated the homecoming queen, she turned out to be a bitch.

My God, she's beautiful!

"You didn't call me," she accused.

"I . . . uh . . ."

"What have you been doing?" Dorotéa demanded, and then, noticing the beer bottles and the wine cooler full of iced beer, answered her own question. "You've been swilling beer!"

"Guilty," he said.

"I have been waiting by the telephone for hours!"

"I . . . uh . . . didn't think I should call," he said. "Your father —"

"Didn't what I told you mean anything to you?" Dorotéa asked, now closer to tears than an expression of shocked indignation.

"Jesus Christ, Princess," Clete said. It came out a moan.

She looked into his eyes for a long moment and then laughed.

"If you're afraid to just *call* me because of Daddy, what are you going to do about *telling* him?"

"I don't know," he confessed. "How did you get away?"

"Mother helped," she said. "I started to cry when Daddy called your Uncle Humberto and said we wouldn't be going out to Estancia Santo Catalina after all for the mass for your father."

"You were going to Santo Catalina?"

With Ramírez, Rawson, and most of the G.O.U. there? What the hell is that all about? How many people did Claudia say are going to be there, forty? Maybe some of them have nothing to do with the G.O.U.; they'll be there to make it look like all that's going on are people visiting Claudia out of sympathy.

"*Were* going. Henry couldn't wait to tell Daddy he'd seen you kissing my fingers."

"Jesus!"

"I'm supposed to be at the movies. There's a new Bing Crosby and Bob Hope flick — *Road to Morocco* — at the Belgrano. It's supposed to cheer me up."

"Oh."

"What are we going to do, Cletus?"

"What are we going to do about what?"

"What do you think?" Dorotéa asked, exasperated.

"What are my options?"

"You bastard!"

"Would you like me to get down on my knees?"

"That would be nice," she said.

"Jesus, I almost forgot," he said.

"Forgot what?"

He went into the bathroom. After a moment, curiosity got the better of her and she followed him. He was rooting around in his toilet kit.

"What on earth are you doing?" Dorotéa demanded.

He handed her a ring. She looked at it dubiously.

"What's this?"

"It's my mother's," Clete said. "My grandfather gave it to me. Her high-school ring. I . . . uh . . . when he gave it to me, I thought maybe you'd like to have it."

"It's beautiful," she said, not very convincingly. "It looks Catholic."

"Yeah. Sacred Heart Convent in New Orleans. About as Catholic as you can get. All the nice girls in New Orleans go to Sacred Heart."

"I thought your mother was Church of England."

"She *was* Episcopalian. More or less the same thing. She converted to Catholicism when she married my father."

And it killed her.

"I want to be married in the Anglican Church. I want our baby to be raised as an Anglican."

"I haven't even asked you to marry me yet."

She slipped the ring on her finger.

"It fits," she said. "And it was your mother's. I'll never take it off." She immediately had second thoughts, and took it off. "*After* you talk to Daddy. After that, I'll never take it off. I don't want to get him hysterical before you talk."

She pulled her sweater up and put the ring into

her white brassiere, which was all she had on under the sweater. Cletus found the act excruciatingly erotic.

"Until then, I'll keep it next to my heart," she said, and looked at him, read his mind, and announced: "They're swelling."

"Really?"

"They're swelling, and they're tender. Would you like to see?"

"Christ!"

"Not until you've proposed properly," she said.

"You first," Clete said.

"Me propose?"

"Show me first," he said.

"You are really a very wicked man," Dorotéa said. "My father's probably right about you."

Then, her eyes locked on his, she very deliberately pulled the sweater over her head, dropped it onto the floor, then reached behind her back and unfastened her brassiere.

The telephone on the bedside table rang.

"Who the hell can that be?" Dorotéa snapped. "Don't answer it, Cletus!"

She was lying naked on top of him, with her face on his chest. When she spoke, he could feel the warmth of her breath.

Antonio maybe doesn't know exactly what's going on up here, but he knows I don't want to be disturbed. That call is probably important.

He picked up the telephone.

"A gentleman insists on speaking with you, Señor Frade," Antonio said. "He says he's from 'Texas A and M.' "

From the way Antonio pronounced the phrase, it was clear that he had no idea what it was.

"Put him through," Clete ordered. Dorotéa snorted.

"Just checking in," Commander Delojo said. "I'm — temporarily — at the Plaza Hotel. I'd hoped we could get together soon."

"Not before Tuesday or Wednesday, I'm afraid. I'll get word to you through our friend."

"Fine," Delojo said. "Good to hear your voice." The line went dead.

"I hope that was important," Doroféa said.

"Yes, it was."

"More important than us? Wouldn't it have waited?"

She lowered her head and nipped him on the nipple, then suddenly pushed herself off him.

"Oh, my God!" Doroféa cried. "What time is it? How long have we been here?"

"Not nearly long enough."

"By now Daddy will have called the Belgrano, found out what time the movie was over, and be sitting by the front door with his watch in his hand."

"He's going to have to find out sooner or later that we've been up to more than finger kissing. Preferably sooner, under the circumstances."

"Not today, thank you," she said, and pushed herself off him and slipped out of bed.

She bent over to reclaim the clothing strewn all over the floor and trotted naked into the bathroom.

"You are the most beautiful thing I have ever seen in my life," Clete called after her.

"After we have our baby, I will be fat and ugly and you won't even want to look at me."

"Jesus, Doroféa!"

"I wish women could just lay eggs, like chickens," Doroféa called from the bathroom. "You know, just sit on a nest."

"You're a lunatic!" he called as she closed the bathroom door.

He put his hands under his head and looked around the room.

I probably should have some sort of guilty feeling, making love to her in my father's bed on the day I buried him, but I don't.

"You want me to take you home?" he asked in nearly a shout.

"God, no!" Dorotéa called back. "Put me in a taxi!"

He got out of bed, pulled on his clothes, and reached for his battered pair of cowboy boots.

She came out of the bathroom — much sooner than he expected — as he was stomping his feet in the boots.

"Those boots are a disgrace," she said.

"I like them."

"What and when are you going to do about telling Daddy?"

"What, I don't know. When, next week. I really have to go to the estancia."

"Why don't you talk to your Uncle Humberto? Or Claudia?"

"You want them to know?"

"Everybody is going to know, darling, sooner or later," Dorotéa said with unanswerable logic.

"OK. You're right. Claudia, I think."

"Call me when you have something to tell me," she said. "And now, put me in a cab."

"I love you, Princess," Clete said.

"I should hope so. I don't do what we just did with just anybody."

She kissed him, rather chastely, on the lips, and walked to the door and waited for him to open it.

"Antonio will know what we've been up to," he said mischievously.

"Everybody will soon know what we've been up to," she said. "But I would rather that Daddy learned it from you."

Holding hands, they descended the stairway to the foyer.

"There are cars here," he said. "Hell, I can send you home in a Rolls Royce."

"A taxi will do nicely, thank you just the same," she said.

As they reached the door, Enrico, now in a suit, appeared from nowhere.

"Señorita Mallín requires a taxi," Clete said.

"I will have the chaffeur take her. Or if you wish, Señor Clete, I will take her myself."

"A taxi, please," Dorotéa said.

"Sí, Señorita," Enrico said. He turned toward an umbrella stand, and when he turned back, Clete saw he was holding a double-barreled twelve-bore vertically beside his leg.

"Is that necessary?" Clete asked.

Enrico ignored the question.

"I'll find a taxi. You and the Señorita wait here."

He crossed the narrow area between the house and the fence, went through the gate, stepped out onto Avenida Coronel Díaz, and flagged down a taxi, a Model A Ford with the upper body painted yellow.

When the door was open, he motioned for Clete to bring Dorotéa.

"Why did I have to fall in love with a man people are trying to kill?" Dorotéa asked. She did not seem at all frightened. "Darling, telephone me just as soon as you talk to Claudia."

"OK."

She kissed him quickly and chastely on the cheek, then ran to the taxi and stepped in.

Clete watched the taxi drive off, then walked back into the foyer and went back upstairs.

X

[One]

1728 Avenida Coronel Díaz
Palermo, Buenos Aires
2055 10 April 1943

With his shotgun leaning on the paneled wall behind him, Enrico had been half dozing in an oversize dark-red leather armchair in the foyer. He almost jumped to his feet when Clete came off the elevator.

"I suppose you're going with me?" Clete asked.

Clete was now wearing a glen plaid suit, a stiffly starched white shirt, a somewhat somber tie, and wing-tip shoes. Khakis, boots, and a sweater were not the proper uniform to meet the head of the FBI in Buenos Aires — if only to politely tell him to go fuck himself.

"Where are we going?"

"To the Café Colón, near the opera."

"I will drive you."

"I'll drive myself, thank you," Clete said. "I am a big boy. I can even tie my own shoes."

The brilliant wit sailed over Enrico's head.

"I will go with you, of course," he said.

They went to the basement garage through the kitchen. The keys to the Buick were in the ignition,

302

and it started immediately. But as Clete was about to put it in gear, Enrico touched his arm and opened the glove compartment and pointed.

The garage was dimly lit, and it took Clete a moment to recognize that Enrico was pointing at a .45 pistol.

It's an Argentine copy, not a Colt 1911A1, he thought. *But essentially the same gun.*

"OK, Enrico," he said. "Gracias."

Enrico closed the glove compartment, and Clete put the car in gear and drove out of the garage and headed downtown.

Avenida 9 de Julio, which dead-ends at Avenida del Libertador at the tracks leading to the main railroad station, is one of the widest streets in the world. Like Libertador, it commemorates Argentine Independence. While he was in Washington Clete couldn't help comparing that city to Buenos Aires. Libertador was something like Constitution Avenue, he concluded. But Washington didn't have a main avenue called The Fourth of July. He wondered why not.

There was another difference, too. Washington was "browned out." This meant that signs were not illuminated, that the lights which in peacetime shone on government buildings were no longer turned on at dusk, and that by law the top half of automobile headlights were painted over.

Theoretically, this was to deny German submarines reflected light that would allow them to more easily torpedo ships in the Atlantic. There was even a hint that it was a protective measure against German bombers attacking the nation's capital.

These measures might have made some sense in New York City, or Miami, but Washington was too far from the ocean for its night lighting to be seen there. In other words, he concluded, it was a propaganda action, to remind the American people they were at war. This also explained the Air Raid Wardens and the patriotic citizens who spent their nights on building roofs prepared to call the alarm when the first German bomber was sighted.

The lights were on on Avenida 9 de Julio, and the huge advertising signs mounted on the buildings lining both sides of the street were brilliantly illuminated.

So far as he could tell, they had not been followed from the house.

He found both the Teatro Colón and a place to park the Buick without trouble, but they had to circle the theater — which occupies most of a city block — before he found the Café Colón, a not very impressive establishment literally in the shadow of the opera building.

Tony had said Leibermann would be in the basement, so he looked for and finally found a narrow curving stairway leading downward. There were perhaps twenty tables in the dimly lit room, half of them occupied.

He looked around the room. At a table halfway across it, a plump, rather dowdy-looking bespectacled man made an "over here" gesture with his hand, and Clete walked to the table. Clete signaled for Enrico to sit at another empty table. Without rising, the man put out his hand and said, in perfect Spanish, "Dr. Livingston, I presume?"

"And you must be Señor Stanley," Clete said. "How nice to see you here in the heart of darkest Argentina."

Leibermann laughed. "Thank you for coming. I

wasn't sure you would. I was sorry to hear about your father."

"Thank you," Clete said, somewhat abruptly. "I'm not sure I should have come. What's on your mind?"

A waiter appeared. Clete ordered a beer, and Leibermann pointed at his wineglass to order another.

Leibermann handed him a small black-and-white photograph. It showed a young, small but well-muscled young man in a skivvy shirt and cutoff utilities. He was posing ferociously with a Thompson submachine gun in one hand and a K-bar knife in the other.

"My son," Leibermann said. "Sidney. Corporal, First Raider Battalion, U.S. Marine Corps."

"Nice-looking young man," Clete said.

"I had a very nice letter from a lieutenant colonel named Merritt Edson," Leibermann said evenly. "He said that he felt privileged to have commanded such a fine young man; that he had been proud to recommend him for a Silver Star; and that his grave site has been very carefully marked, so that when the battle for Guadalcanal is over, they can recover his remains."

"I'm sorry," Clete said.

"I have the letter with me. Would you care to see it?"

God, no, I don't want to see it!

Leibermann handed him the letter. Clete read it and handed it back.

"The point I'm trying to make, Major Frade, is that you and I — if not everybody in the OSS and the FBI — are on the same side in this war."

"It's not Major anymore. I've been discharged

from the Marine Corps," Clete said, and waited for Leibermann to go on.

"I heard about that," Leibermann said, making it clear he didn't believe it. "But what is it they say, 'Once a Marine, always a Marine'? I didn't hear that you're out of the OSS, and this conversation will go easier if we don't waste time bullshitting each other."

Clete nodded.

There's something about this guy that I like. And I don't think that it's because his son got blown away on Guadalcanal.

"My orders — nothing written, of course," Leibermann said, "but I know an order when I get one — are that I am to have as little contact with the OSS as possible. That goes for the people who work for me, as well."

"I've got the same kind of orders," Clete said.

"Let me give you a little background on me — unless you already have it?"

"I never heard your name until a couple of hours ago," Clete said.

"I'm from New York. I have a BS in accounting from the City College of New York. When I graduated, took the exam, got certified, there was not much of a demand for CPAs, especially Jewish ones. But the FBI was accepting applications for CPAs — in those days, you had to be either a lawyer or a CPA to get in the FBI — and there wasn't much they could do to keep me out. I was Phi Beta Kappa at CCNY."

"What do you mean, 'keep you out'?"

"There's a couple of jokes about Jews in the FBI. One: There are so few of us that we can hold our convention in a phone booth. And the second: The last time we had a convention, we voted to petition

J. Edgar Hoover to treat us the way Hitler treats the Jews in Germany, as it would be an improvement."

The waiter delivered the wine and beer. Leibermann raised his glass to Clete and took a very small sip.

"OK. So I got in, surprised everybody by making it through agent's school, and got myself assigned to the Manhattan Field Office. I went to work as an accountant. I was happy — I never saw myself as a Jewish Elliott Ness — and the FBI was happy, because I am a good accountant. When I caught people manipulating their books, they usually went to jail. Twice a year I shot my pistol, and then put it away in a drawer. You getting the picture?"

"I suppose," Clete said.

"After 1940, the FBI became really involved in South America. I hear they're recruiting Latins now, but in the old days there were about as many Spanish-speaking FBI agents as there were Jews. Anyway, they ran everybody's records and came up with the fact that Leibermann, Milton, spoke a little Spanish —"

"Your Spanish is pretty good," Clete interrupted.

"I took it for three years at CCNY, but most of what I have I picked up in Spanish Harlem. My father had a dry-cleaning store on 119th Street. Your Spanish is pretty good, too."

"I got mine from a Mexican lady who kept house for us in Midland, Texas," Clete said.

"Surprising. You could pass for an Argentine," Leibermann said. "Anyway, I got a form letter telling me I was being considered for a foreign assignment. I figured that would happen the next time it snowed in Miami on the Fourth of July, and didn't pay any attention to it."

"I don't understand," Clete confessed.

"Quote, legal attaché, unquote, jobs in places like Buenos Aires usually went — still do — to nice young WASPs from Princeton, nice Mormon boys from Brigham Young, and once in a while, maybe even an Irisher from Notre Dame, but almost never to Jewish accountants from CCNY."

"You're here," Clete argued.

"The SAC here . . . You know what I mean?"

Clete shook his head, "no."

"The Special Agent in Charge. The Argentines caught him doing something he shouldn't have been doing and persona non grata-ed him. Their BIS . . . You know what that means, of course?"

Clete nodded.

". . . is pretty good," Leibermann went on. "OK, so they made the ASAC, which means Assistant Special Agent in Charge, the SAC. He fired off a cable saying he absolutely had to have a Spanish-speaking ASAC as of yesterday. Scraping the bottom of the barrel, guess who they send down here as ASAC?"

"Leibermann, Milton," Clete said, chuckling.

"Right. I was here two weeks when guess who else got himself persona non grata-ed?"

"The SAC?" Clete said, chuckling again.

"And to make it three in a row, can you guess who they made, temporarily, the new SAC?"

"His last name begins with L?"

"Right. I figured that would last for as long as it would take to get a real SAC on the Panagra flight out of Miami, but that didn't happen. I don't know why. Nobody ever came down to replace me, and

308

about six months ago, about the time you came down here the first time, they made the appointment official."

"Maybe somebody decided you're doing a good job," Clete said.

"I try. I figure that the FBI is supposed to be down here developing information, not, for example, blowing up boats and things like that."

"People blow up ships down here, do they?"

"So the story goes. A lot of people — Colonel Martín of the BIS, for example — think that the OSS is down here to do things like that . . . things that violate Argentine neutrality."

"I've met el Teniente Coronel Martín," Clete said. "He has a suspicious nature."

"He's a nice fellow," Leibermann said. "We have an understanding. I make sure the FBI doesn't go around trying to blow ships up, and we tell each other things. Like, he called me the night you shot the, quote, burglars, unquote, in your house on Libertador."

"That was nice of him."

"And when somebody blew up that Portuguese ship — what was it called?"

"I have no idea what you're talking about," Clete said.

"The *Reine de la Mer*," Leibermann said. "It was called the *Reine de la Mer*. I called him and gave him my word I had no idea that was going to happen."

"Why should you?"

"Right. I shouldn't. I didn't. And if anything like that happens again, I don't want to know about that either."

"That shouldn't be any problem for either of us," Clete said.

"It's turned into a pretty good relationship, Martín and me. We tell each other interesting things all the time."

"For example?"

"For example, just today he told me that there was a very interesting passenger on the Lufthansa flight. A man named Goltz. He's a Standartenführer — that's like a colonel — in the German SS."

"How interesting."

"It was to me. What's an SS colonel doing in Argentina?"

"I have no idea."

"If you hear, would you let me know?" Leibermann asked. "What I'm suggesting is that we, you and me, have the same sort of arrangement I have with Teniente Coronel Martín. I hear something interesting, I'll pass it on to you, unofficially, of course. And vice versa — you hear something interesting, you pass it to me unofficially."

"If I ever hear something interesting, you'll be the first to know," Clete said. "Unofficially, of course."

"Like, for example, what goes on at the G.O.U. convention this weekend."

"The G.O.U. convention? I have no idea what you're talking about," Clete said.

"At Estancia Santo Catalina," Leibermann said. "They're going to sit around, drink a little vino, cook some steaks, sing, maybe do a little dance around a sombrero" — he snapped his fingers — "and when they can find a couple of minutes, decide who's going to be the next President of Argentina, now that your father's no longer available, and maybe even decide *when* to give Castillo

310

the boot. You can understand why I'd like to hear anything you happen to pick up."

"I didn't hear about any convention," Clete said. "And, if there is going to be one, I didn't get invited."

"Just so you don't think I'm as dumb as I look," Leibermann said, "one of the colonels who'll be there is a tall drink of water named Juan Domingo Perón. He was a real close pal of your father's. He came back from Germany yesterday on the same plane with the SS colonel. There are a lot of people, including me, who think the sonofabitch is a real Nazi. And I would like to know — the U.S. government would like to know — the role the Nazi sonofabitch is playing in the coup d'état, and the role he will play in the new government if your father's cronies get away with it. Any information you could pass on to me would be greatly appreciated."

He took out his wallet and handed Clete a card with three numbers written on it.

"My office, my apartment, and a number that's answered twenty-four hours a day. Your code name is 'Cowboy' if you don't want to use your real name."

" 'Cowboy'?"

"Cowboy," Leibermann confirmed. "Did they teach you in OSS school that the best way to handle numbers like that is memorize them and then burn the little piece of paper?"

"I didn't go to OSS school," Clete said.

"Why doesn't that surprise me?" Leibermann said wryly, then suddenly stood up. A broad smile appeared on his face, and he put out his hand.

"Well, it's been a real pleasure meeting you, Señor Frade," he said, raising his voice so it could be heard all over the room. "Welcome back to Argentina!"

He pumped Clete's hand enthusiastically, then walked toward the stairwell.

[Two]

Bureau of Internal Security
Ministry of Defense
Edificio Libertador
Avenida Paseo Colón
Buenos Aires, Argentina
0915 11 April 1943

The Chief of the Bureau of Internal Security of the Ministry of National Defense, el Almirante Francisco de Montoya, liked to gaze out of the window of his ninth-floor office. His office windows looked out over the River Plate. On a clear day, one could just make out the coast of Uruguay, near Colonia del Sacramento, across the river.

The Admiral was especially fond of peering out the window at the ships on the river through a high-powered, tripod-mounted binocular, a gift from Captain Sir Bernard Jules-Wiley, Royal Navy, the British Naval Attaché. Montoya had once joked to el Teniente Coronel Alejandro Bernardo Martín, of whom he was both fond and a little afraid, that if only his office windows looked back toward the city, instead of out over the Plate, he could probably peer into high-rise apartment windows and see some of Buenos Aires's most lovely ladies in their unmentionables, or less.

The Admiral, resting his buttocks on his desk, was peering through his Royal Navy binoculars when Martín put his head through the door.

"You sent for me, Sir?"

It was unusual for Montoya to send for him, and that made Martín a little nervous. Normally, Montoya was satisfied with a briefing by Martín whenever he had interesting information to report. Summoning him to his office happened only rarely, usually only when Montoya had a specific question he wanted answered, or even more rarely, when he himself came up with something that he thought Martín should know.

What concerned Martín now was that Montoya might somehow have learned of the existence of OUTLINE BLUE. On the one hand, this knowledge would make him look like an incompetent for not discovering it himself. On the other hand, it would put in question — with every justification in the world — his loyalty.

Even worse, it was possible that Montoya had learned not only of the existence of OUTLINE BLUE, but that OUTLINE BLUE was missing, and in considerable risk of falling into the hands of President Castillo's supporters.

Martín had worked for Almirante Montoya long enough to have a very good idea how his mind worked. He did not have a great deal of respect for Montoya's intelligence. Indeed, he was sometimes capable of demonstrating great stupidity. And yet — like many other senior officers and officials Martín had come to know who were not generously endowed by their maker with brainpower — he frequently demonstrated almost astonishing cunning.

This should not have been surprising — one

313

could not rise to the rank of Almirante without being either highly intelligent or unusually cunning — but in fact it was.

Martín knew Montoya had not made up his mind whether the planned coup d'état would succeed or not. If it succeeded, he wanted to be able to truthfully state that although he could not, of course, have openly supported Frade, Ramírez, Rawson, or any of the others, he had lent what support he could to their noble cause. For example, he had ordered Teniente Coronel Martín not to place any of them under surveillance.

If the coup d'état failed, he wanted to be in a position to truthfully state that he had ordered Teniente Coronel Martín to immediately bring to his attention any evidence whatever suggesting that Frade, Ramírez, or Rawson, or anyone else, was planning a treasonous coup d'état.

The only way he could accomplish this dance was not to ask Martín too many questions. He really did not want to know, Martín understood, that the Grupo de Oficiales Unidos had come up with a plan — OUTLINE BLUE — for their coup. Rather, he wanted Martín to approach him and tell him that there was going to be a coup d'état and whether it was going to fail or succeed.

At that point, he could take action.

Martín had not, therefore, informed Almirante Montoya that the plan for OUTLINE BLUE existed, or that it was missing and liable to wind up on President Castillo's desk. If he had, that information would almost certainly have been enough to cause Montoya to come down on the side of the present regime.

And finally, if Castillo did know about OUTLINE BLUE, and it succeeded even so, Montoya could reasonably argue that under the circumstances he had no choice but to do his duty. And yet in order to assist the coup d'état, he held off doing it as long as he possibly could.

"Ah, Bernardo," the Admiral said. "We don't often see you in uniform."

"I wear it from time to time, mi Almirante, to remind myself that I was once an honest cavalryman."

While that was quite true, it was not the actual reason he was wearing his uniform this morning. He was bound for El Palomar airfield — in fact, if Montoya hadn't sent for him, he would already be halfway there — where a light army airplane from Campo de Mayo* was to pick him up. Questions would almost certainly be asked by some diligent official at El Palomar if an Army airplane picked up a civilian, and Martín preferred not to call any more attention to himself than was absolutely necessary.

Today, in particular. Though his credentials gave him unquestioned access to any Argentine military base or government-controlled facility, authority to requisition any personnel or equipment he felt necessary to accomplish his duties, and almost incidentally authorized him to wear mufti on duty, they also stated that any questions concerning his activities should be directed to the personal attention of el Almirante Francisco de Montoya. He didn't want Montoya to know where he was going, or why.

* The huge Argentine military complex just outside Buenos Aires. In 1943, Campo de Mayo held a Cavalry Regiment, an Infantry Regiment, and Engineer Battalion, the School for Equitation, the Artillery School, the Military Prison, a number of support units, plus the campus of the Military Academy and the buildings and airfields of what was later to become the Argentine Air Force.

"You don't think you are anymore?" Montoya challenged jokingly.

"An honest cavalryman, mi Almirante, does not begin his days by asking ladies of the evening the preferences of their last night's patrons."

"Did you really?"

"The agent who was supposed to deal with gathering this information fell ill, and I thought it best not to wait until he recovered."

"And who were the patrons of the ladies?"

"Gradny-Sawz and the visiting German coronel."

"Oddly enough, I called you in here to ask about him. Who is he, and what is he doing here?"

"I don't know much, only that he and Gradny-Sawz are old friends; that Gradny-Sawz moved him out of the Alvear and into his house; and that according to the ladies, both of them were perfect gentlemen."

"Really?"

"There was champagne, and dancing to phonograph records. Later, Gradny-Sawz's houseman put them into a taxi, generously compensated for their labors."

"And the ladies heard nothing of interest?"

"They were told that Vienna is the most romantic city in the world. Apparently, Goltz and Gradny-Sawz knew each other there."

"How odd."

"Frankly, I was relieved. I find it distasteful to compile dossiers about strange sexual preferences."

"Distasteful, but sometimes very useful."

"I find using such information even more distasteful," Martín said.

"Has it ever occurred to you, Bernardo, that you might be in the wrong line of work?"

"Many times, mi Almirante. The last time as recently as two minutes ago."

"Unfortunately, Bernardo, you are very good at what you do. Anything on young Frade?"

By God, he doesn't know about OUTLINE BLUE. Or that it's missing. If he did, the subject would be on the table by now!

"He met with Leibermann at the Café Colón. He went there alone — except of course, for Suboficial Mayor Rodríguez. The agent on him said he skillfully eluded him in traffic — I'm not sure I believe that or not. But, anyway, the man on Leibermann picked up on him and telephoned the office to tell the other one where he could be found."

"And their conversation?"

"Nothing could be heard. They were together less than half an hour, and then parted. Leibermann went to his home, and so did young Frade."

"In your mind, does this meeting between the head of the American FBI and Señor Frade confirm that Frade is back here as OSS Station Chief?"

"Leibermann tells me that the new Naval Attaché is the new OSS Station Chief. His name is Delojo, Commander Delojo, and he arrived yesterday. When I asked Leibermann the relationship between Frade and Delojo, he shrugged his shoulders."

"Meaning he doesn't know, or doesn't want to tell you?"

Martín chuckled. "Meaning he either doesn't want to tell me, or doesn't really know."

"You trust Leibermann, don't you?"

"He has never lied to me."

"We can presume, I think, that Frade still has some connection with the OSS."

317

Yes, and we can presume that the sun will probably come up again tomorrow, and that winter will follow fall again. God, did he really have to think about that?

"Yes, mi Almirante. But whether he takes his orders from this man Delojo, or vice versa, is still a question. Leibermann says Delojo is an experienced Naval intelligence officer. I would like to think he has been sent here to control Frade, but I'm always afraid of what seems to be the obvious answer."

Montoya grunted, and shrugged.

"I really would like to know what the German coronel is up to."

Don't you think I know that?

"It's entirely possible that it is a routine visit. On the other hand, if it is not precisely a routine visit, then it probably has something to do with German plans to send a replacement for the *Reine de la Mer*."

"You have an opinion?"

"That was it, mi Almirante."

"Anything else?"

"El Coronel Juan Domingo Perón will join General Rawson and some of the others at Estancia Santo Catalina this weekend."

"To console Señora Carzino-Cormano, presumably?" Montoya said.

"There will be a requiem mass for el Coronel Frade at the Chapel on Estancia San Pedro y San Pablo," Martín said. "She has naturally been invited, and so have a number of her — and el Coronel's — old and close friends."

"Argentina will miss Jorge Guillermo Frade, and so will I," Montoya said, then: "How did you come by Perón's weekend plans?"

"He is staying at the Frade guest house on Libertador. Capitán Lauffer telephoned him there last night to ask for a convenient time for General Rawson to pick him up this morning. Since I knew that General Rawson —"

"I thought I suggested, and you agreed, that there would be no telephone surveillance of either General Ramírez or General Rawson?"

"The line surveilled, mi Almirante, is the line in the Frade guest house. I installed it in the belief that young Frade might return to Argentina, as indeed he has."

Montoya appeared to be giving the situation some thought. And then, when he spoke a few moments later, he moved to another subject.

"Now that Perón has returned from Germany, it could mean they are prepared to act."

"Yes, it could."

"But you don't think so, Bernardo?"

"I have not formed an opinion."

"Even if we can't break their code, I think it might be interesting to see if there is an increase in transmissions from the American radio station on Estancia San Pedro y San Pablo during or immediately after this weekend."

"I have ordered round-the-clock monitoring of the frequencies they are using, mi Almirante."

"The big question, Bernardo, isn't it, is how much contact there has been between the G.O.U. and the norteamericanos. If any. If there is a sudden increase in radio traffic . . . ."

"I take your point, mi Almirante."

"Keep me advised, Bernardo," Montoya said. "About this, and about this German coronel."

"Of course, mi Almirante."

"Thank you, Bernardo. That will be all."

He doesn't know *anything. I don't think he's even* heard *anything. But that damned cunning again — it's animal-like — he* senses *that something important is going on.*

[Three]

The Embassy of the German Reich
Avenida Córdoba
Buenos Aires, Argentina
0920 11 April 1943

As he came into the Ambassador's office, Standartenführer Josef Goltz raised his right arm from the elbow, palm outward, in a casual Nazi salute.

"I very much appreciate your finding time for me on the weekend, Herr Ambassador," he said.

"I am at your service, Herr Standartenführer," Ambassador Manfred Alois Graf von Lutzenberger replied. He neither rose from his seat nor returned the salute. Instead he offered his hand, then waved Goltz into a chair.

"May I request that First Secretary Gradny-Sawz and Oberst Grüner join us?" Goltz asked.

Von Lutzenberger picked up his telephone.

"Will you ask Herr Gradny-Sawz and Oberst Grüner to come in, please?" he ordered. "And bring in a kleines fruhstück for all of us, please?" (Kleines fruhstück, "little breakfast": pastry and coffee.)

He smiled at Goltz.

"Gradny-Sawz has some difficulty with the Argentine version of the kleines fruhstück," he said.

"As a Viennese, he naturally believes Viennese pastry is the best in the world. More cream, more butter."

"And?"

"They make the same pastry here. *Viennese* make the same pastry here. Even the names in Spanish are the same. Except that if the Viennese recipe calls for six eggs, and two hundred grams of butter, here they use a dozen eggs and half a kilo of butter. It not only does terrible things to Gradny-Sawz's waistline, but causes him to question his most sacred belief in the superiority of all things Viennese."

Goltz smiled. "I knew Gradny-Sawz in Vienna," he said. "Before the Anschlusse."

"So I understand," von Lutzenberger said, and then, as the door opened, "Ah, here he is!"

Gradny-Sawz came into the room and gave a somewhat more correct Nazi salute than Goltz had done earlier.

"Heil Hitler!" he said. "Good morning, Herr Ambassador Graf."

Oberst Karl-Heinz Grüner, in civilian clothing, was on his heels. His only greeting was a curt bow of his head to the Ambassador.

"I've ordered coffee and some cake," von Lutzenberger said, neither acknowledging Gradny-Sawz's greeting nor returning his salute.

Gradny-Sawz then walked to a couch and settled himself comfortably on it. Grüner sat down beside him.

"Josef," Gradny-Sawz said, "you won't believe the pastry here. It's quite as good as in Vienna. Probably because it's made by Viennese."

Goltz and von Lutzenberger smiled at each other.

321

Von Lutzenberger's secretary, Fräulein Ingebord Hässell, wheeled in a cart loaded with pastries and a silver coffee service.

Gradny-Sawz looked it over without paying much notice to Fräulein Hässell. She was a middle-aged spinster who wore her graying hair drawn tight against her skull and gathered in a bun at the nape of her neck.

"And even Schlagobers" — whipped cream — he said. "It's almost like being in Vienna."

The secretary went to the Ambassador first and then to each of the others in turn and poured coffee, adding sugar and spoonfuls of Schlagobers as directed. Finally, after awaiting pointed finger instructions, she slid pastries on plates and served them.

"That will be all, Fräulein Hässell, thank you," von Lutzenberger said when she was finished, "and no interruptions of any kind, please."

Fräulein Hässell smiled tightly and left the room.

Goltz set his coffee cup down, stood up, and went to von Lutzenberger.

"The first question we Germans always ask is 'by whose authority?' " he said with a smile. "This is my authority, Herr Ambassador Graf."

He handed him the envelope he had received from Reichsleiter Martin Bormann at Wolf's Lair.

Von Lutzenberger opened the envelope, read the letter without any visible reaction, refolded it, replaced it in the envelope, and handed it back to Goltz.

"A remarkable document, Herr Standartenführer," he said.

Goltz handed the envelope to Grüner.

Not to Gradny-Sawz, von Lutzenberger thought. *Which means that Gradny-Sawz has already seen it.*

"It should go without saying that what is said in this room goes no further," Goltz said.

"It's really a pity this is a secret document," Grüner said, handing it back to him. "With those signatures on it, it would bring a hell of a price from a dealer in signatures of the powerful."

"I'll keep it," Goltz said, "with that in mind, Herr Oberst. Perhaps after the war . . ."

There were polite chuckles. Gradny-Sawz's chuckle came a little after the Ambassador's.

"How may we assist you in your mission, Herr Standartenführer?" von Lutzenberger asked.

"Let me give you a little of the background, if I may. Historical and philosophical," Goltz began. "The point to consider, to always keep in mind, is that we are all privileged to be participants in the early days of the Thousand Year Reich. The *Thousand* Year Reich. That's a long time. If I suddenly should travel through time to A.D. 2943 — *'The Year of Our Lord'* — I personally would not be surprised to find that the calendar was no longer calculated from the date of birth of a Hebrew carpenter in Palestine, but rather from 1933, the year the Führer took power, and that I was now in A.H. 1000 — 'The Year of Our Führer.' "

I really think this idiot believes what he's saying, von Lutzenberger thought. *And there is really no one more dangerous than an idiot, a zealot, with power.*

"With that thought in mind, that we are not dealing with years here, or with decades, or even with centuries, but with a millennium," Goltz said, "it has been necessary for our leaders — the disciples, if you like, of our Führer — to think about matters most ordinary Germans would consider unthinkable."

"Why not?" Gradny-Sawz asked thoughtfully.

"Why not start dating things from the time the Führer assumed leadership?"

Why not? von Lutzenberger thought. *After all, we already have, in* Mein Kampf,* *the* New *New Testament. The Gospel According to Adolf.*

"I don't think the Herr Standartenführer, Anton, has come all this way to discuss a possible revision of the calendar," von Lutzenberger said. "What unthinkable things, Herr Standartenführer?"

"That brings us to history," Goltz said. "History all of us in this room are familiar with. The Armistice of 1918, and the Versailles Conference of 1919."**

"I don't think I'm quite following you, Standartenführer," Grüner said.

"To put a point on it, let's think about the Armistice of, say, 1944, followed by the Washington

---

* *My Struggle* was written by Adolf Hitler while he was imprisoned in Landsburg Prison following the failed Munich coup d'état. It was in as many German homes as the Bible, and the royalties therefrom were the major source of Hitler's personal wealth, used, among other things, for building his mountain retreat in Berchtesgaden.

** Under the Versailles Treaty of June 18, 1919, Germany lost 25,550 square miles of its land and 7 million of its citizens to Poland, France, and Czechoslovakia. Its major Baltic port, Danzig, became a "Free Port" administered by Poland. Most of the Rhineland was occupied by Allied troops. The Saar was given "temporarily" to France, and the Rhine, Oder, Memel, Danube, and Mosel rivers were internationalized. Austria was prohibited from any future union with Germany.

All German holdings abroad, including those of private German citizens, were confiscated. Almost the entire merchant fleet was expropriated. More than 140,000 dairy cows were shipped out of Germany as reparations, as well as heavy machinery and entire factories. And vast amounts of iron ore, coal, and even livestock were requisitioned by the Allies.

Billions of marks were assessed annually as reparations, and German colonies in Africa and elsewhere were seized by the League of Nations and then mandated to the various Allies, excluding the United States.

Conference of 1945."

"Now *I* don't follow you, Herr Standartenführer," von Lutzenberger said.

"Our leaders, the men who have given me this mission, had the duty to consider the unthinkable. An Armistice of 1944, not very different from the Armistice of 1918, followed by another conference like Versailles in 1919."

"You're not saying, are you," Grüner challenged, "that an Armistice of 1944 is a possibility?"

"Personally, of course not. I believe in the ultimate victory. What has had to be considered here is that *if there should be* an Armistice of 1944, it cannot — *cannot* — be followed by a repeat of the Versailles Conference of 1919."

"Frankly, Herr Standartenführer," von Lutzenberger said indignantly, "if you had not come here cloaked in the authority of our leaders, I would consider such talk as dangerously approaching defeatism and perhaps even treason!"

I was expected to react that way, and I think I did so convincingly. What is this SS slime up to?

"Herr Ambassador Graf," Gradny-Sawz said kindly. "I must tell you that until the Standartenführer explained this to me, my reaction was very much like yours."

"I should hope so!" von Lutzenberger said.

"Let me try to put it this way, Graf von Lutzenberger," Goltz said. "Let us be realistic. The war has not been going entirely our way in recent times. And of course our leaders must deal with cold facts. Consequently — while by no means demeaning the courage and self-sacrifice of the Sixth Army at Stalingrad — the cold fact is that the Sixth Army, six hundred thousand men strong, was wiped out there."

"As I understand it, they did their soldier's duty to Germany to the end," Grüner said.

"Indeed. And it would be senseless to deny that the situation in Africa is grave; that Allied bombers are causing great damage to the Fatherland; and that the Führer has not been able to provide the next level of weaponry as quickly as he hoped. Let me digress by saying that I was privileged to witness, at Peenemünde,* the testing of weapons I believe will not only sweep Allied aircraft from the skies but bring England to its knees. To *our* conference table, if you like, begging for *our* terms for an armistice."

And somewhere in the Bavarian Alps, von Lutzenberger thought, *there is a pig who really can whistle the* Blue Danube Waltz.

"Really?" Grüner asked.

"Rockets, Herr Oberst, traveling at near the speed of sound," Goltz said. "And there are other weapons, propellerless aircraft, for example, faster than anything now flying. And we have under development new tanks — a whole arsenal of weapons — I feel sure will change the tide. But the point is that these weapons may not be available in time. Our leaders have had the duty to consider the unpleasant alternatives. Which, if I may, brings us back to the Armistice of 1944."

"I have faith in the Führer," Gradny-Sawz said.

"We all do," Goltz said, an impatient tone in his voice. "But pray let me continue. Considering the impossible: Let us say, hypothetically, that in 1944 the Führer decides that seeking an armistice is best for Germany."

---

* German V-1 and V-2 rockets were developed at Peenemünde under Wernher von Braun.

326

"The British, Americans, and Russians at Casablanca called for our unconditional surrender," von Lutzenberger said.

"Rhetoric. If we offer an armistice, they will jump at it," Goltz said. "But the postwar conference following an Armistice of 1944 will be far worse for Germany than the Versailles Conference. Roosevelt is owned by the Jews. His Secretary of the Treasury, Morgenthau, *is* a Jew. England's not much better, and France, as we all know, is far worse. And Russia!"

"Then we should not seek an armistice!" Gradny-Sawz said firmly.

"Here our leaders have been looking at the longer time frame, the millennium of the Thousand Year Reich," Goltz said. "It is possible — I don't say likely, I say *possible* — that the Führer may decide that a few years of German humiliation now is a price that has to be paid to ensure that the Thousand Year Reich triumphs in the end."

"May I ask, Herr Standartenführer, what this has to do with Argentina?" von Lutzenberger asked.

"That will be self-evident in a moment, Graf von Lutzenberger," Goltz said. "Let us say there is an Armistice of 1944, with a postwar conference following. Almost certainly, the Allies would insist on occupying all of Germany, not just the Rhineland, as they did after World War One. What's left of Germany, that is. We could expect to lose more of our territories this time than we did in 1920. The Russians will steal anything and everything they can lay their hands on. The Americans and the French and the English will debase our currency, and otherwise ruin our economy. Our technology will be stolen. Conditions in Germany will be twice, three times, *ten times* as bad as they were after World War One."

"It's difficult to imagine anything so terrible for Germany!" Gradny-Sawz said, horrified.

Well, that's the first thing you've said that I agree with, von Lutzenberger thought. *But that's what will happen. We brought this war on ourselves, and now we have to pay for it.*

"But after a few years," Goltz went on, "the Allies will tire of the expense of occupying Germany. And, having stolen all they can from us, they will know we can't pay for the expense of keeping their soldiers on our soil."

"And what will happen then?" von Lutzenberger asked evenly.

"They will leave Germany," Goltz said. "Convinced that they have stripped us to the bone."

And are you now going to tell us how Adolf will turn this defeat into victory?

"Now," Goltz said, as if he were lecturing to children, "let us suppose that there was a sanctuary, a safe place, where not only large amounts of money but German technology, even German leaders, could be moved, secretly, before the Armistice of 1944."

Why am I surprised? I should be surprised that it took them this long to think of what we've already been doing for six months, moving real money out of Germany so that it can be sent back to salvage what can be salvaged from the ashes.

"You mean here?" von Lutzenberger asked evenly.

"Yes, of course here," Goltz said.

"Have our leaders come up with a means to do this?"

"The primary concern is for secrecy," Goltz said.

"If there is an Armistice of 1944, there can be no trail left for the Allies to discover."

"A trail of money, you mean?" Grüner asked.

"In addition to other things," Goltz said.

"You're thinking of secret bank accounts in Switzerland?" Grüner asked.

"Switzerland is a nation of bankers," Goltz replied. "Banks are controlled by Jews. They have no secrets from each other. And with Germany on its back, funds in Swiss banks would be no safer than funds in the Dresdenerbank."

"You think the banks here would be any different?" von Lutzenberger asked.

"If they were unaware of the source of the funds, they would be," Goltz said. "These funds would not be secret funds. They would be in the hands of Argentine citizens, indistinguishable from any other funds on deposit by Argentine citizens."

Which is exactly what Duarte and I have been doing with von Wachtstein's money. Why should I be surprised that someone else has figured this out?

"I just arrived, of course," Goltz said. "But already I have met — your driver, Oberst Grüner — a good German, a good National Socialist, who happens to hold Argentinian citizenship. I mention this just to start your thinking. What if — what's that boy's name?"

"Loche, Herr Standartenführer," Grüner furnished. "Günther Loche."

"What if the Loche family's sausage business started to prosper? Began to increase their bank deposits, opened other bank accounts, acquired farm property in the country? Who would be suspicious?"

"I see what you mean," Grüner said.

"But there would be records in Germany," von

Lutzenberger argued. "We're obviously talking about very large sums of money here."

"In the immediate future, approximately one hundred million U.S. dollars," Goltz announced, paused, and went on, "of which, I assure you, Graf von Lutzenberger, there is no record anywhere."

I think he means that figure. But one hundred million dollars, with no record? Where did they find that much money? With no record of it?

"In addition to that, there is something like twenty million U.S. dollars now in Uruguay," Goltz said, "which will have to be incorporated in our arrangements here."

What the hell is he talking about?

"Twenty million in Uruguay?" von Lutzenberger asked.

"I'll come to that in due time, Graf von Lutzenberger," Goltz said. "Our immediate problem is the reception of the one hundred million, and providing safe and very secret storage for it once it enters the country. Until it can be disbursed and invested."

My God, he's talking about money stolen from the Jews! There is no other place that much money could have come from!

"The money will be brought in by diplomatic pouch?" he asked. "I have to tell you, Herr Standartenführer, that I consider that a great risk."

"The funds are aboard the *Comerciante del Océano Pacífico*, a Spanish-registered vessel already on the high seas," Goltz replied.

"Forgive me, Herr Standartenführer," Grüner said. "But *there's* a trail. There will be manifests. . . ."

"The *Pacífico*'s ostensible mission — obviously a well-guarded secret itself — is to replace the *Reine* de la Mer," Goltz said. "The last-minute addition of half a dozen more crates of engine and radio parts to her cargo, taken aboard under the personal supervision of her captain, caused no raised eyebrows at all."

"I wondered what they would do about replacing the *Reine de la Mer*," von Lutzenberger said.

"When the *Pacífico* is on station in the Bay of Samborombón," Goltz went on, "I will board her. Her captain has been told that someone will present special orders to him when he arrives. When the crates are placed in my custody, that will be the end of the trail."

"Six crates, you said?" Grüner asked. "Full of money?"

"Six crates, Herr Oberst, containing engine and radio parts, *and* the special funds. They are not all in the form of currency. There is gold, and gemstones, and even some negotiable securities. All of which, of course, will have to be converted into cash here."

"I see," Grüner said.

If there is gold, von Lutzenberger thought, *it came from the dental work and wedding rings of murdered Jews; and the gemstones from the fingers and necks of murdered Jewish women.*

Does this slime really believe this Thousand Year Reich rising phoenixlike from the ashes of Berlin nonsense, or is he simply a criminal?

"At the time I remove the crates from the *Océano Pacífico*, I will confide in her captain that they contain weapons and other matériel necessary for the accomplishment of my mission here," Goltz said.

"Excuse me?" von Lutzenberger said.

Goltz smiled at him smugly.

"Which mission — personally authorized by the

331

Führer — is to free and return to Germany the interned officers from the *Graf Spee*. As you know, this is also of personal interest to Admiral Canaris. And when we do in fact deliver, say, twenty *Graf Spee* officers to the *Océano Pacífico*, for subsequent transfer to a submarine, that should remove any lingering curiosity the captain might have about the six crates."

"Very clever," Grüner said.

" 'Brilliant' is the word, my dear Grüner," Gradny-Sawz said.

"I presume the implications of taking the *Graf Spee* officers from their place of internment has been considered," von Lutzenberger said. "The Argentines will be offended."

"We presume, of course, Graf von Lutzenberger, that the Argentines will make a *pro forma* fuss about it. That will be fine. First, it will further obfuscate my — our — primary mission. Second, their protests should create nothing extraordinary for you to deal with, Herr Ambassador. And after a week or two, I think they will rather admire our audacity."

"I'm not so sure about that," von Lutzenberger said. "About it being easy to deal with. When the word spreads that the *Graf Spee* officers have broken their parole — and there is no way we can keep that out of the newspapers — no matter what his personal feelings on the subject, President Castillo will feel compelled to do more than register a *pro forma* complaint. And if the coup d'état planned by the Grupo de Oficiales Unidos succeeds — and in my judgment, it will — the escape of the *Graf Spee* officers could very well be the excuse the new President needs to radically alter the status quo. Perhaps to go so far as to recall their ambassador to Berlin. And conceivably, even to seek a declaration of war."

"The ramifications of Argentine indignation, Graf von Lutzenberger, have been considered at the highest level, and it was decided it was the price that had to be paid," Goltz said. "Frankly, I think you are overly concerned. For instance, when I spoke with Oberst Grüner about the Frade assassination, he told me he felt the Argentine officer corps would deeply resent that."

"I shared that opinion," von Lutzenberger said.

"Yesterday, I sensed no resentment at all," Goltz said. "Either at the Edificio Libertador, or even at the Duarte house. My God, Frade's sister even invited von Wachtstein to that private funeral service!"

Beatrice Frade de Duarte, von Lutzenberger thought, *is quite mad. Even more insane than Herr Hitler.*

Neither he nor Grüner replied.

"Vis-à-vis Oberst Frade," Goltz went on, "I am convinced that there is an understanding on the part of the Argentine military that we did what had to be done, and, more important, that our audacity in the matter is respected. And vis-à-vis the repatriation of the *Graf Spee* officers, I feel that the same thing will happen. Do you disagree, Graf von Lutzenberger?"

"There probably is something to what you say," von Lutzenberger said. "I would suggest the resentment from Frade's close friends will be the greater problem . . ."

"It will pass," Goltz said firmly.

". . . we are going to have to deal with," von Lutzenberger went on, "magnified, of course, if one of his friends, General Rawson, for example, became President of Argentina. Do I correctly infer from your orders, Herr Standartenführer, that I am forbidden to ask for reconsideration of the plan to break the interned officers out?" von Lutzenberger said.

"You and I, Graf von Lutzenberger, are forbidden to do anything about our orders but carry them out."

"The highest priority, as I understand it, is to move these funds ashore?" Grüner asked.

Ah, the military mind, von Lutzenberger thought. *When you receive an order, you start to plan to carry it out. Never consider the morality; that is a question for your betters.*

"*Safely* ashore," Goltz said.

"Then the major problem, in my opinion, would be to find some absolutely secure place to store these funds once they are ashore. Taking them off the ship will be a relatively simple matter. Perhaps it would be better to attempt to find two, or three, or even six places to store the material. So that, in case one location is detected, all would not be lost —"

"Herr Oberst," Goltz interrupted. "I appreciate your enthusiasm. But I think we all need now to take some time — twenty-four hours, perhaps even forty-eight — to think all of this over. Afterward, we shall meet again, and discuss specifics. I caution you to discuss any of this with no one not present here." He paused. "Unless there is someone?"

"I was thinking of Major von Wachtstein," Grüner said. "I think we will need him. For one thing, he is very friendly with the man who runs the Anglo-Argentine bank. For another, his Spanish is impeccable."

"Can he be trusted?" Goltz asked.

"I would say so, Josef," Gradny-Sawz said. "He is a fine young officer of an old Pomeranian family. He received the Knights Cross of the Iron Cross from the hands of the Führer himself."

"Graf von Lutzenberger?"

"He is a trustworthy officer," von Lutzenberger said. "And I agree with Grüner. I'm sure we'll need him, if we're to be involved in a matter of this kind. He flies our Storch, and I can see where —"

"All right, then," Goltz cut him off. "You may bring him into this, Graf von Lutzenberger."

"I don't mean to challenge your authority in any way, but I would suggest that Oberst Grüner deal with Major von Wachtstein. For one thing, they are both soldiers."

That distances me from Peter, and if he learns anything from Grüner, he'll tell me.

"Yes, perhaps it would be best if he did," Goltz said. He stood up.

"Thank you for your time, gentlemen," he said. "Have a pleasant weekend. I will look forward to hearing your further thoughts on this operation on Monday." And then he thought of something else: "Your secretary, Graf von Lutzenberger?"

"A reliable woman. A good National Socialist."

"We'll need someone to keep records, of course, but someone who is absolutely trustworthy."

"Fräulein Hässell is reliable," Grüner said.

"Well, then, we seem to have taken the first step in carrying out our orders, haven't we? We have chosen the members of our team," Goltz said. "Anton is going to give me a tour of the city."

He walked to and opened the door.

"Ready, Anton?"

"At your service, Josef," Gradny-Sawz said.

"Oh, one more thing," Goltz said, closing the

door. "I made contact over the weekend with one of our agents here. He tells me that one of the OSS agents has been asking dangerous questions — the Jew, his name is Ettinger —" He interrupted himself to look at Grüner. "Not one of your agents, Herr Oberst. A special agent reporting directly to Reichsprotektor Himmler. His identity must remain a secret."

"I understand, Herr Standartenführer," Grüner said. "Should I know, however, the nature of the dangerous questions?"

"In due time, Herr Oberst. Not now. For now, with great care, but as quickly as possible, I want you to eliminate Herr Ettinger. What do you know about him?"

"He's a Spanish Jew, whose family had a branch in Berlin. He and his mother left Germany and went to the United States, where he was apparently recruited by the OSS. He came here under cover, as some sort of an oil-storage-terminal expert in the employ of Howell Petroleum. After the *Reine de la Mer* incident, when Frade and the other agent returned to the United States, he remained here. He has an apartment — 4B — at Calle Monroe 127. . . ."

"Well, then, since you know so much about him, eliminating him shouldn't be much of a problem, should it?"

"Would the Herr Standartenführer like to review my plans when I have made them?"

"Yes. And I'm glad you brought that up. From now on I wish to review any plans for this sort of thing."

"Jawohl, Herr Standartenführer."

Goltz opened the door again and passed through it.

PART
TWO

Brunner Still at Large

Paris

French police said yesterday that they hunted in vain in Argentina for Alois Brunner, the most notorious Nazi war criminal still at large, after tips he had left his longtime refuge in Syria.

"He's not there, at least we didn't see him," said Gerard Bronne, head of the manhunt section of the Paris Gendarmerie after his trip to a remote region of northern Argentina near the borders of Paraguay and Brazil last month.

He told French television TF-1 he had tried to follow up reports from neighboring Uruguay that Brunner, now 83, had settled in Argentina along with other Nazi war criminals wanted by the international police agency Interpol.

Brunner, WWII deputy to fellow Austrian Adolph Eichmann, is wanted in connection with the deaths of 130,000 Jews whom he had deported to death camps during World War II (Reuters).

Page 1
The *Buenos Aires Herald*, Buenos Aires, Argentina
August 3, 1995

XI

[One]

4730 Avenida del Libertador
Buenos Aires, Argentina
0925 11 April 1943

"I wonder why that worries me?" General Arturo Rawson asked softly of his aide-de-camp, Capitán Roberto Lauffer, who sat beside him in the rear seat of Rawson's personal Packard. Both were in civilian clothing.

Rawson pointed at the official Mercedes-Benz of General Pedro P. Ramírez, which was parked at the curb in front of the Frade guest house.

"Interesting," Lauffer said.

"I better go in with you."

The driver, a sargento, also in civilian clothing, pulled up behind the Mercedes, stopped, and ran quickly around the front of the Packard to open Rawson's door.

By the time they reached the gate in the high fence, a maid had come quickly from inside the house to open it for them.

"El Coronel Perón asks that you join him for coffee in the sitting," she said, and then trotted ahead of them to hold open the door to the house.

The maid, trotting ahead of them again through the foyer, knocked politely at the door to the sitting, but pulled it open before there was time for a reply to her knock.

Juan Domingo Perón, wearing a tweed jacket with an open-collared shirt, and Ramírez, in uniform, were seated side by side in identical armchairs drinking coffee. Mayor Pedro V. Querro, Ramírez's diminutive aide-de-camp, perched on the cushions of a matching couch, his feet not quite reaching the floor.

"Mi General," Rawson said to Ramírez.

"I wanted to see you, you and Juan Domingo, before you leave for the country," Ramírez said.

"Is everything in order, mi General?" Rawson asked.

"It will be if you can get into Jorge's safe before anyone else does."

Rawson moved his arm around the room, asking with his eyes if their conversation was likely to be overheard.

"Martín had the place examined yesterday, and has had it under surveillance since then," Perón said.

"Claudia Carzino-Cormano told me that no one knows the combination to the safe," Rawson said. "We thus have —"

"Juan Domingo tells me he finds it hard to believe that Suboficial Mayor Rodríguez does not have the combination," Ramírez interrupted.

"Claudia told me she asked Rodríguez — or rather the son did, in her presence — and Rodríguez claimed he didn't know where the combination is."

"Juan Domingo believes he has the combination," Ramírez repeated.

341

"Where does that leave us?" Rawson asked.

"Juan Domingo believes he can talk to Rodríguez, explain the situation."

"I have known Rodríguez since . . . Jorge and I joined the Second Cavalry in Santo Tomé as Sub-Tenientes," Perón said. "Asking him to give the combination to me is not quite the same thing as asking him to give it to Claudia."

"Where is Rodríguez?" Ramírez asked. "In the hospital?"

"I don't think so, mi General," Lauffer said. "I'm sure he's . . . wherever Mayor Frade is."

"You mean in Jorge's house on Coronel Díaz?" Ramírez asked.

"I believe Mayor Frade is driving out to Estancia San Pedro y San Pablo today, mi General," Lauffer said.

"Wonderful!" Ramírez said sarcastically. "And what do you think Suboficial Mayor Rodríguez would do if Mayor Frade asked him for the combination to the safe — presuming Perón is correct and Rodríguez knows it?"

"Give it to him, mi General," Lauffer said. "Sir, I spent some time with them. Rodríguez has transferred his loyalty for el Coronel Frade to his son."

"Why did Jorge's son suddenly show up down here?" Perón asked. "After all these years?"

"Obviously the Americans thought he could influence his father," Rawson said. "And some suspect he is an agent of the OSS."

"*Suspect?*" Ramírez snorted. "My God! He blew up the *Reine de la Mer.*"

"Jorge's son?" Perón asked in disbelief. Ramírez and Rawson both nodded. "And everybody knows this?"

"Everybody is pretending the *Reine de la Mer* was not a replenishment vessel for German submarines, which makes it easier for everybody to pretend she sank as a result of a spontaneous explosion in her fuel bunkers," Ramírez said.

"The Germans know better," Perón said. "They know it was blown up by the United States in an outrageous violation of Argentine neutrality!"

"So, Juan Domingo, was resupplying German submarines in Argentine waters 'an outrageous violation of Argentine neutrality,' " Rawson said.

"Argentina has done no more for the Germans than the Americans did for the British," Perón said. "I find it impossible to believe that Jorge had a part in this!"

"And I think, gentlemen," General Ramírez said, "that the less said about the *Reine de la Mer*, the better."

Perón could not be silenced: "I refuse to believe that Jorge had any hand in sinking that ship!"

"Let me put it to you this way, Coronel," Rawson said. "Before the 'spontaneous combustion' of the *Reine de la Mer*'s fuel bunkers, Jorge had an airplane . . . 'the stagger-wing,' you remember?"

Perón nodded.

"There were reports that such an aircraft was seen near the *Reine de la Mer* shortly before the explosion, and other reports that it crashed into the sea. Jorge never reported the loss of his aircraft to either the authorities or his insurance company."

"His son could have taken it without his knowledge, stolen it!"

"For what I really hope is the last time, gentlemen, I will suggest that the less said about the *Reine de la Mer*, the better. I can't think of a clearer way to say that."

"Sí, mi general," Rawson and Perón said, almost in unison.

"There is another problem with the son," Perón said. "Somewhere he's acquired the odd idea that the Germans were responsible for the death of Jorge."

"He's not the only one who believes that," Rawson said.

"Nonsense!" Perón said.

"And there is one other problem vis-à-vis Jorge's safe," Rawson said. "Claudia tells me the money's in there, too."

"What money?" Perón asked.

"The money which will ensure the success of OUTLINE BLUE would be a polite way to phrase it," Rawson said. "The funds to bribe certain officers would be more accurate."

"I don't even like the sound of the word 'bribe,' " Perón said. "And as a practical matter . . ."

"As a practical matter, Juan Domingo," Ramírez said, "our first consideration is to take power bloodlessly. We've all been over this. A vote was taken by the Executive Committee of the G.O.U. Certain payments will have to be made. In cash. For several months, we have been gathering the necessary funds and placing them in Jorge's hands."

"At the time," Rawson said, "it seemed the obvious way to handle it, and not only because three-quarters of the money raised was from Jorge. We had no idea he would be murdered."

"And now we find ourselves *begging* a norteamericano OSS agent to give us *our* money?"

Perón asked, his tone making it clear that he found this at least as distasteful as the subject of bribing officers.

"Unless we can get into Jorge's safe before he does, and that seems very unlikely," Ramírez said.

"Perhaps Claudia can appeal to him. To carry out something his father began," Rawson said. "Or we could appeal to him as an Argentine."

"At what price?" Perón asked.

"From what I have seen of him, I like him," Ramírez said, ignoring the question. "I think he would trust Claudia Carzino-Cormano in this matter."

"And if he doesn't?" Perón asked.

Rawson shrugged.

"The two of you," Ramírez said, "plus Claudia Carzino-Cormano will have to meet with him. There is no other choice. If he has a price, pay it."

"Perhaps, if — as Roberto says — Suboficial Mayor Rodríguez is with Mayor Frade all the time, he would be helpful," Ramírez said. "I wish I could be there, but . . ."

"May I ask why you won't be there?" Perón asked.

"At my suggestion," Rawson answered for him. "To alleviate the suspicions of Almirante Montoya that OUTLINE BLUE is about to be executed. Not that I think it will do any good."

"Is Montoya with us or not?" Perón asked.

"I really don't know," Rawson said. "And I really don't think we will know until we put the plan in operation."

"What do you *think*, mi General?"

"I think el Almirante will fall, very late in the game, toward the side he thinks will win," Ramírez replied.

"Isn't it already very late in the game?" Perón asked.

Ramírez shrugged.

"The other question to be decided, preferably over this weekend, is who will assume power when we have taken action," Rawson said.

"Presuming we have the money to take action," Perón said, bitterly. "Money to bribe fellow officers! I —"

Rawson interrupted him. "How would you like to be President, Juan Domingo?" he asked.

Perón's face stiffened.

"Don't joke about something like that," he said. "Someone who doesn't know better might take you seriously."

"Maybe I am serious," Rawson said. "It's something to think about."

Perón shook his head in disbelief.

"My candidate is General Rawson," Ramírez said. "I have given General O'Farrell my written proxy vote."

"I never said I wanted to be President," Rawson said.

"Many people, not only me, consider you to be the logical choice," Ramírez said. "Now that Jorge Frade is no longer available to us."

"Why not you, mi General?" Perón asked.

"I do not wish to be considered. I am doing what we must do for the good of Argentina, not to assume political office," Ramírez said.

"For what it's worth, the Germans would be pleased if you were to assume the presidency, mi General," Perón said.

"You haven't mentioned any of this to any of your German friends, have you, Juan Domingo?" Rawson asked softly.

"You know better than that, Arturo," Perón said. "This is our business, no one else's. Which is not to say that the Germans won't heave a sigh of relief when we do it."

"Why, do you think?" Rawson asked softly.

"What's wrong with Argentina now, what has been wrong with Argentina all along, is a lack of order, a lack of efficiency, a lack of respect for authority. The Germans understand that."

Rawson shrugged.

"You don't agree?"

"The means by which the Germans have achieved order, efficiency, and respect for authority is more than a little frightening."

"You were delighted when National Socialism took power, as I recall," Perón said.

"That was before I came to understand what Señor Hitler really had in mind for Germany."

"You said — you gave a speech, I was there — you said 'only Germany can stem the spreading cancer of godless communism.' "

"I think the Germans will be pleased if we succeed," Ramírez said. "Because it will probably accrue to their advantage. They would rather deal with someone they can trust. And like us, they have learned one cannot trust Castillo."

"Is there anything wrong with that, mi General?" Perón asked.

"Not if that's as far as it goes," Rawson said. "The only thing I can imagine worse for Argentina than Castillo staying in power is Argentina joining the Axis."

"The Germans will win this war, Arturo," Perón said firmly.

Rawson shook his head from side to side in disagreement.

"Let's not discuss that now, for God's sake," Ramírez said. "The sooner you reach Estancia Santo Catalina, the better. Call me when you learn anything."

[Two]

Route Nacionale Two
Outside La Plata, Buenos Aires Province
1005 11 April 1943

"Piss call time, Enrico," Clete announced, glancing at Enrico, beside him in the front seat of the Buick.

When they left Buenos Aires it was too cold to put the Buick's top down, and for a while Clete even turned on the heater. Clete was happy with his impulsive decision at the last minute before leaving The Museum to wear his new Stetson. His head would have been cold without it.

And also, he admitted to himself, it was somehow comforting to have something of Uncle Jim's with him. James Fitzhugh Howell bought the white curled-brim Stetson with a rattlesnake band the morning of the day he died at the Midland Petroleum Club.

"Señor?" Enrico said, confused.

Clete pointed out the windshield to a truck stop.

"Coffee time," Clete said as he slowed to make the turnoff.

"Here, Señor Clete?" Enrico replied, making it clear he felt that stopping at a truck stop was beneath the dignity of a Frade.

"Time and the call of nature wait for no man,"

Clete intoned sonorously, mimicking the announcer on "The March of Time."

Because he was as unfamiliar with the movie-theater newsreel program as he was with the Marine Corps expression giving permission to void one's bladder, Enrico looked at him curiously but said nothing.

Clete pulled the Buick into a parking spot beside a Ford stake-body truck and got out. The truck was grossly overloaded with bags of carrots, each as large as his wrists.

"Leave that in the car," he ordered, pointing to Enrico's double-barreled shotgun.

Enrico reluctantly stowed the shotgun under the seat and got out.

The large, noisy, simply furnished restaurant was crowded with people, most of them there because it was also the local bus depot. Clete found a table and ordered hot chocolate, which was his solution to Argentinian coffee strong enough to melt one's teeth. Enrico was made uncomfortable by this, too. The waiter, apparently agreeing with Enrico's conviction that men drank coffee, women and children hot chocolate, asked him to repeat the order.

Clete went in search of the baño. It was clean but not very sophisticated. A concrete wall served as the urinal; water trickled down it. Flat porcelain fixtures at floor level, with a hole and places to place one's feet, served those who had to move their bowels. The odor was not pleasant.

Don't be a snob. This is far more elegant than the slit trenches on Guadalcanal. And it's at least inside.

When he returned to the table, he saw that he and Enrico were the subject of great interest to their fellow patrons.

What did the waiter do? Tell everybody that the guy

in the funny hat and boots ordered chocolate?

He smiled warmly at an enormous truck driver with bad teeth and three days' growth of beard. After a moment the man gave him a somewhat uneasy nod of the head.

When they left the restaurant, he put the convertible's top down but left the windows rolled up. Enrico was visibly relieved that they were leaving the truck stop.

He drove past Lake Chascomús to the Pila turnoff, then down it to and through the town of Pila, a sleepy village lined with stone houses that looked as if they were built a century or more before.

A mile out of town, they reached a brick and wrought-iron sign at the side of the road, reading "San Pedro y San Pablo." A moment later they bounced over eight railroad rails laid closely together across the road as a cattle barrier. On both sides of the road, the grassy pampas rolled gently off to the horizon. It looked something like the Texas prairie, except the grass was greener and here and there were stands of trees. Except for water tanks and their windmill-powered water pumps, no buildings or other signs of human life were in sight. Cattle roamed, in small groups or alone, as far as the eye could see.

Ten minutes later — at sixty-five m.p.h., a bit less than ten miles past the sign — he had his first glimpse of the windbreak — a triple row of tall cedars — which surrounded the main buildings of the ranch. And a minute or so after that, he was able to pick out the sprawling, two-story, white-painted stone house, sitting with its outbuildings in a three-hectare manicured garden, and then, just outside the windbreak, the landing strip, with two Piper Cubs parked on it.

I really don't want to go looking for that goddamned replenishment vessel in one of those puddle-jumpers.

As he came closer, he could see that the doors of the hangar where the Beechcraft stagger-wing used to be kept were open, and he could just make out the nose of a third Piper Cub.

Why not? The stagger-wing's on the bottom of Samborombón Bay.

Even if somehow I get that C-45, could I land it on this strip? Why not? I have all the room I need to make a slow, low-level approach. And I brought the stagger-wing in and out of here without any trouble, so why not a C-45? The problem will not be taking off, but the landing roll coming in. If I land long here, I'll run out of runway. You can't stop a C-45 as easily as you can a stagger-wing.

His attention on the landing strip, he drove without paying much attention through the cedar windbreak and found himself on the cobblestone drive inside.

Suddenly he became aware that there were people lining both sides of the road, men, women, and children. Many of the gauchos — Clete thought of them as cowpokes — held the reins of horses in their hands, and all of them had removed their hats and were holding them in their hands.

Christ, it's a reception committee. Paying homage to the new Patrón. The Patrón is dead; long live the Patrón!

And they knew I was coming. I didn't see anybody as we came in here, but somebody damned sure saw us, and called here and let them know we were coming.

What the hell am I supposed to do, wave at them?

Made uneasy by the unabashed humility, he raised his left hand and waved it somewhat stiffly as he fixed his eyes straight ahead and drove to the house.

The household staff, half a dozen maids, three women in cook's aprons, and a middle-aged woman he recognized as the housekeeper — *What the hell is her name?* — were lined up on the steps of the shaded verandah behind three priests. Two of them were in — *whatever the hell they call that skirt-like costume* — and one wore a black business suit — *I recognize the old priest and the young one from Señora Pellano's funeral, but who's the one in the suit?* Antonio, his father's butler, stood beside the priests. *What the hell did Antonio do? Get up at four in the morning to get down here before me? Or drive down here last night after I finally went to bed?*

One of the maids ran down to the car and pulled open Clete's door.

"Thank you," he said, and stepped out.

The older priest, apparently taking advantage of his seniority, walked up to Clete.

"God bless you, my son," he said.

Clete offered his hand. It was ignored as the priest made the sign of the cross.

"Good to see you, Father," Clete said, and nodded to the younger priest, who also responded by making the sign of the cross.

The priest in the business suit, who looked to be in his forties, walked up to Clete and offered his hand. He was a bespectacled, slim, fair-skinned man who had lost most of his light-brown hair. Clete's immediate impression of him — his well-cut black suit didn't come off a rack in a cheap clothing store; there were gold cuff links on his shirt; and something about him suggested, if not arrogance, then unusual self-confidence — was that he was anything but a simple parish priest.

"I'm Father Welner, Mr. Frade," he said in only slightly accented British English. "On those — too rare, I am afraid — occasions when your father felt it necessary to seek absolution, I was his confessor."

"How do you do?"

"There wasn't the opportunity, the time, for us to talk in Buenos Aires. Perhaps we can find time here."

"I'd like that," Clete said.

I know who this guy is. The only lowly priest in that squad of bishops and monsignors at the church. What does he want to talk about?

"Fathers Denilo and Pordido would like your approval of the arrangements for the requiem mass for your father tomorrow," Welner said.

"I'm sure whatever they've laid on will be fine," Clete said.

" 'Laid on'? Set up? Arranged?"

"Yes."

"I think Father Denilo would be grateful if you were to review what he's *laid on*," Welner said.

"I would be honored, Father Denilo," Clete said, switching to Spanish and smiling at the older priest. "If you and Father Pordido would take a coffee, or a glass of wine, with me while you tell me of the arrangements you have made for the mass."

The old priest beamed.

"Where do we go, Antonio?" Clete asked.

"I suggest the library, Señor Cletus."

"Father, I will be with you in just a moment," Clete said. "There is something that requires my immediate attention."

"I understand," Father Denilo said.

Clete motioned the priests to proceed ahead of him into the house. They insisted that he go first.

Clete went with them to the library, and then motioned Antonio to follow him back into the corridor.

"Has Señora Carzino-Cormano been here? Last night, or this morning?"

"No, Señor."

"That will be all, Antonio, thank you," Clete said, and walked down an interior corridor with Enrico on his heels.

"Where's the safe?" Clete asked.

"In el Coronel's study."

"Christ, we may need a key!"

Enrico went into his pocket and came up with a single key on a key ring. Most of the keys to doors at Estancia San Pedro y San Pablo were old-fashioned, large and simple. The key Enrico held up was small and modern; the lock it fit could not be picked by an amateur burglar with a screwdriver.

El Coronel's study had been off limits to just about everybody, and kept carefully locked. Clete was not surprised to find it locked now.

"I'll need my own key, Enrico," Clete said.

Enrico stepped past him and put his key in the lock.

"Sí, Señor," Enrico said, and pushed the door open for him, and flicked on the lights. The heavy metal blinds on the window were down. Enrico looked to Clete for orders about the blinds.

"Leave them down for now," Clete said.

El Coronel's study was furnished simply. There was a comfortable-looking, thickly upholstered dark-red leather armchair with a matching footstool. Beside it was a table holding a cigar humidor and a large ashtray. Two smaller, cloth-upholstered armchairs that showed no signs of use faced a large wooden desk, behind which was a high-backed, red leather office chair, the cushions showing signs of much use. A library table held four leather-bound photo albums. A large oil portrait of Elizabeth Ann Howell de Frade with her infant son, Cletus, in her arms hung over the fireplace.

Jesus, I'd swear I saw that hanging in Uncle Willy's house. Are there two of them?

Clete walked to a small table holding a large photograph in an ornate silver frame and looked at it. He had seen it once before, on the only previous time he had been in his father's study. It had been taken before the altar of the Cathedral of St. Louis on Jackson Square in New Orleans. It showed Elizabeth Ann Howell de Frade in her wedding dress standing beside her new husband, in formal morning clothes. They were flanked by His Eminence, the Archbishop of New Orleans; Mr. James Fitzhugh Howell; and Miss Martha Williamson, his fiancée. At opposite ends stood Mr. Cletus Marcus Howell, whose smile was visibly strained; and a tall, erect, olive-skinned young man in morning clothes, whom Clete had not previously been able to identify. Now he was sure he could.

"Enrico?" he asked. Enrico came to him. Clete pointed.

"Sí, Señor Clete. Juan Domingo Perón."

"He was my father's best man?"

Enrico looked confused.

"El Coronel Perón — he was then, as your father was, Capitán — stood beside your father. Had the rings. Is that 'best man'?"

"Yes, it is," Clete said.

I'll be damned!

"Open the safe, Enrico, please," Clete ordered. One of the walls in the study was covered with framed photographs of Clete. At age nine, taking first place in the Midland FFA Sub-Junior Rodeo Calf-Roping Contest. As Cadet Corporal Cletus Frade in the boots and breeches of the Corps of Cadets of the Texas Agricultural and Mechanical College. In sweat-soaked whites, looking as if he had already had at least three post-tournament Sazeracs, with the rest of the Tulane Tennis Team . . .

The photo albums on the table were full of photographs and newspaper clippings, mostly from the Midland, Texas, *Advertiser* and the New Orleans *Times-Picayune*. Since there was no other way for Jorge Guillermo Frade to keep up with the activities of his son, he had hired a lawyer in Midland, and the lawyer had hired a clipping service. Every time Clete's name was mentioned in the newspapers — for example, when he was a guest at some six-year-old's birthday party — it was clipped out and sent to Argentina.

Clete's eyes teared, and his throat was tight.

What the Old Man did to you, Dad — what he did to me — was wrong. You were my father, and I was your son, and he should have let us get to know one another.

He didn't kill my mother. She killed herself. When she converted to Catholicism, she went whole hog — not surprising, considering who her father was — and swallowed that horseshit about birth control being a mortal sin — murder — and got herself in the family way even after she was told it would very likely kill her.

And you lied to me, every time the subject came up. My father did not *simply put me out of his mind as if I never happened. The proof of that is all this crap in this room. He never got in touch with me because you did everything in your power to keep him from even*

356

writing me a goddamned letter.

And he told me, and I believe him, that he considered having me kidnapped and brought here. And the only reason he didn't was that if he did, his sister would have raised me, and she's as nutty as a fruitcake. He didn't have me kidnapped because he thought Martha raising me was better for me than having Beatrice raise me. And he was right.

He didn't forget me. For Christ's sake, the only reason he didn't marry Claudia was because it would have posed problems about my inheritance. He wanted me to have everything he owned.

Another wall of el Coronel Jorge Guillermo Frade's private study was a bookcase. *Books that he actually read,* Clete had decided the first time he saw them, *not books bought by the yard to look good.*

When Clete raised his eyes from the leather-bound photo albums, Enrico was tugging at one of its shelves. A four-shelf section of the bookcase swung slowly outward, revealing a substantial-looking safe. There was a combination dial and a small, spoked, stainless-steel wheel. On the safe was the legend HIMPELL G.M.B.H, BERLIN in gold letters.

Enrico leaned over to work the combination.

"While I think of it, you'd better give me the combination," Clete said. "Wait till I find a pencil and some paper."

He went to his father's desk, opened the center drawer, and found both.

"OK?"

"Señor Clete, you are going to write the numbers down?" Enrico asked dubiously.

"Let's have them," Clete ordered.

"Right two times, then stop at eleven," Enrico reported reluctantly. "Left, past eleven, to eighteen. Right past eighteen to twenty-two. Left past twenty-two to nine."

Clete wrote the numbers down.

"Let me see if I can work it," he said, and went to the safe. He showed Enrico what he had written down: *Right 12. Left 27. Right 26. Left 13.*

"That is not what I told you," Enrico said, his curiosity showing.

"It is if you add the year 1943 to it," Clete said. "Eleven and one is twelve; eighteen and nine is twenty-seven, et cetera. Get the idea?"

"Sí, Señor Clete," Enrico said. "Clever!"

"I am a clever fellow with a lousy memory," Clete said. "That little trick is very helpful."

He had done the same thing with the telephone numbers Leibermann gave him in the Café Colón.

Clete bent over the safe and, reading from the notepaper, worked the combination. The dial turned very smoothly; there was no audible or tactile sensation as he moved the dial to the numbers.

I'm going to look like a fool if this thing doesn't open.

He stopped on thirteen and turned the spoked, stainless steel wheel. Again there was no sound or tactile sensation, but when the wheel had turned its limit, and he pulled on it, the safe door swung smoothly open.

There were two shelves in the safe, dividing it into thirds. The upper shelf held an inch-thick stack of paper held together with a metal fastener, obviously a document of some sort. Clete started to reach for it, then stopped when his eye fell on the butt of a Colt .45 ACP pistol nearly concealed under a large light-blue manila envelope on the second shelf.

What the hell is the .45 for?

A melodramatic scenario came into his mind.

El Coronel, forced to open the safe at gunpoint, does so, and suddenly turns, blazing automatic in hand, and puts a round right between the eyes of the bad guys. Oh, horseshit!

He pushed the manila envelope to the side and picked up the pistol. The hammer was cocked and the safety was off. He ejected the clip, then worked the action. A stubby, glistening .45 cartridge arced though the air, bounced on the tile floor, and came to rest on a rug.

Jesus Christ! Loaded, cocked, and safety off! And obviously on purpose. El Coronel was not the sort of man to leave a loaded, cocked pistol around, safety off, through carelessness.

Enrico picked up the cartridge and handed it to Clete. Clete put the cartridge into the magazine, then inserted the magazine into the pistol, letting the slide slam forward, chambering a round. He put the safety on, then carefully laid it on the rug. After that, he picked up the envelope and untied the string holding it closed.

It contained two Argentine passports made out in names he didn't recognize, but carrying the photographs of Dave Ettinger and Tony Pelosi. He glanced at them quickly, put them back in the envelope, then put the envelope on the floor beside the pistol.

Then he reached into the safe and took out the document. When he did so, he saw that it had been lying on half-inch stacks of currency.

What the hell is all that money doing in there?

He started to pick up one of the stacks of money, then changed his mind.

I don't think Claudia would be all that concerned about money, not even this much money.

He looked at the document. Its light-blue — *like*

the blue in the Argentine flag, he thought — cardboard covers were blank. He turned to the first page. Neatly typed in the center were the words "ESQUEMA AZUL" — OUTLINE BLUE.

Jesus! What the hell is this?

He turned to the next page. It was once as neatly typed as the title page, but there had been a number of corrections since, in both pencil and ink. He had little doubt, however, that it was an index to the rest of the document. Turning to page three removed any doubt about what he was holding in his hands.

PART ONE

STATEMENT OF PURPOSE

The purpose of OUTLINE BLUE is the seizure, in the name of the people of Argentina, by the Group of United Officers of all elements of the Government of Argentina; to depose the incumbent President of the Republic and all officials holding appointed power under him; and to govern the Republic of Argentina under Martial Law until, at the earliest feasible time free, honest and democratic elections may be held.

Jorge Guillermo Frade

Jorge Guillermo Frade
Coronel, Cavalry, Retired
President, Grupo de Oficiales Unidos

No wonder Claudia wanted to lay her hands on this before I did!

But if she knew about it, that means she's involved with this, too, and up to her ears!

I wonder where, if at all, Humberto fits in. I don't think he knows about this.

He quickly flipped through the folder. It wasn't exactly like an American Operations Order, but it was organized very much like the last Operations Order Clete had seen — *"Movement of VMF-221 From Ewa Marine Air Station, Territory of Hawaii, to Guadalcanal, Solomon Islands."*

Who was to do what and when was spelled out in numbing detail. The consequence of the "who" listed in OUTLINE BLUE was that it was a list of all the officers, all over Argentina, Army and Navy, who were involved in the planned coup d'état. Officers who could be tried for treason, if this document fell into the wrong hands and OUTLINE BLUE was nipped in the bud.

"Did you know what this was?" Clete asked.

"Sí, Señor Clete."

"You think Señora Carzino-Cormano did?"

"Of course."

"Humberto Duarte?"

"I don't think so."

"Is there someplace else we can hide this?" Clete said. "She's liable to show up here any moment. And I want to read it."

And decide what, if anything, I'm going to do with it.

"I know where to put it," Enrico said. "The money, too, Señor Clete?"

"What's that money for?"

"To pay some of the senior officers," Enrico replied, making it clear he thought that should have been self-evident.

"I think we'll leave the money there," Clete said,

thinking aloud. "I may even let Señora Carzino-Cormano into the safe. But I want to put OUTLINE BLUE someplace else — someplace safe — until I make up my mind what I'm going to do about it, understand?"

Enrico nodded.

Clete laid OUTLINE BLUE on the floor and reached for the three large manila envelopes inside the safe. The first two held legal documents, including several deeds.

These were obviously the documents Humberto was concerned about. The records involving the investment of the money Peter von Wachtstein had brought from Germany.

There's no time to look at these now, and even if there was I wouldn't know what I was looking at.

The third envelope contained only another, letter-size envelope. The rear flap was embossed, SCHLOSS WACHTSTEIN, POMERN.

Wachtstein Castle, Pomerania. A year ago, six months ago, when I heard the word castle, *I thought of King Arthur, or maybe Frankenstein. It never occurred to me that anybody I would ever know would have grown up in a castle . . . considered it his home. And when I heard "Pomerania," I thought of some ugly snarling mutt sitting drooling on a fat lady's lap.*

He remembered Peter trying without success to control his voice and to ignore his tear-filled eyes when he read the letter aloud, translating it for him as he did so.

And he remembered his father reading the letter shortly afterward, and then, turning to Peter with tears in his eyes and with great difficulty finding his voice, finally saying, "I can only hope, my friend, that one day my son will have reason to be half as proud of me as you must be of your father."

Well, I'm proud as hell of you, too, Dad. It took balls to sign this OUTLINE BLUE thing. You damned well knew your signature was all Castillo would need to convict you of treason and stand you in front of a firing squad. Maybe signing it wasn't smart, but it was the honorable thing to do.

His own eyes watery, he replaced the small envelope in the larger one, tied it, and put it on the floor with everything else. Then he walked to his father's desk, sat down in his father's chair, and started to read OUTLINE BLUE.

"Señor Clete, the good fathers are waiting for you," Enrico said.

"Damn!" Clete said. He closed OUTLINE BLUE and held it out to Enrico. "Wherever you take this, Enrico, put it someplace where I can look at it later."

"Sí, Señor."

[Three]

Estancia San Pedro y San Pablo
Near Pila, Buenos Aires Province
1105 11 April 1943

"May I?" Father Welner asked, holding up a fresh bottle of wine and a corkscrew.

Fathers Denilo and Pordido had just left them, after two glasses of wine each and a fifteen-minute briefing on the requiem mass. It was apparently going to be nearly as elaborate as the service in the Basílica of Our Lady of Pilar; all that was missing was the casket and the Húsares de Pueyrredón.

"Of course," Clete said, and slid his glass across the desk. "I could use another sip myself."

"Was that difficult for you?" Welner asked, and then interrupted himself. "This is very nice. It comes from one of your vineyards. Your father was very fond of it."

"*One* of *my* vineyards?"

"San Bosco, in Córdoba. It's essentially a varietal cabernet."

Welner pulled the cork out, sniffed it, and then poured wine into Clete's glass before filling his own.

"That wasn't difficult," Clete said. "*Odd.* I'm not a Catholic, and having a Catholic priest seek my approval, of anything, is a little strange."

"Oh, but you are a Catholic," Welner said.

"I'm an Episcopalian, Father," Clete said. "An Anglican, I guess you say down here. A communicant of Trinity Protestant Episcopal Church, Midland, Texas."

"You were baptized here into the Roman Catholic Church," Welner said. "So far as we're concerned, you're a Roman Catholic."

"So far as I'm concerned, Father, I'm not."

"Would it offend you if I continue to think of you as a *Christian?* There is even some talk in Rome that Anglican holy orders are valid."

"You can think of me any way you want to, Father."

Welner smiled and nodded.

"You made Father Denilo happy when you approved of the arrangements he made. Your approval is very important to him. I know he would like to stay on here at Estancia San Pedro y San Pablo. He's been here for almost thirty years."

"What have I got to do with him staying on or not?"

"In one sense, nothing. He is a diocesan priest, assigned here on the sole authority of his bishop. On the other hand, if it came to his bishop's attention that the Patrón of Estancia San Pedro y San Pablo wished that Father Denilo was assigned elsewhere, I'm sure the Bishop would consider that the Patrón of Estancia San Pedro y San Pablo provides — I would guess — somewhere between forty and fifty percent of his budget."

" 'Money talks,' huh? You sound like my grandfather."

"Should I take offense at the comparison? Your father was not an admirer of your grandfather, of whom he often talked."

"No offense was intended. I'm very fond of, greatly admire, my grandfather."

I even admire his capacity to hate, his ruthlessness. So what does that make me? A chip off the old blockhead?

"Your father described him as a hardheaded man who saw things only in black and white. Which could have been a description of himself."

Clete chuckled.

"Where are you assigned, Father? I guess I'm asking how come you were my father's priest . . . what did you say, 'his confessor'?"

"I'm a member of the Society of Jesus."

"A Jesuit?"

Welner nodded. "I am educated in the law, canonical and temporal. I teach in Buenos Aires, at the University of St. Ignatius of Loyola. We're not really as bad, as Machiavellian, as we are sometimes painted, Mr. Frade."

"What makes you think I think you're Machiavellian?" Clete asked with a smile.

"Your eyes. When your mouth said 'Jesuit,' your eyes said, 'OK, that explains everything.' "

"Am I that transparent?"

"You are your father's son, Mr. Frade. You are no more opaque than he was. And I was his friend — as well as his confessor — for many years."

"You said you wanted to talk to me. What about?"

"I am, of course, first and foremost a priest. I thought I might be of some service under the circumstances. How are you handling your father's death, for example?"

"Frankly, Father, with a good deal of anger."

"The classic dichotomy between the 'eye for an eye' of the Old Testament and Christ's admonition to 'turn the other cheek' in the New."

" 'Thou shalt not murder,' " Clete quoted.

" 'Vengeance is mine, saith the Lord,' " Welner responded.

"How did we get into this?" Clete asked.

Welner picked up the wine bottle.

"This may have something to do with it," he said. *In vino veritas.*"

"Well, let's get off the subject," Clete said.

"As you wish," Welner said. "There is nothing else you would like to talk about?"

"Not a thing, thank you," Clete said, and then heard himself saying: "Well, there is something."

"What?" Welner asked.

Clete picked up his wineglass. It was nearly empty. He drained it, reached for the bottle, poured more, and then offered the bottle to Welner, who nodded.

"I need a little *cultural* advice," Clete said as he filled the priest's glass. "Not moral."

"When faced with more tableware than you know what to do with, the best thing to do is work inward," Welner said, straight-faced. "The outer fork first, then the —"

"My Aunt Martha taught me all I need to know about knives and forks, thank you very much, Father," Clete interrupted, chuckling.

"I'm surprised. According to your father, norteamericanos are savages who handle their food with sharpened sticks," Welner said. "I was apparently misinformed."

"Actually, most of the time we just use our fingers," Clete said.

"What is your *cultural* problem?"

"I think the wine got to me," Clete said. "Now I'm sorry I started this."

"Your father once told me — we had been drinking some wine — that the only reason he tolerated me at his table was that I was the only priest he ever knew who didn't pry," Welner said. "We'll leave your cultural problem at that."

He took a swallow of his wine and set the glass down.

"I'll leave you to get settled," he said. "Thank you for your kindness to Father Denilo."

Clete had a sudden insight.

"Is that why you were here to greet me?"

"One of the reasons. Father Denilo is a good man, a good priest, but I wasn't sure you would understand him. Or he you."

"Tell the bishop that if he transfers him, I *will* shut off the money," Clete said.

"I won't do that," Welner said. When Clete looked at him in surprise, Welner went on: "According to your father, you are, or were, a very fine officer. Doesn't the U.S. Army teach its officers to conserve their ammunition against the time when they will really need it?"

"I was a Marine, not a soldier," Clete said. "But thank you for the advice."

"Thank you for the wine," Welner said, and started to walk out of the room. "I'll see you again, soon."

"I'll look forward to it," Clete said, feeling somewhat hypocritical.

He heard the sound of an airplane engine, low, over the house, distracting him.

That's not one of el Coronel's Piper Cubs.

Two of them are J-3s with a 40-horsepower Continental A-40-4 engines; the third one is a J-4 with a 75-horsepower Continental A-75-8.

All of which are now mine, of course.

There's a much bigger engine in whatever that is.

I wonder what it is?

The sound of the engine changed as the pilot throttled back for landing.

I wonder who it is, landing on my strip?

He returned his attention to Father Welner and saw that the priest had just about reached the door.

"Father," Clete called out, and when the priest stopped and turned to look at him, Clete heard himself blurting, "Father, I've . . . uh . . . I've made a girl pregnant."

Welner looked at him for a long moment.

"You don't consider that a moral problem?"

"The morality of it will have to sort itself out. What I'm ignorant about is how to tell her father."

"You love her?"

"Yes, I love her."

"You intend to marry her?"

"Of course."

"Who is she?"

"I'm reluctant to give you her name."

"You may not like this, but in my mind you've come to me as a priest. What you tell me will go no further. At least tell me, is she of your background?"

The already faint sound of the aircraft engine died as the pilot shut it down, and then there was a backfire.

What the hell is that engine? Who is that?

"Dorotéa Mallín," Clete heard himself saying. "Her father is Enrico —"

"I know him well," Welner said. "He will not like this at all."

"He's a hypocritical sonofabitch," Clete was shocked to hear himself blurting. "Great wife, great family, and he was keeping a mina" — mistress — "on the side."

" 'Judge not,' et cetera," Father Welner said. "I must say I admire your taste. And, now that I think about it, I can see why Dorotéa was attracted to you."

"I think they call that 'stupidity,' " Clete said. "For one thing, she's just a child . . ."

"Not any longer," Welner said.

". . . who really had no comprehension of what she was letting herself in for."

"Because of your connection with the OSS?"

"Where did you hear about th— What was that you said, 'OSS'? Never heard of it."

"Where do you think?"

"Yeah," Clete said.

"You might consider that in the United States, there are probably many thousands of young women with child, whose husbands are off fighting a war. Is Dorotéa's situation so different?"

"Hell, yes, it's different. I don't want her, or our

369

baby, killed because the Germans are after me."

"Then you will have to make provisions for her. Bring her out here, for example, after you're married."

"The immediate problem is to *get* married," Clete said. "How do I go about that? Show up at his door? *'Buenos días, Señor Mallín, you're about to be a grandfather, and I'm the sonofabitch who did it'?*"

Welner chuckled.

"You're asking for my advice?"

"I guess I am," Clete said after thinking it over.

"Well, then, I would suggest you first tell your uncle Humberto, and then Señora Carzino-Cormano. Overlooking the missing sacrament, she is de facto your father's widow. She would want to know; she would be deeply hurt if you didn't tell her. If that bothers you, I'll be happy to talk to them for you."

"And then what?"

"And then Humberto and Claudia and I will call upon Señor Mallín to discuss the problem we have regarding the children."

" *'The children'?* And then what?"

"What can he do, Cletus?" Welner asked. "Shoot you . . . ?"

That's the first time he called me by my Christian name.

"Throw Dorotéa out on the street? You and Dorotéa are not, you know, the first two young people in history who let their glands overwhelm their brains. He loves Dorotéa, and in time he may even learn to tolerate you."

"That'll be a cold day in hell," Clete said.

"A newborn, they say, can melt stone hearts."

"You really think there won't be a problem?"

"There is a problem. We can deal with it. And

I'm sure the bishop, after prayerful consideration, would be willing to accept my suggestion that he waive the customary banns for the Patrón of Estancia San Pedro y San Pablo. You could be married here at the chapel. Possibly as soon as next week."

"By a Catholic priest? The Old Man will shit a brick when he hears about that!"

"Now, there's a colloquialism I never heard before," Welner said. "'The 'Old Man' — presumably you mean your grandfather — will 'shit a brick'?"

Clete nodded, smiling.

"A little vulgar, I suppose, but accurately descriptive."

"I am sure that Dorotéa, or her mother, knows one of my erring brother priests of the Anglican persuasion who could be induced into performing, quietly, one of your pagan rituals. You could tell your grandfather about that ceremony."

"I'll be damned," Clete said.

"Not for getting married, I wouldn't think."

"I mean, that's all there is to it? It can be arranged?"

"It can be arranged, because it has to be arranged. Would you like me to speak with Claudia and your uncle Humberto?"

Clete nodded. "I'd be grateful. I'm a coward."

"No," Welner said. "A confused young man, perhaps, but not a coward." He looked at his watch. "I'll have to telephone Buenos Aires and break an appointment," he said. "No problem. I really didn't want to drive in there and then have to drive right back. Humberto and your aunt Beatrice will probably arrive here in time for tea. I'll go see Claudia now, and come back in time to be here when they arrive."

"I'm very grateful," Clete said. "Thank you."

"That's what priests are for, you know. Trying to help people follow God's commandments."

He shook Clete's hand firmly and walked out of the library.

That's one clever sonofabitch, Clete thought. A used-car salesman in a clerical collar. I should check to see if I still have all my fingers after that politician's handshake, and then see if I still have my wristwatch and wallet. I don't have the foggiest idea what, but he wants something *from me.*

That said, why do I feel a hell of a lot better right now than I have since I came down here? Because he said he's going to fix things about Dorotéa. And I think he will. And if he can, he can have anything he wants.

Within reason.

XII

[One]

Estancia San Pedro y San Pablo
Near Pila, Buenos Aires Province
1125 11 April 1943

Enrico rose to his feet when Clete came out of the library. He had been sitting in one of the massive wooden armchairs that lined the wide corridors of the house, spaced every ten feet in nearly military precision, like soldiers guarding a perimeter. They were nearly square, and their only upholstery was thick, deeply tooled cowhide saddle leather nailed to the backrests, seats, and armrests.

"Whose airplane did I hear landing?" Clete asked.

"I have sent Rudolpho to find out."

The logical thing is to be patient. Rudolpho will be back in a minute with an explanation. What difference does it make, anyway?

To hell with it.

Enrico caught up with him as he walked down the verandah steps.

"Are there any more airplanes around here that I don't know about?"

"That was not one of our airplanes, Señor Clete."

"Who the hell could it be?"

Enrico shrugged.

"Tell me about my father and Padre Welner," Clete said.

Enrico looked uncomfortable, reminding Clete of Welner's statement that he was "no more opaque" than his father.

"Come on, Enrico!"

"El Coronel did not treat the Padre with the proper respect," Enrico said. "They often argued. Many times, your father raised his voice to him. He even called the Padre by his Christian name, sometimes even in my presence."

"What did they argue about?"

"Matters that a man should not argue about with a priest," Enrico said.

"Such as?"

"Heaven, Hell, absolution. The sacraments. What happens between men and women."

In other words, el Padre and el Coronel were friends.

They were through the garden now, and through the windbreak.

A high-wing monoplane, a two-seater, painted in something like olive drab, with an Argentine military insignia — a blue bull's-eye with a white center — on its fuselage was parked alongside two of the Piper Cubs, dwarfing them.

What the hell is that thing? It looks like the Cadillac version of a Piper Cub. Christ, that's what it is. A military observation airplane. Probably German. I've never seen anything like it before, and they don't make airplanes in Argentina.

Standing beside it, their passage barred by Rudolpho, who was carrying a shotgun, were two men. One, in a baggy flight suit, was obviously the pilot. The other was wearing a cavalry officer's uniform, complete to highly polished riding boots. Clete recognized him immediately, although he had seen him only twice before in his life.

What the hell is el Teniente Coronel Martín doing here? The first thing that comes to mind, of course, is that he's after OUTLINE BLUE, and the money. I can't think of any other reason he'd be here. But who does he want it for? *He's Internal Security — read counterintelligence — charged with protecting the government from operations like OUTLINE BLUE. If he's working for Castillo, and I turn that over to him, that's the end of OUTLINE BLUE, and all the players are going to find themselves blindfolded and tied to a stake in front of a wall.*

Jesus, why did he show up here now? *I need time to think.*

When he saw Clete and Enrico walking toward them, the pilot nudged Martín, who looked toward them.

The first time Martín met Clete was the night of the incident at the Frade guest house on Avenida del Libertador. After being advised of the shooting by agents he had assigned to surveille the house, and by Frade himself, he had rushed to the house. He arrived on the heels of the Policía Federal, who by then had arrested the OSS agent. They were about to take him to police headquarters for questioning, but Martín used the superior authority of the BIS to take the "incident" under BIS control, which did not endear him to the Policía Federal officer-in-charge.

In the kitchen he found the Frade housekeeper with her throat cut, bathed in her own blood. Upstairs he found two dead men, both shot to death by the man they had come to murder. From the evidence, he judged that one of them had been shot — killed instantly — by the OSS agent in self-defense. The second assassin was wounded in the first confrontation. Frade then went to check on the woman, found her with her throat cut, and then returned upstairs in a rage to dispatch the second assassin. Which he did with three shots — all that remained in the pistol — one of which blew the assassin's brains all over the bathroom, where he had crawled.

It was rather a surprising loss of control by a professional, he thought at the time.

The "incident" forced Martín to abandon his neutral status as a BIS officer and choose sides between the government of President Castillo and the Grupo de Oficiales Unidos, led by el Coronel Jorge Guillermo Frade, who were plotting Castillo's ouster.

He still sometimes wondered if by choosing the latter he had righteously selected the forces of good over the forces of evil; or whether the notion that the Castillo-controlled Policía Federal were charging with murder the intended victim of an assassination paid for by the Germans had so outraged his sense of right and wrong that he just couldn't stand idly by.

Or, even less appealing, he wondered if he had chosen sides because he was aware that el Coronel Frade was likely to be the next President of the Argentine Republic and in a position to punish anyone who had assisted those responsible for the murder of his housekeeper and the arrest of his only son. Or to reward those who had been helpful.

After a good deal of thought, Martín was able to conclude only that he had no one reason to act as he had. It was a combination of several reasons. He could only hope that time would show he'd acted in the best interests of Argentina.

What he did was summon an Army ambulance from the Dr. Cosme Argerich Military Hospital and order the OSS agent confined there, incognito, until further notice, for "medical examination."

Afterward, it took some creative investigative techniques to develop the evidence necessary to support the conclusions in his Official Report of Investigation that Victim Frade had acted in self-defense and had broken no laws. But two days later, Martín was able to visit Frade in the hospital and inform him officially that the incident was closed and he could now leave the hospital. He also suggested then, unofficially, that Frade leave the country as soon as possible.

Clete walked up to Martín and put out his hand.

"How are you, mi Coronel?" he asked. "What a pleasant surprise."

"Please forgive the intrusion," Martín said. "I wouldn't be here if I didn't think it was necessary."

"No intrusion at all," Clete said. "Very interesting airplane. What is it?"

"A Fieseler Storch, Señor," the pilot said. "German."

"Forgive me," Martín said. "Mayor Frade, may I present Capitán Birra?"

"A sus órdenes, mi mayor," the pilot said politely.

"I can't seem to get anyone down here to accept the fact that I am no longer a serving officer," Clete said.

"Is that so?" Martín said.

"That's so," Clete said.

"At one time, Capitán, *Señor* Frade was an aviator in the norteamericano Corps of Marines," Martín said. "Why don't you show him around the plane?"

"It would be my pleasure, Señor," Capitán Birra said, and motioned Clete toward the airplane.

"It was in this type aircraft, I believe, *Señor* Frade, that the late Capitán Duarte lost his life in Russia," Martín said.

Clete was already sorry he had started the whole business, and it got worse. Capitán Birra was justifiably proud of his airplane. It was designed for the same purpose — liaison and artillery spotting — as aircraft used by the Army and the Marine Corps. The difference was that the aircraft more or less affectionately called "puddle jumpers" used by the Corps were Piper Cubs right off the civilian assembly line. This thing, Wildcat pilot Frade could not honestly deny, was a *real* airplane. It wasn't a Wildcat, of course, but neither was it a Cub.

And Capitán Birra lost no time in politely telling him the Storch had a 240-horsepower engine, a range of 800 miles, and a cruise speed of 115 m.p.h. The Cubs Clete had flown several times on Guadalcanal had 75-horse engines and a range of no more than whatever two hours at about 70 miles an hour added up to. Then Capitán Birra politely asked if it was really true that "Americans used 'little civilian planes like the Piper' in combat."

"If you are free, Señor Frade, I would be happy to give you a ride."

"That's very kind of you, Capitán," Clete said.

"But I'm sure el Coronel Martín is pressed for time."

"Perhaps some other time, Señor Frade," Martín said. "Is there somewhere we could talk?"

"Certainly. Why don't we go up to the house?"

"May I offer my condolences on your loss?"

"Thank you very much."

Clete led him back through the windbreak and garden into the house. He told Rudolpho to see that Capitán Birra had whatever he needed, then took Martín into the library. Enrico followed them in and stationed himself in a chair near the door.

Clete waved Martín into one of the armchairs and sat down in another.

"I've never seen you in uniform before, mi Coronel."

"I wear it from time to time to remind myself that I am an officer, not a policeman," Martín said. "I'm glad to find you here, Señor Frade."

"There's a memorial Mass for my father tomorrow. I had to be here for that, of course."

"I meant, arriving unannounced, that I was afraid that you might be out at your radio station," Martín said. "And I don't have much time."

I'm going to pretend I didn't hear that. That casual matter-of-fact reference to my supposedly secret radio station was purposefully made by a real professional, and this goddamned amateur doesn't know how to reply.

"How may I be of service, mi Coronel?"

"General Rawson and Coronel Perón are coming to see you," Martín said. "Probably before, but possibly after, your father's memorial service."

"I've heard something . . ."

"What they want is OUTLINE BLUE . . ."

"Excuse me?"

"OUTLINE BLUE," Martín repeated, "and the money that has been collected in connection with OUTLINE BLUE."

"I really have no idea what you're talking about," Clete said.

Martín did not even acknowledge the denial.

"The reason I wanted to see you before they came was to suggest to you — as one reasonable professional to another — that it would be in everybody's best interest for you to hand it over to them."

"Not, to repeat, that I have any idea what you're talking about, but if I did have something like that, why would it be in my best interests to hand it over to you?"

"What I said, Mayor Frade —"

"*Señor* Frade, if you don't mind, mi Coronel."

"Excuse me. My memory seems to be about as bad as yours. What I actually said, *Señor* Frade, was that it would be 'in *everybody's* best interests,' not just yours, to turn over OUTLINE BLUE and the money to General Rawson. I can understand why you wouldn't want to turn it over to me."

"Not to you? I mean if I knew what you're talking about, and if I had it."

"You're a professional, as I am. You don't know who I'm really working for. If I were in your shoes . . ."

Clete remembered then that Enrico had said that Martín "was now one of us."

Does this guy really think I'm a professional? Or is that el soft soapo?

"Tell me why it would be in everybody's best interests. Yours for example, mi Coronel."

"At half past nine this morning, General Ramírez

380

went to your house on Libertador to meet with General Rawson and el Coronel Perón. The subject of their conversation was to be how to retrieve OUTLINE BLUE, and the money, from your safe."

"You seem pretty sure it's in my safe. How is that? And what safe are we talking about, mi Coronel?"

Martín smiled at him and shrugged.

"I didn't think this would be easy," he said. "But if you insist . . . Since OUTLINE BLUE and the money are not in the house on Coronel Díaz, or in the Libertador House, or in any of your father's safety-deposit boxes."

"You looked, did you?"

"Let us say I am confident about what I just said," Martín said. "So, by the process of elimination, *and* because keeping it here would have made more sense to your father than keeping it anywhere else, I think we can all reasonably presume that it's here. Specifically, in the safe in your father's private study."

"Is that the safe Señora Carzino-Cormano was asking you about, Enrico? The one you said only el Coronel had the combination to?"

"Sí, Señor Mayor."

"Forgive me, Suboficial Mayor," Martín said. "But not only do I think that you know the combination to the safe, but el Coronel Perón thinks you do, too. He told General Ramírez that last night."

Enrico looked very uncomfortable.

"You were telling me why it would be in your best interests if I gave it to Rawson, if I had what you're talking about," Clete said.

"Again, I said, 'everybody's best interests,' " Martín said.

"OK, everybody's," Clete said.

"A good many officers, friends of your father's, who feel as he did that the present government of Argentina must be replaced . . ."

"Let's stop the fencing," Clete said. "What's in it for you, mi Coronel, if I hand over OUTLINE BLUE, and the money, to you?"

Martín met Clete's eyes.

"It would keep me from receiving an order I would much prefer not to carry out."

"What order would that be?"

"To take whatever steps are necessary to obtain OUTLINE BLUE and the money."

"And what would be in it for me?" Clete asked.

"Aside from my profound gratitude, you mean?" Martín asked, smiling.

"Aside from your profound gratitude."

"What did you have in mind?"

Christ, he called my bluff. He's a professional, and he knows when to call a bluff. So what do I say now? Think, for Christ's sake!

That SS colonel!

"An SS colonel arrived on the same plane as el Coronel Perón from Germany —" Clete said.

"Goltz," Martín interrupted. "Josef Goltz. What about him?"

"I'm a curious man, mi Coronel. Who is he, and what does he want here?"

"He's in the secret service of the SS," Martín said. "I have no idea what he's doing here. What's your interest in him?"

"I'm wondering if he's the man who ordered my father's murder."

"A moment ago you suggested we stop fencing. Very well. I don't really know if he ordered your father's assassination, but it's probable. I do know

382

that early this morning he ordered the assassination of your man Ettinger. I learned that just before we took off."

Ettinger? And not me? What the hell is that all about?

"I don't suppose you'd want to tell me who told you that? From General Ramírez?"

Martín shook his head and smiled. "A reliable source," he said.

"I don't suppose your reliable source had any specifics on when and where? Or, for that matter, why?"

Martín shook his head.

"Only the sooner the better. I would regard the threat as very real if I were you, Señor Frade."

I believe him. And if he knows about that, it's one more proof that he's a professional, and I am out of my league trying to match wits with him. I don't have any choice but to trust him.

"Where is it, Enrico?" Clete asked.

"Where is what, Señor?"

"OUTLINE BLUE."

"In el Coronel's . . . in your apartment, Señor Clete."

Clete gestured with his hand for Martín to rise, then led him out of the library, down the corridor, and into what was now his room.

"Is there a safe in here, too?" Clete asked.

"No, Señor," Enrico said.

He went to the bed, pulled up the bed cover, and shoved his hand under the mattress. He came out with the blue folder, walked to Clete, and handed it to him.

Martín chuckled.

"Since I can't believe that el Coronel Frade really hid that under his mattress, would it be reasonable for me to assume you've been in the safe?"

Clete didn't answer. He simply handed Martín OUTLINE BLUE.

"Thank you," Martín said. "Believe me. This is the right thing to do."

"I hope so," Clete said.

"The money?"

"That's in the safe."

"Is it all still there?"

"I would suppose so. I don't think anybody else has been in there."

I know nobody else has been in there. If anybody had, the money would be gone, and so would Peter's papers and money.

"Have you read this?"

"Just glanced through it."

"But enough to tell you how dangerous this would be in the wrong hands?"

Clete nodded.

"I really am grateful," Martín said. "So will a number of other people be grateful."

"Just keep me up to date on Colonel Goltz's plans for Ettinger," Clete said, "and we'll call it square."

"I would have done that anyway," Martín said. "I am offended at the notion of a foreigner coming into my country, cloaked in diplomatic immunity, and ordering someone killed. Are you sure there's nothing else I can do for you?"

"How good are you at obtaining import permits?"

"What kind of import permits?"

"For an airplane, for example."

"What kind of an airplane?"

"My father's airplane seems to be missing."

"A rumor is going around that it's on the bottom

of Samborombón Bay, near where the *Reine de la Mer* blew up."

"I hadn't heard that," Clete said. "Anyway, I need an airplane."

"Why?"

"For someone obviously aware of the advantages of having a light airplane at your disposal, that's an odd question, wouldn't you say?"

"Indulge me."

"I have recently learned that I have a vineyard in Córdoba. . . ."

"Of course, San Bosco."

"And other property around the country."

"And you'd like to be able to fly around and look at it from time to time, is that it?"

"Right."

"Well, import permits are a little out of my line, but I'll look into it for you."

"Thanks."

"What kind of a plane did you have in mind to import? Another stagger-wing?"

"They don't make stagger-wings anymore, unfortunately. But I happen to know where I can lay my hands on a twin-engine Beech — same manufacturer — in Brazil."

"In Brazil? You mean you could fly it in? It wouldn't have to be brought in by ship?"

"It could be flown in."

"That might make things a good deal simpler. Let me ask some questions."

"Discreet questions, please, mi Coronel."

"Of course, discreet questions," Martín said. "And now I am somewhat embarrassed to find myself imposing on your generosity again."

"How is that?"

"Do you think you could find a briefcase, or a

small suitcase, to carry OUTLINE BLUE in?"

"Enrico?"

"Sí, mi Coronel," Enrico said. "There are several briefcases here. There's probably one in the sitting closet here."

"See if you can find one, would you, please?" Clete asked.

Enrico nodded and left the bedroom.

"Do you want the money, too?" Clete asked.

"I've been thinking about that," Martín said. "If you don't mind, I'll leave it where it is for the time being. Money by itself is not incriminating."

"Whatever you say," Clete said. "What if General Rawson asks for it?"

"I'd give it to him, or if he should send his aide for it, Capitán Lauffer — you've met him — I'd give it to him. No one else, I would think."

Clete nodded. Enrico came back into the room carrying a somewhat worn-looking briefcase.

"Perfect," Martín said, taking it from him. "I'll return it, of course."

"Enrico tells me that money is to 'ensure the success' of OUTLINE BLUE."

Martín looked at him coldly.

"If you're asking, politely, if it's bribe money, yes, I'm afraid it is," he said. "That offends you?"

" 'We mutually pledge to each other our lives, our Fortunes, and our sacred Honor,' " Clete quoted. "That's from our Declaration of Independence. . . ."

"I know," Martín said. "I'm familiar with it."

"In our revolution, our guys took a chance. I saw where my father signed OUTLINE BLUE. He took a chance. But I didn't see anybody else's signature on OUTLINE BLUE. And everybody seems perfectly comfortable with the idea of bribing people."

"I wouldn't say anyone involved in this is comfortable with it. It's necessary."

"Why?"

"There are two kinds of officers in the Argentine Army and Navy," Martín said. "Those like your father, perhaps ten, fifteen percent, who have no need to concern themselves with a salary or pension. For the others, losing their commissions and their pensions, as they would if OUTLINE BLUE fails, would mean the end of their livelihoods. Understandably, they want to protect their families —"

"As a practical matter, has anybody considered what these 'patriots' you're buying are going to do if somebody comes along with more money?"

"For what this is worth, Señor Frade, your father had similar moral objections. The issue was debated at some length. It was decided that at whatever cost, the revolution should be bloodless. Having said that, I do not wish to discuss it further. Forgive me, but it's really none of your business, is it?"

"I don't know if it is or not," Clete said. "If they can't carry off OUTLINE BLUE, I might be in a little trouble myself."

"I wouldn't worry about that," Martín said. "You're a norteamericano."

"Oh, but I'm not. I'm an Argentine."

"That's right, isn't it?" Martín said. "I keep forgetting that. I try, but I guess it's hard for me to think of you as an Argentine."

"Maybe you should try harder, mi Coronel. I'm going to be around awhile."

"I promise you I will," Martín said. He closed

the briefcase, then offered his hand to Clete. "Thank you for all your courtesies."

"My pleasure, mi Coronel," Clete said. "Any time."

[Two]

Estancia San Pedro y San Pablo
Near Pila, Buenos Aires Province
1140 11 April 1943

Clete stood with Enrico on the verandah, waiting for the Fieseler Storch to take off.

He could hear the pilot test the magnetos, and then the roar as he pushed the throttle to takeoff power. Much sooner than he expected, the airplane appeared above the cedar tree windbreak in a slow, incredibly steep climb.

He's showing off, of course, the sonofabitch. But look at that thing climb!

The pilot dipped the wings, waving good-bye, and then passed over the house.

Christ, the flaps are as big as the wings. No wonder he could get it off that way!

"What do you think of Martín, Enrico?"

"For a clown, he is not so bad. Of course, he is a cavalry officer."

"There is no such thing as a bad cavalry officer, right?"

"That is not what I said, Señor Clete."

"How do you feel about aviators, Enrico?"

"El Coronel wondered why you did not go into the cavalry, Señor Clete."

"We don't have cavalry anymore," Clete said. "But in the Marine Corps, we sort of think of airplanes as flying horses."

Enrico considered that carefully but didn't reply.

"I'm going to take a ride," Clete said.

"To see el Jefe" — the Chief — "I will go with you, Señor Clete."

"And Ettinger," Clete said. "You are not going. You are full of holes, and I don't want you bleeding all over a horse. It will attract flies, and annoy the horse."

Enrico looked at him long enough to decide that argument would be futile.

"Rudolpho will go with you," he announced.

"OK. If either Señora Carzino-Cormano or my Uncle Humberto arrives before I come back, do not tell them where I am."

"Sí, Señor Clete."

With Enrico on his heels, Clete turned and walked down the corridor toward the entrance foyer, where Antonio intercepted him.

"Is there anything I can do for you, Señor?"

"I'm going for a ride."

"I will lay out riding clothes for you."

"Antonio, I'm a Texas Aggie. This is all the riding clothes a Texas Aggie needs."

He pulled up his khakis to reveal his boots.

"Whatever you wish, of course, Señor Cletus," Antonio said.

As they walked across the garden to the stables, Enrico asked, "Señor Clete, what is a 'Texas Aggie'?"

"A despoiler of virgins, Enrico. A drinker of hard whiskey, and above all, a superb horseman."

Enrico nodded.

Twenty or more saddles were in the tack room,

neatly straddling leather padded sawhorses. There were two sidesaddles and a half-dozen hornless saddles, apparently for polo. The rest were *recados,* hornless, long-stirruped saddles that were used with a thick sheepskin pad under the rider.

Clete impulsively chose one of the latter, hoisted it onto his shoulder, and went into the stable. There was room for forty animals, each in an individual stall. Nearly all the stalls held horses. Clete noticed that Enrico was no longer with him.

"Where the hell are you when I need you?" he asked aloud. "One of these animals is a vicious sonofabitch who would toss Gene Autry on his ass, and that's the one I'll pick."

Enrico appeared a moment later, followed by Rudolpho, who had a *recado* over his shoulder. Enrico carried a short-barreled bolt-action Mauser rifle in his hand.

"What do I ride, Enrico?"

"Your father was fond of Julius Caesar, Señor Clete," Enrico said, pointing to an obviously high-spirited black stallion that had put its head out of its stall and was looking at them curiously.

"Fine," Clete said, and started for the stall.

Rudolpho's eyebrows rose, and Enrico picked up on it.

"Señor Cletus is a fine horseman," he said. "He is a *Texas Aggie.*"

That being said, I'll get on him, and he will toss me before we get out of the yard.

"I will saddle him for you," Enrico said.

"No, you won't," Clete said.

As he saddled Julius Caesar, the horse tried to bite him. And when he led him out of the stables into the yard and tried to mount him, Julius Caesar not only shied but tried to bite him again. A few moments later, he swung into the saddle and moved across the yard to establish who was in charge. When Clete jerked on his bit, Julius Caesar reared.

Clete kept his seat, but Uncle Jim's Stetson came off.

Julius Caesar put his front feet back on the ground, took two or three delicate steps, and then reared again.

"Goddamn you! If you stepped on that hat, you sonofabitch, you're cat food!" Clete told him, as he jerked hard on the bit and kicked him hard in the ribs.

Julius Caesar came down from his rear again — then, as if he had decided that Clete was a horseman worthy to ride him, suddenly gentled down.

Enrico picked up the Stetson and handed it to Clete, who saw approval and amusement in the old soldier's eyes.

"*Cat food*, Señor Clete?"

Jesus, if Enrico understood that, I must have cussed him out in Spanish!

Rudolpho, on a wiry roan, moved beside him. He held the Mauser easily, vertically, its butt on his leg.

They rode out of the yard, through the garden, and started down the road. They passed a dozen workers, each of whom took off his hat when he saw Clete and stood waiting for him to pass.

I feel like Don Pancho Spaniard, father of the dark-eyed beauty Gene Autry's got the hots for, on his hacienda down Mexico way in the movie of the same name, accepting the humble salute of his people.

I should feel embarrassed, the way I was in the car. But now I don't. How come?

He nodded at each man and smiled.

Five hundred yards down the road, Rudolpho turned off it and onto the pampas. Clete nudged Julius Caesar with his heels and the animal broke into a canter. Just to see what the horse would do, Clete applied the pressure of his left knee and made as faint a tug on the reins as he could manage. Julius Caesar immediately turned to the left. And a moment later, when Clete applied right-knee pressure — no reins — the horse turned in the other direction.

Damned well-trained horse. No wonder my father liked him. Did he train him himself? Is this a polo pony? Aren't they smaller than this?

I'm going to have to try polo, real polo. Why not? There's two polo fields here, and it can't be all that difficult. I don't care how small the ball is, I can probably learn to whack it with a little practice.

The polo Clete had played, on Big Foot Ranch outside Midland and at College Station, was played with brooms, a volleyball, and on cow ponies, and, every once in a while, on a well-trained quarter horse, just for the hell of it.

What the hell are you thinking about? Playing polo, for Christ's sake?

Without thinking about it, he touched the reins. Julius Caesar, who had been trying to push his nose ahead of Rudolpho's roan, obediently moved behind him.

"Rudolpho, is it safe to gallop here?" he called.

"Sí, Señor."

"Let's go, then," Clete said.

Rudolpho touched the roan with his spurs and shouted something to him Clete couldn't understand. The roan broke into a gallop. Julius Caesar's ears stood up. Clete touched his heels to him, and the animal broke into a gallop.

Julius Caesar was larger and faster than Rudol-pho's roan, and a minute later, passed him. Clete saw that at a full gallop the only change in Rudol-pho's seat was that he no longer supported the Mauser on his knee. Now he had it cradled in his arm, like a hunter. He looked as comfortable as someone sitting in his armchair.

Well, that shatters your foolish belief that you really know how to ride a horse about as well as anybody, doesn't it?

Five minutes later, now moving at a walk to cool the horses, Clete realized that he had no idea where he was. There was nothing from horizon to horizon but the rolling pampas, dotted with cattle and groves of eucalyptus and pine trees. No sign of a road, or even a power line or a fence.

He had a sobering thought: *If I had come out here by myself, and damned fool that I am, that's exactly what I intended to do, I not only couldn't have found the station, but I would have been lost, and they would have had to send somebody to find me.*

Twenty minutes later, they topped a small rise and Clete scanned the horizon. There was a glint of reflected light high in a stand of pine trees several hundred yards directly ahead. It disappeared, and then reappeared. He shielded his eyes with his hand and looked again. It was gone.

He looked again a minute or so later, and it was again visible. He had just decided it was white, and a couple of inches long — and thus probably man-made — when there was proof. There was a faint but unmistakable glint off copper wire.

A radio antenna. They were approaching the station.

It was only when they were no more than fifty yards from the thick trees that he could see through them far enough to pick out automobiles and trucks. Three of them — immaculately maintained Ford Model A pickup trucks — belonged to the estancia. And there was a 1940 Chevrolet business coupe and a 1941 Studebaker sedan. Tony Pelosi's and Dave Ettinger's cars, he decided, although he didn't know which car belonged to which.

They entered the trees, and a hundred yards inside came to a small clearing that held three buildings made of reddish sandstone. A large, somewhat florid-faced man in a gaucho's Saturday-Night-Go-to-the-Cantina costume emerged from the largest building. His flat, wide-brimmed black gaucho's hat was at a suitably cocky angle. He wore a red bandanna rolled around his neck, a flowing white blouse, topped with a black, red-embroidered vest, billowing black trousers, and soft, thigh-high black boots. There was a menacing-looking, silver-handled dagger in a leather sheath on his belt. And he held a silver Mate* jar with a silver straw in his hand. He smiled at Clete.

"Buenos tardes, Señor."

He looks more like a gaucho than Rudolpho. The only thing he won't do is get on a horse.

Clete smiled at him, then touched his right hand to his temple in a crisp salute.

"Permission to come aboard, Chief?"

Chief Radioman Oscar J. Schultz, USN, returned the salute crisply.

"Permission granted, Sir," he said. "Welcome aboard."

Clete slid off Julius Caesar.

---

* An herbal tea, also favored by Arabians, who for well over a century have been the best export customers of the Argentine Mate plantations in Corrientes Province.

"I like the hat," Chief Schultz said, offering his hand.

"Thank you."

"If I'd had a little warning, I could have arranged for side boys," Chief Schultz said, and then, remembering, added soberly, "I'm sorry as hell about your father, Mr. Frade."

"Thank you. It's good to see you, Chief."

"You're just in time for lunch," Chief Schultz said, pointing inside the house. "Mr. Pelosi and Sergeant Ettinger are here. They told me you would be coming, but not when."

Tony and Dave Ettinger — a tall, dark-eyed, sharp-featured man in his late twenties, in his shirtsleeves — were seated at a wooden table. There were bowls of tomatoes, onions, and red and green peppers, and what looked like ten pounds of two-inch-thick New York strip steaks on a wooden platter.

They were being served by a dark-haired woman in her thirties, wearing a white blouse, a billowing black skirt, and what Clete thought of as gaucho boots. She smiled nervously at Clete and looked between him and Chief Schultz.

I wouldn't be at all surprised, Clete thought, *if the lady keeps the Chief warm on cold pampas nights — at least when Tony and Ettinger aren't here.*

The Chief attributed his near-perfect Spanish to the "sleeping dictionary" he had known during a tour at the Cavite Naval Base in the Philippines.

"Buenos tardes," Clete said, smiling at her.

"Buenos tardes, Patrón," she said.

"That's Dorothéa," Chief Schultz said.

Well, that's nice. I'll have to be careful to see the two ladies are not confused.

"She's helping you perfect your Spanish, Chief?"

Clete said as he slipped into a chair and offered his hand to Ettinger.

"Yeah, and she's a not half-bad cook, too," Chief Schultz said.

"I'm sorry about your father, Major," Ettinger said.

"Thank you," Clete said. "And just for the record, I'm out of the Marine Corps."

"Tony was telling me something about that."

Dorothéa extended the platter of New York strip steaks — called *bife de chorizo* — to Clete and he took one. Dorothéa filled a second plate with tomatoes, onions, and pepper.

"Señorita," Clete began.

"Señora," Chief Schultz corrected him. "She's a widow."

"And you're the answer to a widow's prayer, right?" Clete said in English, and then, in Spanish, went on, "Señora, please find Rudolpho and tell him I said to come in and eat."

"Sí, Patrón."

"Tony wasn't very clear about the nature of our relationship to Commander Delojo," Ettinger said.

"I thought I made it pretty clear, Tony," Clete said, "that I remain in command of this team — and that includes you, Chief Schultz. That means you have no relationship to Commander Delojo except through me. That answer your question, Dave?"

"Not precisely," Ettinger said. "Tony said you met Mr. Leibermann." Clete nodded. "I've been passing some things I've developed to Leibermann. Shall I do the same sort of thing for Commander Delojo?"

Clete felt a surge of anger. Ettinger was a damned good man, but he seemed unable to grasp that he was in the military — he was in the Army Counterintelligence Corps, on 'detail' to the OSS — and that in the military one is not permitted to disobey orders that seem inconvenient or with which you disagree.

"What sort of things have you been passing to Leibermann, David?" Clete asked coldly.

"I've been working with the Jews here, the Argentine Jews and the refugees. . . ."

"I know that. What I want to know is what you've been passing to Leibermann."

"Nothing that has any connection with anything we're doing. I know how you feel about that."

"Then what, for Christ's sake?"

"The Argentine Jews are deeply involved in the shipping business. They've been giving me shipping manifests, sailing times, that sort of thing, for ships bound for Spain and Portugal, or allegedly bound for Spain and Portugal. Leibermann wants this sort of information, and — I don't mean to sound flip, but we *are* on the same side in this war — I can't see any harm in giving it to him."

Neither can I. And I would be wasting my breath to order Ettinger to stop.

"My orders — which are of course, your orders — are to have as little to do with the FBI as possible," Clete said.

"You're telling me to stop passing him this sort of information?"

"I'm telling you to have as little to do with the FBI as possible. And I would strongly suggest you do not, repeat not, ever let Commander Delojo become aware that you even know Leibermann."

"OK," Ettinger said. "That answers my question about what to tell him about Uruguay."

"Tell him what about Uruguay?"

"I'm just getting to the bottom of it," Ettinger said. "I haven't even told Tony about it."

That was my cue to sternly remind Ettinger that Tony is Lieutenant *Pelosi, that in my absence* Lieutenant *Pelosi becomes Team Chief, and that* Sergeant *Ettinger is duty bound to tell* Lieutenant *Pelosi anything and everything of interest.*

But that, too, would be a waste of breath. Ettinger long ago figured out that the only reason Tony is down here is because he knows a lot about explosives and demolition, and that everything he knows about espionage and intelligence gathering can be written with a grease pencil inside a matchbook. And the truth is, Ettinger would probably make better Team Chief than I am, and for that matter, a better Station Chief than Delojo. The only reason he's not an officer is because he's a Spanish national, and the U.S. Army is not commissioning Spanish nationals.

"Tell us now," Clete said.

"I can't prove this. I can't get anybody to come out and say this is being done — all I get is doors slammed in my face, conversations suddenly ended —"

"Prove what?" Clete asked in exasperation as he put another piece of *bife de chorizo* in his mouth.

"I think, if you have a relative in Sachsenhausen, or Belsen — probably any concentration camp, but those are the only names I've heard —" Ettinger said, "that, if you go to the right man in Uruguay, carrying with you a lot of dollars or Swiss francs, you can get him, her, the whole family out."

"I'll be damned," Clete said. "Are you sure about this?"

"No. Not in the sense that I can prove it. But I believe it."

"Who's the right man in Uruguay? Somebody at

the German Embassy? Do you have a name?"

"No. No name. But I don't think it's someone at their Embassy. I think the connection is from the right man in the Jewish community here, to the right man in the Jewish community in Montevideo, or maybe Colonia, and from there to whoever they're dealing with in the German Embassy. Or, for that matter, the Spanish Embassy or the Swedish Embassy. I told you, Clete. Nobody wants to talk about it."

"Not even to you?" Clete said. "Sorry, I had to ask that."

Ettinger's entire family had been taken into concentration camps in Germany . . . except for his mother, who had managed to escape from Germany with her son because they still had their Spanish passports. There had been official word from the SS that his grandfather and grandmother had "died of complications from pneumonia," but there had been no other word of anyone else.

"I picked up on this whole operation when an old man I knew in Berlin told me it was a pity I went to New York instead of here, 'where something might have been done.' "

"You think he meant you could have brought your family out?"

"This fellow was brought out," Ettinger said. "I saw the SS tattoo, the SS numbers, on his arm."

"And he won't tell you anything more?"

Ettinger shook his head, "no."

"The big mistake I made when we first came down here was telling Ernst Klausner, somebody else I knew in Berlin, that I was in the American Army; he's apparently spread the word. My feeling is that they have this system going, and they don't want anything to happen that will threaten it."

"Christ, don't they know we're fighting the goddamn Krauts?" Tony said.

"They don't want whatever is going on to be threatened," Ettinger repeated. "American interest in what's happened, is happening, to European Jews, Tony, is a relatively new thing."

"What happens to the people who get out of the concentration camps?" Clete wondered aloud.

"Apparently, they're provided with documents that take them out of Germany. To Sweden, maybe, or Spain. And then either to here or Uruguay. I don't know. The old man is here; he got out of a concentration camp, and then out of Germany somehow. He couldn't have done that without papers."

"Have you said anything to Leibermann at all about this?" Clete asked.

"No," Ettinger said, and added: "I was waiting for you to come back, and to find out more, if I can."

"I don't want you to say anything at all about this to Leibermann, David."

Ettinger nodded, accepting the order.

"I think we have to pass this to Colonel Graham," Clete said.

"I was afraid you'd say that," Ettinger said.

"That bothers you?"

"It's a moral problem for me," Ettinger said. "If there is a system, and people are getting out, I don't want to be the one responsible for shutting that system down."

"There may be, almost certainly is, something here that you and I don't know how to deal with," Clete said.

Ettinger, looking very unhappy, shrugged.

"What David just told us doesn't go anywhere,"

Clete said, looking at Tony and Chief Schultz in turn. Both nodded.

"There's something I have to tell you. I just got, from a source I trust —"

"Meaning you're not going to tell us who, of course?" Tony interrupted.

"No, I'm not," Clete said sharply. "And you know why. We operate on the premise that if any one of us is interrogated by a professional, sooner or later, and probably sooner, we'll tell him everything he wants to know. If you don't know something, you can't give it up, OK?"

"Sorry, Clete," Tony said, sounding genuinely remorseful.

"A German officer, an SS colonel named Goltz, came here on the Lufthansa flight the same day I did —"

"SS, or SS-SD?" Ettinger interrupted.

"SD. Does that mean something to you?"

"SD means Sicherheitsdienst. The Secret Police, so to speak. The real bastards."

"OK, this guy is SD. And we already have the proof that he's a bastard. This morning, this bastard issued orders to have you killed."

"No shit?" Tony asked. "Just Dave?"

"That would suggest, wouldn't it," Ettinger said, "that maybe I'm asking the right questions?"

"Just for the sake of argument, yes," Clete said. "And it would also suggest that this Colonel Goltz is connected with this business. He comes here, somebody tells him you're asking questions, and he says, 'eliminate him.' "

"I've been operating on the premise that such an order would be standard operating procedure. Eliminate anybody who's asking the wrong questions. Or stumbles onto something," Ettinger said.

"The Sicherheitsdienst is ruthless, and killing someone to keep a secret like this would be normal routine. You think this is something new?"

"According to my source — who I think is reliable — the order to eliminate you was issued this morning, by this Colonel Goltz. Maybe it's a coincidence — they didn't know you were asking questions until just now — but I don't think so."

"No," Ettinger said after a moment, "neither do I."

"Dave, do you have a gun?" Clete asked.

Ettinger nodded.

"He's got a little .38," Chief Schultz said. "I tried to get him to carry a .45, but he says he can't shoot a .45."

"I can't," Ettinger argued. "And a .45 is hard to conceal."

"It's your neck, Dave," Clete said. "Do what you think you should."

Ettinger nodded.

"Are we on the air, Chief?" Clete asked.

"Five by five," Chief Schultz replied.

"David, write down everything you know or suspect about this ransoming operation. Right now. Before I ride back to the estancia, I want to send this out."

Ettinger nodded his acceptance of the orders.

"Everything, David," Clete emphasized. "I want to tell Colonel Graham everything you know. And ask him if you should look deeper. For all we know, as far down on the totem pole as we are, they already know about this. They may just tell us to butt out."

"I've considered the possibility that Leibermann is aware of it. He's a very clever fellow."

Clete nodded in agreement.

"In the meantime, you don't go back to Buenos Aires until I tell you to."

"I can't ask very many questions here," Ettinger replied.

"We may get orders telling you not to ask any more questions, period."

"Clete, if you're right that the order to kill me was issued only this morning, I don't think they'd have time to set anything up. And I have a couple of people I'd like to talk to."

Christ, he simply does not know how to take an order!

"And there may be two guys outside your apartment this minute, waiting for you to show up. I don't want you killed. I need you. You stay here until I tell you otherwise, you understand?"

Ettinger threw up his hands in a gesture of surrender.

Clete turned to Chief Schultz. "Chief, in Washington they were really concerned about losing the station. I must have had six lectures on triangulation."

"No problem here, Mr. Frade," Chief Schultz said. "You know how that works?"

Clete nodded, and started to say "Yes, a little," but Chief Schultz went on without giving him the chance.

"First of all, they have to catch us on the air," he explained. "By two, preferably three, directional antennae mounted on trucks. One receiver won't cut the mustard. If they do happen to catch us, they won't be close. To really pinpoint a transmitter, you have to get close."

"And they can't get close here?"

"You know how big this place is? I got a map of it. And Mr. Pelosi stole an almanac from the embassy for me. This place takes in more than eighty thousand hectares. A hectare is about two point seven acres. That makes it more than two hundred thousand acres. *That's* three hundred twenty-five square miles. You know how big Manhattan Island is? Twenty square miles. This place is one-quarter the size of Rhode Island."

"We've got counties in Texas that big," Clete heard himself arguing. "Hell, I think the King Ranch takes in more than two hundred thousand acres."

Chief Schultz looked at him for a moment with the tolerant look a veteran chief petty officer gives young officers who cannot seem to grasp a simple explanation.

"Without coming on the property, Mr. Frade — and they can't do that without us hearing about it — they can't get close enough to us to get a good triangulation fix," he said. "In addition to which, I made the transmitter mobile."

"What?"

"I mounted one of the transmitters and a receiver on one of the Model A's, and a generator on another one. So what I can do is go three, four miles from here, rig a straight-wire antenna, fire it up, send the traffic, and then haul ass. Even if they got a triangulation fix on that site — which, like I say, is damned unlikely — by the time they got there there'd be nothing there but trees and cows."

"What about the antenna I saw in the trees?"

"That's a *receiver* antenna, Mr. Frade," Chief Schultz said tolerantly. "What we hear people calling *us* over."

Clete looked at Ettinger, who was an electrical engineer. Ettinger nodded. Chief Schultz was telling the truth.

"Well, perhaps not all chief petty officers are as

404

retarded as Marine officers are led to believe," Clete said. "Could I have a look at this mobile transmitter of yours?"

"You don't want to hear what Chiefs have to say about Marine officers, Mr. Frade," Chief Schultz said. "You just want a look at it, or do you want me to fire it up for you?"

"A look now, and after Mr. Ettinger has finished his report, I'd like to see it in operation."

"They're right out in back, Mr. Frade."

"Tell me about radar, Chief," Clete said after Schultz had completed his demonstration of his truck-mounted radio station.

"They're really sending one down here?"

"It's in Brazil, with a team to set it up and operate it."

"I think they're pissing into the wind," Schultz said.

"Tell me why."

"You know how it works?"

"Tell me."

"They found out — at Bell Labs, in New Jersey — that at the higher frequencies, radio waves bounce. So they send out directional radiation. You know what I'm talking about?"

Clete shook his head, "no."

"You try to narrow the radiation field. Like, a civilian broadcasting system tries to get a wide radiation pattern. Like a stone dropped in the water, you know? Expanding circles? So the signal can be picked up by as many receivers as possible?"

Clete nodded.

"With radar, you try to do the opposite. Send out as narrow a field of radiation as you can. Then you've got a receiving antenna. It looks like a great big saucer. The signals from the transmitter bounce back to the saucer. Still with me?"

Clete nodded again.

"The antenna moves, sometimes through a 360-degree circle, sometimes just through a part of the circle. OK. So if you're using the radar at sea, for example, the signals will *not* bounce back to the antenna, unless they hit something — a ship — that they can bounce off. When that happens, and the signals bounce back, all you have to do is figure how long it took them to do that."

"How do you do that?"

"Radio signals move at the speed of light. That's the constant. The radar can tell — this is the theory — how far away whatever the signal bounced off of is by how long it took the signal to come back. Then they can put that up on a cathode-ray tube. You know what that is?"

Clete shook his head, "no."

"Remember at the 1940 World's Fair in New York, when they broadcast pictures of people? What you saw the pictures on was a cathode-ray tube. So anyway, you mark on the screen the distances. So many microseconds for the signal to bounce back from whatever it hits — they call that the 'target' — and it's, say, two miles away. So many more microseconds, and it's, say, five miles away. And because you're pointing the receiving antenna — like the radio direction finder on airplanes — you know in what direction the target is. That's the theory, Mr. Frade."

"What's the reality?" Clete asked.

"They had radar at Henderson Field, right?"

"Yeah."

"What did it do?"

"When it worked, it told us when Jap airplanes were coming."

"That it'll do. And it'll tell you the direction. But not the distance with any precision. Mr. Pelosi said they told him they can locate something within a hundred yards. I'll believe that when I see it."

"And you don't expect to see it?"

Schultz shook his head, "no."

"Chief, what if the radar they sent down is absolutely the latest thing?"

"I'll believe it can locate something within a hundred yards when I see it."

"Where are we going to put it?"

"It works line of sight," Schultz said. "Which means the target has to be between the transmitter and the horizon. So it has to be on the highest ground you can find. On ships, they mount it as high aloft as they can get it. That's another problem here. The land here, by Samborombón Bay, is flat. There are only a couple of hills. If the Germans anchor their ship more than thirty miles offshore, then it will be over the horizon, and the radar won't work."

"The radar at Henderson Field spotted Jap planes a lot further away than thirty miles."

"When you aim at the sky, there's no horizon," Schultz explained. "The limiting factor there is really the strength of the bounced-back signal."

"In other words, you don't think this thing will work?"

"I'll believe it when I see it."

"If we can get it into the country, have you located a place where they can put it up?"

"Yes, Sir. And I got everything we need — concrete, timber, even a generator — to put it in operation."

"I really hope you're wrong, Chief," Clete said. "I don't want to have to locate that damned ship with a Piper Cub."

"Yeah," Chief Schultz said. "Well, I been wrong before, Mr. Frade."

Clete sensed that this was one of those times when Chief Schultz did not think he was wrong.

"Let's go back and see if Dave's finished his report," he said.

XIII

[One]

Office of the Minister of War
Edificio Libertador
Avenida Paseo Colón
Buenos Aires
1445 11 April 1943

Major Pedro V. Querro pushed open the left of the twelve-foot-tall double doors leading to the office of Teniente General Pedro P. Ramírez, waited until he had the attention of the Minister of War and then announced, "El Teniente Coronel Martín is here, mi General."

Like Querro, Ramírez was in civilian clothing. An hour before, Martín had called to tell him that it was important to see him immediately, and Ramírez directed Martín to meet him in his office. His home in the suburb of Belgrano — like those of other senior government officials — was patrolled by the Policía Federal, and he thought it likely that a note would be made if anyone saw the BIS counterintelligence chief paying him a Saturday-afternoon visit. He had been waiting for Martín for fifteen minutes, and he didn't like to wait for anyone.

Ramírez impatiently signaled for Querro to show

him in. Martín marched into the office, his brimmed cap under his left arm. At the last moment, he remembered his right hand was holding a briefcase, making it difficult to render the called-for salute.

Ramírez smiled as Martín hastily transferred the briefcase to his left hand, therefore causing the brimmed cap to be dislodged. Martín managed to catch it with the side of his arm before it fell to the carpet, and saluted. The maneuver fell somewhat short of the precision expected.

"Good afternoon, mi Coronel," Ramírez said as he returned the salute.

"May I suggest, mi General, that we close the door?" Martín said.

Ramírez again made an impatient gesture with his hand.

Querro started to close the door.

"Will my presence be required, mi General?" he asked.

"Martín?" Ramírez asked.

"I think it would be best, mi General," Martín said.

Querro closed the door, then marched across the room and took up a position behind Ramírez's desk.

"May I?" Martín said, holding the briefcase above Ramírez's desk.

Ramírez signaled that he could.

Martín set the briefcase on the desk, opened it, and handed OUTLINE BLUE to Ramírez.

Ramírez opened OUTLINE BLUE to the first page to confirm it was what he thought it was, then looked up at Martín.

"Where did you get this, Coronel?"

"From Señor Frade, mi General."

"I thought he was supposed to have gone to his estancia?"

"He did, mi General. I went down there."

"And the money?" Ramírez asked.

"In the safe at Estancia San Pedro y San Pablo, mi General."

"He wouldn't give it to you?"

"I thought it best to leave it in the safe, mi General."

"Your reasons?"

"I thought the money would be secure there until arrangements can be made to transport it. I went down there in a Fieseler."

"Hence the uniform? We don't often see you in uniform, Coronel."

"Sí, Señor."

"Two questions: Are you sure we can have the money when we want it, and how would you recommend transporting it?"

"I am sure the money will be available when we ask for it, mi General, and I would recommend transporting it by auto, suitably protected."

"When?"

"I don't think there would be time to make the necessary arrangements today. So tomorrow, during the memorial service for el Coronel Frade."

"Mi General," Querro said. "I can take half a dozen men down there this afternoon. I could be back by perhaps ten."

"And you don't think questions would be asked if my aide showed up down there, accompanied by half a dozen soldiers?" Ramírez said patiently. "Thank you, but no, Pedro. Let's leave this in the hands of an expert. Please go on, Coronel Martín."

"My recommendation, Señor, would be to send two officers —"

"Your men, Coronel?"

"No, Sir. I had in mind officers, majors or teniente coronels, who are members of Grupo de Oficiales Unidos. Officers who knew el Coronel Frade and whose presence at the memorial service would not attract curiosity. They would travel in one auto, and be accompanied by two other automobiles, each containing an officer and three men, preferably senior sub-Oficiales who are reliable, and who would of course be armed."

"You think Frade would turn the money over to an officer he's never met before, mi Coronel?" Querro asked.

Martín gave him a mildly sarcastic look that suggested he did not like to be questioned by any officer junior to him. Ramírez picked up on this and extended his left hand, palm outward, as a signal for Querro to shut up.

"I frankly didn't think that Frade would just turn OUTLINE BLUE over to me, mi General," Martín said. "My hope was that I could convince him to give it, and the money, to either General Rawson or Coronel Perón."

"I want to talk about that in a moment," Ramírez said. "But go on."

"In that circumstance, I presumed that General Rawson would have made provision for the safe transport of both OUTLINE BLUE and the money."

"Are you familiar, Pedro, with anything like that?"

"No, Señor."

Ramírez looked at Martín and shrugged.

"When Señor Frade gave me OUTLINE BLUE, mi General, I did the only thing I could think of at the time. I brought OUTLINE BLUE here, and I left the money in the safe. By now General Rawson

412

has learned that I have OUTLINE BLUE and that the money is in the safe."

"They're at Señora Carzino-Cormano's estancia. Did you go there?"

"No, Señor. But I sent word to General Rawson."

"How?"

"One of the pilots at Estancia San Pedro y San Pablo is a retired officer. I saw him just before I took off to come back to Buenos Aires."

"A retired officer who works for you, you mean?"

Martín didn't reply to that question.

"I now suggest, mi General — presuming you agree with my suggestion that the money should be entrusted to G.O.U. officers?"

Ramírez nodded. Martín went on: "I suggest that late tonight, or very early in the morning, we send the officers I mentioned to Estancia Santo Catalina with instructions to report to General Rawson. When I left Señor Frade, I suggested that he give the money to either General Rawson or his aide, Capitán Lauffer, if either should ask for it. Both General Rawson and Coronel Perón are more familiar with Estancia San Pedro y San Pablo than I am; and they will be there in any event for the memorial service."

"Leave the method up to them, right?"

"Sí, Señor."

"Very shortly, Major Querro and I will pay a surprise visit to the First Regiment of Cavalry at Campo de Mayo," Ramírez said, "where I will have a discreet word with several officers of my acquaintance. They will be at Estancia Santo Catalina first thing in the morning, in the manner you propose, in other words, accompanied by armed and trustworthy personnel, and will report to General

413

Rawson for specific orders."

"Sí, Señor."

"General Rawson will give them specific instructions about how to carry out their mission, and, in one way or another, they will go to Estancia San Pedro y San Pablo and take charge of the funds in question."

"Sí, Señor."

"There is one potential problem area in this outline, Coronel. Do you know what it is?"

"I don't think I understand, mi General," Martín said.

"It all depends on your faith in Frade. How do we *know* that he will turn the money over to us tomorrow? That he will not, for example, change his mind tonight? For that matter, remove the money from the safe tonight?"

"We have no way of knowing that for sure, mi General."

"I can go down there and get it myself, mi General, and be back by ten tonight," Major Querro offered again.

Ramírez ignored him completely.

"Tell me why you believe that Frade will not change his mind, Coronel."

"In my business, mi General, it is sometimes necessary to trust your intuition," Martín said.

"In the Infantry, we use our intuition based on the facts we have," Ramírez said. "I'm curious about Frade's motives. Why did he turn it over to you? For all he knew, you could be working for Castillo. What did he want in return?"

"I believe his primary motivation was that he saw his father's signature on the Purpose Page of OUTLINE BLUE, mi General."

"That might explain his turning it over to me,

414

or General Rawson, or Juan Domingo Perón, but not to you. From all we've heard of him, he's a professional intelligence officer."

"Sí, mi General, he is that."

"And professional intelligence officers, I have been told, don't trust anyone without reason. Good reason. Does Frade have some reason, some good reason, to trust you?"

"Sí, Señor."

"Would you like to tell me what that is?"

"I would prefer not to, mi General."

Ramírez considered that for a long moment.

"Very well, Coronel. But can you assure me Frade's cooperation was not based on your promise of cooperation in the future?"

"Mi General, it is not at all uncommon for intelligence officers to make arrangements with their counterparts," Martín said. "But I have offered Frade nothing more than that. I would not tell him anything I don't think he should know, and he would not expect me to."

"He asked for nothing?"

"He asked about an import permit for an airplane to replace the Beechcraft which is missing."

Ramírez grunted. "This 'arrangement' between intelligence officers fascinates me. Could you give me an example?"

"It has come to my attention that the Germans have ordered the assassination of one of Frade's men. I told him that."

"How did you come by that?" Querro asked.

Martín did not reply to Querro but looked at Ramírez.

"I would say, Pedro," Ramírez said, "that you don't have the need to know that," he said, and turned to Martín and asked, "You believe the Germans will kill this man?"

"Sí, Señor, I believe they will try."

"Certainly, you can do something to keep that from happening?"

"Not very much, Señor. Only by providing him with protection, overtly, or covertly, mi General. And there would be no guarantee at —"

"Do so."

"Excuse me?"

"Do so, Coronel. Do whatever you have to do to keep Frade's man from being assassinated."

"Señor, I couldn't provide one-fourth the protection that would be the minimum required without it coming to el Almirante Montoya's attention. It would require many people, and a good deal of money."

"The last Bureau of Internal Security budget I saw, Coronel, was anything but parsimonious."

"Señor, what I was suggesting is that I could not order such an operation on my own authority. And to report that I was doing so on your orders . . ."

"Would tell Montoya that we have been in touch? Is that what you're saying?"

"Sí, mi General."

Ramírez considered that for a moment.

"Pedro, get el Almirante on the telephone, please. I'll tell him, Martín, that I have learned of this threat and authorize him to authorize you to do whatever is necessary to reduce the threat to zero."

"Señor? Permission to speak, mi General?" Martín said.

"Frankly, Coronel, I am rapidly tiring of debating this with you. But go ahead."

"Señor, I have reason to believe that the Germans have someone in BIS. If Almirante Montoya is aware that we know about this German decision, the Germans will learn that he knows."

"The Germans have someone inside BIS?" Ramírez asked incredulously.

"I believe so, Señor."

"Well, so what if the Germans know we know? It might make them reconsider."

"It would also let them know we have someone in . . . in their embassy, Señor. My source would be compromised."

"An important source? Important to the security of Argentina?"

"Sí, Señor."

"Shall I get el Almirante on the phone for you, mi General?" Querro asked. He had a telephone in his hand.

Ramírez waved his hand, "no," and Querro replaced the receiver in its cradle.

"With Argentina's interests as the criterion, Coronel, is this source worth this man's life?"

"Sí, Señor. That would be my very reluctant conclusion."

"You have no one you could assign to this?"

"I had already planned to increase the surveillance on Frade and the others, mi General. But beyond that . . ."

"And you have warned him, haven't you?"

"Sí, Señor. And if anything else comes to my attention that I can tell him without putting my source at risk, I intend to tell it to him."

"That would seem to be about all you can do under the circumstances," Querro volunteered.

"Thank you very much, Mayor, for that astute observation," Martín said, icily sarcastic.

Ramírez looked between them.

"About this aircraft import license Frade asked

417

for," he said. "Would the import of an airplane for him, his use of an airplane, pose a serious threat to Argentine security?"

"No, Señor. And there are other aircraft available to him."

"Can you obtain the permit for him?"

"It might be difficult, mi General," Martín said. "And it would be impossible to keep quiet. There would be curiosity about BIS asking for an aircraft import permit for Señor Frade."

"So you're saying it would be ill-advised."

"On the way here from the estancia, in the airplane, I thought of an irregular way to accomplish it."

"By 'irregular' you doubtless mean 'illegal,' " Ramírez said.

"Sí, Señor."

"How illegal?"

"Aircraft registration numbers are painted on the tail and on the wing. When an aircraft lands somewhere, the airport authorities write down these numbers and put them in a file. Afterward, they are seldom, if ever, seen again by human eyes."

"Oh?"

"It occurred to me that if someone wished to paint the registration numbers of an already registered aircraft on another aircraft — in other words, to substitute aircraft — I very much doubt anyone would notice."

"Unless the original aircraft showed up," Ramírez said thoughtfully.

"I don't think that's likely in this case," Martín said.

"Wouldn't the name of the manufacturer of the aircraft appear somewhere?"

"Both el Coronel Frade's missing aircraft and

the aircraft Señor Frade wishes to bring into Argentina were manufactured by Beech."

"Then there would be no problem at all, is that what you're saying?"

"There is one small problem. El Coronel Frade's missing airplane had one engine. The other aircraft has two."

"Well, you're a very resourceful fellow, Coronel," Ramírez said. "A little thing like the number of engines shouldn't be too difficult for you to deal with."

"Another thought occurred to me, mi General: If something goes wrong when OUTLINE BLUE is executed, an aircraft that can fly six, and in a pinch, eight, people to Uruguay might be nice to have."

"Your resourcefulness never ceases to amaze me, Coronel," Ramírez said.

[Two]

Office of the Director
The Office of Strategic Services
Washington, D.C.
1930 11 April 1943

"Come on in, Alex," Colonel William J. Donovan, a stocky, well-tailored man in his fifties, said, looking up from his desk. "What have you got?"

Colonel A. (Alejandro) F. (Fredrico) Graham, USMCR, laid a large, torn-open manila envelope on Donovan's desk and settled himself in a green leather armchair.

419

Donovan went into the envelope and extracted a slightly smaller envelope, also recently torn open. It was stamped TOP SECRET in red letters, top and bottom, on both sides. From this he extracted three stapled-together sheets of paper.

The first sheet of paper was a U.S. Government Inter-Office Memorandum. It was from the Chief of Naval Intelligence and addressed to the Deputy Director for Western Hemisphere Operations, Office of Strategic Services, and announced that transmitted herewith by officer courier was nondecrypted message N-45-7643 (no copies made) of a communication received from Station Aggie at 1505 hours 13 April 1943.

The second sheet of paper contained many lines of apparently meaningless five-letter words (e.g., AKLQE MXCBI PISLA TDEQF).

The third sheet of paper was stamped TOP SECRET in red, top and bottom, and was headed: DECRYPTION OF USN # N-45-7643. Donovan tore that from the top two sheets and dropped them, plus the two manila envelopes, into one of two wastebaskets at the side of his desk. This one held a white paper bag on which was printed in several places, in four-inch-high red letters, the phrase BURN TOP SECRET BURN.

Donovan's expression clearly intended to convey to Graham the idea that his time was too valuable to waste tearing unimportant pieces of paper from important pieces of paper, and that Graham should have performed this bureaucratic task himself.

If Colonel Graham felt rebuked, he offered no apology. And there was no sign on his face that he regretted annoying Colonel Donovan.

Donovan started to read the decrypted message:

```
TOP SECRET

DECRYPTION OF USN #N-45-7643

URGENT TOP SECRET

FROM STACHIEF AGGIE
1555 GREENWICH 11APR43

  MSG NO 0001

  TO ORACLE WASHDC

  EYES ONLY FOR DDWHO GRAHAM

  1. SARNOFF HAS DEVELOPED HIGHLY
RELIABLE INFORMATION THAT AT
LEAST ONE GERMAN-JEWISH MALE IN-
CARCERATED IN SACHSENHAUSEN CON-
CENTRATION CAMP WAS RELEASED AND
PERMITTED TO LEAVE GERMANY AND
PROCEED TO ARGENTINA POSSIBLY VIA
URUGUAY FOLLOWING PAYMENT OF SUB-
STANTIAL AMOUNT OF MONEY TO GERMAN
AGENT, OR REPRESENTATIVE OF GER-
MAN AGENT, IN URUGUAY.
```

"This is from Argentina, right? Judging from that very cute 'Station Chief Aggie' business?"

"Right."

"This just came in?"

"It was sent at five minutes to four Greenwich time. That's one in the afternoon Buenos Aires time, and eleven in the morning our time. For once the Navy brought it over here in a hurry."

"You're not going to change that 'Aggie' business now that we have a new station chief down there?"

"(a) We don't have a new station chief down there, for one thing. (b) I don't think I'd change it if we did. What's wrong with it?"

"What do you mean we don't have a new station chief down there? What's Delojo?"

"Commander Delojo is the *titular* station chief," Graham said. "And I have — we have — complied with Roosevelt's order that we identify the station chief to the Ambassador and the FBI, also known as the Legal Attaché."

"And Frade?"

"Frade is Frade. I was a little vague about who has the actual authority. If the Ambassador and the FBI think Delojo's the station chief, fine. I think we can also safely assume that someone down there will let the Argentines know — by accident or on purpose — that the Naval Attaché, Delojo, is the OSS station chief. With a little bit of luck, the Argentines may decide he really is, which would take some of the pressure off Frade. But I want Frade running things."

"You can't do that, for God's sake, Alex. You can't be a 'little vague' about who has the actual authority."

"Wait a minute, Bill," Graham said coldly. "After the fiasco your pals caused running their own war down there, we made a deal. So long as I tell you everything I'm doing down there, which is what I'm doing now, Argentina is my pie, and nobody — including you — puts their fingers in it. I either run it, or you get somebody else to run it, and I go back to running my railroad."

Before he went on active duty, Colonel Graham

was the president of either the second- or the third-largest railroad in the United States — depending on the factors used to make the determination. While he had a good deal of respect for Colonel Donovan, he was no more awed by him than by any other lawyer who had made a fortune on Wall Street.

"Don't be touchy, Alex," Donovan said.

"Sometimes you have a short memory span," Graham said. "Read on."

Donovan dropped his eyes to the message, and almost immediately asked, "Who's Sarnoff?"

"His name is Ettinger. Detailed to us from the Army's CIC. He's a Spanish Jew whose family had a Berlin branch. Or vice versa. Before he went into the Army, he worked for Dave Sarnoff at RCA. Electrical engineer, and according to Dave, a damned good one."

"Yeah," Donovan said, and resumed reading.

> 2. SARNOFF HAS REASON TO BELIEVE THAT AS MANY AS SEVERAL THOUSAND JEWS HAVE BEEN RANSOMED. DEVELOPMENT OF INFORMATION IS EXTREMELY DIFFICULT. MEMBERS OF REFUGEE AND PREEXISTING ARGENTINE JEWISH COMMUNITIES ARE EXCEEDINGLY RELUCTANT TO TALK, EVEN THOUGH MEMBERS OF REFUGEE COMMUNITY WERE WELL KNOWN TO SARNOFF IN GERMANY, AND ARE AWARE MOST OF HIS FAMILY HAS GONE INTO CONCENTRATION CAMPS.

" 'Several thousand' have been gotten out?" Donovan said. "You believe this, Alex?"

"Ettinger is a very clever fellow," Graham said.

"Yeah, I believe it, and so does Cletus Frade, or he wouldn't have sent that."

"If Mr. Hoover has heard anything about this, he hasn't felt the urge to say anything about it to me," Donovan said.

"Or anybody here I asked — at least anyone here who felt I had the need to know," Graham said.

Donovan dropped his eyes to the message again.

3. INFORMATION DEVELOPED SO FAR INDICATES RANSOM OPERATION (HEREAFTER LINDBERGH) OPERATING WITH SACHSENHAUSEN (POSITIVE) AND BELSEN (PROBABLE) BUT SARNOFF BELIEVES OTHER (PERHAPS ALL) CONCENTRATION CAMPS MAY BE INVOLVED.

4. INASMUCH AS VACUUM HAS CLOSE TIES TO BUENOS AIRES JEWISH COMMUNITY STRONG POSSIBILITY EXISTS THAT VACUUM IS AWARE OF LINDBERGH. POSSIBILITY EXISTS THAT FURTHER INVESTIGATION BY SARNOFF MIGHT HINDER VACUUM INVESTIGATION. REQUEST DIRECTION.

"Vacuum is Hoover, right?" Donovan asked. "The FBI?"

"Right," Graham said. "As in Hoover vacuum cleaner, sucking things up down there. That very cute code name was your idea, as I recall."

This earned him a dirty look from Donovan, who for a moment seemed about to respond, then changed his mind and resumed reading.

5. SS-SD STANDARTENFUHRER JOSEF GOLTZ (HEREAFTER BLACKSUIT) ARRIVED BUENOS AIRES BY LUFTHANSA 9 APRIL. SARNOFF BELIEVES HIGHLY PROBABLE THAT BLACKSUIT MISSION INVOLVES LINDBERGH WHICH COULD NOT OPERATE WITHOUT INVOLVEMENT OF HIGHLY PLACED GERMAN OFFICIALS.

6. RELIABLE SOURCE (HEREAFTER CAVALRY) INFORMED STACHIEF BLACKSUIT TODAY ORDERED ELIMINATION OF SARNOFF ONLY REPEAT SARNOFF ONLY AS PRIORITY PROJECT. CAVALRY BELIEVES BLACKSUIT PROBABLY ORDERED ASSASSINATION OF WHITEHORSE.

"Whitehorse is . . . was . . . Frade's father, right?" Donovan asked. "Who's this reliable source, 'Cavalry'?"

"I can only guess. The Ambassador messaged that the red carpet was really rolled out for Frade when he arrived in Argentina. The War Minister, General Ramírez, met his plane and took him to the place where they had his father laid out in state. It could be Ramírez, but I doubt it. Ramírez was Infantry, and Frade's calling whoever it is 'Cavalry.' Maybe General Rawson. He was Cavalry, and he and Colonel Frade were close. Whoever it is, it's somebody high enough up to have access to their intelligence about German activities. Which also means they must have somebody in the German Embassy."

Donovan considered that, nodded, and went on reading.

425

```
7. STACHIEF BELIEVES BLACKSUIT
SPECIAL INTEREST IN SARNOFF MAY
ALSO BE DUE SARNOFF'S QUESTIONING
SHIPPING INTERESTS WHICH MIGHT IN-
VOLVE NEW GROCERYSTORE ACTIVI-
TIES.

8. IF FURTHER INVESTIGATION OF
LINDBERGH BY SARNOFF IS DIRECTED
REQUEST AUTHORITY TO DISCUSS AND
POSSIBLY EXCHANGE INFORMATION
WITH VACUUM. ABSENT DIRECTION TO
CONTRARY SARNOFF WILL CONTINUE IN-
VESTIGATION OF LINDBERGH.

9. STACHIEF BELIEVES OPERATION
OVERTURN WILL CONTINUE DESPITE
LOSS OF WHITEHORSE. MEETING OF
OVERTURN LEADERS THIS WEEKEND SUG-
GESTS STRONG POSSIBILITY OF EXE-
CUTION IN NEAR FUTURE.


STACHIEF  END
```

"Do we have anything on this Blacksuit?" Donovan asked.

"We have Goltz listed as Himmler's liaison officer to Martin Bormann — to the Nazi party," Graham replied. "Longtime Nazi. I think we have to presume that (a) Frade's source is reliable and (b) this fellow has given orders to take out Sarnoff . . . Ettinger. I'm surprised."

"Why are you surprised? They took out the entire team we sent down there before we sent Frade's team."

"I'm surprised that Blacksuit ordered the elimi-

nation of Ettinger only. You picked up on that?"
Donovan nodded. "Why not the whole team? The
team poses the same threat it did before to their
replenishment vessel. So why only Ettinger?"

"You tell me."

"By meeting Frade with that delegation of brass
hats — which included Rawson, who is likely to
become President if Ramírez doesn't — it looks to
me that Ramírez went out of his way to send a
message to the Germans that he (a) didn't like what
happened to Colonel Frade, (b) he's not afraid of
the Germans, and (c) neither are a great big bunch
of the other brass."

"I wish we knew who 'Cavalry' is," Donovan
said. "I don't like this."

"You believe this ransoming business?"

Donovan nodded.

"Neither Frade nor Ettinger are investigators,"
he said. "Ettinger is a radio engineer. Frade is a
pilot. If they turned this up, I think we have to
presume that the FBI guy down there already
knows all about it. *More* about it than Ettinger
does. Would you agree?"

Graham nodded.

"I can just see J. Edgar going in to see the President with this ransom business — that is, if he
hasn't *already* been in to see him," Donovan said:
" 'I told you all along, Franklin, that the only thing
the Oh So Social* is doing down there is spending
money and assets and spinning its wheels. My
trained investigators, following my mandate to handle all intelligence gathering in the Western Hemisphere, have known about this business from the

---

* So called by detractors of the OSS, a reference to the fact that
many OSS senior officers and agents had been recruited from the
upper echelons of business, the Ivy League schools, and society.

beginning. The nation would be better served if you left this sort of thing to the professionals, to the FBI.' "

Graham smiled and chuckled.

"We took out the *Reine de la Mer*," he said. "How will Hoover get around that?"

"In the Gospel according to Saint Edgar, the Navy took out the *Reine de la Mer*. If it hadn't been for the subcommander's After Action Report, we would have had a hard time getting Frade and Pelosi Good Conduct Medals, instead of what they got."

Graham nodded again, remembering the words: When the President read them — Graham had personally taken the After Action Report to him — he ordered the award of the Navy Cross to Frade, and the next-highest award for conspicuous valor, the Silver Star, to Pelosi.

19. THE UNDERSIGNED DESIRES TO STATE IN CONCLUSION THAT ACCOMPLISHMENT OF THIS MISSION WOULD HAVE BEEN IMPOSSIBLE HAD IT NOT BEEN FOR BOTH THE PROFESSIONAL SKILL AND PERSONAL VALOR OF FIRST LIEUTENANT C. H. FRADE, USMCR, AND SECOND LIEUTENANT A. J. PELOSI, AUS, WHO, IN ORDER TO ILLUMINATE THE TARGET, FLEW THEIR SMALL UNARMED AIRCRAFT DELIBERATELY INTO RANGE OF THE HEAVY MACHINE GUN AND AUTOMATIC CANNON ANTIAIRCRAFT WEAPONRY ABOARD THE REINE DE LA MER IN THE CERTAIN KNOWLEDGE THAT THEIR AIRCRAFT WOULD BE HIT, AND PROBABLY DESTROYED, WHICH IN FACT PROVED TO BE THE CASE. THEIR DEDI-

CATION TO DUTY AND PERSONAL COURAGE
IN THE FACE OF WHAT APPEARED TO BE
NEAR-CERTAIN DEATH WAS INSPIRA-
TIONAL, AND IN KEEPING WITH THE HIGH-
EST TRADITIONS OF THE NAVAL SERVICE
AND THE UNITED STATES ARMY.

BRYCE J. STEVENS
COMMANDER, USN
COMMANDING, USS DEVIL-FISH

"What do you want me to tell Frade, Bill?" Graham asked.

"What do you think? (a) Continue the investigation as a matter of the highest priority. (b) Do not communicate to the FBI in any manner whatsoever anything remotely involved with the ransoming. (c) Identify the source he calls 'Cavalry.' "

"What do you think this whole thing is all about, Bill? You think it's a matter of policy? And if so, why haven't we heard anything about it here in the United States?"

"I really don't know. My suspicion is that it's some sort of a private operation. Some high-ranking SS sonofabitch has decided there's money to be made, personally, and is in a position to make it. Why not here? Because it's *not* German policy, and he doesn't want his private operation to get back to the top-level people in the SS. Or maybe they're involved, the top-level Nazis, and are worried about public opinion. I just don't know, Alex. The only thing I know is that the more we learn about this, and the quicker, the better."

Graham grunted again.

"We call it 'Lindbergh,' right? And how do we classify it?"

"Top Secret — Lindbergh. Eyes Only, you and me. And I mean that. Just you and me. We can't afford somebody with a large mouth on this one."

"Right," Graham said, and stood up.

"When I go to the President with this, Alex, I want facts, not suppositions."

"Right," Graham repeated, and walked out of his office.

[Three]

Estancia San Pedro y San Pablo
Near Pila, Buenos Aires Province
1730 11 April 1943

As Clete and Rudolpho rode back to the main house, Clete's mind kept jumping back and forth —

I probably should not have given OUTLINE BLUE to Martín before reading it thoroughly. I am, after all, an intelligence officer, and there was certainly something in OUTLINE BLUE which would interest Graham. Consciously, I know everything is the OSS's business, but did I decide, unconsciously, that since the Grupo de Oficiales Unidos are not any kind of a threat to the United States, it's really none of our business. And just to satisfy Graham's idle curiosity does not justify putting Ramírez and Rawson at risk?

What the hell is Henry Mallín going to do when that Jesuit shows up at his door with Claudia and Humberto and tells him the Virgin Princess is pregnant. And who did it?

I have to get in touch with Peter and tell him I have

his father's letter and the records. I didn't tell Graham about that, either, and I know damned well the OSS would be interested in a German general who plans to assassinate Hitler.

But there are some dangerous sonsofbitches in the OSS, like the two who sent me down here hoping the Germans would kill me so that my father would be pissed off. Those two are gone, but there are probably others who would want to help assassinate Hitler, and that "help" just might get Peter's father killed. If they didn't worry about getting me killed, for the greater good, they certainly wouldn't worry about getting a German general killed. If Peter's father wanted American help, he would have asked for it.

Is marrying Dorotéa really the right thing to do, presuming the Jesuit can do something? Or is marrying me going to get her killed? Her and the child she's carrying?

What the hell is going on with this ransoming of Jews from concentration camps? Is Ettinger onto something? Is that the reason that Nazi bastard ordered him killed?

Maybe, if the Jesuit can fix things with Henry Mallín, and we can get married, I can send Dorotéa to the States to have the baby, and to wait there until this fucking war is over. Martha would be happy to have her, and she wouldn't be in the line of fire on Big Foot Ranch.

There was something very unreal about thinking all of these thoughts while he was cantering across the pampas on a beautiful afternoon, with nothing in sight but cattle and groves of trees.

He remembered the Solomon Islands. It was beautiful and peaceful there too, at 15,000 feet over Guadalcanal. Blue sky and white clouds, with the blue ocean and the nice bright green vegetation of the island far below.

Until the first Japanese planes appeared. Then, all of a sudden, there was no more peace or beauty.

That's going to happen here, too. All of a sudden everything here is going to turn to shit, too. The difference was that in the Solomons, I was at least a pretty good Wildcat pilot. Here I didn't know shit from Shinola.

When they rode up to the house Enrico was waiting for them, sitting in one of the rattan chairs on the verandah. A nice-looking blond-haired kid, thirteen or fourteen years old, sat below him on the wide verandah steps. Each was wearing a loose, white, long-sleeved shirt, black vest, billowing black trousers, and a wide leather belt; and each had a silver-handled knife in the small of his back. Enrico also had a .45 automatic jammed inside his belt, and his shotgun was resting against one of the pillars.

There's no question in his mind that sooner or later he's going to need a gun to protect me. And he's probably right.

Jesus, why couldn't we just keep riding? But I can't do that, any more than I could have just kept circling 15,000 feet over Guadalcanal.

The nice-looking kid rose to his feet and came off the steps.

"Buenos tardes, Patrón," he said, reaching up to take Julius Caesar's bit.

Clete swung out of the saddle. The kid mounted Julius Caesar — who, Clete noted with some chagrin, immediately sensed an expert horseman and behaved like a lamb — and reached over to take the reins of Rudolpho's roan. Rudolpho slipped easily out of his saddle, and the kid rode toward the stables.

Even in that gaucho suit, Clete thought, *that kid*

looks more like an Englishman or a German — or maybe a Pole or some other kind of Slav, a Latvian or something — than a Spaniard or an Italian.

He remembered his father telling him there was a massive immigration of Germans at the turn of the century, and another wave of immigrants after World War I — Germans running from the postwar depression in Germany, and Lithuanians, Latvians, Poles, and Russians fleeing the Russian Bolshevik revolution.

Antonio was also waiting for him to return.

"Are Señor Duarte or Señora Carzino-Cormano here?"

"No, Señor," Antonio replied as he opened the door to Clete. "Señor and Señora Duarte are expected any moment."

"Well, that gives me time for a shower," Clete thought aloud. "Where did you put my things, Antonio?"

"In your room, Señor," Antonio said. There was a slight tone of disapproval in his voice.

Ask a dumb question, get a dumb answer. Where else would he put my things?

Oh, God! My room is not where I stayed before. My room is el Coronel's room.

Well, that's the way it is. I better get used to it. El Coronel's gone, and what used to be his is now mine. Including his room and his bed.

Clete turned to look at Enrico. He was pushing himself out of his chair.

With effort, Clete saw. *And tough old soldier or not, you're in pain, pal. And tough old soldier or not, are you in any shape to try to protect me? Am I going to get you killed, too, just because you're around me?*

Antonio led him to the apartment of the late el Coronel Jorge Guillermo Frade — unnecessarily,

433

since Clete knew where it was. It consisted of a bedroom, a sitting, and a bath at the rear of the house. The windows opened on a garden.

In the room there was another sign of Antonio's none-too-subtle snobbery. A clothes tree held a tweed jacket, an open-collared shirt — *that's a* polo *shirt, a* real *polo shirt, for people who play* real *polo* — and a pair of gabardine riding breeches. A pair of highly polished riding boots stood beside it.

Christ, I hope that stuff's not my father's!

"Your father intended that clothing as a Christmas present for el Capitán Duarte," Antonio said. "He never had a chance to wear it. El Capitán was about your size. . . ."

I would just as soon not wear any clothing made for my dead cousin, not to mention clothing which would make me look like an Englishman about to go chase a fox, but thank you very much, Antonio, just the same.

"Thank you," Clete said. "I'll see if it fits."

The seeds of curiosity were sown, however, while he was taking a shower and shaving: *I wonder how I would look in that outfit? The Princess would probably think it made me look — what's that Limey word she uses? — smashing!*

And why not wear it? It's new. And you're wearing Uncle Jim's Stetson. And you brought Sullivan's Half Wellingtons home from Guadalcanal and you wear them. So why not wear Cousin Jorge Alejandro's fancy English riding boots and the rest of it? Waste not, want not, as Aunt Martha always says.

A sudden, very clear, and very painful image came into his mind and was still there when he came out of the bathroom in his underwear: First Lieutenant Francis Xavier Sullivan, 167th Fighter Squadron, U.S. Army Air Corps, flying his P-40 in support of the Marine Raiders; going into Edson's Ridge on fire from the nose to the vertical stabilizer.

As Clete walked into the bedroom, he was startled — even frightened for a moment — to find Capitán Roberto Lauffer, in civilian clothing, sitting in an armchair near the bed, his very nice, highly polished jodhpurs crossed on a matching footstool. Clete then noticed that Enrico was also there, leaning on the wall beside the closed door to the sitting.

Lauffer quickly pushed himself out of the chair and offered Clete his hand.

"I thought, mi Mayor," Enrico said, "that it would be all right to bring el Capitán here. Señor and Señora Duarte are in the reception."

One Cavalryman taking care of another, huh? Spare a fellow horse soldier from Beatrice? Well, at least it shows Enrico likes him.

Clete nodded at Enrico to show him he approved, and then looked at Lauffer.

Very sporty, Clete thought, *that's a damned nice tweed jacket, a classy polo shirt, and he's even got one of those whatchamacallits around his neck.*

"Of course," Clete said. "How are you, Roberto?"

"I'm afraid you're stuck with me again," Lauffer said. "General Rawson wants me to stay close to something you're holding for him . . ."

"The money, you mean?" Clete said, but it was not a question.

". . . until he can make arrangements, tomorrow, to safely transport it elsewhere. Señora Carzino-Cormano said you would understand the necessary imposition this will cause."

"Sure," Clete said. "No imposition at all. When can I expect her?"

"She said that you would understand why she can't call today, but that she looks forward to seeing you tomorrow."

I wonder what that's all about?

Clete started to get dressed.

Cousin Jorge Alejandro's — the late Capitán Duarte's — polo shirt fit him perfectly. The breeches were maybe half an inch too large in the waist, and the jacket was a little loose. But once he managed to work his feet into them, the boots also seemed to fit perfectly.

One other item of clothing was left on the clothes horse, a whatchamacallit like Roberto Lauffer was wearing. Roberto's was yellow. Cousin Jorge Alejandro's whatchamacallit was red.

Foulard! It's a foulard!

Maneuvering the silk foulard in place, and making it stay in place, proved more difficult than he thought looping some red silk around his neck would be, but he finally made the thing work.

"Very elegant," Lauffer said.

"I'd feel a lot more comfortable in it if my father's butler hadn't told me my father bought it as a Christmas present for my cousin, the late Capitán Duarte."

"I'm the youngest in a large family," Lauffer said. "I think I was sixteen before I received anything but shoes that weren't previously 'hardly worn at all' by one or more of my brothers. Be grateful it fits. And it is elegant!"

"You look pretty elegant yourself. I never saw you in civvies before."

"One never knows, does one, where one might come across an attractive member of the gentle sex with an eye for a man's clothes," Lauffer said.

"And then, all dressed up, you get yourself

screwed by the fickle finger of fate? You get sent over here, where the only female is going to be my Aunt Beatrice."

" 'Fickle finger of fate'? That's good," Lauffer chuckled. "Well, there's always tomorrow." Then, visibly embarrassed: "Forgive me, I was not thinking of what will happen tomorrow. No disrespect was intended."

"I know that," Clete said. "I'm just going through the motions. I'm told the people who work here expect it." He turned to Enrico. "You did find the Capitán someplace to sleep, Enrico?"

"I told Antonio you would wish for el Capitán to be well cared for," Enrico said. "He is the third door to the left."

"Speaking of Aunt Beatrice," Clete said, "Antonio said she'll be here any minute, Enrico. I think el Capitán and I need a little liquid courage before we face her. Is there anything — strong — in here we can drink?"

"Scotch whiskey, mi Mayor?"

Clete looked at Lauffer, who nodded.

"Please, Enrico."

"My pleasure, mi Mayor," Enrico said, and walked out of the bedroom.

He's never *going to stop calling me "Major,"* Clete thought. *To hell with it.* And then he had another thought: "It's liable to be worse with my aunt than you think," Clete said.

"She is a very charming lady."

"Tonight, she will almost certainly regale you with the details of a wedding we hope will be held here sometime in the near future."

"Oh, really? Whose?"

"Mine."

Lauffer's eyebrows went up.

"I didn't know you . . . I hadn't heard that you were engaged."

"At the moment, actually, I'm not," Clete said.

"I don't understand," Lauffer confessed, a little uncomfortably.

Enrico came back into the room carrying not the expected whiskey glasses, but a telephone, a large French-looking instrument.

"It is Padre Welner, Señor," he said as he walked to a plug mounted on the wall beside the bed and plugged it in.

He took the receiver from its cradle and held it out to Clete. Clete walked to the bed, sat down, and took the receiver from Enrico.

"What can I do for you, Father?"

"I have been busily taking care of my pastoral duties, and I thought you might be interested in learning the result," the priest announced cheerfully.

If he had bad news, he wouldn't be so cheerful!

"Absolutely!"

"First of all, I called on the Bishop, to explain the role you and Father Denilo would like him to take in the mass tomorrow. And the subject somehow turned to the waiving of the banns of marriage, which is permitted under canonical law when a bishop determines there are extraordinary circumstances. In these extraordinary circumstances —"

"You told him the circumstances?" Clete interrupted.

"Not in specific detail. I think the Bishop formed the impression that I had learned of the extraordinary circumstances through the confessional booth; and of course, he could not ask me to reveal matter I had learned in my role as confessor. In any event, the Bishop feels that he can in good conscience

438

permit your marriage in fourteen days. He also indicated that if you asked him to officiate, he would grant your request."

"And what do we do about her father?"

"That proved less of a problem than I thought. After I spoke to Claudia, she telephoned him and asked him to reconsider his decision not to come to Estancia Santo Catalina. She told him that I was here and wanted to speak to him about you and Dorotéa." The priest laughed.

"That's funny?"

"Señor Mallín responded that Claudia should thank me very much indeed for my interest, but to tell me there was no longer cause for my concern. He was already aware of your regrettable and impossible interest in Dorotéa and had taken the necessary steps to bring the situation under control."

"And?" Clete asked, chuckling.

Why am I laughing?

"At that point, Claudia told him that I was standing beside her, and why didn't he tell me that himself?"

"And?"

"He did so. I had to correct his belief that the situation was under his control, and to explain his options, as I saw them."

"Which are?"

"The one he chose is to accept your invitation to stay with you at Estancia San Pedro y San Pablo tonight. Tomorrow, his family will be seated in the family pews — to the right of the altar — of La Capilla Nuestra Señora de los Milagros. With the exception, of course, of Dorotéa."

"They're coming out here?"

Welner ignored the question.

"During the mass, Dorotéa will be seated beside

439

you on the chairs — in front of the family pews — reserved for el Patrón of Estancia San Pedro y San Pablo and his wife. When the service is over, she will take your arm and the two of you will lead the exit procession of the laity. Immediately afterward, she will stand beside you at the head of the reception line, as you greet your guests."

"He went along with this?" Clete asked incredulously. "You said they're coming out here today?"

"They are at this moment en route and should be here within the hour. But let me finish. I told Señor Mallín that Dorotéa's prominent role in the ceremony should suggest to just about everyone present that the relationship between you and Dorotéa is long-standing, has had all along the approval of the respective families, and that because of your recent loss, there is nothing really extraordinary in your electing to have a small, private wedding in two weeks here at the Estancia."

"You're an amazing fellow, Padre."

"So I have been told. I prefer to think of myself as a simple priest, a simple shepherd, encouraging the erring members of my flock to do the right thing," Welner said with outrageous piety, then added: "And Señor Mallín didn't really have much of a choice, did he?"

"He could have said no," Clete said, laughing. "Not only no but 'over my dead body.' "

"But that, my son, might have been misinterpreted by some people — as matters of this kind often are. The word might have been whispered around the Jockey Club that 'there goes poor Henry Mallín. Foolish chap, thinking he was onto a good thing, practically threw his daughter at Cletus Frade, who, after sampling the merchandise decided he'd rather not endow the young lady with all his worldly goods.' He would, I knew, find something like that hard to take."

"Good God! You didn't say anything like that to him, did you?"

"Let us say that I suggested to Señor Mallín that it would really look better all around if you appeared eager to take his daughter as your bride. You are prepared to do that, aren't you, Cletus? To eagerly endow Dorotéa with all your worldly goods?"

"Of course," Clete said, chuckling.

"Good. Now that you've had a chance to consider how many worldly goods you now possess, I was a little concerned that you might have had second thoughts."

"I hope you're kidding."

"Another reason I called, Cletus, is that Claudia suggested there is probably a ring which might be suitable for Dorotéa in your father's strongbox."

"What strongbox?" Clete asked, and turned to Enrico. "Is there a strongbox around here?"

"In the library, Señor Clete."

"Enrico says there's a strongbox in the library."

"That's probably it. Why don't you have a look? I think it would be nice when I come for dinner — Did I mention that Claudia suggested you ask me to dinner?"

"Why don't you have dinner with us, Father?"

"Thank you very much. Very kind of you. It would be nice, as I was saying, if when I come over there, Dorotéa had an engagement ring on her finger. And even more for people to notice tomorrow morning."

"Christ, you're something."

"I'll be over there, probably, before your fiancée

and her family arrive," the priest said, and the line went dead.

Clete put the receiver back in its cradle and stood up.

"Show me the strongbox, Enrico," he said, and then turned to Lauffer. "I have just been informed that my fiancée and her family will be joining us for dinner. I know, a moment ago, I told you I was not engaged. A moment ago, I wasn't. Now I am."

"Well, then let me be the first to offer my congratulations," Lauffer said.

XIV

[One]

Estancia San Pedro y San Pablo
Near Pila, Buenos Aires Province
1805 11 April 1943

The strongbox turned out to be just that, a metal box reinforced with thick wrought-iron bands, and closed with two enormous padlocks. It was concealed in a huge leather trunk set against one wall of the library. After Enrico showed it to Clete, he retrieved the padlock keys from behind a set of *Compton's Picture Encyclopedia.*

The strongbox held two small wooden boxes, resting on top of what appeared to be legal documents. Clete picked up the first box and started to open it.

"Where's that whiskey you promised us, Enrico?" he asked.

Inside was a collection of discarded male jewelry, cuff links, studs, pocket watches, wristwatches, tie pins, tie clips, and rings. The watches and rings had tags tied to them, identifying their owners. Clete looked at several of them. There was one huge gold ring with maybe a dozen half-carat diamonds surrounding a deeply engraved Frade family crest; its tag read GUILLERMO JORGE FRADE.

That looks just like something Uncle Willy would wear.

He put the ring back in the box and picked up the second box. It contained discarded female jewelry — broaches, necklaces, rings, pendants, and wristwatches. Rolling around loose on the bottom of the box were what looked like several hundred pearls. He saw the rotted-through strings they had escaped. More than two dozen rings were each tagged with a name. But only three could pass for engagement rings. He read the tags. Only one name — MARIA ELENA PUEYRREDÓN DE FRADE — meant anything to him, and that tag was attached to the least impressive of the three rings. It was old and worn thin, and the stone was tiny compared to the stones in the other rings.

That's a pity. It would have been nice if that one, in particular, had been the sort of thing I could give Dorotéa. The reason "the blood of Pueyrredón" flows through my veins. And now of our baby.

Well, hell, I'll show her these, and tell her to pick one just for the circus tomorrow. I'll tell her I'll buy her any damned ring she wants later.

He untied the tags and slipped the three rings in his pocket.

Enrico was holding out a whiskey glass to him. Clete took it.

"Close it up, Enrico," he ordered.

Thirty minutes later, Antonio came into the library to announce the arrival of the Mallín family.

Clete rose quickly out of his chair and started to walk to the library door. The action caused him to realize that his belief thirty-five minutes earlier that Cousin Jorge Alejandro's English riding boots fit perfectly was grossly in error.

"Christ!" he exclaimed, surprised at the intensity of the pain in his feet.

"New boots, eh?" Roberto asked innocently.

By the time he reached the foyer, maids were carrying in the Mallín luggage, Enrico Mallín was himself in the doorway, and Clete was hobbling in pain.

Enrico Mallín's eyebrows rose questioningly as Clete limped across the tile floor and put out his hand to him.

"Thank you for coming, Señor Mallín," he said.

"How good of you to ask us," Mallín replied, with a smile that Clete thought deserved the all-time, all-category prize for insincerity. The hand-shake conveyed the same message.

"Have you met el Capitán Lauffer?" Clete asked as Pamela Mallín came through the door.

She laid her hands on his arms and moved her face to his ear.

"I don't know whether I want to kiss you or kill you," she said. "How could you, Cletus?"

His attention was distracted when he saw Dorotéa pass through the door. She was wearing a sweater and a skirt, and her hands were folded modestly in front of her. Her head was bent shyly. She looked very quickly at Clete and then lowered her head again.

Christ, she's beautiful!

"How could I what?" Clete asked absently.

"You know very well —" Pamela said, and then, blushing, interrupted herself.

Little Henry came in the door.

"Little Mr. Big Mouth," Clete said.

That earned a faint smile from Dorotéa.

"May I see you a moment, Dorotéa?" he asked.

Her father glowered at him.

He walked to her, fishing for the rings in his pocket. He held the three of them out to her, displayed in his palm.

"Pick one," he said. "Just for tonight and tomorrow. I'll get you another one later."

"Are you trying to give me a ring or loan me one?" Dorotéa demanded.

"They're all yours, if you want them," he said. "I didn't think you'd like —"

"This is exquisite!" she said, picking up one of the rings. "You *can* be such a bloody fool, Cletus!"

She slipped the ring on her finger, met his eyes defiantly for a moment, and then called, "Daddy, look at the exquisite ring Cletus gave me."

Her father examined the ring for all of half a second.

"How nice," he said.

"That's old," Pamela Mallín said, an observation, not a criticism.

"It belonged to my great-grandmother," Clete said. "Maria-Elena Pueyrredón de Frade."

"Then it belongs in a museum," Pamela said. "The National Museum, not on Dorotéa's finger."

"It's mine," Dorotéa said. "Cletus gave it to me. It'll go into a museum over my dead body!"

[Two]

Estancia San Pedro y San Pablo
Near Pila, Buenos Aires Province
2010 11 April 1943

Humberto and Beatrice Duarte arrived twenty minutes after the Mallín family. By then Enrico Mallín had had two stiff drinks of whiskey.

It was a very long twenty minutes.

Once Enrico Mallín had inquired into the well-being of el Capitán Lauffer and his wife, little seemed available to talk about, at least that either he or his wife had to say to Cletus H. Frade, at least in front of Lauffer.

Sensing this, Lauffer raised an eyebrow and gave his head a tilt, asking Clete if he should leave the library. Clete placed his hands together as if in prayer and shook his head, meaning that he would very much prefer for Lauffer not to leave him alone with his father-in-law-to-be.

When Humberto came through the door, Clete felt an enormous sense of relief. That, however, did not last long.

With tears in his eyes, Humberto wrapped his arms around Clete and wetly kissed both his cheeks. Feeling another male's stubble against his own made Clete uncomfortable.

"God is good," Humberto announced emotionally. "The Lord taketh away, and the Lord giveth. A new life! I will pray that it will be a son."

Dorotéa looked very uncomfortable.

The face of Roberto Lauffer, who was standing beside Clete, made it quite clear that he understood the meaning of the term "new life."

At the same moment, Enrico Mallín's face made

it quite clear that he did not regard the new life as a manifestation of the generosity of the Supreme Being. He allowed himself to be embraced by Humberto, then held out his glass to one of the maids for a refill.

"I found those documents you were concerned about," Clete said.

It took a long moment for understanding to register on Humberto's face.

"Oh, good," he said finally.

Since he is anything but stupid, he must be drunk. I didn't think that was aftershave I smelled when he kissed me. And that "God is Good!" speech!

"What documents are those?" Beatrice asked.

"Some business dealings I have with von Wachtstein," Humberto replied, "nothing to concern yourself about, my dear."

And he has a big mouth. My God!

"Oh," she said, and put the subject out of her mind.

As soon as she walked in, it was immediately apparent to Clete that Beatrice was again — still? — detached from reality, heavily dosed with what Humberto euphemistically called her medicine. The odds were remote that she would ever remember the exchange, Clete decided.

But Enrico Mallín and Roberto Lauffer both heard von Wachtstein's name, and it caught their attention.

It soon became apparent that while Father Welner had apparently told both Humberto and Beatrice that Clete and Dorotéa were to be married, he apparently told them separately, and left Dorotéa's pregnancy out of the version for Beatrice.

The minute the priest showed up, just before

they were going into dinner, Beatrice went after him.

"I don't want to talk about it at dinner," Beatrice said, "but I don't want to hear one more word about a small wedding here, and in the next few weeks. That's simply out of the question. What would people think?"

The faces of Señor and Señora Mallín made it clear they had already considered what people were going to think.

"I agree," Welner said, "that it is not a matter we should talk about at dinner."

Beatrice then talked about nothing at dinner but the wedding she thought Dorotéa and Clete should have, starting with a detailed account of her own wedding, and moving through weddings she thought had been "done well," and then on to the relative merits and disadvantages of celebrating the Frade-Mallín nuptials at Estancia San Pedro y San Pablo or in the city.

Hardly touching her food, Dorotéa sat through it all with her head bent.

It was only with a great effort, buttressed with pity, that Clete was able to keep himself from taking Humberto into the corridor and asking him, for Christ's sake, to shut his blabbering wife up.

And seeing the looks she was getting from Enrico Mallín, he was surprised that Mallín didn't say something to her.

It was Mallín, however, who finally ended it.

The coffee had just been served, and with it snifters of cognac. Antonio moved to each of the men, offering cigars from a humidor.

Mallín suddenly pushed himself away from the table and lurched to his feet, knocking over his chair, his wineglass, his water glass, and his untouched cognac snifter. The heavy crystal water glass fell onto the snifter, smashing it. He didn't seem to notice; but his wife's humiliation showed on her face. Little Henry giggled.

"With your kind permission, Cletus," Señor Enrico Mallín said, carefully pronouncing each syllable, "we will ask to be excused. It has been a long day, and we have a busy day tomorrow."

"Of course," Cletus said, rising to his feet.

The perfect end, Clete thought, *to a perfectly lousy dinner.*

The Mallíns left the dining room. Dorotéa didn't even look at Clete.

"I think Beatrice and I should get our rest too," Humberto said.

"But I'm talking to Cletus about his wedding!" she protested.

"You can talk to him tomorrow, darling," he said, and stood behind her chair until finally she got up.

"Poor woman," Father Welner said after they were gone. And then he rose out of his chair. "I'll pass on the brandy, Cletus. I've had a busy day myself."

He touched Cletus's shoulder, nodded at Roberto Lauffer, and walked out of the dining room.

"It would appear, mi amigo," Clete said, "that we get all the cognac."

"I don't think, mi amigo, that we should drink all of it, but one . . . a stiff one . . ."

"Thank you for . . ."

"Poor woman," Roberto said, obviously quoting the priest.

He raised his glass to Clete, and Clete clinked glasses with him.

"Roberto, I would like to ask you a favor."

"Anything within my power."

"Could you forget hearing the name von Wacht-stein here tonight?"

Lauffer's eyebrows rose.

"It's very important to me," Clete said.

"Whose name?" Lauffer said. "I have such a hard time remembering names. . . ."

"Thank you."

"May I say that I admire your taste? Dorotéa is quite beautiful."

"I noticed," Clete said.

Lauffer stood up.

"It should go without saying that I wish you every happiness," he said.

"Thank you," Clete said, and then chuckled. "That was the first word of congratulations I've received, incidentally."

"Then I'm glad it came from me," Lauffer said, and put out his hand. "We're all going to have a busy day tomorrow. Thank you for a . . . I was about to say 'memorable,' but that wouldn't be accurate. Thank you for your hospitality."

"Good night, Roberto."

Lauffer left Clete alone in the room.

Clete picked up his snifter and took a sip.

Jesus, he thought. *I'm going to have to tell the Old Man and Martha, before they hear about it someplace else.*

He put the glass down and stood up.

"Will that be all, Señor?" Antonio asked.

"Yes, thank you, Antonio," Clete said. "Please thank the cook for a . . . wait a minute. Is there a typewriter around here someplace?"

"A typewriter, Señor?"

"A typewriter."

"The housekeeper has —"

"Will you bring it, and some paper and envelopes, and a pot of coffee, to my room, please?"

"Of course."

Writing the Old Man was even more difficult than Clete imagined, and not only because the venerable Underwood had a Spanish keyboard with the keys in the wrong places.

He had just ripped from the typewriter his sixth failed attempt to write the Old Man a letter when there was a knock at the door.

Now what?

"Come!"

The door opened. One of the maids was standing there. Behind her, in his gaucho costume, stood Chief Schultz.

"The Señor, Señor insisted on . . ."

"We got a reply to your radio, Major," Chief Schultz said. "I thought I'd better bring it over."

"Come on in, let's have it. You want a cup of coffee? Something stronger?"

"I never turn down a little taste," Schultz said.

"Scotch?"

"You wouldn't have a little cognac around here someplace, would you?"

"Bring cognac, please," Clete said. "There's a bottle on the table in the dining." He turned to Schultz.

"How'd we get this reply so quick?" he asked. "I thought you said you had an oh one thirty net call?"

"Oh one thirty, oh nine thirty, and seventeen thirty, three times a day," Schultz explained. "But we *monitor* the frequency all the time when someone's there. We just don't *acknowledge*, unless they

452

ask for it special. Once a day, at oh nine thirty, if they've sent something, we acknowledge. Or, if we have something for them — like your 0001 — we acknowledge everything we got, starting with their oh one thirty. The idea is for *us* to go on the air as little as possible. You understand?"

"They monitor us all the time?"

"Sure. And when we send something off the schedule, I add a service message to any Navy station asking them to copy and relay. I did that with your 0001."

Clete opened the envelope Schultz had handed him and read the message.

```
TOP SECRET
LINDBERGH
URGENT
DUPLICATION FORBIDDEN

FROM ORACLE WASHDC

MSG NO 2545 DDWHO 0030 GREENWICH
12 APRIL 1943

TO STACHIEF AGGIE

REFERENCE YOUR NO. 0001

   1. PROCEED WITH LINDBERGH INVES-
TIGATION AS HIGHEST PRIORITY.

   2. LIAISON WITH VACUUM IN ANY
ASPECT OF LINDBERGH IS FORBIDDEN
REPEAT FORBIDDEN.

   3. INTELLIGENCE DEVELOPED IS TO
```

BE CLASSIFIED TOP SECRET LINDBERGH
EYES ONLY DDWHO AND TRANSMITTED BY
RADIO ONLY. FACILITIES OF USEMBASSY
ARE NOT REPEAT NOT TO BE UTILIZED.

4. IDENTIFY SOURCE CAVALRY, IN-
CLUDING MOTIVATION FOR HIS COOP-
ERATION.

5. PERSONAL TO SARNOFF FROM OR-
ACLE QUOTE GOOD JOB UNQUOTE.

6. ACKNOWLEDGE DELIVERY THIS
MESSAGE TO STACHIEF BY TRANSMIS-
SION OF PHRASE GOT IT. REPEAT GOT
IT.

GRAHAM END

"I wonder why we're not supposed to use the
Embassy's radio?" Clete asked. "Or the diplomatic
pouch?"

"I guess Graham figures the FBI gets its nose in
just about everything around the Embassy,"
Schultz said. "Tony . . . Mr. Pelosi . . . got to the
Army crypto guy, I guess he told you. That place
is a fucking sieve, security-wise."

Clete grunted.

"Do you write home, Chief?"

Schultz looked at him strangely for a moment.

"I got a sister in Milwaukee," he said. "Once a
month, like, I drop her a note. Send her a couple
of bucks. She's married to a bum."

"How?"

"Through the Embassy. They put a pouch —
you know this — on all the Pan American flights.

You just write your name and serial number and 'free' where the stamp is supposed to go on the envelope, and that's it."

"I'm no longer in the service. . . ."

"Yeah, so you keep saying."

"Would you put your name and serial number on a couple of letters and get them in the mail for me?"

"Sure. You got 'em?"

"I'm going to have to write them. Is Tony still out there?"

"He said he would stick around in case you wanted to say something about it when you got this."

"Then he's going back to Buenos Aires?"

"Right."

"Make sure Ettinger does not go to Buenos Aires, Chief. If you have to chain him to a tree. He's a good man, but he hasn't quite grasped the idea that an order is an order. He ignores those he doesn't like."

"Well, Mr. Frade —" the Chief interrupted himself. "I was about to say he's got a personal interest in this war we don't have. But now you've got one too, don't you?"

"Ettinger told you about his family?"

"His family, and a lot more. I hate to admit it, but before I got to know Dave, I thought all this business about the shit the Nazis are doing was propaganda bullshit — the concentration camps, putting people in rooms and gassing them, just because they're Jews. You know, like in World War One, they said the Germans were bayoneting babies in Belgium."

"It's not bullshit. What they do is so bad your mind doesn't want to accept it. And when it hits you personally . . . I understand Dave, Chief. But I can't permit him to wage a private war. For one thing, we can't afford to lose him. You keep him out here until you personally get the word otherwise from me."

"Aye, aye, Sir."

"Have another little taste, Chief. This won't take long. And tell Mr. Pelosi to make sure they go out with tomorrow's pouch."

He sat down at the venerable Underwood with the Spanish keyboard, rolled a piece of paper into it, and started to type.

Clete walked Chief Schultz through the house and out to where he had parked his Model A on the drive.

"I thought maybe you would have learned to ride while I was gone," Clete said.

"Don't hold your fucking breath, Mr. Frade," Chief Schultz said. "Horses is dangerous."

He put the car in gear and drove off.

Clete walked back to his apartment. There was an untouched cognac snifter on the desk in the sitting.

Well, it's done now. In three, four days the Old Man'll have that letter, and what will happen will happen.

He picked up the snifter and drained it, then pushed open the door to his bedroom.

Just enough light was coming through the open window to make out the bed, so he didn't turn on the light.

He sat down at the bed and grunted as he pulled off the boots.

I wonder what happened? The goddamned things weren't so tight when I first put them on. But then I

456

couldn't walk. Did I have that much to drink? Or was it the charming company?

"I wondered if you were ever coming to bed," a voice behind him said. "What in the world were you doing out there anyway with that bloody type-writer? And who was that with you?"

He turned. His eyes had now adjusted to the light.

"Hello, Princess," he said.

She was sitting up in the bed, wearing a white nightgown.

"Hello, yourself, and don't call me that, please."

She sat up suddenly, then started to bounce on the mattress.

"I think I'm going to like sleeping here," she said. "This mattress is wonderful!"

"What did you do, climb in through the window?"

"I could hardly walk down the corridor, could I?" she asked reasonably. "What would people *think?*"

Then she held her arms open for him.

[Three]

La Capilla Nuestra Señora de los Milagros
Estancia San Pedro y San Pablo
Near Pila, Buenos Aires Province
0940 12 April 1943

A large, badly hand-tinted photograph of el Coronel Jorge Guillermo Frade in a gilded wooden frame sat on an easel in the center aisle of the chapel.

457

It was probably taken, Clete decided, shortly before his father retired from command of the Húsares de Pueyrredón. His father — wearing a ribbon-bedecked green tunic and a brimmed cap with an enormous crown — was photographed standing beside a horse, holding its reins. The saddle blanket carried the Húsares de Pueyrredón regimental crest and the insignia of a colonel.

Without conscious disrespect, he wondered where his father had gotten all the medals, and remembered Tony's crack that the Argentine Army passed out medals for three months' perfect attendance at mass.

There was plenty of time to examine the photograph, for two reasons. For one thing, the requiem mass had begun at eight. That was because work on Estancia San Pedro y San Pablo had to go on, and no one was going to work until the mass and the reception following it were over.

The second reason was that Clete had only limited success keeping his eyes off Dorotéa. The best he could do was focus his attention on either his father's photograph or the ceremony itself. Dorotéa was sitting beside him, her legs modestly crossed, on a slightly smaller version of his own thronelike, high-backed, elaborately carved chair.

She was wearing a black suit with a white lacy blouse, the lace covering most of her neck. She wore a black hat with a veil, and her black-gloved hands held a missal in her lap. In other words, she was the picture of respectable, demure, virginal young Christian womanhood.

Whenever he glanced at her, and she smiled demurely at him, his mind's eye flooded with images of Dorotéa wearing absolutely nothing at all, cavorting with enthusiastic carnal abandon

458

in his father's bed.

While it was probable that they at least dozed off momentarily sometime between the moment she held her arms open to him and the time she crawled out the bedroom window as the first light of day began to illuminate the bed (which would be rightfully theirs in the sight of God once the goddamned wedding was over and done with), he could not remember it.

These kinds of thoughts — not to mention the physiological reaction they caused in the area of his groin — did not seem appropriate within the Chapel of Our Lady of the Miracles during a service honoring his father's life, so he tried to hard to devote his attention to his father's portrait and the ceremony.

Behind what he thought of as his and Dorotéa's thrones, Humberto and Beatrice Duarte and the honored guests were seated in red-velvet-upholstered pews. The honored guests were Señora Claudia Carzino-Cormano and her two daughters; Suboficial Mayor (Retired) Enrico Rodríguez; Antonio LaVallé, el Coronel Frade's lifelong butler; Major Freiherr Hans-Peter von Wachtstein, a houseguest of Señora Carzino-Cormano; and el Capitán Roberto Lauffer, aide-de-camp to General Arturo Rawson, who had been assisting the late el Coronel Frade's son during the final services honoring his father.

Finally, the Bishop — who spoke after Fathers Denilo, Pordido, and Welner — concluded his "talk." Clete was not sure if it was a homily, a eulogy, or a thinly veiled plea for the new Patrón of Estancia San Pedro y San Pablo to continue the generous support of the diocese and its clergy that had been a longstanding tradition of previous God-fearing and commendably devout Patróns of the estancia.

The Bishop climbed down from the pulpit and took his place to lead the recessional parade. Father Welner, taking his place behind Fathers Denilo and Pordido, discreetly signaled Clete that it was time for him and Dorotéa to stand up and be prepared to join the recessional, immediately behind the crucifer.

The crucifer was the nice-looking blond kid who had taken Julius Caesar and Rudolpho's roan back to the stables the day before. Clete was reminded of his own service as a crucifer at Trinity Episcopal in Midland, Texas. He had been "promoted" to crucifer following an unfortunate incident in which he, functioning as one of two acolytes, had lost the taper from the candle-lighting device and set the altar cloth gloriously aflame.

The procession moved through the church, out, and then down the paths of the English garden until it reached the house. There the Bishop, the priests, and the deacon lined themselves up on the lower step of the verandah. The crucifer and the other acolytes marched off down the drive.

Clete and Dorotéa, and then Beatrice and Humberto, joined the clergy on the wide verandah step. Father Welner shifted position so that he was standing next to Clete.

Not on the ground, Clete thought, *but on the step. Was that on purpose? I've had about all of this I can take.*

First the Mallín family shook everybody's hand in the reception line.

That handshake and smile, Henry, are even more magnificently insincere than yesterday. Have you been practicing, or are you just hung over?

Henry Mallín next kissed his daughter, then subjected himself to the effusive greeting of Beatrice Frade de Duarte, who was obviously enjoying the reception line.

Pamela Mallín kissed him.

It's nice when Pamela kisses me that way, sort of motherly.

El Kid Brother is a little sheepish. He knows I'm pissed. Good. I am. Nobody likes a squealer.

"A beautiful service, I thought," Claudia Carzino-Cormano said, both shaking his hand and kissing him. "And the two of you were handsome."

You've lost just as much as I did, Claudia. Maybe more. You spent most of your life with him, and he never married you. Because of me. And then he got killed, also because of me. If I were you, I don't think I'd like me. You should have been sitting where Dorotéa sat, and we both know it.

"I'd like to talk to you, if we can find time, Claudia."

"We'll make time."

Isabela Carzino-Cormano kissed his cheek with about as much enthusiasm as Henry Mallín shook his hand.

The feeling is mutual, Señorita. Go fuck yourself.

"I felt a little better when I saw Dorotéa sitting there with you," Señorita Alicia Carzino-Cormano said.

"You're very sweet. Did I ever tell you that?"

"Again, my condolences, Señor Frade," Major Freiherr Hans-Peter von Wachtstein said, clicking his heels and bowing as he shook Clete's hand.

"I found that letter we were looking for," Clete said softly. "Don't leave before we have a chance to talk."

Peter nodded and moved on. El Capitán Roberto

461

Lauffer was next in line.

He heard what I said to Peter. And so did the Jesuit.

"When it's convenient, I would like to take that material off your hands."

"Just as soon as this is over."

And Welner heard that, too. I wonder how much he knows?

It was half an hour before the last of the guests and estancia workers had made their way through the line, and Father Welner could tug on the Bishop's vestments.

"Señor Frade suggests that you might like to have a coffee with him whenever you're ready," Welner said.

The Bishop beamed at Clete and then went into the house, trailed by the others.

"Thank God that's over," Dorotéa said. "I need to find a loo in the worst way."

"The worst way is probably blindfolded," Clete said solemnly.

It took her a moment to understand what he considered to be humor.

"And I'm going to marry you and spend the rest of my life with you?" she asked incredulously, and went quickly into the house.

When Clete saw Beatrice turn to him, a dazzling smile on her face, he moved quickly after Dorotéa.

The house was full of people; each of them had something to drink in one hand and something to eat in the other. He saw General Rawson and Colonel Perón.

I don't remember Perón coming through the line.

He saw Lauffer, who inclined his head in the direction of the safe and asked with his eyebrows if Clete was free to go there. Clete nodded.

Two well-dressed men — *Army officers?* Clete

462

wondered, *majors, maybe* — were in civvies standing in the corridor by the door of the private study. Two large leather briefcases rested on the floor beside them. And both men obviously carried pistols under their jackets.

Clete was fishing through his pockets for the key to the room when Enrico walked past him, his key in his hand.

Lauffer did not introduce Clete to the two officers, and they did not volunteer their names.

"Open it, Enrico," Clete ordered, and Enrico pulled the bookcase away from the safe and worked the combination. Then he spun the spoked wheel and pulled the safe door open.

Clete looked at Lauffer and saw one of the briefcases in his hand.

"Help yourself," Clete said.

"I wouldn't wish to take anything I shouldn't," Lauffer said.

Clete went to the safe and handed Lauffer bundles of currency. They all would have fit easily into one of the briefcases, but when Lauffer apparently decided Clete had handed him about half, he put out his hand to stop Clete, then motioned for the second briefcase.

The entire business didn't take two minutes.

"That's it," Clete said.

"Gracias, Mayor Frade," one of the two men said.

"I will inform el Coronel that we have finished our business," Lauffer said.

OK, el Coronel is obviously Perón. The reason I didn't see him in the reception line, or, for that matter, in church, either, now that I think about it, is that he and these two guys were sitting on the safe.

"You're leaving, Roberto?" Clete asked.

That was dumb. Both of these guys picked up on my calling him by his first name.

"When it pleases el General Rawson to leave, Señor Frade."

"Well, if I don't see you again, thank you for everything you have done for me in the past few days, Roberto."

"It has been my privilege to be of service, Señor Frade."

I think we did that perfectly. Roberto was properly formal with me, and I was the typical ill-mannered norteamericano who calls people he hardly knows by their first names.

The two men nodded to him and left the room. Clete now had no doubt they were officers. Lauffer left last.

Why do I have the idea I've made friends with that guy? Trust him? Feel comfortable that he's not going to run off at the mouth to anyone about Peter? Is that what you call masculine intuition? Or gross stupidity?

He gave in to his curiosity ten seconds after they left the room. He went out into the corridor in time to see them leaving the house by a door at the end of the corridor. He went into one of the rooms on the corridor and started to haul quickly on the canvas strip that raised the vertical wooden shutters.

He gave it one quick pull, and was about to give another, when Enrico stopped him.

"What?" Clete demanded impatiently.

Enrico gave him his El Winko Famoso, as Clete now thought of it, then showed him that if you pulled the canvas strip just a few inches, the shutter rose enough so you could see through the cracks. The message was clear. He could see out, and no

464

one would notice an open shutter, or one being opened.

"Gracias," Clete said, and peered through a crack.

Three cars were parked on the service road that ran past the kitchen, two 1941 Chevrolets and a car of about the same size sandwiched between them — he thought it was an Opel. The Chevrolets each held four men.

The two officers with the briefcases got in the backseat of the Opel. For two or three minutes, nothing happened. Then a Mercedes sedan appeared on the road. Clete saw the lanky form of el Coronel Juan Domingo Perón in the backseat. It drove on the lawn to move around the three cars on the road. Then they started after it.

Soon what was now a small convoy — a small, *armed* convoy, Clete thought — disappeared around the corner of the house.

"Where are they taking that money?" Clete asked.

Enrico shrugged.

Clete thought it interesting that el Coronel Perón had assumed responsibility for the money. That fixed Perón's place in the G.O.U. hierarchy; he was somewhere near the top.

Enrico lowered the shutter all the way and followed Clete into the corridor.

Peter von Wachtstein was standing by the open door to the private office.

"Captain Lauffer said he thought you would be back here," Peter said.

"Go on in," Clete said. "Don't let anybody else in here, Enrico."

He followed Peter into the study and closed the door.

"Lauffer came *looking* for me," Peter said. "To tell me you would be back here. What was that all about? How much does he know, in other words?"

"He was being a nice guy," Clete said. "He knew where I was, and that I wanted to see you. He doesn't know anything he shouldn't, and what he suspects he will keep to himself."

Peter did not seem convinced.

"Your father's letter is in there," Clete said, pointing over his shoulder toward the safe. When Peter looked confused, Clete turned and saw that the movable section of the bookcase was back in place.

He went to it and swung it outward.

"You saw it?" Peter asked.

"And the documents."

"Then you might as well leave it where it is," Peter said. "I certainly don't have a better place to hide it."

"Maybe Alicia does," Clete said. "You can leave it here, of course. But . . ."

"I'll ask her," Peter said. "I hadn't thought about her."

"Or Claudia may have a place," Clete said as he swung the bookcase closed.

"Claudia's up to her ass in this coup d'état," Peter said. "Half the General Staff of the Argentine Army is, or has been, at her place in the last twenty-four hours."

"I don't suppose you heard anything interesting?"

"Is that personal curiosity, or is the OSS interested?"

"Both."

"I'll tell you something I heard," Peter said, meeting his eyes. "That should get your personal

attention. We have a visitor. A Standartenführer —
do you know what that is?"

Clete nodded.

"Yesterday morning Standartenführer Goltz ordered Grüner to have your man Ettinger killed. As
soon as possible."

"Who told you that?"

"Von Lutzenberger. You better tell your man to
watch his back, Clete."

I wonder if von Lutzenberger also told Martin?
And do I tell Peter I already heard about it?
No. I don't know why no, but no.

"I'm interested in this SS guy. Why is he here?"

"That sounds like the OSS asking," Peter said.

"You sound like you're trying to straddle a fence,
Peter," Clete said softly.

"You have to understand, my friend, that I have
this large yellow streak running down my back,"
Peter replied. "I don't want Goltz finding out about
it, as he's likely to do if he learns you — the Americans — are onto him, and starts wondering who
could have told you. He's SS-SD. They follow the
charming Nazi philosophy that it's better to gar-
rote, or castrate, one hundred innocent men than
have one guilty one get away."

Clete didn't reply.

"Not only am I not used to — what's that charming phrase in international law? 'giving aid and
comfort to the enemy'?" Peter went on, "but I
don't like the odds that Goltz will hear about it
and order Grüner to have somebody cut *my* throat
and blame it on burglars. Not only would it foul
up what my father wants me to do, but I think it
might hurt."

"So what's the SS guy up to?" Clete asked.

Peter looked at him and chuckled.

"Believe it or not, according to von Lutzenberger, the same thing I am. We are. Making safe investments in Argentina. For different people, I'm sure, but the same thing."

"Tell me more," Clete said.

"As Mata Hari said to the nice young Spad pilot?"

Clete chuckled.

"I thought what Mata Hari said to the young Spad pilot was 'why don't you let *me* play with your joystick?' "

"God, that's terrible!" Peter said. "Your sense of humor is not only juvenile, but vulgar beyond —"

"So what's the SS guy up to?" Clete asked again.

"I don't know much — von Lutzenberger didn't have time to tell me much — but there's apparently a lot of money on the way here — plus jewelry and negotiable securities."

"How on the way here? And how much is a lot of money?"

Peter hesitated.

"This is difficult for me, you understand," he said. "There is a difference in being philosophically opposed to what the Nazis are doing and in giving information to the enemy who will use it in such a manner as to cause the deaths of one's countrymen, many of whom are not Nazis, and some of whom are as opposed to Hitler as I am."

Clete did not reply.

"A replacement for the *Reine de la Mer* is en route," Peter said, finally. "A Spanish ship called the *Comerciante del Océano Pacífico*."

"If it makes you feel any better, we already knew that," Clete said.

That's not the truth. What the OSS knows is that a replacement ship is en route. This is the first I've ever heard her name. Why did I lie — and so automatically — to Peter? As a good intelligence officer, wanting to keep his source feeling less guilty? Or as his friend?

"You did?" Peter asked, surprised.

Clete ignored the question. "The money you're talking about is aboard that ship?"

Peter nodded. "He didn't say — von Lutzenberger didn't say — how much money. But he did say Goltz told him they already have twenty million of your dollars in Uruguay. That reminds me of something my father told me —"

"Tell me about the twenty million dollars in Uruguay," Clete interrupted.

"That's all I know about it," Peter said. "Why are you interested?"

"There's a story going around that for enough money, paid in Uruguay, you can ransom people out of concentration camps."

"Where'd you hear that?"

Clete held up hands, palms outward, to show that he didn't want to reveal his source.

"If they have twenty million in Uruguay, it could be ransom money."

"I don't believe it."

"Keep your ears open."

"You're serious about this, aren't you?" Peter asked, surprised.

"Yes, I am."

"I don't believe it," Peter said. "Not that they aren't capable of it morally; they are. Most of the SS would sell their mothers. But I just can't believe it could be done. The risks would be enormous."

"Unless it was being done by some very senior people, or under their authority," Clete said. "Does this guy Goltz fit those shoes?"

Peter looked thoughtful. "Von Lutzenberger told

469

me he's the liaison between Himmler and Bormann."

"I don't know what —"

"Reichsführer-SS Heinrich Himmler runs just about everything in Germany connected with the SS, the police, the Gestapo, counterintelligence . . .'"

"Including concentration camps?"

"Including, of course, concentration camps. Martin Bormann is the Party Chancellor."

"What's that?"

"He runs the Nazi party. He's Hitler's private secretary. I don't mean he takes shorthand. It's half a dozen one way and six the other who is second in power to Hitler between them."

"I thought Göring was Hitler's Number Two."

"The last time I saw *Der Grosse Hermann,* he was wearing his uniform as Chief Hunter of the Reich, which included lederhosen — short leather pants — and a Robin Hood hat with a long feather. . . ."

"You're kidding!"

Peter spread his hands to show the length of the feather.

"Not at all. And more makeup than Marlene Dietrich."

"In public?" Clete asked, not sure if he should believe Peter or not.

"I saw him dressed that way at his estate. Karin Hall. The Commander in Chief of the Luftwaffe has the custom of inviting all pilots who earn anything more than the Iron Cross First Class for a weekend at Karin Hall, where, more often than not, he tries to get them in bed."

"He's homosexual?" Clete asked incredulously.

"You really are naive, aren't you?" Peter said. "Queer as he can be. And he's also a drug addict."

"And Hitler knows this?"

"Of course, which is why Göring is not Hitler's Number Two, no matter what is being put out for public consumption. Bormann and Himmler are swine, but they don't make themselves up like women, and, more important, they don't take drugs. Whatever else my Führer is, he's not a fool."

"You ever meet Hitler?"

"Oh, yes. Many times. When he hung my Knight's Cross on me, he told me I was the future of Germany. Fascinating man. Charming. Spend ten minutes in his presence, and you'd volunteer to follow him into Hell. Which is, of course, what has happened to a lot of people. They have done just that."

"The Commander in Chief of the Luftwaffe didn't find you attractive, Peter? Or did he?"

Peter smiled. "I'm sure he did. Why not? I'm a handsome fellow."

"Jesus!"

"My father is on the OKW staff," Peter said, turning serious. "Making advances to me might have had consequences. Göring, and others like him, generally leave the aristocracy and the officer class alone. They have thousands of others to choose from."

"If this guy, Goltz, is connected to Bormann and . . . what was the other one's name?"

"Himmler," Peter said, his tone making it clear he found it odd Clete could not remember the name. "I take your point. Between those two, anything could be arranged in Germany. But why? They all have more money than they know what to do with. What would they do with more money if they had it?"

471

"Buy property in Argentina," Clete said. "Wait a minute. . . ."

Peter looked at him curiously.

"*Why* would they want to buy property here?" Clete asked. "Think about it."

Peter looked at him without comprehension.

"You tell me," he said, finally.

"Why are you buying property here?"

"So that something can be salvaged from the ashes," Peter said.

"You just said your Führer is no fool. Maybe he's figured out he's already lost the war and is looking for a place to go when it's over."

Peter considered that.

"If he wanted to do that — just for the sake of argument — he'd simply send money to von Lutzenberger and tell him to buy property."

"There would be a record of that," Clete said. "Roosevelt and Churchill called for unconditional surrender at the Casablanca Conference. We would find the records of something like that, declare that it was property of the former German government, and therefore belonged to us."

Peter considered that a long moment.

"I'm not saying that's impossible, but it's hard to believe."

"I find it hard to believe that the Commander in Chief of the Luftwaffe is a drug addict and a faggot who goes around seducing his pilots dressed up like Robin Hood."

Peter looked at him again for a long moment, and Clete saw acceptance come into his eyes.

"I'll see what I can find out."

"If I'm right, that means that you and Uncle Humberto will have to be damned careful to make sure what you're doing here isn't lumped together

472

with the Nazi property."

"I'll see what I can find out," Peter repeated.

"When are you going back?"

"Tonight," Peter said. "Von Lutzenberger said Goltz will probably want to go to Uruguay first thing Monday morning. I told you he wants me to fly him over in the Storch."

"When are you coming back?"

"Maybe the same day. But I'd bet no later than Tuesday."

"I'd like to know who Goltz sees in Uruguay."

"I'll see what I can find out."

"I won't be back in Buenos Aires before Tuesday at the earliest. You want to meet at The Horse — The Fish — Wednesday night?"

"We better set up a time now," Peter said. "That would save a telephone call. Ten o'clock? If either of us can't make it, say by ten-thirty, we'll try something else."

"Ten's fine with me," Clete said.

"Is a personal question in order?" Peter asked.

"Certainly."

"Dorotéa?"

"The idea of having Dorotéa sit beside me on the royal thrones — that is what you're asking?" Peter, smiling, nodded. ". . . was to convey the idea to our loyal subjects and the upper strata of Argentinian society that we have been engaged for some time, with the blessing of our parents. That will further explain why we will be married here, quietly, in about two weeks."

"I heard that much from Alicia, who heard it from her mother," Peter said, but it was a question.

"She's pregnant, Peter."

"In that case, congratulations."

"Yes, it was, Peter."

"Yes, it was what?"

"Grossly irresponsible of me."

"I didn't think that."

"Yes, you did."

"Yes, I did," Peter confessed. "And it puts me on a hell of a spot, you understand."

"Alicia wants to get married?"

"Yes."

"I'm in no position to offer anyone any advice."

"Or me," Peter said, and put out his hand. "Good luck, my friend."

XV

[One]

The Reception
Estancia San Pedro y San Pablo
Near Pila, Buenos Aires Province
1645 12 April 1943

Clete was standing with Humberto Duarte, holding a cup of coffee, in a circle of seven men. Each of them, he had come to understand, either managed one Frade enterprise or another or had business dealings with it. They had come from all over Argentina to pay their final respects to el Coronel, and of course to meet the new Patrón.

It was something like a one-man reception line, the difference being that those passing through it felt they had either the right or the obligation — he wasn't sure which — to join the half dozen or so standing around el Patrón for a cup of coffee and four or five minutes of conversation. As one man joined the group, and a maid offered him a tiny white gold-rimmed coffee cup and saucer, another left the group and placed his coffee cup and saucer on the maid's tray.

There was a steady stream of them all afternoon, either employees of what Clete had started to think of as El Coronel Incorporated, or representatives of businesses that bought from, or sold to, one El Coronel Inc. subsidiary or another.

Humberto, for example, introduced him not only to the man who ran the San Bosco vineyards in Córdoba, but the men who sold San Bosco the wine bottles; the corks that sealed San Bosco's bottles; and the bottle labels — this one also sold San Bosco the cases in which the wine bottles were packed. One man told him his father had begun carting San Bosco wine with horse-drawn wagons. And a somewhat effete gentleman told him that with the exception of Buenos Aires Province, he handled distribution of San Bosco products throughout the country.

The same thing was true of the people connected with Estancia San Pedro y San Pablo itself, and with the other estancias and enterprises of El Coronel Inc. around the country. In some place called Bariloche — he had never previously heard of it — he learned El Coronel Inc. owned both a trout farm and a dairy farm, which also manufactured cheese. He found the trout farm fascinating, for he had previously believed the only way to harvest trout was by standing in a stream with a fly-casting rod.

Several people blurted that they had not known that el Coronel had a son. Yet there was an almost universal surprised relief that el Patrón spoke Spanish. Which meant, of course, that everyone knew that he was a norteamericano. He wondered if any of them had heard the rumors that el Coronel was killed by the Germans because his son was an American OSS agent. If anyone had, no one was tactless enough, or careless enough, to make reference to it.

Humberto stood at his side throughout the ordeal. Claudia had left an hour after the requiem mass with what Clete thought of as the Military Delegation . . . but only after telling him what was expected of him in "receiving" the managers and the businesspeople. Humberto, she went on to explain, would suggest how to deal with "the people in Buenos Aires" — he inferred she meant lawyers and bankers and their ilk. He would have to start doing that no later than Wednesday.

He had only a rare glimpse of Dorotéa. She and her mother mingled in the reception with the wives of the men who spoke to Clete. But he didn't have a chance to talk to her. Earlier he had sent Little Henry off riding with the good-looking kid — whose name, he learned, was Gustavo, which almost certainly confirmed that Gustavo was German. He firmly admonished Gustavo to put Little Henry on a horse he would have minimal chance of falling from. He didn't see Henry Mallín, and wondered if this was because Dorotéa's father didn't want to see Cletus H. Frade, or whether he was sleeping off the effects of the night before.

Clete sensed that Antonio had walked up behind him.

"Señor, your guests are leaving," Antonio said.

"Excuse me, gentlemen, please," Clete said, and placed his coffee cup on the maid's tray.

When Clete reached them, the Mallín family was already on the verandah, their luggage stacked around them, waiting for someone to bring their car. Little Henry, Clete noticed, showed no signs of a fall from a horse. Dorotéa had changed from the black suit she had worn all day into a skirt and blouse.

"Thank you for coming, Henry," Clete said.

"So kind of you to have us," Mallín replied with a smile that would freeze a West Texas water hole in the middle of August.

"I suppose we'll see you very soon, Cletus," Pamela said. "We really have no time at all, do we?"

"I'm going into the city either Tuesday or Wednesday," Clete said. "Claudia said she'd help with things out here."

"That's my responsibility — mother of the bride — but it was sweet of you to think of asking her, and I will need her."

"Thank you for the ride, Clete," Little Henry said.

"What ride?" Henry Mallín asked.

"Clete sent Henry riding with one of his gauchos," Pamela replied. "Wasn't that nice of him?"

Henry did not reply.

Rudolpho pulled up before the verandah in the Mallíns' Rolls Royce drophead coupe, stepped out, and started to load the luggage in the trunk.

"Thank you for my ring, Cletus," Dorotéa said, and with her father watching in evident discomfort, kissed him on the lips with slightly less passion than she might have kissed Little Henry.

Henry Mallín walked around the front of the car. Clete went to the passenger side with Dorotéa, ushered Little Henry into the backseat, and waited for an opportunity to kiss Dorotéa again. It did not present itself. She slumped against the seat and smiled at him demurely.

"Oh, damn," she said. "I think I left my compact on the roof!"

"Great!" her father said.

Clete surveyed the roof. Dorotéa moved forward on her seat to see if he could locate the compact. This movement placed her close to Clete's midsection in such a way that her body concealed the movement of her hand, which she used to possessively squeeze Clete's reproductive apparatus.

"It's not here!" Clete cried, referring to Dorotéa's compact.

"Well, perhaps I was mistaken," Dorotéa said, sliding back onto the seat. From there she smiled demurely at Clete again, waved her fingers at him, and admonished him to "be a good boy, Cletus."

"Goddamn," Clete blurted, "you're really something!"

"Would you please close the door?" Henry Mallín asked impatiently.

Clete watched the Rolls Royce until it was out of sight, then turned to reenter the house.

"Excuse me, Señor Frade," a short, muscular man of about forty asked. "Do you remember me? Capitán Delgano?"

Oh, yeah, I remember you, you sonofabitch! You were my father's pilot, and he trusted you, and you were all the time working for Martín and the goddamned BIS!

"I remember you," Clete said.

"I wonder if I might have a moment of your time, Señor Frade?"

"I can't think of a thing we might have to say to one another, Capitán," Clete said coldly.

There was hurt in Delgano's large dark eyes.

"I would prefer to talk with you somewhere we would be less likely to be overheard," he said, and gestured toward the English garden.

"I have nothing to say to you," Clete repeated,

and started up the steps. Enrico was standing by the door.

"I am here at the direction of Coronel Martín," Delgano said softly.

Clete turned and looked at him, then gestured toward the garden.

Delgano walked down the red-gravel path until almost at the center of the garden, then stopped.

"Martín sent you? You're still working for him?"

Delgano did not reply directly, but the question was answered.

"I would ask you to consider that people in our profession are sometimes required to do things that are personally repugnant, Mayor Frade. Your father, for whom I had the greatest respect, came to understand that I was, and am, a serving officer, carrying out my orders."

"I thought you were supposed to be retired," Clete challenged.

Why am I talking to this sonofabitch?

"And you are supposed to have been discharged from the Corps of Marines, mi Mayor."

"What did Martín send you out here to say, Delgano?"

"I have been here all along, mi Mayor."

Clete's surprise, or disbelief, showed on his face.

"Your father reemployed me a week after you went to the United States," Delgano said. "At the request of Coronel Martín, after your father understood that Coronel Martín had allied himself with the Grupo de Oficiales Unidos."

That's what Enrico meant when he said "Martín is now one of us."

"What's on your mind, Capitán?"

"I have two missions," Delgano said, "which should make you believe me. The first is to provide any protection I can for your man Ettinger against the German problem."

"How will you do that?"

"If you will let me know when he leaves the estancia, I will see that he is not alone," Delgano said. "The more notice you can give me, of course, the better. The second is to deal with the problem of the aircraft you wish to import. We have to reach an understanding about the airplane."

He could have heard about the assassination order someplace else, but the only place he could have heard about the airplane is from Martin.

"What's the understanding? That every time I get in it, you're my copilot?"

Delgano smiled.

"I'm sure our mutual friend would like that, and I am equally sure he realizes that would not be possible," he said. "My orders are to assist you in bringing the airplane here from Brazil, on condition that you teach me how to fly it, and that the airplane be placed at Coronel Martín's disposal at a time he has specified — he has a three-day period in mind."

What the hell is that all about? OK!

"In case OUTLINE BLUE goes wrong? To take certain people out of the country in a hurry?"

Delgano held up both hands, palms outward, and shrugged.

What did I expect him to say?

"Are those conditions acceptable, mi Mayor?"

Clete nodded.

"Then let's try to bring the airplane here," Delgano said. "Where is it now?"

"Somewhere in Brazil."

"You don't know where?"

Clete shook his head, "no."

"But you can find out? We'll need to know that."

"I can find out."

"The scheme is to put the registration numbers of the stagger-wing on the new plane. And then to change the fuselage serial number — and the number of engines — on the Argentine registration documents. The numbers can be put on here, or where the aircraft is now. The question then becomes how to fly the aircraft from where it is in Brazil to an airfield in Argentina. That airfield will obviously depend on where the aircraft is in Brazil and its range."

"Changing the registration papers will be that easy?"

"I don't know how easy, but I'm sure Coronel Martín can arrange it."

"I don't know the stagger-wing's numbers."

Delgano reached in his pocket and handed him a slip of paper.

"If it could be done, it would be helpful to have the aircraft painted the same color — which I understand is called 'Beechcraft Stagger-wing Red.' "

"Yeah," Clete said. "Let me look into that."

Delgano put out his hand.

Clete looked at it.

"The sooner this can be done, the better," Delgano said. "Can I tell Coronel Martín that I expect to hear from you soon?"

"We're about to have a revolution, are we?" Clete asked.

Then he took Delgano's hand.

"I really didn't expect you to answer that," he said, then turned and walked away from Delgano.

Enrico was standing at the entrance to the path through the garden.

"Why didn't you tell me Delgano was here?" Clete asked.

"You didn't ask me," Enrico replied.

[Two]

```
Office of the Director
The Office of Strategic Services
Washington, D.C.
0830 13 April 1943
```

"This came in overnight, Bill," Colonel A. F. Graham, USMCR, said to OSS Director William J. Donovan, and laid a large manila envelope on his desk. "I thought you better have a look at it."

Donovan took the manila envelope, removed from it a slightly smaller white envelope stamped TOP SECRET in large letters, from that took two sheets of neatly typed paper, and then started to read them.

To judge by his expression, his initial reaction was not favorable.

```
                 TOP  SECRET

LINDBERGH
URGENT
FROM STACHIEF AGGIE
1605 GREENWICH 12APR43
MSG NO 0002
TO ORACLE WASHDC
EYES ONLY FOR DDWHO GRAHAM


   1.  IN RE LINDBERGH.

   A. RELIABLE SOURCE (HEREAFTER
GALAHAD) REPORTS REINE DE LA MER
REPLACEMENT IS SPANISH REGISTERED
COMERCIANTE DEL OCÉANO PACÍFICO
(HEREAFTER GROCERYTWO) EN ROUTE
ARGENTINA CARRYING LARGE AMOUNTS
OF MONEY AND VALUABLES (UNCONFIRM-
ABLE FIGURE 100 REPEAT 100 MILLION
DOLLARS) PURPOSE ACQUIRING SAFE
HAVEN FOR FUNDS AND/OR ACQUIRING
REAL ESTATE FOR POSSIBLE POSTWAR
HAVEN FOR SENIOR NAZIS. INVESTI-
GATING.
   B. POSSIBILITY EXISTS LINDBERGH
RANSOM FUNDS INTENDED FOR SAME
PURPOSE. INVESTIGATING.
```

"There he goes again," Donovan said.

"Excuse me?"

"Another unidentified 'reliable' source. Who the hell is 'Galahad'?"

"He doesn't say," Graham said.

Donovan ran his eyes down the rest of the message.

"And he hasn't identified the other one, 'Cavalry,' either. You *did* ask for that information, didn't you?"

"Yes, I did."

"Do you think he forgot to send it?" Donovan asked sarcastically. "I would hate to think he's ignoring you, Alex."

"Frade may have his reasons."

"For example?"

"It comes immediately to my mind that he doesn't want the others on the team to know the identities of these people in case they find themselves interrogated."

"And what if something happens to Frade and nobody else knows who Cavalry or Galahad are? They would then be lost to us."

"I'm sure he's considered that."

"And decided not to tell you?"

Graham nodded. "That's possible. Maybe even likely. I think I have to give Frade the benefit of the doubt on something like this."

"You understand the implications of that 'safe haven,' Alex?"

"It suggests someone high up in Berlin isn't quite as sure of the 'Final Victory' as they would have people believe?"

"I'd like to go to the President with this safe haven business, but I'm not doing that on the basis of a 'reliable source' without a name."

"I'll ask him again," Graham said.

"No. You will *tell* him again."

They locked eyes for a long moment, then Graham shrugged.

"You're the boss," he said.

"Yes, I am," Donovan said, and resumed reading.

"Are you going to the President with the name of the German vessel?" Graham asked.

"If we board, much less sink, a Spanish ship on the high seas," Donovan said, visibly annoyed at the interruption, "we'll have to have a more reliable source than somebody we know only as 'Galahad.' No. I'm not going to the President with that."

"The *Comerciante del Océano Pacífico* is one of the ships on our list," Graham said.

"You're not listening, Alex. We need to know who Galahad is, how he came by this information, and why he's telling us. Now, can I finish reading this, please?"

```
    2. IN RE AIRCRAFT: REQUIREMENTS
TO MOVE AIRCRAFT HERE FOLLOW:


    A. ENTIRE AIRCRAFT IS TO BE
PAINTED IN COLOR KNOWN AS BEECH-
CRAFT STAGGER WING RED.
    B. REGISTRATION NUMBERS Z DASH
5 8 4 3 REPEAT Z DASH 5 8 4 3 ARE
TO BE PAINTED

    (1) EIGHT INCH BLACK BLOCK
LETTERS ON OUTWARD FACING SUR-
FACES VERTICAL STABILIZERS AP-
PROXIMATELY ONE FOOT FROM TOP
    (2) TWENTY-FOUR INCH BLACK
BLOCK LETTERS CENTERED ON TOP
SURFACE RIGHT WING
    (3) AS (2) ABOVE EXCEPT UNDER
SURFACE LEFT WING

    C. LOCATION OF AIRFIELD FROM
WHICH COVERT TAKEOFF PREFERABLY IN
```

HOURS OF DARKNESS CAN BE MADE. WOULD APPRECIATE ONE HOUR OF COCKPIT FAMILIARIZATION AND TOUCH AND GOES.

D. AIRCRAFT SHOULD BE AVAILABLE IMMEDIATELY ON ARRIVAL OF UNDERSIGNED AT AIRFIELD THEREFORE WILL NEED NAME OF 24 HOURADAY CONTACT OFFICER WITH AUTHORITY TO TRANSFER AIRCRAFT TO UNDERSIGNED AND CLEAR COVERT TAKEOFF.

E. WILL REQUIRE 48 TO 72 HOURS FROM RECEIPT YOUR NOTIFICATION FOR TRAVEL TO AIRFIELD. URGE SOONEST POSSIBLE ACTION YOUR PART.

STACHIEF END

TOP SECRET

LINDBERGH

"Well, it looks as if he's figured out how to take the airplane into Argentina, doesn't it?" Donovan asked. "Can we handle what he wants, painting it?"

"That shouldn't pose a problem," Graham said.

"He wants it painted. Painted red. 'Beechcraft Stagger-wing Red.' That's a color? What the hell's that all about?"

"I have no idea. But I'm sure he has his reasons."

"Wait a minute," Donovan said. "There was something about that airplane!"

"What about it?"

"Helen!" Donovan raised his voice. "Can you lay your hands on the file about that airplane we sent to Brazil, Direction of the President?"

Donovan's middle-aged but still very attractive secretary laid a file folder stamped TOP SECRET on his desk two minutes later. Donovan flipped through it quickly.

"Yeah, I knew there was something," he said, a slight triumphant tone in his voice. "It was not a Beechcraft. They couldn't come up with a Beechcraft on such short notice."

"And?"

"When we asked the goddamned Air Corps for an airplane, they said they could give us a C-45. We said fine. Then they said they couldn't give us a C-45, after all, how about a C-56?"

"What's a C-56?" Graham asked. "I can't keep those model numbers straight."

"The Air Corps man I asked," Helen offered, "said they were about the same thing. Both twin-engine small transports."

"How small?" Donovan asked. "Compared to the C-47, for example?"

"Smaller," Helen said. "The Air Corps man, I can't think of his name offhand, he was a brigadier general, it should be in there somewhere, said they were both smaller than the C-47."

"Is that a problem?" Graham asked.

"Not for me, Alex," Donovan said. "For you. You'll have to find this Air Corps general's name, and then, without telling him why, tell him he has to arrange for the Air Corps in Brazil to paint this C-56, or whatever the hell it is, fire-engine red, and then have somebody available around the clock down there who can show Frade how to fly it. But you can't, of course, tell him who Frade is, when he's showing up, or where he's going with the airplane. Good luck!"

"Thank you," Graham said, chuckling.

"I'm not really trying to be funny," Donovan said. "After we go through all this, how do we know that Frade can really fly this airplane? Have you considered that?"

"He's a Marine aviator, Bill," Graham said. "Of course he can fly it!"

"Oh, God!" Donovan groaned. "Get out of here, Alex, and let me do some work."

[Three]

Above Nueva Helvecia
Uruguay
1105 13 April 1943

Major Freiherr Hans-Peter von Wachtstein turned and looked into the backseat of the Storch to see if Standartenführer Josef Goltz was awake.

He was. He was wearing a gray flight suit, a coverall-like garment that he had reluctantly crawled into at La Palomar airfield an hour and a half before. He had earphones on his head.

Peter gestured with his hand out the window and down. When he saw that Goltz was looking at the small town under their right wing, he picked up his microphone.

"New Switzerland, Herr Standartenführer," Peter said.

It took Goltz some time to locate his microphone and push its transmit button.

"What?"

"New Switzerland, Herr Standartenführer," Peter repeated. "They call it Nueva Helvecia. A little further up the river, there is Nueva Berlin."

Goltz did not seem grateful for this recitation of travel lore.

"How far to Montevideo?" Goltz asked impatiently.

"Approximately fifty minutes, Herr Standartenführer," Peter replied, then gave in to the impulse and added, "unless we pick up some more headwinds, which may delay us another twenty minutes or so."

There were no headwinds. Peter had invented them for the same reason he'd made a full-flaps, full-power takeoff from La Palomar, which he knew would cause an unpleasant sinking feeling in the Herr Standartenführer's stomach. Likewise, whenever he'd glanced in the rear seat and noticed that the Herr Standartenführer was about to doze off, he'd made sudden small attitude and directional changes that he knew would wake him up.

We would be touching down right about now at Carrasco, Schiesskopf, if you hadn't insisted we fly the overland route.

He'd taken off from La Palomar and headed north — Montevideo was to the east. Avoiding the Restricted Zone around Campo de Mayo, he'd flown over El Tigre and the Delta, then turned east and crossed the Río Uruguay into Uruguay, south of a small town called Carmelo.

"Have we sufficient fuel?" Goltz asked.

Peter looked at the fuel gauges and did the mental arithmetic. They had at least two hours to make the airfield at Carrasco, ten miles or so east of Montevideo.

"I'm sure we'll make it all right, Herr Standartenführer," Peter said with what he hoped was a detectable lack of conviction in his voice. "But there's nothing to worry about, Herr Standartenführer. I can set this thing down almost anywhere, on the road or in a field."

He then picked up his chart and studied it carefully — and wholly unnecessarily. He was going to use Uruguay's Route Nacionale Number One, below him, to find Montevideo. But with a little bit of luck, Herr Schiesskopf might think they were lost.

When he lined up with the one paved runway of Carrasco's airfield, it occurred to Peter that this was the ninth time he had been to Uruguay. But it would be the first time — Goltz said he was going to spend the night — that he would be able to see more of it than the airport.

Most of his previous flights had been to deliver or pick up a diplomatic pouch or other correspondence between the Embassy in Buenos Aires and the German Embassy here. There had been only a few passengers. Most of the Embassy staff of sufficient importance to have access to the Storch preferred the comfort of the overnight ship to Montevideo to the un-upholstered backseat of the Storch. Always before, Peter had landed at Carrasco, turned over or picked up his cargo, refueled, and flown back to Buenos Aires.

The Condor Dieter von und zu Aschenburg had flown in on Friday carried a pouch for the German Embassy in Montevideo. Ordinarily, Peter would have flown it across the river the same day; but Gradny-Sawz's insistence that Peter attend the services for Oberst Frade had delayed that until today. That pouch was now under Goltz's seat. And tomorrow, when he returned to Buenos Aires, he would almost certainly have a pouch — two or more pouches, he hoped, heavy ones that he could look at with great concern as Goltz watched — to take to Buenos Aires and put aboard the Condor when it returned to Germany tomorrow afternoon.

He taxied to the terminal, and Uruguayan Customs and Immigration officers came out to the plane. There was no problem. They had diplomatic status and were immune to all local laws.

"Your orders, Herr Standartenführer?" Peter asked as he waited for Goltz to take off the flight suit.

"What do you normally do, von Wachtstein?"

"Ordinarily, Herr Standartenführer, I exchange packages with whoever comes out here from the Embassy, refuel the aircraft, and fly back to Buenos Aires."

"So you will need someplace to stay tonight, is that it?"

"Oberst Grüner suggested I stay at the Casino Hotel here in Carrasco, Herr Standartenführer."

"And the diplomatic pouch, what do you plan to do with that?"

"Ordinarily, Herr Standartenführer, someone from the Embassy is here to take it off my hands."

"I wish I had given thought to that damned pouch before this," Goltz said. "Arranged for someone to meet you here."

"Is there a problem, Herr Standartenführer?"

"I hadn't planned to visit the Embassy. My business here is with the Security Officer of the Embassy, an old friend. My plan was to conduct our business at his home, and then spend the night with him."

"I'm sure I could take a taxi to the Embassy, Herr Standartenführer, and then another to the Casino Hotel, if that meets with your approval."

"No. I know what to do. I'll telephone him that I'm here. He will come out to meet me. Presumably, you can turn over the pouch to him?"

"To the Security Officer? Of course, Herr Standartenführer."

"And then he can drop you at the hotel, we can go about our business, and we will pick you up at the hotel in the morning. How does that sound?"

"Whatever the Herr Standartenführer wishes."

"Where is a telephone?"

"Just inside the terminal, Herr Standartenführer."

"Well, I'll make the call, and you do whatever you have to do to the airplane."

"Jawohl, Herr Standartenführer!"

While they waited, Peter took the opportunity to refuel the Storch. As he was doing that, he wondered why Goltz's old friend the Embassy Security Officer, or at least someone from the Embassy, was not waiting for them at the airport when they landed. Thirty minutes later a canary-yellow 1941 Chevrolet convertible, roof down, raced up to the entrance of the terminal building.

A nattily dressed, somewhat portly man in his forties, sporting a neatly manicured full — à la Adolf Hitler — mustache jumped from behind the wheel and walked quickly to Goltz.

"Herr Standartenführer, how good it is to see you!"

"Werner, how are you?" Goltz said, enthusiastically shaking his hand, then asking admiringly, "Where did you get that car?"

"Inge saw it," the portly man said, gesturing to the woman stepping out of the car. "Said it matched her hair, and absolutely had to have it."

"My dear Inge," Goltz said. "As lovely as ever!"
Christ, I know her!

"Josef, how good to see you. Welcome to Uruguay."

"May I present Major Freiherr Hans-Peter von Wachtstein?" Goltz said. "Sturmbannführer von Tresmarck and his lovely bride."

"I believe," Frau von Tresmarck said coyly, "that the Major and I have met. Isn't that so, Herr Major?"

Frau von Tresmarck was a tall, slim blonde perhaps fifteen years younger than her husband.

Indeed, we have met — if memory serves, in the bar at the Hotel am Zoo — and then spent two days in the Hotel am Wansee, leaving bed only to meet the calls of nature. I returned to the Squadron with just barely enough energy to crawl into the cockpit.

"I believe we have, Frau Sturmbannführer," Peter said, bobbing his head and clicking his heels. "I've been trying to recall where."

"Me too," she said. "It'll come to me, where we met."

Peter offered his hand to von Tresmarck, who smiled when he took it but looked at him oddly.

Are you aware, Herr Sturmbannführer, that your wife has probably taken to bed one in four of the fighter pilots in the Luftwaffe? Is that why you're looking at me that way?

"We have a small problem, Werner," Goltz said. "Von Wachtstein has a pouch for the Embassy, and presumably there will be another for him to take back to Buenos Aires tomorrow. . . ."

"That shouldn't be a problem, Josef," Inge von Tresmarck said. "When we reach the house, Werner can call the Embassy and have someone come for it."

"Unfortunately, Inge," Goltz said, "arrangements have been made for von Wachtstein to stay at the Casino Hotel. He has business of his own to transact."

You either know the Gnädige Frau von Tresmarck fucks like a mink and are trying to avoid Inge and me causing a social problem, or you don't want me around with you and von Tresmarck. One or the other. Or both.

"What a pity," Inge said.

"I can take the pouch off your hands, von Wachtstein," von Tresmarck said. "And we can drop you at the Casino Hotel. It's not far from here."

"You're very kind, Herr Sturmbannführer."

"And we'll work out how to deal with the outgoing pouch sometime today," Goltz said.

"I am at your orders, Herr Standartenführer."

Peter took the receipt form for the pouch from his jacket pocket and gave it to von Tresmarck to sign. When he put the signed receipt in his pocket, he saw that Inge had climbed back into the car, into the rear seat.

"My dear Inge," Goltz said, "I will ride in the back with von Wachtstein."

"No, you're our honored guest," Inge said.

Von Tresmarck gave Peter another strange look as he climbed in the back with Inge.

As soon as they were moving, Inge slid forward on her seat and rested her elbows on the back of the seat between her husband and Goltz.

"I can't tell you how delighted I am to see you, Josef," she said. "Now, don't go running to the Ambassador to tell him I said this, but those Foreign Ministry people are dull, dull, dull."

"This isn't Berlin, is it?"

"And one feels . . . oh, I don't know how to say

this, and I know Werner is doing important things, but I feel . . . *guilty* I guess is the word . . . guilty about being away from the home front, where I could do something for the cause!"

"But my dear Inge," Goltz said. "You are doing something for the cause! Your very presence here helps Werner in the accomplishment of his responsibilities."

"I wish I could do more," Inge said.

She pushed herself off the seat back and slid back into the rear seat. The fingers of her right hand moved slowly and provocatively up Peter's leg.

With a little bit of luck, we are almost at the Casino Hotel, and I can bid auf wedersehn *to the lovely Frau Sturmbannführer von Tresmarck before anything happens.*

Ten minutes later, after passing through a residential area that reminded Peter of the Zehlendorf section of Berlin, they came to a large, ornate, stone, balconied, turn-of-the-century building. It sat alone, where three streets converged in a half-circle.

"There it is!" Inge announced, squeezed his inner thigh almost painfully, and withdrew her hand.

As von Tresmarck drove up to the main entrance, Peter saw a sandy beach and a large body of water on the other side of a four-lane divided highway.

Muddy brown water, which probably means that's still the Río de la Plata.

A doorman and a bellboy — a boy; he looked about twelve or thirteen — came down the wide marble stairs to the car.

Goltz opened his door for Peter to get out, and von Tresmarck went to the trunk to reclaim Peter's small canvas bag.

"I will leave word what time I'll be here in the morning," Goltz said.

"Thank you, Herr Standartenführer," Peter said, and clicked his heels. "And thank you, Sturmbannführer." Von Tresmarck nodded but did not say anything. "It was a pleasure to see you again, Frau Sturmbannführer," Peter concluded, clicked his heels again, and marched up the stairs after the bellboy.

He did not look back at the car.

The lobby of the hotel was crowded with well-fed, well-dressed, prosperous-appearing people. There seemed to be fewer blond, fair-skinned people here than in Buenos Aires, but he wondered if this was just his imagination.

He was shown to a suite on the second floor, a foyer, a sitting room and room with a large double bed. When he opened the vertical blinds, he saw there was a balcony overlooking the water. He went out on it.

A few moments later he left the room, descending to the main-floor corridor by a wide flight of carpeted marble stairs, rather than by the elevator. He had just decided that the place reminded him somewhat of the gambling casino in Baden-Baden when, glancing down a side corridor, he saw the hotel casino.

He went in. He was not a gambler, but he was curious. Three-quarters of the casino's tables were in use. He watched roulette for a few minutes, then baccarat, and that was enough.

When he left the casino, he passed through the hotel dining room, which was in the center of the building. It was a large, somewhat dark room from whose three-story-high ceiling hung four enormous crystal chandeliers. There was a grand piano at one end of the room, beside the bar, and a pianist was playing Johann Strauss. The bar was crowded.

A headwaiter offered him a table but he declined.

He left the hotel and walked around the street across from it. The smell of burning beef caught his nostrils, and he followed it to a small restaurant where an amazing amount of beef was cooking over glowing wood ashes.

He had a steak, french fried potatoes, a tomato and lettuce salad, and washed it down with a bottle of the local beer. He was surprised that the bill was so small.

On the way back to the hotel he stopped at a newsstand, where there was an array of American magazines. There was nothing in German except for yesterday's Buenos Aires *Frei Post*. He bought copies of *Time, Look, The Saturday Evening Post,* and a man's magazine, with a racy picture of a woman in a bathing suit on the cover, called *Esquire*.

He carried them back to the Casino Hotel, nobly decided against quenching the thirst his first beer had caused by having a second in the bar, and walked back up the stairs and down the wide corridors to his suite.

There, he called room service and ordered three bottles of the local beer on ice in a wine cooler. That much beer would last him until he finished reading the magazines. By then it would be time for supper. He would then go back to the small restaurant, have another steak and perhaps another beer. He would then return to the hotel stuffed and sleepy.

He took off his trousers and shirt and hung them neatly in the closet beside his jacket. He jerked the bedspread off the bed, arranged pillows against the headboard, took off his shoes and socks, laid the magazines out, and settled himself comfortably in the bed to wait for room service.

The knock came just as he opened *Esquire.*

"Come," he said as he reached for the money on the bedside table to tip the waiter.

"You must have been rather sure that I would come!" Inge von Tresmarck called from the door.

He turned to look at her.

"The last thing I expected you to do was come," he said, truthfully.

"But you are glad to see me?"

"Delighted," he lied.

She walked to the bed and sat down on it. She laid her hand on the magazines.

"You really didn't expect me, did you?"

"No. What about your husband?"

"I don't think we have to worry about him," Inge said. "Not this afternoon, anyway. They went right in Werner's study and closed the door."

"They may have already opened the door and are wondering where you are."

"I'm shopping," she said. "Where else would I be?"

"Your husband looked at me strangely at the airport."

"Werner looks that way at every good-looking young man," she said.

There was a knock at the door.

"Oh, you *were* expecting someone," Inge said petulantly. "Not *me*. But *someone.*"

"That's probably my beer."

"Your *beer?*"

"I ordered beer."

"Well, let him in, and order champagne," she said. "I don't drink beer. Don't you remember?"

She stood up and walked to the bathroom.

"Come!" Peter ordered.

A waiter entered carrying three bottles of beer in an ice-filled silver cooler.

"I've changed my mind," Peter said. "What I really need is a bottle of champagne. Is that going to cause any problem?"

"No, Señor," the waiter said, and walked to the desk, taking from it a leather-bound wine list. He opened it and handed it to Peter.

Over the waiter's shoulder, Peter could see Inge in the bathroom. Smiling naughtily, she was working her skirt down over her hips.

He didn't recognize one name among the twenty different champagnes on the list. He ordered by price, selecting one twice as expensive as the cheapest listed, but considerably cheaper than the most expensive.

Inge ducked behind the bathroom door a split second before the waiter turned to leave. When she heard the door close, she reappeared, now naked, posing in the door with her hand on her hip.

He felt a stirring in his groin.

She is a good-looking woman. And it is apparently true that a stiff prick has no conscience.

"Please tell me you don't think I'm fat," she said.

"I don't think you're fat," Peter said. "Foolish, perhaps, but not fat."

"Why foolish?" she said, walking to the bed.

"You have a husband," Peter said. "I would guess a jealous husband."

She sat down on the bed and rested her hand on his leg, just below his shorts.

"Werner worries that I will succumb to the attentions of some tall, dark, and very rich Uruguayan rancher, and that there would be talk," Inge said. "There aren't very many blondes here, and a great many tall, dark, and very rich Uruguayan ranchers seem to be fascinated with us."

Her hand moved under his shorts.

"Oh, you *are* glad to see me, aren't you? I wasn't really sure."

"I don't know how soon the waiter will be back with the champagne," Peter said.

"I don't want to start something and then be interrupted," she said. "So we will just tease each other until the waiter comes and goes."

She moved her hand on him, then took it out of his shorts.

"Tell me about Werner," Peter said. "Was he around when we knew each other?"

"He's been around forever," she said. "He used to work for Goltz in the Office of the Reichprotektor."

"You were married to him?"

"No. Let me think. Was I? No, I wasn't. I was then Frau Obersturmbannführer* Kolbermann," she said. "I would have thought I would have told you about Erich."

"You didn't."

"Erich was then on the Eastern Front with the Waffen-SS" — the military branch of the SS — "He was killed shortly before von Paulus surrendered the Sixth Army at Stalingrad."

"I'm sorry."

"I needed another husband, of course," Inge said, matter-of-factly. "Someone who could keep me out of the hands of the Labor Ministry."

"Excuse me?"

Inge lay down on the bed beside him.

* The SS rank equivalent to lieutenant colonel.

"Liebchen, do I look like the sort of girl who should spend ten hours a day sewing shoes together — or worse, in a shoe factory?"

"No, you don't," Peter said, chuckling.

"I was safe for a while," Inge explained. "Daddy had me on the payroll at the mills. I was 'constructively employed in industry essential to the war effort.' Then the mills were bombed out, and Albert Speer* decided they weren't worth rebuilding. Which put Daddy and me on the 'available labor' list. Daddy — who doesn't know the first thing about steel; he spent his entire life at the mills — was sent to the Saar, where he's living in one room and working as sort of a clerk in the Kruppwerke. The Labor Ministry ordered me to report to Gebruder Pahlenberg Schuhfabrik in Potsdam as a 'trainee.'"

"What kind of a trainee?"

"I never found out. Erich came along *right then* and swept me off my feet — he was on a twenty-day furlough from the east. A whirlwind romance. He had friends in the police side of the SS who could deal with the Labor Ministry. The wife of a Waffen-SS Obersturmbannführer heroically serving the Fatherland on the Eastern Front certainly could not be expected to do something as undignified as working in a shoe factory. It would be terrible for his morale."

"An older man, was he?" Peter asked.

"Older than you and me, Liebchen, younger than Werner. Actually, he was rather nice. I felt sorry for him. He was a Hamburger, and had lost his wife and two children in the bombing. And his apartment, too, of course."

* Reichs minister for Armaments and War Production.

"Why the older men?"

"Well, for one thing, younger men tend to be lieutenants and captains — you're an exception, of course, Peter. And they don't seem to be able to afford drinking at the Hotel am Zoo, much less to take on the responsibility of a wife with expensive tastes."

"And Werner can, I gather?"

"I don't think he really could," Inge said. "Now, of course, it's different."

"How?" Peter asked.

There came another knock at the door.

"Ah, the champagne," Inge said, "that was quick."

She jumped out of bed and ran into the bathroom. Peter went to the door, took the champagne in its cooler and two glasses from the waiter, and signed for it, without letting the waiter into the room.

Inge came out of the bathroom as he was unwinding the wire around the cork.

"The champagne's not bad here," she said. "The wine's very nice. And the food is marvelous!"

"I've noticed," Peter said.

He worked the cork out with his thumb, and poured champagne into the glasses.

"I would have preferred to marry someone like you," she said. "But you weren't available, were you?"

"No, I wasn't."

"You were my first failure," she said. "Perhaps that's why I was — am — so fascinated with you."

"How a failure?"

"You didn't fall in love with me, and beg me to be faithful to you when you went back to the war."

"Everybody else did?"

"Everybody else I took to the Hotel am Wansee did," she said. "I saved the Wansee for special people."

"I thought I took you to the Hotel am Wansee," he said.

"You usually took girls from the Hotel am Zoo to the Hotel am Wansee?"

"Only special girls," Peter said. "From the am Zoo *and* the Adlon."

"Was I special for you?"

"Of course."

"No, I mean, *really* special?"

"Of course really special."

"Tell me the truth, Peter. Was that why you loaned me the money? Because I was special?"

What money? I loaned her money? I don't remember that.

"I'm going to pay you back," Inge said. "That's the first thing I thought when I saw you. No. The second thing. The first thing was, 'Ach du lieber Gott, that's Peter. And he's alive. And here.' The second thing was, 'I can repay the loan.' "

"I don't remember a loan, Inge," Peter said. "Truthfully, I don't."

"You probably thought of it as a payment," she said. "I showed you a good time, and then I asked for a loan, and you 'loaned it' to me."

"I really don't recall anything about money," he said. "But if I did, forget it."

"No. I'll pay you back," she said. "It's important to me. If we're going to be here for a long, long time — and thank God, it looks like we will be — I don't want you looking across a dinner table at me ten, fifteen years from now and thinking, *'That old woman was once an amateur prostitute I took to the Hotel am Wansee. I say amateur prostitute because she didn't ask for the money first, the way a professional prostitute would. She asked for a "loan" afterward, complete with a complicated explanation of her financial predicament.' "*

"Your apartment had been burned out," Peter said, remembering. "You couldn't go to the housing people for another one, because you didn't have permission to live in Berlin. You did know a place you could get on the black market, but you didn't have quite all the money you needed. . . ."

"I needed five thousand Reichsmarks," she said. "And you gave me a check."

You're right, Peter thought, remembering. *I did think you were an amateur prostitute. And I felt sorry for you for having been forced into it by the war — and that was when I was having a premonition of death about once a week — so I wrote you a check, thinking I wouldn't need the money anyway.*

"I didn't think you were a prostitute, Inge, amateur or otherwise," Peter said. "I thought you were a nice girl, alone, and in trouble. And I had the money, so I gave it to you. *Loaned* it to you."

"See?" she said. "You said 'gave' and then corrected yourself. You did think I was a prostitute, didn't you?"

"I told you what I thought."

"You never thought you'd see the money again, did you?" Inge said. "Tell the truth, Peter!"

"I didn't care if I did or not," Peter said. "And I don't care now."

"Why, then, did you think I let you pick me up? And take you to the Hotel am Wansee?"

"I thought you were dazzled by the Knight's Cross," Peter said, truthfully.

Later, when you asked for the loan, I thought you were an amateur prostitute. That was not good for my

505

ego. Fighter pilots aren't supposed to pay whores. So I forgot it.

"When I thought about you — and I often thought about you — I used to think that it wasn't your medal that dazzled me, or the aristocratic 'von,' or even your looks, but the fact that the bartender served you French cognac from an unmarked decanter kept under the bar and normally reserved for generals. That meant you were somebody special — the bartenders there are notorious snobs — and that was what attracted me to you."

"Really?" Peter asked. The conversation was beginning to make him uncomfortable.

"But today, on the way from the airport, I realized that wasn't it at all."

"Wasn't it?"

What the hell is she talking about?

"It was subconscious," she said. "It was because we were two of a kind."

What the hell does that mean?

"Two of what kind?"

"Survivors," she said. "I sensed you were a survivor, too. And I was right, wasn't I? We're both here, aren't we? We're among the first survivors."

"The first survivors of what?"

"The Thousand Year Reich, of course," Inge said. "That's why I finally married Werner. There were practical considerations, of course. He told me he was being assigned here, and I think I would have married a gorilla if he promised to take me somewhere away from the bombing, somewhere with fresh eggs and meat with no ration coupon, somewhere warm. But the real reason was that I sensed — this subconscious thing — that Werner was also a survivor."

"Werner's a survivor?" Peter asked.

"If he wasn't a survivor, Liebchen, Werner would be *in* Sachsenhausen wearing a pink triangle,* instead of in Montevideo making himself rich getting Jews *out* of Sachsenhausen."

What did she say, "making himself rich getting Jews out of Sachsenhausen"?

"Werner's a little light on his feet?" Peter asked, as nonchalantly as he could.

She nodded.

"Do you think Goltz knows?"

"Of course he does," Inge said. "That's why Werner is here."

"I don't understand that."

"You can trust someone who knows you know you have something on him that can send him to the gas chambers," Inge said. "What does Herr Standartenführer Goltz have on you, Peter? Or is it the other way around?"

"I don't have anything on him, God knows, and I don't think he has anything on me."

"Then how are you involved in this?"

"In what?"

"I hope you're being discreet," she said.

"Discreet about what?"

Inge looked at him intensely for a long moment.

"You *don't* know, do you?" she asked. "God, I think I'm going to be sick to my stomach!"

"I don't know about what?"

"Peter, tell me honestly — look into my eyes — what are you doing in Montevideo?"

"I flew Goltz here in the Embassy Storch," Peter replied. "In addition to my other duties, I'm the Storch pilot."

* Homosexuals in concentration camps were required to wear a pink triangle affixed to their clothing in the same manner as Jews were required to wear a yellow six-pointed star.

507

"And you don't know what Goltz is doing here?" she asked.

"Haven't the foggiest idea."

"You do know who Goltz is?"

"He's the liaison officer between Reichsprotektor Himmler and Parteileiter Martin Bormann."

"Would you believe me if I told you that if one word I said about Werner being pink, or Goltz knowing it, not to mention about Jews and Sachsenhausen, got back to Goltz, you and I would be dead?"

"Yes," Peter said simply. "I'm aware that Goltz is a very dangerous man."

"I can't believe I have been this stupid," Inge said. "I simply presumed . . . How did you get out of Germany?"

"An Argentine officer, an observer with von Paulus, was killed at Stalingrad. I brought his body home. And was assigned as Assistant Attaché for Air at the Embassy."

She looked intently into his eyes, and then he saw something in them.

"You told me your father was a general, didn't you?"

"I don't remember if I did or not," he said.

"Is he?"

Peter nodded.

"Where is he stationed?"

"With the OKW."

"All right. He got you out of Germany. Maybe he has something on Goltz."

"I can't imagine what that could be."

"Then maybe Goltz has plans for you here, using your father in Germany to make sure you do what you're told."

"Aren't you being just a little melodramatic?"

"When I came here with Werner, Herr Standartenführer Goltz told me that if I went an inch out of line, the next I would hear from my father would be one of those postcards saying Reichsprotektor Himmler desired to inform me my father had died of pneumonia in Sachsenhausen."

"You didn't think coming to my room was out of line?" Peter asked.

"He wasn't talking about my sex life, so long as I don't make Werner look like a fool. He was talking about . . ."

"Making yourself rich getting Jews out of Sachsenhausen?" Peter asked.

"You'll get us both killed, Peter, and my father killed, and maybe even yours, if you ever let those words out of your mouth again. Here, or anywhere else. Do you understand that?"

"Yes. We never had any of this conversation. You were never here."

She shook her head.

"I was here. I may have been followed. Or the car was seen. If I'm asked, I'll say I was here. And you too."

"All right," Peter said. "So what do we do now?"

She turned and took the bottle of champagne from the cooler, filled her glass, and walked to the bed.

"What do you think we do now, Liebchen?" Inge asked.

She got into the bed, rested her back against the headboard, met Peter's eyes, and deliberately tilted the champagne glass and spilled champagne down her breast.

"Remember this, Peter?" she asked, and motioned for him to come to her.

XVI

[One]

Estancia San Pedro y San Pablo
Near Pila, Buenos Aires Province
0230 14 April 1943

The lights went on in the apartment of el Patrón, startling him. He sat up quickly in bed and saw Chief Schultz and Enrico.

"You scared the hell out of me," Clete confessed. "What's up?"

"You got a reply on the oh one thirty call," Chief Schultz said. "Should I have waited until morning?"

"No, of course not," Clete said, pushing himself up against the headboard and reaching for the sheet of paper Schultz extended to him.

TOP SECRET
LINDBERGH

URGENT

DUPLICATION FORBIDDEN

MSF NO 2545 DDWHO
1650 GREENWICH 13APR43

FROM ORACLE WASHDC

TO STACHIEF AGGIE

REFERENCE YOUR NO. 0002

1. ORACLE DIRECTS YOU FURNISH QUICKEST MEANS IDENTITY CAVALRY AND GALAHAD AND PROVIDE REASONS YOU BELIEVE THEY HAVE ACCESS TO INTELLIGENCE DESCRIBED.

2. AIRCRAFT (HEREAFTER PARROT) WILL BE AVAILABLE PORTO ALEGRE BRAZIL AIR STATION (HEREAFTER BIRDCAGE) AFTER 1700 GREENWICH 16 APR43. COLONEL J.B. WALLACE USAAC (HEREAFTER BIRDDOG) WILL RELEASE PARROT TO YOU ON YOUR FURNISHING HIM YOUR NEW ORLEANS TELEPHONE NUMBER.

3. BIRDDOG ADVISES PARROT WILL BE MARKED AS REQUESTED AND PAINTED APPROXIMATELY DESIRED COLOR; HAS

```
1600 MILE RANGE; CIVILIAN ONLY
REPEAT CIVILIAN ONLY RADIO AND
NAVIGATION SYSTEM. REQUESTED ON
SITE TRAINING AVAILABLE FOR YOU
AND COPILOT.

4. ADVISE UNDERSIGNED QUICKEST
MEANS WHEN PARROT MOVEMENT COM-
MENCED AND COMPLETED.

GRAHAM END
```

"Looks like you got your airplane, Major," Chief Schultz said when Clete looked up at him.

"All I have to do is fly it into Argentina from Pôrto Alegre, wherever the hell that is, right?"

"It's on the Atlantic Coast, maybe a third of the way between Buenos Aires and São Paulo," Schultz said. "I got a chart."

He handed it to Clete.

"Is that typewriter still in there?" Clete asked, jerking his thumb toward the sitting room of the apartment.

Schultz nodded.

"Do me a favor, Chief," Clete said, swinging his feet out of bed. "While I'm getting dressed and Enrico is going to get Capitán Delgano out of bed, extract enough from this message so that I can show it to Delgano without telling him anything that's none of his business."

"Aye, aye, Sir."

"Be so kind as to present my compliments to el Capitán Delgano, Suboficial Mayor," Clete said. "And ask him to join me at his earliest convenience."

"Sí, mi Mayor," Enrico said, smiling.

512

"See if you can rustle up some coffee on your way," Clete added.

"Coffee, mi Mayor? Not chocolate?"

"I'm glad you thought of that, Enrico. I'm jumpy enough the way I am. I don't need any coffee. Chocolate, please."

"Chocolate for me too, please, Enrico," Schultz said. "I can't handle Argentine coffee."

Enrico shook his head in disbelief and then followed Schultz out of the bedroom.

Clete went into the bathroom and took a quick shower, hoping it would wake him up.

When he came out, Schultz had already finished the extract. Clete read it, then started to get dressed.

```
AIRCRAFT AVAILABLE AT PORTO ALEGRE
BRAZIL NAVAL AIR STATION AFTER
1200 LOCAL TIME 16 APR 1943

AIRCRAFT HAS ARGENTINE REGISTRY
NUMBERS FURNISHED AND IS PAINTED
SAME COLOR AS STAGGERWING.

AIRCRAFT HAS 1600 MILE RANGE AND
CIVILIAN ONLY RADIO AND NAVIGATION
SYSTEM.

REQUESTED ON SITE TRAINING AVAIL-
ABLE FOR YOU AND COPILOT.
```

"I didn't know if you were planning on taking Delgano with you or not, is why I left that training business in."

"This is just what I wanted, Chief," Clete said. "And I'm not taking Delgano with me. He's an

Argentine intelligence officer. Getting the airplane is a temporary truce, nothing more. I'm sure he would be fascinated to have a look at a Brazilian Navy Base. And I don't want to piss the Brazilians off by bringing an Argentine officer with me. If I didn't have to, I wouldn't even let him know where the airplane is."

"You don't need him to help you fly it?"

"No. It's not much of an airplane. A little twin-engine aerial taxi, is all it is. I can handle it by myself."

"How about navigating it by yourself? I could go along with you."

"You stay here and make sure Ettinger stays here," Clete said. "But thanks for the offer, Chief."

Schultz shrugged to indicate thanks were not required, then asked, "While we're waiting for Delgano, you want to write your reply to the message?"

"No big deal. The next time you're in contact, tell them I expect to be at Pôrto Alegre shortly after the airplane is ready."

"What I meant is that they want you to identify Galahad and Cavalry," Schultz said. " 'Quickest means' is what they said."

"I'm not going to identify them," Clete said. "I don't want to run the risk of having either of them exposed."

"The Luftwaffe guy and Colonel Martín, right?"
Clete didn't answer.

"Mr. Frade, I work for you," Schultz said. "That was just to keep things straight in my mind. If anybody else asks me, I don't have a clue who Galahad and Cavalry are."

"How did you pick up on Martín?"

"I figured it had to be either him or Captain Lauffer, but Delgano works for Martín. Two and two usually makes four."

"Usually," Clete said, chuckling.

"I don't think you can just ignore them," Schultz said. "I think you have to tell them you have reasons not to identify them."

"You really think so?"

"Either that or make up names," Schultz said.

"Oh, shit," Clete said, and walked out of the bedroom and sat down in front of the typewriter. He rolled a sheet of paper into the machine and looked thoughtful for a long moment. Then he typed a single sentence, tore the paper from the machine, and handed it to Schultz.

```
Regret that to obtain absolutely re-
liable intelligence from galahad and
cavalry it was necessary to give my
word of honor that their identities
will not be furnished to third par-
ties.
```

"You really want me to send this?" Schultz said, chuckling.

"It's more polite than 'fuck you, I ain't gonna tell you,' isn't it? Send it word for word."

"Aye, aye, Sir."

A sleepy-eyed maid entered the room carrying pots and cups and saucers. A moment later, Capitán Delgano, in a bathrobe, and Enrico came in.

Clete handed him the extract Schultz had prepared.

"I would prefer to discuss this subject in private, Señor Frade," Delgano said.

"I prefer that Chief Schultz stay," Clete said. "Sorry."

"Very well," Delgano said. "I rather suspected the aircraft would be at Pôrto Alegre. It's a major Brazilian base, and both U.S. Navy and Army Air Corps units are stationed there."

"Is that so?"

"With that in mind, I did a little preliminary planning," Delgano said. "May I show you on the map?"

"Of course."

Delgano laid Chief Schultz's map on the desk beside the typewriter and pointed with his finger.

"This is Santo Tomé, in Corrientes Province," he said.

Christ, Graham said Corrientes Province is where they're going to infiltrate the new team into Uruguay!

"It's across the Río Uruguay from São Borja, Brazil. It's approximately five hundred fifty kilometers from Pôrto Alegre to Santo Tomé. Since your aircraft has a range of sixteen hundred miles, we should have no difficulty —"

"Wait a minute," Clete said. "Now that I think of it, I don't think the C-45 has a sixteen-hundred-mile range. That's probably a typo. A thousand seems more like it, and it may be as little as six hundred."

"Six hundred miles seems a short range for a transport aircraft," Delgano said.

"It's not a transport aircraft," Clete said. "It's a liaison aircraft, a small twin-engine aerial taxi."

Delgano looked at him dubiously. "In any event, even if it has a range of only six hundred miles it's no problem. Six hundred miles is nearly a thousand kilometers. We should have no trouble making it."

"I'm going alone, Capitán Delgano," Clete interrupted. "There's no way I'm taking you to Brazil with me."

Delgano considered that for a moment.

"In that case, actually," he said finally, "things may be less complicated than I thought at first. Let's talk about Santo Tomé."

"Why Santo Tomé?" Clete asked. "Why couldn't I just fly directly here?"

"Across Uruguay?"

Clete nodded.

"It would be better to avoid crossing Uruguay at all," Delgano said. "The Uruguayans patrol their border with Brazil, and we patrol our border with Uruguay, at least in the Río de la Plata estuary. Your chances of being detected would be far less if you crossed directly from Brazil into Argentina, and into Corrientes Province, not into Entre Ríos or Buenos Aires Province."

That's the reason Graham ordered the team to be infiltrated through Corrientes Province. They'll probably have to paddle across the river, but the idea is the same, less chance of being caught crossing the border.

"OK," Clete said. "Tell me about Santo Tomé."

"The Second Cavalry Regiment is stationed at Santo Tomé," Delgano said. "The commanding officer is a member of Grupo de Oficiales Unidos. More important, there is an airfield, of sorts, there."

"Of sorts?"

"When your father was a teniente coronel, Mayor Frade, he was the Deputy Commander of the Second Cavalry. It is a tradition that an officer serves as the Deputy Commander of the First or Second Cavalry Regiments before being promoted coronel."

"Is that so?"

" 'Santo Tomé,' your father used to say, 'is two hundred kilometers from nowhere.' It was during his assignment at Santo Tomé that he became very interested in the potential value to the army of liaison and observation aircraft. It was by then generally understood that he would be promoted, as in fact he was — when he assumed command of the Húsares de Pueyrredón. Thus, when he requested that an airstrip be built at Santo Tomé, and that an Army aircraft be assigned to the Second Cavalry for experimental purposes, the request was granted. An Army aircraft, a Piper Cub, incidentally, was assigned to the Second Cavalry, together with a pilot — me — and a small detachment of mechanics.

"Under my supervision, a dirt field was laid out adjacent to the Second Cavalry barracks. At your father's 'suggestion,' the runway was made somewhat longer than it had to be to accommodate a Piper Cub. He wanted it long enough for a Beech stagger-wing to use it safely. He had just purchased such an aircraft, and it was en route from the United States. When he was summoned to the Edificio Libertador, it would permit him to travel to Buenos Aires in a matter of hours, instead of the twelve or fourteen hours the trip took by automobile, or the overnight trip by train."

"The Army went along with this?" Clete asked. Delgano nodded.

"And you were the pilot of the stagger-wing?"

"The delivery pilot from Beech taught me how to fly the stagger-wing," Delgano said. "And I also found myself flying one of the Piper Cubs your father kept on his estancia — San Miguel — near Posadas."

"What was that all about?"

"Your father found the quarters provided at Santo Tomé for the Deputy Commander of the

Second Cavalry inadequate. He spent his weekends — the weekends he did not spend in Buenos Aires or here — at Estancia San Miguel."

"Was this before or after you went to work for Coronel Martín?"

"El Coronel Martín assumed his duties after your father was promoted and had assumed command of the Húsares de Pueyrredón," Delgano said. "I had worked for the man he replaced."

"In other words, you were spying on my father all the time?"

"I prefer to think of it as performing my duties as an officer of the Bureau of Internal Security," Delgano said. "Your father came to understand that, Mayor Frade."

"OK," Clete said after a moment. "So this airfield you built so my father could spend his weekends in Buenos Aires is still there?"

"It was not used much after your father was promoted and transferred, but it is still there. Recently, the commanding officer was told to make sure it is still capable of accommodating an aircraft such as the stagger-wing."

"When was he told this?"

"Immediately after we came to our understanding of the terms under which you are importing the aircraft from Brazil."

I get it. If the coup d'état fails, Delgano will fly Ramírez, Rawson, and the others in my airplane to this airstrip — which will be in the hands of the Second Cavalry. It will then be refueled and flown either into Brazil or, more likely, into Paraguay.

"In other words —"

"I think you understand the situation, Mayor Frade. I don't think we have to discuss the specifics."

"What about fuel?" Clete asked.

"That's been taken care of," Delgano said. "I'm suggesting that you and I drive to Santo Tomé today. It's fifteen or sixteen hours from here . . ."

"I have business in Buenos Aires today."

"The overnight train leaves Buenos Aires at ten P.M. and arrives in Santo Tomé the next morning at nine. Can you finish your business in Buenos Aires in time to take the train?"

"Yes."

"Very well. I will drive to Santo Tomé. Tonight. It's already morning, isn't it? When we finish here. I will meet your train at Santo Tomé and take you out to the Second Cavalry. You and I will inspect the airstrip and ensure that the fuel is there. I will then take you to the ferry across the Río Uruguay. I think I can pass you through Customs and Immigration without having your passport stamped, or any questions being asked. It would then be up to you to travel from São Borja to Pôrto Alegre. Would that pose any problem?"

"No," Clete said. "Wait. I'll need some Brazilian money."

"I'll have that for you in Santo Tomé. I suggest you buy a ticket to Posadas and make the announcement you're bound for Estancia San Miguel, which is near Posadas, and then simply leave the train at Santo Tomé."

"OK," Clete said. "I don't suppose this airstrip at Santo Tomé is lighted?"

"The Brazilians, I gather, will not be aware of your flight? You have to cross the border in the hours of darkness?" Delgano asked.

Clete nodded.

"No, it's not lighted," Delgano said. "I will have a fire, in the shape of an arrow, burning during hours of darkness. When you overfly the arrow, I will have the gasoline lights ignited. We can go over this in detail together in Santo Tomé."

"OK."

"Is that it for now?" Delgano said.

"I think so," Clete said.

"Anything you need me to do, Mr. Frade?" Chief Schultz asked.

"Send that radio we talked about," Clete said. "And make sure Ettinger stays here."

"Aye, aye, Sir."

[Two]

1728 Avenida Coronel Díaz
Palermo, Buenos Aires
0815 14 April 1943

By coincidence, Clete happened to be about to descend the wide marble staircase from the "first" floor — in the States, it would be the second — to the foyer of The Museum when he saw Antonio start to open the front door, apparently in response to a ringing in the kitchen, or someplace, that Clete had not heard.

Clete stopped to see who it was. If it was not Tony and Delojo, he was going to turn and get out of sight.

It was Tony and Delojo, both in civilian clothing.

Tony looks pretty classy, Clete thought a little smugly.

In Washington, after he learned that Tony's idea of "dress-up" clothing was a two-tone jacket, pastel-colored trousers, and a colored shirt worn tieless, with its collar spread over the two-tone jacket collar, Clete took him to the Men's Store in Woodward & Lothrop and supervised the purchase of his wardrobe. Tony was now wearing a single-breasted gray flannel suit, a white, button-down-collar shirt, and a red-striped necktie.

His suit fits better than Delojo's.

"Up here," Clete called, adding to Antonio, "Bring us some coffee and rolls, will you, please?"

Tony came bounding up the stairs, taking them two at a time.

When Clete had knocked at his door in La Boca an hour before, Tony was awake, bright-eyed and bushy-tailed. Then Clete had the somewhat unkind thought that Tony, *like a good paratrooper, has been up since oh dark hundred and has run five miles and done a hundred and fifty squat jumps before he even thought about breakfast.*

Commander Delojo walked up the stairs one at a time, a wan smile on his face, looking like someone who had just reluctantly left his bed, showered, and shaved.

"You look like an advertisement in *Esquire*, Tony," Clete said.

"I see you took off your cowboy suit, Major, Sir."

"I had no choice. I am meeting my mother-in-law-to-be for lunch," Clete said, then offered his hand to Delojo. "Good morning, Commander. I ordered coffee. Would you like something else? It's no problem."

"Coffee will be fine, thank you, Frade," Delojo said. "I don't think we were followed, but . . ."

"There's a couple of BIS guys in an apartment across the street," Clete said. "Go on the presumption that they will know you two have been here."

"I don't understand. Shouldn't we have met someplace —"

"There would have been BIS agents on each of us. I don't think we could lose all of them. So why bother to try?"

He led them into the master's apartment.

"We can talk here," he said. "There are no microphones."

"How do you know that?" Delojo challenged.

"Enrico found the one cleverly concealed in the chandelier," Clete said. "And tells me there's no other place they could put one."

"Whose microphone?"

"Probably the BIS's," Clete said. "Tony said you wanted to talk to me."

Delojo looked dubiously around the room.

"I wish I shared your faith in your man's ability to sweep a room," he said.

"What's up?" Clete said impatiently.

"The team chief has been successfully infiltrated across the Río Uruguay into a town called Santo Tomé, in Corrientes Province."

"Just the team chief?"

"It's a five-man team. The team chief infiltrated. Two more men are in a town called São Borja just across the river in Brazil. The other two, and the radar and other equipment, are still at the Pôrto Alegre Naval Base. The team chief's infiltration was sort of a trial run, to see how difficult the infiltration was going to be. The Río Uruguay is a wide river."

"How did he cross the river?"

"Presumably in a boat. I would guess they have a rubber boat, rubber boats."

"How much does this radar weigh? Will it fit through the door of the C-45? How much other equipment do they have? Same questions — what does it weigh, and will it fit through the door of the C-45?"

"Presumably you have a reason for asking?"

"I'm going to Santo Tomé tonight. Then I'm going to Pôrto Alegre, and will fly the C-45 to Santo Tomé. I'll be alone in the C-45. If I can get this stuff in it, that makes more sense than trying to smuggle it across the river in a rubber boat."

"This is the first I've heard any of this," Delojo said.

"Most of it just happened," Clete said. "I intended to see you sometime today — even before I heard the team chief is already in Argentina."

"Why Santo Tomé?" Delojo asked.

"I've made a deal with . . . certain people. They are helping me bring the airplane into Argentina. Specifically, into an airstrip at Santo Tomé."

"What kind of a deal?"

"I have the feeling, Commander, which I don't like, that you think I'm supposed to ask your approval of my actions."

"You are supposed to coordinate your actions with mine, Major. I presume Colonel Graham is aware of your plans?"

"He knows that I'm going to pick up the airplane at Pôrto Alegre two days from now. That's all."

There was a knock at the door, and a maid came in carrying a tray with two pots on it. She laid it on the desk.

Clete was pleased when Tony, helping himself from one of the pots, said, more in surprise than indignation, "Shit, this is hot chocolate!"

"Paratroopers don't drink sissy chocolate, right?"

"This one does. The coffee here dissolves my stomach."

Commander Delojo waited until the maid left the room, poured himself a cup of coffee, diluted it with cream and added sugar, and then asked, "You are bringing the C-45 in black, is that it?"

"Let's say 'covertly.' Not black."

"I don't think I understand the distinction."

"Let's say that I'm confident I can get the airplane from Pôrto Alegre into Argentina via Santo Tomé, and from Santo Tomé to Estancia San Pedro y San Pablo, without any trouble."

"This has something to do with Galahad and/or Cavalry?"

"I'm surprised you're familiar with those names."

"I have a radio from Director Donovan asking me to identify them."

"When did you get that?"

"Last night."

"From Donovan? Not Graham?"

"From Director Donovan. Who are they?"

"I'm not at liberty to tell you," Clete said.

"Doesn't the fact that Director Donovan has directed me to identify these people give you the 'liberty'?"

"I'm afraid not."

"You understand that I will have to reply that I asked you for their identities, and you refused to give them to me?"

"I've already informed Oracle that I cannot identify these people," Clete said. "Look, I'm offering to help you get the team and their equipment into Argentina. If you don't want me to help, fine."

"I really can't understand your attitude, Major," Delojo said. "You're not being at all cooperative."

"Does that mean you don't want my help?"

"How do you propose to help?"

"How are you communicating with Pôrto Alegre? I mean, who at Pôrto Alegre?"

"We have an agent there."

"Birddog?"

"I never heard that name."

"Your agent does know about the C-45?"

"Of course."

"Well, then I suggest you contact your man — he's either Birddog by another name, or he knows who Birddog is — and find out if the radar and the other equipment, and the other two guys on the team, will fit on the C-45. If so, have the equipment and the two guys ready to go when I get there. If they won't, that's too bad. We tried."

"I think I would need authorization from Colonel Graham to do that."

"There's not time to ask Graham's permission."

"The ramifications of you being discovered bringing the C-45 in black, with the radar and two agents aboard . . ."

"There's not time to ask Graham's permission," Clete said. "I'm leaving here at ten o'clock tonight, and there's no way we can get a reply by then."

Delojo shook his head as he considered the ramifications of that.

"OK," Clete said impatiently. "Let's leave it this way: It's your responsibility to get Ashton's team and their equipment into Argentina, and from Santo Tomé to Estancia San Pedro y San Pablo. You worry about that, and I'll worry about getting the C-45 to Estancia San Pedro y San Pablo."

"You would fly everybody from Santo Tomé to Estancia San Pedro y San Pablo? Is that what you're saying?"

Clete nodded.

Delojo exhaled audibly.

"This can't be delayed a couple of days until we coordinate everything with Oracle?" he asked.

"I'm on the ten-o'clock train tonight to Santo Tomé," Clete said. "Where's Ashton?"

"At the Automobile Club of Argentina hotel in Santo Tomé."

"When you message Oracle, Commander," Clete said, "you can ask him to relay to Graham that I plan to cross into Brazil either tomorrow night or early the next morning."

"What makes you think I'm going to message Oracle?"

"Unless I've misread you completely, Commander, as soon as you get to the Embassy, you are going to radio Oracle all of this, so that if Oracle doesn't 'authorize' what I'm planning on doing, there will be time for him to have the whole operation stopped by the time I get to Pôrto Alegre."

"That would not be necessary, Major Frade, if you were willing to delay your operation for seventy-two hours," Delojo said. "We could have authorization, or denial of authorization, within that period."

"I don't have seventy-two hours," Clete said. "Have you got anything else for me?"

"I think that's all," Delojo said. "I suggest that when you meet with Ashton you make it clear to him that the pickup of his two men and the radar at Pôrto Alegre is a tentative plan."

"In case you can't make contact with him before I do, you mean?"

"I really don't understand you at all, Frade," Delojo said.

"Stay behind a minute, will you, Tony?" Clete said, adding to Delojo, "I mean just a minute, Commander. You can wait for him."

He went to the door and held it open for Delojo, then closed it after he had gone through.

"What the hell was that all about?" Tony asked.

"He would have liked to stand me at attention and order me to do what he thinks should be done, but he's not sure he has the authority."

"I picked up on the way he kept calling you 'Major.' "

"Tony, I don't trust Dave."

"Excuse me?"

"To stay at Estancia San Pedro y San Pablo, I mean."

"You want me to sit on him?"

"Can you get away from the Embassy?"

"Yeah. Delojo has apparently had a little talk with the Military Attaché. Now he disappears when he sees me, instead of handing me shitty little details."

"Go to Estancia San Pedro y San Pablo and sit on Dave until I get back," Clete said.

"Right," Tony said. "Unless you want me to go with you and get the airplane?"

"I thought about that. But you're on a diplomatic passport. . . ."

"Yeah," Tony said, then put out his hand. "Good luck, Clete. Don't do anything foolish."

[Three]

The Embassy of the German Reich
Avenida Córdoba
Buenos Aires, Argentina
1025 14 April 1943

Major Freiherr Hans-Peter von Wachtstein had been in his small, high-ceilinged office — it was taller than it was wide, he once decided — no more than thirty seconds, just long enough to take off his jacket and start to put it on a hanger, when Günther Loche came in.

"Good morning, Herr Major Freiherr," Günther said cheerfully, placing a stack of newspapers and several magazines on Peter's somewhat battered desk. "Did the Major Freiherr have a pleasant flight from Montevideo this morning?"

Very nice, thank you for asking. Herr Standartenführer Goltz had his balls in an uproar about flying back here in a hurry, so we flew over the water. I managed to make the engine backfire and splutter three times when we were out of sight of land, and if the Herr Standartenführer didn't actually piss his pants, to look at the expression on his face, he came close.

"Very nice, thank you," Peter replied. "And you, Günther, are disgustingly cheerful this morning. Been pulling wings off flies again, have you?"

"Excuse me, Herr Major?" Günther asked, confusion all over his handsome, if somewhat vacant, face.

Peter took pity on him.

"I said you seem very cheerful," Peter said. "Some good news?"

"Oberst Grüner told me he is looking into a

529

scholarship for me, Herr Major Freiherr," Günther said.

"Is that so? What kind of a scholarship?"

"Diesel-engine technology, Herr Freiherr Major. In the Fatherland. The Herr Oberst says that diesel engines are the wave of the future."

In the Fatherland"?

"And when did you have this discussion with the Herr Oberst, Günther?"

"This morning. He told me that Standartenführer Goltz talked to him about it."

"Really?"

What the hell is this all about?

"Over the weekend, I was driving the Herr Standartenführer and First Secretary Gradny-Sawz, Herr Major Freiherr. The Herr Standartenführer was kind enough to report to the Herr Oberst that he was favorably impressed with my performance of duty, and that I was worthy of being trained to accept greater responsibilities."

"Fascinating," Peter said.

"For a very important man, Herr Freiherr Major, the Herr Standartenführer is very friendly."

What is that sonofabitch Goltz up to? Is he a faggot? God knows there's enough of them in the SS, including his good friend Werner von Tresmarck in Montevideo.

"Yes, I have noticed," Peter said.

"Oberst Grüner said Ambassador Graf von Lutzenberger will have to give his approval, Herr Freiherr, but he sees no problem in arranging for a scholarship. The Herr Oberst told me he will tell the Herr Ambassador that I am a reliable, hardworking employee, with promotion potential."

"And you would go to Germany on this scholarship?"

"Yes, Herr Major Freiherr. For six months or

so. To the Daimler-Benz Technical Institute in Stuttgart."

"Stuttgart, eh?"

"And the Standartenführer says there is even a possibility that a passenger space might be available on a Condor flight, Herr Major Freiherr."

And the minute you step off the plane, you poor idiot, you will be told there is a slight change in plans. First, you will go to the Eastern Front as a rifleman. And later, after you have helped stem the Communist Horde, then you can go to the Daimler-Benz Technical Institute in Stuttgart.

What the hell is Goltz up to? Is this some sort of perverse joke? Is he really thinking of sending Günther to Germany? Why?

"Well, good luck, Günther."

"Thank you, Herr Major Freiherr!" Günther said, coming to attention and then marching out of the office.

Peter sat down at his desk and took a quick look at the front pages of the *Frie Presse*, *La Nacion*, *La Prensa*, the *Buenos Aires Herald*, and several of the magazines. He opened one of the latter, *La Vida!*, a weekly magazine devoted mainly to rotogravure photographs of younger members of Buenos Aires's upper class attending social functions. Then he reached into his trousers pocket and came up with a three-by-five-inch file card he had been given by Humberto Duarte at the reception following the interment of the late el Coronel Jorge Guillermo Frade in Recoleta Cemetery.

He placed it on the open copy of *La Vida!* so that if someone came unexpectedly into his office, he could conceal it quickly simply by turning a page of the magazine.

Handlesbank Zurich 0405567

Privatebank Gebruder Hach
Zurich 782967

Banque De Suisse Et Argentina
Zurich 45607

Anglo-suisse Banque De Commerce
Basel 970012

Peter wasn't at all sure that he had completely understood what Humberto had told him, although he had asked as many questions as he could think to ask. As best he could remember, Humberto told him he had experienced difficulty transferring money from Generalleutnant von Wachtstein's numbered account in the Handelsbank to the merchant banking firm of Hach Brothers. Previous transfers had gone smoothly. What happened this time, no one seemed to know.

Neither Humberto personally nor the Anglo-Argentinian Bank had a "correspondent relationship" — whatever the hell that meant — with the Handelsbank. But Humberto did have a "personal relationship" with Hach Brothers, which apparently meant they would do what he told them to do without asking questions or making records.

However, Handelsbank informed Gebruder Hach that there were "administrative problems" that would "briefly delay" the transfer of the funds requested from account number 0405567.

"I think, Peter, that they are just exercising due caution," Humberto said. "Exercising due caution also permits them to hold on to the money for, say, another two weeks. And interest accrues daily, as you know."

There was also the possibility that the Nazis were onto the secret account, which was painful to consider.

Humberto went on to explain that the Anglo-Argentine Bank had a "correspondent relationship" with both the Bank of Switzerland and Argentina and the Anglo-Swiss Bank of Commerce, as did the Handelsbank. "Less due caution," he said, "is exercised between banks which have correspondent relationships, Peter, as you can well understand, than with banks, especially private merchant banks, where no correspondent relationship is in place."

Thus, after some thought, he concluded that the best way to handle transfers in the future was for Generalleutnant von Wachtstein to instruct Handelsbank to move the funds to either the Anglo-Swiss Bank, where he — Humberto — controlled account number 970012, or to the Bank of Switzerland and Argentina, where he controlled account number 45607. Humberto would then direct those banks to transfer the funds to the Hach Brothers private bank, which would then transfer the funds to his personal account at the Anglo-Argentine Bank in Buenos Aires.

Even with Humberto leading him patiently by the hand through all this, Peter remained confused. This problem was compounded by the necessity of leading Dieter von und zu Aschenburg, the Condor pilot, through this maze. Dieter had to commit everything except the bank names and account numbers to memory, and then pass it on to Generalleutnant von Wachtstein when he reached Germany.

Ordinarily, when Dieter flew a Condor into Buenos Aires, they got together — as two veterans of the Condor Legion in the Spanish Civil War could be expected to do — and there was plenty of time to handle this sort of thing. But this time, getting together had been impossible. The only time Dieter was free of the company of Karl Nabler, the copilot, Peter was at the Carzino-Cormano estancia or in Uruguay with Goltz.

Peter had considered, and decided against, writing everything down and having Dieter smuggle it into Germany for transmission to his father. Although he knew Dieter would have done that without question — and not only because some of the funds in the Handelsbank had been entrusted to Generalleutnant von Wachtstein by the von und zu Aschenburg family — that would have not only been too risky for Dieter and for his father, but, if the data fell into the wrong hands, for the entire operation.

The only way to handle the problem was to give Dieter the card with the bank names and account numbers, and then try to make him understand what Humberto Duarte, without complete success, had tried to make him understand.

He picked up the filing card, looked at it for a long moment — *there is absolutely no way Dieter could memorize all this; he'll have to carry it with him and hope he doesn't find himself searched by the Gestapo before he can burn it or swallow it* — and then put it in his pocket and picked up the *Buenos Aires Herald*.

He had just settled himself comfortably — pulled down his necktie and rested his crossed feet on an open desk drawer — when Standartenführer Josef Goltz, in civilian clothing, walked in without knocking.

Peter immediately began to untangle his feet and rise.

"Oh, keep your seat, von Wachtstein," Goltz said.

"How may I be of service, Herr Standartenführer?" Peter asked, getting to his feet anyway.

"I just dropped in to ask you your plans for the day," Goltz said.

"Nothing specific, Herr Standartenführer, until four this afternoon, when I will take the diplomatic pouches out to El Palomar and give them to the Condor pilot."

"Curiosity prompts me to ask if you always begin your duty day by reading the English newspaper."

"The English newspaper, Herr Standartenführer, and *La Nacion* and *La Prensa* and . . ." He pointed to the newspapers and magazines Günther had laid on his desk. "I go through them to find information of interest to Oberst Grüner."

"Of course, I should have thought of that. What have the English to say today?"

"That they have achieved glorious victories on all fronts, Herr Standartenführer."

"Oh, really?"

"The war will be over sometime next month, Herr Standartenführer, and we will lose. If one is to believe the *Herald*."

"I suppose that is to be expected," Goltz said, smiling. "Do you ever find anything — anything you can believe — that is of interest?"

"Every once in a while, Herr Standartenführer, there is something. Most often in the personals, oddly enough. The assignment of Anglo-Argentines to various British units, for example, which often furnishes the location of the unit. I believe Oberst Grüner forwards them to the Abwehr for the use of their Order of Battle people."

"The Condor is leaving . . . when?"

"Probably at about six, or a little later."

"When we left Berlin, we left very early in the morning."

"Did you?"

"I'm curious why the Condor is leaving at nightfall. Why not early this morning? Or tomorrow morning?"

"In this case, Herr Standartenführer — and I don't know this — I would think it is so they can fly off the coast of Brazil in the hours of darkness."

"Why is that?"

"The Brazilians now have Maritime Reconnaissance aircraft, Herr Standartenführer. They are looking for our submarines, but they would be pleased to come across the Condor."

"Could they shoot it down?"

"It's unlikely. The Condor is faster than the Brazilian aircraft — they're using Catalinas, American Navy aircraft — but under the right circumstances —"

"The 'right' circumstances, or the 'wrong' ones?"

"I suppose, Herr Standartenführer, that I was thinking as a fighter pilot. I am trained to shoot planes down, not avoid a confrontation."

"Yes, of course you were," Goltz said with a smile. "The reason I asked for your schedule, von Wachtstein, is that I promised your father to have a little chat with you — you are apparently not much of a letter writer . . ."

"I'm afraid not, Herr Standartenführer."

". . . and relay his paternal disapproval."

"Paternal disapproval duly noted, Herr Standartenführer."

"I'm thinking now — it would fit in with my schedule — that I will ride out to the airfield with you. It will give us a chance to chat on the way, and perhaps we could have dinner . . ."

"The Argentines don't even begin to think of dinner, Herr Standartenführer, until nine o'clock."

"Well, then, a drink or two, and if we're still able to think of food at nine o'clock, perhaps we can think of dinner then."

"I am entirely at your disposal, Herr Standartenführer."

"Well, then, why don't you come by First Secretary Gradny-Sawz's office when you have the pouches and are ready to go out there? That would be about four?"

"Whenever it would be convenient for the Herr Standartenführer, of course, but I was planning to leave at half past four."

"At half past four, then," Goltz said. "I'll look forward to it."

He raised his hand in the Nazi salute.

"Heil Hitler!"

Peter snapped to attention and returned the salute.

"Heil Hitler!" he barked.

[Four]

The Director's Room
The Anglo-Argentine Bank
Calle Bartolomé Mitre 101
Buenos Aires, Argentina
1315 14 April 1943

"Gentlemen," Humberto Valdez Duarte announced from the far end of the twenty-five-foot-long ornately inlaid table, "I'm afraid Señor Frade and I have an appointment that cannot be broken or delayed, and we'll have to stop right where we are."

Thank God! I can't take much more of this! thought Señor Frade, who had been seated at the other end of the twenty-five-foot-long ornately inlaid table since half past nine.

Between the two were seven assorted accountants and attorneys, two *escribanos*, and a secretary. The function of the *escribanos*, Clete had finally figured out, was something between that of a notary public and a lawyer. The table was littered with paper, much of it gathered together in sheafs, tied together with what looked like shoelaces.

The only thing that Clete had really understood was that his father's business interests were even more extensive than he had suspected, and more complicated. He understood that he would have to come to understand what it was all about.

More than once, he heard the Old Man's voice: *"What you never can forget, Cletus, is that for every dollar a rich man has, there are three clever sonsof-bitches trying to cheat him out of it."*

And that, of course, had caused him to wonder how the Old Man was going to react when he got the letter telling him he was going to marry an Argentine.

It had been difficult to concentrate on anything that was explained to him. His mind kept wandering from details of finance and real estate to the problems of making a cross-country flight in an airplane in which he had a total of maybe five hours' time — and that in the copilot's seat. And he was doing it at night, navigating by unfamiliar radio direction signals — and thus most probably by the seat of his pants — all the time avoiding detection by both Brazilians and Argentines.

"Perhaps," Humberto went on, "we can meet tomorrow . . ."

No way!

". . . or the day after. I will get word to you."

With a little luck, the day after tomorrow I will be in Brazil. And what am I going to tell Humberto about that? "Sorry I can't make the meeting, I have to smuggle an aircraft into Corrientes Province"?

It took five minutes to shake the hands of all the participants in the conference, five of whom said, "We can't really discuss all the details in a conference like this; we will have to meet privately just as soon as possible," or words to that effect.

But finally he and Humberto walked together out of the Anglo-Argentine Bank Building onto Calle Bartolomé Mitre, where Enrico was waiting at the wheel of Clete's Buick.

Clete moved quickly to climb in the back, to give Humberto the front seat.

"Claridge's Hotel, por favor, Enrico," Humberto ordered.

The streets in Buenos Aires' financial district were lined with banks, and the narrow sidewalks were crowded with well-dressed men, most of them carrying briefcases. As the car moved slowly through the narrow, traffic-jammed streets — Enrico sat on the horn — Clete looked up and saw the American flag flying from an upper story of the Bank of Boston Building, where the U.S. Embassy had its offices. He saw buildings housing the National City Bank of New York; La Banco de Galacia; and the Dresdener Bank.

Just as Clete noticed a brass sign reading "Claridge's Hotel" on a building, Enrico turned off the street in the drive and stopped.

"Here we are!" Humberto announced.

The restaurant was on the ground floor. The paneled walls, heavy furniture, and long bar reminded Clete of the Adolphus Hotel in Dallas.

Humberto was greeted, in English, by the headwaiter. Picking up on that, Clete noticed that the snippets of conversation he overheard as they were led past the crowded bar to the dining room were also in English.

English English, not American.

Seated at a table, waiting for them, were Señorita Dorotéa Mallín; her mother; Señora Claudia Carzino-Cormano; and three gentlemen of the cloth, only one of whom, Father Kurt Welner, he could identify by name.

Dorotéa was in her demure mood, he saw immediately. He was not surprised, when he went through the Argentine kissing ritual, that she moved her head in such a way as to absolutely preclude any accidental brushing of their lips.

"Beatrice sends her regrets," Humberto announced. "She has a migraine."

Pro forma expressions of regret were offered, but Clete saw relief on everyone's face.

The clergymen were introduced. The tall, thin,

balding one was the Very Reverend Matthew Cashley-Price of the Anglican Cathedral, and the jovial Irishman was Monsignor Patrick Kelly, who was one of the squad of clergy participating in his father's funeral at Our Lady of Pilar.

The look the Very Reverend Mr. Cashley-Price gave Clete made it quite clear that while God might have forgiven a repentant Cletus Howell Frade for despoiling one of the virgins of his flock, he was not quite ready to do so.

"There is very good news —" Father Welner said, then interrupted himself. "Would you like something to drink?"

"I think a little whiskey would go down nicely," Clete said.

"When you hear the good news," Monsignor Kelly said, "you might wish to have champagne."

"Whiskey now, champagne later?" Clete asked.

"Poor Cletus has had a bad morning," Humberto said. "Business, you understand."

He raised his hand with two fingers extended.

"So have we all," Dorotéa said.

"You spoke to the Cardinal Archbishop, Father?" Humberto asked Father Welner.

"His Eminence has graciously granted permission for the Very Reverend Cashley-Price to assist me in the nuptial mass," Monsignor Kelly answered for him.

"It will be necessary for you, Cletus —" the Very Reverend Mr. Cashley-Price began, and interrupted himself. "You don't mind if I call you 'Cletus,' do you?"

"No, Father," Clete said, deciding it was five-to-one Cashley-Price was High Church and would prefer that form of address.

"It will be necessary, of course, Cletus, for you

and Dorotéa to go through our premarital counseling. The Bishop was quite firm about that."

A waiter delivered two glasses dark with whiskey and set them before Clete and Humberto.

"I'll have one of those, please," Claudia Carzino-Cormano said. "If you don't mind. Pamela?"

"I think I'll wait for the champagne," Pamela Mallín said.

"Bring some champagne," Humberto ordered. "Something very nice."

Clete held up a hand to keep the waiter from adding ice or soda to his glass, picked it up, and took a deep swallow.

"With the . . . uh . . . how shall I put it?" Cashley-Price went on, "*time constraints* placed upon us by the situation, we shall have to take care of that right away. I have an hour free tomorrow at three. We could have our first session then. Would that be convenient, Cletus? Dorotéa?"

"I'll be out of town tomorrow," Clete said.

"You can't be out of town tomorrow," Dorotéa said.

"It's unavoidable, Dorotéa," Humberto said. "He really has to go. Business, you understand, that just can't be put off."

Thank you, Uncle Humberto!

"Where is he going?" Dorotéa demanded.

"Posadas," Clete said.

"To Estancia San Miguel," Humberto added. "Business."

"And when will you be returning, Cletus?" Cashley-Price asked.

"Why don't I call you the minute I get back?" Clete said.

"We are going to be very pressed for time," Cashley-Price said.

Waiters appeared with Claudia's drink and champagne.

The first waiter held back until the second waiter had poured the champagne before passing out menus.

Humberto ordered a second bottle of champagne.

Two of Humberto's acquaintances stopped at the table to shake his hand.

Clete glanced at Dorotéa, who was scowling at him.

"Cletus, I know what you're thinking," she said. "We *have* to meet with Father Cashley-Price."

"I know that," Clete said, and smiled at her.

"They do a very nice rack of lamb in here," Humberto announced.

"May I toast the happy couple?" Father Welner said, raising his glass.

"If we have a morning ceremony," Pamela Mallín said, "people won't expect to be asked to stay over."

"Well, some people will have to stay over anyway," Claudia argued. "And afternoon ceremonies are so much nicer."

"I'm not hungry at *all*," Dorotéa said.

"You have to eat, dear," Pamela Mallín said.

"I'm eating for two, is that what you're saying, Mother?"

"That's not what I meant at all."

"The lamb sounds good to me," Clete said.

"There is one question, Cletus, I have to ask," Monsignor Kelly announced. "You have been baptized as a Christian, haven't you?"

"You're missing the whole point, Father," Father Welner said. "Of course he has. The Church regards him as one of ours. There is no question about that. Actually, I really think that the reason His Eminence granted the dispensation was because he agrees — as do many people in Rome — with the idea that Anglican Holy Orders, and certainly those of Father Cashley-Price — are valid. If that is the case, then —"

"Will you excuse me, please?" Clete said. "I have to wash my hands."

There were caricatures of Emperor Hirohito, Adolf Hitler, and Benito Mussolini inside the white china urinals in the men's room.

Clete wondered idly if there were caricatures of Franklin Roosevelt, Winston Churchill, and Charles de Gaulle in the urinals of the Kempinski Hotel across town.

"Giving Adolf a good *Spritz,* are you?" a somewhat familiar voice asked behind him. "Or did that double scotch you just tossed down so fast affect your aim?"

Clete looked over his shoulder and saw Milton Leibermann.

"Take your time, Tex," Leibermann said. "When a man's got to go, he's got to go."

Clete's initial annoyance disappeared. He had to smile.

Leibermann, moving very quickly, pushed open all the doors to the toilet stalls in the men's room to make sure they were empty, then walked to the men's room door and jammed his furled umbrella into the chrome pull-handles. He tested it to make sure the doors could not be opened, then turned and smiled at Clete.

"What did you do, Sherlock, follow me?"

"You wouldn't believe I eat here all the time?"

"Of course I would. Would anybody in your line of business lie?"

"So what's new, Tex?"

"Not much, Milton."

"Strange, I thought that over the weekend you might have heard something I'd like to know."

"Not a thing."

"Not even that they're going to have their little revolution? I keep hearing things that make me think it's going to be damned soon."

"I didn't hear a thing. Maybe they're trying to keep it a secret."

"And maybe you wouldn't tell me if you knew," Leibermann said. "Tell you what I'm going to do, Tex. I'm going to give you the benefit of the doubt."

"Thank you."

"I'll even tell you something I heard that you will want to know."

"What's that?"

"That SS colonel we were talking about? He put out a contract on your man Ettinger."

"What's a contract?"

"Murder Incorporated? Lewis 'Lepke' Buchalter? Ring a bell? Nice Jewish boy who went bad?" Buchalter was an infamous assassin for hire in New York City."

"I've heard the name."

"I used to spend a lot of time with his income tax records," Leibermann said. "Anyway, a contract means you pay somebody to murder somebody else. Colonel Goltz put out a contract on your man Ettinger."

"Is that so?"

"Either you don't give a damn or you already heard."

"I already heard," Clete said. "But . . . honest, Leibermann, thank you."

"I thought it very interesting. Just Ettinger. Not you and the paratrooper who blows things up. Just Ettinger. Was that because Ettinger's a Jew, do you think? Or do you have him doing something the Germans don't like, Jew or no Jew?"

"The latter," Clete said. "Or that's what I think."

"You want to tell me what?"

Clete shook his head, "no."

"Maybe I already know about what he's looking for," Leibermann said.

"I can't. I'm sorry."

"Maybe I could tell him something that would keep him alive," Leibermann said. "You were lucky, what happened to you. They got people down here who could give lessons to Buchalter."

"I met a couple," Clete said. "Not nice people."

"Tell him to be careful."

"I have."

"Your friend von Wachtstein flew Goltz to Montevideo yesterday, and flew him back today. You don't happen to know what that's all about?"

" 'My friend von Wachtstein'?"

Christ, I'm supposed to meet Peter tonight at The Fish. I'll be on my way to Santo Tomé instead.

"He was a guest of honor at your father's requiem mass at your estancia."

"You must have friends all over," Clete said. "Von Wachtstein was there for good manners. He's running around with one of the Carzino-Cormano girls."

"So I heard. You ever think of trying to make friends with him?"

"He's a German officer, for Christ's sake."

"You see *Boys' Town*? Spencer Tracy said

'there's no such thing as a bad boy,' meaning Mickey Rooney. I figure maybe that *all* Germans aren't bad. As a matter of fact, I know a couple of good ones. Maybe von Wachtstein's one of the good ones. You ever hear the phrase 'turning an agent'?"

"No. But I can guess what it means."

"Think about it, Tex," Leibermann said. "And think about telling me why the Germans, the bad ones, they call them 'Nazis,' want Ettinger dead."

He walked to the door and pulled his umbrella free.

"Oh. I almost forgot. Mazel tov. That means congratulations, good luck."

"What for?"

"Isn't that a happy bridal party out there? Should be a hell of a wedding, with three priests."

He pushed the door open and walked out.

Clete washed his hands and then rejoined the happy bridal party.

XVII

[One]

El Palomar Airfield
Buenos Aires, Argentina
1725 14 April 1943

Standartenführer Goltz and Peter von Wachtstein came to be on a — one-way — first-name basis moments after they stepped into Oberst Grüner's Mercedes at the Embassy. Peter thought it interesting that Goltz did not make the overture of friendship — if that's what it was — while they were in Uruguay.

"Which do you prefer your friends to call you, von Wachtstein?" Goltz asked with a smile, " 'Hans-Peter' or 'Hans' or 'Peter'?"

" 'Hans,' Herr Standartenführer."

That was not true. From the age of six, he had learned to increasingly loathe the connection people seemed too frequently to make between Hansel — the affectionate diminutive of Hans — von Wachtstein, and the sweet little boy in the "Hansel & Gretel" fairy tale. Since it proved impossible to punch the nose of everyone who, after fair warning, called him "Hans," he adopted the reverse philosophy. Since only assholes would call him "Hans," he would encourage all assholes to do so.

"You wouldn't mind if I called you 'Hans,' would you, von Wachtstein?"

"Not at all, Herr Standartenführer."

"There is a time, wouldn't you agree, when a certain informality between officers is not only permissible but desirable?"

"I have often thought so, Herr Standartenführer."

"The secret, Hans, is for the junior in such circumstances to correctly predict when the senior is not in the mood for informality. I speak from experience. I once made the mistake — when I myself was a Sturmbannführer,* by the way — of calling Brigadeführer** Max Ruppert . . . Do you know him, by the way?"

"I have not had that privilege, Herr Standartenführer."

"Fine chap. Splendid officer. For a time, he commanded the Liebstandarte Adolf Hitler. Anyway, he was not at the time in a mood to be addressed as 'Max' by a lowly Sturmbannführer, even one he'd known for years. He gave me a dressing-down I still recall painfully."

Peter laughed dutifully.

If that little vignette was intended to caution me not to call you by your first name, it was unnecessary.

Goltz chatted amiably all the way out to the airport, saying nothing important. But also nothing, Peter realized, that seemed in any way unusually curious or threatening, just idle chatter.

But from the moment Goltz suggested "they have a little chat" with drinks and dinner to follow, Peter felt uncomfortable. Not only was the very

---

* The SS rank equivalent to major.
** The SS rank equivalent to brigadier general.

idea that Goltz would go along with him to El Palomar unnerving — it would almost certainly interfere with the talk he must have with Dieter — but there was certainly a reason for Goltz's charm, and Peter wondered what it was, what Goltz wanted from him.

As they approached the passenger terminal, the Condor came into view.

"There it is," Peter said. "It's a beautiful bird, isn't it?"

The Condor was sitting, plugged into fuel trucks and other ground-support equipment, on the tarmac in front of the passenger terminal.

"You miss flying, Hans?" Standartenführer Goltz asked.

"Very much, Herr Standartenführer," Peter replied.

Günther pulled the car into one of the spaces reserved for the Corps Diplomatique, jumped out, and pulled the door open for Goltz.

"I'm going to have a word with Nabler, Hans," Goltz said when Peter had gotten out of the car. "A personal matter. Is there somewhere we could have a coffee while you're dealing with the diplomatic pouches?"

"There is a small restaurant in the terminal, Herr Standartenführer."

"Well, then why don't you see if you can find Nabler for me, and tell him where I'll be?"

"Of course, Herr Standartenführer."

What's the connection between him and Nabler? When Dieter warned me to watch out for Nabler, I thought it was simply because he was an enthusiastic Nazi. If Goltz wants a word with him, he's more than that. What? Is he keeping an eye on Dieter specially, or is it just that the SS likes to keep an eye on everybody who's able to spend time out of Germany? What Dieter said when he couldn't get away from Nabler was that Nabler was following him around like a horny dachshund chasing a Great Dane in heat. Was that coincidental, or is Nabler watching Dieter? And if so, why?

He watched Goltz walk toward the terminal and then went to the back of the car to help Günther with the diplomatic pouches. There were four. Three were mailbag-type pouches and the fourth was a steel box.

"I can manage these, Herr Major Freiherr," Günther said.

"Your offer is tempting, Günther, but unfortunately I'm not supposed to let them out of my sight."

He grabbed two of the pouches and started dragging them to the gate in the fence. When he was through it, he saw Dieter and Karl Nabler walking around under the Condor, doing the preflight.

He walked toward them, looking over his shoulder to see that Günther was following him, staggering under the weight of the third pouch and the steel box.

"Christ," Dieter said, "that's all I need. What the hell is in that steel box, Peter?"

"They don't confide in me."

"What do you figure all that crap weighs?"

"I know precisely what it weighs. A hundred forty point two kilos," Peter said. "Hello, Nabler."

"Herr Major," Nabler replied.

"That's going to put me, with fuel aboard, about three hundred kilos over max gross," Dieter said.

"You should have thought about your intended cargo before you loaded your fuel," Peter said. "We of the Luftwaffe call that 'flight planning.' "

"Thank you so much for the advice," Dieter said

sarcastically. "Kiss my ass, Peter."

"Standartenführer Goltz wants a word with you, Nabler," Peter said. "He's in the . . . Günther, would you take First Officer Nabler to Standartenführer Goltz?"

"Jawohl, Herr Major Freiherr!"

"Let's get these pouches into the bird," Peter said as Nabler started to follow Günther.

"We of Lufthansa have something called 'pre-flight inspection,' " Dieter said. "Won't your god-damned pouches wait?"

Peter shook his head, "no."

Dieter picked up the steel box and pouch Günther had set on the ground and announced, "I can pick this crap up, but I damned sure won't be able to climb the ladder with it."

He put everything down, picked up the third pouch, and started up the ladder to the passenger compartment. Peter looked at the ladder and picked up only one of the two pouches, then climbed the ladder.

Dieter stopped just inside the door and raised his voice.

"Willi?"

Peter looked down the cabin to the cockpit, where a man was sitting at the flight engineer's position.

"Kapitän?" the man asked.

"There's a box and a pouch under the wing. Would you get them for me, please?"

"Jawohl, Herr Kapitän!"

"Put them in the aft storage," Dieter said, then turned to Peter and softly said, "Willi's very oblig-ing. He doesn't want to be sent back to the Luft-waffe. Luftwaffe Condor flight engineers spend a lot of time in Russia."

"Are there many Condors left?"

"Not many. Our beloved Führer has four for his personal use. I suppose, all over, there's another four or five. Maybe six. But not many. I wonder how long they'll be able keep up this charade. You know how many passengers are on the manifest? Five."

"If they cancel these flights, what will you do?"

"Spend a lot of time in Russia, I suppose."

"I have something to go over with you," Peter said. "It's important."

He took the file card with the bank names and account numbers from his pocket. Dieter didn't ask many questions, and Peter wondered how much he understood and could reliably pass on to his father.

"Are you running any risk carrying that card around?" he asked as Dieter slipped the filing card into his shirt pocket.

"The risk I'm worried about is, say four hours from now, looking out the window to find a B-24 pilot waving at me."

He made a gesture of pointing down, an order to land.

"A B-24?" Peter asked, surprised.

"The Americans gave the Brazilians a Navy version of the B-24. They're as fast as the Condor, and they have multiple half-inch Browning machine guns in turrets. Four turrets, if memory serves, plus a couple of single gun positions in the fuselage."

"If that happens, what will you do?"

"Try to keep Nabler from trying to ram the B-24 while I head for the nearest Brazilian airfield — waving a white flag."

"What's Nabler's connection with Goltz?"

"I used to think he was watching me, and Christ knows, he does that, but now I think there's something more than that."

"Any idea what?"

"You're the intelligence officer, Peter. I'm just a simple airplane pilot."

Peter heard a noise, and looked at the door to see Karl Nabler starting up the ladder.

"Have a nice flight, Dieter," Peter said.

"The station manager, Herr Kapitän, asks when you plan to make your departure," Nabler said.

"Just as soon as we can wind up the rubber bands," Dieter said. He offered his hand to Peter. "I'll tell your father how bravely you are holding up in this hellhole far from the comforts of home," he said. "That is, presuming I can get this overloaded sonofabitch off the ground."

He held his right arm up vertically from his belt elbow.

"Heil Hitler!" he said.

Peter returned the salute.

"Good flight, Dieter," he said. "Heil Hitler!"

[Two]

The Horse Restaurant
Avenida del Libertador
Buenos Aires, Argentina
1905 14 April 1943

As they passed the Argentine Army Polo Fields on Avenida del Libertador across from the Hipódromo, Major Freiherr Hans-Peter von

554

Wachtstein slid forward on the seat of Grüner's Mercedes.

"Günther, just this side of the bridge," he ordered. "The Horse. The parking lot is in the back."

"Jawohl, Herr Major Freiherr!"

"What's this, Hans?" Standartenführer Josef Goltz asked.

"A bar I sometimes come to, Herr Standartenführer. It has been my experience that fast horses attract beautiful women."

"Ah-ha!" Goltz said.

Peter originally planned to take Goltz to the men's bar at the Plaza Hotel for a drink. The decision to go to The Horse was impulsive.

He wondered if he was being clever. He didn't know how closely he was being watched by either the Argentine BIS or Oberst Grüner's agents, but there was no doubt that he was frequently under surveillance. Given that, if someone had seen him enter The Horse with Cletus Frade, or saw him do that again with Cletus tonight, or at some other time in the future, there would be some confusion if he was also seen entering The Horse with Standartenführer Goltz.

The more likely reason for his change of mind, he decided, was that he suddenly needed a drink. Maybe two drinks. Not more than two, which would be foolish in Goltz's company. But he wanted a drink, and right then, not fifteen minutes later when they would reach the Plaza Hotel.

What happened at El Palomar had disturbed him. For one thing, though Kapitän Dieter von und zu Aschenburg was as good and experienced a pilot as Peter knew, he had a very hard time getting Lufthansa flight 666 off the ground. For several very long seconds before the Condor finally staggered into the air, it looked as if he would run out of runway.

There was no wind; the wind sock hung limply from its pole atop the control tower. Dieter, he had reasoned, was probably counting on *some* wind for his takeoff roll, and there was none.

That was bad enough, but when Peter got in the Mercedes beside Goltz he remembered Dieter's gesture, the hand signal to land or be shot down he was likely to get if the Condor was intercepted by one of the B-24s the Americans had given to the Brazilians.

And that triggered a sudden very clear memory of Hauptmann Hans-Peter von Wachtstein of Jagdstaffel 232 making the same gesture from the cockpit of his Focke-Wulf 190 to a B-17 pilot near Kassel.

The B-17 had almost certainly been hit by anti-aircraft either before or after he dropped his bombs on Berlin. The damage to his fuselage and wings did not come from machine-gun fire. He had lost his port inboard engine — the prop was feathered — and his starboard outboard engine was gone. The starboard wing was blackened from an engine fire.

He was staggering along at less than a thousand feet, trying to keep it in the air until he was out of Germany. He probably knew that he wasn't going to make it home, but was hoping he could make it to Belgium or the Netherlands, where there was at least a chance the Resistance would see him go down and take care of him and whoever was still alive in his crew.

Peter throttled back and pulled up beside him and gave him the land or be shot down signal. By then he had no desire to add one more aircraft to his shot-down list by taking out a cripple.

The pilot looked at him in horror, then very deliberately shook his head from side to side, asking either for an act of chivalry on Peter's part, or mercy. Peter repeated the land or be shot down signal, and then the question suddenly became moot. The B-17's starboard wing burst into flame and then crumpled, and the B-17 went into a spin. Twenty seconds later, it crashed into a farmer's field and exploded.

Until Dieter made the land or be shot down signal, Peter had been able to force from his mind the memory of the B-17 pilot slowly shaking his head from side to side. Now it came back.

The B-17 pilot, he thought, was probably a young man very much like Cletus. Well, maybe not exactly. Cletus was a fighter pilot, but a pilot. A pilot like himself, and Dieter. He had no doubt that Dieter would like Clete if he knew him, and vice versa.

Why the hell are we killing each other?

Günther jumped out from behind the wheel and held the door open for Standartenführer Goltz. Peter stepped out of the other side of the Mercedes and led Goltz into The Horse.

"One has the choice, Herr Standartenführer: One can sit at the bar, or at a table; or one can go into the balcony. The view is better from the balcony, but at the bar one might have the chance to strike up an acquaintance with one of the natives."

Goltz thought that over.

"I think the balcony, Hans," he said. "I want to have a word with you that won't be overheard."

Peter followed him up the stairs to the balcony, where Goltz selected a table by the railing. A waiter appeared immediately and took their order. Resisting the temptation to order a whiskey, Peter ordered a beer. After a moment's indecision, Goltz ordered whiskey.

When the waiter left them, Goltz looked unabashedly at the women at the bar below.

"The sometimes painful cost of duty," he said. "Look at that one!"

"The natives are attractive, aren't they?"

"Spectacular! I could spend the next three days with my nose buried in those breastworks!"

Peter laughed.

"If it makes you feel any better, Herr Standartenführer," Peter said, "it has been my experience that ninety-nine percent of the native females carry a sign you don't at first notice around their necks reading, 'Look, But Do Not Touch!' "

"Really?" Goltz replied, sounding genuinely disappointed.

"It may be their Spanish heritage," Peter said. "I always thought we were on the wrong side in Spain. I have been reliably informed that the Spanish Communists believed in free love. That was not true of the ladies who supported El Caudillo.* Like their Argentine cousins, they believed in saving it for the marriage bed."

"And you couldn't overcome that unfortunate situation?"

"The competition to fly a Fokker on a supply run to Germany was ferocious, Herr Standartenführer. The girls who hang around the bar at the Hotel am Zoo, or the Adlon, are far more appreciative of, and generous to, dashing airmen resting

---

* General Francisco Franco, the Spanish fascist leader, was known as "El Caudillo," "The Leader," much as Adolf Hitler was known as "Der Füher."

from the noble war against the communist menace."

"I've noticed that. Some of the girls I've seen in the am Zoo and Adlon even seem to prefer shallow young Luftwaffe lieutenants to more senior, and better-looking, SS officers."

"I am sure the Herr Standartenführer is not speaking from personal experience, about the ladies of the Adlon preferring shallow Luftwaffe lieutenants to senior officers of the SS."

"Oh, but I am, Hans." He paused, then asked, "Is that where you previously had the pleasure of Frau von Tresmarck's acquaintance?"

Well, I guess I was wrong again. He is not a faggot after Günther's firm young body. So what is that scholarship in the Fatherland all about?

"My experience, sadly, was the opposite," Peter said. "The one thing wrong with those bars — I hope the Herr Standartenführer will forgive me — is that senior officers frequent them. The young ladies prefer senior officers to junior ones."

"My question was, was it at the Adlon or the am Zoo that you knew Frau von Tresmarck?"

"I was hoping that the Herr Standartenführer would forget he had asked the question."

"That, meine lieber Hans, confirms what I suspected from the smiles on your faces when you met again at the airport," Goltz said.

"I hope Sturmbannführer von Tresmarck —"

"I wouldn't worry about him," Goltz said with a smile. "Unless, of course, he smiles warmly at you."

"I'm not sure I understand the Herr Standartenführer."

"Oh, I think you do, Hans. You're a man of the world. Von Tresmarck's reaction, I'm sure, is better someone like you, who presumably knows and will follow the rules of the game, than someone else." Then, reacting to the look on Peter's face, he added, "Don't look so surprised. I came to know our Inge rather well myself in Berlin before she married von Tresmarck," Goltz said. "You might even say that I was their Cupid."

"Excuse me?"

"A man in Werner's position needed a wife," Goltz said. "And I was very much afraid that our Inge would be caught in one of the periodic sweeps the police made through the Adlon, and places like it, looking for those who could be put to useful work and who don't have permission to live in Berlin. Our Inge would not be happy in jail, I don't think, or, for that matter, running a lathe in some factory."

"You don't consider improving the morale of lonely officers useful work, Herr Standartenführer?"

"A commendable *avocation*, Hans. One I suspect our Inge continues to practice here. How did you pass your time waiting for me?"

"May I respectfully request that we change the subject, Herr Standartenführer?"

"After one final word," Goltz said. "A word to the wise. Don't let your . . . friendship with Inge get out of hand. Moderation in all things, meine lieber Hans."

"I hear and obey, Herr Standartenführer," Peter said with a smile.

"I'm not at liberty, at this time, to tell you how, but von Tresmarck is engaged in quite important work, and nothing, nothing can be allowed to interfere with that."

"Jawohl, Herr Standartenführer."

"Now, we can change the subject," Goltz said. "What shall we talk about?"

"Günther said something about a scholarship at Daimler-Benz?" Peter said. "Is that a safe subject?"

"Oh, he told you about that, did he?"

Peter nodded.

"I'm going to arrange that, Hans, to show my appreciation to his family."

"I don't think I understand, Herr Standartenführer."

Goltz looked around the balcony to assure himself that no one was close enough to eavesdrop on the conversation.

"One of the reasons I'm here, von Wachtstein, is that Admiral Canaris wants to bring the officers from the *Graf Spee* back to Germany. It is a matter of personal importance to him. You know, of course, that the Admiral was himself interned here during the First World War and escaped?"

"Yes, I do, Herr Standartenführer. When we learned I was coming here, my father told me that story."

"Your father and the Admiral are quite close, I understand?"

"I don't think close, Herr Standartenführer. They know each other, of course, but I don't think they could be called close friends."

Why do I think that question wasn't idle curiosity?

"Anyway, the preliminary thinking — Oberst Grüner and I were talking about this earlier today — is that the repatriation of the *Graf Spee* officers will be accomplished in three stages. First, get them out of their place of imprisonment, which should not pose much of a problem. Second, find a location where they can be kept safely until transportation can be arranged for them. And, of course, third, getting them from their refuge out of the country and to the Fatherland."

"There's a lot of them," Peter said. "That will have to be quite an operation."

"There's something near two hundred of them. That's the second problem. Obviously they can't all be moved at once. So we're thinking right now that we will move them in groups of, say, twenty or twenty-five. A single truckload, in other words."

"Herr Standartenführer, excuse me, but my understanding is that the officers have given their parole. They were offered the choice: They would be confined under guard. Or they would give their parole that they would not attempt to escape, and thus would undergo their internment in a hotel, without guards."

"That was in 1939, von Wachtstein," Goltz responded. "The situation is different in 1943."

"I understand, Herr Standartenführer. But once the first group of officers disappears, I was wondering whether the Argentine authorities will then place all the others under greater restrictions."

"We'll have to deal with that when it happens," Goltz said impatiently. "Oberst Grüner did not seem to consider that an insurmountable problem."

"I was trying to be helpful, Herr Standartenführer."

"I understand, Hans," Goltz said.

We're now back to "Hans," are we?

"I had a long chat with our friend Günther over the weekend. I learned that not only is he a good National Socialist, but that his father and many of his father's friends are also."

"That has been my impression, too, Herr Standartenführer."

"I also learned that his father has a small estancia near a place called San Carlos. Are you familiar with San Carlos?"

"No, Herr Standartenführer, I am not."

"San Carlos de something . . ."

"San Carlos *de Bariloche.* Yes, Herr Standartenführer, I know it. It is commonly called simply 'Bariloche.' It's in the foothills of the Andes."

"Near the Chilean border," Goltz said.

"There's a very fine new hotel there," Peter said. "Strange name: Llao Llao. But a first-class hotel. I had a chance to visit there. Hauptmann Duarte's father has an interest in it, and he —"

"I want to talk to you about your relationship with the Duarte family, Hans, but right now —"

"Excuse me, Herr Standartenführer."

"The Loche family has a small estancia near San Carlos de Bariloche. They manufacture some of their sausage products there. The sausage is transported to Buenos Aires, and elsewhere —"

"In their truck, which could carry, say, twenty or twenty-five people without attracting any attention at all?"

"Oberst Grüner said you were a bright and perceptive young officer," Goltz said approvingly, and then went on: "If Herr Loche is willing to assist the Fatherland, his estancia would offer a good refuge for the *Graf Spee* officers until arrangements for their movement to the Fatherland can be arranged. Perhaps through Chile."

"Fascinating."

"Since this operation has approval at the highest echelons — I have been told the Führer is personally aware of it — there is no question regarding money. We will generously compensate Herr Loche for the use of his truck, and for the room and board of the officers while they are under his care."

"And also arrange a scholarship for Günther to Daimler-Benz," Peter said.

"And Günther's presence in Germany might reinforce Herr Loche's patriotism, if you take my meaning. Grüner tells me the Argentine counter-intelligence people . . . What do they call themselves?"

"The BIS. Bureau of Internal Security."

". . . the BIS is not as incompetent as generally believed. If they should ask questions of Herr Loche, it is important for him to give the right answers. Or the wrong ones, which would depend on your perspective, as we talked about this morning."

"Excuse me?"

"You said, 'under the right' circumstances the Brazilians might actually be able to shoot down the Condor. The semantics are interesting, wouldn't you say?"

"I'm sure the Standartenführer took my meaning correctly this morning."

"Of course," Goltz said, smiling. "Now, you're going to have a role in this . . ."

"I would be honored, Herr Standartenführer."

". . . but just what role has not been decided. I'm having dinner with Herr Loche tomorrow, and I'll broach the subject to him then. If that goes well, perhaps it would be a good idea for you to visit Bariloche. . . . You said you've been there. How did you travel?"

"By train, Herr Standartenführer."

"Well, perhaps you might drive to Bariloche, reconnoiter the road, examine the facilities at the Loche farm. . . ."

"I understand, Herr Standartenführer."

"As I say, I have not yet had a chance to make firm decisions."

"I will hold myself in readiness, Herr Standartenführer."

"If things work out well with Herr Loche . . . ," Goltz said carefully. "What I'm driving at, Hans, is that it might be very useful to us to have a place, perhaps more than one place — I'm talking about somewhere in the country, what do they call their farms?"

"Estancias, Herr Standartenführer."

"If we had an estancia, several estancias, I can see where that would be very useful to us in the future. Not only in connection with the repatriation of the *Graf Spee* officers, but in connection with other operations. There are two operations, which I'm not at liberty to discuss, which come immediately to mind. And I'm sure there will be others."

"Is the Herr Standartenführer talking about buying an estancia?"

"Should we decide to acquire an estancia or two — and perhaps even the controlling interest in a business, a trucking firm, for example — it would be absolutely essential that our ownership be kept secret."

"I understand, Herr Standartenführer."

"The *legal* owner could be someone like Herr Loche or one of his friends, Argentine nationals who are good Germans. People we can trust."

"I see."

"But questions might be asked if Herr Loche were suddenly to start acquiring property. His business, as I understand it, while successful, is not successful to the point where he can buy another estancia."

"I see the problem."

"Bankers would be curious, is what I'm driving at. Which brings us to your relationship with the late Hauptmann Duarte's father. One would think that someone who had lost his son at Stalingrad would be interested in helping Germany in any way he could. But on the other hand, Herr Duarte is the Managing Director of the Anglo-Argentine Bank. How would you judge Herr Duarte's feeling toward Germany?"

"His nephew is an American, Herr Standartenführer," Peter said. "And I think he believes we were connected with the death of his brother-in-law."

"That's unfortunate. You know, of course, the nephew is an American OSS agent."

"So I have been told."

"It may be necessary for him to join his father," Goltz said. "Which would, in your judgment, further tilt Herr Duarte toward the Allies? He is close to the nephew?"

"Frade is going to be married shortly . . ."

"Oh, really?"

". . . to the daughter of the man who runs SMIPP, Enrico Mallín."

"What?"

"It stands for Sociedad Mercantil de Importación de Productos Petrolíferos. They import petroleum and petroleum products from the Howell Petroleum Company, which is owned by Frade's family."

"How did you learn this?"

"I've spent a good deal of time with the Duarte family, Herr Standartenführer. One hears things."

"And Frade is marrying the daughter of this firm?"

"One of the things I heard this weekend, Herr

Standartenführer, was that Herr Duarte — rather emotionally — feels that since God has taken both his son and his brother-in-law, God is now making things right by giving the family a baby."

"You did not hear what I said a moment ago about young Frade joining his father, Hans. And from this moment on, you will not hear another word about it. If that becomes necessary, I want you to be outraged."

"Excuse me?"

"Let me try to explain. We have right now a situation in which they regard you with a certain fondness. We want to encourage that."

The waiter appeared at the table, interrupting Goltz.

"I think we should have one more," he said, nodding at the waiter, "and then think about dinner."

He waited for the waiter to leave.

"What I'm thinking is this, Hans. At some point in the future, you approach Herr Duarte and tell them you are not only disenchanted with Germany —"

He interrupted himself.

"The more I think of this, the more it seems to be a splendid solution to our problem," Goltz said.

"I'm afraid, Herr Standartenführer, that I'm not following you."

"*Even before* something unfortunate happens to young Frade, you approach Herr Duarte and tell him that you are disenchanted with Germany, that you are convinced Germany will lose the war, and that you wish to invest your family's money in Argentina. Naturally, this would have to be done in the greatest secrecy. . . ."

"Herr Standartenführer, the von Wachtstein

family doesn't have any money to invest anywhere. And if we did, sending money out of Germany is considered treason."

"And rightly so. Hence the reason for secrecy. It's all very credible," Goltz said. "The money you would invest here — in an estancia, or estancias, or to acquire the controlling interest in a trucking firm, for example — would be from the funds available to me for the Argentine operations I alluded to a moment before. Someone like Herr Duarte would be able to keep such activities very quiet, and certainly no one would suspect the Anglo-Argentine Bank would be conducting secret operations on behalf of the German Reich!"

"I don't know what to say," Peter said.

"You have your choice between a simple 'Jawohl, Herr Standartenführer,' " Goltz said, smiling broadly, obviously very pleased with himself, "or, if you agree, 'what a clever line of thought, Josef.' Either will suffice."

"It does seem like a brilliant idea, Herr Standartenführer."

"Sometimes the best ideas" — Goltz snapped his fingers — "come from out of the blue like that," Goltz said. "Our Führer has often said that impulsive action is often better than anything else."

"Permission to speak, Herr Standartenführer?"

"Permission granted, Major."

"The possibility must be considered, I respectfully suggest, Herr Standartenführer, that the elimination of young Frade might cause Herr Duarte to dislike all Germans, including me."

"No, Hans. . . . No, don't you see, if you went to Duarte immediately and allied yourself against the Third Reich now, then when Frade is eliminated, and you are outraged, it will make it all the

568

more credible that you wish to disassociate yourself from Germany."

Peter nodded, thoughtfully, as if accepting Goltz's reasoning.

"Another thought," Goltz said. "What is your relationship with Frade? You must see him from time to time."

"Correct, Herr Standartenführer. We are officers of belligerent powers on neutral soil."

"While there is still time, it might be a good idea for you to cultivate him. Doing so would make your indignation at his passing more credible."

You slimy, amoral, miserable sonofabitch!

"I see your reasoning, Herr Standartenführer," Peter said. "I don't know how —"

"If the situation comes up where you can, Hans," Goltz said, "don't be too obvious about it."

The waiter appeared with their drinks.

"I'm sorry now that I ordered this," Goltz said. "I would really like champagne."

"Well, we can have champagne with our dinner, Herr Standartenführer."

"Hans, about dinner . . ."

"Yes, Herr Standartenführer?"

"The point is, we have actually covered all the matters I wanted to discuss with you over dinner. In point of fact, a good deal more. And Gradny-Sawz has promised a *diversion,* if you take my meaning, if I could conclude our business at an early hour. Could I renege on my offer of dinner? Save it for another time?"

"Of course, Herr Standartenführer."

"Do I detect a tone of relief in your voice, Hans?"

"Perhaps regret, Herr Standartenführer. I was looking forward to having dinner."

"What I meant was that I thought perhaps after

how you spent yesterday afternoon and evening, you might wish to make a very early night of it. Our Inge can be exhausting."

"I don't think I will be up until the wee hours tonight, Herr Standartenführer."

"Can I drop you somewhere?"

"I can find a taxi, Herr Standartenführer."

"You're sure?"

"I live in the opposite direction from Herr Gradny-Sawz's house, Herr Standartenführer."

"Well, then. The least I can do is pay for the drinks," Goltz said. He laid money on the table and put out his hand to Peter.

"Bon chasse, Herr Standartenführer," Peter said.

"And the same to you, Hans. After you regain your strength, of course."

Goltz walked to the balcony stairs. Peter watched him descend and leave The Horse. He caught the waiter's eye and signaled that he wanted the check. When he had paid it, he left The Horse and walked up Avenida del Libertador past the polo field.

When he was satisfied that he wasn't being followed, he flagged down a taxi and gave the driver the address of Humberto Valdez Duarte's mansion on Avenida Alvear.

[Three]

1420 Avenida Alvear
Buenos Aires, Argentina
2025 14 April 1943

Major Freiherr Hans-Peter von Wachtstein was kept waiting in the foyer of the mansion while the butler went to determine if Señor Duarte was at home.

Humberto, in his shirtsleeves, appeared immediately through the door Peter had learned led to the dining.

"I'm sorry to come like this. . . ."

"Don't be silly," Humberto said. "I'm always glad to see you."

"Something has come up that I thought I should tell you about right away," Peter said. "And I really need to talk to Cletus."

Humberto looked at his watch.

"Cletus is taking the ten-o'clock train to Corrientes," he said. "He's probably at the Avenida Coronel Díaz house. I'll call."

"Thank you."

"I'm just having a little dinner," Humberto said. "My wife is . . . indisposed. Can I offer you something?"

"I don't like to impose."

Humberto took him into the dining room, ordered a maid standing there to set a place for Peter — only one place was set at the huge table, which Peter thought was sad — and then dialed the telephone.

Peter could hear only one side of the conversation.

"Cletus, I think it's important that we have a

word before you board the train," he said. "Could you come here?"

"It's not that at all. I promise."

"The sooner the better."

"Thank you."

He hung the telephone up.

Peter's curiosity got the better of him.

"What's 'it's not that at all, I promise'?"

"Cletus had a very bad day," Humberto said, smiling. "Business all morning, then a long, long lunch discussing wedding plans, followed by a long, long afternoon doing the same thing. He told me that he had all the wedding plans he could stand for one day. I had the feeling he has had a couple of recuperative drinks."

"Why's he going to Corrientes?"

"He didn't say, Peter," Humberto said. "Let me get you a glass of wine."

"Can I offer you something to eat, Cletus?" Humberto asked when Clete walked into the dining twenty minutes later, trailed by Enrico.

"Enrico said the food is pretty good on the train," Clete said. "But yes, I will have a little whiskey and soda, thank you for asking." He turned to Peter. "Not that I'm not glad to see you, amigo, but if we keep meeting like this people will talk."

Humberto was right. Cletus has been drinking.

"I wasn't followed," Peter said. "I wanted you to hear about Standartenführer Goltz, and I wasn't sure you would be at The Fish — The Horse — tonight."

"I wouldn't have been," Clete said. "Duty calls. I'm on my way to Corrientes."

"Why?"

"I could say I am going to inspect Estancia San

Miguel, but I'm at the point where I am forgetting which lie I told to which person," Clete said. "Actually I'm going to bring a C-45 in from Brazil."

"What's a C-45?" Peter asked. "An aircraft?"

"A light twin," Clete said. "Liaison, it has six or eight seats in the back. They also use it as a trainer for navigators."

"How are you going to bring it into the country?" Humberto asked.

"Fly it across the border into a strip at Santo Tomé," Clete said, "and from there to Estancia San Pedro y San Pablo."

"Cletus, isn't that dangerous?" Humberto asked. "They patrol the border."

"I made a deal with the BIS," Clete said. "They help me bring the airplane into the country, and I make it available to them in case they don't get away with their coup d'état."

He looked at his watch.

"I don't have much time," he said.

"Two things," Peter said. "I want to tell you both about a conversation I just had with Standartenführer Goltz. And I want to tell you, Cletus — it might be better if Humberto didn't know about this — what I found out when I was in Montevideo."

"Perhaps it would be best if I was familiar with everything," Humberto said.

"I think maybe Peter's right," Clete said. "You probably shouldn't, for your own good, know about —"

"For the common good," Humberto said, very seriously. "The more I know, the better." When neither Peter nor Clete seemed convinced, he added, "When I became involved in this business, I knew it was going to be like pregnancy."

"Excuse me?" Peter asked.

"One cannot be a little bit pregnant," Humberto said. "So if there is not some valid reason not to tell me everything . . ."

"The two are connected, Cletus," Peter said.

"OK, Humberto," Clete said. "Your choice. Let's have it, Peter."

"I've heard rumors," Humberto said after Peter finished, "about money being paid to help people *immigrate* here, or to Uruguay, from Germany. I didn't hear much, and this is the first I've heard that they were being released from concentration camps. I thought it was simply bribe money, paid to obtain visas."

"There's one more thing," Peter said, "now that I think about it. Inge said that her husband was 'making himself rich' getting Jews out of concentration camps. That sounds personal — I'm sure she meant it that way — so how does that fit in with the money in Uruguay being used to buy property, et cetera?"

"Perhaps your friend's husband," Humberto said, "is taking a small commission for himself."

"Wouldn't that be more than a little dangerous?" Clete asked.

"Illicit moneys have a way of sticking to people's fingers," Humberto said.

"The SS is full of thieves," Peter said matter-of-factly. "When I think about it, I think Humberto's probably right."

"You're sure about what your lady friend said?" Clete asked.

Peter nodded.

"When are you going to see her again?" Clete asked.

"Never, I hope," Peter said.

"Maybe she can tell us something else," Clete said, then looked at his watch again. "I've got to get out of here."

"There's plenty of time for you to make your train," Humberto said.

"I can't risk missing it," Clete said. "We drove here. Can I leave my car in your garage?"

"If you'd like, Cletus, I can have my chauffeur take you to the station. Either in my car, or yours, in which case he could take it to Avenida Coronel Díaz."

"You use your car to take Peter to his apartment," Clete said. "Enrico and I will take a taxi."

"Whichever you prefer," Humberto said.

"Thanks, Humberto," Clete said. "For everything."

Humberto hugged him.

"I will pray for your safe return," he said.

Clete looked at Peter.

"What are you going to tell Alicia about — what's her name? *Inge.*"

"You sonofabitch!" Major Freiherr Hans-Peter von Wachtstein said.

At the Central Train Station, Clete called Tony from a pay telephone, gave him that number, and ordered him to call him as soon as possible from any other telephone.

"And bring paper and a pencil with you. You're going to have to write down my message."

It took Tony fifteen minutes to call back. By that time four indignant people were lined up to use the pay telephone, and there were only six minutes left to board the train.

"Sorry," Tony began. "I had a hell of a time finding a phone."

"I want you to send this off to Washington as soon as possible. Can you drive out there tonight?"

"Sure."

"You ready?"

"Shoot."

"This goes as Lindbergh."

"Got it."

"One. Galahad confirms absolutely Lindbergh exists."

"No shit?"

"Two. Montevideo operation run by SS Major Werner von Tresmarck, security officer of German Embassy."

"You're going to have to spell that for me."

"Whiskey Easy Roger Nan Easy Roger," Clete spelled quickly. "You know how to spell 'von.' Tango Roger Easy Sugar Mike Able Roger Charley King."

"Got it."

"And when you get to the estancia, stay there and make sure Dave doesn't go anywhere until I get back."

"Where are you going?"

Clete hung up without replying and ran to catch the train.

When Antonio informed Clete that he "had been packed," it didn't enter Clete's mind to see what had actually gone into his suitcase. Antonio would certainly, he reasoned, include his toilet kit, plus several changes of underwear, a couple of fresh shirts, maybe a spare jacket and trousers, and whatever else necessary for a three- or four-day trip.

Thus, when he went into his compartment aboard the train, he was a little surprised — and a little amused — to see that Antonio's idea of clothing for a trip of no more than four days filled two large suitcases. The identical saddle leather suitcases were nearly new. He was not surprised to see a burnished spot on both cases where he could just make out what was left of his father's initials.

They had two adjoining compartments in what Clete recognized from movies as the English version of an American Pullman car. He remembered his father telling him that the English had built Argentina's railroads. He wondered idly if this car was made here from an English pattern or imported.

When he went into his luggage for his toilet kit, he found a complete riding outfit.

"No wonder he needed two suitcases," he mused aloud. "I wonder where he expects me to wear the riding costume?"

"Señor Clete," Enrico said. "I told Antonio to pack that. We are going to the Second Cavalry."

"We're going riding at the Second Cavalry?" Clete asked.

My God. If he heard me wonder out loud where I'm going to wear this costume, I must have been speaking in Spanish!

"I feel sure the Coronel Commanding will ask you to ride with him as he shows you the regiment. Excuse me, Señor Clete, but I must say this: It would not be fitting for you to accompany him in your Texas Aggie boots."

"I stand corrected, Suboficial Mayor," Clete said. "I will even shave in the morning, and close my fly, so I will not embarrass you."

"In the morning, Señor Clete, it would be best if you put on the appropriate clothing."

"You mean this?"

"Sí, Señor Clete."

XVIII

[One]

Bureau of Internal Security
Ministry of Defense
Edificio Libertador
Avenida Paseo Colón
Buenos Aires
0930 15 April 1943

El Teniente Coronel Alejandro Bernardo Martín answered the red security telephone on his desk before it had a chance to ring a second time.

"Martín," he said.

"Bernardo," the familiar voice of el Almirante Francisco de Montoya said, conversationally, "just as soon as you have a free minute, would you step in, please?"

"Immediately, mi Almirante."

"Thank you," Montoya said, and the line went dead.

Martín was familiar enough with Admiral Montoya to know when the Admiral was deeply upset — despite an outward aura of calm. "That tone" was in Montoya's voice just now.

He pulled open the center drawer of his desk and slid into it everything he had been working on, making no attempt to organize it. Then he locked the drawer carefully and left his office.

"El Almirante expects you, mi Coronel," Montoya's secretary said when he entered the outer office. "Go right in."

Montoya was peering through his Royal Navy binoculars when Martín entered the office. He continued to peer through them for another thirty seconds after Martín politely wished him a good morning.

Martín understood this action, too. It signaled three messages. First, it reminded the caller that he was a subordinate — seniors kept subordinates waiting. Second, it gave the caller the impression el Almirante was not upset — otherwise he would not be looking out the window. And finally, it gave el Almirante time to consider how he would begin the interchange to follow.

Martín waited patiently, his hands folded in the small of his back, until el Almirante turned around.

Montoya looked at Martín for ten seconds and then nodded, as if in approval.

"El Presidente of the nation sent for me this morning, Coronel," he announced. "I have just returned from the Casa Rosada."

Martín didn't reply.

"Presidente Castillo has been informed by a source he considers very reliable," Montoya said, "that the Grupo de Oficiales Unidos is not dissolving, as he hoped they would, following the tragic death of el Coronel Frade. They are in fact planning the overthrow of his government."

Does that mean what it sounds like — that we have been betrayed — or did Castillo finally wake up? And does Montoya's careful choice of words — suggesting this is the first he has heard the Grupo de Oficiales

Unidos is planning the coup — mean that he has chosen sides against us?

"Mi Almirante, did el Presidente identify the source of his information?"

"Of course not."

"Do you believe el Presidente's source to be reliable, mi Almirante?"

"I would think so. Among other things, el Presidente's source provided him with a complete list of the officers who were at Estancia Santo Catalina over the weekend. According to that source, General Arturo Rawson has replaced el Coronel Frade as President of the Grupo de Oficiales Unidos."

So we do have a traitor in our midst. Or, from Castillo's perspective, a patriot. And I have no idea at all who it could be.

"I hadn't heard that, but I am not surprised. I thought it would be either Rawson or General Ramírez."

"Apparently, you were not able to place anyone at Estancia Santo Catalina?"

"At the estancia, of course," Martín said. "You will recall that on Monday morning I furnished you with a list of the officers who were at Estancia Santo Catalina. . . ."

For precisely this purpose, in case someone else out there was counting noses and making lists.

"Fortunately, I was able to present el Presidente with your list. If it wasn't for that list, I would have looked — we would have looked — more incompetent than otherwise."

"I was unable, mi Almirante, to place a source inside the meeting of the G.O.U., if there was such a meeting."

"Of course there was a meeting. At which

581

Rawson was elected, or appointed, to replace Frade."

"Appointed by whom, mi Almirante?"

"I was thinking Ramírez."

"General Ramírez was not at Estancia Santo Catalina over the weekend, mi Almirante."

"Juan Domingo Perón was. He was almost certainly Ramírez's proxy."

"That is a possibility."

"Putting together all the intelligence you have gathered, Coronel, what is your assessment of the chances that the G.O.U. will succeed if they attempt to depose Presidente Castillo?"

"I think they will succeed, mi Almirante," Martín said.

Although he looked carefully, Martín could not see any reaction to that on Montoya's face.

But if I told him I thought the coup would fail, the next time he opened his mouth he would have ordered me to arrest everybody on the list, and probably Ramírez as well.

"And when do you think they will try?"

What they did talk about at that damned meeting was when they would execute OUTLINE BLUE. And they didn't make a decision. The foot draggers triumphed. "Let's wait until there is the absolute minimum chance that something will go wrong!" It is one thing to talk about, even plan, a coup d'état, and entirely something else to vote to try it. And if whoever among them knew that Rawson was elected president of G.O.U. — and who is that sonofabitch? — he also knew that no date was decided upon. Does Montoya know that?

"I can only guess, mi Almirante."

"Guess."

"Once the decision was reached to try to over-

582

throw the government, I would think it would take a minimum of two weeks to coordinate everything and issue the execution order."

"That quickly?"

"That is my opinion, mi Almirante. It could be longer. Three weeks or a month. Any coup would require that all military and naval bases all over the country be part of the coup, or that they be neutralized."

"For the sake of argument, Bernardo, let's say the decision to proceed was made at the Estancia Santo Catalina meeting. You're saying that the attempt could not be made before" — he consulted his desk calendar — "the twenty-eighth of this month?"

"At the absolute minimum, mi Almirante. *If* such a decision was made over the weekend. And I would really think it would take longer than two weeks, which would move any such action into the first week in May."

"You would stake your professional reputation on that?"

"I stake my professional reputation whenever I present something I know to be a fact. What I just said is an opinion, nothing more."

"Calling in all your sources, Coronel, could you find out, as a fact, if the decision to attempt to overthrow the government was made at the Estancia Santo Catalina meeting, and if so, when?"

"That's two questions, mi Almirante. Within, say, three or four days, I should be able to tell you, as a fact, if the decision to go ahead has been made or not. I would have had that information in that time frame in any case. The second question, when, is more difficult. My sources may not be privy to that information. If they are not, it would certainly take more time to obtain it. Presuming it could be obtained at all."

Montoya obviously was not pleased with the reply.

"That's the best you can do?"

"I'm afraid so, mi Almirante."

"Presidente Castillo won't be pleased when I tell him that," Montoya said. "If you had additional funds, would that speed things up?"

"Additional funds probably would."

"Spend whatever you have to," Montoya said. "The country is in a crisis. This is no time to economize. But bring back information I can take to el Presidente!"

"Did el Presidente give you any idea how he plans to deal with the situation, mi Almirante?"

"He didn't discuss that with me, Coronel. Possibly because he believes I am familiar with the penalties the law provides for treason."

"What I meant to ask, mi Almirante, is whether Presidente Castillo plans to alert the Army — or certain Army officers he believes loyal to him — to the possibility of a coup. Or the Policía Federal."

"He did not discuss any of that with me," Montoya said. "But there are a number of officers whose loyalty to el Presidente is beyond question, and I'm sure he has had discussions along these lines with them."

"If that's all, mi Almirante?"

"That's all. I expect to be kept fully abreast of any developments, Bernardo."

"Sí, Señor," Martín said, saluted, and left Montoya's office.

[Two]

Office of the Minister of War
Edificio Libertador
Avenida Paseo Colón
Buenos Aires
0950 15 April 1943

"The question, Martín, it seems to me," Teniente General Pedro P. Ramírez said, "is whether Montoya accepted your claim that it would take two weeks to execute OUTLINE BLUE from the time we give the order."

"I believe he did, Señor," Martín answered.

The door opened and el Coronel Juan Domingo Perón passed through it, saluted Ramírez, and then stood at attention.

"Have a chair, Juan Domingo," Ramírez said. "You're probably going to need one."

"Mi General?"

"Let's wait until the others arrive, then we won't have to say everything twice," Ramírez said.

General Arturo Rawson; his aide, Capitán Roberto Lauffer; and Mayor Pedro V. Querro, Ramírez's aide, entered the room a moment later.

"O'Farrell?" Ramírez asked.

"General O'Farrell is not in the building, mi General," Querro said.

"Then we'll have to do without him," Ramírez decided aloud. "El Coronel Martín has just come from el Almirante Montoya. Castillo called Montoya into the Casa Rosada this morning, where he told him: first, that he was disappointed that the G.O.U. did not fold its tent when Jorge Frade was killed; second, that the G.O.U. is planning to depose him; and third, that he knows this because

585

someone at the meeting where Arturo was elected G.O.U. president told him."

"Who?" Perón said.

"I have no more idea than you, Coronel Perón," Ramírez said. "But I suspect an olive branch was concealed in Castillo's message: we fold our tent, and all is forgiven. Which gives us two options, as I see it. We either fold the G.O.U. tent; or we don't fold it, which means we issue the Blue Sky message this morning, right now, and carry out OUTLINE BLUE."

"Do we have time?" Perón asked. "If Castillo had someone at the meeting, and it's clear that he did . . ."

"Martín believes he has convinced Montoya that it will take at least two weeks to take action from the time we order it."

"And if Castillo decides to act today?" Perón asked. "For all we know, there may be Policía Federal on their way right now to arrest us."

"I don't see where we have any choice but to issue Blue Sky," Rawson said. "We should have issued it over the weekend."

"We were seeking unity," Perón said. "We can't afford for people to have second thoughts at the last minute."

"If the order is issued, there won't be time for anyone to have any second thoughts," Rawson said. "Unless there is objection from you, mi General, I will order Blue Sky issued."

"We are never going to be any more ready than we are now," Ramírez said. "Issue Blue Sky, Mayor Querro."

Ramírez's diminutive aide came to attention, said, "Sí, Señor," and dialed a number from memory on one of the telephones on the desk.

586

"Querro," he said when someone answered. "Blue Sky. Blue Sky."

Then he hung up.

Ramírez looked at his watch.

"If things go according to OUTLINE BLUE — and if they do it will be the first time in my military career that anything has gone as planned — in a hundred and twenty hours, this distasteful duty will have been accomplished, Castillo will be gone, and Arturo will be running the country. May God forgive us all if we are doing the wrong thing."

"Martín," General Rawson asked. "Where's that airplane we were talking about?"

"Young Frade went to Corrientes last night on the train. We have made arrangements for him to land it at the airstrip on the Second Cavalry Reservation in Santo Tomé. With a little bit of luck —"

"My experience," General Ramírez interrupted, "is that it is better not to plan on anything going right. We better proceed on the assumption that if we fail, we will *not* have an airplane to fly us to Paraguay."

"Does the General wish to call off the arrangements vis-à-vis the airplane?" Martín asked.

"That's not what I said, Coronel. What I said was that we should not *count on* the airplane. By all means, continue that operation."

"I have a man in Santo Tomé, mi General," Martín said. "When he receives the Blue Sky message, he will understand the need for quick action."

"Presuming I can leave this building without being arrested," Rawson said, "you know where I will be for the next ninety-six hours."

"The moment Castillo learns we have all disappeared," Perón said, "he will know what we're up to."

"With a little bit of that luck Coronel Martín seems to have such faith in, Castillo may decide that the message he gave Montoya has reached us, and that we have decided not only to fold the tent, but to take the precaution of fleeing the country," Ramírez said. "But in any event, I don't think he will be looking for Arturo and Lauffer in the Italian Rowing Club in El Tigre."

"Unless, mi General," Martín said. "Unless the person who was there when General Rawson was elected president of the Grupo de Oficiales Unidos was also there when it was decided where General Rawson would go once Blue Sky was issued."

Ramírez considered that thoughtfully.

"If Arturo is arrested, that will considerably reduce the number of people who could be betraying us, won't it?" he asked. "Where did you say O'Farrell was?"

"I was told he was inspecting the First Infantry Regiment," Querro said.

"I don't think Castillo's source is General O'Farrell," Martín said.

Ramírez shrugged, then asked, "And where will you be, Coronel Martín, for the next ninety-six hours?"

"I'll be in touch by telephone, of course," Martín said. "I really don't know where I'm going to be. But I don't think I'll be missed."

"Why not?"

"It will be presumed I'm out looking for you, mi General," Martín said. "May I suggest that we all leave now — you, General Ramírez, fifteen minutes after General Rawson, and you, Coronel Perón, fifteen minutes after that?"

"And you, Martín?" Perón asked.

"I'll make sure you are all gone before I leave," Martín said. "If you are arrested, I may be able to have you turned over to me."

[Three]

The Office of the Military Attaché
The Embassy of the German Reich
Avenida Córdoba
Buenos Aires, Argentina
1005 15 April 1943

Oberst Karl-Heinz Grüner did not rise to his feet when Standartenführer Josef Goltz walked into his office. He raised his right arm from the elbow in a casual Nazi salute, which Goltz returned as casually.

"Have you a minute for me?" Goltz asked.

"Of course. Would you like some coffee?"

He waved Goltz into a brown leather couch against the wall.

"Thank you," Goltz said. "Yes, as a matter of fact, I would. I think I'm going to get coffee nerves. I'm still taking advantage of drinking all the coffee I want."

"They truck it in from Brazil. It's not only good, but it's cheap," Grüner replied. He raised his voice: "Günther! Would you bring the Herr Standartenführer and me some coffee, please?"

"Jawohl, Herr Oberst!" his driver called from the other office.

"I presume you have heard about the *Comerciante*

del Océano Pacífico, Grüner?"

"Not officially," Grüner said.

"Excuse me?"

"When the radio came in, it was classified 'Most Urgent For Ambassador Only.' Since the cryptographic officer was at the dentist, I was pressed into service decoding it."

Goltz chuckled. "Herr Oberst, you may now presume you have the Right to Know what you already know."

"Thank you, Herr Standartenführer," Grüner said, smiling.

"I would, of course, like her to discharge the cargo we're interested in as soon as possible after she drops anchor in Samborombón Bay. If that is in six or seven days . . ."

"I think I can be ready for that. I've already done a little preliminary planning," Grüner replied, indicating the papers on his desk. "There's one bit of information I'd love to have."

"Which is?"

"In the ideal situation, the *Océano Pacífico* carries aboard a boat suitable for our purposes."

"I'm not sure I understand you. You're talking about lifeboats?"

Grüner shook his head, "no."

"She will anchor over the horizon from the shore. The horizon is approximately eleven kilometers. If I were her captain, I would probably at least double that distance, which would mean she will anchor somewhere between twenty and thirty kilometers offshore. The engines in lifeboats — where in fact they have engines — propel them at no more than five or six kilometers per hour. That's a very long voyage from ship to shore. At thirty kilometers offshore, five to six hours."

"And acquiring a much faster boat here would pose problems?"

"I know where I can get a boat," Grüner said. "In a little town called Magdalena. One capable of about thirty-five kilometers per hour. But we don't gain much time."

"Explain that, please."

"For the sake of argument, say the *Océano Pacífico* is anchored thirty kilometers offshore, the boat would have to put out from Magdalena to the *Océano Pacífico*."

"That would take an hour," Goltz said.

"Presuming the *Océano Pacífico* was thirty kilometers offshore from Magdalena. She may not be so conveniently anchored. She may be further down in Samborombón Bay. Another twenty-five or thirty kilometers distant."

"I see what you mean."

"So if I utilize the boat in Magdalena, we have at least an hour's trip to the *Océano Pacífico* — probably more. Then a trip of approximately the same length to the place where we will discharge the cargo — which I think you will agree should *not* be at Magdalena — and then however long it takes to travel from the discharge point to Magdalena. Unless, of course, there are other potential problems."

"Which are?" Goltz asked, forcing himself to smile. He was torn between impatience at Grüner's methodical listing of all problems, and admiration for his methodical mind.

"The boat I have available in Magdalena has a captain," Grüner said. "He would of course know how we have used the boat. He'll have seen us take the cargo from the *Océano Pacífico* and land it under suspicious conditions. He might talk, of course."

"That could be dealt with, couldn't it?"

"Of course, but dealing with the captain might attract attention in itself. And there's another problem tied in with that: Who will physically unload the cargo at the discharge point?"

"Seamen from the *Océano Pacífico*," Goltz said impatiently.

"In that event, they would have to be carried back to the *Océano Pacífico* before the boat returned to Magdalena."

"How would you deal with these problems, Oberst Grüner?"

"They would all be solved if there was a suitable boat already aboard the *Océano Pacífico*. Failing that, I would suggest that we acquire a boat which could be taken aboard the *Océano Pacífico* — if only temporarily. Then that boat, loaded and crewed by *Océano Pacífico* seamen, would go directly to the discharge point, unload the cargo into our waiting truck, and return directly to the *Océano Pacífico*, greatly reducing the chance of interception."

"You want to buy the boat in . . . where was it?"

"Magdalena. But no. I would suggest keeping that in reserve."

"You want to buy another boat? Buy another boat."

"That raises the question of the captain again. Who would command the boat?"

"Von Wachtstein," Goltz said. "If he can navigate an airplane across the River Plate, he certainly should be able to navigate twenty or thirty kilometers in a boat."

"He would need a crew."

"He can get a crew from the *Océano Pacífico*."

"*After* he initially gets the new boat to the *Océano Pacífico*, he could," Grüner said. "Pursuing that line of thought: We acquire a boat here. In El Tigre. Using a minimum crew — Günther comes immediately to mind — von Wachtstein takes it out to the *Pacífico*. A crew from the *Océano Pacífico* then takes von Wachtstein and Günther ashore, and returns the boat to the *Océano Pacífico*, where it will be taken aboard."

"Fine," Goltz said, his patience worn thin. "Buy the boat."

Grüner was not through.

"Then, when you decide the time has come to bring the cargo ashore, the boat in Magdalena will take you out to the *Océano Pacífico*, and then return —"

"Why do I have to do that?"

"I had the impression only you could authorize her captain to release our cargo," Grüner said.

"Correct," Goltz said, just a little embarrassed. "And then I would come ashore with the cargo to the discharge point, correct?"

"Right. I will be there, of course," Grüner said. "And once the cargo is discharged, the boat will return to the *Océano Pacífico* and be taken aboard for later use in connection with the *Graf Spee* officers."

"Well, that should solve everything, shouldn't it?"

"We don't know if von Wachtstein knows anything about boats," Grüner said. "And then, of course, there is the problem of funds to purchase a boat. And someone to purchase it. I don't think it wise for someone connected with the Embassy to buy a boat. There would be questions."

"I'm having dinner with Günther's father tonight. I will suggest that he purchase the boat. Do you know where you can find one?"

"I'm sure I can find one in El Tigre," Grüner said.

"How much money will be required? In American dollars or Swiss francs?"

"In dollars or francs?" Grüner asked dubiously.

"In dollars or francs," Goltz said.

Grüner did the necessary arithmetic on a sheet of paper.

"Fifteen thousand dollars," he said. "In francs . . ."

"I will give you fifteen thousand dollars this afternoon," Goltz said. "From my special funds."

"Fine."

The fifteen thousand dollars was not in fact from any official special fund. It was part of the just over fifty thousand dollars — (in U.S., English, and Swiss currency) — he had brought back from Montevideo. It represented his 60–40 share of the commission Sturmbannführer Werner von Tresmarck had waiting for him. Before depositing the balance to the Special Fund Reichsprotektor Himmler and Partieleiter Bormann knew about, Von Tresmarck had deducted a 10 percent commission from the money he received from those who wished their relatives to be permitted to immigrate to Uruguay.

Goltz thought it was possible he could be reimbursed from the Special Fund. But even if he couldn't, it wasn't a major problem. There would be more money as his share of the commission von Tresmarck was charging.

"I'm relying on you, Oberst Grüner, to take care of all this."

"I understand, Herr Standartenführer," Grüner replied. "When you have the time, I would like your opinion of the preliminary plans I have drawn up concerning the *Graf Spee* officers."

"For the moment, the priority is to transport our special cargo safely ashore. We can deal with the *Graf Spee* officers afterward."

"Of course."

[Four]

Second Cavalry Regiment Reservation
Santo Tomé
Corrientes Province, Argentina
1145 15 April 1943

As the son of the late el Coronel Jorge Guillermo Frade, Señor Cletus Frade was given the position of honor beside el Coronel Pablo Porterman, Colonel Commanding the Second Cavalry, as they rode out to inspect the landing strip. Coronel Porterman was in a pink and green uniform. A cavalry saber in a sheath was attached to his saddle. His saddle blanket carried gold-thread-embroidered representations of his rank and the regimental crest.

Behind them, alone, rode Capitán Gonzalo Delgano, Air Service, Argentine Army, Retired, who was dressed almost identically to Señor Frade in riding breeches, boots, a tweed jacket, an open-collar shirt with a foulard, and a woolen cap.

Behind Capitán Delgano, Suboficial Mayor Enrico Rodríguez, Cavalry, Retired, similarly dressed, rode beside Suboficial Mayor Annarana of the Second Cavalry, who wore a khaki-colored woolen uniform, was also armed with a saber, and who could have been Enrico's brother.

Though Señor Frade was raised on a West Texas

ranch and was once a member of the horse-mounted Corps of Cadets at the Texas Agricultural and Mechanical College, he had never seen so many horses in one place in his life.

Earlier, he had asked Coronel Porterman, a tall, good-looking man who looked uncomfortably like Clete's father, how many troopers there were. Approximately 1,200, Coronel Porterman told him, and, he added, approximately 1,600 horses, following the Argentine Army standard of 1.3 mounts per officer and trooper.

As they rode out to the landing strip, which was about two miles from the barracks and stables, Clete watched for a time the troopers of the Second Cavalry at their routine training.

Some were doing mounted drill, moving their horses in precise parade-ground maneuvers. Some were going through what looked like an obstacle course for horses, jumping over barriers, and moving the animals through mazes of stakes. Some were actually engaged in saber practice, riding past what looked like blanket-wrapped stakes and taking swipes at them.

They were, Clete decided, magnificent cavalrymen. He wondered if any of them knew that the magnificent cavalry of the Polish Army, with dash, élan, and courage, sabers flashing, had charged the tanks of the German Army and were wiped out in a matter of minutes by machine-gun and cannon fire.

He wondered if they were aware that at that very moment, at some place in the world, tanks were fighting each other, and that horse cavalry as a viable tool of warfare was a thing of the past.

The landing strip was, of course, dirt. At Clete's suggestion, their little cavalry detail formed a line and rode the length of it six or eight feet apart, looking for holes or rocks that would take out landing gear.

Though there were only a few holes, and no rocks, there were a number of cattle skeletons, some of them posing, in Clete's judgment, a bona fide threat to aircraft operation.

Coronel Porterman promised to send a troop of his cavalry out that very afternoon to fill the holes, remove the cattle skeletons, and examine the field with greater care.

"You can land here, Señor Frade?" Delgano asked. "More important, can you take off from here?"

"I don't see any problem landing or taking off," Clete said. "The problem will be finding this place at night."

"Mi Coronel?" Delgano asked.

Coronel Porterman rode up beside them on his magnificent horse, and standing at the threshold of the dirt strip, the three of them discussed where the locating fire would be located — it would burn all night as a beacon — and the precise location of the gasoline-in-sand-in-clay-pots "runway lights."

Then they rode past the troops of the Second Cavalry, who were practicing using their sabers and bolt-action carbines on enemy cavalry, and back to the barracks and stable area. From there they proceeded to the officers' mess.

The mess was crowded with the regiment's officers, and Señor Frade was introduced to each of them as the son of the late el Coronel Jorge Guillermo Frade, onetime Deputy Commander of the Second Cavalry.

Señor Frade was shown the trophy cases, containing silver cups won by his father for one equitational competition or another. These began with his first assignment to Second Cavalry as a Sub-Teniente fresh from the Military Academy, and ended with trophies won during his assignment to the regiment as a Teniente Coronel.

On the wall were framed photographs of a young Teniente Frade and his peers, among whom Señor Frade recognized Teniente Juan Domingo Perón and a chubby smiling character who was probably Capitán Arturo Rawson.

El Coronel Porterman led the procession into the dining room, where Señor Frade again was given the position of honor and seated beside Porterman.

The table was elaborately set with silver bearing the regimental crest, and fine china and crystal. There were three glasses for every place, and waiters promptly began to fill glasses with wine.

Clete thought of the "officers' mess" on Guadalcanal. It consisted of crude plank tables. The tableware was steel mess trays; the "silver" was knives, forks, and spoons from mess kits; and the china was heavy Navy-issue mugs.

An officer appeared and whispered in el Coronel Porterman's ear. He rose, excused himself, and left the dining room. A minute or two later, the same officer appeared and whispered in Capitán Delgano's ear, and he rose and left the dining room.

Then they returned, without explaining why they had left. The five-course luncheon continued for another thirty-five minutes. And then el Coronel Porterman rose to his feet, excused himself again, motioned to Delgano, and turned to Clete.

"Will you come with me, please, Señor Frade?"

They went to a corner of the bar.

Porterman looked at Delgano as if he wanted him to begin.

"Word has just reached us that makes it very important to have the airplane here as quickly as possible," Delgano said.

Well, that can only mean they've ordered the execution of OUTLINE BLUE.

"It will be available to me in Brazil as of noon the day after tomorrow," Clete said.

"There's no way you can have it any earlier?"

"I'm not even sure I can get where I have to go by noon of the day after tomorrow," Clete said.

"You have made no plans to reach Pôrto Alegre?" Delgano asked, incredulous and annoyed.

"I have to see someone here," Clete said.

"Who?"

Clete shook his head, "no."

"When do you have to see this person?"

"Whenever I can."

"You know where to find this person?"

"Yes, I do. I'll need a car."

Delgano looked at el Coronel Porterman, who nodded.

"Not an Army car," Clete said.

"Of course not an Army car," Delgano said. "When can you see this person?"

"Now."

"You will see him, and then return here?"

"If possible."

"You believe he will have instructions for you? How to travel to Pôrto Alegre?"

"I thought you were going to get me across the border?"

"We are prepared to do that," el Coronel Porterman said.

"Where is Suboficial Mayor Rodríguez?"

599

"At the suboficiales' mess."

"Where's the car?"

"I will borrow a car from one of my officers," el Coronel Porterman said. "You wish Rodríguez to drive you?"

"No. I don't want to take him with me. Now, *or* when I cross the border. That may pose problems."

"I will deal with Suboficial Mayor Rodríguez," el Coronel Porterman said. "It will not be a problem."

"Would you get me a car, please?"

[Five]

The Automobile Club of Argentina Hotel
Santo Tomé, Corrientes Province
1430 15 April 1943

Finding the Automobile Club Hotel was simply a matter of asking an old woman walking along the side of the road to Santo Tomé where it was. Feeling somewhat foolish, he took the borrowed car — a 1939 Ford Fordor — on a trip up and down the streets of Santo Tomé until he was sure he wasn't being followed, then drove to the hotel.

It wasn't what he expected. The name had suggested an Argentine version of a motel built on the side of a road, with both economy and easy automobile parking as the design criteria. This was a new building on the outskirts of town, overlooking a sweeping curve of the Río Uruguay. It was surrounded by a large lawn studded with tall palm trees. It looked, more than anything else, like one of the small, exclusive, oceanfront resorts north of Miami.

It had two wings extending from a central core housing a restaurant and bar. Each was two stories tall, with a palm-shaded parking lot. To the right were tennis courts, and when he entered the lobby, he saw that on the far side a large swimming pool surrounded by umbrella-shaded tables sat overlooking another gardenlike area extending down a slope to the river.

His eye was caught by a statuesque olive-skinned woman whose more than ample breasts and rear end were barely concealed beneath a bathing suit whose brevity would have certainly caused her arrest in the United States.

He took a chance that Ashton was using his own name, and asked the desk clerk for the room number of Señor Maxwell Ashton.

Señor Ashton and Party, the desk clerk told him, were in Apartment 121.

"And Party"? What the hell is that all about? Delojo said he was alone.

Clete found 121 — what looked like a three-room suite, with a private patio, overlooking the swimming pool — without difficulty; but there was no answer to his knock. He knocked louder, and when that failed to get a response, looked around for someone who might be an OSS agent.

There was no one at the pool except a diminutive mustachioed cigar-smoking Latin in bathing trunks and a flowered shirt who was unabashedly watching the statuesque olive-skinned woman in the scant bathing costume climb the diving board ladder.

Neither was there anyone who remotely looked like an American among the half-dozen men he saw in the restaurant, bar, or on the tennis courts.

601

Just to be safe, he asked a dour-faced man in his late forties if his name happened to be Ashton, and received a curt "No, Señor" in reply.

What the hell do I do now? Where the hell could he be? If he has his team with him, where the hell are they?

He made one more sweep of the place, then returned to the borrowed 1939 Ford sedan.

The diminutive mustachioed Latin who had shared his fascination with the statuesque lady in the revealing swimming costume walked up to the car as Clete was unlocking it.

"Why do I have this feeling that you are looking for me?" he asked in English.

Clete stared at him in utter surprise.

"Excuse me, Señor," the little man said in Spanish. "I obviously have made a mistake."

"You're Ashton?" Clete asked.

"Major Frade?"

Clete nodded.

"Why don't we have a beer by the pool?" Ashton said. "I don't think I'm being watched, but you may be."

Clete followed him to one of the umbrella-shaded tables by the pool.

Clete had no sooner settled himself in one of the chairs than the statuesque lady, smiling invitingly, walked up and sat down.

"Consuelo," Maxwell Ashton said in Spanish, "this is Señor Smith, the business associate I told you I would probably meet."

"I'm very happy to know you, Señor," Consuelo said, almost coming out of the bathing suit as she leaned over to offer Clete her hand.

"The pleasure is entirely mine, Señorita," Clete said.

"Why don't you go take another dive, Consuelo," Maxwell Ashton said, "while Señor Smith and I transact our business?"

She smiled and stood up and strolled toward the diving board. As she walked, she rearranged as well as she could her bathing costume over her left buttock, which had escaped.

"Fantastic ass," Maxwell Ashton said, switching to English. "And all muscle!"

A waiter appeared, and Ashton ordered beer in Spanish.

"You're not what I expected, frankly," Ashton said. "You don't look old enough to be either a major or a hotshot pilot."

"You're not what I expected, either," Clete said. "Is she the 'party,' as in 'Señor Ashton and Party'?"

"You have a problem with that, *mi Mayor?*"

"I thought maybe you had your team here."

"They're in the transient officers' BOQ in Pôrto Alegre, unless Colonel Wallace has confirmed his suspicions that three of them are enlisted swine and he has them in his stockade awaiting trial for impersonating officers and gentlemen."

"I somehow don't think you're kidding."

"You know el Coronel Wallace?"

"I know who he is. He's my contact at Pôrto Alegre."

"You're a pilot, right? When *you're* wearing a uniform, do you carry a riding crop?"

"No," Clete said, chuckling.

"Wallace does. Getting the picture? Regular Army. Very starchy. He made it very clear to me he wishes he'd never heard of the OSS. He can't find any regulation in his book on how to deal with us."

"You told him everybody on your team was an officer?"

"He somehow got that impression, after he told me that the officers would be billeted in a hotel off the base, and the enlisted swine in barracks on the base."

"How many enlisted swine?" Clete asked, chuckling.

"Three. Good guys. One's a German Jew. Seigfried Stein. Buck Sergeant. He's my explosives expert. Tech Sergeant Bill Ferris is our weapons and parachute guy, and Staff Sergeant Jerry O'Sullivan is the radar operator. Plus, of course, the gorilla. My executive officer. First Lieutenant Madison R. Sawyer the Third. He went to the parachute school at Fort Benning before he came to OSS. At Benning, they tell people that parachutists are tougher than anybody else, and being a Yalie, Sawyer believes it."

Ashton looked at Clete, saw that Clete was smiling, and went on.

"Truth to tell, mi Mayor, you've been wondering what somebody who looks like me is doing with a name like Maxwell Ashton, haven't you?"

"You look more like a Pedro type," Clete said. "Or maybe a Pablo."

"Actually, it's Maxwell Ashton the Third, Captain, Signal Corps, Army of the United States. What's your date of rank, Major?"

"Two months ago."

"If I were a betting man — and unfortunately, betting's another of my serious vices — I would lay five to one I outranked you before you got promoted. You got promoted, right, because of that John Wayne–type stunt you pulled on the first submarine-supply ship?"

"I was promoted because I am an absolutely perfect officer," Clete said, chuckling. "They wanted to make me a general, but I am also modest to a fault and declined. Is who ranks who going to be a problem between us?"

"Not unless you start giving me or anybody on my team orders to do something like you and that Army paratrooper did. Heroism is not my strong suit. I want you to understand that."

"Mine either," Clete said.

"Bullshit," Ashton said. "I got into your file at the National Institutes of Health, and I know all about you. Most of what I read scares me, frankly."

"Why?"

"So far you've been shot down twice in the Pacific and once here," Ashton said. "And the Germans tried to kill you — and damned near did — in Buenos Aires. And your father was killed. Assassinated. Graham told me. It looks to me like you're a dangerous man to be around. I don't want to be an innocent bystander."

"My middle name is Coward, all right?" Clete said, and added, "You don't look old enough to be a captain yourself."

"I'm twenty-nine," Ashton replied, "which I know is considerably older than you. But let's get this personal history business out of the way. Tit for tat."

"Why not?" Clete said.

"I'm half Cuban and half American. Educated in the States. Choate and then MIT, where I took a degree in electrical engineering. Good schools, and people were very kind there to the poor mixed-blood kid from Cuba —"

"You don't have to tell me all this!"

"I think I do. I think it's important that we understand one another. Anyway, with the draft board breathing down my neck, I applied for a commission. I was working for Bell Laboratories in New Jersey, and that was good enough to get a captain's commission. I thought I would spend the war at Fort Monmouth, doing what I was doing at Bell Labs." The Army's Signal Corps Center was at Fort Monmouth, New Jersey.

"Which was?"

"Radar. You know what radar is?"

"Yeah, we had radar on Guadalcanal. It usually didn't work."

"The stuff you had in the Pacific was garbage, probably designed by the Limeys," Ashton said. "The stuff we have now is a hell of a lot better."

"That's encouraging," Clete said. "Presumably, you have one of the good ones with you?"

"Por favor, mi Mayor, don't interrupt me when I'm talking."

"I am overwhelmed with remorse for my bad manners."

"You should be," Ashton said. "As I was saying, two bad things happened to me at Fort Monmouth. The first was that my wife left me. She didn't want to live on what they pay captains. I really couldn't blame her."

"And the second bad thing?"

"A Navy guy came to see me. A lieutenant commander. A fellow Latino. By the name of Frederico Delojo."

"I know the gentleman," Clete said.

"I figured if you can't trust a fellow Latino, who the hell can you trust, right?"

"Right," Clete said.

The waiter delivered three large bottles of beer.

Ashton poured beer into their glasses.

"You *can* handle a beer, right? You're not going to start doing something heroic? And/or start making eyes at Consuelo?"

"I will do my best to control myself," Clete said.

"So Delojo hands me this line of bullshit, in Spanish, of course: His 'organization,' about which he can't talk but which is in Washington, has been looking for someone just like me, an electrical engineer at the cutting edge of radar technology, who also speaks Spanish. I can make significant contributions to the war effort, et cetera, et cetera. So I volunteer, which was about the dumbest thing I have ever done."

"Why was that?"

"You know goddamn well why was that," Ashton said. "The next thing I know, I'm at the Country Club, where a bunch of crew-cutted gorillas got their rocks off throwing me over their shoulders and bouncing me off walls and teaching me all sorts of things I didn't want to know, like how to blow things up and stick knives in people. How the hell did you manage to escape going through the Country Club, by the way?"

"I'm a Marine. All Marines know how to stick knives in people and blow things up."

"The *pièce de résistance* of all this was taking me up, not once, *but five fucking times,* and throwing me out of an airplane."

"You and Lieutenant Pelosi will have a lot to talk about," Clete said. "Before he found a señorita in Buenos Aires, that's how he got his rocks off, jumping out of airplanes."

"Or getting shot down in one, like he did with you, right?"

"He really liked that. The first thing he said when

607

we pulled him out of the water was 'Jesus, that was fun! Can we do that again?' "

Ashton smiled at Clete.

"Then Delojo shows up and says he's got good news for me. I have been given command of a team. And they are going to *parachute* us into Argentina with a radar set."

"Did he tell you why?"

"Yeah. To find a ship that's supplying German submarines. He told me the first team they sent down here disappeared, and that the second team got shot down while they were locating the ship for a submarine. So the next thing I know we're on an airplane headed for Brazil, three very nice guys and the gorilla. I finally figured out what the gorilla is supposed to do. I think he has orders to shoot me the minute he sees me pissing my pants, providing I've got the radar up and working. You know where it goes, right?"

"Yeah, we have figured that out," Clete said. "How did you get here, Ashton? I mean, to this place?"

"I came down here to see if there wasn't some other way besides by parachute to get the radar set across the border," Ashton said. "If I never jump out of an airplane again, it will be too soon."

"By 'other way' you mean by rubber boat?"

"Just when I was beginning to think that maybe you weren't as dumb as I thought, you ask a question like that," Ashton said. "Come with me, por favor, mi Mayor."

He picked up his beer glass and led Clete to the far side of the swimming pool. From there they could look down at the Río Uruguay.

"That sonofabitch is at least three-quarters of a mile wide, and the current is at least six knots,"

Ashton said. "The radar set is broken down into four crates, each weighing two hundred pounds. Maybe the Marine Corps can paddle something like that across that river in little rubber boats, but *I* have no intention of trying."

"How did you get here?" Clete asked.

"On the ferry," Ashton said.

"No trouble getting across the border?"

"They gave us all phony Brazilian passports," Ashton said. "No problem."

"Tell me about Consuelo," Clete said.

"The Brazilian town on the other side of the river is São Borja. I went to a bar there, and in the interests of international friendship struck up a conversation with Consuelo. We had a couple of drinks, and I asked her where a poor lonely businessman could go for a good time. Consuelo said she knew just the place — she meant here; this is the NoTellMotel of choice for the local sportsmen on both sides of the border — but it was expensive. I asked her how expensive. You would be surprised, Major, how far the American dollar goes down here."

"How far?"

"Twenty dollars a day for Consuelo — plus rations and quarters, of course, say another fifteen bucks — and another fifteen a day for her cousin's Fiat."

"That sounds like a bargain," Clete said. "And aside from watching the diving demonstrations, how have you passed the time?"

"I passed the word, very discreetly, that I had four crates of tractor parts I would like to get into Argentina without anybody official noticing."

"And?"

"The only nibble I got was from a character who

might as well have had 'Cop' written on his fore-head. You have any ideas, mi Mayor?"

"There's an airplane waiting for me at Pôrto Alegre," Clete said.

"Were you paying attention before when I said I am not about to parachute me, or the radar, or anybody on my team except the gorilla — you're welcome to him — into anywhere?"

"I just came from checking out the airstrip where I'm going to land the airplane," Clete said.

"On this side of the border?"

Clete nodded.

"You're an officer and a gentleman, so you don't lie, right?" Ashton said.

"Not about this."

"On the other hand, Delojo is a Regular Navy officer and gentleman, and look what happened to me when I trusted him."

"He took advantage of your innocence," Clete said. "I wouldn't do that."

Ashton looked at him thoughtfully.

"How'd you arrange for someplace to land?"

"That I can't tell you. It's arranged."

"How are you going to get across the border into Brazil?"

"That's arranged, too."

"And from São Borja to Pôrto Alegre?"

"How much do you think Consuelo would want to take me, maybe take the both of us, to Pôrto Alegre?"

"I don't think that's such a good idea," Ashton said. "I think the 'smuggler' will be watching us. He's a little too obliging."

"Is there a train, or a bus, from São Borja to Pôrto Alegre? Or could I rent a car there?"

"It's not much of a town. I'm not sure you could

rent a car at all, and even if you could, it would attract attention. And how would you get it back, if you fly back here?"

"Then it's a train or a bus?"

"Unless you can think of something else," Ashton said. "When do you want to go?"

"As soon as possible."

"The last ferry leaves at six-thirty, unless it's full. If it's full, then it leaves whenever it's full after five. Can you make that?"

Clete looked at his watch.

"I'll give it a hell of a try. If I can't make it tonight, I'm sure I can be on the first ferry in the morning. I suggest you go to Pôrto Alegre, tell Colonel Whatsisname that I'm on the way, and get your people ready."

Ashton looked at him thoughtfully again.

"You're sure you'll have an airplane when you get there?"

Clete nodded.

"Jesus, I hate to tell Consuelo to put her clothes on," Ashton said. "But I guess I have to."

Clete looked at his watch.

"It's not quite three," Clete said. "That gives us two hours to make the ferry. I'll try to be on it."

"I was really looking forward to tonight," Ashton said. "You understand what a sacrifice you're asking of me? Sweet girls like Consuelo don't come down the pike very often — Consuelo means 'consolation,' by the way."

"Neither does an offer that will keep you from jumping out of an airplane or paddling across that river."

"That's true," Ashton said.

"Where do I go when I arrive in Pôrto Alegre?"

"The Gran Hotel de Pôrto," Ashton said.

"That's now the Air Corps BOQ. It's not far from the Navy base. I think it would be better to check in with me before you go see Colonel Wallace."

"OK. As soon as I can get there, I'll see you there."

Ashton nodded.

"One thing, mi Mayor. I think you should know that I got a Gold Star to take home to Mommy when I went through the knife-fighting course," Ashton said. "If we reach Pôrto Alegre and you tell me 'Sorry, there's been a change of plan' and we have to do the parachute bit, I will, mi Mayor, with my razor-sharp instrument of silent death, turn you into a soprano."

"I'll bear that in mind," Clete said. "My very best regards to Señorita Consuelo, Capitán."

[Six]

The Port
Montevideo, Uruguay
1430 15 April 1943

Although he was in fact an agent of the Office of Strategic Services — and before that an agent of the U.S. Army Counterintelligence Corps — David Ettinger rarely thought of himself as a real-life version of the secret agents Humphrey Bogart, Alan Ladd, and other film stars portrayed in the movies.

Earlier, he was assured that his employment at the RCA Laboratories was "essential to the war effort" and would thus exempt him from the draft. Even so, he enlisted in the Army because putting on the uniform of the country that had given him and his mother refuge seemed the right thing to do.

At the time, however, he thought there was very little chance he would be handed a rifle and sent off to fight the Nazis and the Germans in the trenches. Indeed, David Sarnoff, the head of RCA, for whom he worked, had used that argument when he tried to talk him out of enlisting:

"One of two things will happen to you, David. They will make you a rifleman and you will get killed, which would be a terrible waste and not nearly as great of a contribution to the war as you can make here; or they will send you to the Signal Corps Laboratories at Fort Monmouth, where they will have you doing the same thing you're doing here, except with a good deal less freedom, and on a private's pay."

At the time Sarnoff tried to dissuade him from enlisting, Sarnoff was himself about to become Colonel David Sarnoff of the Signal Corps, so David concluded that Sarnoff's arguments to him were *pro forma* at best. Meanwhile, other sources told him that a man with his background and experience would qualify for a commission. Thus he imagined that after he went through the horrors of basic training, he would be commissioned a lieutenant. And then, more than likely — as Colonel Sarnoff suggested — he would be assigned to the Army's Signal Laboratory to work in his specialty — high- and ultrahigh-frequency radiation.

He applied for both a direct commission and for Officer Candidate School during his second week of basic training at Camp Polk, Louisiana. By the time both applications returned — within days of each other in his seventh week of basic training —

he had decided that being an enlisted man was not the most pleasant way to serve one's newly adopted country. Unhappily, the returned applications stated that inasmuch as he was a Spanish National, he was not qualified to be commissioned as an officer in the Armed Forces of the United States.

A week later he was summoned from the Live Hand Grenade Range to meet a gentleman from the Counterintelligence Corps — he still remembered holding a bomb, fuse ticking, as the most terrifying aspect of his basic training. It had come to the attention of the CIC, the gentleman in civilian clothing told him in a thick Munich accent, that he spoke both German and Spanish. Was this true?

"Auch Französisch," Private Ettinger replied.

They chatted for ten minutes, long enough to convince the CIC agent — also a Jew who had escaped from Nazi Germany — that he wasn't a Nazi spy. And then the CIC agent told him that the CIC needed someone like him. A large number of Germans lived in the Yorktown district of New York City — and elsewhere. And the Army wished to keep an eye on them. And Private Ettinger seemed to have the necessary linguistic and educational qualifications for that.

Private Ettinger volunteered for the Counterintelligence Corps for several reasons. For one thing, it would keep him from being sent to the then forming Ninety-fifth Infantry Division for training as a radio operator. For another, he would probably be assigned to New York City, where his mother lived. And finally, he was told that after graduation from the CIC School in Baltimore, he would be designated a Special Agent of the CIC, which carried with it the pay of a staff sergeant. CIC agents, he was told, worked in civilian clothing, and their rank was not made public.

That seemed to be the next-best thing to getting the commission he was denied because of his Spanish nationality.

After graduating from the CIC School at Camp Holabird in Baltimore, Special Agent Ettinger was retained there as an instructor in shortwave radio telephony. This allowed him to travel to New York City to see his mother just about every other weekend. The Pennsylvania Railroad's tracks went past Cherry Hill, New Jersey, where, had he not been overwhelmed with patriotic fervor to serve his adopted country, he would still be employed by RCA at a vastly greater compensation than he was now being paid.

While he was stationed at the CIC Center, another civilian with interesting credentials visited him. This man was an agent of the Office of Strategic Services, an organization about which Special Agent Ettinger had heard very little.

This interview was conducted in a dialect of Spanish Ettinger recognized as Tex-Mex — in other words, spoken by people of a Mexican background who lived in Texas. In this interview the OSS agent told him that the OSS needed someone qualified to set up and operate a clandestine shortwave radio station in a not-then-identified South American nation, and that Ettinger seemed to have the qualifications they were looking for. It was some time later that Ettinger learned that he had been interviewed by a man who was not only a full colonel of the U.S. Marine Corps, but Assistant Director for Western Hemisphere Operations of the OSS.

A week later, Ettinger found himself in a place

that before the war had been the Congressional Country Club in Virginia, not far from Washington. The training there was something like a repeat of basic training and CIC training — in a sense, ludicrous, considering what he had been told was planned for him. He was going to Argentina, by Pan American Airlines, ostensibly an expert on oil-industry tank farms, to operate a radio station. He thought it highly unlikely that he would ever be called upon to parachute from an airplane, or engage in a knife fight, or follow someone down city streets without being seen, or pick a lock.

Once he was in Buenos Aires, Argentina, he did find himself on the fringes of warlike acts, but only on the fringes. He wore civilian clothing and lived in an apartment. He ate in restaurants. He even had a maid to do his laundry, and an automobile to get around town and to drive out to the radio station. His role in the sinking of an ostensibly neutral merchant vessel engaged in the clandestine resupply of German submarines was indisputably noncombatant.

Nevertheless, he took a private pride in knowing that without his radio station, there would have been no way to tell the submarine where to find the ship it would torpedo.

Although he sensed that if he gave either of them the slightest hint of this, they would be embarrassed, David Ettinger was thrilled to be closely associated with men like Cletus Frade and Anthony Pelosi.

More than that, they had given him the resolve — he didn't think of it as courage — to do what he was doing now. He realized that in a manner of speaking he was indeed now in the trenches, facing the Nazis personally.

And he was doing work that Cletus Frade and Tony Pelosi could not do, no matter how courageous they were, or how skilled at things like flying airplanes or rigging explosive charges. They didn't have his background or, frankly, his intelligence. Nor did they speak German, nor were they Jews.

There was no telling what the Naxis were up to with their ransoming operation. He had no idea whether it was simply one more turn of the screw to squeeze more money out of Jews inside, or outside, Germany, or a far more complex operation. But whatever it was, it had certainly attracted the attention of Colonel Graham back in Washington.

And this problem — this, if you will, contribution to the war effort, to the war against the Nazis — was his to solve. His alone. He had been *ordered* not to even mention anything about it to Milton Leibermann. At first he thought this was preposterous. Leibermann was after all FBI, and thus presumably skilled in investigation and interrogation. But then he wondered about that. If Leibermann was so skilled in investigation and interrogation, then why was it David Ettinger, and not FBI agent Milton Leibermann, who uncovered the Nazi ransom operation?

While of course he wasn't doing any of this for credit, if Leibermann was brought into it, the "investigation," if that's what it could be properly called, would have become Leibermann's — the FBI's — investigation. David Ettinger, after all, was officially only a staff sergeant radio technician detailed to the OSS.

Furthermore, it was entirely possible that the very presence of Leibermann, or one of his FBI agents, would be counterproductive. It had taken him a good deal of time, and all of his psychological insight, to persuade any of the people involved to talk to him at all.

The sudden appearance of someone else asking questions would very likely result in all the just-be-ginning-to-open doors being very firmly slammed shut again.

And he was getting close to finding out how the money was being moved. The fact that the Sicher-heitsdienst colonel had ordered his assassination was clear enough proof of that.

He was, of course, concerned about that. But the time of greatest danger for him was when he was still on the estancia. It was possible, if not very likely, that the German hired assassins would try to do to him what they had done to Cletus Frade's father, ambush him on the road to Pila.

Not only was that unlikely, but he was being protected on Estancia San Pedro y San Pablo — and as far as that went, anywhere in Argentina — by two men from the Bureau of Internal Security. He had heard Pelosi telling the Chief about that.

And so, feeling rather clever about the whole thing, he made sure that once he had sneaked away from the house, with lights in the Chevrolet turned off so that neither Pelosi nor the Chief would wake up, he turned the lights on, so that the BIS men would see him and follow him.

Which they did. All the way into Buenos Aires. There they stationed themselves on Calle Monroe outside his apartment. If any assassins were lying in wait on the estancia, or at his apartment, the sight of two men in an obviously official car was enough to discourage them from trying anything.

In the apartment he took a shower and shaved, then called the ferryboat terminal and reserved space for the 8:30 departure. Then he dealt with the problem of his gun. He had two holsters for the Smith & Wesson .38 Special snub-nose, a shoulder holster and one that strapped on his belt. It was, of course, illegal to take any firearm across the border. It was unlikely, he thought, that he would be searched passing through Uruguayan Customs, but it was better to be safe than sorry.

He decided he didn't need the holster. The Smith & Wesson was small enough to carry in his pocket. He wrapped the pistol in a small face towel, then put the package in his toilet kit under his razor and other toilet articles. He put the toilet kit itself in the small suitcase he was taking with him, carrying only a change of linen and a spare set of trousers. He didn't plan on being in Uruguay long.

At 7:45 he left his apartment, got in the Chevrolet, and, trailed by his BIS protectors, drove to the port. He was early — on purpose — which meant that his early on-loaded car would be off-loaded early in Montevideo.

When the ferry moved away from the pier, he saw the men from the BIS standing on the quay, and resisted the temptation to wave at them. They would not, of course, follow him across the border.

He paid some attention to his fellow passengers on the ferry, but none of them looked like assassins for hire. They looked like businessmen off to Montevideo for the day — in other words, he hoped, much like he did.

Uruguayan Customs and Immigration officials performed their function aboard the ferryboat. An Immigration officer took a quick glance at his passport, saw that it bore the stamps of a dozen or more short trips back and forth between Buenos Aires and Montevideo, added one more stamp, and waved him on to the Customs officers standing at the ramp.

They asked him to open the trunk, and after finding nothing in it but a spare tire and a jack, didn't even ask him to open his one small suitcase.

He drove off the boat, then drove to the Casino in Carrasco by the Rambla, the road that follows the coastline.

He was completely unaware of the somewhat battered and rusty 1937 Graham-Paige sedan that followed him to Carrasco, possibly because it never came closer than two cars behind him, and possibly because he wasn't looking for it. He did not expect to be followed in Uruguay.

He had not telephoned the Casino Hotel for a reservation, to obviate the possibility that the desk clerk, the concierge, or someone else in the hotel hierarchy had been paid to notify someone if he should again come to Montevideo.

He felt just a little smug about this, too. It seemed to prove that he had paid attention to the instructors in Camp Holabird and at the Country Club.

The Casino Hotel had a room for him, a nice two-room suite on the second floor. He went to the room, left his bag, and then went back downstairs and to the car. He drove it into the basement garage and went back up to the room.

If there was any basis to think that the Germans, or Uruguayans in German employ, had arranged to be notified if he appeared again, then obviously they had already been notified, or would be shortly.

He took the Smith & Wesson snub-nose from his toilet kit and checked it for operation. He even went so far as to put a match head in his jar of Vaseline and lubricate the wear points.

He had confidence in the pistol and in his ability to use it. He was not, of course, a shot like the Chief and Tony Pelosi were shots. He used to watch them a little enviously as they shot their .45 automatic pistols on Estancia San Pedro y San Pablo. They would shoot at tin cans, more to kill time than anything else, burning up case after case of Argentine Army ammunition provided by Frade's father through his sergeant.

They just didn't shoot the tin can. The object was to make it jump in the air, and keep jumping, as long as any ammunition was left in the pistol.

Ettinger knew that no matter how much he practiced, he could never become that sort of pistol shot. But he had paid attention at the pistol ranges at Camp Holabird and the Country Club. They shot at life-size silhouette targets at seven yards. The object was to fire rapidly and hit what were called "vital" areas on the silhouette targets.

Using a pistol identical to one he had now, over time he became rather proficient. Three times out of four, firing five shots as rapidly as possible, he put four bullet holes in the vital areas of silhouette targets.

When he was really feeling good about his shooting, he aimed all shots at the silhouette's head. Two or three times, he put all five shots in the head.

He didn't telephone the man he wanted to see. You couldn't dial the number directly. You had to give it to the operator, who did the dialing for you. If you accepted the possibility that the concierge was paid to telephone someone that he was in the hotel, then it followed that the telephone operator was probably keeping a record of the numbers he called.

It wasn't really a problem. He knew where the

man he wanted to see was going to be at seven-thirty. He stopped in for a going-home glass of beer at a bar on Avenida Foster, less than a dozen blocks from the Casino Hotel. Ettinger had met him there three times before. The bar was crowded at that time of day, and it was relatively easy to exchange a few words about how and where they could meet in privacy.

Ettinger hadn't had much to eat in the restaurant on the ferryboat, and it was possible that dinner might be delayed by the business he had to do tonight.

There were a half-dozen cafés and restaurants within easy walking distance of the Casino Hotel. The restaurants would probably not yet be open, but you could generally find a small steak at any café.

He experimented with the best place to carry the Smith & Wesson, finally deciding that the right rear hip pocket offered the most concealability.

He had a bottle of beer, a small steak, and a small salad. For dessert, there was a very nice egg custard, called "flan."

Then he walked back to the hotel and went down into the basement.

It took him several minutes to find the light switch to illuminate the cavernous basement garage. He walked to the Chevrolet and slipped behind the wheel.

David Ettinger's last conscious thought before the man in the back of the Chevrolet twisted his neck and shoved an ice pick through his ear into his brain was that he remembered locking the car when he parked it.

XIX

[One]

The Santo Tomé-São Borja Ferry
Corrientes Province, Argentina
0730 16 April 1943

A long line of vehicles, trucks, pickup trucks, motorcycles, and even two two-wheeled horse-drawn carts were waiting on the dirt road to the ferry when the official Mercedes of el Coronel Pablo Porterman drove up. Colonel Porterman's car was followed by a well-polished 1937 Buick Limited four-door convertible sedan, its top down. In the backseat of the Buick rode, somewhat regally, el Patrón of Estancia San Miguel, Señor Cletus Frade, and Suboficial Mayor Enrico Rodríguez, Retired.

Both cars drove past the vehicles waiting their turn to pass through Customs and Immigration to the head of the line.

The senior Customs officer and the senior Immigration officer on duty came out of the Customs and Immigration Building to present their respects to the Commanding Officer of the Second Cavalry. They then walked to the Buick, where they were introduced to Señor Frade.

One of them announced that he had been privileged to know the late el Coronel Jorge Guillermo Frade both as el Patrón of Estancia San Miguel and when el Coronel was assigned to the Second Cavalry. Both expressed their condolences for Señor Frade's recent tragic loss.

Señor Frade then shook el Coronel Porterman's hand and expressed his gratitude for all the courtesies the Coronel had rendered. The Buick was then passed to the head of the line of vehicles, without troubling Señor Frade with the routine Customs and Immigration procedures. From there it rolled onto the ferry.

The Buick was Enrico's solution to the problem of getting from São Borja to Pôrto Alegre. A telephone call was placed to Estancia San Miguel, and the Buick, kept at the estancia for the use of el Patrón, was dispatched to Santo Tomé.

After that, of course, Clete was unable to tell Enrico that he wanted him to stay in Santo Tomé. He thought he might be able to talk him into returning to Santo Tomé with the car when it returned, but he was aware that was probably wishful thinking.

Before the ferry left the shore, the driver took a rag from the trunk and wiped the dust from the Buick.

Clete left the car and stood in the bow of the open ferry as it moved away from the shore.

With something close to alarm he saw there was no more than ten inches of freeboard. The river was smooth but the current was fast-running, and it looked to him as if it wouldn't take much — running against a sandbar, for example — to cause water to come on board and send the ferry to the bottom.

Ashton was right. Trying to paddle across this in a

*rubber boat carrying boxes that weighed two hundred
pounds apiece would have been idiocy.*

Ten minutes later, when the Buick rolled off the
ferry on the Brazilian side of the Río Uruguay, the
Brazilian Customs and Immigration officials who
came to the car also elected not to trouble the
passenger of such an elegant chauffeur-driven vehicle with routine administrative procedures.

The road on the far side of São Borja was wide,
well-paved, and straight. The driver proceeded
down it at a steady forty miles per hour.

"Enrico," Clete said, "I would like to drive."

"It would not be fitting, Señor Clete."

"Can you ask him to drive any faster?"

"Ernesto wishes to impress you with his reliabil-
ity, Señor Clete."

"I'm impressed," Clete said, and raised his voice.
"A little faster, Ernesto, por favor."

"Sí, Patrón," Ernesto replied, and raised the
speed no more than two miles per hour.

"Much faster, por favor, Ernesto."

"Sí, Patrón," Ernesto said, and shoved the accelerator to the floor.

[Two]

Big Foot Ranch
Midland, Texas
0945 16 April 1943

While it was not the custom of Mrs. Martha Williamson Howell — who was, among other things,
Chairman of the Ladies' Guild of Trinity Episcopal

Church — to partake of spirituous liquors often — rarely before the cocktail hour, and never before noon — today was to prove an exception.

The Old Broad, she thought as she sat down to eat her breakfast at the kitchen table, *needs a little pick-me-up. Martha's got a bad case of the I-Feel-Sorry-For-Poor-Old-Martha.*

She had, she thought, justification for her low spirits. Primarily, of course, she missed Jim. Everybody told her — and it seemed logical — that time heals all wounds, and that her grief over the loss of her husband would pass.

It didn't pass. It changed. Though she no longer wept herself to sleep, the realization — a black weight on her heart — that Jim wouldn't be back seemed to grow by the day.

She had originally been angry, at God primarily, for doing that to Jim, taking him when he was still a relatively young man, depriving him of a long and full life. Now she was angry at God for taking Jim from her, for leaving her alone. She was too young to lose her man.

And that wasn't all that was wrong with her life. Every time — this morning included — she walked into the kitchen, she was flooded with memories of the kitchen full with Jim and Clete and the girls, of spilled orange juice, pancakes laid carefully atop fresh fourteen-year-old coiffeurs, French toast seasoned with Tabasco in the maple syrup, and all the rest of it.

The girls were gone, too. Beth was twenty-one and about to graduate from Rice. There was more than that, too. The way Beth and the latest Beau behaved when she saw them just before Clete went off to South America again, Martha knew that Beth and Whatsisname were more than just good friends. Phrased delicately, Beth was now a woman, and Whatsisname, whose father was in the drilling business in East Texas, was the one to whom she had given the pearl beyond price.

She was reasonably sure that Marjorie was still a girl, but she wouldn't have laid heavy money on that, either. Marjorie had always been precocious. If she hadn't been with some boy, it was because she hadn't met one she really liked. And one she really liked was likely to be the next one through the door.

So they were gone, too, as Clete was gone.

The family would never have breakfast again in the kitchen.

Never.

She was alone, and it looked as if she was going to be alone from now on. Getting married again seemed absurd. Jim had been one hell of a man, and it was damned unlikely that she would find anyone who came close.

So when Juanita — who didn't really have a hell of a lot to do herself anymore with everybody gone — went in the back of the house to make up the bed, Martha poured herself a tall glass of tomato juice, then added horseradish and Tabasco and salt and a large hooker of gin.

Then she went out on the porch to wait for Rural Free Delivery. The mail would probably be all bills, she thought. Or invitations she wouldn't want to accept. Or another communication from the Texas Railroad Board or the Internal Revenue Service, or more likely both, to cause her trouble. The odds against a letter from Marjorie or Beth were probably a hundred to one, and the odds against a letter from Clete were astronomical.

The astronomical long shot came in.

"Got a special-delivery letter for you, Miss Martha," Henry the Mailman announced. "From some Navy chief petty officer."

What the hell can that be?

"Are you sure it's for me?" she asked as she took the envelope. It was indeed addressed to her. She tore it open.

"It's from Clete," she said.

"Back in the Pacific, is he?" Henry asked, and stayed around until she had read it.

"Not bad news, I hope, Miss Martha?"

"No. Not bad, Henry."

"You tell him I was asking for him, you hear?"

"I surely will, Henry," Martha said.

She waited until Henry's old Ford had disappeared from sight, then picked up the letter and read it again.

Estancia San Pedro y San Pablo
Midnight, 11/12 April 1943

Dear Martha:

I don't have much time, so this will get right to the point.

The Old Man will get a letter, about the time you get this, in which I told him that in two weeks, more or less, I'm getting married.

I think you will take me at my word when I say that I am doing the right thing, and that when, sometime in the future, you meet her — she's Dorotéa Mallín, Henry and Pamela's daughter — you will wonder how in the world a nice girl like that got stuck with a bum like me.

I will probably have a big favor to ask of you,

628

but not right now.

What I'm worried about now is the Old Man. He hates all things Argentine, and you know what kind of a hater he is. I don't want him to start hating me, or Dorotéa, before he even gets a chance to meet her. And I don't want him trying to stop me for my own good, or anything like that. And I don't want him to have a heart attack, and that's not a joke.

I will really appreciate anything you can do. I'll leave telling the girls about this up to you. If you don't want to tell them, I'll understand.

Let me know how he reacted. You have the address, Box 1919, National Institutes of Health, Washington, D.C.

Love,

Clete

"It's Mrs. Howell for you, Mr. Howell," Mrs. Portia Stevens announced, putting her head into the door.

Cletus Marcus Howell was standing at the plate-glass window of his twenty-sixth-floor office atop the Howell Petroleum Building, looking out at the traffic on the Mississippi River. Without turning to look at her, he replied, "Please tell her that I'm tied up and will call her later."

Mrs. Stevens, who had been Mr. Howell's personal secretary for thirty-two years and had known Cletus Howell Frade for most of his life, did not feel the slightest reluctance when slicing open the morning's mail to take out and read the letter bearing the return address *C.H. Frade, Box 1919, Na-*

tional Institutes of Health, Washington, D.C. She was quite sure she knew why her employer did not wish to talk to his daughter-in-law.

She entered the office, picked up one of the telephones on his desk, walked to the window, and handed it to him.

"I told you to tell her I would call her later."

"So you did," Mrs. Stevens said, and walked out of the office.

"Good morning, Martha," the Old Man said. "How are you? The girls?"

"I just got a letter from Clete," Martha said.

"Did you?"

"And from the tone of your voice, so did you."

"As a matter of fact, I did," the Old Man said.

He walked to his desk, put the telephone base on it, and picked up the letter.

Estancia San Pedro y San Pablo
Midnight, 11/12 April 1943

Dear Grandfather:

I hope you're sitting down when you open this.

In about two weeks, I'm getting married. To Henry Mallín's daughter, Dorotéa.

That's the bottom line. It's not open for discussion. I'm doing what I think is the right thing, and that's it.

I don't expect you to understand. And I don't want you calling Henry and threatening him. He's about as unhappy about this as you will be when you get this letter, and there's nothing he can do about it either.

I'm telling you because I love you, and figure

---

you have a right to know.

If you haven't already figured this out, you're going to be a great-grandfather.

Somebody told me yesterday that a newborn melts stone hearts. I really hope he's right.

Love,

Clete

"It came special delivery," the Old Man said. "Mrs. Stevens apparently read it, and then laid it on my desk. Cletus has apparently lost his mind. A genetic defect, I suppose, dormant all these years."

"I suppose I should have known you would say something like that."

"What did you expect me to say?"

"I told myself when I put in the call that I wasn't going to get into a fight with you, and I won't. I called because I need something."

"What do you need?

"I called Pan American Airlines and they told me there's a waiting list with three hundred names on it of people who want to fly to Buenos Aires and don't qualify for a government priority."

"Martha, do you think you can talk some sense to him if you go down there?"

"I need three tickets, Marcus, and I don't want to wait my turn on the waiting list."

"Who's going with you?"

"Who would you guess?"

"You're not taking the girls down there? What-ever for?"

"So they can see Clete getting married."

"Did he tell you why he feels he has to marry this Argentine female?"

"What's that supposed to mean?"

"He didn't tell you, then. He was too ashamed to tell you."

"He told you that she's . . . in the family way?"

"The way he put it was that I am about to be a great-grandfather," the Old Man said. "I can't believe you would want to humiliate the girls, my granddaughters, by forcing them to —"

"Not one more goddamned word, Marcus!" Martha flared. "Are you going to get me three tickets or not?"

"And if I don't?"

"Then it will be a cold goddamned day in hell before me, or my daughters, ever talk to you again."

"That sounds like a threat! Nobody threatens me!"

"I just did," Martha said. "Oh, go to hell, you nasty old bastard! I'll get the tickets myself!"

There was a click as the line went dead.

The Old Man hung the telephone up and then stood looking down at it for a long moment.

"Mrs. Stevens," he called, "would you see if you can get Mrs. Howell back for me, please?"

"All right."

"And then see if you can get Juan Trippe on the line for me."

"Where is he?"

"I have no idea. Call Pan American Airways, tell them you're calling for me, and ask."

Two minutes later, Mrs. Stevens reported the telephone at Big Foot Ranch was busy, but that she had a Mr. Walpole at Pan American Airways on the line.

The Old Man snatched up the telephone and

demanded, "Who's this?"

"Ralph Walpole."

"My name is Cletus Marcus Howell. Does that mean anything to you?"

"We've met, Mr. Howell. Good to hear your voice, Sir."

"I was trying to talk to Mr. Trippe."

"He's not available at the moment, Mr. Howell. Is there any way I can be of service?"

"You're connected with Pan American?"

"Yes, I am," Mr. Walpole said, somewhat stiffly. "As a matter of fact, I happen to be Vice-President, Operations."

"Well, Mr. Walpole, I need four seats on your Buenos Aires flight the day after tomorrow."

"Well, that may be somewhat difficult, Mr. Howell. Those planes are invariably full."

"I'm not concerned with how difficult it is, Mr. Walpole."

"Well, let me take your priority information, and I'll be happy to look into it for you, Mr. Howell. I'm sure that something can be worked out, if not — being completely honest with you — as soon as the day after tomorrow."

"I don't have a priority," the Old Man said.

"Excuse me, Mr. Howell? Did I understand you to say you haven't arranged for your priority yet?"

"What I said was, 'I don't have a priority.'"

"In that case, may I suggest you call me back when you do have the priority? And then we'll see what we can work out for you."

"Listen to me carefully," the Old Man said. "One of your airplanes is going to take off from Miami the day after tomorrow, bound for Buenos Aires. Unless I am mistaken, it will make its first fuel stop at Caracas, Venezuela."

"That is correct, Mr. Howell."

"If there are four people named Howell — myself; my daughter-in-law, Mrs. Martha Howell; and my granddaughters, Miss Elizabeth and Miss Marjorie Howell — on that airplane when it lands in Caracas, then Howell Petroleum Venezuela will furnish you whatever quantity of 110–130-octane aviation gasoline you require. If we all are not on that airplane, then you had better be prepared to paddle it to Buenos Aires, because I won't pump one drop of aviation gasoline, and neither will anyone else in Caracas."

"I can't believe you're serious, Mr. Howell."

"Find Mr. Trippe and ask him if I have ever made an idle threat," the Old Man said, and hung up.

[Three]

Office of the Director
The Office of Strategic Services
Washington, D.C.
1105 16 April 1943

"This just came in." Colonel A. F. Graham, USMCR, handed OSS Director William J. Donovan a large manila envelope with TOP SECRET stamped on it.

Donovan took it wordlessly and read it.

```
          TOP  SECRET
          LINDBERGH


URGENT


FROM  AGGIETWO  AGGIE
0400  GREENWICH  15APR43


MSG  NO.  0003


TO  ORACLE  WASHDC


EYES  ONLY  FOR  DDWHO  GRAHAM


  1.  IN  RE  LINDBERGH


    A.  GALAHAD  CONFIRMS  ABSOLUTELY
LINDBERGH  EXISTS.


    B.  MONTEVIDEO  OPERATION  RUN  BY
SS  MAJOR  WERNER  VON  TRESMARCK,
SECURITY  OFFICER  OF  GERMAN  EM-
BASSY  HEREAFTER  BAGMAN.


  2.  AGGIE  EN  ROUTE  BIRDCAGE  AS  OF
1700  GREENWICH  14APR43.


AGGIETWO  END


          TOP  SECRET

          LINDBERGH
```

"Interesting," Donovan said.

"Somehow I thought you would be pleased," Graham said. "Am I missing something here, Bill?"

"Well, for one thing, we don't know who Galahad is," Donovan said. "It would really be helpful to me if I could tell the President that the reason we really believe there is an ongoing operation down there ransoming concentration-camp inmates is that we are getting our information from somebody who knows what he is talking about for the following reasons, one, two, three, and is motivated to tell us all this for the following reasons, one, two, three. Galahad won't cut the mustard, Alex. FDR has a very droll sense of humor. If I go to him and tell him what we have learned from Galahad, he'll ask me what we have heard from King Arthur and the rest of the Knights of the Round Table."

"I messaged Frade to identify Galahad and Cavalry," Graham said.

"And he has decided he doesn't want to tell us," Donovan said.

"We don't know that," Graham said.

"Oh, but we do," Donovan said, and went into the side drawer of his desk and came up with two other messages.

"The one from Frade came in while you were in Havana," Donovan said.

```
          TOP  SECRET

          LINDBERGH

URGENT
FROM  STAFCHIEF  AGGIE
0830  GREENWICH  15  APRIL  1943
MSG  NO  0003

TO  ORACLE  WASHDC
EYES  ONLY  FOR  DDWHO  GRAHAM


   REGRET  TO  OBTAIN  ABSOLUTELY  RE-
LIABLE  INTELLIGENCE  FROM  GALAHAD
AND  CAVALRY  IT  WAS  NECESSARY  TO
GIVE  MY  WORD  OF  HONOR  THAT  THEIR
IDENTITIES  WILL  NOT  BE  FURNISHED
TO  THIRD  PARTIES.

STACHIEF  END

          TOP  SECRET

          LINDBERGH
```

Donovan waited until Graham had a chance to read it before he spoke:

"I can't believe that word-of-honor business," he said. "What the hell does Frade think the OSS is? The Boy Scouts?"

"I don't have any trouble with it," Graham said. "I think they call that 'honor.' "

"Jesus!" Donovan said. "You don't really think he thinks he doesn't have to tell us, do you, because he gave his 'word of honor'?"

"I think that's exactly what he thinks," Graham said.

"And he gets taken out, which is a real possibility, we then lose both Galahad and Cavalry because nobody else knows who they are. Did you think about that?"

"No, but I'm sure Frade took that into consideration," Graham said.

Donovan shook his head in disbelief.

"The second one just came in. Take a look at it, Alex, and then tell me you still think you were right to leave who gives orders to who down there a little vague."

Graham took the message and read it.

```
             TOP  SECRET

URGENT
FROM  STACHIEF  BUENOS  AIRES
1315  GREENWICH  15APR43
MSG  NO  0007

TO  ORACLE  WASHDC

   1.  IN  RE  YOUR  545.  TEX  INFORMED
BY  UNDERSIGNED  THAT  ORACLE  DESIRES
IDENTIFICATION  OF  GALAHAD  AND  CAV-
ALRY.  TEX  STATED  HE  HAD  ALREADY
INFORMED  ORACLE  HIS  UNWILLINGNESS
TO  DO  SO.

   2.  TEX  STATED  HE  IS  DEPARTING
BUENOS  AIRES  TONIGHT  FOR  PORTO
ALEGRE  PURPOSE  FERRYING  AIRCRAFT
PLUS  PERSONNEL  AND  MATERIEL  AT
PORTO  ALEGRE  BLACK.  ATTEMPTED  TO
EXPLAIN  THAT  ENORMOUS  RISK  OF
BLACK  FLIGHT  BEING  DETECTED  UNDER
```

THESE CIRCUMSTANCES INDICATED NECESSITY OF AUTHORIZATION BY ORACLE AND UNDERSIGNED REQUESTED SEVENTY-TWO HOUR DELAY PURPOSE DOING SO. TEX DECLINED TO DELAY DEPARTURE.

3. TEX DECLINED TO FURNISH UNDERSIGNED DETAILS OF BLACK INFILTRATION, STATING UNDERSIGNED DOES NOT HAVE NEED TO KNOW AND FURTHER STATED HE DOES NOT CONSIDER HIMSELF OBLIGED TO HAVE APPROVAL OF UNDERSIGNED FOR ANY OF HIS OPERATIONS.

4. UNDERSIGNED RELUCTANTLY PROVIDED TEX LOCATION OF TEAM CHIEF ALREADY IN COUNTRY. BLACK INFILTRATION OF TEAM PERSONNEL AND MATERIEL FROM PORTO ALEGRE TO ARGENTINA WILL THUS PROCEED AS DESCRIBED UNLESS ORDERS TO CONTRARY FURNISHED STACHIEF PORTO ALEGRE.

5. UNDERSIGNED STRONGLY FEELS THAT EFFICIENCY OF ALL ARGENTINA OPERATIONS WOULD BE GREATLY ENHANCED IF COMMAND STRUCTURE MADE ABSOLUTELY CLEAR TO ALL PERSONNEL.

STACHIEF END

TOP SECRET

Colonel Graham handed the message back to Donovan and met his eyes.

"I still think that leaving who gives orders to who down there a little vague was the right thing to do," he said.

"You do?"

"And this proves it. If I told Frade that he took his orders from Delojo, he would not be on his way to take the airplane, and Ashton, and Ashton's team and the radar, into Argentina. He would be sitting with his thumb up his ass waiting for Delojo to think of some way to do the same thing in a manner that would absolutely guarantee that if something went wrong, he couldn't be held responsible."

"You must be angry, Alex. The only time you're vulgar is when you're angry."

"I don't like Delojo going over my head to you to complain about Frade."

"This may come as a big surprise to you, Alex, but neither did I," Donovan said, and went into his desk drawer again and came out with another message.

TOP   SECRET

URGENT

FROM ORACLE WASHDC

MSG NO 2602
0605 GREENWICH 16APR43

TO STACHIEF BUENOS AIRES

REFERENCE YOUR NO. 0007

  1. REGRET COMMAND STRUCTURE AND MISSION PRIORITIES NOT MADE CLEAR. HIGHEST PRIORITY OF BUENOS AIRES STATION IS TO SUPPORT TEAM AGGIE. STACHIEF AGGIE AT HIS SOLE DISCRETION WILL DETERMINE STA-CHIEF BUENOS AIRES'S NEED TO KNOW DETAILS OF ANY MISSION.

  2. INASMUCH AS STACHIEF AGGIE IS UNDER DIRECT CONTROL OF ORACLE FURTHER COMMENTS FROM YOU CON-CERNING HIS ACTIVITIES ARE NOT DE-SIRED.

COPY TO STACHIEF AGGIE

DONOVAN END

TOP   SECRET

"I don't think I quite understand," Graham said.

"That looks pretty clear to me," Donovan said. "That just went out. I wanted to have my reply to show you at the same time I showed you Delojo's message."

"You messaged Delojo to find out who Galahad and Cavalry are?" Donovan nodded. "Isn't that my job?"

"I don't need your permission to message anybody," Donovan said. "But I don't — and you know I don't — if there's not a good reason. In this case, you were in Havana when I sent that to Delojo."

Graham considered that, nodded, and then asked, "And then you jump all over him for asking Frade?"

"I didn't tell him to ask Frade. I told him I wanted to know who they are. That's all. He — perfectly naturally, as far as I'm concerned; he does outrank Frade — misconstrued that into thinking he had authority over Frade. And when Frade told him no, he considered it insubordination. I had to straighten that out, Alex. You *were* wrong to be 'a little vague.' "

Graham didn't reply.

"I'm meeting you more than halfway, Alex," Donovan said. "I need Galahad and Cavalry identified. Galahad in particular. I have to go to the President with Lindbergh."

"All I can do is order him again," Graham said.

"No. That's not all you can do."

"You want me to go down there?"

"I want to know who Galahad and Cavalry are. I don't care how you find out."

"It's that important?"

"Yeah, it is," Donovan said simply. "If J. Edgar

Hoover beats me to the President on this, it will hurt us badly."

"And the reverse is true, right? That's what this is all about? Your little war with Hoover?"

"Just find out who Galahad and Cavalry are, Alex. OK?"

Graham looked at him for a moment, then walked out of the office.

[Four]

Bachelor Officers' Quarters
2035th U.S. Army Air Corps Support Wing
Pôrto Alegre, Brazil
1930 16 April 1943

"I'm really going to miss her," Captain Maxwell Ashton said as Consuelo drove off in her cousin's Fiat, leaving Ashton, Clete, and Enrico standing on the sidewalk in front of what before the war had been The Gran Hotel de Pôrto.

"I can understand that," Clete said.

"I seriously considered asking her to spend the night. With a little bit of luck, you would have been caught sneaking across the border and tossed in a cell. I hope you realize, mi Mayor, what a sacrifice I am making for the common good."

"Your devotion to duty is inspiring, Capitán Ashton," Clete said.

"I know, I know. It's another character flaw I can't seem to get rid of. Come on in, mi Mayor, we'll get you a room, and then you can meet the team. The gorilla's all excited about meeting a

643

genuine hero face-to-face."

"Por favor, Capitán, kiss my ass."

The Army Air Corps technical sergeant who was the Bachelor Officers' Quarters manager was polite but firm; he could not assign a room to anybody who didn't have orders.

"These gentlemen are with me," Ashton said. "Colonel Wallace arranged for our quarters."

"They still have to have orders," the Air Corps sergeant said.

A telephone call was made to Colonel Wallace's office. He had gone for the day, and it was necessary to establish contact with him at the bar of the Officers' Club on the Navy base.

"Colonel Wallace."

"This is Major Frade, Sir."

"I wasn't expecting you until tomorrow, Major."

"I got in a little early, Sir."

"Come to my office at twelve hundred tomorrow."

"I'm at the BOQ, Sir. Two of us are."

"Come to my office at twelve hundred tomorrow," Colonel Wallace repeated somewhat impatiently.

"I'm having a little trouble getting a room, Colonel."

"How is that?"

"The problem seems to be my orders."

"What's wrong with your orders?"

"I don't have any orders, Sir."

"You don't have any orders?" Colonel Wallace asked incredulously.

"No, Sir."

"That's very unusual, you understand."

"Yes, Sir. I realize that. I was hoping, Sir, you

would have a word with the sergeant."

"Very well," Colonel Wallace said after giving the subject a full thirty seconds of thought. "Put him on."

"Thank you very much, Sir."

The price of each room was one dollar and twenty-five cents, United States currency only. Major Frade had to borrow the money from Captain Ashton.

First Lieutenant Madison R. Sawyer III did not physically resemble a gorilla. He was a good-looking, large, well-muscled young man wearing a well-cut tweed jacket and a button-down-collar shirt and gray flannel slacks. His blond hair was closely cropped in a crew cut.

"It's a privilege to meet you, Sir," he said enthusiastically, shaking Clete's hand in a bone-crushing grip.

"Easy on the hand, Lieutenant!"

"Sorry, Sir."

Staff Sergeant Jerry O'Sullivan, who was dressed in a cotton zipper jacket and a turtleneck shirt, was a wiry little man with sharp features and intelligent eyes. Sergeant Siegfried Stein, who wore a rumpled suit, was almost as large as Lieutenant Sawyer, but did not look muscular. Technical Sergeant Ferris was average-size, with a lithe build.

"I've explained to Lieutenant Sawyer and the men, Major," Ashton said, for the first time sounding like an officer, "that you believe that the infiltration can be best accomplished by flying us across the border into Argentina in your aircraft."

"It's a C-45," Clete said, looking at the team.

"The Air Corps uses them as liaison aircraft, and to train navigators. I've flown one a couple of times, and I have seen the strip where we can land in Argentina . . ."

"Permission to speak, Sir?" the gorilla asked.

Clete nodded.

"Parachute infiltration has been decided against, Sir?"

"You're asking the wrong man, Lieutenant. I don't command your team."

"But you are the senior officer of the line present, Sir," the gorilla argued.

Clete's glance fell on the enlisted men. From their faces it was clear they shared the opinion of their executive officer held by their commanding officer.

"Let the major continue, Lieutenant Sawyer," Ashton said. "Perhaps he will be good enough to hold a question-and-answer period when he's finished."

"Yes, Sir. Thank you, Sir," the gorilla said, then looked at Clete and added, "Excuse me, Sir."

"As I said, I just had a look at the landing strip where I'll land. I don't see any problem in getting a C-45 in there."

"Excuse me, Sir," Lieutenant Sawyer said. "It's not a C-45, Sir, it's a C-56 —"

"Shut up, Sawyer!" Ashton snapped.

"Going by plane would solve a lot of problems," Clete said. "Starting with getting everybody and all the equipment across the Río Uruguay. And then from Corrientes Province to —" Clete interrupted himself and looked at Ashton.

"Have you discussed your destination?"

"No, but this is as good a time as any."

"Your radar will be installed on the shore of Samborombón Bay. My men have already selected the site. If we travel by plane, we can fly directly there from Corrientes. Otherwise, obviously, you'd have to get a truck to carry the radar. There would be a damn good chance of running into trouble at a police or military checkpoint if you moved by truck."

"Are we being given a choice here?" Sergeant Stein asked.

"Of course not," Lieutenant Sawyer said incredulously.

"Yeah, Siggie, you are," Captain Ashton said.

"I vote for the airplane," Stein said.

"Anybody have any objections?" Ashton asked.

There were no objections.

"Are there any questions?" Clete asked.

"When would we go?" Sergeant Stein asked.

"The aircraft is supposed to be available to me as of noon tomorrow," Clete said. "If that happens, they've promised me an hour's cockpit familiarization and an IP to ride with me while I shoot some touch-and-goes. Unless something goes wrong, we could break ground right after nightfall tomorrow. It's about a three-hour flight, maybe three-thirty, to Santo Tomé."

"What's a 'touch-and-go'?" Sergeant Stein asked.

"Practice landing. You touch down, but instead of stopping, you apply throttle and take off again."

"Am I allowed to ask where we're going to land where we'll set up the radar?" Technical Sergeant Ferris asked.

"On an estancia, a ranch. The radar will be installed on property belonging to the estancia."

"Whose ranch?" Ferris pursued.

"Actually, it's mine," Clete said.

There was no response to that.

"Permission to speak, Sir?" Lieutenant Sawyer inquired.

"Granted."

"Firearms and explosives, Sir?"

"How are you armed, Captain Ashton?" Clete asked.

"Side arms. We also have Thompsons. Is that a problem?"

"We're not invading Argentina. We'll be landing at an Argentine Army base. I don't want them to see armed men."

"Ferris, is there room in the radar crates to hide the weapons?" Ashton asked.

"Yes, Sir."

Ashton looked at Clete. "OK?" he asked.

"What kind of explosives?"

"Are you familiar with plastic explosive, Major? C-3?" Clete nodded. "I have fifty pounds."

"Can you put it with the submachine guns?"

Stein nodded.

"Do that," Clete said. "I'd be happier if the side arms were also out of sight."

"Ferris, you and Stein go out there now and put all the weapons and all the plastic explosive in with the radar."

"Yes, Sir."

"Sergeant, do you think you could load the crates aboard the aircraft tonight?" Clete asked.

"I'd have to talk somebody out of a truck to move the stuff from the warehouse to the hangar and talk somebody into letting me into the hangar. I think it would probably be better if I had an officer with me."

"I'll go with Sergeant Ferris," the gorilla said.

"No," Ashton said. "You will stay here and see that the Major and Mr. Rodríguez get their dinner. I'll go with Ferris and Stein."

[Five]

Headquarters
2035th U.S. Army Air Corps
Support Wing
Pôrto Alegre Naval Base, Brazil
1205 17 April 1943

Colonel J. B. Wallace, U.S. Army Air Corps, who commanded the 2035th Training Wing, was informed at 1155 hours by the Brazilian Navy officer in charge of base security that two Argentinian gentlemen — a Señor Frade and a Señor Rodríguez — were at the main gate, seeking permission to enter the base for the purpose of visiting Colonel Wallace.

"I'll send a car for them," Wallace replied.

"They have a car, my Colonel. Shall I pass them in?"

"Please."

Colonel Wallace then made a note in his pocket notebook: *1159 17 Apr43 — Major Frade, accompanied by an Argentine named Rodríguez, admitted to Base.*

The notes he had been keeping would be later typed in draft, and edited, and then retyped. Colonel Wallace had every intention of keeping a detailed record of everything that happened with regard to these OSS people. Irregular was a monumental understatement. There was no question in his mind that questions would be asked about this whole mess, and he wanted to be prepared.

Colonel Wallace's office was on the ground floor of a single-story building that reminded him very much of the buildings at Maxwell Air Corps Base in Alabama. Obviously, since Brazil drew its culture from Portugal, it was "Portuguese-style" architecture, but Colonel Wallace could not help but think of it as Spanish. The buildings at Maxwell were always thought of as Spanish-style.

He walked to the window and peered around the edge of the heavy curtain for his first look at Major C. H. Frade of the Office of Strategic Services. It was always helpful to have a look at someone with whom one was to deal before actually meeting them.

A 1937 Buick Limited convertible touring sedan, which looked as if it had rolled off the showroom floor that morning, came down the street and pulled into the curved drive in front of the building. It was chauffeur driven, and when it came to a stop, it was close enough for Colonel Wallace to read the license plate. It was an Argentine plate, reading "Corrientes 11." It was obviously the property of some prominent Argentine.

The chauffeur ran around the rear of the car and opened the rear door. A very young man stepped out. Colonel Wallace thought he was no older than twenty-two or twenty-three. He was wearing a tweed jacket, a yellow polo shirt with a red foulard filling the open collar, riding breeches, and glistening boots.

He did not look like a field-grade Marine Corps officer detailed to the Office of Strategic Services,

Colonel Wallace decided. The older man with him, who had a pronounced military bearing, was probably Major Frade. The young man — Señor Rodríguez — was probably somehow connected with the chauffeur-driven Buick with the low-numbered license plate.

The more he thought about it, the more he was pleased. Not only was Major Frade obviously competent in what he was doing — establishing a good relationship with prominent natives was obviously both useful and difficult to accomplish — but Frade would likely be very interested to learn that Captain Maxwell Ashton had such contempt for military customs that he had installed his enlisted men in officers' quarters.

And Frade would very possibly, at least unofficially, tell him what this whole irregular operation was all about.

Two minutes later, Colonel Wallace's sergeant knocked at the door and informed him that Mr. Frade and another gentleman wished to see him.

"Show the Major in, Sergeant," Colonel Wallace said as he walked from the window toward the door.

"Welcome to Pôrto Alegre, Major Frade," Wallace said, offering his hand to Suboficial Mayor Enrico Rodríguez, Cavalry, Argentine Army, Retired.

"I'm afraid Enrico doesn't speak English, Colonel," Clete said. "I'm Major Frade."

"Who is he?" Wallace blurted.

"My friend," Clete said.

Enrico came to attention.

"A sus órdenes, mi Coronel," he said.

"What did he say?" Wallace asked.

"It's the Argentine military custom when a

junior meets a superior to say that," Clete said. "It means, 'at your orders.' Enrico spent some time in the Argentine Cavalry before he became a pilot."

"May I see your identification, Major Frade?" Wallace asked.

"I've got an Argentine passport," Clete said. "But I was told that I was to identify myself by giving you a telephone number."

"Quite right, quite right," Wallace said, and took out his notebook and found the number he was told would identify the OSS agent to whom he was going to turn over the C-56.

"Ready, Major," he said.

"CANal 5-4055," Clete said.

"Correct," Colonel Wallace said.

"I was also told that someone would be here who could give me an hour's cockpit familiarization in the C-45, and then let me shoot a few touch-and-goes."

"Yes. That is correct. Under the circumstances, Major, I thought it would be best if I performed that service. But it's a C-56, not a C-45."

What the hell is a C-56?

"I stand corrected, Colonel."

"What I thought we could do, Major, is have luncheon in the Officers' Club, a working luncheon, so to speak, to make sure all the paperwork is in order, and then go to the flight line."

What paperwork?

"That's very kind of you, Sir."

"How much time do you have in the C-56?"

I don't even know what the hell a C-56 is. Maybe it's like that business with the Bell fighter the Air Corps had on Guadalcanal. The one Sullivan was flying when he went in was a P-39. Another model of the same airplane, for reasons known only to God and the Army Air Corps, was called the P-400. It has to be something like that. Graham wouldn't have sent a plane down here he knew I couldn't fly.

"Not very much," Clete said. "I'm a fighter pilot by trade. But there were a couple of them at Ewa, in the Hawaiian Islands, and two at Henderson Field. We used them as sort of aerial taxis, and I got to fly a couple of them."

"As aerial taxis?" Colonel Wallace asked incredulously.

"Yes, Sir."

"You have not gone through a standard C-56 transition course?"

"No, Sir."

"That's very unusual. Presumably, this gentleman will function as your copilot?"

I never had any trouble flying a C-45 by myself, but I suspect that is something I should not confide in this guy.

"Yes, Sir."

"Well, let's go have our lunch. They do a very nice luncheon steak."

"Thank you, Sir."

There were a half-dozen Marines having their lunch in the Officers' Club, four of them wearing wings. None of them looked familiar. In other circumstances, this would not have bothered Clete; he would have walked over to them and said hello, and played Who Do You Know?

Going over to them now was obviously out of the question. What would happen ran through his mind:

"Hey. Clete Frade's my name. Used to fly Wildcats with VMF-221 on Guadalcanal."

"Really? What are you doing here? And how come you're in civvies?"

"Well, I'm in the OSS, and I'm here to pick up a C-56 I'm going to smuggle into Argentina so we can find a neutral ship that's supplying German subs, and/or, depending on how the coup d'état goes, maybe to fly some Argentine generals out of the country. You don't want to wear a uniform when you're doing stuff like that. People would ask questions."

"What are the Marines doing here, Colonel?" Clete asked.

"They're probably either Naval Air Transport Command pilots, IPs for the Catalinas we've given the Brazilian Navy, or they're ferry pilots who've brought aircraft down from the States."

"Colonel, I want you to do something for me," Clete said.

"What is it?"

"I want to have a word, in private, with the Marine Captain. You're going to have to identify me as a Marine major; I don't have an ID card."

Colonel Wallace looked at him, uncomfortably, for a long moment and then stood up and walked to the table where the Marines were sitting. He spoke to the Marine Captain, who rose to his feet and followed Wallace far enough from the table so they couldn't be overheard, and spoke to him again.

The Captain looked at Clete with suspicion, but after a moment walked to the table.

"You wanted to speak to me?"

"My name is Frade, Captain. I used to fly Wildcats with VMF-221 on Guadalcanal."

"That Air Corps Colonel said you were a Marine major," the Captain said, his tone of voice making it clear he thought that highly improbable.

The Captain, Clete thought, *was in his thirties.*
"That's right."

"Who was the MAG" — Marine Air Group — "Commander when you were on the 'Canal? Colonel Stevenson?"

"No," Clete said, almost as a reflex action. "Dawkins, Lieutenant Colonel Clyde W., was skipper of MAG-21. I never heard of a Colonel Stevenson."

"Neither did I, Major. Excuse me. I was just checking you out. You don't expect to find a VMF-221 Wildcat pilot in riding clothes in a Navy Club in Brazil. I knew 'The Dawk'; I used to fly R4Ds into Henderson from Espíritu Santo. How can I help you, Sir?"

"What's a C-56?"

"It's the Lockheed Lodestar," the Captain said.

"Oh, shit," Clete said.

He was familiar with the Lockheed Lodestar. It was a seventeen-passenger transport aircraft with a sixty-nine-foot wingspan powered by two 1,200-horsepower Wright Cyclone engines. It had a top speed of 250 m.p.h., a range of 1,600 miles, and a takeoff weight of 17,500 pounds.

"Excuse me, Sir?"

"I was hoping it was another number for the C-45," Clete confessed.

"Pardon me?"

"Remember the Bell fighters the Army had on Guadalcanal?"

"Yes, Sir. Some of them were P-39s and some were P-400s. I never understood that," the Captain said, adding, "I guess you were on the 'Canal, Sir."

"Right at this moment, I almost wish I still was," Clete said. "Do you know how to fly a C-56, Captain?"

"Before I came into the Corps, I flew Lodestars for Transcontinental and Western Airways. Los Angeles to Dallas."

"Are they hard to fly?" Clete asked. "Let me put that another way. How much time would it take you to teach someone who's never even been in one how to fly one?"

"Give me someone with a thousand hours, including a couple of hundred hours' twin-engine time, say, in the C-45, three, four days, including six hours or so in the air."

"How much could you teach me between now and dark?" Clete asked.

"I don't understand."

"And I can't explain very much, except that I'm here to pick up a C-56. I thought I was supposed to pick up a C-45, which I *can* fly. If that Air Corps colonel who's supposed to give me an hour of touch-and-goes sees that I don't know my way around the cockpit, much less how to fly one, he's going to give me trouble. I can't blame him. But a lot depends on me taking off out of here in that airplane as soon as it's dark."

The Captain looked at him for a good thirty seconds.

"You're OSS, right?"

"If I was, do you think I would say so?"

"There's a Lodestar in a guarded hangar freshly painted red with Argentine numbers. There's four guys in the BOQ, three of whom look suspiciously like sergeants, that don't talk to anybody but themselves. And the first thing I heard when I landed here in my R5D was that the OSS was here."

R5D was Navy nomenclature for the Douglas DC-4 (Army C-54), a four-engine, fifty-passenger transport aircraft with a range of 3,900 miles and a takeoff weight of 63,000 pounds.

"Maybe they are. I just wouldn't know."

"What makes you think that Air Corps colonel is going to let me try to teach you how to fly the Lodestar?"

"I'll just tell him you are," Clete said.

"If I were a suspicious man, I would think that you must be OSS. Most majors don't get to tell full bull colonels anything but 'Yes, Sir.' "

"Don't put me on a spot, please. And I'm sorry, but I have to tell you that if anyone hears you saying you think somebody's in the OSS, or about how this C-56 is painted, or who is flying it, you'll probably spend the rest of the war in the Aleutian Islands."

"In four hours, Major, *maybe* I can teach you to make a normal takeoff and a normal landing under perfect conditions. That's all."

"What would you say if I said I have to put that airplane into a dirt strip?"

"I would say don't try it."

"What I said was 'I *have to* put that airplane into a dirt strip.' "

"In that case, I think we should get to the flight line just as soon as we can."

"What's your name, Captain?"

"Finney."

Clete raised his hand and signaled Colonel Wallace to join them.

"Colonel," Clete said, "it turns out that Captain Finney is a C-56 IP. If you have no objection, I'll shoot my touch-and-goes with him."

"Whatever you wish, of course, Mr. Frade."

XX

[One]

```
Bachelor Officers' Quarters
2035th U.S. Army Air Corps Support Wing
Pôrto Alegre, Brazil
1730 16 April 1943
```

Clete found Captain Maxwell Ashton III at the bar of the hotel. Ashton was in a tieless shirt and sweater, sipping a beer and examining with interest and obvious approval the long legs of a waitress as she bent over to deliver a round of drinks to a table across the room.

"We have a problem," Clete said as he slipped onto a bar stool beside him.

"Why doesn't that surprise me?" Ashton said. "You want a beer, or is it the kind of bad news you would rather tell me sober?"

Clete looked around the room and found a table where there was less chance to overhear their conversation than at the bar.

"Let's go over there," he said.

"You want to take a beer with you?" Ashton pursued.

"No, I'm flying," Clete said automatically.

"I'm sorry to hear that," Ashton said, sliding off his stool. "I was hoping the bad news was that something was wrong with the airplane and the operation was called off."

"Nothing wrong with the airplane," Clete said. "The problem is with the pilot."

"What does that make you? The only modest Marine pilot in the Naval Service?"

They sat down at the table. The long-legged waitress appeared. Clete ordered hot chocolate.

"And I, my dear, will have another of this very excellent beer," Ashton said.

He waited until she had walked out of hearing, then said, "Let's have it, mi Mayor."

"I don't know how this happened, but the airplane they sent down here is a C-56, not a C-45."

"What's the problem?"

"The C-45 is a small twin. I know how to fly one. The C-56 is a Lockheed Lodestar. . . ."

"And you don't know how to fly a Lodestar?"

"I just spent three hours in this one with a guy who used to fly them for Transcontinental and Western Airlines. He taught me how to start it, how to taxi it, how to get it in the air. No real problem there. Landing it, however, is something else. This is a great big airplane, Ashton. Almost all of my time is in small airplanes."

"Which means?"

"That I had one hell of a time getting the Lockheed onto the ground. I missed three approaches."

"I don't know what that means," Ashton confessed.

"Three times I came in either too fast, or too high, or both — and it was daylight; I could see the runway. I could not get it onto the wide, long runways here and had to go around."

"Why?" Ashton asked.

"I just told you. I don't have any experience in

airplanes like that; I'm a fighter pilot."

"So what are you telling me?"

"The strip in Santo Tomé is dirt and short. For one thing, I'm not sure if it will handle the weight of the Lockheed. Equally important, since I had trouble here, I'll probably have more trouble at Santo Tomé. Where I'll be landing at night, with jury-rigged runway lights."

" 'Jury-rigged runway lights'?"

"When they hear me flying over the strip, a couple of guys on horses are going to ride down the sides of the runway and light the landing lights, which are clay pots filled with sand and gasoline."

Ashton stroked his mustache with his index finger, then met Clete's eyes.

"I don't know what the word is, maybe 'practice.' If you had more *practice,* could you learn to land the airplane the way you're supposed to?"

"That's not possible."

"What's not possible? Getting any better at landing it?"

"Getting more practice."

"Why not?"

"Colonel Wallace has set up a meeting at 0900 tomorrow with the appropriate Brazilian Customs officials to handle the paperwork for an international flight. There cannot be a record of this flight; therefore, I have to get out of here tonight."

"You can't fix that? Get Graham to fix it?"

"It would take at least twenty-four — more likely forty-eight — hours to explain the problem to Colonel Graham and have him tell Wallace to butt out. I've got to get the airplane out of here tonight."

"So what happens?"

"There's a couple of possibilities. The basic problem is that there is maybe a fifty-fifty chance that I'll wreck the airplane trying to land it. . . ."

"If that's the odds, why are you going to try it?"

"I have to try. I can't just chicken out. I told some people I'd get them an airplane."

"If you crash it, it won't do anybody any good."

"I will have tried. And I may get lucky."

"You are a dangerous man, mi Mayor."

"And we now know that the submarine-supply vessel will be in Samborombón Bay in five or six days."

"And if you wreck the airplane with the radar on it, where will that leave us?"

"No worse off than we are now, unless you can come up with some way to get your team and the radar into Argentina and to Samborombón Bay by yourself."

Ashton considered that a moment, then shrugged.

"One option," Clete went on, "would be to drop the radar — and maybe you and your team — by parachute onto the Santo Tomé airstrip. Then I would try to land it."

"Would getting rid of that much weight make landing it any easier?"

"I've been thinking about that. The simple answer is yes. The less weight, the better. But you've got five people. That's a thousand pounds, tops. You told me you've got five crates . . ."

"Four," Ashton corrected him.

Clete nodded.

". . . weighing about two hundred pounds each. Call that another thousand pounds. Weight of team and radar, two thousand pounds total. This is a seventeen-passenger aircraft, plus a crew of three —"

Clete interrupted himself: "That's something

else. I will not have a copilot. That will make landing it even harder."

"OK," Ashton said. "What was that about a seventeen-passenger aircraft?"

"Seventeen passengers, plus a crew of three. You usually figure weight and balance using two hundred pounds per man. Twenty times two hundred is four thousand pounds. In other words, with everything aboard, we'll have about half a normal load. Less, if you take into consideration that we'll have zero pounds of cargo. I don't really think that dropping you and the crates — in other words, getting rid of two thousand pounds — is going to make a hell of a difference in an airplane with a takeoff weight of about eighteen thousand pounds."

"Parachutes sometimes don't work," Ashton said. "And we're dealing with delicate radio equipment. Aside from my massive cowardice, one of the problems I had with parachuting the radar in was subjecting it to the shock of landing. I need all four of my crates."

"What I said was you and your guys can jump, and I will land with the radar on board."

"I've got a problem with that," Ashton said. "I have no intention of jumping out of an airplane unless the sonofabitch is on fire. If I don't jump, and tell the other guys to jump, they're going to wonder why — except, of course, the gorilla. He would love to jump out of your airplane. Screaming, 'Geronimo!' "

Clete chuckled.

"The problem with that," Ashton went on, "is that he'd probably break his leg, and we'd have to carry him wherever the hell we're going."

"Well, I can leave you all here," Clete said. "And

you figure out some way to get you and the radar across the river — without using a rubber boat. That doesn't seem like such a bad idea, really."

"Was your attention entirely focused on Consuelo's magnificent ass, or did you hear me when I said gambling was among my many vices?"

"Meaning you want to take a chance with me?"

"Look at it this way, mi Mayor," Ashton said. "Unless we get all the crates — in other words, the radar in a functioning condition — and everybody on my team where we are supposed to go, there's no point in the whole operation. Three crates won't work, and I can't afford to do without any member of my team. Let's give Colonel Graham the benefit of the doubt and accept that getting that radar in operation is important; that maybe down the line, if we carry this off, we'll save more lives than the six people who'll be on the airplane. . . ."

"Seven," Clete thought out loud. "I'll have Enrico with me."

"So I don't see where we have any choice but to roll the dice and see what happens. You agree?"

"It's not my decision," Clete said.

"Meaning what?" Ashton asked.

"On Guadalcanal, when I saw the rifle platoon leaders, I was glad I was an aviator. I didn't have to tell people to do something that was likely to get them killed."

"You want to know what I've been thinking?" Ashton asked.

Clete nodded.

"First I thought, 'This goddamned Marine hero is dumping this decision on me. Why doesn't the sonofabitch just have the balls to say, "Captain, get your men on my airplane"?' "

"Because this sonofabitch is not good at telling people to do something that's liable to get them killed," Clete said.

"But you're going, right? Whether or not we go with you?"

"I don't have any choice," Clete said.

"Neither do I, mi Mayor," Ashton said. "I don't want to get on that airplane, and I don't like having to order my team to get on it. And you are a three-star sonofabitch for spelling out everything that can go wrong."

Clete met his eyes and shrugged.

"But if you get us on the ground at Santo Tomé in one piece, mi Mayor, I may forgive you."

"For what this is worth, Ashton, when my ass is exposed I am a very careful airplane driver."

"You better be, mi Mayor," Ashton said. "When do we go?"

"That's another problem," Clete said.

"Oh, shit! What?"

"I didn't know whether you would be going with me or not," Clete said. "So I told Colonel Wallace I wanted to shoot some more touch-and-goes to-night — at night, in other words. The plane's being serviced, and is supposed to be ready at twenty-one hundred."

"So?"

"Colonel Wallace wants to do this by the book. Clear everything with the Brazilians. And he's not stupid. If he sees me loading you and your team aboard the Lockheed tonight, he'll suspect that I have no intention of meeting the Brazilian Customs people tomorrow morning."

"So what would he do?"

"Possibly he would give me a formal order not to leave the local area. . . ."

"Fuck him. Let him write Graham a letter after you've gone. Subject: Disobedience of Direct Order by Frade, Major Cletus, USMCR."

"More likely he would either 'volunteer' to go with me, or send some other pilot with me, to make sure I came back."

"Fuck him again. Take him with us. Let him walk back here."

"That just wouldn't work," Clete said, smiling. "He can stop me from loading the team on the Lockheed. There's two problems. Getting the airplane without Wallace or one of his pilots in it, and getting you and your people on it without Wallace finding out."

"You're not suggesting, are you, mi Mayor, that two intrepid OSS agents, in the noble tradition of Errol Flynn and Alan Ladd, such as you and me, cannot outwit one chickenshit Air Corps colonel?"

"I would really feel more comfortable, Major Frade," Colonel J. B. Wallace, U.S. Army Air Corps, said, "if I went along with you and Colonel Rodríguez."

"What did he say?" Suboficial Mayor Enrico Rodríguez, Cavalry, Argentine Army, Retired, asked in Spanish.

"The Colonel wishes us a safe flight," Clete replied in Spanish, then switched to English: "Colonel Rodríguez feels that it would be best if he were given the opportunity to ride in the right seat while we shoot some landings."

"But he doesn't have any C-56 time," Wallace argued.

"The Colonel has several thousand hours' multi-engine time, Colonel," Clete said. "Mostly in Ford

665

Tri-Motors, to be sure, but he really has more experience than I do."

"What did you say, Señor Clete?" Suboficial Mayor Rodríguez asked.

"I told the Colonel you thanked him for all his courtesies to us," Clete said in Spanish.

Suboficial Mayor Rodríguez saluted.

"Muchas gracias, mi Coronel," he said.

Colonel Wallace knew that much Spanish.

"You're welcome, I'm sure," he said, returning the salute.

"Get in the airplane, Enrico. Walk up in front and sit down in the right seat," Clete said in Spanish, and then switched to English: "I don't think we'll need more than a couple of hours, Colonel. Is there someplace I can reach you if I get some warning lights on the panel and need a mechanic?"

"I'll either be at the Club or in my quarters," Colonel Wallace said as he watched, in obvious discomfort, Enrico climbing into the Lockheed. "Two hours, you say?"

"No more than three, certainly, Sir," Clete said.

He climbed into the Lockheed and closed the door. With the door closed, it was absolutely dark inside the fuselage. He painfully banged his knees twice and his shoulder once as he made his way through the cabin to the cockpit.

There was a little more light in the cockpit — enough for him to see Enrico's bafflement with his seat and shoulder harness — but not enough to be able to read the switch labels anywhere.

With the aid of his Zippo, it took him thirty seconds to find COCKPIT INTERIOR LIGHTS. When he threw the switch, nothing happened. It took another fifteen seconds to find the MAIN

666

BUSS switch. When he threw that, the panel lit up and the cockpit lights came on.

He put the earphones on his head. There was no hiss. Neither was there a hiss when he flipped the RADIO/INTERCOM switch to RADIO. He left the seat, went to the engineer's station and turned on the radio, selected the tower frequency, and returned to his seat.

He leaned over and showed Enrico how the seat and shoulder harness went together, then put the earphones on.

He could hear the tower.

He looked out the window and saw Colonel Wallace, standing uncomfortably by the ground crewman and his fire extinguisher. Clete smiled at both of them, and, raising his voice, shouted, "Clear!"

The left engine started immediately and quickly smoothed down. The right engine didn't seem to want to start at all, and didn't, until Clete noticed the MAIN FUEL switch and moved it from LEFT to BOTH, whereupon the right engine backfired, shot orange and blue flame a good six feet out the nacelle, and caught.

He picked up the microphone.

"Pôrto Alegre tower, Lockheed Zebra Fiver Eight Four Three."

"Go ahead, Eight Four Three."

"Eight Four Three in front of Hangar Seven, permission to taxi to the active runway."

"Eight Four Three, cleared to the threshold of Runway One Four."

"Roger, understand One Four."

He gingerly advanced the throttles, then retarded them, took off the brakes, and gingerly advanced the throttles again. The Lockheed began to move.

Clete waved cheerfully at Colonel Wallace, who smiled unhappily back.

Clete switched to INTERCOM and ordered, "Enrico, go back and get ready to open the door."

Then he reached over, showed Enrico where to put his earphones, and repeated the order. Enrico started to unbuckle himself.

Ground visibility from the cockpit of the Lockheed was unbelievably bad. He had to swing the airplane from side to side to see where he was going.

He stopped at the threshold of Runway One Four.

The tower saw him.

"Zebra Eight Four Three, you are cleared for local area operation only. The winds are negligible. Ceiling and visibility unlimited. The altimeter is two niner niner, the time is five past the hour. You are cleared as number one for takeoff on Runway One Four."

"Tower, Eight Four Three. I'm going to run a mag check."

He put the brakes on, unstrapped himself, left the seat, and went quickly down the cabin aisle, colliding en route with one of the goddamn crates, and made it to the door. Its operation was beyond the mechanical comprehension of Suboficial Mayor Rodríguez.

As soon as he had the door open, Maxwell Ashton's team came running out of the darkness and jumped aboard, Captain Ashton last.

Clete went as quickly as he could back to the cockpit, strapped himself in, and put the earphones on.

"Zebra Eight Four Three, tower."

"Tower, Four Three. Mags check OK."

"Zebra Eight Four Three, do not take off. I say again, do not take off. Return to Base Operations."

It wasn't hard to figure out what happened. Colonel Wallace went up into the control tower and watched Clete taxi, possibly through binoculars. And in the bright lights of the runway threshold, he saw Ashton and his team come running out of the dark and climb aboard.

"Tower, Zebra Eight Four Three rolling," Clete said, advancing the throttles as he lined up with the runway.

"Zebra Eight Four Three, abort takeoff, I say again, abort takeoff, and return to Base Operations."

"Tower, Four Three is rolling. Say again your last transmission. You are garbled."

"Zebra Eight Four Three, abort takeoff, I say again, abort takeoff."

The airspeed indicator jumped from zero to forty knots and began climbing. Clete felt life come into the controls.

"Zebra Eight Four Three, by order of Colonel Wallace, you will abort takeoff and return to Base Operations."

He eased the wheel forward and felt the tail come off the ground. The airspeed indicator climbed to ninety, then one hundred.

He eased back on the wheel. The rumbling stopped. The nose turned to the left, and he made the necessary corrections.

He reached to the quadrant and raised the gear.

"Zebra Eight Four Three, you are directed to land immediately."

Clete took the earphones off his head and reached up and turned the NAVIGATION LIGHTS switch to off.

Pôrto Alegre passed under him.

He looked at Enrico, who had his eyes closed and was making the sign of the cross.

He flew to the edge of the city, then set a course for Santo Tomé.

[Two]

Above Río Grande do Sul Province
Brazil
2145 16 April 1943

Captain Maxwell Ashton, Signal Corps, Army of the United States, got out of his seat and walked to the cockpit door of the Lockheed, opened it, and stood behind the pilots' seats.

"Presumably, mi Mayor, you know where we are," he said to Major Cletus H. Frade, USMCR. "I can't see a goddamn thing down there."

Clete turned to look at him.

"Enrico," he ordered, "let el Capitán have your seat."

Enrico unbuckled himself and got out of the copilot's seat. Clete had the feeling he was glad to go. He motioned Ashton into the seat and gestured for him to strap himself in, and to put on his headset.

"Not entirely," Clete said. He handed Ashton an aeronautical chart. "The last *X* shows where we *should* be."

"Should be?"

"We are navigating by what is known as dead reckoning," Clete explained. "Which means that

I know that we're making about 220 knots indicated about 10,000 feet above sea level and on a heading of 310 true. I also know that we left Pôrto Alegre about thirty-seven minutes ago. That, presuming there are *no* winds aloft, should put us — two minutes ago — where I marked the *X* on the chart."

"OK," Ashton said, after a moment to consider this. "What's the hook?"

"There are *always* winds aloft," Clete said. "The problem is one never knows what sort they are. They may be coming straight at us at, say, twenty knots, which would mean that we've been making 200 knots — not 220 — over the ground. Or they may be coming from behind us, which would mean that we are making 240 knots over the ground. Most likely, they are coming from one side or the other, as well as from the front or back. When there are winds, so to speak, from the side, they will push us off course, to one side or the other."

"I came up here to be reassured, thank you very much, mi Mayor," Ashton said. "When you got this thing into the air, I thought there might be a slight possibility that you actually knew what you're doing."

"What I'm actually trying to do is find the town of Carázinho," Clete said. "It's about a hundred and sixty miles northwest of Pôrto Alegre. You see it?"

Ashton found it on the map.

"Yeah," he said. "And there's nothing around it for miles. What happens if we miss it?"

"*Because* there's nothing around it, that increases our chances of finding it. We'll look for a glow on the horizon, starting about now. If, since there is nothing else for miles, there is a glow, it will probably be Carázinho."

"Then what?"

"Then we change course to 270 true — due west — and start looking for another glow, which, with a little bit of luck, will be either a village named Ijuí or a town called São Ângelo. *If* we hit Carázinho, it will probably be easier to find Ijuí and/or São Ângelo because there is a highway between them, down which, I devoutly hope, there will be a stream of cars, trucks, and buses, headlights on high."

"Is this the way airplane pilots normally steer?" Ashton asked.

"No. Normally, there's a radio direction finder. There's a loop antenna — it looks like a doughnut — which can be turned. You look at a meter, and when the strength of the radio signal is strongest, you can tell the antenna is pointed at the transmitter. So you just steer toward the transmitter."

"We don't have such a clever device? We have to look for buses with their headlights on?"

"The airplane has the antenna. What I don't have is the frequency of any radio station, or its location. When I asked for what are cleverly called 'Aids to Navigation,' Colonel Wallace said he would have them for me by the time I finished clearing Brazilian Customs."

"Do you think Wallace was born a chickenshit sonofabitch, or did he have to go to school?"

"I guess if you spend a lot of time in uniform you get used to doing things by the book, and learn to spend a lot of your time covering your ass."

"When should we be seeing this glow we're looking for?" Ashton asked.

"That may be it," Clete said, pointing with his finger straight ahead.

"Right where it's supposed to be."

"That's almost certainly an accident," Clete said. "Either that, or it isn't Carázinho."

"What else could it be?"

"Dallas, maybe," Clete said. "I'm not too good at dead reckoning."

He put the Lockheed into a shallow turn to the west.

"You're not going to fly over it to make sure?" Ashton asked. "Don't they paint the name of the town on roofs down here?"

"I wouldn't be surprised if the Brazilian Army Air Corps is looking for us," Clete said, growing serious. "By now I think it's entirely possible that Wallace has had time to both decide I'm not going back there and to consider the best way to cover his ass. Telling the Brazilians that we're overdue and probably lost would do that."

"So would telling the Brazilians a crazy Argentine stole one of his airplanes," Ashton said thoughtfully.

"With a little bit of luck, we should find the highway," Clete said. "If I stay a couple of miles to one side, we see them, and they can't see us."

"I'm impressed, mi Mayor," Ashton said.

Five minutes later, Clete spotted lights moving slowly across the terrain. When he got closer, the lights divided into two, and he could just pick out the red glow of running lights.

"I think we just found Route Sixty-six," he said.

Once the glow of Ijuí faded, it was possible to pick up another glow. But as he approached this, it was obvious that it came from the lights in a far smaller town than Ijuí. São Ângelo was larger than Ijuí; the glow it gave off should be larger.

Don't panic. Don't start running around looking for

673

bright lights. You didn't do anything wrong. There is an explanation for this.

The explanation came ten minutes later, when a glow appeared on the ground past the lights he thought had to be São Ângelo.

That's almost certainly São Ângelo. What the other lights were was a small town, a village, not marked on the chart.

Final proof came thirty minutes later, when he saw a large glow where his chart showed him São Luis Gonzaga should be.

And then the glow dimmed, and then brightened, and then dimmed again and vanished.

Christ, there's a low-level cloud cover down there!

"Shit!" he said.

"Something wrong, Frade?" Ashton asked.

"Obviously, we're getting into the soup," Clete said. "Which means I have to drop down so that I can see the ground. The lower I go, the less distance I can see, and that chart doesn't have altitudes on it. I don't want to run into a rock-filled cloud."

"I'm sorry I came up here," Ashton said. "Sitting in the back, I could pretend I was on Eastern Airlines, about to land in Miami. Are we really in trouble?"

"That depends on what we find at five thousand feet," Clete said as he pushed the nose of the Lockheed down into a shallow descent.

They broke out of the soup at 6,000 feet, but into rain, not the clear. The ground was again visible, if not as clearly as before. The problem now was how far the area of rain extended; if it was part of an electrical storm; and — if it was raining in Santo Tomé — what the rain would do to the dirt landing strip.

He leaned forward and looked out and upward through the cockpit window, then confirmed what he suspected by banking steeply and looking out the window by his side.

The three-quarter moon, which had been clearly visible from the time they took off, was no longer clear. They were entering some kind of soup, perhaps even bad weather. He was flying in the clear above clouds at 4,000 or 5,000 feet, and below a layer of clouds at maybe 15,000 feet.

The glow that had to be São Luis Gonzaga appeared again, faintly.

I have two options. I can stay on this course, dropping down to see if I can get under that cloud layer at 5,000, and follow the road — turning onto it — from São Luis Gonzago to São Borja. But to do that, I need the headlights on the road. If I can't see them, I won't know where the hell I am.

Or I can continue on this course, fly past São Luis Gonzaga, and try to find the Río Uruguay. If I can find the river, I can drop down to 500 feet and fly down the river until I hit São Borja and Santo Tomé. And if I get lucky, and there is, say, 1,500-feet visibility under the cloud layer, I can probably find that glow of their lights and just steer toward it until it breaks in two. The glow on the right will be Santo Tomé.

The decision was made for him. As he dropped down, visibility worsened and the glow of São Luis Gonzaga vanished.

Rain began to beat against the cockpit windshield.

There was nothing to do but lose more altitude and pray that the clouds he was flying through were not rock-filled. The needle crept past 5,000 feet to 4,000 to 3,500.

A quick glance at the Hamilton confirmed his

suspicion that by now he had flown past São Luis Gonzaga without seeing it.

He did not to have to remind himself that he was 3,500 feet above sea level, which was not the same thing as 3,500 feet above the ground; a chilling experience in the Hawaiian Islands — a pineapple plantation on Maui had suddenly appeared out of the soup fifty feet below him with his altimeter indicating 2,500 feet — had burned that detail of aviation lore permanently in his brain.

According to Delgano, the field in Santo Tomé was 950 feet above sea level. Call it a thousand. He was actually 2,500 feet above the ground.

Very, very slowly, he lost more altitude, until the altimeter indicated 2,500 feet. It was now getting turbulent, and, if anything, darker.

And then the cloud cover above him opened for a moment, and the light from the moon provided just a little more visibility. For a moment he could make out a light on the ground.

There was nothing to do but see what it was.

I will not go lower than a thousand feet! If I can't get through this, I'll just do a one-eighty and head back for Pôrto Alegre.

With the altimeter indicating a little less than 2,000 feet, the light he was approaching became clearer and then divided into two lights: red and green.

Navigation lights.

A boat! Or a ship!

It didn't matter. If it was a boat or a ship, it has to be the river!

What he could not afford to do was lose those navigation lights. He dropped lower.

There was no longer any reason to look at the altimeter. Altimeters worked on atmospheric pressure, and there was a built-in dampening system. The altitude indicated on the dial was the altitude the aircraft had held two, three seconds — he had heard as many as seven seconds — before.

He could now make out the outline of the vessel he was approaching. It was a freighter, a vessel capable of sailing the high seas. He flashed over it no more than 200 feet over its masts.

"I think you probably scared hell out of whoever was steering that," Ashton said dryly.

Clete considered that.

Hell, yes, he had scared whoever was at the wheel of the freighter. He had turned off his navigation lights as soon as he broke ground at Pôrto Alegre. The people on the ship certainly heard his engines, but they couldn't see anything, and it is virtually impossible to determine the direction of an airplane at night by the sound of its engines.

And then, all of a sudden, this great big sonofabitch with 2,400 unmuffled horsepower roars overhead at 220 knots.

"Serves him right," Clete said idiotically, and then started to chuckle, then giggle.

"I'm glad that someone finds this situation amusing," Ashton said, and for some reason Clete found that hilarious too.

He was laughing uncontrollably.

One part of his brain told him that what was happening wasn't at all funny, that he was experiencing a nerve overload. But that was not enough to make him stop laughing. His eyes started to water.

He lost vision, and that frightened him, and as suddenly as it had begun — the instant he pulled back on the wheel to pick up altitude — the hysterical laughter stopped.

And in that moment he saw a glow ahead. First it was a single, wide glow, and then, a moment later, it separated into two separate glows.

"We'll be landing in just a few minutes, ladies and gentlemen," Clete said. "Please put your seats in the upright position and check your seat belts."

"That's Santo Tomé?" Ashton asked.

"I think so."

"You are an amazing man, mi Mayor!"

"Tell me that again when I get us on the ground," Clete said.

He steered to the right of the glow on the right, and two minutes later saw a small, very bright glow.

"I think that's the outer marker," he said. "The bonfire."

He leveled off at an indicated altitude of 2,000 feet and flew directly over the fire. He punched the button on his Hamilton and watched as the sweep second hand made its way around the dial. When the smaller dial showed that he had flown four minutes, he made a one-minute, 180-degree turn.

He could now see a faint line of small glowing spots stretched off at right angles to the wooden bonfire. He turned and carefully lined up with the "runway." He flipped on the LANDING LIGHT switch, retarded the throttles, and lowered the flaps to twenty degrees.

Where the hell is the little fire that's supposed to tell me where the wind is?

There it is! I'm flying into the wind!

This final approach looks perfect.

That's probably wishful thinking.

What I should do is fly around again and make sure I know what I'm doing.

But on the other hand, I'm not likely to make another accidentally perfect approach like this one if I do.

He reached up to the quadrant and pulled down the lever with the representation of a wheel on it.

He felt the additional drag immediately.

The green GEAR DOWN AND LOCKED indicator light did not go on.

Christ, I'm going to have *to go around!*

I got this far, and now the gear's going to give me trouble?

The green GEAR DOWN AND LOCKED indicator light came on as he flashed over the bonfire, his hand preparing to shove the throttles forward.

He took his hand off the throttles and put it on the wheel.

The wheels touched, and bounced him back into the air.

He flared again, and this time the wheels stayed on the ground.

He applied the brakes and felt the Lockheed start to skid.

He corrected, but not before he had left the "runway." Both lines of pots filled with gasoline burning in sand were to his left.

The rumble from the landing gear was frightening.

He tried the brakes again. They seemed to work for a moment, and then the Lockheed started to skid again.

He looked at the airspeed indicator. As he watched, the needle dropped abruptly to zero.

That doesn't mean we've stopped; it means we're going less than forty miles an hour.

He pushed on the brakes again, and this time they worked.

The Lockheed lurched to a stop, at the last moment turning slightly to the left.

"I'll be damned!" Captain Maxwell Ashton III said.

"Oh, ye of little faith!" Clete said, and started to shut the engines down.

"What this means, you understand, mi Mayor," Ashton said, "and I will *never* forgive you for this, is that I can never again make a long-shot bet. I have used up my lifetime's allocation of long-shot luck in the last two hours."

Clete felt a sudden chill.

He put his hand on his chest and found that he was sweat-soaked. And then his hands and knees began to tremble uncontrollably.

You're a brave and intrepid Marine Aviator? Bull-shit!

"What happens now?" Ashton asked.

"I'm afraid to get up," Clete said. "There is a strong possibility that I have pissed — or worse — my pants."

He became aware that he had not turned off either the landing lights or the main buss. As he reached for the switch he saw a dozen or more horsemen, in rain-slick ponchos, approaching the airplane from the right.

He turned off the main buss, unstrapped himself, and left his chair.

"Wait here a minute," he said. "The people who expect me here do not expect you, and I'll have to come up with some sort of explanation."

When he opened the cabin door, he saw Capitán Delgano walking up to the plane. He was hatless, his hair plastered to his head by the rain, and wearing a poncho.

"I had just told Coronel Porterman that you probably couldn't fly through this," Delgano said,

680

gesturing toward the sky.

"Well, I made it," Clete said.

"This is not a Beechcraft C-45," Delgano said.

"This is a Lockheed C-56," Clete said. "Something got screwed up."

"I see," Delgano said, visibly displeased.

"I have passengers aboard," Clete said.

"Passengers?" Delgano parroted.

"People I am going to fly to Estancia San Pedro y San Pablo," Clete said.

"You said nothing about passengers!"

"No, I didn't."

"You smuggled people into Argentina?" Delgano asked, but it was an accusation, not a question. "An OSS team, no doubt?"

"I have five civilians with Brazilian passports aboard," Clete said.

"I consider that a breach of our agreement," Delgano said. "They will, of course, have to be interned."

"If you intern them," Clete said, "this airplane will not leave the ground again."

"Colonel Martín told me you were dangerous, and that I should not trust you," Delgano said, and then, as if he had just made up his mind, added: "I will intern them."

"The presence of my passengers in no way changes our arrangement. I will teach you how to fly the aircraft . . ."

That's bullshit. That would really be a case of the blind leading the blind.

". . . and make it available to the G.O.U. as I promised."

That's bullshit too. There's no way he could fly this airplane by himself. If the G.O.U. wants this airplane, I'll have to fly it.

"Nevertheless, your 'passengers' will have to be interned," Delgano said. "Or if not interned, sent back across the Río Uruguay. That would be probably be best, for all concerned."

"I think you're overstepping your authority, Capitán. I don't think you have the authority to do anything that will keep this airplane from flying to Estancia San Pedro y San Pablo tomorrow."

Delgano considered that.

"What am I to tell Coronel Porterman?" he asked.

Clete decided Delgano was thinking out loud.

"I suggest you tell him that there has been an unexpected development," Clete said. "That it will be necessary to quarter five people overnight — for reasons that are none of his business."

"You are asking me to lie to a superior officer, Mayor Frade. That is dishonorable."

"How would you categorize your behavior toward my father, Capitán? And what was it you said to me, at Estancia San Pedro y San Pablo, about 'people in our profession being sometimes required to do things that are personally repugnant'?"

Delgano met Clete's eyes. There was cold anger, even hate, in them.

Christ, we got this far, and now this self-righteous sonofabitch is going to screw everything up.

Delgano turned and walked away from the aircraft without saying anything.

So what do I do now?

I can't really refuse to fly this thing to Estancia San Pedro y San Pablo; I gave Martín my word that I would. And if this goddamned coup d'état fails, I don't want Martín and Rawson and Ramírez and the rest of them stood up against a wall because I didn't provide them a means to get out of the country.

682

Delgano said, "send them back across the Río Uruguay." If that happens, it wouldn't be the end of the world. If I can get the radar sent back with them, we wouldn't be any worse off than we were yesterday.

Clete saw Delgano, faintly, standing beside a man on a horse.

That's probably Coronel Porterman.

Delgano walked back to the Lockheed.

"Your 'passengers' will take the horses of the guard detail," Delgano said, "and be accommodated overnight in the transient officers' quarters."

"I'm not sure my passengers know how to ride," Clete thought aloud.

"Excuse me?" Delgano asked, somewhat incredulously.

"Just a moment, Capitán," Clete said, and turned to walk back up the aisle to talk to Ashton.

He immediately bumped into him; he had come down the aisle to see what was going on.

"I've never been on a horse in my life," Ashton said in English.

"You heard all that?" Clete asked.

Ashton nodded.

"And I'm not comfortable with them guarding our stuff," Ashton said. "So what we'll do is that I will stay aboard —"

"No," Clete said. "I don't want Coronel Porterman to get the idea we don't trust him."

"I *don't* trust him," Ashton said.

"If they want to take the radar away from us, there's nothing we can do to stop them," Clete said. "We will accept his hospitality."

"You trust the guy you were talking to?"

"Yes, I do," Clete said, hoping there was more conviction in his voice than he felt.

"OK," Ashton said. "Your call, Major."

683

Thirty minutes later, a wagon drawn by a matched pair of white-booted roans took aboard four passengers and headed through the rain toward the barracks of the Second Regiment of Cavalry.

Saddled horses had been brought from the stables along with the wagon, for Clete, Enrico, and First Lieutenant Madison R. Sawyer III, Infantry, Army of the United States, the only member of Ashton's team who said he could ride.

As they started to ride away from the Lockheed, Lieutenant Sawyer told Clete that he had "played a little polo at Ramapo Valley" while at Yale, and asked if there would possibly be a chance that he could play while he was in Argentina.

"We'll see, Lieutenant," Clete said.

He looked over his shoulder.

Four troopers of the Second Cavalry, short-barreled Mauser carbines hanging muzzle downward from their shoulders, had set up a moving perimeter guard around the tied-down Lockheed.

To one side, maybe a dozen others were squatting around a bonfire under a quickly erected tent fly. A dozen horses stood stoically in the rain, their reins tied to a rope suspended between two tree limbs jammed into the ground.

If it wasn't for the Lockheed, Clete thought, *this could be the plains of West Texas in 1890.*

[Three]

USS *Alfred Thomas DD-107*
26° 35" South Latitude
42° 45" West Longitude
0615 17 April 1943

Lieutenant Commander Paul Jernigan, a neat, thin Annapolis graduate who was six months shy of being twenty-nine years old, pushed himself out of his pedestal-mounted, leather-upholstered bridge chair — the captain's chair — and walked to the navigation room.

His ruddy-faced, Irish, twenty-three-year-old navigator, Lieutenant (j.g.) Thomas Clancy, USN, and Ensign Richard C. Lacey, USNR, a short, somewhat pudgy twenty-two-year-old, who was the communications officer of the *Thomas*, were bent over the chart.

"She appears to be picking up speed, Skipper," Clancy said. "Lacey estimates she's now making twenty-two knots."

"She" was a vessel they hoped was a Spanish-registered merchantman called the *Comerciante del Océano Pacífico*. They had been looking for her for almost four days. There had been an OP-ERATIONAL IMMEDIATE, the highest-priority communication, from the Navy Department.

TOP SECRET

OPERATIONAL IMMEDIATE

FROM CHIEF OF NAVAL OPERATIONS
WASH DC

0440 GREENWICH 13 APR 43

TO USS ALFRED THOMAS DD107

1. REFERENCE MSG 43-100-656
DATED 1 APR 43 SUBJECT LOCATION
AND IDENTIFICATION OF CERTAIN
VESSELS BELIEVED TO BE OPERATING
IN SOUTH ATLANTIC OCEAN.

2. PRIORITY OF SEARCH SHOULD BE
DIRECTED TO LOCATION AND POSITIVE
REPEAT POSITIVE IDENTIFICATION OF
SPANISH REGISTERED COMERCIANTE
DEL OCEANO PACIFICO. SUBJECT VES-
SEL DESCRIBED IN DETAIL IN REFER-
ENCE ABOVE AND IS LISTED WITH
PHOTOGRAPH ON PAGE 123 IN 1938
JANES MERCHANT SHIPS OF THE WORLD.

3. SUBJECT VESSEL BELIEVED BOUND
FOR RIVER PLATE ESTUARY AND WAS
LAST REPORTED 1300 GREENWICH 8 APR
43 AT 8 DEGREES 33 MINUTES NORTH
LATITUDE 26 DEGREES 55 MINUTES
WEST LONGITUDE.

4. ON DETERMINING LOCATION CHIEF
OF NAVAL OPERATIONS WILL BE AD-

VISED PRIORITY OPERATIONAL IMMEDI-
ATE TOGETHER WITH YOUR ESTIMATED TIME
OF ARRIVAL MOUTH OF RIVER PLATE.

5. ALFRED THOMAS WILL NOT REPEAT
NOT BOARD SUBJECT VESSEL OR CON-
DUCT ANY ACTIVITY IN HER REGARD
WHICH MIGHT POSSIBLY BE CONSTRUED
AS VIOLATION OF RULES OF SEA WAR-
FARE IN RE PASSAGE OF NON-COMBAT-
ANT VESSELS BETWEEN NEUTRAL PORTS.

6. ON LOCATION OF SUBJECT VES-
SEL, ALFRED THOMAS WILL MAINTAIN
CONTACT WITH SUBJECT VESSEL UNTIL
FURTHER ORDERS AND WILL FURNISH
POSITION EVERY FOUR (4) HOURS UN-
LESS THERE IS A CHANGE OF HER
COURSE SUGGESTING A CHANGE OF DES-
TINATION.

BY DIRECTION OF THE CHIEF OF NAVAL
OPERATIONS QUIMMER VICE ADMIRAL

The chart over which Clancy and Lacey were
bent traced the course of seven merchantmen they
— and probably every other U.S. Navy vessel operating in the South Atlantic — had been directed
to "monitor."

Skippers of other U.S. Navy men-of-war were
almost certainly wondering what the hell was
going on, and one did not radio the Chief of
Naval Operations to ask for the reason behind
an order.

But Captain Jernigan was sure he knew exactly
what was going on — although he had not been

officially told. He thought the *Alfred Thomas* had been selected from among the other ships on station, not so much because of its location, but rather because the Chief of Naval Operations knew that he would correctly guess what was going on.

The *Alfred Thomas* had been involved in the sinking of the *Reine de la Mer* in Samborombón Bay. A torpedo from the U.S. submarine *Devilfish* had actually sunk the ship, but *Devilfish* could not have gotten into position to fire her torpedo without the assistance of the *Alfred Thomas*.

When they received the first message to "monitor" the seven merchantmen, Jernigan immediately decided that Naval Intelligence — or maybe the OSS — had determined that the Germans were sending a replacement, which they could be expected to do, but were unable to determine which of the seven it was.

And obviously, at least to Captain Jernigan of the *Alfred Thomas*, ONI and/or the OSS now thought the *Comerciante del Océano Pacífico* was probably the ship they were looking for. *Probably* was the operative word. If they were more certain, they would have ordered the *Alfred Thomas* to board the *Océano Pacífico* or, possibly, even to sink her.

When the second message came, Clancy, at Jernigan's orders, set up a sweeping course that would possibly allow them to intercept her — presuming the *Océano Pacífico* maintained her last known course.

Lookouts were ordered aloft around the clock, and of course there was the radar, which was supposed to have a range of fifty miles, and which Captain Jernigan trusted as profoundly as he trusted gentlemen in two-tone shoes and gold bracelets who operated businesses called "Honest Albert's Hardly Used Automobiles."

After days of fruitless search, Jernigan had just about decided that the search course Clancy set was the wrong one — his fault, not Clancy's; he gave the order to follow it — when, to his genuine surprise, two hours after nightfall the day before, the radar operator reported a "target" thirty miles away, on a heading that would ultimately lead to the River Plate estuary.

Jernigan ordered Clancy to set up an interception course that would place them eight miles off the unknown vessel, on a parallel course.

That was just close enough for the lookout to report bright lights on the horizon. Bright lights suggested a neutral vessel — they sailed with flood-lights lighting huge national flags painted on their hulls — but there was no way to further identify her without moving closer, and Jernigan was unwilling to do that at night. The *Alfred Thomas* took up a parallel course ten miles to starboard.

Jernigan then went to bed, in the belief that he should be well-rested when it came time to make decisions in the morning. After at least thirty minutes in his bunk, he realized that falling asleep in these circumstances fell in the category of wishful thinking. He showered and returned to the bridge.

It was now daylight. The vessel, whoever it was, was not visible to the lookouts, but still presented a good target to the radar.

Jernigan realized that it was of course likely that if it was the *Océano Pacífico*, she would also be equipped with radio direction and ranging apparatus, and know that there was a ship just a few miles away.

It was also likely that if it was the *Océano Pacífico*,

she was armed. Putting a submarine-replenishment vessel into position in Samborombón Bay was of critical importance to German submarine operations in the South Atlantic.

With the naval cannon that could be placed aboard a merchantman, the *Alfred Thomas* of course would have the advantage. Unless, of course, the captain of the other vessel decided to take a long shot and opened up without warning with everything he had.

Jernigan glanced at his watch.

The crew had been fed.

"Set a course which will bring us within visual range, Mr. Clancy," he ordered. "How long would you estimate that would take?"

"Presuming they can't run any faster than the twenty-two knots she's now making, Sir, I would estimate fifteen minutes."

"In ten minutes, order Battle Stations," Captain Jernigan ordered. "I'm going to go have my breakfast."

"Aye, aye, Sir."

He did not, in fact, have any breakfast. He instead moved his bowels, and returned to the bridge.

Exactly ten minutes had elapsed. As he stepped onto the bridge, and Mr. Lacey bellowed "Captain is on the bridge" much more loudly than was necessary, Mr. Clancy pressed the microphone switch and bellowed, "Battle Stations, Battle Stations, this is no drill."

Three minutes later, the lookout aloft reported a vessel dead ahead on the horizon. Thirty seconds after that, Jernigan saw the stack of a merchantman.

"All ahead full," he ordered softly. "Make turns for flank speed."

"All ahead full, make turns for flank speed, aye," the talker repeated.

"Charge all weapons," Jernigan ordered.

"Charge all weapons, aye."

"Mr. Clancy, we will pass to starboard."

"Pass to starboard, aye, aye, Sir."

"I want to read her stern board," Jernigan said. "Run right up her ass until I can see it."

"Right up her ass, aye, aye, Sir."

```
OPERATIONAL IMMEDIATE
FROM ALFRED THOMAS DD107
0150 GREENWICH 17 APR 43

TO CHIEF OF NAVAL OPERATIONS
WASHDC

ALL RECEIVING USN VESSELS AND
SHORE STATIONS TO RELAY

  1. MOTOR VESSEL COMERCIANTE DEL
OCEANO PACIFICO LOCATED AND POSI-
TIVELY REPEAT POSITIVELY IDENTI-
FIED AT 0145 GREENWICH 17 APR 43
POSITION 27 DEGREES 25 MINUTES
SOUTH LATITUDE 43 DEGREES 05 MIN-
UTES WEST LONGITUDE.

  2. SUBJECT VESSEL MAKING 22 RE-
PEAT 22 KNOTS ON COURSE 195 REPEAT
195 TRUE. BASED ON FOREGOING, ES-
TIMATED ARRIVAL MOUTH RIVER PLATE
2150 19 APR 43.

  3. ON APPROACH OF THIS VESSEL
SUBJECT VESSEL UNCOVERED FOUR NA-
```

```
VAL CANNON BELIEVED TO BE 5-INCH
OR EQUIVALENT, FOUR MULTIPLE BAR-
REL AUTOMATIC CANNON BELIEVED TO
BE 20 OR 30 MM BOFORS, PLUS SIX
MACHINE GUNS OF UNDETERMINED
CALIBER.

    4. NO REPEAT NO FIRE OF ANY KIND
WAS EXCHANGED AND NO REPEAT NO
CONTACT OF ANY KIND WAS ATTEMPTED
OR MADE BY EITHER VESSEL.

    5. USS ALFRED THOMAS PROCEEDING
IN COMPLIANCE WITH ORDERS.

JERNIGAN, LTCOM USN, COMMANDING.
```

[Four]

**Second Cavalry Regiment Reservation
Santo Tomé
Corrientes Province, Argentina
0700 17 April 1943**

The rain had continued through the night. It was still raining when Capitán Delgano came into the transient officers' quarters to take everybody to breakfast.

Delgano tugged at Clete's sleeve as they walked down a gravel path to the officers' mess. Clete slowed and let the others get ahead of them.

"There's a small problem," Delgano announced.

"The truck with the fuel got stuck on the way to the airstrip. They're transferring the fuel barrels to a wagon."

The first thing Clete thought was that if the ground was so rain-soaked that the truck had gotten stuck, the airstrip itself would also be too soft for takeoff.

But then some Guadalcanal-learned expertise popped into his mind. That wasn't necessarily so. You got mud where there was nothing but dirt, and where the dirt had been chewed up by tires. Before they got all the pierced-steel planking laid at Fighter One on Guadalcanal, he had often taken off from the dirt runway, after heavy rains that had made the roads to Fighter One just about impassable.

Where there was grass, often there was not mud. The airstrip here had not been used, except to graze cattle. The strip itself might be all right.

One criterion to judge by would be how far the Lockheed's wheels had sunk into the ground overnight. It was to be expected that they would sink in some — there was 18,000 pounds resting on maybe two square feet of tire surface — but sometimes that didn't prohibit taxiing and takeoff.

A Wildcat could often be rocked out of tire ruts using the engine alone, or helped by people pushing. But you could *feel* a Wildcat and operate the throttle accordingly. The Lockheed was too heavy to feel, and probably would be difficult to push.

He had a quick mental image of a team of horses pulling the Lockheed out of tire ruts with a rope tied to the gear.

And then he had another thought. The Lockheed no longer weighed 18,000 pounds. It weighed 18,000 pounds less the weight of the fuel consumed between Pôrto Alegre and Santo Tomé, and while he hadn't done what a good pilot should have done — checked to see how much fuel remained — he figured he had burned at least a thousand pounds of AvGas, and possibly more. Maybe even two thousand pounds.

If they topped off the tanks here, that would mean adding that weight back, which very well might spell the difference between sinking into the ground and being able to taxi and take off.

He could also considerably lighten the aircraft by off-loading the ton of radar equipment and not taking anyone with them. That would get the aircraft into the air and to Estancia San Pedro y San Pablo, where it was needed, at the price of worrying how to get Ashton, his team, and the radar to the shore of Samborombón Bay.

"Don't start fueling it until I have a look at it," Clete said.

"We are pressed for time," Delgano said.

"Getting that airplane, fully loaded, off of here may be difficult. Hold off on topping off the tanks," Clete ordered firmly, as another problem entered his mind.

Delgano nodded, agreeing with the takeoff problem.

"And we're probably going to need more runway than I thought we'd need for the C-45," Clete went on. "Which means we have to walk some more to make sure there's nothing out there we'll run into."

"We have to get that airplane to Buenos Aires Province as soon as possible," Delgano said.

"If I can't get it off the ground here, it'll never get to Buenos Aires Province," Clete said. "The lighter it is, the better a chance I have."

Delgano nodded again.

They were now at the door to the officers' mess.

"I'll be in in a minute," Clete called to Ashton, then turned to Delgano: "I'd try to get it off with the fuel aboard, but I know I don't have enough to make Estancia San Pedro y San Pablo. What I'm thinking is going from here to a regular airfield, and taking on fuel there."

"That would call attention to us," Delgano argued.

"The safest thing to do would be to unload my cargo here, leave my passengers here, and you and I take off alone, with the fuel now on board, and refuel somewhere between here and Buenos Aires."

Delgano nodded. "What's your cargo?"

"I don't think you want to know," Clete said.

"Explosives?"

"I don't think you want to know," Clete repeated.

"I think I should know," Delgano said.

"Are you familiar with radar?" Clete asked.

"I know what it is, of course. A radar? What are you going to do with a radar?"

"Guess," Clete said.

"My best information — el Coronel Martín's best information —" Delgano said without missing a beat, "is that there is no German replenishment vessel in Samborombón Bay."

"That was yesterday," Clete said. "If I left my cargo and my passengers here, could you arrange transportation for them and guarantee their safe arrival at Estancia San Pedro y San Pablo?"

"No," Delgano said after some thought. "I could get a truck, but there would be at least a dozen checkpoints on the highway between here and there. Authorization from Colonel Porterman — a shipping manifest — might get them past the Army checkpoints, but not those of either the Policía Federal or the Provincial Police. They would want to check the cargo against the manifest. The only way I could ensure getting through them would be to be there and I have to be with the airplane."

Clete grunted thoughtfully.

"They could stay here until after . . ." Delgano suggested.

"And if the coup d'état fails, then what happens to them?" Clete didn't wait for a reply. "I'm not going to leave them here. That brings us back to two choices: taking off with them aboard, which I'm not at all sure I can do, or leaving them here, to make it by road to some airfield near here where I can get 110–130-octane aviation gasoline."

"Posadas," Delgano said immediately. "It's 130 kilometers from here; two hours, maybe a little less, by truck."

"Long-enough runways? Capable of handling the Lockheed?"

Delgano nodded.

"OK. Posadas it is. Let's get some breakfast."

If the fuel gauges were to be trusted — and Clete had learned from painful experience that this was something wise birdmen did not do — there was just barely enough fuel remaining aboard to get them to Estancia San Pedro y San Pablo.

That was not good news; he would have been happier if the tanks had contained just enough AvGas to get them to Posadas. The Lockheed would have been that much lighter.

He briefly considered pumping gas out of the tanks. That was obviously not practical. It would have been time-consuming in itself. And, since there were no empty barrels at the landing field to

696

pump it into, they would have had to wait until empty barrels could be brought from the barracks out to the strip.

A second truck sent from the barracks to take aboard the radar had made it out to the Lockheed without trouble. By driving across the grass of the pampas, Clete noted somewhat smugly, and staying off the muddy road.

He was almost through giving Capitán Delgano enough of a cockpit checkout to enable him to work the landing gear and flaps controls on orders, and to operate the radio direction finding system, when Captain Maxwell Ashton III came up to the cockpit.

"The radar's on the truck," he announced. "But just between you and me, mi Mayor, I'm more than a little nervous to see my radar going off by itself."

"There will be no awkward questions asked at checkpoints of five happy Brazilian civilians in a civilian car," Clete said. "There would be if you guys were on an Army truck."

"OK," Ashton said. "Good luck!"

"If I can't get this thing out of here, you're on your own," Clete said. "I'm sorry about that."

"Yeah, well, let's see what happens," Ashton said.

He touched Clete's shoulder, then turned and left the cockpit.

Clete looked around the cockpit a moment, then got up and walked through the cabin to make sure the door was closed properly. When he returned to the cockpit, had strapped himself in, and looked out the window, he saw that the thorough Capitán Delgano had arranged for a fire extinguisher to be present against the possibility of fire when the engines were started.

It was not, however, the latest thing in aviation-safety technology. It looked as if it belonged in a museum. It was a wagon-mounted water tank, with a pump manned by four cavalry troopers. Presumably, if there was a fire, and the four of them pumped with sufficient enthusiasm, a stream of water could be directed at it.

But since water does not extinguish oil or gasoline fires with any efficiency, all it was likely to do was float burning oil and/or AvGas out of the engine nacelle over the wing and onto the ground.

Clete threw the master buss switch and yelled "Clear!" out the window.

The four cavalry troopers, startled, took up their positions at the pump handles.

Clete set the throttles, checked the fuel switch, and reached for the LEFT ENGINE START switch.

The left engine started, smoothed down, and he started the right engine.

He looked at Delgano, who smiled, and crossed himself.

Clete took off the brakes and nudged the left throttle forward. The Lockheed shuddered, and then the left wheel came out of the depression it had made during the night. Clete advanced the right throttle, and the right wheel came out.

He straightened the Lockheed out, then taxied back between the clay pots marking the runway, and then down it as far as he could to where he decided the downward slope of the "runway" was going to be too much to handle.

He turned the plane around, and saw that the wheels had left ruts six inches deep.

"Here we go," he announced matter-of-factly, and moved the throttles to TAKEOFF power.

The Lockheed shuddered, and for a moment

seemed to refuse to move.

Then it began to move.

It picked up speed very slowly, and then suddenly more quickly. Life came into the controls. He pushed the wheel forward a hair to get the tail wheel off the ground, then held it level until he felt it get light on the wheels. He edged the control back, and a moment later the rumbling of the gear stopped.

"Gear up!" he ordered.

Thirty seconds later, as he banked to the left, setting up a course for Posadas, he glanced at Delgano.

"This is a fine airplane!" Delgano said.

"I don't know about you, Capitán," Clete said, "but I always have more trouble landing one of these things than I do getting one off."

"I have faith in you, mi Mayor," Delgano said. "For the very best of reasons."

"Which are?"

"Because you are in here with me."

XXI

[One]

Posadas Airfield
Posadas, Missiones Province, Argentina
0930 18 April 1943

It was a twenty-five-minute flight from Santo Tomé to Posados, which turned out to be a recently and extensively expanded airfield shared by Aerolíneas Argentina and the Air Service of the Argentine Army.

Clete managed to put the Lockheed down on the field's new, wide concrete runways without difficulty. A pickup truck flying a checkered flag met them at the taxiway turnoff and led them to a new hangar, where a dozen soldiers of the Air Service, Argentine Army, were waiting to push the Lockheed into a hangar.

The aircraft normally parked in the hangar — a half-dozen Seversky P-35 fighter planes — were parked outside. Clete stared at them with fascination. In high school, he made a tissue-covered balsa wood model of the fighter. He was so fond of it that he was never able to find the courage to wind up its rubber band and see if it would fly.

When Clete was in high school, the Seversky was about the hottest thing in the sky. Dreaming of one day flying it, Clete could still remember its capabilities: It had a Pratt & Whitney 950-horsepower engine, which gave it a 280-m.p.h. top speed; and it was armed with two .30-caliber machine guns firing through the propeller and could carry three 100-pound bombs, one under each wing and the third under the fuselage.

The F4F-4 Wildcat Clete flew on Guadalcanal had six .50-caliber machine guns, and was powered by a 1,200-horsepower Pratt & Whitney engine, which gave it a 320-knot top speed. The F4U Corsair, which was already in the Pacific to replace the Wildcat, had a 2,000-horsepower Pratt & Whitney engine, a top speed of 425 knots, and in addition to its six .50-caliber machine guns could carry a ton of bombs.

Clete had never seen a P-35 before. It was obsolete long before Clete went to Pensacola for basic flight training. There was something very unreal about seeing them parked here, obviously ready for action.

If the Brazilians decided to bomb Argentina with the B-24s I saw parked at Pôrto Alegre, and the Argentines sent up these P-35s to attack them, it would be a slaughter. The multiple .50s in the B-24s' turrets would be able to knock the P-35s out of the sky long before the P-35s got into firing range of their .30-caliber guns.

Why am I surprised? They're still practicing how to swing sabers from the backs of horses in Santo Tomé.

The Lockheed was equally fascinating to the Argentine pilots standing by their Severskys. To judge from the looks on their faces, they had never seen a Lockheed Lodestar before.

As soon as the Lockheed was inside the hangar, the doors were closed. Clete and Delgano walked through the cabin, opened the door, and found a major and a captain waiting for them.

They were introduced to Clete as the commanding officer and the executive officer of the Fourth Pursuit Squadron, but no names were provided by Delgano. He referred to Clete as "Major," without a last name.

It was obvious that the Major and the Captain were participants in OUTLINE BLUE, and that they were not only nervous about having the Lockheed at their field but deeply curious to get a better look at it.

Delgano, sensing that, suggested to Clete that he show them around the airplane. While they were in the cockpit, the hangar door opened wide enough to permit a hose from a fuel truck to be snaked inside, and the tanks were topped off.

The curious pilots and ground crewmen outside the hangar were not permitted inside.

By the time Ashton's team arrived at Posadas — crammed into the same 1939 Ford Clete used to find Ashton in the Automobile Club Hotel — Clete was able to receive a somewhat rudimentary weather briefing and, with Delgano watching over his shoulder, to lay out the flight plan.

The truck with the radar arrived ten minutes after Ashton and his men. The crates were loaded aboard, and then the passengers.

The Major and the Captain shook hands rather solemnly with Clete and Delgano, and then the hangar doors were opened again. Ground crewmen pushed the Lockheed back out onto the tarmac. Two men with a bona fide aircraft fire extinguisher on wheels appeared. Three minutes after Clete started the engines, he lifted the Lockheed off the runway and set course for Estancia San Pedro y San Pablo.

[Two]

Once he found the cluster of buildings around the Big House on Estancia San Pedro y San Pablo, Clete dropped close to the ground and went looking for the radio station. He wanted to see if he could find it — if he could find it from the air, then somebody else also could — and to let Ettinger, the Chief, and Tony, if he was there, know he had returned.

He had a good idea where the station was in relation to the Big House, but still had a hard time finding it. When he did, pleasing him, he could see nothing that would identify it from the air as a radio station. The three reddish sandstone buildings visible in the clearing were essentially identical to other buildings in other stands of trees all over the estancia. Such buildings were used as housing and for any number of other purposes in connection with the operation of the ranch.

He was, in fact, not entirely sure he had found the right buildings until, on his third pass over the clearing, a gaucho he recognized as Schultz came out of one of them and gazed up with curiosity.

Clete dipped his wings and turned toward the landing strip at the Big House.

Clete was not very concerned about putting the Lockheed onto the estancia strip. When he'd flown the stagger-wing into it he had more than enough runway, and he had enough experience with the Lockheed to have a feel for its landing characteristics.

703

But, as he took deeply to heart the saying that a smugly confident pilot is the one who is about to badly bend his airplane, he set up his approach very carefully. He came in low and slow and greased the Lockheed onto the strip within twenty feet of the whitewashed line of rocks that marked the end of the runway. He had a good thousand feet of it left when he brought the Lockheed down to taxi speed.

"Nice landing," Delgano said.

"Thank you," Clete said. "This thing isn't as hard to fly as I thought at first."

Clete turned the Lockheed off the runway and taxied toward the hangar.

I wonder if we can get this great big sonofabitch in that little hangar?

Because Second Lieutenant Cletus H. Frade, USMCR, of VMF-221 had received a truly magnificent ass-chewing on Henderson Field on Guadalcanal for using too much of his Wildcat engine's power in similar circumstances, he now remembered to use the Lockheed's engines very carefully to turn the airplane around so that it pointed away from the hangar without flipping over one or more of the Piper Cubs parked near it.

That done, he started to shut it down. This time he checked the gauges for remaining fuel. He still had enough aboard, he quickly calculated, to make it back and forth to Montevideo, and probably enough to make it one-way to Pôrto Alegre.

He unfastened his harness and started to slide out of his seat.

Delgano stopped him by laying a hand on top of his.

"We must talk," Delgano said.

"Oh? About what?"

704

"If you succeeded in bringing the airplane across the border to Santo Tomé, my orders were to take it directly from Santo Tomé to Campo de Mayo."

"OK," Clete said. "And my having my passengers screwed that up?"

"That and the fact that it is not the C-45 light twin you told us it would be. I thought I would be able to fly the C-45 alone."

"Alone?" Clete asked, not quite understanding what Delgano was talking about.

"You were to become a guest of Colonel Porterman at Santo Tomé for the next four or five days," Delgano said.

"You . . . forgot . . . to mention that."

"Coronel Martín spoke with General Rawson," Delgano said. "Coronel Martín believed that if you flew any airplane into Campo de Mayo, that would have put you in a delicate position — actually, I suppose, a more accurate term would be 'dangerous position.'"

"How so?"

"You would have played an active part in the revolution," Delgano said. "If OUTLINE BLUE failed, and for some reason you could not leave the country, you would almost certainly be one of the dozen or so officers who faced the most severe consequences."

"You mean, they would shoot me?" Clete asked. "Just for loaning you an airplane?"

"For flying the airplane to Campo de Mayo, *and* because you are your father's son," Delgano said, waited long enough for that to sink in, and then went on. "Your execution by Castillo's people under such circumstances would be — is — a real possibility."

"Is?" Clete thought aloud.

"So, on General Rawson's authority, it was decided that I would 'borrow' your airplane at Santo Tomé, and leave you there. Two things, of course, made that impossible. You arrived in an airplane that I could not fly by myself, and you had your 'passengers' and their cargo with you."

"If I had known about this," Clete said, "I would have thought twice about bringing Captain Ashton and his people with me."

"Well, what is the expression? That's water under the dam. The reality I had to deal with is that you arrived at Santo Tomé with an airplane I could not fly by myself, and with your passengers and the cargo aboard."

"OK," Clete said, and waited for Delgano to go on.

"I made a decision at Santo Tomé," Delgano said, "without consulting with el Coronel Porterman, but on my own authority. Based on the facts that I had somehow to get the airplane to Campo de Mayo, that I could not do so alone, and that I could not leave your passengers and their cargo with the Second Cavalry, I decided that everybody would leave Santo Tomé and that en route I would ask you to divert to Campo de Mayo."

"Ask me?"

"Insist."

"How insist?" Clete asked, aware that he was getting angry.

Delgano shrugged, making it clear he was sure Clete knew what he was talking about.

"En route, I decided that brandishing a pistol would not only be melodramatic but probably impractical. Suboficial Mayor Rodríguez would certainly try to stop me, for one thing. In any event, I decided that attempting to take control of the airplane would be at best risky. It would also have been dishonorable on my part."

"If you asked me to divert to Campo de Mayo, I would have flown there," Clete said.

"Knowing that your 'passengers' would certainly be interned the moment we landed?"

"They weren't interned at Posadas."

"I needed you to fly the airplane out of Posadas," Delgano said. "If they appeared at Campo de Mayo, they would have been arrested."

"So now what?"

"The situation is now in your hands," Delgano said.

"In other words, you're asking if I will fly the airplane to Campo de Mayo?"

Delgano nodded.

"Aware of what I said before," Delgano said. "That doing so constitutes more than simply ferrying an airplane."

"Sure," Clete said. "I promised you the airplane. I'll deliver it. A deal's a deal, Delgano."

"Thank you. I really thought that would be your reaction. On my part, unless asked directly, I will not report that we made a passenger stop here."

"Thank you."

"I am, of course, honor bound to inform Coronel Martín. But I don't think that will be a problem for you. He already knows about your radio station, and I'm sure understands the mission of the second OSS team. If he wanted to shut you down, he could have done so before now."

Clete nodded.

"What about the people at Posadas?" Clete asked.

"I may be wrong, but I don't think they will have anything to say. They know nothing except that you and I took on fuel and some unidentified passengers at Posadas in connection with OUTLINE BLUE. They may have thought that Captain Ashton's accent was odd, but he spoke Spanish — and you speak Spanish like an Argentine — and they have no reason to suspect that any of you are norteamericanos."

"And Colonel Porterman?"

"If the airplane appears at Campo de Mayo, he will presume that any problems we faced were solved. He took my word that your passengers and their cargo do not pose any threat to Argentina. He was a friend of your father's. He wishes you no harm."

"OK, Capitán," Clete said, putting out his hand to Delgano. "We have a deal. Now let's get the aircraft unloaded, and then we'll take it to Campo de Mayo."

As Clete was walking Delgano through the preflight check of the Lockheed, Tony Pelosi arrived in the 1941 Studebaker Clete had seen at the radio station. Chief Schultz drove up fifteen minutes later at the wheel of a Model A truck.

Ettinger, Clete decided, *is probably monitoring the radio.*

Then he sensed that something was not as it should be. Neither the Chief nor Tony smiled when they came up. The reverse. They both looked uncomfortable.

"Where the hell is my brass band?" Clete asked.

"Ettinger took off," Tony blurted.

"He did what?"

"He took off."

"Took off to where?" Clete asked.

Tony looked uncomfortably at Delgano, visibly

wondering if he should continue talking in the presence of an Argentine.

"I have two men here who were supposed to keep Sergeant Ettinger on the estancia," Delgano said.

"How much does this guy know?" Tony blurted.

"He knows the Germans are trying to kill Ettinger," Clete said.

"He probably went to Uruguay," Chief Schultz said.

"What the hell for?"

"The Chief thinks it's got something to do with the message where you told Graham the name of the German in Montevideo," Tony said.

"How did he see that?" Clete asked furiously.

"That's my fault, Cle . . . Major," Tony said. "Ettinger was awake when I started to encrypt it. The Chief was asleep. Ettinger's better with that than I am. So, instead of fucking it up, or waking the Chief, I asked Ettinger if he would do it."

"Jesus H. Christ, Tony! I can't believe you were that stupid!"

"Neither can I, now," Tony said. "Anyway, the next morning, he wasn't there. He left this for you."

Tony handed him a sheet of paper, on which Ettinger had typed:

Clete:

I think I can put Bagman's name together with a couple of names I already have. If I can, we'll have just about all the pieces of the chain identified.

I hope your flight went smoothly. See you soon.

David

Clete read it, and then looked at Pelosi.

"I was going to Uruguay to look for him," Pelosi said. "But the Chief said he thought I'd better wait until you got back."

You ever hear about looking for a needle in a haystack, Tony?

Delgano suddenly made an imperious waving "come here" motion in the direction of the tree line behind a hangar. A gaucho stepped out of the trees and walked quickly toward them.

"Who's that?" Chief Schultz asked.

"I told both of you I didn't want Ettinger to leave the estancia," Clete said coldly.

Looking about as uncomfortable as Tony and the Chief, the gaucho approached Delgano and almost came to attention.

"Sí, Señor?"

"The norteamericano?"

"He left the estancia three nights ago, mi Capitán."

"We know that. Where is he?" Delgano demanded impatiently.

"He took the car ferry to Montevideo that same morning, mi Capitán."

"You had people on him all the way to the boat ferry?"

"Sí, Señor."

"And presumably the borders are being watched? We would know if he has returned?"

"Sí, Señor."

"Presumably, mi Mayor," Delgano said, "Sergeant Ettinger is in Montevideo. I did not have authority to send any of my men across the border."

"You tell me what you want me to do, Mr. Frade," the Chief said.

"I don't know what the hell to do," Clete said.

"I can be in Montevideo in the morning, if I leave now," the Chief said.

"We don't know where the hell he is in Montevideo," Clete said. "If he got that far before the Germans got to him."

"Clete, I'm sorry," Tony said.

"You goddamned well should be, Tony!"

Jumping on Tony's ass isn't going to do any good. The sonofabitch in this is Ettinger himself.

If he gets his throat cut, it's his own goddamn fault!

I don't mean that.

What the hell am I going to do?

Oh, yeah!

"Captain Ashton and his team, and the radar, are in the hangar," Clete said. "Get them and their stuff out of here. Our priority is to get that radar in place and set up."

"What do we do about Dave?" Tony asked.

"I'll deal with Dave," Clete said. "You two make yourself useful to Captain Ashton."

"Aye, aye, Sir," the Chief said.

"I'm sorry, Clete," Tony said.

"You said that," Clete said somewhat unkindly, and then turned to Delgano. "I have to make a telephone call," he said. "It won't take long."

Delgano was obviously curious, but asked no questions.

Clete called the office number, the first of the three numbers Leibermann had given him.

The man who answered the telephone did so by reciting the number called in Spanish.

"This is Cowboy," Clete said. "I need to talk to him right now."

"Can he call you back?" the man said, still speaking Spanish.

"No."

"Hold on," the man said, now in English.

A long ninety seconds later, Milton Leibermann came on the line.

"So how's things out in the country, Tex?"

"Ettinger is in Uruguay. Probably Montevideo."

"I thought he planned to stay in the country?"

"So did I. Do you have any friends in Uruguay who could be useful?"

"You're not going over there yourself?"

"I wish I could, but I can't get away."

"You wouldn't want to tell me why not?"

"You remember that party we talked about?"

"The big one? All the important people?"

"Right. I've been invited. Under the circumstances, I can't turn down the invitation."

"You will tell me all about the party, won't you, Tex? Just as soon as you can?"

"What are we doing here, making a deal?"

"You could put it that way."

"OK, Milton. Deal."

"Just for the record, Tex, I would have gone anyway," Leibermann said, and the phone went dead.

[Three]

The pilot of the Douglas R5-D took his microphone from its cradle on the control yoke, checked to see that his transmitter was set on the correct frequency, and depressed the TRANSMIT switch.

"Pôrto Alegre, Navy Seven Niner Niner Seven."

"Go ahead, Seven Niner Niner Seven."

"Niner Seven passing through seven thousand estimate twenty miles northwest your station. Approach and landing, please."

"Niner Seven, you are cleared for a straight-in approach to Runway One Seven. I say again One Seven. Ceiling and visibility unlimited. The winds are from the south at fifteen, gusting to twenty. The barometer is two niner niner. Report when passing through five thousand and when you have the field in sight."

"Niner Seven understands One Seven."

"Niner Seven, that is a Roger."

"Pôrto Allegre, please advise your base commander we have a Code Six aboard."

"Wilco, Niner Seven."

The staff car — a 1942 Chevrolet sedan — assigned to Colonel J. B. Wallace, U.S. Army Air Corps, stopped at the side of the Base Operations building. The driver, a young, crew-cutted sergeant, jumped out. He went quickly to the trunk and removed a checkered flag rolled around a length of aluminum pipe. Unrolling the flag as he walked, he went quickly to the front of the Chevrolet and inserted the pipe into a holder welded to the bumper. The purpose of the checkered flag was to increase the chances that pilots of taxiing aircraft would see the Chevrolet and not run over it.

Then he quickly slipped back behind the wheel, drove onto the tarmac in front of Base Ops, and waited for the Navy Transport that had just landed to turn off Runway One Seven and taxi to the Base Operations building.

After it did that, ground crewmen pushed a flight of stairs up to the door of the aircraft.

"Drive over there," Colonel Wallace ordered.

"Yes, Sir."

The sergeant drove to the rolling stairs, then jumped out and opened the rear door for Colonel Wallace.

Colonel Wallace tugged at the skirt of his green tunic, adjusted his leather-brimmed cap — to signify his status as an active pilot, he had removed the crown stiffener from it — tucked his riding crop under his arm, and stood near the foot of the stairs to officially greet the Code Six passenger that Naval Air Transport Command flight 404, Panama–Brazil, had reported aboard.

A Code Six was a Navy captain, or an Army (or Marine) colonel. Colonel Wallace believed that an officer who had achieved such a high rank, and was bearing the enormous responsibility that went with it, was entitled to the courtesy of being greeted by someone of equal rank when arriving at a military base. If an incoming aircraft, when asking for landing permission, did not volunteer the information that they did — or did not — have colonels or general (or flag) officers aboard, the Pôrto Alegre tower was instructed to inquire.

The passenger door — within the much wider cargo door — opened, and a Marine colonel stepped out onto the landing at the head of the stairs. He immediately turned to the aircraft, and someone inside handed him two leather suitcases.

"Take care of the Colonel's luggage," Wallace ordered, and his driver went quickly up the stairs, saluted, took the suitcases, and motioned for the Colonel to descend the stairs.

Wallace stepped to the foot of the stairs, removed his riding crop from under his left arm, and touched the brim of his cap with it.

"Welcome to Pôrto Alegre," he said with a smile.

The Marine colonel returned the salute. He wore, as Marines did — Wallace thought it was a fine idea — the silver eagles denoting his rank both on the epaulets of his tunic and on the points of his collar.

"Thank you," he said.

The Marine colonel was not wearing any ribbons to indicate where he had served, or what, if any, decorations for valor or outstanding performance he had earned. Colonel Wallace thought the wearing of ribbons should be mandatory, and he did not like to hear them referred to deprecatingly as fruit salad.

"I'm Colonel J. B. Wallace, commanding," Wallace announced.

"Just the man I'm looking for," the Marine said. "My name is Graham."

"How may I be of service, Colonel?"

"You can point me in the direction of the nearest head," Graham said. "And then I would like a few minutes of your time."

"I guess the Officers' Club is as close as any-place," Wallace said, gesturing toward his car. "Unless you would prefer, Colonel, to let me have you set up in the VIP quarters?"

"The Club would be fine, thank you," Graham said.

"Can I still find something to eat here?" Graham asked when he had come out of the restroom and joined Wallace at a table in the barroom.

"Of course," Wallace said, signaling to a waiter.

"All I had on the plane was a bologna sandwich and a banana," Graham said.

"Well, we'll get you something here — the beef is invariably good — and then we'll take you to my office and settle your paperwork with my adjutant. How long will you be with us, Colonel?"

"Not long," Graham said. "I don't think I'll have to get involved with your adjutant."

"Excuse me?"

Graham reached in his pocket, didn't find what he was looking for, and then searched his other pockets until he did. He handed Wallace a some-what battered envelope containing a single sheet of paper.

THE JOINT CHIEFS OF STAFF
THE PENTAGON
WASHINGTON, D.C.

1 January 1943

Subject: Letter Orders
To: Colonel A.F. Graham, USMCR
    Office of Strategic Services
    Washington, D.C.

   1. You will proceed to such des-
tinations as your duties require
by U.S. Government or civilian motor, rail, sea or air transportation as is most expedient. JCS
Travel Priority AAAAAA-1 is assigned. The wearing of civilian
attire is authorized.
   2. United States Military or Naval commands are authorized and
directed to provide you with whatever assistance of any kind you
may require to accomplish your
mission(s).

By Order of The Chairman,
The Joint Chiefs of Staff:

OFFICIAL:

Matthew J. Markham

                Matthew J. Markham
          Lieutenant General, USAAC
                      J-3, JCS

"I don't think I've ever seen any orders like that," Colonel Wallace said, and then blurted: "We had some of your people in here recently, I expect you know."

"That was going to be my first question to you," Graham said, and then noticed the waiter was standing by the table. "You say the beef is good?"

"Excellent."

"I would like a steak, a New York strip, medium rare. French fried potatoes and a sliced tomato. Could I get that?"

The waiter nodded, then looked at Colonel Wallace.

"Just coffee, please," he said.

The waiter nodded and left.

"You said you 'had,' past tense, some of my people in here?" Graham asked.

"Yes, we did. A Marine Major Frade and an Army Captain Ashton, plus four men he identified to me as commissioned officers."

"Did Major Frade pick up the airplane?" Graham asked, and then interrupted himself. "Colonel, there was some confusion about the type airplane. What's the difference between a C-45 and a C-56?"

"A C-45 is what we call a 'light twin,'" Wallace explained. "The C-56 is the Lockheed Lodestar transport."

"The Lockheed Lodestar? The airliner?"

Wallace nodded.

"Major Frade . . . could fly the Lodestar?"

"He flew it out of here," Wallace said, "under somewhat unusual circumstances."

"Which were?"

"He asked permission to make some practice landings," Wallace said. "Which I of course granted. I also volunteered to accompany him — I have a good many hours in large, multiengine aircraft and believed I could impart some of my experience. He declined my offer."

"He did?"

"He then proceeded to the end of the runway," Wallace said, warming to his subject, "where he loaded aboard what I presume were the other OSS personnel, and took off. Against specific orders from the tower to abort his takeoff and return to Base Operations. He did not return. I'm afraid I have no idea where he is now, or the airplane."

"What makes you think he took aboard the other people?"

"They have not been seen since," Wallace said. "This places me in a very difficult position, Colonel, with the Brazilian authorities."

"How's that?"

"I had arranged with the appropriate authorities for them to clear the airplane through Customs, and to commence an international flight."

"Nobody told you to do that. All you were supposed to do was paint it red and paint some numbers on it. You did do that?"

"Yes, of course."

"When did Major Frade leave here?"

Colonel Wallace took his notebook from his pocket, flipped through it, and found what he was looking for.

"At 2126 hours 17 April," he said. He read further: "After ignoring *four* orders from the tower specifically ordering him to abort his takeoff and return to Base Operations."

"Just as soon as I see Major Frade, Colonel, I'll ask him why he did what you said he did."

"How would you suggest I deal with the Brazilian

authorities, Colonel? They are still waiting to clear the aircraft."

"I'll tell you what happened to that aircraft, Colonel," Graham said. "The right engine was about to fall off."

"Excuse me?"

"You tell the Brazilian authorities you discovered the right engine of that airplane was about to fall off. Faulty bolts, or something. You have ordered replacement parts from the United States. Until they arrive, obviously, the airplane isn't going anywhere. When it's ready to go, you will get in touch with them again."

"That would be the uttering of a statement I know to be false."

"Yes, it would," Graham said.

"I couldn't do that without written authority," Wallace said.

"Of course you couldn't," Graham said. "I'll be happy to give you written authority. And then I suggest you prepare a full report of the entire incident, including this conversation, and forward it directly to General Markham at the Joint Chiefs."

Colonel Wallace considered that. From the look on his face, Graham concluded that he found the suggestion satisfactory. Or almost so.

"What will I say to the Brazilians if they should ask, some time from now, whatever happened to the aircraft?"

The waiter delivered Colonel Graham's food.

Graham cut a piece of steak, chewed it appreciatively, and then replied:

"Why don't you ask General Markham what to tell the Brazilians? When you write him?"

Wallace considered that for a long moment, then nodded his head.

"I think that should do it," he said.

"I'm sure it will," Graham said.

"And how may I be of service to you, Colonel?"

"I have to get to Buenos Aires as soon as possible," Graham said. "What would you suggest?"

"The simplest way would probably be for you to go to Río de Janeiro and catch the Panagra flight. They usually have seats — people get off in Río de Janeiro, and there are few people who fly from Río to Buenos Aires."

I flew to Pôrto Alegre on the Navy transport because it was considerably faster than Panagra's sea planes. Now this idiot is suggesting I fly north to Río de Janeiro to try to get a seat on tomorrow's plane, which is the same one I didn't want to board in Miami.

"That'll take too long. Can you get me from here to Montevideo?"

"It would be difficult."

"Why?"

"It generally takes about four days — sometimes longer — to obtain permission from the Uruguayan authorities to land an American military aircraft in Uruguay."

"There's an airstrip, I have been told, in Chuí, on the Brazilian-Uruguayan border," Graham said. "From Chuí, on the other side of the border, it's only a hundred seventy-five miles to Montevideo. Can you put me in there?"

"Are you sure there's an airstrip in . . . where did you say?"

"Chuí," Graham said. "Yes, I'm sure."

"Well, if there is, it would be a small airstrip. You'd have to go in by L-4 — Piper Cub. I'll look into it. When would you like to go?"

"As soon as I finish my lunch and change into civilian clothing," Graham said.

[Four]

Visiting Officers' Quarters
First Cavalry Regiment
Campo de Mayo
Buenos Aires Province, Argentina
1515 18 April 1943

"Where are you?" Dorotéa Mallín demanded, by way of greeting, the moment she came on the line.

"Don't ask," Clete said.

"What does that mean, 'don't ask'?"

"I can't tell you, is what it means."

"What am I supposed to tell Father Matthew?"

"What?" Clete asked as his memory kicked in half a second later and identified Father Matthew as the Very Reverend Matthew Cashley-Price of the Anglican Cathedral. Provided Clete and Dorotéa underwent premarital counseling under his direction, Father Matthew was going to unite them in holy matrimony.

"Cletus, damn you, you heard what Father Matthew said. We have to have premarital counseling. He's called twice a day since you . . . since you disappeared. Where have you been? Where *are* you?"

"Honey, you just have to stall him for a couple of days."

"That's simply out of the question," Dorotéa announced with feminine imperialism. "I don't care where you are or what you're doing, you have to call Father Matthew, *right now*, apologize, and set up an appointment."

"I can't, Princess," Clete said.

Her entire tone of voice changed.

"My God, you're in some sort of trouble."

"No."

That's not the truth, the whole truth, and nothing but. But at the moment, I'm not actually in trouble.

"Yes, you are. I can tell by your voice."

"Honey, I'm not," Clete said. "Really, I'm not. But I'm . . . tied up . . ."

"Tied up how?"

". . . for the next couple of days."

"Tied up how?"

"With rope. To the bed."

"You don't really think you're funny?"

"Princess, you're just going to have to trust me."

"Why should I?"

Clete replied with the truth without thinking much about the possible ramifications of that.

"You don't have any choice, honey," he said.

Doroféa hung up on him.

He was standing with the handset in his hand, his finger holding down the switch, wondering whether it would be better to call her back or not, when he heard the door creak open.

Teniente Colonel Bernardo Martín and Capitán Roberto Lauffer came into the room. Martín was in mufti and carrying a well-worn leather briefcase, while Lauffer was not only in uniform but wearing a Sam Browne belt with a saber hanging from one side of it, an Argentine .45 automatic in a glistening molded leather holster riding high on the other side.

Enrico, who had been sitting on the windowsill, stood up and came to attention.

Lauffer waved his hand at him to stand at ease.

"If I'd known there was a telephone in here, I would have had it removed," Martín said, turning his back to Clete as he closed the door. He turned and asked: "Who were you talking to?"

Clete — just in time — bit off the "none of your goddamned business" reply that came to his lips.

For one thing, who I talk to is his business, and for another, he has enough to worry about without getting into a verbal duel with me.

"My . . . fiancée," Clete said.

"Oh. You didn't happen to tell her where you were, did you?"

"No. Nor where I've been. She was curious about that, too."

Lauffer smiled.

"What was the subject of your conversation?" Martín asked, and Clete saw a faint smile on his face too, before he added, "or is that too intimate a question for a gentleman such as myself to ask?"

"The Very Reverend Matthew Cashley-Price, of the Anglican Cathedral," Clete said, and had to smile, "is apparently greatly annoyed that I have been unable to fit him and his premarital counseling into my busy schedule. And consequently, so is the lady."

"Shame on you," Martín said, now smiling wickedly. "Before taking a serious step, like marriage, one should have all sorts of counseling. How did the conversation end?"

"She hung up on me when I said she had no choice but to trust me," Clete said.

Lauffer chuckled.

"It would appear that your charming fiancée and I have the same problem," Martín said. "We both have no choice but to trust you. As we both do, I'm sure. The question is not *if* we trust you, really, but *how far*, isn't it?"

Clete felt his temper start to simmer.

I'm here, aren't I? With the airplane?

724

"You have no reason not to trust me, Coronel," Clete said.

No longer smiling, Martín looked at him for a long moment.

"I inform you now, Mayor Frade," he announced formally, "that you are a prisoner of the armed forces of the Provisional Government of Argentina, and ask you now, Mayor Frade, if, as an officer and a gentleman, you will offer your parole to me?"

Clete's temper began to boil over.

"A prisoner? What the hell is that all about?"

"A record will be made of your arrest," Martín said. "And of the seizure by the Provisional Government of your aircraft. In the event events do not go as planned, those records will come into the possession of the Castillo government. Possibly, they may —"

"Oh, come on, Martín!" Clete interrupted. "If you can't pull OUTLINE BLUE off, and we all get arrested, Castillo's people will look at my, quote, arrest, unquote, and the, quote, seizure, unquote, of the Lockheed and see it for what it is, a transparent attempt to get me off the hook. Christ, they know damned well my father started the whole goddamned thing!"

"What are you saying?"

"I'm saying that when I landed that airplane here, I knew what I was getting myself into."

"That's what General Rawson thought you would say," Lauffer said emotionally, "as your father's son, as the great-grandson of General Pueyrredón. That you would join us!"

"Don't get carried away, Roberto," Clete said. "I'll fly the airplane, if it comes down to that, but I'm not enlisting in your army."

725

"Actually, the subject of a temporary commission did come up," Martín said. "Would you be willing —"

"I already have a Marine Corps commission," Clete said.

"This would be a temporary commission," Martín said. "It would solve a lot of problems. . . ."

"Would I have to swear an oath? Of allegiance?"

"Yes, naturally. Of course."

"The moment I did that," Clete said, "I would lose my American citizenship."

"That would be difficult for you?"

"Yeah, it would," Clete said without thinking about it. "I don't want to do that."

He happened to glance at Martín's eyes.

And saw in them that he had just closed a door that would never again be opened.

If I had accepted that temporary commission under these circumstances, where accepting it might mean that I would find myself standing in front of a wall with Rawson, Martín, and Lauffer, even if it lasted only three days, they would thereafter have accepted me as a bona fide Argentine. Now that will never happen.

Well, so be it. I'm an American. I don't want to give that up.

"That leaves you, of course," Martín said, cordially enough, "as the English would put it, as neither fish nor good red meat."

"I guess it does," Clete said.

"I'm turning you over to Capitán Lauffer," Martín said. "Until this is over, I want you to be with him. If using the airplane becomes necessary, you will receive that word from him."

"Fine with me," Clete said.

"As an officer and a gentleman, I would like you to give me your parole," Martín said.

"What kind of a parole?"

"That you will not leave Campo de Mayo, nor communicate with anyone outside Campo de Mayo, without the express permission of Capitán Lauffer or myself."

"I've already told you that I'll fly the airplane. But I will need to use the telephone. What if I give you my word I will not mention, in any way, OUTLINE BLUE?"

"I don't think you're talking about telephoning your fiancée," Martín said. "You're concerned about Sergeant Ettinger? Is that what you mean?"

Clete nodded.

"Delgano told you he took the car ferry to Montevideo?"

Clete nodded again.

"I'm sorry, Mayor," Martín said. "You will not be in any position to help Ettinger until OUTLINE BLUE has run its course. If I hear anything, I will let you know. I will require your parole."

"Or what?"

"Or I will place an armed guard at your door."

"OK," Clete said. "I won't try to leave, and I won't communicate with anyone without your permission."

"On your word of honor as an officer and a gentleman?"

"On my word of honor as an officer and a gentleman," Clete parroted.

I wonder if I mean that? What is the really honorable thing to do? Pass up an opportunity to try to keep one of my men alive? Or live up to Martín's adult version of Boy Scout's Honor?

"Suboficial Mayor Rodríguez," Martín said, turning to Enrico, "are you armed?"

Enrico looked at Clete for guidance.

"Tell him, Enrico."

"Sí, mi coronel," Enrico said, patting the small of his back to indicate that he had a pistol concealed there.

Martín picked his briefcase up from where he had set it on the floor, opened it, and produced a .45 automatic.

"I really hope you won't have occasion to need this," he said, handing it to Clete.

Then he nodded at Lauffer and left the room.

[Five]

The Embassy of the United States
of America
Montevideo, Uruguay
2205 18 April 1943

"I will take you there, Señor, of course," the taxi driver at the bus terminal said to the somewhat rumpled-looking middle-aged man, "but it is a long way, an expensive trip, and the norteamericano Embassy is not open at this hour."

"You are very kind, Señor," Colonel A. F. Graham, USMCR — *and have just earned yourself a very nice tip* — "but please take me there anyway. Someone is waiting for me."

That's the absolute opposite of the truth. If I can find Stevenson, he will be the most surprised sonofabitch in Uruguay.

The Embassy of the United States was in a stone villa, inside a tall stone-and-steel-spear fence. A brass sign was on the fence gate pillar, and a painted wooden sign announced the hours the Embassy was open for business. The gate was firmly closed with a heavy chain and a large padlock.

There was also an intercom device with a button.

Graham pushed the button. Thirty seconds later, a voice barely comprehensible through static — but obviously American — announced "Cerrado" — Closed.

Deciding that communication over that device would be impossible, Graham put his finger back on the button and held it there.

There were several more "closed" announcements over the next two minutes, and then there was a flash of light as the door of the Embassy villa opened and an indignant young man in Marine khakis appeared and shouted, "Cerrado! Cerrado!"

Graham kept his finger on the button until the Marine — a corporal — came down to the gate.

"Cerrado, Señor," he said with finality.

"Good evening, Corporal. My name is Graham. I would like to see Mr. Ralph Stevenson, who is the Cultural Attaché."

The Corporal was visibly surprised that the middle-aged man wearing rumpled clothes and badly needing a shave spoke English so well.

"Sorry. We're closed. You'll have to come back in the morning."

"I would like to see either Mr. Stevenson, please, or the duty officer."

"You American?"

"Yes, as a matter of fact, I am."

"Is this some sort of bona fide emergency?"

"Yes, I would say so, Corporal."

"What kind of an emergency?"

"Corporal, listen to me carefully. I may not look

like one, but I happen to be a colonel of the United States Marine Corps."

It was clear that the corporal thought this highly unlikely.

"Is that so? You got anything to prove it, *Colonel?*"

Colonel Graham had with him his Marine Corps identification card, his JCS Letter Orders, and another plastic enclosed card identifying him as the Deputy Director for Western Hemisphere Operations of the Office of Strategic Services. But before leaving Pôrto Alegre, he had placed all of these documents into the false bottom of one of his suitcases.

But, he realized, he was not without the means to convince the corporal that he was a fellow Marine.

"Listen to me, son," he said. "Unless I am inside the Embassy talking to the Duty Officer within the next thirty seconds, you're going to be a buck private on your way to permanent duty cleaning mess-hall grease pits on Parris Island so fast it will take a week for your ass to catch up with you. Now open this goddamned gate!"

"Aye, aye, Sir," the corporal said as he reached for the key to the padlock.

As they reached the open door to the Embassy building, the corporal volunteered the information that Mr. Stevenson was in the building but had left orders that he was not to be disturbed by anybody but the Ambassador.

"That was before I got here, son," Graham said. "Tell him I'm here."

"Aye, aye, Sir," the corporal said. "I'll take you to his office."

"Thank you."

The office of the Cultural Attaché was in the basement of the villa.

The corporal knocked on the door.

It was opened by a nice-looking young man in his thirties whose face bore a look of resigned tolerance.

"Corporal, I said I didn't want to be bothered," he said, and then saw Graham. "Jesus Christ! Colonel Graham!"

"Hello, Stevenson," Graham said.

"You know the Colonel, Sir?" the corporal asked.

"Yes, I do," Stevenson said.

"Yes, Sir. Then I'll just log him in."

"No, Corporal, don't do that," Graham said. "Actually, since you didn't see me, there's no reason to log me in."

The corporal looked at Stevenson.

"You didn't see Colonel Graham, Corporal," Stevenson said. "I'll explain this to the Security Officer."

"Yes, Sir."

"Come in, Colonel," Stevenson said.

There was a man sitting on a battered leather couch in Stevenson's small office.

"Don't tell me this is the legendary Colonel A. F. Graham in the flesh," the man said.

"Who are you?"

"My name is Leibermann, and before you jump all over Stevenson's ass for talking to me, I came to see him."

"Is that so? Why?"

"Has my fame preceded me?" Leibermann asked. "Can I infer from the utter lack of surprise on your face that you know who I am?"

"I know who you are, Mr. Leibermann. What

I'm curious about is what you're doing here."

"Tex Frade asked me to see what I could do to keep your man Ettinger alive. I'm sorry to tell you I failed."

"What are you saying? Ettinger's dead?"

"Dead, and they mutilated the corpse to send a message."

"What kind of a message? To whom?"

"That's what Stevenson and I were talking about," Leibermann said. "But since Stevenson won't tell me what Ettinger was doing over here, we aren't doing very well with our little game of Twenty Questions."

"I told you, Milton, I don't know what Ettinger was doing there," Stevenson protested. "I never heard his name before you walked in here tonight!"

You call him by his first name, do you, Stevenson? That means that (a) you are probably seeing more of him than Wild Bill Donovan would like you to, (b) that you like him, and (c) Leibermann likes you, or else he wouldn't have made a point of telling me he came to see you to keep him out of trouble with me.

"What does this mean, Colonel?" Leibermann asked sarcastically. "That the OSS not only doesn't talk to FBI, they don't talk to each other, either?"

"I think the word is 'compartmentalization,' " Graham said. "Nobody knows anything more than they have to."

"Of course, all I am is a simple accountant, not a secret agent, like you two, so I may be missing the big picture on this, but *my* word for that is 'stupid.' "

"When did this happen?" Graham asked.

"According to the local cops, he'd been dead about thirty hours when they found him."

"Where did they find him?"

"There's a sort of a seaside resort here called Carrasco. They found him in the sand dunes about a mile north of the hotel — actually it's a gambling casino and hotel — where he was staying. His car is in the casino garage. No signs of a struggle in his room."

"How did they kill him? How was he mutilated?"

"Ice pick in the ear," Leibermann said. "And, postmortem, they severed his penis and placed it in his mouth. That's what we were talking about when you showed up."

"Why would they do that?" Graham asked.

"Are we talking to each other to the point where we agree that probable bad guys are the Germans?" Leibermann asked.

"OK, why would the *Germans* do that?"

"I don't think the Germans would," Leibermann said. "They might do something imaginative, like hang a gasoline-filled tire around him and set it on fire, but I don't think they'd cut off a Yiddisher's *schwantz* and stick it in his mouth. They'd have to touch it."

He mimed lifting the penile member erect and then sawing on it with a knife.

"Isn't that sort of thing, the penis in the mouth, associated with gangs in the United States?" Graham asked.

"The true indication of somebody else's intelligence is how much he agrees with you," Leibermann said. "My own theory of what happened is that the local branch of Murder Incorporated was hired by parties unknown but who probably have offices in the German Embassy. The reason for the contract was that Ettinger knew too much and talked. The local cops tell me that's what happens down here, too, to people who talk too much."

"You say Frade asked for your help?" Graham asked.

Leibermann nodded.

"When was that?"

"A little after noon today."

"Do you know where he is now?"

"Hey, *I'm* the FBI. *I'm* supposed to ask the questions. You guys are supposed to blow things up."

"Very funny, Milton," Graham said. "You don't mind if I call you Milton, do you?"

"Not if I can call you Alejandro," Leibermann said.

Christ. He even knows my first name.

"I would be honored if you called me Alejandro, Milton," Graham said. "And very grateful if you would tell me where Frade is."

"He told me he was invited to a party and couldn't turn down the invitation. Clever fellow that I am, I think he was telling me the coup d'état has started."

"Did he happen to mention anything about an airplane?"

"What did you do, get him one to replace the one he put on the bottom of Samborombón Bay?"

Graham happened to glance at Stevenson. From his face, it was obvious that he was hearing a number of things for the first time.

"If I answer that so subtly phrased question, will you answer a question for me?"

"That depends on how subtle your answer is," Leibermann said, smiling at him.

"Yes. We got him another airplane. He picked it up in Brazil, and had aboard another OSS team. It was supposed to be a small twin, but it turned out to be a Lockheed airliner, a Lodestar. Since that was the first time Frade has flown a Lodestar,

734

so far as I know, I have been naturally wondering if he and the people with him made it all right."

"That wasn't evasive at all, Colonel," Leibermann said. "So I will reply in kind. Frade landed at his estancia with the Lockheed. They unloaded five people — almost certainly your OSS team — and some crates, and then took off again. I don't know where to."

"How reliable is that information?" Graham asked.

"The man I have on Frade's estancia is pretty reliable."

"A minute ago, Milton, when I asked about an airplane, you weren't exactly truthful, were you?" Graham said.

"I was *obfuscatory*," Leibermann said. "The first time you asked me about an airplane was before I knew you had really stopped playing games. So I was *obfuscatory*."

"Do the names 'Galahad' and 'Cavalry' mean anything to you, Milton?"

"These sources? Code names for sources?" Leibermann asked, as if he didn't expect a reply. "You got them from Frade?" Now he waited for Graham to nod. "I haven't a clue about who Galahad might be," he went on. "But Cavalry might be Martín. You know who I mean, the BIS guy?"

Graham nodded again.

"I'll ask around, if it's important to you," Leibermann said. "Is it important?"

"Important enough for me to come down here," Graham said. "Which is the next thing on my agenda. I need to get to Buenos Aires. How's the best way?"

"The best way is to catch the eight-o'clock boat ferry in the morning. That'll put you into Buenos

Aires a little before two."

"That's not quick enough," Graham said.

"You're out of luck," Leibermann said. "There's no other way tonight. You missed the boat, to coin a phrase."

"What about driving?"

"There's a ferry across the border into Entre Ríos Province," Stevenson said. "But it stops running at ten. I'm afraid Mr. Leibermann is right, Colonel. You're stuck here for the night."

Graham shrugged.

"Colonel, what about Ettinger's body?" Stevenson asked.

"What about it?"

"What do we do with it when the police release it?"

God forgive me, that subject never entered my mind.

"Ettinger was here as a private citizen. What happens when a private citizen dies down here?"

"I really don't know," Stevenson said. "I'll have to ask one of the diplomats, the Consul General."

"No. You go to the Ambassador. You tell them Ettinger died in the service of his country. I want him put in a casket with a flag on it, and I want him taken to Pôrto Alegre, Brazil, escorted by the Military Attaché and a couple of Marines from the Embassy Guard. They can fly him home from there. You tell the Ambassador I said that's what's going to happen, and all you want from him is to tell his people to do it."

"Yes, Sir."

"Do it now, tonight," Graham said. "And send off a message to Oracle — right now — so somebody can let his mother know what happened."

"Yes, Sir."

"Where can I stay tonight?"

736

"There's room in my apartment, Sir," Stevenson said.

"Where are you staying, Milton?"

"I've got a room in the Casino Hotel I told you about."

"Could I get a room there?"

"Probably. But there's two beds in my room, if there's a problem."

"That might be best of all," Graham said. "Once I have a shower and a shave, and change into clean clothes, I think that you and I ought to have a long talk, Milton."

"I was hoping that's what you had in mind, Alejandro," Leibermann said.

XXII

[One]

Visiting Officers' Quarters
First Cavalry Regiment
Campo de Mayo
Buenos Aires Province, Argentina
0125 19 April 1943

The lights in the room went on. Clete, startled, sat up in the bed.

Capitán Roberto Lauffer was standing just inside the door, by the light switch. He was fully dressed, and wore a blue-and-white-striped band of cloth around his right arm. The door was open, and through it Clete could see two soldiers armed with Thompson submachine guns. They both looked maybe seventeen years old — and terrified. They also had the blue-and-white — the Argentine colors — armbands.

"Sorry to wake you, Cletus," Lauffer said politely. "But something has come up. The order to execute immediately has been given."

Nice choice of words, Roberto! It's really great to have someone waking you up in the middle of the night saying things like "the order to execute immediately has been given."

The door to the other bedroom opened, and

Enrico, in baggy cotton undershirt and drawers, came in. He had his right hand behind his back.

I don't think Enrico's scratching his ass; he's got his .45 back there.

"Buenos días, mi Capitán."

"The order for immediate execution of OUTLINE BLUE has been issued, Suboficial Mayor," Lauffer said formally.

"I will get dressed, Señor," Enrico said.

Clete swung his feet out of bed.

"What are you talking about?" Clete asked. "What's this 'execute immediately' order all about?"

"Castillo knows that Blue Sky was ordered — the command to execute OUTLINE BLUE," Lauffer explained. "He sent messages to every command, stating that General Ramírez has resigned as Minister of War, that any orders Ramírez might issue are to be ignored, and that General Savaronna has taken his place."

"Who's Savaronna?"

"He was Castillo's Minister of Labor," Lauffer furnished, and then went on: "We expected something like that might happen, Coronel Martín predicted it. The only thing that's changed is that General Ramírez has ordered us to move now."

"Instead of when?"

"Instead of tomorrow morning," Lauffer said. "I thought you read OUTLINE BLUE."

"Not that carefully."

"And under the circumstances, General Rawson feels that we should make sure the airplane will be ready. Just in case it's needed."

Clete had put on clean underwear, stockings, and a clean shirt. He stood looking at the closet where Enrico had hung up his clothing. He had his choice of a business suit or the riding breeches and boots he wore flying the Lockheed into Campo de Mayo.

"I don't think my diplomat's uniform is the appropriate uniform of the day," he thought aloud.

"Excuse me?"

"Nothing," Clete said, and reached for the riding breeches.

"I don't know whether you will feel comfortable with these," Lauffer said when Clete had finished — with a loud grunt — pulling on his riding boots. "But General Ramírez said I should offer them to you."

Lauffer extended to him a blue-and-white armband, together with two safety pins and an envelope. Clete opened it. It contained a single sheet of paper:

TO WHOM IT MAY CONCERN:

Campo de Mayo
19 April 1943

Señor Cletus Howell Frade is in the service of the Provisional Government of the Republic of Argentina, acting under the direct orders of the undersigned.

Ramírez

Teniente General Pedro P. Ramírez
Minister of War
Provisional Government of the
    Republic of Argentina

Rawson

General de Division Arturo Rawson
Presidente of the
    Governing Council
Provisional Government of the
    Republic of Argentina

The point of his crack about being comfortable with these is that I turned down that temporary commission.

Clete took his tweed jacket from its hanger, laid it on the bed, and pinned the blue-and-white-striped armband to it. He put it on, then looked at Lauffer.

"Rawson's the new President, huh?"

"Until elections can be held," Lauffer said.

Or until they stand us all in front of a wall wearing

blindfolds and offer us a last cigarette, right? Whichever comes first?

Enrico came into the room, wearing what apparently was the prescribed uniform for field service. This included a leather harness ringed with well-polished leather clip holders for a rifle, a well-polished molded holster for his .45, and a cavalry saber in a scabbard.

"You have one of these armbands for him?" Clete asked.

Lauffer handed Enrico an armband. When it became apparent that Enrico was going to have trouble pinning it on without taking his jacket off — and that meant also unstrapping his leather harness and belt — Clete took it from him and pinned it on for him.

"I have a car outside," Lauffer said.

"Your pistol, Señor Cletus?" Enrico said.

"Well, we can't forget that, can we?" Clete said, and bent over and took the pistol from where he had stored it under the bed.

In a Marine Pavlovian reflex, he ejected the magazine, pulled the action back, saw that the chamber was empty, let the slide go forward, lowered the hammer, and replaced the magazine. Then he looked at the pistol.

What the hell am I supposed to do with this? Not only don't I want to shoot anybody with it, but I don't have a holster.

He remembered that Enrico often carried his pistol in the small of his back. He could not work the pistol under his waistband until he had loosened his belt.

There is a very good chance that this thing will slip down my ass, into my pants leg, and clatter noisily onto the ground. What I should do is just leave it here.

But I don't really want to do that.

Lauffer was waving him through the door.

A 1940 Chevrolet, painted in the Argentine shade of olive drab, was parked by the curb outside the building. The driver held open the door and saluted as Clete, Lauffer, and Enrico squeezed into the backseat. That was not easy, and both Enrico and Lauffer had trouble arranging their sabers.

The two soldiers with Thompsons squeezed into the front seat beside the driver.

It must be even more crowded up there with those tommy guns.

Fifty-round drum magazines, too.

I wonder if either of those kids knows how to shoot a Thompson?

Here lies Major Cletus H. Frade, USMCR, who survived Guadalcanal but died in a South American revolution when he was shot by mistake by a nervous seventeen-year-old who didn't know that unless you let go of the trigger, the Thompson will keep shooting.

The driver turned on the headlights and started off.

"Turn off the lights!" Lauffer ordered sharply.

"Why?" Clete asked as the lights faded.

"We want to mobilize with as much secrecy as possible," Lauffer said seriously, and as if the question surprised him.

Don't you think that Castillo has somebody out here with orders to report immediately when anything out of the ordinary happens?

The Chevrolet crawled to the end of the block and turned right onto a row of two-story barracks.

All the lights in the barracks were on, and soldiers were sleepily forming ranks in the street.

Clete, with effort, said nothing about lights in the barracks.

Five minutes later, they reached the airfield.

The guard detail there was under the command of a nervous infantry major who ordered everybody out of the car. He examined the interior with the aid of a flashlight, and did not seem at all happy with the document signed by the President of the Governing Council of the Provisional Government of the Republic of Argentina and his Minister of War vis-à-vis a Señor Cletus H. Frade.

Finally, however, he passed them through the barricade — fifty-five-gallon drums set in the middle of the street — into the airfield property.

The lights inside both hangers were on, and so were the floodlights mounted on the hangers to illuminate the parking ramp. Clete saw a half-dozen small airplanes, including two Piper Cubs and a Fieseler Storch — *that's probably the one Martín came to the estancia in.* The others he thought were English, but he wasn't sure.

There were also what looked like two platoons of infantrymen, in field gear, armed with Mauser rifles, standing at ease in ranks, with their officers, in riding breeches and high-crowned brimmed caps, standing in front of them, hands on their swords, smoking cigarettes and trying to look calm and nonchalant.

Not one of these guys, including Lauffer, has ever heard a shot fired in anger.

I don't see any bigger airplanes. Are those half-dozen puddle jumpers all they keep out here?

"I don't see any larger airplanes than those Piper Cubs and the Storch," Clete said, making it a question.

"The bombers and transport aircraft are on maneuvers in Tucumán Province," Lauffer said.

"When did that happen?" Clete asked.

"Four days ago," Lauffer said. "Coronel Martín advised General Ramírez that the Air Service was not in sympathy with the G.O.U. General Ramírez then ordered them to Tucumán Province," Lauffer said.

Well, that explains why it was so important to get the Lockheed here, doesn't it? No Lockheed, no way out.

"You think they will stay there?"

"We hope so. Orders were issued at midnight to detain their commanding officers until further orders."

The Chevrolet stopped by the side door of the closest hangar. Everybody got out of the car.

"There are supposed to be men here to push the airplane from the hangar," Lauffer said. "But something may have gone wrong, and they may not have arrived. We may have to push it ourselves."

What's wrong with those infantrymen? Why can't they push the airplane out of the hangar?

Capitán Delgano, in civilian clothing and wearing a blue-and-white-striped armband, walked out of the hangar.

I wondered where you were.

He then had another thought.

"Roberto," he asked finally, and carefully. "Am I allowed to make a comment, a suggestion?"

"Of course," Lauffer said.

"Everybody seems a little nervous," Clete said.

"I think that's to be expected, don't you?" Lauffer replied a little stiffly.

"I was thinking that everybody is already wondering what that Lockheed is doing here in the first place. What I mean is that somebody has probably already figured out it's intended to fly Rawson and Ramírez and the others out of here if this thing goes wrong."

"I'm sure that thought has occurred to some people," Lauffer said.

"Roberto, the moment we roll that airplane out of the hangar, and I start the engines, everybody's going to think the revolution is over and our side lost."

"Why would they think that?"

"That's what I would think if I were them," Delgano said, nodding at the infantrymen.

"What do you suggest, Mayor Frade?" Lauffer asked formally.

"Have you had the tanks topped off?" Clete asked.

Delgano nodded.

"Then there's no point in rolling it out of the hangar and making anybody nervous. If we need it, we can roll it out then."

"General Rawson ordered me to make sure the aircraft is ready," Lauffer said.

"Tell him it's ready, Delgano," Clete said. "All we need to get it out of here is to open the hangar doors." He thought of something else. "It would also be nice if I knew where we're going. Or don't you trust me with that information?"

"You will be informed when —" Lauffer said.

"Asunción, Paraguay," Delgano interrupted. "It's thirteen hundred kilometers. Would you like to see the flight plan I laid out?"

"If Capitán Lauffer thinks I can be trusted with it," Clete said. "I would like very much to see it."

"It's inside," Delgano said, gesturing in the direction of the hangar.

When they started to walk toward the hangar

door, Clete saw the infantry officers watching carefully.

Fifteen minutes later, after checking Delgano's flight plan and walking him through another preflight check, they came out of the hangar. When they did, there was visible relief on the faces of the infantry officers.

But Lauffer was not through.

"You do not wish to test the aircraft's engines? Could that be done inside the hangar?"

"Not without opening the doors," Clete said. "The prop blast would very likely knock the doors off their tracks and then you'd never get it out of the hangar."

"I'll go to General Rawson and tell him that it was my decision not to roll the aircraft from the hangar," Delgano said. "If that's what you'd like."

Lauffer considered that a moment.

"I think it would be best if Señor Frade did that," he said. "I suggest that you stay here and hold yourself in readiness."

"Whatever you say, Capitán," Delgano said, his tone suggesting that he was at least as disappointed with Lauffer as Clete was. Lauffer seemed more interested in making sure no one could criticize his actions tonight than anything else.

[Two]

Officers' Casino
Campo de Mayo
Buenos Aires Province, Argentina
0225 19 April 1943

The muzzles of what looked like .30-caliber air-cooled Browning machine guns poked from upstairs windows in the Officers' Casino (which was what the Argentine Army called their Officers' Club). There were two sandbagged machine-gun positions on the lawn of the club, and there were a number of soldiers — mostly noncoms — guarding the door who looked as if they knew what they were supposed to do with their rifles and submachine guns.

The capitán in charge of the building's guard detail would not pass Lauffer, Clete, and Enrico into the lobby of the building until one of his lieutenants had gone inside the building to "check with el Coronel Perón."

They got inside as far as the door of what looked like the Main Dining Room, converted now to the command post where Ramírez and Rawson were directing the coup d'état, before they were stopped again to wait further clearance.

Clete looked inside, and decided that while this place looked like a command post — there were maps on the wall; batteries of telephones; messengers coming and going and the like — there was something about it that reminded him of the command post training exercises he'd gone through during his officer's training. Then the aviation cadets had played at being squadron and air group commanders and staff officers, and solemnly pre-

748

tended they knew what they were doing. There was somehow the same flavor here. Everybody seemed to be playing a role, and only a few people seemed to act as if they really knew what they were doing.

El Coronel Juan Domingo Perón himself, in an immaculate, splendidly tailored uniform, finally approached the door and waved them inside.

"There is a problem with the aircraft?" he asked.

"It will be available on five minutes' notice," Clete answered.

Perón looked at Clete and then at Lauffer, his attitude making it clear that he wasn't interested in what Clete had to say.

"Is the aircraft available?" Perón asked.

Screw you, Coronel!

"Señor Frade thought it best not to take the aircraft from the hangar," Lauffer said.

"What?" Perón asked indignantly.

"I thought it better to leave it in the hangar . . . ," Clete began, and stopped when he saw General Rawson walking toward them.

"Is there a problem?" Rawson asked.

"No problem," Clete said. "The aircraft is available on five minutes' notice. It will take me that long to get it out of the hangar and warm the engines."

Rawson looked at Clete with his eyebrows raised questioningly.

"My thought, General," Clete said, "was that —"

"Lauffer, why did you bring Señor Frade here?" Perón interrupted.

"Excuse me, Coronel," Clete said, "I was speaking to the General."

Perón glared at him. Rawson made a face and then gestured for Clete to continue.

"If we rolled the airplane out of the hangar and started the engines, it might give people the idea we were about to use it," Clete said. "Which seemed to me to be both unnecessary and unwise."

Rawson considered that a moment, then said, "You're right. I should have thought of that."

Perón's face tightened, but he didn't offer a comment.

"Capitán Delgano is with the airplane?" Rawson asked.

"Sí, mi General," Lauffer said.

"Coronel Perón and I are about to have a final word with Coronel Tarramanno of the First Cavalry," Rawson said. "OUTLINE BLUE calls for them to begin their march at two-thirty. I suggest that you stay here with Capitán Lauffer, Señor Frade, in case we need you."

"Yes, Sir."

"With a little luck, we won't, but I'd like to have you available," Rawson said. "Take a look at the situation map. And if you have any other thoughts, please give them to me."

"Yes, Sir."

Perón's face was now as stiff as a board.

"Your car is outside, Roberto?" Rawson asked.

"Sí, mi General."

"Then we'll use it," Rawson said. "Let's go, Coronel."

The Situation Map was actually a collection of maps, all taped to a sectional sliding wall normally used to break the large dining room into smaller rooms. In the center were large maps of Argentina, one showing the upper half of the country, and the other the lower.

On the maps flag pins located both provincial

capitals and military bases. The pins were either black or red, and Clete wondered about the significance of the colors until he spotted a blue-and-white pin on the map of the upper half of Argentina, looked closer, and saw that it marked Campo de Mayo.

The blue-and-white flag pin obviously identified locations under control of the revolutionaries.

So far, there's only one blue-and-white flag.

Confirmation of the meaning of the flag pins came almost immediately, when a lieutenant stepped to the map and replaced the black pins that marked Santo Tomé and the Second Cavalry post outside Santo Tomé with blue-and-white pins.

Obviously, word had just come in that the Second Cavalry had not only joined the revolution, but had taken over the city of Santo Tomé.

Clete moved to the right of the central maps to one of Buenos Aires and Entre Ríos Provinces. Here more than a dozen blue-and-white pins marked the location of military bases and cities. But there were far more black — "undecided," Clete judged — pins than blue-and-white, and there were two dozen red pins, which probably marked units and locations that were opposed to the ouster of President Castillo's government.

On these maps, too, were grease pencil marks outlining the routes of march the military units controlled by G.O.U. would take from Campo de Mayo and other military bases to the Casa Rosada.

A major politely moved him away from the map and inserted two different pins, one blue and one yellow, both numbered "1" at the gate to Campo de Mayo. These obviously represented the First Cavalry and First Infantry Regiments, which were at this moment preparing to begin their march.

Two minutes later, the major replaced the black pins marking the location of the barracks of the Second Infantry, the Buenos Aires garrison troops, and the cantonment of the Navy's School of Engineering. Clete knew where both military bases were. The Second Infantry's barracks were near the Army's polo fields across from the racetrack (and near Uncle Willy's house) and the Navy School was on Avenida del Libertador several miles closer to Campo de Mayo.

The new flag pin on the Second Infantry was blue-and-white, and the new flag pin on the Navy Engineering School was red. The Navy was apparently staying with Castillo.

What does that mean? Will they fight the First Infantry when they see them coming down Avenida del Libertador? With what? The Navy usually doesn't have many small arms, just enough rifles and pistols to arm Navy guards.

In the next few minutes, with decreasing courtesy, he was moved out of the way to allow a procession of officers and noncoms to replace pins all over the map.

Finally realizing with more than a little chagrin that he was really bothering people, he turned from the wall of maps and got out of the way.

At one side of the room he saw a table tended by white-jacketed waiters, and walked to it. Coffee and pastry was being served. That, like the swords dangling from every officer's Sam Browne belt, seemed grossly incongruous to him, but apparently to no one else.

He took a cup of coffee and a roll and found an armchair, sat down, and stretched out his legs. The coffee was very hot, and he set the cup down on the wide arm of the chair to let it cool.

He was a well-nourished young man in excellent physical condition, and quite naturally excited to be taken out of bed in the middle of the night to witness a coup d'état.

But on the other hand, during the last seventy-seven hours he had traveled from Buenos Aires to Santo Tomé by train; crossed into Brazil by ferry, and then been driven across Brazil by a driver who apparently believed the two speeds of a car were On and Off; received four hours' intense, if rudimentary, instruction in the operation of a Lockheed C-56 Lodestar aircraft; flown that two-pilot aircraft without assistance, using dead-reckoning navigation, illegally across the Brazilian-Argentine border; landed it at night in a heavy rainstorm on a too-short, unpaved landing strip illuminated by gasoline burning in clay pots; flown the aircraft the next morning from Santo Tomé onto another dirt strip at Estancia San Pedro y San Pablo and then from the estancia to Campo de Mayo.

The next thing Clete knew, Enrico was gently shaking him.

"Señor Cletus," the old soldier said, gently reproving him. "You are snoring."

Clete looked at his Hamilton. It was quarter past five.

Jesus Christ!

What did you do in the revolution, Daddy?

Why, son, I slept through it.

He rose quickly out of the chair and walked back to the wall of maps.

General Rawson was there, with Lauffer standing beside him.

Looking over Rawson's shoulder, he could see that almost all of the flag pins on the map of Buenos Aires were now blue-and-white.

Almost *all. Not all.*

There were more than a dozen red flag pins, mostly congregated around the Casa Rosada, but also on the Edificio Libertador, and, surprising Clete, on the Naval School of Engineering. Near that red flag pin was the blue flag pin with the numeral 1, identifying the First Infantry Regiment.

He looked for and found the yellow flag of the First Cavalry. It was on the intersection of Avenida Córdoba and Avenida Pueyrredón, less than a mile from the Casa Rosada. Beside it was the blue flag pin of the Second Infantry.

General Rawson sensed somebody behind him and looked over his shoulder.

"You must have a clear conscience, Señor Frade," Rawson said, letting him know that he had seen him sleeping — or possibly heard him snoring. "Either that, or you have a commendable faith in OUTLINE BLUE."

He's in a good mood. The revolution must be on track.

"The latter, mi General," Clete said. "Judging from the map, it looks like it's going well."

"Not here," Rawson said, pointing at the School of Naval Warfare. "There is resistance here. Machine guns. There have been some casualties. The First Infantry is stalled."

Clete blurted, "Can't they bypass it? Come back later and clean it out?"

"They could, they should, and I have ordered them to do precisely that," Rawson said. "I had to order the First Cavalry and the Second Infantry to stop their advance."

He pointed to those flags.

"I don't understand."

"I am not in communication with the commanding officer of the First Infantry," Rawson explained. "They had a radio truck with them, but it has stopped functioning, and the telephone lines all along Libertador are not working. They were probably disconnected by the Navy; there is a switching station inside the compound."

What about sending a messenger?

Rawson read his mind.

"I've sent three messengers, and they have either been unable to get through, or the legitimacy of the order is being questioned."

"What about dropping them a message?" Clete thought out loud.

"Excuse me?"

"You have three Piper Cubs on the airfield. One of them could be there in ten minutes. Just drop your orders to the commanding officer."

"Drop?" Rawson asked, confused.

"You put the message in a pouch, with something heavy, like a wrench or a brick. You tie a long piece of cloth to the pouch, so that they can see it coming down, and throw it out the window."

"Is that possible?"

"It's routine in the Marine Corps," Clete said.

"How do you keep the message from falling into the . . . wrong hands?"

He almost said "hands of the enemy." But these sailors aren't enemies, they're people who just haven't gotten the word. Which probably explains why the infantry commander hasn't blown them away. They're trying to spill as little blood as possible.

"You fly low enough, and slow enough, over the people you want to get the pouch so you can't miss."

"That's very interesting."

Clete warmed to the subject.

"As far as that goes, there's a couple of soccer fields right next to the Navy School. You could land a Cub there and deliver the message in person."

"Is that possible?"

"Yes, it is."

"You would be willing to do that?"

Oh, shit!

Actually, I was thinking that Capitán Delgano would be just the man for the job. For one thing, he's got a lot more time in Piper Cubs than I do; and for another, I don't think I want to explain to some loyalist Argentine sailor what I'm doing flying an Army airplane for the revolutionaries.

"Yes, Sir," he heard himself saying. "If you'd like me to."

"Excuse me for a moment," Rawson said. "I would like a word with General Ramírez."

He was back in two minutes with Ramírez, who obviously thought the idea had great merit.

"What I was thinking, Mayor Frade," he said, "was that we have two problems which might be solved if you believe you can drop a message to the First Infantry by small aircraft."

Are you ever going to learn to keep your mouth shut?

"Yes, Sir?"

"OUTLINE BLUE called for the two columns to converge simultaneously on the Casa Rosada. The First Infantry would move down Avenida del Libertador, while First Cavalry and the Second Infantry would move down Avenida Córdoba. As I'm sure you'll understand, that will have a certain psychological effect. As a matter of fact, the simultaneous arrival of the two columns was your father's idea."

"Yes, Sir."

"The First Cavalry and the Second Infantry have been halted, as General Rawson told you, at Pueyrredón and Córdoba. Now, if we can send word to the First Infantry to bypass the resistance at the Naval School, we can start the First Cavalry and the Second Infantry moving again. But since they are so much closer to the Casa Rosada than the First Infantry, we again have the problem of arranging for them to move in concert. At the moment, we have communication with the First Cavalry and the Second Infantry, but we cannot count on the telephones continuing to be operational. You see the problem?"

"Yes, Sir."

"Once we start the First Infantry moving, do you think it would be possible to observe it from the air as it moves down Avenida del Libertador?"

"Yes, Sir, of course."

"And then, when they are the same distance from the Casa Rosada as the First Cavalry and the Second Infantry, to drop a message to them to resume their march?"

"There is only one problem I see with that, mi General," Clete said. "Or two. The first is that I'm not qualified to make an assessment like that. I would have no idea when the two columns were, time-wise, an equal distance from the Casa Rosada."

"Oh. I didn't make myself clear. General Rawson would be in the airplane. His presence at the Naval School is essential to the whole idea. So he would be with you; and he would make the decision when to order the First Cavalry and the Second Infantry to resume their march."

"The second problem, Sir, is that while I can fly the Lockheed by myself, should that be necessary,

Capitán Delgano cannot."

"I think by now we can safely say that the success of OUTLINE BLUE is a given," Ramírez said, "and we will not need your aircraft. What we must do now is finish the operation with as little loss of life as possible. What I'm saying is that the honor of the officers defending the Casa Rosada will be satisfied when clearly irresistible force — the simultaneous appearance of the two converging columns — makes further resistance obviously futile and surrender honorable. Lives will be saved!"

"Yes, Sir. I take your point."

"God go with you!" Ramírez said emotionally, and grasped both his shoulders. "Your father would be proud of you, my boy!"

Here lies Major Cletus H. Frade, USMCR, who survived Guadalcanal and slept through most of the Argentine Revolution of 1943, but — for reasons that have never been made clear — died while trying to land a Piper Cub on a soccer field. General Arturo Rawson, who had just been appointed President of the Governing Council of the new military government, was also killed in the crash.

[Three]

The Office of the Military Attaché
The Embassy of the German Reich
Avenida Córdoba
Buenos Aires, Argentina
0525 19 April 1943

Standartenführer Josef Goltz, Oberst Karl Heinz Grüner thought, *looks to be in complete possession of his faculties; Der grosse Wienerwurst looks as if he's about to wet his pants.*

Goltz was shaved and in uniform. First Secretary Anton Gradny-Sawz was unshaved, his hair was mussed, he was not wearing a necktie, and his face was flushed.

"We almost couldn't get through," Gradny-Sawz announced. "There are troops all along Avenida Córdoba. We were stopped —"

"The First Cavalry and the Second Infantry Regiments," Grüner said, directing this information to Goltz. "Obviously headed for the Casa Rosada. I have no idea why they have stopped. If there were resistance, gunfire, I would have heard it."

"Will their coup d'état succeed?" Goltz asked.

"I would think so. These units may be ahead of schedule, and are waiting for others to show up. I haven't been receiving much information — the loyalists have shut down many of the telephone trunks. But what I have suggests that almost all of the troops in the Buenos Aires area have placed themselves under Ramírez and Rawson. I have no idea what's going on in the rest of the country. It's impossible to call in or out of Buenos Aires. I was surprised that I was able to get through to you. I can't reach the Ambassador."

Goltz grunted.

"General Rawson has been appointed — or has appointed himself . . ." Grüner stopped to read from a clipboard where he had written it down: " 'President of the Governing Council of the Provisional Government of the Republic of Argentina.' "

"That's not good news," Gradny-Sawz said.

"Why do you say that?" Goltz asked.

"Oberst Perón told me that Rawson is one of those who believe we were responsible for the death of Oberst Frade. They were close friends."

"Oberst Perón was the late Oberst Frade's *closest* friend," Goltz said. "He understands why the death of Frade was necessary. Believe me, Anton, Rawson will come to understand that, too."

There was a knock at the door.

"Come!" Grüner said.

Major Freiherr Hans-Peter von Wachtstein entered Grüner's office. He, too, was in uniform.

"Heil Hitler!" he said, giving the stiff-armed salute.

"I tried to call you," Grüner said. "The lines were out."

"I saw troops moving — as well as a squadron of the Corps of Mounted Police," Peter said. "I thought the revolution had probably started. I tried to call you, Herr Oberst, at your home, and when I could not get through, decided I had better come here."

"Right," Grüner said. "The correct decision."

"First Cavalry and the Second Infantry Regiments are stopped along Avenida Córdoba at Avenida Pueyrredón. . . ."

"We had trouble getting past them, von Wachtstein," Gradny-Sawz said. "There was a major who had apparently never heard of diplomatic privilege."

"Well, we're here," Goltz said. "And now that we are?"

"The reason I called you, Herr Standartenführer," Grüner said, "was not because of the revolution; all we can do about that is wait to see what happens. There has been a message from Berlin. The cryptographer officer is still ill, and the communications officer called me. About four-thirty I was in the process of decrypting the message when one of my sources telephoned from Campo de Mayo to tell me the troops had left there at half past two."

"It took him two hours to send that word to you?" Gradny-Sawz said incredulously. "That doesn't seem to be a very good source."

"I was pleased that he managed to get through at all," Grüner said. "At that point I telephoned your house, Herr Standartenführer."

"I think we must proceed on the assumption that President Castillo will be removed from office — if he has not been removed already," Goltz said, "and that henceforth we will be dealing with — what was it you said, Grüner? 'The Governing Council of the Provisional Government' — as, it seems appropriate to say, you accurately predicted. What did Berlin have on its mind?"

Grüner went to his safe, worked the combination, opened the safe, and handed Goltz a business-size sealed envelope. On this he had written, "For the Exclusive Attention of Standartenführer Goltz." Goltz tore the envelope open and read the message.

MOST SECRET

URGENT

FROM FOREIGN MINISTRY

TO EMBASSY OF THE GERMAN REICH
BUENOS AIRES

FOR EXCLUSIVE ATTENTION
  (1) AMBASSADOR
  (2) STANDARTENFUHRER JOSEF GOLTZ

BERLIN 18 APRIL 1943 7:05 PM

  1. SUMMARY OF INFORMATION RE-
CEIVED FROM DOENITZ AND CANARIS
FOLLOWS:

    A. ON 13 APRIL 1943 US CHIEF
OF NAVAL OPERATIONS SIGNALED ALL
US NAVY VESSELS OPERATING IN
SOUTH ATLANTIC OCEAN TO LOCATE
AND POSITIVELY IDENTIFY SPANISH
REGISTERED MOTOR VESSEL COMER-
CIANTE DEL OCEANO PACIFICO.

    B. AT 6:27 AM LOCAL TIME 18
APRIL 1943 AT POSITION 27 DE-
GREES 25 MINUTES SOUTH LATITUDE
43 DEGREES 05 MINUTES WEST LON-
GITUDE COMERCIANTE DEL OCEANO
PACIFICO WAS CLOSELY APPROACHED
AT VERY HIGH SPEED AND IN AN IN-
TIMIDATINGLY RECKLESS MANNER BY
US NAVY DESTROYER ALFRED THOMAS.
IMMEDIATELY AFTERWARD ALFRED
THOMAS RADIOED NON-ENCRYPTED

MESSAGE TO US CHIEF OF NAVAL OPERA-
TIONS GIVING POSITION AND ESTI-
MATED TIME OF ARRIVAL (9 PM 20 APRIL
1943) OF COMERCIANTE DEL OCEANO
PACIFICO AT MOUTH OF RIVER
PLATE.

C. US AMBASSADOR MADRID HAS
BEEN SUMMONED TO SPANISH FOREIGN
MINISTRY TO RECEIVE OFFICIAL
PROTEST IN STRONGEST POSSIBLE
LANGUAGE THIS INTIMIDATION AND
HARASSMENT OF A CLEARLY IDENTI-
FIED SPANISH VESSEL ON THE HIGH
SEAS IN BLATANT VIOLATION OF THE
RULES OF NAVAL WARFARE AND THE
RIGHT OF FREE PASSAGE OF NON-
BELLIGERENT POWERS AS OUTLINED
IN THE GENEVA CONVENTION.

2. AMBASSADOR VON LUTZENBERGER
IS DIRECTED TO IMMEDIATELY AND
PERSONALLY REGISTER WITH HIGHEST
POSSIBLE OFFICIAL OF ARGENTINE
GOVERNMENT THE OUTRAGE OF THE GOV-
ERNMENT OF THE GERMAN REICH CAUSED
BY THIS BLATANT VIOLATION OF NEU-
TRALITY BY THE US GOVERNMENT. AM-
BASSADOR WILL REMIND ARGENTINE
GOVERNMENT OF THE SINKING OF THE
PORTUGUESE MERCHANT SHIP REINE DE
LA MER UNDER VERY SUSPICIOUS CIR-
CUMSTANCES IN SAMBOROMBON BAY AND
TO REQUEST IN THE STRONGEST POS-
SIBLE LANGUAGE THAT ARGENTINE NA-
VAL FORCES ASSUME RESPONSIBILITY

FOR THE SAFETY OF THE COMERCIANTE DEL OCEANO PACIFICO WHILE SHE IS IN ARGENTINIAN WATERS. SIMILAR ACTION WILL BE TAKEN BY THE SPANISH AMBASSADOR.

3. AMBASSADOR AND GOLTZ ARE EXPECTED TO TAKE WHATEVER PRECAUTIONS ARE NECESSARY TO INSURE SECURITY OF MATERIEL EN ROUTE IN CONNECTION WITH REPATRIATION PLAN. AMBASSADOR WILL REPORT RECEIPT OF MATERIEL BY URGENT RADIO TO FOREIGN MINISTER.

4. CONTENTS OF THIS MESSAGE, AND ACTION DIRECTED HEREIN HAVE BEEN COORDINATED WITH HIMMLER, BORMANN, CANARIS, AND DOENITZ.

IN THE NAME OF THE FUHRER, ADOLF HITLER!

VON RIBBENTROP

FOREIGN MINISTER

MOST SECRET

Glotz idly handed the message to Gradny-Sawz and looked at Grüner.

"We have another situation, don't we, Herr Oberst, where, thanks to the nonavailability of our delicate cryptographic officer, you already know information you are not authorized to know?"

"It would appear so."

"You are now authorized to know it," Goltz said with a smile. "So what is your reaction to this?"

"May I speak freely, Herr Standartenführer? Offer a professional observation that in another context might be considered disrespectful?"

"Of course."

"The Americans and the English knew the *Océano Pacífico* is the replacement for the *Reine de la Mer* before they dispatched their vessels to find it."

"How could they possibly have known that?" Gradny-Sawz demanded.

"If they weren't sure, they would have shadowed her with discretion. When they 'intimidated' her, they were thumbing their noses at us."

"To what purpose?" Goltz asked.

Grüner did not reply directly.

"And they are by now probably wondering what 'matériel' the *Océano Pacífico* has aboard that merits the attention of the Foreign Minister, after coordination with Canaris, Doenitz, and, *especially,* Bormann and Himmler."

"You're not really suggesting the enemy has intercepted that message, much less have been able to decrypt it?" Goltz asked.

"There's no question that they have intercepted it," Grüner said. "And if they haven't managed to decrypt it yet, it won't take them long."

"I refuse to believe that!" Gradny-Sawz said indignantly. "German cryptography is the best in the world!"

"And I would further suggest, Herr Standartenführer," Grüner went on, ignoring Gradny-Sawz, "that other connections will be made. Your name is listed as a special recipient. 'Who is Standartenführer Goltz?' They have an Order of Battle, Herr

765

Standartenführer. They know who you are. 'What is the SS-SD liaison officer to the Office of the Party Chancellery doing in Buenos Aires? Why is he being made privy to this particular message? Is it because there is a connection between him and this mysterious matériel von Ribbentrop is talking about?' "

"You certainly seem to be greatly impressed, Grüner, with the capabilities of our enemies!" Gradny-Sawz said.

"I am paid, Herr Baron . . . ," Grüner began coldly, but was interrupted by Goltz.

"Anton, ssssh!" he said. "Oberst Grüner is not pleased with what he considers to be his duty to tell me."

"I don't think it reasonable to assume, Herr Standartenführer," Grüner said, "that the Americans or the English have any idea of the nature of the 'matériel' they will correctly suspect is aboard the *Comerciante del Océano Pacífico*, but because of the interest shown by our senior leaders in it they will conclude that it is important. Given that, they may decide it is in their best interests to destroy the 'matériel,' and worry about the indignation of the Spanish and the Argentines later."

"By destroy it, you mean sink the *Océano Pacífico*?" Goltz asked, and then answered his own question. "Why wouldn't they have done that on the high seas when they found her?"

"They found her *before* this message was sent," Grüner replied reasonably.

"Permission to speak, Herr Oberst?" Peter von Wachtstein asked. Grüner nodded. "Herr Oberst, I have the feeling that I am listening to a discussion I perhaps should not be hearing."

Grüner looked at Goltz. Goltz looked at Peter for a moment.

"Give Hans that message, Anton, please," Goltz ordered.

Gradny-Sawz did so reluctantly. Goltz waited until Peter had read the message, and then went on.

"The 'matériel' to which the message refers, Hans," Goltz said, "is for use in repatriating the *Graf Spee* officers. Some of it is military in nature, shortwave radios, that sort of thing, and small arms. Some of it is passports and other documentation. There is even some money. It would be very inconvenient if it were lost, and embarrassing, if the documents, in particular, fell into the wrong hands."

Like hell it is, Herr Standartenführer, Peter thought. *What you're talking about is money. The money von Lutzenberger told me the replacement ship was bringing in. And the loss of a few small arms and radios and "some money" wouldn't even be brought to the attention of Himmler, Canaris, and company.*

"Yes, Sir," Peter said.

"Two things seem evident to me," Goltz said. "The repatriation of the *Graf Spee* officers has come to the attention of our most senior leaders. Perhaps the Führer himself has expressed an interest —"

"Yes, I would not be surprised," Gradny-Sawz interrupted, which earned him a look of disdain from Goltz.

"— and that Oberst Grüner is correct in believing that the Americans are quite capable of sinking the *Océano Pacífico* without concerning themselves with either the Argentine or the Spanish outrage that would cause, simply because attention has been called to the matériel our beloved Foreign

Minister has informed them she has aboard."

Gradny-Sawz was visibly shocked by the sarcastically disrespectful reference to Foreign Minister von Ribbentrop.

"As a matter of fact," Goltz went on, "I think we should consider ourselves fortunate that the Americans did not have a chance to intercept and decrypt Ribbentrop's message. They very likely would have attempted to board the *Océano Pacífico*."

"But Josef," Gradny-Sawz said, "the *Océano Pacífico* is armed. She would have fought rather than submitted to a boarding."

"An armed merchantman is no match for a destroyer," Goltz said. "If the Americans had intercepted that message before they found the *Océano Pacífico*, our matériel would now be on the bottom of the South Atlantic Ocean."

"She's due at the mouth of the River Plate at nine tonight," Grüner said thoughtfully.

"With a little bit of luck, she may arrive a little sooner," Goltz said. "If I were her captain, under the circumstances I would make all the speed I could. And with a little more luck, the Americans will not be able to decrypt Ribbentrop's news bulletin until she is safely inside Argentine waters."

"You don't think the Americans would sink her inside Argentine waters?" Peter asked. "They sank the *Reine de la Mer*."

"One, Hans," Goltz explained, "I don't believe they would send a destroyer into Argentinian waters to sink a neutral vessel, no matter what they suspected of her. A submarine, possibly. Two, I don't think they could set anything up between now and the time the *Océano Pacífico* will enter the River Plate estuary tonight."

"Yes, Sir, I'm sure you're right," Peter said.

"But tomorrow, as a wise man once said, is another day," Goltz said. "And by the day *after* tomorrow, there is no question the Americans could bring a submarine into Samborombón Bay to sink the *Océano Pacífico*. And we certainly cannot place any real hope that by the day after tomorrow the Argentine government will respond to von Lutzenberger's request that the Argentine Navy protect her."

"Not in the present circumstances," Gradny-Sawz agreed solemnly.

"Which means we have three choices," Goltz went on. "We can try to get that matériel off the *Océano Pacífico* tonight, which seems unlikely. Or first thing in the morning, which seems possible but risky — there would be obvious risks in landing a boat during the day. Or as soon after dark tomorrow night as possible, which I think is the solution."

"Yes, I would agree," Gradny-Sawz said.

"Von Wachtstein," Grüner asked, "what's the status of the boat?"

"Herr Loche — Günther's father — took possession of the boat yesterday, Herr Oberst. I believe the both of them — Günther for sure — were going to El Tigre this morning to test the engine, and so forth."

"That may change, because of the circumstances," Gradny-Sawz offered.

"Have you seen the boat, von Wachtstein?" Goltz asked.

"Yes, Sir."

"In other words, you would know where to find it if you went out there?"

"Yes, Sir."

"Anton, I have a mission for you," Goltz said. "You will find Günther — preferably Günther and his father, but Günther in any case — and order him out to the boat, if he's not already there."

"Wouldn't it be better to send von Wachtstein?"

"I will explain, in this instance, that I believe that the First Secretary of the Embassy of the German Reich, in an Embassy Mercedes, stands a better chance of making it through the lines of the revolutionaries than a major."

"Of course, you're probably right," Gradny-Sawz said.

"And I will tell you this just once, Gradny-Sawz: Never question any orders I give you ever again."

Gradny-Sawz's plump face colored.

"Josef, I meant no —"

"For the time being, Gradny-Sawz, I think it would be best if you referred to me by my rank."

Gradny-Sawz swallowed.

"Jawohl, Herr Standartenführer," he said finally.

"Von Wachtstein, do you think you can make it through this revolution we seem to be having out to El Tigre?"

"I'm confident I can, Herr Standartenführer."

"You will go there and take possession of the boat. If Günther and/or his father is there, they will serve as your crew to take the boat to Magdalena. If they are not there by ten-thirty, you will take the boat to Magdalena by yourself and hold yourself in readiness there for further orders."

"Jawohl, Herr Standartenführer."

"You said, Oberst Grüner, that you have someone in Naval Headquarters?"

"Yes, I do."

"Can he be relied upon to notify you of the

arrival of the *Comerciante del Océano Pacífico* within Argentine waters?"

"Not unless I specifically ask him to. I mean, I receive regular routine reports of all shipping activity, but I think you're talking about learning of her arrival immediately."

"We need to know when she enters Argentine waters and more importantly, where she will anchor. Do you think, Grüner, that when the *Océano Pacífico* reports entering the River Plate your man has enough authority to order her to anchor in Samborombón Bay?"

"I would have to go to Naval Headquarters and explain the situation," Grüner said. "My man, unfortunately, owes his allegiance to Castillo."

"You have only one asset in Naval Headquarters?" Goltz asked impatiently.

"Only one in the office of the Harbor Master," Grüner said.

Goltz turned to Peter.

"Oberst Grüner and I will work this out, von Wachtstein," he said. "We really have until, say, six o'clock tonight. You understand what I'm thinking?"

"I think so, Herr Standartenführer. Presuming I can get out of El Tigre, I should be in Magdalena by five or five-thirty. Oberst Grüner will determine the *Océano Pacífico*'s estimated time of arrival and where she will drop anchor, and he will send that information to me at Magdalena. On your orders, I will take the boat out to the *Océano Pacífico*. From that point, we will proceed with the discharge of the matériel aboard the ship as per the original plan."

"You see any problems with that, von Wachtstein? Aside from getting out of El Tigre into the

771

River Plate?" Grüner challenged.

"Only finding the *Comerciante del Océano Pacífico* at night, Herr Oberst."

"If that looks like a problem, you could delay taking the boat out from Magdalena until first light," Goltz ordered. "I'll have to go out to her myself; and if you think there would be a problem finding her at night, I would have the same problem. Grüner, I presume everything else is ready?"

"Yes, it is," Grüner replied. "The only possible problems I can see are von Wachtstein getting out of El Tigre, and then finding the ship from there at night."

"We are presuming your friend can order her to drop anchor someplace where it will be convenient to Magdalena and the landing point."

"Where is that, Herr Standartenführer?" Peter asked.

"You'll be advised, Hans, at the appropriate time," Goltz said. "What I will do now is wait here for the Ambassador to arrive. That will be all, gentlemen, thank you."

Gradny-Sawz gave the Nazi salute, and barked, "Heil Hitler!"

Peter had come to the Embassy by taxi from his apartment. Then, there had been any number of taxis on the street. Now there were none in sight on Avenida Córdoba in either direction. There was no other traffic either, vehicles or pedestrians.

The word was apparently out that the revolution had begun.

Further up Avenida Córdoba, he could see the lead elements of the stalled columns of the First Cavalry and the Second Infantry regiments — riflemen on foot, mounted cavalry, and even some horse-drawn 75-mm howitzers.

He was going to have to get past those lines anyway, he reasoned. Perhaps traffic was again moving in the areas now controlled by the revolutionary forces. He started walking toward the soldiers.

He had walked two blocks when his ears picked up the sound of a light aircraft. A very low-flying light aircraft. He looked up in the sky, trying — without success — to spot it.

And then it came from behind him, very low. It was a Piper Cub, wearing the insignia of the Argentine Army. It was no more than a hundred feet over the roofs of the buildings lining both sides of Avenida Córdoba.

I wonder what the hell that's about?

XXIII

[One]

Office of the Naval Attaché
The Embassy of the United States
The Bank of Boston Building
Avenida Bartolomé Mitre
Buenos Aires, Argentina
0555 19 April 1943

The event that became known in history books as the Argentine Revolution of 1943 first came to the attention of Lieutenant Commander Frederico Delojo, USN, Naval Attaché (and, covertly, OSS representative) of the Embassy of the United States of America at 0452 19 April 1943.

He was later to remember the precise time and circumstances because he not only made a note of the time but also because he was wakened from a sound sleep in his apartment by a horrendous squealing of tortured tires, followed immediately by the scream of metal tearing asunder.

He jumped out of bed and went to the balcony of his apartment. As he suspected, there'd been one hell of an accident, involving a truck and an automobile. The automobile was a police vehicle. It was equipped with a large chrome-plated (and probably American) siren mounted on the roof.

And it had collided with an Army truck, striking the truck as it moved through the intersection.

Then Commander Delojo noticed something odd. There was not just one Army truck, but a number of them, a convoy, presumably under the command of the officer who now appeared, wearing a sword, and accompanied by four soldiers in German-style helmets and field gear. As the officer directed the removal of the injured driver of the police vehicle from his crushed vehicle, another police vehicle, with siren screaming, came racing down the street and very narrowly avoided colliding with the two vehicles now blocking the intersection.

It was followed almost immediately by another police car, siren screaming, which could not stop in time and collided with what Delojo now thought of as Police Vehicle Two.

The intersection was now effectively blocked by the truck and three police vehicles. An Army car, a 1941 Chevrolet four-door sedan, now appeared, and a lieutenant colonel hurried out of the backseat and, with some excitement and waving of his arms, began to order the clearing of the intersection.

Moments later, two sergeants appeared with twenty soldiers in field gear and directed their pushing of the disabled vehicles off the intersection.

As soon as that was accomplished, the convoy of army trucks began to move again. Without thinking about it, Commander Delojo began to count them. Twenty-six trucks passed through the intersection. Each of them was loaded with infantryman in German-style steel helmets sitting shoulder to shoulder and holding their rifles erect between their knees.

This was possibly a routine maneuver, Commander Delojo decided. But on the other hand, it was also possible that the troops were somehow connected with the coup d'état that everybody expected.

It was worth calling the duty officer at the Embassy, Delojo decided. His telephone was dead.

At that point, Commander Delojo put on his uniform, checked to see that he had both his diplomatic passport and the carnet issued to diplomats by the Argentine Foreign Ministry, and left his apartment. Obviously it was his duty to notify the OSS as soon as possible that the long-expected coup d'état was finally taking place.

Nothing now on the street indicated what had roused him from his sound sleep but the first police car. The other police cars and the convoy were nowhere in sight.

A taxi came down the street. He flagged it and ordered the driver to take him to the United States Embassy.

En route to the Embassy the taxi was stopped twice by roadblocks, one manned by half a dozen members of the Corps of Mounted Police and the other by a platoon of soldiers of an Engineer Battalion. The Mounted Police passed him through immediately, but the two Engineer lieutenants held a whispered discussion that lasted ten minutes before deciding they should pass the American diplomat.

While he was waiting for their discussion to conclude, Delojo reconsidered his original idea to urgently message the OSS in Washington that the coup d'état was now taking place.

For one thing, he did not know for a fact that it was. He really should not message Washington unless he could transmit facts. And prudence suggested that just sitting on the nest waiting to see what breed of chick emerged from the egg was the proper course of action.

Yesterday, Vacuum — Mr. Milton Leibermann of the Federal Bureau of Investigation — put his head in the door and in an unexpected and frankly unwelcome spirit of interagency cooperation informed him that he had just learned that one of Frade's enlisted men, Sergeant David Ettinger, was missing from Estancia San Pedro y San Pablo and was very possibly in great danger, and that he thought Delojo should know about it.

Oracle would certainly want to know about that. Theoretically, Frade or his parachutist deputy would have relayed that information to Washington. But that was a dangerous presumption to make. Perhaps Frade didn't know about it, and Lieutenant Whatsisname — Pelosi — could not be relied upon to act in a responsible manner. He was, in fact, a demolitions man, not an intelligence officer.

On one hand, Delojo reasoned, if he messaged Oracle about the missing sergeant, it might make the point that he was staying on top of the situation in Buenos Aires. But on the other hand, doing so raised two potential areas of difficulty. Frade was responsible for reporting on his own men. After that unnecessarily curt message from Donovan about his role with respect to Frade, it might appear that he was trying to put his nose in somewhere it wasn't welcome. Furthermore, if he did inform the OSS that the sergeant was missing, he would be expected to reveal the source of his information, Leibermann. Director Donovan had told him personally that he was to have as little to do with the FBI as possible — preferably nothing.

It was near six A.M. when Commander Delojo reached the Bank of Boston Building. Just before he entered it, he decided that the most prudent course of action was to find out as much about the coup d'état as possible — if that's really what it was — and to see if he could learn anything about the missing sergeant, but not to message Oracle unless he had facts to report.

As Delojo entered the narrow corridor where his office was located, one of the cryptographic section's enlisted men was approaching from out of the corridor. He was a large, tall, corn-haired Iowa farm boy to whom Commander Delojo had been introduced — the Embassy Security Officer thought it a good idea for cryptographic clerks to be personally acquainted with officers authorized to dispatch or receive TOP SECRET material — but he could not at the moment recall his name.

"Morning, Commander," the sergeant said. "I was just looking for you."

"Is that so?"

"Poop from the group for you," the sergeant said, extending a clipboard to Delojo. "Just came in. If you'll sign that, please?"

Commander Delojo held the opinion that the U.S. Army did not instill in its enlisted men a proper respect for commissioned officers — enlisted Army personnel were, if anything, worse than their Marine counterparts — but he did not think this the place or the time to have a word with the sergeant about his informality.

He took the clipboard and signed for Message 3002, TOP SECRET NO COPIES, handed the clipboard back, and reached for the message's envelope.

"What the hell's going on outside, Commander?"

"I don't know, but I wouldn't be surprised to learn the Argentines are staging a coup d'état," Delojo said.

"No shit? Against who?"

That did it. The next time I see the cryptographic officer I will *have a word with him about this young man.*

"By definition, Sergeant, a coup d'état is made against the existing head of state. Here that would be President Castillo."

Commander Delojo carried the envelope to his office, closed and locked the door after him, then tore open the envelope.

```
                 URGENT
              TOP  SECRET


  NOT  TO  BE  COPIED

  FROM  ORACLE  WASHDC

  MSG  NO  3002  DIR
  0050  GREENWICH  19  APRIL  1943


  TO  STACHIEF  AGGIE

    STACHIEF  BUENOS  AIRES

    1.  ADDRESSEE  WILL  REPLY  QUICKEST
  MEANS  GIVING  TIME  RECEIPT  THIS
  MESSAGE

    2.  RELIABLE  INTELLIGENCE  GIVES
  ETA  GROCERYSTORE  TWO  MOUTH  RIVER
  PLATE  1600  GREENWICH  20  APRIL
  1943.
```

3. DETERMINE AND ADVISE QUICKEST
MEANS:

   A. LOCATION AGGIE.

   B. LOCATION TEX AND PARROT AND
OPERATIONAL STATUS OF PARROT.

   C. LOCATION SNOOPY AND TEAM
AND EQUIPMENT AND OPERATIONAL
STATUS EQUIPMENT.

   4. QUERY SOURCE GALAHAD POSSIBLE
REASON SPECIAL INTEREST AT HIGH-
EST LEVELS BERLIN IN SECURITY OF
QUOTE REPATRIATION PLAN MATERIEL
ENDQUOTE POSSIBLY ABOARD GRO-
CERYSTORE TWO.

   5. WHOEVER ESTABLISHES FIRST
CONTACT WITH AGGIE WILL RELAY FOL-
LOWING: PRESIDENT DESIRES EARLI-
EST POSSIBLE IDENTIFICATION AND
MOTIVATION OF GALAHAD.

DONOVAN END

            TOP SECRET

       NOT TO BE COPIED

"Damn!" Commander Delojo said, realizing that the message placed him in an even more difficult position than having to decide whether or not to message Oracle vis-à-vis the coup d'état and Sergeant Whatsisname.

Obviously, if he was to locate Aggie — Colonel A. F. Graham, USMCR — that meant he was down here somewhere.

Why? Has something else gone wrong that I'm not aware of?

Delojo had no idea where Tex — Major Cletus H. Frade, USMCR — was except that he had left Buenos Aires by train five days ago.

The last word he had from Snoopy — Captain Maxwell Ashton III, AUS — was that he was in Santo Tomé and his team and their equipment were in Pôrto Alegre, Brazil.

Pôrto Alegre was the last known location of Parrot — the airplane that Frade had gone to Pôrto Alegre to pick up and, against Delojo's objections, bring into Argentina black, while carrying the rest of Team Snoopy and their radar equipment with him.

Since he had no idea of the identity, much less the motivation, of Galahad, he obviously could not locate him and query him regarding the " 'repatriation plan matériel' possibly aboard grocerystore two," whatever the hell that might be.

But an order was an order, and there was nothing to do but reply to Oracle's 3002, even though he was quite sure it was going to make him look like a fool.

He sat down and rapidly typed his reply on a blank sheet of paper:

TOP SECRET

URGENT

FROM STACHIEF BUENOS AIRES
0010 GREENWICH 19 APR 43

TO ORACLE WASH DC

REFERENCE YOUR 3002

1. RECEIVED 1050 GREENWICH 19 APR 43.

2. HAVE BEGUN EFFORT TO LOCATE AGGIE.

3. LOCATION TEX UNKNOWN LAST RE-PORTED ENROUTE BIRDCAGE. NO IN-FORMATION AVAILABLE RE SNOOPY, TEAM, OR EQUIPMENT. HAVE BEGUN EF-FORT TO DEVELOP REQUESTED INFOR-MATION.

4. CANNOT QUERY GALAHAD INASMUCH AS IDENTITY UNKNOWN.

5. UNUSUAL MILITARY AND POLICE ACTIVITY EARLY THIS AM SUGGESTS POSSIBILITY COUP DETAT MAY BE UN-DERWAY. PRESENTLY AVAILABLE IN-TELLIGENCE INSUFFICIENT TO PREDICT OUTCOME.

6. UNCONFIRMED INTELLIGENCE RE-PORTS SARNOFF MISSING.

END

STACHIEF BUENOS AIRES

TOP SECRET

He carefully read what he had typed, then took it to the cryptographic officer and instructed him to dispatch the message immediately.

Of all the missions Oracle had ordered, he decided, the priority mission was the location of Colonel Graham. The problem was that he had absolutely no idea where Colonel Graham might be.

The best thing to do, he concluded, was stay right where he was. For one thing, if Colonel Graham were here and became aware the coup d'état was probably taking place, he would either contact the Embassy or telephone. If that was true, it was his place to be available. Furthermore, the Embassy was probably the best place to gather additional information about the coup d'état.

Delojo returned to his office, left it to pick up a cup of coffee from the machine in the room housing the typing pool, and returned to his office.

He stepped out on the balcony and gazed down at the street. A group of natives was in the process of rocking a bus. As Delojo watched, they succeeded in turning it onto its side. Gasoline began to spill from the fueling mouth. Someone tossed a match, and the gasoline caught fire.

A minute or so later, the gas tank exploded.

Delojo stepped back from the edge of the balcony. There was no point in making oneself conspicuous in a situation like this.

An Argentine Army Piper Cub flew overhead, from the direction of the Casa Rosada. Delojo had several questions about it. Was it a loyalist, so to be speak, aircraft, or aligned with the revolutionaries? And what was it doing? Delojo had had several conversations with the Army Attaché about such aircraft. For the Attaché had discussed with his Argentine Army counterparts the concept of direction of artillery fire by airborne forward observers, and had been told that this would be quite impossible until Argentine Army artillery units were equipped with radios capable of communicating with aircraft.

Commander Delojo set out to find the Army Attaché. This was an interesting development, and discussing it with the Army Attaché would be a fruitful way of passing the time until something happened.

[Two]

```
Aboard Argentine Army Air Service
Light Aircraft Type 42 #6
Above Plaza San Martín
Capital Federal
Buenos Aires, Argentina
0615 19 April 1943
```

After a brief period of considerable — and visible — uneasiness and uncertainty, General of Division Arturo Rawson, President of the Governing Council of the Provisional Government of the Republic of Argentina, quickly became not only a believer in the amazing capabilities of light aircraft, but quickly applied those capabilities toward the execution of OUTLINE BLUE.

General Rawson had of course previously flown in Type 42 Aircraft (a high-wing monoplane powered by a 75-horsepower Continental A-75-8 engine and known commercially as the Piper J-4

Cub); but on those flights the pilots were Argentine Army Air Service officers with a deep interest in doing nothing that would make a general officer feel uncomfortable or give him any cause whatever to suspect that they were anything but sober, careful airmen devoted to all aspects of aviation safety.

Today, he was being flown by a pilot who had soloed, illegally, in a Piper Cub at thirteen years of age, after six hours of illegal, if careful, flight instruction by his uncle. Later, Marine Aviation Cadet Frade, C.H., had three times come very close indeed to being dropped from the program at the United States Navy Aviation Training Base, Pensacola, Florida. Cadet Frade's problems with the program had nothing to do with his ability, or inability, to fly the Stearman "Yellow Peril" basic training aircraft, or with the academic portion of the training syllabus, but with his difficulty in learning to fly "The Navy Way" at the Navy's pace, while paying strict attention to the Navy's deep concern for flight safety.

For example, some improvised variations from normal procedures during his first solo cross-country flight in the Stearman brought him for the first time before a board of stern-faced Naval Aviators who were considering his possible expulsion from the program.

The flight plan called for him to fly from Saufley Field to an auxiliary field just across the Florida-Alabama border, shoot a touch-and-go, and then return to Saufley Field.

He did that. But he was also observed en route by a flight instructor who reported that Cadet Frade not only engaged in twenty minutes of unauthorized aerobatic maneuvers in the Stearman, but followed this outrageous deviation from his authorized flight plan by returning to Saufley Field via the Gulf Coast beaches, along which he flew at no more than 200 feet above the surf, while waving at female civilian sunbathers on the beach.

After his third appearance before the Elimination Board, Cadet Frade realized that any further infractions against the Navy's Flight Regulations, particularly those involving unsafe flight maneuvers, would almost certainly keep him from receiving his wings of gold and second lieutenant's commission.

No more infractions of any kind were laid against him during the rest of his Primary Flight Instruction, nor during Advanced Flight Training, nor — after he was rated a Naval Aviator and commissioned second lieutenant, USMCR — while undergoing the prescribed courses of instruction which saw him rated as an F4F "Wildcat" pilot.

Things changed slightly when he was assigned to VMF-221 at Ewa, Territory of Hawaii. The Marine Air Group Commander, Lieutenant Colonel Clyde W. Dawkins, greeted him there with a speech. Its most pertinent point developed the notion that now that Second Lieutenant Frade had learned to fly a Wildcat safely, it was his duty, before entering combat, to learn how far he personally "could push the Wildcat's envelope."

"The Envelope" was defined as the limits (in terms of speed, various maneuvers, stress, and so forth) to which the Navy Bureau of Aeronautics had determined the Wildcat could be safely subjected.

Second Lieutenant Frade accepted this order with enthusiasm. By the time he landed his Wildcat on Guadalcanal on the just-captured airfield — not even yet named "Henderson" after a Marine aviator who had died in the Battle of Midway — he had proved to himself that the Wildcat's actual envelope permitted, among other things, close-to-the-ground maneuvering at speeds far beyond those given in the official BUAIR envelope.

The day after First Lieutenant Frade became an ace by downing five enemy aircraft in his Wildcat, he was summoned before Lieutenant Colonel Dawkins, the Marine Air Group Commander. Colonel Dawkins told him he had seen his flight records, which included civilian flying experience, and reported that Cletus H. Frade had passed the Civil Aviation Administration's Flight Examination in a Piper Cub; and had received his private pilot's license in the second week of his fourteenth year; and had subsequently acquired 930 hours of time in the Piper Aircraft Company's Model J-4.

Colonel Dawkins then explained that there had been unexpected losses of Marine aviators, mostly Flying Sergeants, who had been flying the First Marine Division's Piper Cubs, aircraft that were used for artillery spotting, liaison, and aerial ambulance purposes. Dawkins then asked him if he would be willing to fly a Piper Cub until replacement pilots could be brought to Guadalcanal from the States.

On one hand, stepping down from a Wildcat to a Cub was obviously beneath the dignity of a Marine fighter pilot; but on the other, Lieutenant Frade had been in the Corps long enough to understand that when a lieutenant is asked to do something by a lieutenant colonel, the expected response is "Aye, aye, Sir."

Before strapping General Rawson into the backseat of the Argentine Army Air Service Light Aircraft Type 42 #6, Major Frade's last significant

787

flight experience in a Piper Cub had been to locate, and then drop messages and essential supplies, to the First Raider Battalion operating in mountainous jungle terrain some fifty miles behind Japanese lines.

General Rawson, of course, knew nothing of any of this. All he knew was that the Cub he was flying in now was being flown in a different manner — a frighteningly different manner — than he was accustomed to.

For one thing — because Clete had decided the best way to find the Argentine Navy's School of Naval Engineering was to find and then fly down Avenida del Libertador — their altitude between Campo de Mayo and the place where the Navy was holding up the progress of the First Infantry Regiment never exceeded 300 feet and was often considerably less. Frade often flew the Cub around — rather than over — brick smokestacks and other high structures in his flight path.

For another, when they approached the School of Naval Engineering, without really thinking about it, Clete began to move the Cub in a manner that would make the Cub a more difficult target for anyone inclined to shoot at it.

For another, General Rawson's orders to Clete had been to land on the soccer fields adjacent to the School of Naval Engineering, "if possible." In his mind, he would evaluate the situation, the location of the opposing elements, and then authorize Frade to determine, as Step Two, whether he could safely land the airplane on the field.

Clete took one look at the soccer field, decided it was obviously possible to land there — all the Navy weaponry, mostly light machine-gun positions, were emplaced to oppose the First Infantry's movement down Avenida del Libertador — and did so.

By the time he taxied back to a takeoff position, three officers of the First Infantry — one of them had actually unsheathed his sword — galloped onto the soccer field to investigate the astonishing landing of an airplane.

General Rawson climbed out of the Cub, discussed the situation with the officers, and issued his orders. After leaving a few men in place facing the Navy, the regiment would bypass the School of Engineering and resume its march down Avenida del Libertador.

When they had moved far enough down Libertador so that simultaneous movement of the First Cavalry and the Second Infantry would bring both columns to the Casa Rosada at the same time, the First Cavalry and the Second Infantry would be ordered to resume their march.

"I am now going to reconnoiter by air," General Rawson announced, "to ascertain the exact location of the First Cavalry and the Second Infantry."

He then climbed back into the Cub.

The First Infantry officers saluted and began to trot back to their troops.

General Rawson laid a hand on Clete's shoulder, and Clete turned to look at him.

"Is there any way we can communicate when we are up in the air?"

Clete showed General Rawson the earphones and microphone — with which he had mistakenly believed General Rawson would be familiar — and Rawson put them on.

"You may depart," Rawson ordered.

Clete pushed the throttle forward and took off. Once they were airborne he started to look for the

First Cavalry and the Second Infantry, which he had been told were stopped at Pueyrredón and Córdoba.

"It will take twenty minutes for the orders to be passed and for the First Infantry to make any measurable progress," Rawson announced over the intercom. "Would it be possible, without extraordinary risk, to observe what's going on at the Casa Rosada?"

"Yes, Sir," Clete said, and for the next twenty minutes Clete flew back and forth over Buenos Aires.

As he flew down Avenida Córdoba he noticed a man in a strange uniform, and he was almost convinced it was Peter von Wachtstein. When they flew over Plaza de Mayo, they saw an overturned bus in flames, and he could see the faces of people inside Casa Rosada watching it burn.

Twenty-five minutes after taking off from the soccer fields, General Rawson decided the First Infantry had moved far enough so that the First Cavalry and the Second Infantry could be ordered to resume their march.

Clete flew down Avenida Córdoba again and dropped the order to the First Cavalry and the Second Infantry to get moving.

Thirty minutes after that, as both columns converged onto the Plaza de Mayo, white flags — probably sheets, Clete decided — appeared in the windows of the Casa Rosada.

"General, you want me to try to land down there? I'm a little worried about that burning bus. I don't know what debris's liable to be on the street."

"You mean land in Plaza de Mayo?" General Rawson replied, a touch of incredulity in his voice. And then, without giving Clete a chance to reply, he went on: "I think we should return now to Campo de Mayo. It would be more fitting if General Ramírez and I accepted the capitulation together and arrive at Casa Rosada together. By automobile. With a suitable escort."

On the fifteen-minute flight back to Campo de Mayo, General Rawson pushed his intercom mike switch one more time.

"I think I should tell you, my friend, that when your father talked about all the amazing things one could do with a small airplane, I was one of those who simply didn't believe him. How nice it is that his son should be the one to prove us all wrong."

[Three]

The Officers' Casino
Campo de Mayo
Buenos Aires Province, Argentina
1845 19 April 1943

Teniente Coronel Alejandro Bernardo Martín rolled up the curved driveway to the Officers' Casino in the chauffeur-driven official Mercedes assigned to the Chief of the Bureau of Internal Security of the Ministry of National Defense.

During the day there had been well over one hundred proclamations issued in the name of the Governing Council of the Provisional Government of the Argentine Republic. Of these, three personally issued by the President had a direct effect on Teniente Coronel Martín:

El Almirante Francisco de Montoya, Chief of the

BIS, had been relieved of his duties, placed on leave, and would be retired.

Until a successor to Almirante de Montoya was named, Teniente Coronel Alejandro Bernardo Martín would assume the duties of Chief, BIS.

Teniente Coronel Alejandro Bernardo Martín was brevetted Coronel until further orders.

Coronel Juan Domingo Perón wanted Montoya dismissed from the service and placed under house arrest. But Martín prevailed against him. Martín argued before General Rawson and General Ramírez (who retained his post as Minister of War) that Montoya had done his duty to Argentina as he had seen it and had taken or not taken a number of actions that had benefited the Grupo de Oficiales Unidos and the execution of OUTLINE BLUE.

Martín also refused permanent appointment as the Chief of BIS. The offer was colored, he believed, by emotion on the part of General Rawson, who would later come to regret his impulsiveness. He also believed the appointment of another admiral to the post would go a long way toward pouring oil on the troubled waters that now existed between the Argentine Armada and the Argentine Army.

On the other hand, Martín was rather sure that his brevet promotion to Coronel would be made permanent within the next few days. As a Coronel known to have both the ear and the gratitude of the President and the Minister of War, he would have no trouble dealing with the new Chief, BIS, no matter who that might be.

The sandbag machine-gun emplacements in front of the Casino were still there, but the weapons and their crews were gone. So were the machine guns that had earlier been visible in upper-floor windows of the building, and the guards who had been stationed at the Casino's doors.

General Ramírez was now back in his office at the Edificio Libertador — Martín had just come from there — and the maps that had been hung in the early hours of the morning on the movable wall of the Main Dining Room were now hanging in the Situation Room in the Edificio Libertador.

The Officers' Casino of Campo de Mayo was now just that again.

Martín marched through the door of the club — he was in uniform, still bearing the badges of a teniente coronel. *Perhaps,* he thought, *there will one day be a brass plaque affixed to the wall, commemorating the use of the Casino as the headquarters of the coup d'état. But perhaps not. It might be better not to have such an historical marker. It might be better if the coup d'état, and the reasons for it, and the deaths of Argentine soldiers and sailors it caused, just faded from memory.*

As soon as he was in the lobby, he saw Major Cletus H. Frade, of the norteamericano Office of Strategic Services. Frade, who had obviously and understandably been waiting for him, rose out of a leather-upholstered armchair and started walking toward him, closely followed by Suboficial Mayor Enrico Rodríguez, Retired.

I wonder, Martín thought somewhat unkindly, *if the old soldier thinks Frade needs protection in the men's room and follows him in there?*

"Ah, Mayor Frade," Martín said, smiling and putting out his hand. "I understand that you have been flying our new President around."

"That was twelve hours ago," Clete said, "and since then I have been sitting around here with my . . ." He stopped himself just in time from completing the rest of the sentence that came to his lips; it had to do with the insertion of the short thick opposable digit of his hand into his anal orifice. He finished,

". . . nothing to do."

Martín's smile faded but did not entirely disappear.

"I don't know if there's dancing in the streets or not," Clete went on. "But I just heard General Rawson on the radio delivering a speech from the balcony of the Casa Rosada, which suggests to me the coup d'état was successful."

I know what's bothering him: his Sergeant Ettinger. I don't want to break that bad news to him here, like this.

"And so it has been," Martín said. "I was about to have a drink. I would be honored if you would join me."

"I'm not sure I should have a drink," Clete said. "I might say something rude with just a little alcohol in me."

"Please," Martín said. "I will buy. It is a custom in our Army for newly promoted officers to buy drinks for their friends. And the invitation of course includes you, Suboficial Mayor."

"You got promoted?"

"Are you all that surprised?"

"No. Not at all," Clete said. "I didn't mean to be so . . ."

"But you have been unable to understand why you have been . . . asked to stay here . . . when it became apparent that we have a new government?"

"Yeah," Clete said. "And 'asked' isn't the word."

He pointed to a major, still in field uniform, who was watching them.

Martín gestured for the major to join them.

"Señor Frade, Mayor," Martín said, "will no longer require your protection. You may consider yourself relieved of that responsibility."

"Sí, mi Coronel," the Major replied, and then after a moment's hesitation offered his hand to Clete. "I hope, Señor, you can understand my position."

"No hard feelings, Major," Clete said, taking his hand. "I know who gave you your orders."

"I considered it necessary," Martín said, acknowledging he had given the orders. "Not only because I wanted to have a word with you before you took off . . ."

"It's too late to take off," Clete said. "I don't want to try to land that Lockheed at Estancia San Pedro y San Pablo at night."

". . . but for other reasons as well," Martín concluded. "Will you have a drink with me? I'll explain."

"Yes, of course. Thank you. And congratulations, mi Coronel. It's a well-deserved promotion."

"For saying that, I will buy you two drinks."

He touched Clete's arm and propelled him to the bar, which was crowded with the successful members of the Revolution of 1943 not needed at the Edificio Libertador.

"Would you bring us a bottle of Johnny Walker Black, please? And three glasses?" Martín ordered.

When it was delivered, he waved the barman away, poured the whiskey himself, and handed Clete and Enrico their glasses.

"If you will indulge me further, gentlemen, I have three toasts to offer."

"Don't take too long," Clete said.

"To the new government of Argentina," Martín said seriously.

Clete raised his glass.

"Hear, hear," he said.

"To the officers and other ranks of the Argentine Armada and Army on both sides of this unfortunately necessary change of government who died for their country today."

Clete's face showed that the toast surprised him, but after a moment he said, "Hear, hear," raised his glass, and took another sip of his whiskey.

"And to Technical Sergeant David Ettinger, United States Army. I am very sorry indeed, Mayor Frade, to have to tell you that he also died in the service of his country."

"Oh, shit," Clete said. He looked at his half-empty glass of scotch, drained it, and then looked at Martín.

"When did that happen? How?"

"Excuse me, mi Coronel," Enrico said. "Did you say Ettinger is dead?"

"I'm afraid so, Suboficial Mayor," Martín said, then looked at Clete. "I received the word just two hours ago. When the telephones to Montevideo were restored. Sergeant Ettinger's body was found on the beach at Carrasco two days ago. In the morning. He had been stabbed to death."

Martín saw that Clete's face was white, and his lips bloodless.

With either pain or rage or both. This is not the time to tell him Ettinger was mutilated. Or how.

"By party or parties unknown, right?" Clete asked bitterly.

"My sources tell me the murder has all the marks of a killing for pay."

"And we know who paid, don't we? That god-damned Goltz!"

" 'Goltz,' Señor Clete?" Enrico asked.

"That German SS Colonel, Enrico. He ordered Ettinger's murder, and he got it. He's the same sonofabitch who ordered my father killed. I'll get that sonofabitch, somehow!"

"I understand your feelings, Frade," Martín said, "but it would help nothing if you took any —"

"It would be unprofessional, right? Conduct unbecoming an intelligence officer? Well let me tell you, mi Coronel, if I ever get a bead on that Kraut sonofabitch — and I'm damned sure going to try — I'll drop him in his tracks!"

"A 'bead,' Señor Clete?" Enrico asked.

"A 'bead'?" Martín parroted.

Clete, looking at the confusion on their faces, smiled.

"I guess that doesn't translate into Spanish very well, does it?" he said. "In English — or American, I suppose — when you line your rifle sights up on a deer, you say you're 'taking a bead.' I guess it comes from the little brass balls the old Winchesters used to use for front sights; they looked like beads."

"You shot many deer in the United States, did you?" Martín asked.

"Asked the professional intelligence officer, cleverly tactfully trying to change the subject," Clete said, smiling at him. "Don't worry, Martín. When I drop that sonofabitch, I will make a real effort to do it so you won't get involved."

Martín smiled at him.

In Frade's shoes, I would certainly feel exactly the same way.

"I ask you, my friend, not to act in haste or

anger," Martín said.

"Is there any longer any reason I have to stay here?" Clete said, then smiled and added, "Asked the amateur intelligence officer, tactfully trying to change the subject."

"The original reason I asked Capitán Delgano to . . . make sure you were available . . . was of course the possibility that the Lockheed would be needed."

"That, I understood. But why until now?"

"El Presidente considered for a while offering your aircraft to former Presidente Castillo and members of the former government. It would take them out of the country."

"Oddly enough, I thought that might be it," Clete said. "I had a lot of time to think, you understand."

Martín looked at Clete, smiled, and shook his head.

"In any event, former Presidente Castillo, and some others, have been placed aboard a boat in El Tigre which will take them to Uruguay. You are free to leave. With the gratitude of the government, and my personal gratitude."

He offered Clete his hand.

"Where will you go?" Martín asked.

"I don't know," Clete said. "What I'm wondering is how I will get anywhere. I flew in here."

"The least we can do for you is provide you with a car and driver," Martín said.

"How about a ride into Buenos Aires?" Clete asked. "I've got cars there. I want to make a telephone call. . . ."

"I took the liberty of telephoning Señorita Mallín — actually I spoke with her father — and told him that, although you were unavoidably detained, you were not in any danger."

"Jesus H. Christ!" Clete said, and then added, thinking out loud: "That was damned nice of you."

"It was nothing," Martín said.

He looked around the room, found the major who had been Clete's oh-so-courteous guard, and waved him over.

"Mayor, I want you to find a car and a driver, and then escort Señor Frade anywhere he wishes to go in Buenos Aires."

"Sí, mi Coronel."

"Thank you," Clete said. "I *am* free to take the airplane?"

"Of course, but you said you . . ."

"Tomorrow," Clete said, thinking aloud. "I'll have somebody drive me out here. Or, if I decide to go to the estancia, I'll fly a Cub here, pick up the Lockheed, and worry about getting the Cub back later."

"I will order Capitán Delgano to make himself available to you at your convenience."

"Thank you very much, mi Coronel, but I won't need Capitán Delgano."

"I would feel so much more comfortable if he were with you."

"Thank you for your concern, but no thank you."

Martín looked at him for a long moment before saying, "Whatever you wish, of course."

From the windows of the Army Mercedes on the way into Buenos Aires, Clete saw absolutely no signs whatever that the country had just undergone a revolution.

The flow of traffic was normal. The restaurants and cafés were open and apparently doing a good business. When they drove down Avenida del

Libertador past the Navy School of Engineering, nothing suggested that a regiment of infantry had been held up there, or that there had been a skirmish in which people had died.

He realized he was going to have to do something about Ettinger. Starting with finding out what happened to him. The question was how to do that. Tony and the Chief would probably have no more information than when he'd flown the Lockheed out of the estancia. If he was killed in Uruguay, any information the police there passed on to norteamericanos would have been passed on to the Embassy in Montevideo, not the Embassy here.

There was probably an OSS station chief in Uruguay, but he had no idea who he was, and he doubted if Delojo did either, or if he did, that he would give that information to him without argument.

Leibermann probably had contacts in Montevideo, but how much they knew — if anything — about an American getting himself stabbed to death in Carrasco was a big question.

The one person who almost certainly had more information than anyone else was Coronel Martín, and he had already told him everything he knew, or at least wanted him to know.

The only way to find out what he had to know was to go to Montevideo himself, and somehow find the OSS guy there and get him to find out what he could.

That was obviously impossible tonight. And tied in with that difficulty was the Lockheed. He wanted to fly the Lockheed out of Campo de Mayo and back to the estancia. Martín did not at all like it when he refused Capitán Delgano's services. And Clete didn't at all like it that General Rawson had considered using the Lockheed to carry the deposed President out of the country. He might decide it would be useful for other purposes — a flight around the country, for example, to show himself off to the people. Clete needed the plane to deal with the *Comerciante del Océano Pacífico*, and that might be as soon as within the next couple of days. Or tomorrow.

And he wanted to see Dorotéa.

The priorities, therefore, were to see Dorotéa and get the Lockheed out of Campo de Mayo. And since he could not move the Lockheed tonight, that meant he could see Dorotéa tonight.

He could of course visit her at her house, where he could see Dorotéa, and her mother, and Señor Mallin, and even Little Henry. And they could talk about getting together with the Very Reverend Matthew Cashley-Price for premarital counseling.

With a little bit of luck I might even get Dorotéa alone for twenty seconds and put my arms around her.

Or, when the Mercedes drops us off at The Museum — No. Uncle Willy's house would be better — I could telephone Dorotéa from there, tell her I can't leave there, I expect an important telephone call or something, and suggest that she come to Uncle Willy's house . . . alone.

Dorotéa is a very intelligent girl. If she agrees to come, she'll understand what I have in mind. After all, as they say, there is no point in closing the barn door after the cow's gotten out, is there?

He turned to the major sitting beside him.

"Mayor," he announced, "now that I think about it, I would rather go to my house on Libertador. The address is 4730. It's right across from the racetrack."

"Whatever you wish, Señor Frade."

"Why are we going to the Libertador house, Señor Clete?" Enrico asked, turning from the front seat.

"I have my reasons," Clete said.

Enrico looked confused for a moment, and then understanding dawned.

He nodded with comprehension and approval.

"You can find something to do to occupy your time, can't you, Enrico?"

"Yes, of course, Señor Clete."

Señora Lopez, the housekeeper, opened the door.

She is not only surprised to see me, but she doesn't seem to be too happy about it, either.

"You will be spending the night, Señor Frade?"

"I think so, yes," Clete said.

She's uncomfortable with that reply, too. What the hell's going on? Oh, hell, she probably was going to take the night off, go to a movie or something, and I'm screwing that up for her.

"I will need nothing tonight," Clete said. "I'm going to bed early" — *I devoutly hope* — "and there's no point in you staying around, if you've made other plans."

"Sí, Señor," Señora Lopez said.

Oh, to hell with her.

"Let's see what cars are here, Enrico," Clete said. "You may have to go over to Avenida Coronel Díaz and get one."

Enrico nodded.

Three cars were in the basement garage: Señora Lopez used the 1939 Ford station wagon to run the house, and in it, it was to be hoped, she would drive to the movies before Dorotéa arrived. Next to it there was the old, immaculately maintained Rolls Royce. And next to that was the bullet-shattered Horche in which his father had been murdered.

"Does that thing work?" Clete asked, pointing at the Rolls. "Specifically, will it make it out to Campo de Mayo in the morning?"

"Of course," Enrico said as if he considered the question very strange.

"OK. Then we'll use that."

Enrico nodded.

Clete walked to the Horche and ran his fingers over the bullet-shattered windshield and the bullet holes in the fenders and doors.

"I want to have this repaired, Enrico. Made like new. Is that going to be a problem?"

"No. It can be done."

There was the sound of an automobile horn, close, a signal.

Enrico walked to the garage door, slipping his .45 automatic from the small of his back and holding it parallel to his leg as he did so. He pushed a button, and the garage door rose.

An Argentine Army staff car with a sergeant at the wheel rolled into the basement.

Jesus Christ, Perón! I forgot that sonofabitch is staying here!

Are you calling him a sonofabitch because he just ruined your carnal plans for the evening?

He was your father's best friend. Be gracious to the sonofabitch!

Clete walked to the car and opened the rear door.

El Coronel Juan Domingo Perón was not alone in the backseat of the car. A girl, fourteen, fifteen, sixteen, no older than that, was sitting beside him. A shy girl, who glanced at Clete, then blushed and looked away.

"Buenos tardes, mi Coronel," Clete said with a smile.

Perón looked a little embarrassed himself.

Probably because you showed your ass to me this morning at the Officers' Casino. You should be embarrassed, you bastard. That wasn't called for.

"I fear, Señor Frade," Perón said, "that I am still imposing on your hospitality."

"Not at all, mi Coronel. My house is your house for as long as you wish."

"You are very kind, but I am —"

"Suboficial Mayor Rodríguez and I were just about to leave," Clete said. "We just came here to pick up the Rolls Royce."

Perón nodded.

"I hope to see you soon, mi Coronel," Clete said, smiled, and walked to the Rolls Royce.

"You better drive, Enrico," Clete said. "I think this thing was made before I was."

He climbed into the front passenger seat and waited for Enrico to get behind the wheel.

Neither Perón nor the girl got out of the car before Enrico drove the Rolls out of the garage.

"Who was the girl, Enrico? His daughter? I thought Perón wasn't married."

"He is not, Señor Clete."

"What is she, then, his niece?"

"Not his niece, Señor Clete. Where are we going, Señor Clete?"

Interesting question. What do I do now? Go to The Museum and call Dorotéa from there? Why call her? She might have come to Uncle Willy's house, but she won't come to The Museum.

"Oh, Christ. To hell with it. To the Mallíns' house, please."

Enrico nodded, and at the next intersection

turned left off Avenida del Libertador.

"If that girl wasn't Perón's niece, who was she?" Clete asked.

Enrico did not answer.

He's not answering that question. Why not? Because he would be embarrassed by the answer? Or because the answer would embarrass Perón? That's what it has to be.

Jesus, is what I am now starting to suspect possible? Obviously, truth being stranger than fiction, it is.

"My God, Enrico, that girl was only fourteen, fifteen years old."

After a significant pause, Enrico said, "Your father, Señor Clete, used to say that to have true friends, you must accept in each one a character flaw of some kind."

"I'll be goddamned," Clete said, chuckling. "El Coronel Juan Domingo Perón is a dirty old man!"

Enrico was not amused. Clete wondered why he himself — he was still smiling — had thought it, literally, laughable.

"Enrico, you don't think there's something strange about somebody his age fooling around with young girls?"

"It is not for me to judge, Señor Clete."

"Has he been doing this long?" Clete asked, naughtily.

He got a look from Enrico that told him there would not be a reply.

[Four]

```
23 Calle Acros
Belgrano, Buenos Aires
1930 19 April 1943
```

Enrico pulled the Rolls Royce up and stopped before the door of the Italian-style mansion that occupied the eastern corner lot at the intersection of Calle Arcos and Virrey del Pino. He did not get out of the car, as he usually did, to open the door for Clete. He sat, both hands on the wheel of the Rolls, looking straight ahead out the window.

He's pissed at me. Jesus, why? Because I think there is something funny — sick but funny — that the oh, so dignified Coronel Juan Domingo Perón has got a thing for little girls?

"Norteamericanos are different, Enrico," Clete said. "We think there is something funny —"

"It is not funny, Señor Clete," Enrico said, dead serious, and still not looking at him. "God made him that way."

"Did God make you that way, too?" Clete asked gently, thinking he had a sudden insight.

"You have to ask me a question like that?" Enrico demanded indignantly.

"Well, what the hell was I supposed to think?"

"El Coronel Perón was your father's best friend. Your father never laughed at —"

"Well, get this straight, Enrico. El Coronel Perón is not my best friend, and I think he ought to be ashamed of himself!"

He had to smile when he heard what he had said.

"I am sure he is," Enrico said, seriously, rationalizing: "I would be. But he was el Coronel's best friend, and you should not mock him."

"OK. I'm sorry."

"No, you are not, Señor Clete."

"No, I am not," Clete said. "Screw you, Enrico."

He got out of the car and walked to the double doors of the Mallín mansion. Failing to find a doorbell, he raised the clapper and let it fall.

It sounds like somebody knocked over a garbage can.

A maid answered the door, but Dorotéa came running past her.

"Hey, Princess!"

"Cletus, damn you, I've been frantic!"

"I'm sorry."

"Where have you been?" she demanded, then she saw the Rolls. "Where did you get that?"

"It's mine. It was the only thing available." He had a sudden thought. "Would you like to go for a ride? Before your parents learn I'm here and we get all involved with the wedding?"

"They're not here," she said. "Why should we go for a ride?"

"Because we have to talk," he said. "Where are your parents?"

"They went to dinner. I refused to go."

"Why?"

"Because I didn't want to miss your call, if you called. I've been out of my mind, not knowing where you were, not that you give a damn."

"I'm sorry, Princess."

"A Colonel Martín called Daddy and told him that you were all right. All that did was convince Daddy that you were up to your ears in this damned revolution. Were you?"

"Yes."

"I don't think you should see Daddy tonight," she said. "He's furious with you."

"Why?"

"At the moment, because he thinks you went off and got yourself killed just so our baby won't have a name and he'll be embarrassed. When he finds out you're still alive, he'll think of something else. What do we have to talk about?"

"Excuse me?"

"You just said we have to talk."

"Well, I was thinking about Father Whatsisname . . ."

"Father Matthew, you mean?" Clete nodded. "What about him?"

"Well, I know how important —"

"Don't lie to me, Cletus."

He looked at her helplessly, then blurted the truth: "Honey, I just want to be alone with you."

She threw herself into his arms, put her mouth to his ear, and whispered, "Me too."

He thought his heart was going to jump out of his chest.

"Can we go to your place on Libertador?" she asked, her mouth still at his ear.

"No."

"I don't want to go to the other house," she said, now pulling her face back so that she could look at him. "Why can't we go to Libertador?"

"You don't want to know," he said.

"Yes, I *do*," she said.

"Because Coronel Perón is there with a lady friend," he said.

"A lady friend, or one of his little girls?"

"You know about that?" he asked incredulously.

"Everybody knows about that, silly," she said. "What about going to the estancia?"

"I suppose we could. I have some things I've got to do at the estancia . . ." He paused as reality interjected itself into his mental image of the last time she was in his bed at Estancia San Pedro y San Pablo: "How the hell would you explain being with me at the estancia to your father?"

"I'll leave a note saying that I'm spending a few days with Claudia."

"Your father won't believe that," Clete argued.

"No. But he'll pretend he does. Mother will understand why I have to be with you."

"You're serious, aren't you?"

"Of course I'm serious. Give me a few minutes to throw some things in a bag," she said.

"I told you, I have some things to do at the estancia," Clete said. "I won't —"

"Things you have to do tonight?"

"Not tonight. But in the morning . . ."

"Then we'll have tonight, at least," she said. "Before you showed up here, I had convinced myself that I was never going to see you again. I asked God to please, please let me see you just once more, just for a little while. . . ."

"Baby . . ."

She kissed him very gently on the lips.

"I'll only be a minute," she said. "And if you're not here when I come back down, I swear, I'll kill you!"

She turned and ran into the house and up the stairs.

XXIV

[One]

Puerto Magdalena
Samborombón Bay
Buenos Aires Province, Argentina
2115 19 April 1943

The voyage of the good ship *Coronel Gasparo* from El Tigre to Magdalena took just over seven hours. They tied up at five minutes to six, as darkness was falling.

During the voyage, there was plenty of time for Major Freiherr Hans-Peter von Wachtstein, holder of the Knight's Cross of the Iron Cross, to consider the morality of what he was doing and of what he intended to do.

It was, of course, a question of honor. Intellectually, from the day he received the letter from his father, there was no question in his mind that he was honor bound, as an officer, as a von Wachtstein, to follow the path his father had decided honor required.

Germany was in the hands of a collection of unbelievably evil men. These men were not only guilty of unspeakable crimes against the Jews and other people — including Germans — but were also prepared to see Germany itself destroyed.

Clearly, a Christian nobleman of the officer class was honor bound to do whatever was required to take Germany back from the Nazis.

That was the intellectual argument, and he had no doubt that it was valid.

Emotionally, however, he had a good deal of trouble personally engaging in activity that was clearly treason, and would very likely cause the deaths of other Germans who were no more Nazis than he was.

It wasn't simply a question, either, of the Americans' moral justification — of his friend Cletus Frade's, in particular — in sinking the *Comerciante del Océano Pacífico*. By replenishing German U-boats in protected neutral waters, while flying the flag of neutral Spain, the *Comerciante del Océano Pacífico* had given up any claim to be other than what it was, a vessel in the service of a combatant power.

And when he helped the Americans sink the *Océano Pacífico*, which they obviously intended to do, it would obviously hurt the German ability to wage war, and in some measure contribute to the ending of the war, and thus the Nazi regime.

Peter von Wachtstein intellectually understood this, and was intellectually prepared to accept the inevitable death of much of the *Océano Pacífico's crew*.

On the other hand, the submarine crews bothered him. There were a dozen or more submarines somewhere in the South Atlantic who were depending on being refueled and resupplied by the *Océano Pacífico*.

An hour or so out of El Tigre, as he steered the *Coronel Gasparo* through nasty choppy waters far enough offshore to avoid being clearly visible, a number of Untersee officers he knew came to mind. And one — Kapitänleutnant Wilhelm von Dattenberg — in particular.

He knew von Dattenberg at Philip's University in Marburg an der Lahn, and ran into him again in Berlin at the Adlon Bar after he himself had just returned from a tour on the Eastern Front. At that time he had the private belief that fighter pilots had seen as much of the horror of war as could be reasonably expected of any human being, including one whose family had been fighting Germany's wars for centuries.

Von Dattenberg quickly disabused him of that notion. From the moment he saw von Dattenberg's eyes, Peter knew that he had seen more than his fair share of horror. And Peter saw even deeper into that horror as they got drunk and von Dattenberg talked about service in U-boats.

It didn't take Peter long to realize that he simply did not have the courage, the moral fiber, to endure what von Dattenberg had endured, and what he would again endure when his fifteen-day End of Patrol leave was over and he would take his boat out again.

Like Peter, Willi von Dattenberg was a member of the officer class whose family had been either admirals or generals for generations. Willi shared Peter's moral values, including the sense of responsibility he felt for the men placed under his command.

The moral responsibility for the lives of other men was obviously greater for a U-boat commander than it was for a fighter pilot, even for a fighter pilot given command of a Jaeger Squadron. It had occurred to Peter that he was able to discharge his responsibility to the pilots of his squadron — and in the Luftwaffe, only those who flew fought — by doing his best to see they were properly trained and that their equipment was properly maintained.

He of course regretted the loss of any of his pilots — often he privately wept for them. But — because it was at least partially true — it wasn't hard to rationalize their deaths by thinking it was either simple bad luck or a bad decision on their parts that had caused them to go down.

On the other hand, literally during every waking moment, Willi von Dattenberg was aware that any decision he made was liable to cause not only his own death but the deaths of every member of his crew.

And it was entirely possible that Willi von Dattenberg was now floating around somewhere in the South Atlantic, low on fuel, running out of food, and praying for word over the radio that it was now safe to head for the River Plate estuary for replenishment.

From a ship that his old friend was about to help the Americans sink.

It was his own crew on the *Coronel Gasparo*, blissfully unaware that they were doing so, who caused Peter to emotionally understand what he was doing, what he would do, what he was honor bound to do, even though that might mean the death of Kapitänleutnant Wilhelm von Dattenberg and any number of other good Germans.

Peter's first reaction to Herr Gustav Loche, Günther's father, was unkind, if understandable, given that Peter had been raised to never forget he was a member of the aristocracy. If anything, he thought the father was even more of a fool than the son, a typical member of the German laboring class.

This perception stemmed from the first time Peter met Herr Loche, when he was both embarrassed and repelled by the man's servility. The plump, balding, ruddy-cheeked sausage maker did everything but tug at his forelock as he made it clear that he felt deeply honored to be in the very presence of a man who was not only Baron von Wachtstein but also a hero of German National Socialism who had received the Knight's Cross of the Iron Cross from the hands of the Führer himself.

Loche fancied himself a loyal German, honored to make whatever contribution he could to the furtherance of German Nationalism as defined by Der Führer Adolf Hitler. He was thus deeply appreciative of the generosity of an important man like Standartenführer Josef Goltz of the SS-SD, manifested in Goltz's offer to send Günther to Stuttgart. It never entered his mind that Goltz could entertain an ulterior motive.

Peter's contempt for Herr Gustav Loche grew at first, as the idiot prattled on and on while the *Coronel Gasparo* moved down the shoreline of the River Plate into the ever-widening mouth of the estuary; but gradually, the contempt turned to pity.

They weren't bad people, he realized, simply stupid. The father obviously loved the son and presumably had Christian morals. For instance, even though it was financially difficult for him — as he proudly informed Peter — he saw to it that Günther had a Catholic education under the good Jesuit fathers in San Carlos de Bariloche, as opposed to the free, secular education offered by the government.

It therefore followed, Peter reasoned, that Gustav Loche would be outraged if he became aware that the Nazis were rounding up human beings in Russia and forcing them to dig pits, and then standing them on the edge of those pits and shooting them in such a way that their dead and dying bodies fell back into them . . . not to mention gassing women and children by the thousands.

But Loche was unable to accept that anything like this was possible. He regarded as Anglo-American propaganda the stories about concentration camps and death squads and the rest of it that had begun to appear in newspapers and on the radio, ludicrous tales the Allies designed to keep the world in the hands of the Jews from whom the Führer intended to rescue it.

Thus it would simply be beyond Gustav Loche's ability to comprehend that the benevolent Standartenführer Goltz was involved in a scheme wherein people who had done nothing to harm Germany (yet were nevertheless being starved to death — or awaiting murder — in Nazi extermination camps) could, on payment of a sum of money, be released. Much less could he realize that the money raised was to be used to buy sanctuary for high-level Nazis so they would escape being called to account for their monstrous crimes when the war was lost.

Neither could Loche believe that the so correct Oberst Grüner and the so charming Gradny-Sawz could also be involved in such a fantastically evil undertaking.

Loche saw himself simply as a good, patriotic German doing all he could for the Thousand Year Reich. Of course, in its gratitude for his loyalty, the Thousand Year Reich was going to advance him the money to expand his business, acquire an estancia, and send his beloved son to the Fatherland to further his education.

To his surprise, Peter found with little difficulty the mouth of the harbor at Magdalena, and then the pier of the fisherman — Lothar Steuben, another good, loyal, expatriate German who was going to charter his boat to Oberst Grüner. By then Peter had decided that while Loche and his son could not really be held accountable for what they were doing, Standartenführer Goltz — and by extension, all Nazis — could. And there was no longer any question in his mind whether what he would do next was honorable or not.

The problem then became how.

Steuben, a large sunburned man, was a second-generation Argentinian whose family came from near Hamburg. If anything he was more obsequious than Gustav Loche.

He conducted everyone to his small but comfortable home overlooking the harbor. There his wife had laid out coffee and pastry. After introductions — she was a stout woman with blond hair braided and coiled at her ears and she was holding a child on each hip, which made her look like one of the oil paintings Hitler had commissioned to honor Fertile German Womanhood — she shyly inquired if the Herr Baron happened to like sauerbraten, which is what she had prepared for supper. He told her he did.

Despite his promise to contact Peter by six, there was no word from Grüner. And there was none by seven, or by eight. By the time the sauerbraten was eaten, Peter began to wonder whether something had gone wrong.

Maybe the Americans decided the smartest thing to do was sink the Océano Pacífico *before she got into*

Argentine waters? The Spanish would howl in outrage, but what could they actually do about it? Send another division to the Eastern Front? Bomb Washington, D.C.?

At 8:25, the telephone rang.

"Herr Baron Major," Steuben said, handing the telephone to Peter. "It is Herr Oberst Grüner."

Peter took the telephone and said one word: "Yes?"

"I doubt if it would do any good, Peter," Grüner said. "But when we get off the line, why don't you see if you can't at least ask him to consider the possibility that sometimes people listen to other people's telephone calls?"

"I'll certainly do that."

"He has a map," Grüner said. "Tell him to bring it to you."

"One moment," Peter said, covered the mouthpiece with his hand, and asked Steuben for "the map."

"Apparently what you asked for is being stored under the bed," Peter reported. "But I am promised it will appear momentarily."

"Ach, Gott! How was your ride down there? Get plenty of fresh air? Your mount didn't throw you?"

"Actually it was very pleasant. The horses ran well, and Günther was only slightly sick to his stomach. He hasn't had much chance to do much riding."

Steuben appeared with a map, a sheet of paper, and a freshly sharpened pencil.

Without explanation, Grüner gave a list of letters and numbers, which Peter wrote down. He then compared these with the map, the markings on which had been changed.

"That make sense to you, Peter?" Grüner asked.

817

Obviously, he had been given the position where the *Comerciante del Océano Pacífico* had been ordered to drop anchor in Samborombón Bay.

"Yes."

"They may not be valid until later than we thought, if you take my meaning, but they should be good by, say, midnight, and certainly by the morning."

"I understand," Peter said.

"There has been a slight change in plans."

"Oh?"

"Frankly, I prevailed in this," Grüner said, a smug tone in his voice. "I suggested to our friend that there was merit in the principle that the fewer people who know — or think they know — what's going on, the slighter the chance that it will become public knowledge."

"I agree with that completely," Peter said.

"You will therefore have a companion when you take your ride in the morning. Which I suggest should be at first light."

What the hell is that all about? Oh. Either he or Goltz is going with me. Goltz. *Goltz has to go out to the* Océano Pacífico. *The captain won't turn over the "special matériel" to anyone else. So now Steuben remains in the dark. Even if the BIS grabs him, they can't get any information from him, because he won't know.*

"I think I know who you mean," Peter said. "And therefore, we will need one less horse, am I right?"

"Absolutely. You really are becoming quite good at this game, Peter."

"Thank you very much, I'm trying."

"Somewhere along the path, I'll probably meet up with you and take your companion off your hands."

"I think I understand."

"I'd be more comfortable if I knew you understood."

"The only thing I'm a little fuzzy about is what happens to me after we meet up with you."

"With a little bit of luck, some of the people you will have with you will be able to lead your horse back to the stable, and then you and I can lunch together."

The translation of that is if the Océano Pacífico *turns out to be able to take the* Coronel Gasparo *aboard after we unload the "special matériel" — if they have the right kind of davits for that, and, of course, if she can take the strain of being lifted out of the water — her crew will take her from the beach to the ship and take her aboard. In that case, I can stay on shore and go with Goltz and Grüner.*

If the Océano Pacífico *can't take the* Coronel Gasparo *aboard, then Günther and I will have to take her back here.*

"What I suggest is that you have your dinner and get some sleep, and be ready to start out there at first light. Our friend will be there as soon as he can."

"Certainly."

"The truck is ready?"

"I have been assured, a half-dozen times, that everything, including the truck, is in readiness."

"Don't fault enthusiasm, Peter. It is to be encouraged. But, of course, at the same time, controlled. Don't let it get out of hand."

"I assure you I won't."

"Well, then I look forward to seeing you, perhaps even to have lunch with you, tomorrow."

"I'm looking forward to it."

The line went dead.

Peter put the handset back into its cradle.

"There has been a change of plans," he announced. "You, Herr Steuben, will, from five A.M., hold yourself in readiness to comply with any orders Oberst Grüner may issue."

"Jawohl, Herr Baron Major!"

"You, Herr Loche, will make sure the truck, ready for operation, is at the prescribed place at the prescribed hour. I suggest you leave shortly to make sure all is in readiness."

"Jawohl, Herr Baron Major!" Gustav Loche replied, taking his cue from Steuben.

Peter picked up the map, motioned for Herr Loche to follow him, and walked across the room to a floor lamp.

"Indicate where your part in this operation is to take place, if you please, Herr Loche."

Loche's face went white and showed acute discomfort.

"Excuse me, Herr Baron Major," he began hesitantly.

"You have forgotten already? You are not sure, is that what you're saying?"

"Herr Baron Major, both Herr Standartenführer Goltz and Herr Oberst Grüner made it quite clear to me that the landing site was not —"

"— to be revealed to anyone who did not have a need to know?" Peter interrupted.

"Yes, Herr Baron Major."

"Herr Steuben does not have the need to know," Peter said. "Which is why I brought you over here with me, so that he cannot see where you will point at the map. And your diligence is appreciated, Herr Loche, and I will mention it to Standartenführer Goltz. But did you really think that I was not privy to this information?

That the Herr Standartenführer would send me down here not knowing where I am to meet you and the truck? What I am doing here, Loche, is making sure there is no confusion in *your* mind about where you are to be."

"Excuse me, Herr Baron Major," Loche said. "I was not thinking. You will have to understand that I am . . ."

"Where, Loche?" Peter demanded impatiently.

Loche pointed to a small inlet on the shoreline of Samborombón Bay. There were no villages near it, but the coastal highway was no more than half a mile away.

"There, Herr Baron Major. Right there."

"There is no question in your mind?"

Loche considered that.

"None, Herr Baron Major."

"Very well," Peter said.

He folded the map and put it in his pocket and walked back across the room to Günther.

"You, Günther . . ."

"Yes, Herr Baron Major?"

"You and I will take the *Coronel Gasparo* on our mission."

"Jawohl, Herr Baron Major!"

"I have some other business in Magdalena," Peter announced. "If you will be so good, Herr Steuben, you will wait for me to return in case I need you. Günther, you may go to bed."

"Of course, Herr Baron Major," Steuben said.

"Thank you, Herr Baron Major," Günther said.

"Presumably, Herr Loche, you have a car here to take you to the rendezvous site?"

"Yes, of course, Herr Baron Major. Actually a small truck."

"You can take me partway to my destination, then," Peter said.

"It will be my pleasure, Herr Baron Major."

"If by chance, Herr Steuben, either the Herr Standartenführer or the Herr Oberst calls, you will tell them I am about our business, and will return their call on my return."

"Jawohl, Herr Baron Major."

"Let's go, Herr Loche," Peter said.

No questions will be asked. These are good Germans. Authority — me — has spoken, and good Germans do not question authority.

Now all I have to do is figure out where I'm going.

Two kilometers from Steuben's house, they came to a truck stop.

Truck stops have telephones.

"You can drop me there, Loche," he ordered.

With a great deal of difficulty, he reached Buenos Aires three times.

The butler at the Frade mansion on Avenida Coronel Díaz told him that Señor Frade was not at home, and politely refused to say any more than that.

The housekeeper at the house on Libertador told him that Señor Frade had been there earlier but had left, and suggested he try to call the mansion on Avenida Coronel Díaz.

Señor Humberto Valdez Duarte told him that he had no idea where Cletus was, but if he wasn't at the house on Coronel Díaz or the Libertador house, the only thing he could think of was that he might be at the estancia. He added that he knew Cletus was back from Brazil, because there was a telephone call from Capitán Lauffer, General Arturo Rawson's aide-de-camp, telling him privately, and not for publication, that Cletus had been a hero of the revolution.

Although it was only sixty or seventy kilometers from Magdalena, he got through to Estancia San Pedro y San Pablo with much greater trouble. Señor Frade was not at home, but there was a possibility he might be at home later.

"You might try again in an hour or two, Señor, or perhaps in the morning."

Does that mean Clete is going to be there, or not?

If Standartenführer Goltz arrives at Steuben's house and I'm not there . . .

What if, somehow, I can get to Estancia San Pedro y San Pablo and Cletus is not there?

I know his men are there, probably at the radio station. If that is the case, and Cletus is not there, I could give this information to his deputy, if his deputy is there. But where *is* there? *I have no idea where on the estancia Cletus has placed his radio station — and I doubt very much that anyone will tell me. Estancia San Pedro y San Pablo is about as big as Pomerania, and I can't just wander around looking for it.*

What is left?

Getting to Estancia San Pedro y San Pablo somehow. If Cletus is not there, I'll write down the position where the Comerciante del Océano Pacífico *will drop anchor, and the place on the shoreline where I will unload the* Coronel Gasparo, *and leave it for him. If he's not there, they will probably deny knowing where he is; but after I leave — and I will have to leave, praying that I can get back to Magdalena before the good Standartenführer shows up — they will very likely make an effort to reach him or his deputy. Getting in touch with the deputy would be just about as good as getting my message into Cletus's hand.*

That suggests the very real possibility that an American submarine, having been provided with Océano Pacífico's *location by Kapitänmajor Hans-Peter von Wachtstein, will arrive at the scene at just about the moment Kapitänmajor Hans-Peter von Wachtstein sails the good ship* Coronel Gasparo *up to the* Océano Pacífico, *and that she will fire her torpedoes just as the master of the* Océano Pacífico, *Standartenführer Goltz, and I are exchanging pleasantries.*

Maybe that would be appropriate.

How do I reach Estancia San Pedro y San Pablo from here?

He made one more telephone call, getting through on the fourth attempt.

"Estancia Santo Catalina."

"Señorita Alicia Carzino-Cormano, please. Señor Cóndor is calling."

"One moment, por favor, Señor. I will see if the lady is at home."

"Oh, my God, Peter, where are you?"

"Magdalena."

"Magdalena?" she parroted incredulously.

"I need some help, Liebchen. If there was any other —"

"What do you need?"

"I need you to come here and pick me up, take me to Estancia San Pedro y San Pablo, and then bring me back here."

"Why?"

"I can't tell you."

"Where are you in Magdalena? The Hotel San Martín?"

"I'm at the truck stop on the highway."

"I know it," Alicia said. "It will take me an hour. Is that all you have to say to me?"

"Liebchen, if I knew any other way . . ."

"I was thinking along the lines, of 'Te amo, Alicia.' "

"Te amo, Alicia," he said, and for some reason his voice broke.

"An hour, mi vida," she said, and hung up.

[Two]

Estancia San Pedro y San Pablo
Near Pila, Buenos Aires Province
2245 18 April 1943

When el Patrón arrived at Estancia San Pedro y San Pablo in the rear seat of the ancient Rolls Royce, he was in a state of sexual excitement and frustration. He also felt somewhat ashamed of himself.

After they drove away from her father's house, their several minutes of tender embraces quickly turned passionate. And Señorita Dorotéa Mallín realized that unless she took immediate action, there was going to be activity on the leather seats that would not only be improper but that could not escape the attention of Suboficial Mayor Enrico Rodríguez, who was driving.

"Stop, Cletus!" she firmly ordered. "Not *here!*"

They broke apart and took up positions at opposite ends of the wide, dark-red leather seat. Dorotéa placed her hand in the space between them, and Clete took it.

They rode along that way for perhaps half an hour. Then Clete became aware that Dorotéa had dozed off. He thought this was very sweet but

825

quickly changed his mind. The way she was sitting, every time her head dropped below a certain position it clearly caused her discomfort, and she would suddenly snap her head erect.

With absolutely innocent motivation, Clete gently pulled the dozing Dorotéa to him and let her head rest in his lap. He gently and lovingly stroked her hair for several minutes, marveling that this sweet and gentle creature loved him, was bearing his child, and — as soon as they received that goddamned counseling from the Very Reverend Matthew Cashley-Price — was going to be his bride, his wife, to have and to hold from that day forward until death did them part.

With that certainly decent and arguably perhaps even noble line of thought in his mind, he then dropped off to sleep himself.

He awoke two hours later to find Dorotéa's head still innocently in his lap, but its weight was delivering surprisingly sharp pain to what was the father of all erections.

He tried to endure the pain. He looked out the window. He couldn't see much.

"Where are we?"

"About five minutes from the house," Enrico replied, adding, "You were snoring again, Señor Clete."

"Thank you very much, Enrico," Clete said, and then yelped in pain.

"Señor?"

"It is nothing," Clete said.

He tried to gently waken Dorotéa. All that did was make her shift her head, with a concomitant painful reaction in the physiological symbol of his gender.

"Sweetheart," he cried cheerfully — trying to

sound cheerful required a good deal of effort —
"wake up, we're almost there!"

He had to repeat the message three times before
he broke into Dorotéa's peaceful slumber. By then,
he could see the lights of the big house.

She then pushed herself erect, and in doing so,
her hand quite innocently found the source of his
discomfort.

"Cletus," she said naughtily. "You should be
ashamed of yourself!"

For reasons he could not imagine, she then gave
it a good squeeze.

"Jesus, Dorotéa!"

Enrico blew three short blasts on the horn.

As they turned onto the drive before the big
house, the verandah lights came on. Clete saw
Rudolpho, his short-barreled cavalry Mauser carbine slung from his shoulder, come quickly off the
verandah toward the car.

*Good. I can send him to the radio station and have
him tell Tony I need to see him. Maybe he knows more
about David Ettinger than Martín did. And in any
event, I should radio Graham that the airplane is here,
and, for that matter, that the new President of Argentina is General Rawson.*

*Come to think of it, I don't know how much attention
Rawson will pay to anything I have to say, but I don't
think there's much doubt that he'll listen to me. We
became buddies in the Piper Cub.*

"Buenos tardes, Patrón," Rudolpho said.
"Señorita."

Clete shook Rudolpho's hand.

"Could you go out to the radio station and tell
Teniente Pelosi I have to see him?"

"El Teniente is in the house, Patrón."

Great. And that explains what he's doing here carry-

827

ing the carbine, doesn't it?

"Honey, do you want something to eat?" Clete asked.

Dorotéa smiled sweetly at him.

"It's been a long day," she said. "Why don't we just turn in?"

One of the maids came down to the car.

Thank God, nobody's here but Tony. We don't have to go through that nonsense of pretending we're not sleeping together.

"Put the Señorita's luggage in my room, please, and draw a bath for her."

"Cletus!" Dorotéa protested.

"Nobody's here, why not?"

Dorotéa shook her head but did not protest any further.

"I need a minute or two with Tony, and then I'll be right along."

"You'd better be," Dorotéa said. "I'm going to hold you to the promise you made in the car."

"What promise?"

"You've forgotten already?" she asked.

He finally took her meaning, and his face reddened.

"Where's el Teniente?" Clete asked.

"In the library, Patrón."

"I'll just say hello to him," Dorotéa said, and followed Clete to the library. He held the door open for her and she walked in ahead of him.

"Ah, Señorita Mallín," a familiar male voice. "What an unexpected pleasure! How nice to see you again."

Jesus, who the hell is that? Whoever it is, he sounds just like Colonel Graham.

"And Major Frade himself!" Colonel A. F. Graham, USMCR, said. "What a coincidence! We were just talking about you."

"I told the Colonel you'd probably show up here sooner or later, Tex," Mr. Milton Leibermann said. "And tell us all about the revolution."

"What's going on?" Clete said.

"You'll have to excuse my bad manners, Señorita Mallín," Graham said, ignoring the question. "You've met Lieutenant Pelosi, I know. But not these other gentlemen, I believe. May I present Commander Delojo, our Naval Attaché here, and Mr. Milton Leibermann, who is the Legal Attaché of the American Embassy in Buenos Aires?"

What the hell is all this about?

Commander Delojo and Milton Leibermann shook Dorotéa's hand. Leibermann told her that she was even more beautiful than Pelosi had told him she was.

". . . and Mr. Ralph Stevenson, who is the Cultural Attaché of our Embassy in Montevideo, and Captain Maxwell Ashton III. Gentlemen, Señorita Dorotéa Mallín, Major Frade's fiancée." He paused and looked at Clete. "When Tony told us that wonderful news, Clete, frankly I was a little hurt that you hadn't let me know. I would have sent a present, or something."

Clete didn't reply.

Enrico came into the room, looked around, and then at Clete.

"And this gentleman," Graham said, "is Suboficial Mayor Enrico Rodríguez, Argentine Army, Retired, sometimes introduced as Colonel Rodríguez."

Graham has obviously heard from that Air Corps Colonel at Pôrto Alegre, Clete thought.

Or maybe he's been there?

And obviously, behind that little mask of perfect

manners he's wearing, he's pissed at me.

Why?

What the hell have I done wrong, except getting one of my men killed?

Well, if that's what's pissing him off, he's entitled.

"I realize this is an imposition, Señorita Mallín," Graham said, "but I'm afraid that we have to speak to Cletus now, and alone."

She looked at Clete, then at Graham, then turned and left the library without a word.

Clete looked at Graham.

"I accept full responsibility for the death of Sergeant Ettinger," Clete said. "I should have made sure that he would not leave the estancia."

"I'm not surprised that you would say that, Clete," Graham said, "but I am surprised that you know. Who gave you that information?"

"It's not important."

"I decide what's important."

"I decide what I tell you."

"That's not the way it works."

"Yes, it is," Clete said.

Commander Delojo looked at Graham, anticipating a satisfactory reaction to Clete's insubordination.

"If you tell me what you know, about Ettinger, I mean," Graham replied, the reply disappointing Delojo, "I — or Stevenson — will fill in any blanks from what we know."

"In front of Milton Leibermann?" Clete asked.

"In front of Milt," Graham said.

"Including why Ettinger felt he had to go to Montevideo?"

"Yes," Graham said simply. "Milt knows what Ettinger was up to; I told him."

Maybe, if the OSS had been talking to the FBI all

along, David would still be alive, Clete thought angrily.

He looked at Leibermann.

"I was told that Ettinger was found dead of stab wounds in the sand dunes on the River Plate beach north of Carrasco. The murder was probably done for hire, by Uruguayan gangsters, and the murder was paid for by Standartenführer Goltz, or somebody working for him. But at Goltz's orders. Goltz is also the guy who gave the orders to have my father killed."

"You must have a pretty good source of information," Graham said. "That's about all we have. Except why the Uruguayan police believe the murderers were Uruguayan criminals. Do you want to hear that?"

"Please."

Graham looked at Stevenson and gestured for him to furnish the information.

"They severed Sergeant Ettinger's penis and placed it in his mouth," Stevenson said. "In the . . . How do I put this? This is what the gangsters down here do to stool pigeons. The idea, apparently, was to send a message to people."

"What kind of message? To who?"

"To the German Jewish community in Montevideo and here," Stevenson went on. "That Ettinger — in his role as a German Jew, not an OSS agent — had talked too much, which means at all, about the ransoming operation the Germans are running. The message is that anyone who talks about it will be killed, and in that manner."

"I think we ought to send the Germans a message," Clete said. "That anybody who orders the killing of one of us gets a rifle bullet between the eyes."

831

"Shoot Standartenführer Goltz, you mean?" Graham asked.

"Or blow his brains out," Tony Pelosi said. "If Clete had let me do that when I wanted to, maybe Dave would still be alive."

"Tell me about that," Graham said evenly.

There was something in his voice Clete didn't like, and he tried to signal Tony to button his mouth, but Tony had his attention focused on Graham and didn't see him.

And probably wouldn't have understood me anyhow.

"I came up with a way, Colonel," Tony said, not at all reluctant to show off his expertise, "to blow the bastard's brains out his ear. I even tested it on a cow's head Enrico got me from the slaughterhouse. All you need is a piece of plastic explosive about as big as the first joint on your thumb. You put it in the earpiece of a telephone. I can rig it to blow five seconds, whatever, after you pick the phone up, or on command, sending house current down the existing telephone wire pair. Two-twenty-volt current fucks up the whole phone system, but who cares?"

"This testing you did, Lieutenant Pelosi," Graham asked, and now there was ice in his voice, "was that before or after Major Frade told you you were not to try to kill Standartenführer Goltz?"

Tony now sensed he was in trouble.

"I thought maybe I could talk Cl— Major Frade into changing his mind, Sir," he said.

"Let me tell you something, Lieutenant Pelosi," Graham said, and paused, framing what he was about to say. "First, Sergeant Ettinger is dead because he disobeyed Major Frade's order to stay on the estancia. Get that clear in your head. Second, you are an officer in the United States Army, not a thug working for Al Capone in Chicago. Standartenführer Goltz is not an Italian gangster who may be killed according to the Mafia Code of Honor as it applies to revenge. Are you with me so far?"

"Yes, Sir," Tony said, coming to attention. He was now on the carpet and knew it.

"Good!" Graham went on. "Third, the OSS is a military organization. On occasion it may be necessary for us to eliminate people, but we only do so when there is an unmistakable military necessity to do so — and revenge never meets that criterion. In this situation, the elimination of Standartenführer Goltz would be counterproductive."

"What did he say, Señor Clete?" Enrico asked.

"He says Tony cannot blow Goltz's brains out his ears," Clete said.

There was something in Major Frade's flippant sarcasm — which was enough to cause Captain Maxwell Ashton to chuckle — that caused Colonel Graham to turn his wrath to Major Frade.

"This applies to you, too, Frade," he said angrily. "I find it difficult to believe that you are unaware of the importance of Operation Lindbergh to the degree that you would even think, much less seriously suggest, that we assassinate the man who is the key to it, Standartenführer Goltz."

Enrico glared at Graham.

"What did he say?"

Clete's mouth ran away with him.

"He says I can't shoot Goltz between the eyes, either," Clete replied.

Captain Ashton chuckled again, which was enough to ignite the Latin temper of Alejandro Fredrico Graham, Colonel, USMCR.

"I've had about all I intend to take from you,

Frade!" Graham flared, turned to Ashton, pointed his finger at him, and nearly shouted, "This is not funny, goddamn it, Ashton!"

"Sorry, Sir," Ashton said, but he did not seem genuinely contrite.

Commander Delojo looked pleased, having decided that Major Frade was about to receive his long-overdue comeuppance.

But when Graham turned back to Clete, he had regained control of his temper.

"I should not have to spell this out for you, Clete, but I will," he said reasonably. "The elimination of Goltz would cause the people he works for to ask themselves who did that and why. They would quite logically conclude that it was probably you. Since they are aware that you are OSS, they probably would wonder how much you — and the OSS — have learned about what we are calling Operation Lindbergh. They would therefore take greater pains in the future to ensure the secrecy and security of Operation Lindbergh, which, of course, they will continue to operate. Are you with me so far?"

"Yes, Sir."

"The way things are now, we know — and the Germans do not know, or at least aren't sure that we know — about the operation, and that Goltz is running it, with the assistance of whatsisname — what's Bagman's name?"

"Von Tresmarck, Sir," Clete said.

". . . of von Tresmarck in Montevideo," Graham went on. "Between you here, and Stevenson in Montevideo, plus Milt and Milt's people here, and the FBI in Montevideo, we can keep an eye on Lindbergh and von Tresmarck until the decision is made what to do about it."

"I don't understand that, Colonel," Clete said. "What decision?"

"That'll come from the President," Graham said. "Who so far hasn't been told about it. We're dealing with the lives of thousands of Jews in the concentration camps as well as the sanctuaries the Germans are trying to set up here and, maybe, in Uruguay, Paraguay, Chile, and who knows where else. Deciding what to do about it is a decision I'm glad I don't have to make."

"Why hasn't the President been told?" Clete wondered aloud.

"Because Director Donovan doesn't wish to go to the President without more facts. Including the identity of Galahad, how come Galahad has knowledge of Lindbergh, and his motivations for telling us. I was sent down here specifically to obtain that information, Clete. That's how important Donovan thinks it is."

"Milton, you didn't know about this before?" Clete asked.

"I heard whispers," Leibermann said. "I asked around. The Jews know I'm from the Embassy, and almost certainly who I work for. A wall is up. And I'm the only Jew in the FBI down here, and the Jews here are not about to tell some norteamericano Irisher or Mormon about something like this."

"You heard what I said, Clete, about the primary reason I'm down here?" Graham asked.

"I'm sorry, I can't tell you any more about Galahad than I already have."

"We have to talk about that," Graham said without rancor, which almost visibly disappointed Commander Delojo.

Clete shrugged.

"Or, for that matter, Cavalry, either," he said.

"We'll have to talk about him, too," Graham said. "But right now, we have to radio Oracle and report what we know about the new government. Where the hell were you, Clete, when the revolution was going on? I think you'd better start with telling me about the arrangements you made to get that airplane into the country so easily."

"It wasn't easy," Clete said. "It was supposed to be a C-45, not a Lockheed Lodestar."

"I heard about that." Graham chuckled. "What I was talking about, though, is how did you arrange for the Argentine Army to allow you to land it at Santo Tomé? Your friend Cavalry have anything to do with that?"

"OK. Yeah."

"And where did you go with it when you left here?"

"The deal I made was that in exchange for getting the airplane into Argentina, I would make it available to the Grupo de Oficiales Unidos to take them out of the country in case OUTLINE BLUE went bad. So I took the airplane from here to Campo de Mayo."

"Obviously, they didn't need it. Which is fortunate. The Ambassador would have had a hard time explaining to President Castillo why an American OSS agent flew a planeload of traitors out of the country. Presumably you thought about that?"

"No, they didn't need the airplane, and no, I didn't think about what would happen if they had to. I had to have the airplane to deal with the *Océano Pacífico*; and getting Ashton and his radar into the country seemed important."

"You don't think you should have asked for guidance, for authorization, before making a decision like that?" Commander Delojo asked.

"Who was I supposed to ask?" Clete flared. "You?"

"Take it easy, Clete," Graham said warningly, and then went on, "What did they do, just keep you waiting out there, away from a telephone, until they were sure they wouldn't need the plane? And where is it now, by the way?"

"Not exactly," Clete said.

"Not exactly what?"

"I'm not sure that you want to know," Clete said.

"Oh, but I do!"

"They had a little problem communicating with the columns that were moving from Campo de Mayo to the Casa Rosada. So I helped them with it."

"Don't be evasive."

"I flew a Piper Cub for them."

"You participated in the coup d'état?" Delojo asked incredulously. "Took an active role in it?"

Graham ignored him.

"Where did you fly the Piper Cub?" he asked.

"I flew General Rawson around," Clete said. "One of the columns was stalled at the School of Naval Engineering. So we landed there, and he told them to bypass it. And then we flew to the other column, which had stopped because the first column was stalled, and dropped a message to them telling them to start moving. And then we flew over the Casa Rosada and watched both columns converge on it."

"General Rawson was with you?" Graham asked.

"Yes, he was," Clete said, and then added, "They offered me a commission. I turned it down."

"You would have lost your citizenship. You would have . . . ," Delojo fumed.

"I thought about that," Clete said. "Which is why I didn't take the commission."

"Where's the airplane now?" Graham asked.

There was a knock at the door. Clete thought that it was very likely Dorotéa, wondering what was holding him up.

It was a maid.

"Señor Frade," she announced. "Señorita Carzino-Cormano is here and asks to see you."

"Enrico, see what that's all about, will you?" Clete said, and then replied to Graham. "I wasn't turned loose until after dark. I didn't want to try to land the Lockheed here at night. So I asked them to take me into town, picked up the car, and came out here."

"Stopping only long enough, correct, to pick up your fiancée?" Commander Delojo asked sarcastically.

"Why didn't you stay in Buenos Aires?" Graham asked quickly, in time to shut off Clete's reply to Delojo. "So that you could deal with the plane in the morning?"

Clete hesitated, obviously considering the wisdom of saying something rude to Delojo, and then replied, his voice showing that his temper was simmering close to the surface:

"The reason I came out here was to see if anybody here knew any more about what happened to Dave Ettinger than I did. And I thought Ashton might need me for something. And I even thought about messaging you, back in the States, to tell you that OUTLINE BLUE worked. I'll fly over there in one of the Cubs in the morning and pick up the plane."

Enrico put his head in the door — surprising Clete, for he had been gone only a moment.

"Señor Clete?" he said, and motioned for him to leave the room.

Clete walked through the door and closed it after him.

"If you don't mind my saying so, Colonel, I don't like his attitude," Commander Delojo said.

"I don't mind you saying so, Commander — frankly, I'm not thrilled with it myself — but when he comes back in here, you're directed not to open your mouth until I tell you to," Graham said.

"If your purpose in sending Frade down here, Alejandro," Leibermann said, "was to see if he could get close to the new government, that has certainly succeeded."

Graham nodded.

"If he hadn't flown us here on that plane," Ashton said, "my team and I and the radar would still be in Pôrto Alegre."

"Sir," Tony Pelosi said, "I want to make it clear that when I told Major Frade I wanted to rig Goltz's telephone, he told me right away to forget it."

"Apparently the Cletus H. Frade Fan Club is holding its annual convention?" Graham said, but there was a smile on his lips. He then added, "God, wait till I tell Donovan that he was flying Rawson around during the revolution."

Clete and Enrico came back in the room three minutes later.

"What was that all about?" Graham asked.

"I have the position where the *Océano Pacífico* will drop anchor in Samborombón Bay. If she's not already there."

"Where did you get that?" Graham asked.

"And the location of the place where Goltz will

839

land what is probably all that money we've heard about from the *Océano Pacífico*."

"What's your source?" Graham asked.

"The landing will take place tomorrow morning. A boat will leave Magdalena at first light, go out to the *Océano Pacífico*, take on the cargo, and then head to shore. So it will land however long after daybreak it takes the boat to go out to the *Océano Pacífico* and back. Figure forty minutes each way, eighty minutes, an hour and twenty minutes, make it an hour and a half, make it any time between an hour and a quarter to two hours after sunrise."

"I need to know your source, Clete," Graham said.

"This is from the horse's mouth, Colonel, but that's all I can tell you and still look myself in the mirror when I shave."

Graham looked as if he was about to reply, then changed his mind.

"How long will it take you to fly that airplane here . . . or over this position in Samborombón Bay in the morning?"

"About an hour from here to Campo de Mayo, figure twenty, thirty minutes on the ground there, and then thirty minutes to fly the Lockheed back here."

"And over the *Océano Pacífico*?"

"About the same time."

"One thing I know for sure is that we have to have our hands on that airplane. So that's settled. You be ready to take off at first light for Campo de Mayo."

"Aye, aye, Sir."

"That's all, Clete," Graham said. "Get a good night's sleep. Set your alarm so you're up in time to have breakfast and be ready to take off at first light."

Clete nodded.

Christ, I've been dismissed!

He looked at Graham, who made it official.

"That will be all, Major, thank you," Graham said. "You are dismissed."

Clete's face reddened, but he kept his mouth shut and walked out of the room. Enrico followed him.

[Three]

Colonel A. F. Graham glanced in turn at all the officers remaining in the room, and finally settled his gaze on First Lieutenant Anthony J. Pelosi.

"I think you should take one more trip out to the radio station, Pelosi," he ordered, "to see if anything new has come in. After that, I don't think we'll need you any more tonight. Set your alarm early, too. I want you up when Frade gets up."

"Yes, Sir."

"So far as you're concerned, Commander, I can't see any reason for you to stay out here, now that we've found Frade. Or vice versa. So you can go back to Buenos Aires."

"Yes, Sir. Sir, I'm willing to stick around —"

"What I want you to do is make sure that I can get in contact with the Ambassador at any time tomorrow," Graham cut him off. "It's entirely possible that it will be necessary to do just that."

"Aye, aye, Sir."

"Both of you can go," Graham said, and they left the room.

"Ashton, presumably your radar can verify the existence of a vessel — not necessarily the *Océano Pacífico* — at the position we got from Frade?"

"Yes, Sir, if there's a vessel there, we will have already picked it up."

"Where's the camera?"

"At the radar site, Sir."

"OK. You go out there, check to see if a vessel is where Frade says it is — stick around until say oh three hundred if there isn't one there when you get there — and then come back here with the camera. You can use the camera in the Lockheed?"

"Yes, Sir. I'll have to take a side window out for the best results."

"But you can use the camera in the Lockheed?"

"Yes, Sir."

"Be prepared to do so."

"Aye, aye, Sir."

"You're dismissed, Captain."

"Aye, aye, Sir."

Graham waited until he had left the room and then turned to Mr. Ralph Stevenson, the Cultural Attaché of the Embassy of the United States of America in Montevideo, Uruguay.

"I want to ask you an off-the-record question, Ralph," he said, "which I promise you I will never remember asking. If I weren't here, and because of the three team chiefs we have down here, you're the only one who comes close to being what a team chief should be, you were faced with making the decision, what would you do?"

"Decision about what?"

"Let's give Frade the benefit of the doubt a moment. Let's say his source is good. Early tomorrow, the Germans will attempt to smuggle into Argentina a large sum of money — I have trouble with that one-hundred-million-dollar figure, but let's say a very large sum of money. *Five* million. *Ten* million. This money we know has been stolen in some despicable way from Jews in Germany. Not only that, but it will be used to purchase safe houses for — an infrastructure designed to give sanctuary to — any number of characters for whom skinning alive is too good. What do we do about that? Try to prevent them from smuggling it in? Try to grab the money? If we do that, we are probably also going to interfere with Lindbergh. Lindbergh is filthy, but on the other hand, people otherwise doomed to be shot in the head or gassed or starved to death, including, of course, women and children, are getting out of the camps. The third option is to do nothing, let them bring the money into the country and try to keep an eye on what happens to it, in the hope that when the war is over we can make things right."

"I'd rather not answer that question, Colonel," Stevenson said immediately.

"Answer it. What would you do in my shoes?"

Stevenson met Graham's eyes for a moment, then shrugged.

"Let it in," he said. "Try to keep an eye on it. Spend whatever it takes to have enough FBI accountants and whatever else is needed to follow the money trail sent down here. Otherwise the people in the camps won't get out. Isn't life worth more than money?"

Graham didn't reply directly.

"This conversation never took place," he said. "You're welcome to stick around, of course, Ralph.

But if you want to return to Montevideo . . .”

“I think I’ll wait and see what happens tomorrow morning,” Stevenson said.

“In that case, good night, Ralph,” Graham said. “Sleep well.”

Graham walked with him to the door and then turned to face Milton Leibermann.

“That makes it two to one, doesn’t it?” Leibermann said.

“Maybe three to one. But I have other thoughts. If we grabbed this money, wouldn’t it let them know we’re onto them?”

“To what end?”

“It might make them consider that this sanctuary nonsense is a dream,” Graham said.

“I’m not sure it is,” Leibermann said. “Money talks, to coin a phrase.”

“Could you follow the money trail Stevenson talked about?”

“Yes and no. Yes, if I had enough people, and we could — the U.S. government could — put sufficient pressure on the government of Argentina — on all the governments down here — to let us into their banking records. I don’t think either is likely.”

“So your objection to grabbing the money is based on this filthy scheme saving some lives?”

“Yeah. But I’m not sure if that’s Milton Leibermann, Philosopher, talking, or Milton Leibermann, Jew.”

“That doesn’t make it two to one, Milton. It makes it one for letting the money in because it saves lives; one for letting it in because things can be made right later — which is unlikely; and one for grabbing the money and letting the bastards know we know what they’re up to.”

"I still count that two to one for letting it in," Leibermann said. "So what are you going to do about Frade?"

"You mean about Galahad and Cavalry?"

Leibermann nodded.

"Galahad is obviously the Luftwaffe pilot. The confirmation of that we got tonight. Frade leaves the room to see the Carzino-Cormano girl. He comes back three minutes after seeing her with the location of the *Océano Pacífico* and the information that the Germans are going to smuggle the money ashore in the morning, *and where* they're going to land it. And you tell me she is running around with a Luftwaffe pilot — what's his name?"

"Hans-Peter von Wachtstein."

". . . named von Wachtstein."

"Yeah," Leibermann agreed.

"Von Wachtstein tipped Frade that they were going to try to kill him, and Frade figures he owes him his life. He doesn't want to give me his name because — with good reason, I'm sorry to say — he doesn't trust Donovan, and figures if the OSS was willing to consider him expendable, they wouldn't hesitate to use von Wachtstein to manipulate his father, which is likely to get von Wachtstein, *pere et fils,* killed. You heard that couldn't-look-himself-in-the-mirror business."

Leibermann shrugged, clearly meaning he agreed with the identification.

"And Cavalry?"

"I'm not sure about Cavalry. One moment I think it's the BIS guy, Martín, and the next moment I think, really think, that it's Rawson. He and Frade's father were great buddies. . . ."

"So were Frade's father and el Coronel Juan Domingo Perón."

"Rawson obviously trusts Frade enough to let him get close to the coup d'état, not to mention letting him fly him around during the revolution. And who but somebody like Rawson would have the authority to let Frade land his airplane at Santo Tomé?"

"Martín," Leibermann said. "Either at Rawson's bidding, or on his own authority."

"Bringing me back to square one," Graham said. "Go directly to jail, do not pass go, do not collect two hundred dollars."

"So what happens if you take a chance — you understand Frade is not going to identify either one of them, don't you?"

"You'll notice I didn't stand him at attention and order him to tell me," Graham said.

"So what happens if you take a chance and tell Donovan what you think, that Galahad is von Wachtstein . . ."

"I *know* von Wachtstein is Galahad."

". . . and Cavalry is Rawson. Or Martín. And Frade finds out about it?"

"You tell me."

"You know what I really think? That it would be the first time in history that a Marine major with the Navy Cross told you 'fuck you all, I quit.' "

"You really think he'd do that? That would be desertion in time of war. That would mean he could never go back home."

"Where's home, Alejandro? Down here he's a great-grandson of Pueyrredón, which is like being the great-grandson of Washington or Jefferson. And this is all his. . . ." Leibermann gestured around the library. "And, very important, he's going to marry that gorgeous blond."

"He's an honorable man. He swore an oath as a

Marine officer," Graham argued.

"He's an honorable man with a clear conscience. He didn't get all those medals running away from the Japanese. And he came down here and did his Marine officer's duty — *after* he found out the OSS considered him expendable — and nearly got himself killed lighting up the *Reine de la Mer* so the sub could torpedo it."

"It would still be desertion. Maybe even treason."

"Yeah. And none of the usual things that happen to deserters in time of war would happen to him. Even if you could get him back to the States to try him — and I don't see how you could; among other things, the Argentines consider him a citizen — even if you did, do you really want to try for desertion or treason a man who won the Navy Cross? You couldn't keep it out of the papers. And his grandfather would hire a half-dozen U.S. Senators to defend him. The whole story would come out."

Graham grunted.

"You can't even eliminate him," Leibermann said. "And not only because of Cletus Marcus Howell. Rawson — if you're right about him being Cavalry, and I think you are — would be furious. Not only would Frade's window into what's going on down here be slammed shut, but there's no telling the damage that would do to Franklin Roosevelt's diplomatic plans for South America. And we would get not one more item, period, from von Wachtstein. And Frade's family here . . ."

"Eliminating Frade was never one of my options," Graham said.

"So what are you going to do?"

"The President of the United States wants to know the identity of Cavalry and Galahad. What do I do about that?"

"You know what I do when I have problems like this?" Leibermann said. "Problems with no solution? I go to bed and get a good night's sleep. Then in the morning, when you wake up, the problems might still be there, but you've had a good night's sleep."

"What is that, Yiddish wisdom?"

"Go to bed, Alejandro," Leibermann said. "Let's see what happens tomorrow."

XXV

[One]

Estancia San Pedro y San Pablo
Near Pila, Buenos Aires Province
0445 19 April 1943

Señorita Dorotéa Mallín came into the library with Clete. She was wearing a man's silk dressing robe, and her hair was done up demurely in a loose braid hanging down her back.

Beautiful girl, Colonel A. F. Graham thought. *Even at this hour of the morning, with no makeup, just out of bed, she sort of glows.*

With that came insight: *My God, she's pregnant! Of course. That's why Clete's marrying her, and now, rather than after the expected year of mourning for the late el Coronel Jorge Guillermo Frade.*

And home for Clete Frade, he thought, remembering his conversation with Leibermann, *is where the woman who will bear his child is.*

"I didn't mean to disturb your sleep, Miss Mallín," Colonel A. F. Graham said. "Only Marines have to rise at this ungodly hour."

She met his eyes.

"I don't mind, Colonel. I thought I'd see that everybody had breakfast," Dorotéa said.

"I'm sure Clete's —"

"I don't mind, Colonel," Dorotéa repeated, smiling sweetly. "In fact, I insist."

Clete Frade looked amused.

"How much does Dorotéa know?" Graham asked.

"We had a long talk last night," Clete said.

"That wasn't wise, Major," Graham said.

"Well, it occurred to me that since Goltz and Grüner might try to kill her, I thought she had the right to know why."

He didn't say "Sir" or "Colonel." Obviously, he has been thinking about the same things Milt Leibermann talked about. He may already have made up his mind — certainly, that pregnant young woman has not spent the night encouraging him to go out and do something that may get the father of their unborn child killed — and the worst thing I can try to do right now is order either one of them around. Or even order her out of the room. This is his house, and she's, for all practical purposes, his wife. All I can do is hope that when I tell him what I want him to do, he's willing to do it.

"On the strength of your assurance that your information about German activities this morning is accurate, Major, I've developed our plan of action," Graham said.

"My information is good," Clete said.

"In addition to the radar Captain Ashton brought with him, there is an aerial camera," Graham said. "The latest word in aerial cameras, and in high-resolution film."

Clete didn't reply.

Suboficial Mayor Enrico Rodríguez entered the library.

What took you so long, Sergeant Major? Graham wondered. *You usually appear no longer than sixty seconds after your master. Oh, I see now, you stopped for a quick shave.*

"Good morning, Suboficial Mayor," Graham said.

"Buenos días, mi Coronel," Enrico replied, and took up what Graham had come to expect as his usual stance, leaning against the wall.

"If at all possible," Graham went on, "the United States government does not wish to again violate Argentine neutral waters by sending in a submarine to sink a ship flying a neutral flag," Graham said. "Even a ship like *Comerciante del Océano Pacífico* that is itself violating Argentine neutrality."

Clete nodded.

"If I have to say this, this operation was decided upon before we learned about Lindbergh, and about your source's information that the Germans intend to bring into Argentina an enormous sum of money."

"One hundred million dollars, according to my source," Clete said.

Captain Maxwell Ashton III and First Lieutenant Anthony J. Pelosi of the Army of the United States entered the room, both in civilian clothing.

"Have a seat, gentlemen," Graham said. "Señorita Mallín's arranging for breakfast."

Dorotéa smiled sweetly at him again.

"I asked the housekeeper to lay a buffet," she said. "I hope that will be all right?"

"That will be perfect, thank you," Graham said. "I was just telling Major Frade about the camera," Graham said. "You've checked it out, I hope?"

"Seems to be working perfectly, Sir," Pelosi said.

"When did you become an expert?" Clete asked.

"I don't know about being an expert, but I know how to operate it," Tony said. "I told you I went

851

to photo school in Washington."

"Let's talk about the camera a moment," Graham said. "The problems with aerial photography are threefold. First, the vibration of the aircraft causes obvious problems, in proportion to the distance between the camera and the subject being photographed. Second, the instability of the camera is magnified by aircraft movement, again in proportion to the distance between the camera and the subject being photographed. The third problem is enlargement of the negative. The more enlargement necessary, the more the granules of silver on the film become apparent. The term used is 'grainy.' " He paused and looked at Dorotéa.

"I'm afraid I'm boring you with this, Dorotéa."

"Not at all. I'm fascinated."

"Nice try, Colonel," Clete said. "But you might as well give up, she's not going to leave."

"That was the furthest thought from my mind, Major," Graham said.

Clete chuckled. "Yes, Sir," he said. "I'm sure it was."

"As I was saying," Graham went on. "Eastman Kodak's experimental laboratory has come up with two kinds of new film. Both considerably reduce the granularity problem in enlargement. The slower film we have is really extraordinary in that regard. But that's daylight film. The second film is much more sensitive; it can record an image in very little light, in almost total darkness. It works well, for example, in moonlight. But the price paid for that is higher granularity. You understand all this, Major?"

"I get the general idea."

"Now, the Signal Laboratories at Fort Monmouth, working with Sperry-Rand, the gyroscope people, have come up with a platform for the camera which is both heavily damped against aircraft vibration and gyroscopically stabilized. The camera platform is designed to mount on a standard U.S. Army Air Corps fuselage floor."

"I remember that," Clete said. "But the floor we were talking about was a C-45 floor. What about the floor in the C-56?"

"Captain Ashton checked the floor in the Lockheed," Graham said. "There is no problem there. A window will have to be removed, however. Will that be a problem?"

"I don't know," Clete said after a moment. "Can it be unscrewed?"

"We can cut a hole, I suppose, if it won't," Tony said.

"What this gives us, then, is the capability to photograph the *Océano Pacífico* from a considerable distance."

"How do you define 'considerable distance'?" Clete asked.

"Two miles," Ashton replied. "Maybe a little more."

"The idea was to keep the aircraft far enough away from the *Océano Pacífico* so it won't appear to be a threat," Graham said.

"But not beyond the range of its antiaircraft, right?" Clete challenged.

"If they don't consider the airplane a threat, they won't fire on it," Graham said.

Clete said nothing, but shook his head in either resignation or, possibly, contempt.

"To continue," Graham went on. "From a two-mile distance, using telephoto lenses and the new film, we have the capability of making photographs, which, when enlarged, will permit us to see a man's mustache."

"Where do you plan to develop and enlarge this super film of somebody's mustache?" Clete asked. "Did anybody think of that?"

"The original idea was to have it developed at Pôrto Alegre," Graham said. "The Navy has a photo lab there. Ashton brought a supply of the special chemicals with him. The original idea, of course, was to have photographic evidence that we were aware of the location of the *Comerciante del Océano Pacífico*. This would be presented to the Argentine government in the hope that they would then order the *Océano Pacífico* to leave its waters."

"Simply for anchoring in Samborombón Bay?" Dorotéa asked. "Why would we do that?"

"Why would we do that" is what she said.

"Because, Dorotéa," Graham said, desperately trying to keep his annoyance at her question out of his voice, "because they would correctly infer that it was a subtle warning that unless they ordered the ship from their waters, the United States would take other action."

" 'Other action' meaning what you did — as Cletus did — with the first ship?"

"Yes."

"That might work," Dorotéa said.

Thank you very much. It warms the cockles of my heart to know that a nineteen-year-old girl approves of the best idea the Assistant Director for Western Hemisphere Operations of the OSS — and a half-dozen other people all old enough to be your father — could come up with after a hell of a lot of thought. And your beloved, Little Lady, didn't sink the Reine de la Mer *all by himself. There was a destroyer and a submarine who made a little con-*

tribution to sending the Reine de la Mer *down.*

"I said, before, 'the original idea.' All of this planning, of course, was before we became aware of Lindbergh, and of the intelligence Clete came up with last night," Graham went on. "Now there are two issues involved here. The, quote, neutral status, unquote, of the *Comerciante del Océano Pacífico,* and the money Clete's source says they are going to smuggle ashore this morning."

"I don't quite understand," Dorotéa said.

Graham glanced at Clete.

"What's the new idea?" Clete said.

"Maybe killing two birds with one stone," Graham said. "Or at least with one set of photographs. Tell me about this Air Service Captain . . . Delgano?"

"Delgano," Clete confirmed. "What about him?"

"I have the feeling he's more than just a pilot," Graham said.

"He's BIS," Clete said. "He works for Coronel Martín."

"You're sure?"

"He told me."

"OK. New plan. Tell me what you find wrong with it," Graham said. "You go pick up the Lockheed. Digression: Presumably Captain Delgano is going to help you fly it here, right? You cannot fly the Lockheed alone?"

"No. I mean, yes, I can fly the Lockheed alone. And I got Martín to agree that I didn't need Delgano's help. It took some doing. He wanted Delgano to see what I planned to do with the Lockheed."

Is that one more proof, Graham wondered, *that Cavalry is el Coronel Martín?*

855

"So do I," Graham said. "Damn!"

"I'm not following any of this," Dorotéa announced.

"What I wanted to do, Dorotéa," Graham said, "was have Capitán Delgano aboard the Lockheed when we took the pictures of a boat leaving the *Océano Pacífico* to smuggle something into Argentina. Of the boat leaving the *Océano Pacífico*, of the boat landing on the shore of Samborombón Bay, and returning to the *Océano Pacífico*. Lieutenant Pelosi would take two photographs of everything, giving us a duplicate set of negatives. One set of negatives would be given to Capitán Delgano, together with the necessary special chemicals to develop them."

"Yeah," Clete said appreciatively. "He goes to Martín and says, 'I know these are legitimate. I was there when they were taken.' "

"And the Americans have copies," Graham said. "So they couldn't simply ignore them — 'What photographs?' Actually, it gives them a way out. Nobody has mentioned the other reason why the *Comerciante del Océano Pacífico* is in Samborombón Bay resupplying German submarines. The Argentines could then go to the Spanish ambassador and tell him they were ordering the *Océano Pacífico* out of Argentine waters because it was caught in the act of smuggling, and here's the photographs to prove it."

"Delgano's probably still at Campo de Mayo," Clete said. "For two reasons: to keep people from getting curious about the Lockheed being there in the first place, and because I told Martín I would probably fly over there in one of the Cubs here to pick it up. I'm sure, to be a nice guy, he was planning on flying the Cub back here to see if the

Lockheed was here. And/or see what else he could find out."

"And you could politely ask him to help you fly the Lockheed?" Graham asked.

"Yeah."

"You'll have to come here to load the camera platform on the Lockheed," Graham said. "Will you have any trouble persuading him to go with you from here?"

"Oh, I don't think I'll have any trouble at all," Clete said.

"And then you'll go out and photograph this ship, the same way you photographed the first one, when you were shot down?" Dorotéa asked.

Uh-oh, Graham thought, *this is where she's going to say, "Over my dead, pregnant body you will!"*

"If we're two miles away, honey," Clete said, "I don't think they'll start shooting at us."

"And if they do?" Dorotéa asked.

"Then I leave," Clete said, as much to Graham as to Dorotéa.

"You promise?" she challenged.

Clete hesitated before replying. "Honey, I promise you I won't do anything stupid out there."

Please, God, Graham thought, *let that be enough to satisfy her.*

"You understand, Colonel," Dorotéa said, "that this is the last time Cletus is doing anything like this?"

"If this works, Dorotéa," Graham said, hoping he sounded far more sincere than he felt, "there won't be anything more like this for him to do."

"You could be expected to say something like that," she said.

"The truth, Dorotéa, is that Clete is far more valuable to the United States government for his influence on General Rawson — on the new Argentine government — than as an OSS agent. If something like this comes up again, we'll send other people in to do it."

"You don't know my . . . Cletus very well, obviously, Colonel," she said. *She almost said "my husband,"* Graham realized. "If 'something like this comes up again,' Cletus will play the damn fool again. I want you to understand, Colonel, that the next time, I'm fighting you tooth and nail."

"Fair enough," Graham said.

"And in Dorotéa, mi Coronel," Clete said, smiling, obviously proud of her, "you can expect to meet your match."

"I have already figured that out, Major Frade," Graham said. "OK, let me get into the rest of it. The matériel the Germans will unload from the *Océano Pacífico*."

"We're letting them unload the money?" Clete asked, surprised.

Graham didn't reply directly.

"Leibermann has the entire staff of the Office of the Legal Attaché of the Embassy — and some of their local hires — on the way out here. They'll follow the matériel from the beach to its ultimate destination."

"You're letting those bastards bring that dirty money into Argentina?" Clete demanded incredulously. "You know what they're going to do with it!"

"I decided there was a strong possibility that if we grabbed the money today, there would be several unfortunate consequences," Graham said. "And I don't mean only that the only escape route I've ever heard of from German extermination camps would probably be closed for good."

Clete considered that a moment and grunted.

"And, aside from that, I decided that it posed an unacceptable risk to Galahad," Graham went on. "There would be questions asked, on their side, about how we knew precisely where and when the matériel — the money — was to be landed. Only a few people were privy to that information, among them, obviously, Galahad. The Germans have the nasty habit of eliminating people they suspect are guilty. I don't want Galahad eliminated."

"So you can use him again, right?" Clete said bitterly.

"Right."

Their eyes met for a moment, and then Graham went on: "When Lieutenant Sawyer was at Yale —"

"Lieutenant Sawyer?" Dorotéa interrupted. "Who's he?"

"Lieutenant Madison R. Sawyer the Third," Clete furnished, his tone mocking Sawyer's *Oh, So Social*-sounding name. "He's on Ashton's team. Ashton calls him 'the gorilla.' "

"When Lieutenant Sawyer was at Yale, he was a photographer for the *Yale Daily News*," Graham went on. "He tells Ashton, and we have no choice but to take him at his word, that he will have no problem photographing, on the ground, the landing of the matériel from the *Océano Pacífico*. With a little bit of luck, we will furnish your friend Martín not only photographs of the matériel actually being unloaded on the beach, but of our friend Standartenführer Goltz and/or Colonel Grüner supervising the unloading. That will give the Argentine government sufficient cause to persona non grata either of them, hopefully both."

"What does that mean?" Dorotéa asked.

859

The idea of having Grüner booted out of the country didn't seem to bother Clete at all, Graham thought, *thereby eliminating Grüner as Galahad, and confirming, if it needed confirming, that Galahad is von Wachtstein.*

"When someone on a diplomatic passport does something wrong," Graham said, "such as smuggling, the host government declares him persona non grata — a person not welcome — and asks him to leave the country."

"It will also tip the Germans that we know about the money," Clete challenged.

"Why? So far as they're concerned, the money will have safely arrived, still in its crates, wherever they take it."

"They will wonder how someone just happened to be taking pictures where they were landing the money," Clete argued.

"Look," Graham said, "an amateur photographer is walking along the beach and happens to see the strange activity of people unloading crates from a boat and takes pictures of it with his Brownie. If Lieutenant Sawyer's photographs don't naturally look like the work of an amateur photographer, they can be made to look that way." He paused, then went on. "Actually, Leibermann has a local cop on his payroll who can turn them in. That's just between us."

"Why don't we just tell Leibermann's cop what's about to happen? Let them grab the money?"

"I thought about that. I decided that one cop stumbling across the unloading would not arouse undue suspicion; a dozen cops waiting for the boat would."

Clete shrugged. He could not fault Graham's logic.

"There are several problems involved with getting Lieutenant Sawyer to the proper place at the properly appointed time in the properly appointed uniform — civilian clothing — to take his pictures," Graham said. "For one thing, he's in Argentina illegally. For another, despite his protestations to the contrary, the Germans are liable to see him. He would not be able to defend himself, because I don't want him carrying a weapon."

"I could send Enrico with him," Clete thought aloud. "Enrico and Rudolpho."

"Señor Clete?" Enrico asked, having heard his name.

Clete switched to Spanish.

"This morning, Enrico, you and Rudolpho are going to go riding along the beach."

"Where will you be, Señor Clete?"

"I'll be flying the airplane," Clete said. "And you can't go with me." He waited to deal with the expected objections to that; and when — surprising him — there were none, went on. "You will take el Teniente Gorilla with you. He will be taking photographs of the Germans unloading crates from a boat."

"And what do we do about the Germans?"

"Nothing, absolutely nothing. We don't even want them to see you. If they do see you, you're to leave immediately. But I don't want them to see you. This is very important. What I want you to do is put el Teniente Gorilla in a position to take his photographs, and when he's finished, bring him back here. Only if necessary, and I mean absolutely necessary, are you to use your guns to protect el Teniente Gorilla. No dead Germans, you understand, Enrico?"

"Sí, Señor Clete," Enrico agreed with obvious reluctance.

"If you do what Señor Clete asks you to do, Suboficial Mayor," Graham said, "it will result in the deaths of far more Germans than the ones you will see on the beach."

Enrico considered that idea and seemed to like it.

"Sí, mi Coronel," he said.

"Unless anyone has anything else?" Graham asked, looking around the room, and then finished, "I think we should, quickly, take advantage of Dorotéa's buffet breakfast."

[Two]

Aboard Motor Vessel
Comerciante del Océano Pacífico
Samborombón Bay
River Plate Estuary, Argentina
0810 19 April 1943

Capitán Jose Francisco de Banderano, master of the *Océano Pacífico*, was, of course being generously compensated for his services — as was his crew. There had been a generous sign-on bonus, and a promise of an equal amount at the conclusion of the voyage, even if the ship was lost. In addition, each month an amount equal to, and in addition to, his monthly pay would be delivered to his wife, in cash — and thus tax-free. If things should go really wrong, his wife would receive a generous death benefit, plus a pension for the rest of her life. The German Naval Attaché in Madrid had made similar provisions for every member of his crew.

But the generous pay was not the reason he had accepted the commission. He believed in the German cause.

Like his father and grandfather before him, Capitán de Banderano was a graduate of the Spanish Royal Navy Academy. He graduated at eighteen, was appointed a midshipman, and then, on attaining his twenty-first birthday, was commissioned a Lieutenant in the Royal Spanish Navy.

By the time the Communists started the revolution, he had risen to Lieutenant Commander and was in command of the frigate *Almirante de Posco*. Before the revolution, he hoped to rise in rank to Capitán — as his father had — or possibly even to Almirante — as his grandfather had.

The revolution changed all that. He was early on detached from the *Almirante de Posco* to serve on the staff of General Francisco Franco, El Caudillo, when that great man saw it as his Christian duty to expel the godless Communists from Spain and restore Spain to her former greatness.

As the Civil War dragged on and on, his duties had less and less to do with the Navy, but they took him to all fronts and gave him the opportunity to see what the Communists had in mind for Spain. And they were godless, the Antichrist. He saw the murdered priests and the raped nuns.

Hitler, "Der Führer," and Benito Mussolini, "El Duce," were deeply aware of the nature of the Communists, and of the threat communism posed to the very survival of Christian civilization; and they sent help. Der Führer more than El Duce, to be sure, but both came to the aid of a Christianity that once again had infidel hordes raging at her gates.

Without the help German weapons provided to General Franco's army, without the aerial support of the German Condor Legion, it was entirely possible that the war could have been lost.

The English and the Americans remained "neutral," but that in practice meant they were helping the loyalists. The Americans even sent soldiers, formed into the Abraham Lincoln Brigade, to aid the Communists.

Capitán de Banderano was frankly baffled by the behavior of the English and the Americans. The usual answer to this conundrum was that they were not Roman Catholic, and their "churches" had been infiltrated and corrupted by Communists; but he thought that was too simple an answer. A large number of the Germans who came to help Spain were Protestant. He also thought the other answer was too simple: that the Jews controlled both England and America.

Too many good Spanish Jews had fought as valiantly as anyone on the side of El Caudillo to believe that all Jews were allied with the Antichrist.

But whatever their reasons for opposing Hitler, for refusing to accept that the war Hitler was waging against the Communists was their own war, the fact was that England and America were fighting Germany, and that was sufficient cause for him to do whatever he could to oppose them.

The notion of violating the Rules of Warfare by violating Argentine neutrality would have deeply offended him before the Civil War. Now it seemed only right. The actions of the English during the Civil War were blatantly antagonistic to neutrality. And later, the actions of the Americans after the beginning of the current war, but before they themselves joined the hostilities, were equally contrary to neutrality.

There was no command for Capitán de Banderano in the post–Civil War Royal Spanish Navy. Spain was destitute — and not only because the Communists stole literally tons of gold, almost the entire gold stocks of the kingdom, and took it to Russia. There was hardly enough money to operate — much less construct — men-of-war. The once proud Spanish navy was on its knees, again, thanks to the Communists.

Thus, his service during the Civil War was rewarded with a command in the Spanish merchant navy. He saw with his own eyes and heard with his own ears American Navy ships roaming the North Atlantic searching for German submarines — which had every right under international law to sink vessels laden with war matériel and bound for England. When the American ships found one, they reported their positions by radio, in the clear. "In the clear" meant that radios aboard English men-of-war were given the positions of their enemy by "neutral" American men-of-war.

In Capitán de Banderano's opinion, the English and the Americans were absolutely hypocritical in their denunciation of anyone else who violated neutrality.

And it was the further judgment of Capitán de Banderano that the captain of the American destroyer *Alfred Thomas* deserved to be brought before an international tribunal for reckless endangerment on the high seas and put in prison.

He almost wished the American destroyer put a shot across his bows then, or took some other action. He thought there was a good chance he could have blown her out of the water with naval cannon carried aboard the *Océano Pacífico* in false superstructure.

He had always been skilled with naval artillery. He suspected — but did not know — that someone who knew him in the Admiralty had recommended him to the Germans for command of the *Comerciante del Océano Pacífico* because of this skill.

In any event, he was approached about taking command of the *Océano Pacífico* on a "special mission" — and of course he suspected that mission was to replace the *Reine de la Mer* that the Americans had sunk. When the command was offered, he made up his mind to accept the commission even before the generous emoluments were mentioned.

Even if there was, so to speak, no command of the Royal Navy available to him, even if he was technically a civilian, he knew in his heart that he would be fighting the Antichrist, the godless Communists.

Capitán de Banderano was in his cabin shaving when the Second Officer knocked and announced that a small boat was approaching the *Océano Pacífico* from the port.

"How far?"

"A mile or so, Sir. I would say she will come close in five minutes."

"Thank you, I will be there directly."

Capitán de Banderano finished shaving, put on his tunic, and went to the bridge. He picked his binoculars from its rack and walked out on the flying bridge, where he found the binoculars unnecessary. He could quite clearly read the gold-lettered name of the vessel on its bow with his naked eye — *Coronel Gasparo.*

His first thought was that a boat of that type had no business so far out in the bay. She was a river craft, lean, narrow, and long. In a moment he recognized her for what she was: one of the river craft that plied the maze of waters of El Tigre, north of Buenos Aires.

What in the name of all the saints is she doing out here in the first place, so far from the sheltered waters of El Tigre? And in the second place, why is she pulling alongside me?

She had neither bridge nor wheelhouse. She was controlled internally by her coxswain — or more likely by some sheltered water seaman who proudly called himself "Capitán" — from inside her superstructure.

She took water over her bow as she turned to draw alongside — not enough to be dangerous, he judged. And when the light was right, he could see into the interior of her single cabin.

A young blond-haired man was at her wheel. Beside him, hanging on for dear life, was a man very likely wearing the uniform of the SS.

"Capitán, our accommodation ladder is half-raised," his Second Officer informed him.

"Have it lowered. Have someone on the platform throw her a line. Have an officer arm himself and be prepared on my orders to deny the use of the ladder to anyone."

"Aye, aye, Sir."

It took five minutes for the accommodation ladder to be lowered to the surface of the water, then for an officer — de Banderano was surprised to see it was the Second Engineer — to find a submachine gun and come to the rail, and finally for two seamen to find a coil of line and descend to the ladder's platform with it.

During this period, the *Coronel Gasparo* circled, dipping her bow in the swells and leaning almost alarmingly as she waited for the completion of the preparations to receive her.

The first time she approached the ladder, only a last-second desperate maneuver kept her from colliding with the *Océano Pacífico*. This, of course, forced her to make yet another dipping and swaying turn.

Two of her crew — a middle-aged man and a younger one, who looked like his son — were now outside the cabin. The middle-aged man aft caught the second tossed line, tied it to a stanchion that was not very substantial-looking, and the two sailors on the ladder physically dragged the *Coronel Gasparo* back to the ladder.

The SS officer appeared on the aft deck. De Banderano could now see him clearly. He was not only an SS officer, but a Standartenführer. De Banderano had been told he would be contacted by a senior German official, but had expected this would be someone from the German embassy, a diplomat, not a Standartenführer.

Very carefully, the Standartenführer jumped from the *Coronel Gasparo* onto the ladder and started up it.

When he reached the deck, he looked around until he saw Captain de Banderano.

His arm shot out in the Nazi salute.

"Heil Hitler!" he barked in German. "You are Captain de Banderano?"

De Banderano nodded. His German was adequate but not fluent; he used it only when he had to.

"Standartenführer Goltz," Goltz announced. "I am the officer you were told to expect."

"What can I do for you, Standartenführer?" de Banderano asked in his halting German.

"This is my authority," Goltz said, and handed him the letter on the stationery of the Nazi party and signed by all the senior members of the German government except Adolf Hitler himself.

Capitán de Banderano had just finished reading it — and being suitably impressed by it — when Peter stepped off the ladder onto the deck.

"Buenos días, Capitán," Peter said, and rendered a military salute.

"Major Freiherr von Wachtstein, Captain," Goltz said. "My assistant in this undertaking."

There was something about the young major that de Banderano liked.

"You apparently have had a rather rough voyage," de Banderano said in Spanish. "Could I offer coffee? Perhaps with a little something to sweeten it?"

"The Capitán's understatement is exceeded only by his generosity," Peter said. "I accept with the most profound thanks."

Goltz looked at Peter for a translation.

"The Capitán has just offered us coffee," Peter said.

"I think that would be a splendid idea," Goltz said.

"If you'll come this way, gentlemen?" de Banderano said, and then added: "You speak Spanish very well, Mayor."

"Thank you. I spent some time in Spain," Peter said.

"During the war?"

"With the Condor Legion," Peter said.

Goltz picked up on the Condor Legion and guessed what they were talking about.

"Major von Wachtstein received the Knight's

Cross of the Iron Cross from the hands of the Führer himself," he offered.

"For service in Spain?" de Banderano asked.

"For service in the East," Peter said.

De Banderano now had the satisfaction of confirming his snap judgment of the young officer. He was a fellow warrior in the war against the Antichrist Communists.

He waved them to seats around the wardroom table and ordered the steward to bring coffee, sweets, and brandy.

"Curiosity overwhelms me," he said. "What are you doing in that river craft out here?"

"What did he ask?" Goltz asked.

"It was all we could find on short notice," Peter said, and then translated for Goltz both de Banderano's question and his reply.

"We are pressed for time," Goltz said to de Banderano.

"How may I be of service?" de Banderano asked.

"Shortly before you sailed from Sweden, Captain, several crates were loaded aboard your vessel by Obersturmbannführer Hasselmann. . . ."

Goltz paused until this was acknowledged — de Banderano nodded his head — and then continued.

"I tell you now, in confidence, Captain, that they contain certain matériel which will be used to repatriate the officers of the *Graf Spee* now interned in Argentina. These officers will be brought — probably in groups of twenty or so — from their place of internment to your ship, and then transferred to submarines."

De Banderano had been very curious about the crates brought aboard the *Océano Pacífico* under heavy guard at the last moment before he sailed. And once they were under way he went so far as to enter the hold to look at them. He actually considered opening them for a look. But they had been sealed with lead-and-wire seals that could not be broken without detection.

"Major," he said in German, "my German is not that good. This is obviously of great importance. Would you please translate what the Herr Standartenführer just said?"

Peter did so.

"The *Comerciante del Océano Pacífico* is at your disposal, Herr Standartenführer," he said when Peter finished. "And may I say, as a former Naval officer, that I am delighted to make a contribution to such an undertaking?"

"This project, of course," Goltz said, "has the personal support of Admiral Canaris, who was himself interned in Argentina — and escaped — during the First World War. And I have reason to believe that the Führer himself has a personal interest."

"What would you like me to do?" de Banderano asked.

Goltz took a map from his pocket and laid it on the table.

The steward arrived with the coffee, pastry, a bottle of Spanish brandy, and three gold-rimmed crystal glasses. He filled the glasses.

"Have we time for a toast?" de Banderano asked, picking up his glass.

"Of course," Goltz said.

"To Adolf Hitler, our leader in the war against godless communism," de Banderano offered.

They sipped their cognac.

"To El Caudillo, Der Führer's ally in that noble enterprise," Goltz said.

They sipped again.

"To my comrades in the war against the Communists in Spain," Peter said.

De Banderano was touched by the young major's toast.

Goltz pointed to the map.

"I have arranged for a truck to be at this point, Captain," he said, and interrupted himself. "Hans, you better have a look at this. It's time for you to see where we're going."

"Jawohl, Herr Standartenführer," Peter said, and looked at the map.

"By now, Captain," Goltz said, "Oberst Grüner and the others are already in position. All that remains is for us to bring those special matériel crates ashore and into their hands."

In that absurd little river craft? It wouldn't be exactly landing through the surf — this is, after all, a bay — but that boat probably draws a meter or a meter and a half, and they're very likely to run aground fifty meters offshore. If they can make it in without capsizing.

"I have aboard a boat, Herr Standartenführer, which is probably more suitable to land on a beach than your vessel."

"Splendid!" Goltz said. "Now let me ask you this: Can you take our boat aboard your vessel?"

"I don't know. I'd have to look at it," de Banderano said. "Why would you want me to do that, if I may ask?"

"I thought it would be useful when we bring the *Graf Spee* officers from shore," Goltz said.

"With respect, Herr Standartenführer, the *Océano Pacífico*'s boat could do that more efficiently," de Banderano said. "All I would have to know is where and when you wanted our boat available."

"In that case, Hans," Goltz said. "We would not need your boat. You could return it to El Tigre. If we weren't using it, obviously, it would not arouse suspicion."

"You're absolutely right, Herr Standartenführer."

"Let me propose this course of action, Hans, and you tell me what you think is wrong with it. We will use the *Océano Pacífico*'s boat —" He interrupted himself. "I presume your offer, Captain, includes a crew for your boat?"

"Of course. I will send my First Officer . . . No, I will take you ashore myself."

"That's very gallant of you, Captain."

"It is the very least I can do."

"Let me continue," Goltz said thoughtfully. "We will land the matériel in Captain de Banderano's boat. I will stay ashore. You will then return to the *Océano Pacífico*, pick up your boat, and return it to El Tigre. I will have a word with Herr Loche and see if we can't sell the boat back. Or perhaps it might be a good idea to hold it in reserve. That can be decided later."

"I hesitate to . . . ," de Banderano said.

"If you have something to say, Captain, by all means do so."

"There is no reason for Major von Wachtstein to go with us. What I meant to suggest is that if anyone sees your river craft tied alongside, it might seem odd. There was an airplane flying over earlier. . . ."

"What kind of an airplane?" Goltz asked quickly.

"Oh, I am sure this airplane is no cause for alarm," de Banderano said. "It was an airliner, painted bright red, and it passed at least a mile away, probably at five thousand feet or more. But it made me think that the Argentines probably have patrol aircraft."

"I understand your concern," Goltz said after a minute. "That sort of problem was the reason why I asked if our boat could be taken aboard." He hesitated again. "But I still would like Major von Wachtstein to go with us."

"Of course," de Banderano said.

"But as soon as you return here, Hans," Goltz ordered. "You start for El Tigre."

"Jawohl, Herr Standartenführer."

"How long will it take, Captain, for you to prepare your boat? And to load the crates aboard it?"

Capitán de Banderano smiled.

"In my professional judgment," he said. "It will take almost exactly as long as it will take for you to have a nice breakfast."

[Three]

Samborombón Bay
River Plate Estuary, Argentina
0940 19 April 1943

Although he had been standing on the roof of the truck looking out into Samborombón Bay through very good 7 x 57-mm Ernst Leitz-Wetzlar binoculars for fifteen minutes, Oberst Karl-Heinz Grüner did not see the power launch of the *Comerciante del Océano Pacífico* until after it was seen — and photographed — by First Lieutenant Madison R. Sawyer III, USAR.

This was primarily because Sawyer, Suboficial Mayor Enrico Rodríguez, Argentine Army, Retired, and Sarjento Rudolpho Gomez, Argentine

874

Army, had stationed themselves just behind the military crest* of a rise in the land that placed them sixty feet above the beach.

They were thus able to see farther out into the bay. And they, too, were equipped with very fine optical viewing devices. Enrico was looking out into the bay with an 8 x 75 binocular el Coronel Jorge Guillermo Frade had personally purchased at the Leitz plant in Wetzlar while he was in Germany attending the Kriegsschule. Enrico spotted the power launch first.

Lieutenant Sawyer was equipped with Bausch & Lomb 8 x 57-mm binoculars Enrico had found in Señor Clete's luggage when he returned from the United States. Señor Clete told him that this instrument had been stolen from the U.S. Navy and that he had bought it in New Orleans.

After finding the boat with the stolen U.S. Navy binoculars, Lieutenant Sawyer then found the boat in the viewfinder of his telescopic lens–equipped, tripod-mounted, Leica Model I-C camera, also a product of the Leitzwerk.

When the boat came closer to the beach, Suboficial Mayor Rodríguez changed his means of surveillance to the adjustable 2–10-power Zeiss telescopic sight mounted on the Lowe-Berlin Model 95 7-mm sporting rifle, which was also a souvenir of el Coronel Frade's time in Germany.

There were only a few telescopically equipped rifles in el Coronel Frade's gun room. Rudolpho was furnished with the next best, a Remington Model 70 caliber .30-06 sporting rifle equipped

---

* The military crest of terrain is that point closest to and immediately below the actual crest at which soldiers cannot be seen (and thus fired upon) by the enemy.

with a nonadjustable Bausch & Lomb 4-power telescopic sight. It took him a little longer than Enrico
to clearly see the power launch approaching the
beach.

But shortly after Colonel Grüner spotted the
launch in his binoculars, Rudolpho, too, was able
to see it. And shortly after that, when Enrico asked
him if he could identify the German pilot who came
to Estancia San Pedro y San Pablo the night before,
Rudolpho was able to reply in the affirmative.

The launch moved closer to shore.

Lieutenant Sawyer exhausted the thirty-six-im-
age roll of 35-mm film in the Leica and changed
film. For reasons he could not imagine, this caused
him a good deal of difficulty finding the launch
again in the Leica's viewfinder. The mystery was
explained when he saw that one telescoping leg of
his tripod — not properly tightened — had closed
on itself while he was changing film cartridges. He
tightened the leg firmly and had no further trouble.

He very carefully conserved his film, so that by
the time the launch ran aground on the shore he
had twenty-eight remaining images to photograph
the actual off-loading of the crates from the boat,
and the loading of the crates aboard the waiting
truck.

He was very pleased with himself. He was going
to get everything Colonel Graham had asked him
to get. When the film was processed and printed,
there would be absolute proof that a boat from the
Comerciante del Océano Pacífico — the legend was
clearly painted in black on her sides — had landed
on the shore of Samborombón Bay, and had there
off-loaded what appeared to be six wooden crates.
And all of this activity was clearly under the supervision of an officer wearing an SS uniform and

another in civilian clothing, but whom Enrico had identified as the German Military Attaché.

Since there was no amplification in the viewfinder of the Leica, Sawyer raised the binoculars to his eyes with his right hand and watched the SS colonel jump out of the boat and wade the last few feet ashore. There he triumphantly gave that absurd Nazi salute before enthusiastically pumping the hand of the German Military Attaché.

The Leica was equipped with an automatic film-advance device that permitted him to make shot after shot simply by pressing a thumb-operated shutter-triggering device.

Sailors from the *Océano Pacífico* then jumped out of the boat and started to manhandle the first of the crates out of the boat.

There was a sudden, wholly unexpected, painfully loud explosion in Lieutenant Sawyer's ears, followed immediately by another.

Sawyer looked at the two Argentinians who had escorted him here. Both were quickly working the actions of their just-fired rifles.

"What in the name of God are you doing?" Sawyer asked in both surprise and indignation.

They both took fresh sight pictures.

"Stop that!!" Sawyer ordered as he put the binoculars to his eyes again.

He saw that both the SS officer and the Military Attaché were down on the beach. Both looked as if their heads had exploded.

A blond-headed man jumped out of the launch and ran to one of the downed men. Sawyer decided he was probably an officer from the *Océano Pacífico*.

There came again the crack of the rifles, and Lieutenant Sawyer saw the body the officer was kneeling over jump as a second high-powered bullet struck it.

"My God, what have you done?" Sawyer asked.

Both old soldiers had pulled themselves down from their firing positions at the military crest of the hill.

Sawyer looked at the beach again. But not for long. He was knocked off his feet by the Argentine called Enrico, and dragged off the crest of the hill.

"We go now," Enrico said in heavily accented English.

"My God, man, do you realize what you have done?"

Enrico did not speak English, but he understood the question nevertheless.

"My Coronel, mi Teniente," he said, "and my beloved sister may now rest among the saints in peace throughout eternity. Their murders have been avenged."

"What? What?"

"We go now, Teniente," Enrico repeated, and started to walk down the hill to where they had tethered their horses.

[Four]

The Embassy of the German Reich
Avenida Córdoba
Buenos Aires, Argentina
1650 19 April 1943

"Captain, we have of course spoken with Major von Wachtstein," Ambassador Manfred Alois Graf von Lutzenberger said, "but he is — with good reason — upset about the tragic events of this morning, and we thought you might be able to tell us something he didn't."

And I pray God that your story won't give Gradny-Sawz grounds to suspect that Peter is somehow involved in what happened.

"There really isn't much to tell, Herr Ambassador," Capitán de Banderano said. "We had just reached the shore. Major von Wachtstein wasn't even out of the boat when the Communists struck —"

"The Communists?" Gradny-Sawz interrupted.

"You don't think this is the work of the Communists?" de Banderano asked.

"I'm prone to think the Americans are the ones responsible," Gradny-Sawz said, just a little sarcastically, and then had a thought: "Tell me something, if you please, Captain. Did Major von Wachtstein do anything at all to suggest he expected trouble when you landed?"

The question visibly surprised de Banderano.

"No," he said. "He didn't know where we were going until Standartenführer Goltz told him."

"And when was that?"

"At the time he showed me his map," de Banderano said, "he said something to the effect that it was time von Wachtstein should know where they were going."

Gradny-Sawz grunted.

"You're not suggesting that Major von Wachtstein had something to do . . ." de Banderano said.

"I made no such suggestion," Gradny-Sawz said.

"Baron von Gradny-Sawz is simply doing his duty, Captain. Until we find out who is responsible for this, all are suspect."

"All I know is that Major von Wachtstein risked his life to aid Standartenführer Goltz and Oberst Grüner," de Banderano said. "And to guard the special matériel. I could not leave the helm of the launch, of course, and I am ashamed to say that my crew did not behave admirably. It was von Wachtstein —"

"How do you mean, your crew did not behave admirably?" Gradny-Sawz interrupted.

"When Standartenführer Goltz was struck, it was in the forehead. The shot — forgive the indelicacy — opened his head like a ripe melon. There was blood and brain tissue all over. My men jumped back into the boat. Major von Wachtstein, on the other hand, jumped out of the boat while the firing was still going on, and rushed to help."

"How many shots were fired?" Gradny-Sawz asked.

"I don't know. At least six, possibly eight or more."

"Odd," von Lutzenberger said. "Von Wachtstein said there were only four shots."

"How exactly did von Wachtstein help?" Gradny-Sawz asked.

"He went first to Standartenführer Goltz, saw that he was dead, and called that fact to me. Then he went to the other officer. . . ."

"Oberst Grüner," von Lutzenberger supplied.

"Yes. And while he was bent over him, there was another shot. In my mind clearly intended for von Wachtstein. He didn't let it bother him. He showed great presence of mind."

"What did you mean the second shot was 'clearly intended for von Wachtstein'?" von Lutzenberger asked.

"The Oberst had been shot in the head also. And

was clearly dead. There would have been no point in shooting him again. And the shot didn't miss von Wachtstein by the width of my hands when it struck the Oberst for the second time."

"And the great presence of mind?" von Lutzenberger asked.

"Again, excuse the indelicacy. But von Wachtstein, who had every reason to be terrified — this was moments after the bullet missed him by the width of my hands — never let the importance of the special matériel out of his mind. Before he carried the bodies to the launch — and I am ashamed to say not one of my men had the courage to leave the launch to help him — he reloaded the one crate that had been off-loaded. A lesser man, knowing the two were dead, would have been content to leave them on the beach. But von Wachtstein insisted that we had to take them with us."

"He is a courageous officer," Gradny-Sawz said. "He received the Knight's Cross of the Iron Cross from the hands of the Führer himself, you know."

"Standartenführer Goltz told me that. I had the feeling that they were fond of one another. I could tell how difficult it was, on the way back to my ship, for von Wachtstein to retain his composure."

"The special matériel is intact?" von Lutzenberger asked. "Berlin will want to know about that."

"It is safe in my hold," de Banderano said.

"Well, Anton, what do you think?" von Lutzenberger asked after de Banderano had left.

"I think we have a spy in our office, a traitor. The Americans knew where that boat was going to land."

"And you think it's von Wachtstein? Is that it?"

"Herr Ambassador Graf, I said nothing of the kind."

"You gave me that impression, I'm afraid."

"That was not my intention. I mean, after all, Herr Ambassador Graf, one does not quickly question the courage or loyalty of a holder of the Knight's Cross. And then we have Captain de Banderano's testimony to von Wachtstein's courage under fire."

"Well, that may be. I find it quite difficult to even wonder if the traitor is von Wachtstein, but you're right, Anton, we have one."

"We will smoke him out. Or *her* out."

"You really think it could be Fräulein Hässell?"

"As you yourself said, Herr Ambassador Graf, until we know for sure, everyone is suspect."

"Yes, that's so."

"I wonder what Berlin's going to say?" Gradny-Sawz asked.

"I suppose, Anton, they will most likely name you to replace Standartenführer Goltz in carrying out this project. They'll probably send in another military attaché —"

"Do you really think so?" Gradny-Sawz interrupted. "Place me in charge of this operation?"

"Yes, I do," von Lutzenberger said.

"They'd almost certainly ask for your recommendation about that."

"And I would certainly give it."

Praying, meanwhile, that they would be so stupid as to actually do it.

What they will do, probably, is send in someone to take Grüner's place as Attaché, and someone else to be the security officer, and keep an eye on Gradny-Sawz. And, of course, on me and von Wachtstein.

[Five]

Estancia San Pedro y San Pablo
Near Pila, Buenos Aires Province
1730 19 April 1943

Colonel A. F. Graham replaced the telephone handset in the cradle and turned to Major Cletus Frade and the Legal Attaché of the United States Embassy, Mr. Milton Leibermann.

"The Ambassador — that was his Excellency himself — has been given an appointment to see the Foreign Minister at nine-thirty tomorrow morning," he said. "He was unofficially given to understand that the Foreign Minister has seen some photographs in the possession of Colonel Martín of the BIS, and was led to believe that the Foreign Minister wishes to personally inform him that the new government of Argentina intends to scrupulously observe the provisions of neutrality."

"Which means, of course," Leibermann said, "that the *Océano Pacífico* will sail off into the sunset with all that money on board."

"Which they will find another way to bring into the country," Clete said.

"Having a lot of money on board does not give us the right to sink her, unfortunately," Graham said. "And I think — I know — they will bring it in some other way. I think when I go back to Washington I can get Milton some more money, some more people, to keep track of it. We're that much ahead.

"And if the *Océano Pacífico* is ordered out of Argentine waters, she won't be able to supply any submarines. It'll take the Germans another six weeks, maybe longer, to get another replacement here. So we won, maybe."

"Dave Ettinger is dead," Clete said. "How's that winning?"

"So are Standartenführer Goltz and Colonel Grüner," Leibermann said.

"And my father and Enrico's sister. That makes it three to two. Does that mean I can send Enrico out to even up the score?"

"Don't do that, please," Graham said. "I wouldn't want him to shoot von Wachtstein — excuse me, Galahad — by mistake."

Clete looked at him coldly.

"Relax," Graham said. "That goes no further than this room. I have decided that since Milt and I know who Galahad is, and can guess at his motives, Donovan doesn't have to know. I won't tell him."

"Thank you," Clete said sincerely.

"There's a hook in that," Graham said.

"I should have known," Clete said, his relief instantly replaced with bitter anger.

"If something happens to you, Clete, the deal is off. So don't do anything dangerous — like falling out of your wedding bed — or anything else risky down here. Go on the canapé-and-small-talk circuit. Keep your ears open. Say a kind word for our side when you get the chance."

"Get rid of Delojo," Clete said.

"We have enough on an Argentine in Washington to persona non grata him," Graham said. "We will. They will tit for tat, and Commander Delojo gets sent home from here. I think Ashton's the man to replace him, but I'm going to have to sell that to Donovan."

The door opened and a maid put her head in the door.

"Excuse me, Patrón," she said. "But the Señora insists on seeing you this very moment."

"Jumping the gun a little, isn't she?" Graham said.

"What's the word for that?" Leibermann chuckled. "Hen-pecked?"

"Tell Señorita Mallín I am occupied and will be with her directly," Clete said.

"Patrón, the lady says her name is Señora Howell."

"And that's what it is," Martha Williamson Howell said, pushing into the room. "Nice spread you have here, Clete. How are you, honey?"

"I'll be goddamned!"

"Watch your mouth!"

He ran to her and put his arms around her.

"God, I'm glad to see you!" Clete said.

"Where is she?" Martha asked.

"Where's who?"

"Who do you think?"

"Would you ask Señorita Mallín to come in here, please?" Clete said to the maid.

"Well, look who's here," Martha said, spotting Graham. "What brings you down here?"

"Clete's wedding, what else? How nice to see you, Mrs. Howell."

The door opened again and the Misses Howell passed through it, followed by Cletus Marcus Howell.

He spotted Graham.

"God, what are you doing here? What the hell's going on around here?"

"Not much," Graham said. "How are you, Mr. Howell?"

"I've spent thirty-six hours on an airplane without sleep and four hours in a twenty-year-old Ford

885

taxi driving here. How do you think I am?"

He looked at Cletus.

"Have you nothing to say to your grandfather, Cletus?"

"That depends on what you're doing down here."

Dorotéa Mallín entered the room.

"This must be her," the Old Man said.

"That's her."

The Old Man fished in his pocket.

"This is what I'm doing here," he said to Clete, and then turned to Dorotéa. "Miss Mallín, I am Cletus Marcus Howell."

"I know who you are," Dorotéa said. "Cletus has told me all about you, and so has my father."

"This is now properly yours," the Old Man said, and handed her a square of folded tissue.

She unfolded it. It was an engagement ring, with what looked like a four-carat emerald-cut diamond.

"I don't understand," Dorotéa said.

"What the hell is that?" Clete asked suspiciously.

"It's your mother's engagement ring," the Old Man said. "Jorge Guillermo Frade gave it to your mother, and now I'm giving it to this young lady. What she sees in you is beyond me, but if she's going to marry you, she damned well deserves it, and a lot more."

"Thank you," Dorotéa said, and then kissed him.

The Old Man looked embarrassed. But pleased.

Priebke Extradited to Italy Today

San Carlos de Bariloche

On the eve of his extradition to Italy to stand trial for allegedly participating in a massacre of 335 civilians, former SS Captain Erich Priebke said in an interview yesterday the Vatican had tried to stop the killings.

"The Vatican requested clemency in every way possible and even appealed to the German Embassy," Priebke told the *La Mañana del Sur* daily.

Priebke, 82, will be extradited to Rome today to await trial. The massacre, in the Ardeatine Caves outside Rome in 1944, was ordered by Hitler to avenge the killing of 32 German soldiers in an ambush.

Priebke has been under house arrest in Bariloche for 17 months since admitting a role in the killings. He has said his task was to cross out the names of victims as they were led into the caves to be executed.

"I was just obeying orders," he said in the interview. "All I knew was that they (the victims) belonged to the Italian Resistance in some way."

Argentina's Supreme Court ordered Priebke's extradition to Rome on November 2.

An Italian delegation, including Interpol officers and a military doctor, arrived yesterday in Bariloche.

According to unconfirmed local press reports, the officials were expected to fly back to Rome with Priebke today at 8 A.M. Argentine authorities will hand over Priebke to Italian authorities at the local airport, the report said.

Priebke had lived openly in Argentina since escaping from a British prison camp in 1946. He worked as a waiter in Buenos Aires before moving to Bariloche, where he ran a delicatessen.

Priebke's attoney Pedro Bianchi said yesterday that the case was historically significant because it involved "the last Nazi." Today marks the 50th anniversary of the Nuremberg trials in which Nazis were tried for committing crimes against humanity during World War II.
(Reuter-NA)

The *Buenos Aires Herald*, Buenos Aires, Argentina
November 20, 1995

Priebke Gone, Hugs Cops, Latter in Trouble

Argentina extradited former Nazi officer Erich Priebke to Italy yesterday to face trial for his role in that country's worst World War II atrocity — the Ardeatine Caves massacre of 335 men and boys.

The former SS captain, now 82, was taken from his home in Bariloche to an airplane sent by Italy to take him to Rome.

He looked serene as he smiled and waved goodbye from the tarmac before boarding the Falcon DA 90 aircraft.

A preliminary committal hearing to determine whether there was sufficient evidence to proceed to a full trial is scheduled in Rome for December 7.

Priebke shook hands with police and hugged some of those who escorted him to the local airport, witnesses said. Interior Minister Carlos Corach later asked that the young officer who was caught by television cameras hugging Priebke be stripped of his police duties. The police suspended him and the officer in charge.

In an interview published yesterday by a local newspaper Priebke expressed grief at having to leave his family behind and hope that his captors will set him free.

He said his wife Alicia was not accompanying him because of her poor health.

"She suffered a shock the day I was arrested," he said.

Several Italian Interpol members and at least two doctors also boarded the plane. Priebke has a heart condition but an Argentina judge ruled last week he was fit for the flight.

He has been under house arrest in Bariloche since confessing his part in the atrocity to a US television interviewer last year. The extradition put an end to a year and a half of legal wrangling.

Priebke, who spent the weekend with relatives and friends, said in a newspaper interview on Sunday that he had rejected repeated Vatican pleas to avoid the massacre.

"Between March 23 and 24 (1944), Pope Pius XII tried to avoid the reprisal. A great number of Vatican envoys were sent everywhere," Priebke told *La Mañana del Sur.* He said the Vatican appealed to the German Embassy in Rome and to military leaders, including himself and his superior Herbert Kappler. (DYN-Reuter)

The *Buenos Aires Herald*, Buenos Aires, Argentina
November 21, 1995

The employees of G.K. Hall hope you have enjoyed this Large Print book. All our Large Print titles are designed for easy reading, and all our books are made to last. Other G.K. Hall books are available at your library, through selected bookstores, or directly from us.

For information about titles, please call:

(800) 223-2336

To share your comments, please write:

Publisher
G.K. Hall & Co.
P.O. Box 159
Thorndike, ME 04986

LANCASTER COUNTY LIBRARY SYSTEM

3 0339 43214 3150

LANCASTER COUNTY LIBRARY
LANCASTER. PA